some kind of perfect

KRISTA & BECCA RITCHIE

ADDICTED SERIES
Recommended Reading Order

A NOTE FROM THE AUTHORS

It is highly recommended to read this book after *Long Way Down*. Otherwise, it will spoil the entire series. *Some Kind of Perfect* is meant to be the 10th book in the series. The epilogue novel. The conclusion.

2018

"I'm always going to be a sex addict, but I'm more than just sex."

- Lily Hale, We Are Calloway

(Season 1 Episode 01 — Pilot)

{ 1 }

June 2018
HALE CO. LOBBY
Philadelphia

Lily Hale

I've never been punched in the face before, but I imagine this is how it feels. Below my eye, the skin puffs and swells with constant throbbing pain. I cover the right one with my palm, afraid if I drop my hand, half of my face may fall apart altogether. Just like Mrs. Potato Head.

That's me.

Lily Potato Head Hale.

For the moment at least. I'm a mess, and it's not even my fault.

Lo clutches my wrist, attempting to tug my hand down, but I don't relinquish that easily. *Lest my eyeball pop out of the socket.*

"Let me see, Lil." His amber irises rage hot between concern and anger.

We're not in private. We stand in the very center of Hale Co.'s pristine lobby, the waxed marble floors reflecting my discomfort back at me. I can't hide behind the fiddleleaf fig plants, their ceramic pots stationed on either side of the shiny elevators.

I'm not a botanist or suddenly fascinated by foliage, but Connor mentioned their specific name one day. Apparently Cobalt Inc. has English Ivy in their lobby. I didn't know someone could find a way to be conceited about houseplants, but Connor has lots of talent in making his belongings seem superior.

Maybe because they are.

I shake out the thought. I don't need the fiddleleaf figs or Connor's English Ivy. I can stand here. Right here. Out in the open. I know I can.

At the sleek entrance desk, a pretty blonde receptionist watches us like she's tuned into a television show. She doesn't even care as my sole eye meets her eye. And she's not the only one. Hale Co. employees push through the revolving doors and depart from the beeping elevators, and their wandering gazes plaster onto us.

Loren Hale might be the boss, but I don't show up at his offices that often. Let alone flanked by *three* bodyguards. They do their best to subdue the crowds outside, which start dispersing. Younger teens hoist posters like: **KISS ME, LOREN HALE!** and **MY CINNAMON ROLL LOREN HALE** and **WE LOVE YOU, LILY!** They wait by the curb on the chance that we'll exit, but they can't see us through the tinted windows.

It's not their fault my eye swells either.

My bodyguards couldn't prepare for the *one* hostile stranger. It's usually just one bad apple.

And this apple happened to throw a plastic penis at my face. Which, granted, has happened before, but none have ever made contact.

Now I'm suffering from being literally smacked in the face with a penis, and I'm not sure what hurts more: my face or my dignity.

Probably my face.

It fucking hurts.

Lo cups my cheeks, his features contorting through a series of emotions. "Are you crying?"

"No…my one eye is just watering." I sniff before my watery eye morphs into full-fledged tears.

His cheekbones cut sharp. "That asshat is road kill."

It sounds less like a threat and more like a character description. When Lo realizes that I am in no way dropping my hand, he tucks my gangly frame closer to his hard chest.

My tense shoulders nearly melt, but my palm stays its course, keeping my face together. I am one step away from a Picasso painting.

Lo fumes beneath his breath, "A goddamn disgrace to human kind." His fury is radiating so much that I almost expect flames to shoot out of him like Cannonball from *X-Men*.

For some reason, I decide now's a great time to bring it up. "You look like Cannonball."

"I didn't realize I have blond hair…oh wait, I don't," he says dryly. "And I haven't checked my ass recently, but I'm really fucking positive fire isn't shooting out of it."

Talk of his ass distracts me. I almost sneak a peek, but my long-time bodyguard approaches us. Bald, burly, and extremely tall, Garth is the most experienced bodyguard of them all. As the head of the fleet, he has the unique job of ordering Rose and Connor's bodyguards around. It's one of the few things I can hang over their heads with pride.

My bodyguard is better than your bodyguard, ha!

Lo speaks first, his eyes narrowing to scalding pinpoints. "Did security get him?"

Garth nods. "They're calling the police now." To me, he asks, "Do you need to go to the hospital?"

Before Lo insists, I blurt out, "No! I'm fine. Seriously I just got punched." *By a penis.* What is my life?

Lo stares down at me like I've lost my mind. I haven't. I'm completely sane. None of the guys would go to the hospital for this, and I don't want to either just because I'm the girl. *So there.*

Lo can't read my mind though. "If you don't need a hospital, then let me see." He grabs my wrist again, and his other hand coyly slides down the length of my hip. *Where is that going?*

I watch it, sort of distracted by his jawline, which is closer to me—really his entire *body* is close to me. His black slacks, black V-neck shirt, arrowhead necklace, soft skin and light brown hair. Just all of him: the entirety of Loren Hale. Ice and whiskey.

But the metaphorical whiskey.

His hand continues to dip down my cotton black dress, which resembles an extra long T-shirt. I feel his palm slip to my lower back, descending and descending—he squeezes my butt!

I startle enough that I surrender. Public displays are frequent between us, but surprise ass-grabs still do *surprise* me.

With both of my hands clutched to his belt loops, he has free view of my whole face. I watch his expression grind through more dark and stormy sentiments. Then his throat bobs, and his eyes lose all trace of anger.

"Lil," he breathes, holding my cheek again.

"It's that bad?" I pat the tender skin with my fingertips. It stings, so I lower my hand.

He shakes his head slowly and then forces out a sharp, "No." Lo has started doing this thing when he lies: his eyes dart to the side for a millisecond before returning to me. He adds, "Don't give me that look."

"What look?"

"The one that says, *you're a lying liar, Loren Hale.*"

"Then tell me I look like the best Lily Hale you've ever seen." I try to straighten up to appear like the best version of Lily. I can't recall what version I'm on. Maybe Lily 8.2.

He grimaces at my eye. "You're the best Lily—but your eye looks like shit, which is *not* your fault."

"I know."

He nods, more to himself. "Can you see out of it?"

My eyelid droops, and it hurts to lift it up. "A bit."

Lo nods again, but this time, his gaze flashes murderously. He turns to Garth. "We're pressing charges for assault. You can stay here with the other bodyguards and wait for our lawyers. When you're finished, you can meet us at my office." Lo is so assured, no indecisiveness or need to turn to his father or a friend.

After Garth agrees, we walk to the elevators, and Lo's confidence never vanishes. I inspect my face in the shiny elevator door while we wait.

It's worse than I thought. A giant red welt covers half my face. The bottom of my eye took the brunt of the impact. I run my fingers through my shoulder-length hair, at least hopeful that the strands aren't greasy today.

You're not a total mess. See.

Lo comes up behind me—and I blink back most thoughts that could easily turn into sexual fantasies. *Don't space out.*

It's not like I have in a while, but I still need to remind myself. He wraps his arms around my waist and sets his chin on my shoulder. I ease back into his chest. "Mmmm." I freeze. *Did I make that sound aloud?*

Lo whispers in the pit of my ear, "You doing alright?"

He means about sex. In stressful situations, I cope *with* sex—but everyone already knows this by now, unless you like to skip our sad stuff.

"I think I'm overthinking," I say honestly. I'm clutching onto his bicep, basically saying *don't let go of me.*

He doesn't.

But he does kiss my temple and then straightens up, holding me tighter.

The elevator dings, and we slide inside. He pushes one of the buttons, and the doors shut, finally granting us a sliver of privacy.

I face him and grab onto his belt loops again. "I can't believe that happened...pinch me."

He pinches the skin on my elbow.

"Ouch." I wince and rub my arm. "Why can't this be a dream?"

"Come on, Lil. You wouldn't want this in your dream. There are no cocks or mind-blowing orgasms."

He's right. "You're so right."

His gaze finds my swollen eye again. "Next episode of *We Are Calloway*, I'm speaking about this fucking idiot—see how he likes to be called the dick-thrower for the rest of his life."

The docu-series reminds me of Daisy, and for about five months, my first incoming thought attached to my little sister has been *Daisy is alive.*

My eyes start welling.

Daisy is alive.

I wasn't certain I'd ever see her again. She almost died giving birth, and that day in the hospital hit all of us like a comet slamming into Earth. Rose, the backbone of our sisterhood, was inconsolable. I couldn't speak. I remember feeling like someone destroyed a link in my life. I'd spent my high school and college years pushing my sisters away, and now I could barely function at the thought of Daisy being ripped away.

I blink back tears. Before Lo notices my glassy gaze, I sweep out the morose thoughts and try to recall what he said. *The docu-series.* We've only released one episode of our new docu-series so far, but all the articles have been positive since it aired. We're all eager to film more soon.

"All the other fans were nice outside." A girl started crying when I smiled and complimented her poster. As though my acknowledgment of her existence made her year. I never thought *I* could bring someone that level of happiness.

It felt good.

Lo wraps his arm across my shoulders, and we watch the numbers increase on the elevator monitor. Swanky jazz music plays softly, and my mind starts taking detours.

I wonder, "You're not going to be embarrassed to have me walk through your offices, right?"

Lo looks at me like I've grown antennas.

"I mean," I say quickly, "it's just that I've obviously been punched." I point to my face. "And in a few minutes, the news will relay how it was a penis that punched me. Not to mention, I'm your wife, so all of your employees will see me and be thinking *his wife was just punched by a penis*."

The elevator suddenly halts, and the doors spring open. A forty-something man in a suit and two women in business-casual dresses stand on the other side. Waiting.

Lo says bitingly, "These are taken." He taps the *closed doors* button incessantly, and when they shut, he hits the *stop elevator* button.

My eyes widen like *he's* the crazy one here. "Now they're going to think we're having sex on the elevator." The fact that I'm a sex addict is so much a part of me that I don't shy from it anymore. I only care because I don't want to make it harder for Lo to be respected by his colleagues. I know none of us can escape gossip, but I just want to be a positive force in his life.

As Lo looks at me and as I look at Lo, I see the little boy who chased me around my family's parlor. I see the teenager who relentlessly teased me, who stuck his tongue in my ear. Who pinched my cheeks. Who said mean things after drinking bourbon. Who held me as I fell fast asleep.

I see my best friend.

With his sharp features and daggered gaze, he snaps, "First of all, no one is thinking *his wife was just punched by a penis*."

"I am."

He cocks his head. "You're Lily Hale. Ninety-nine percent of your thoughts are certified original."

I smile. "What about the one percent?"

"That's when you and I are thinking the same thing." He draws me to his chest, his hands on my shoulders.

His strength courses through vital parts of my soul, and I inhale a heartier breath. We're so much better together than we are separate. I wouldn't have said that at our beginning, but now, it's truer than anything I know.

"Secondly," he says with that familiar edge to his voice, "you did not get *punched* by a penis. Some dipshit threw it at you. And it was *fake*."

"Solid point." I nod and then cringe. "I do feel kind of badly though. Like, your dick has been the only one to touch my face in so long and…"

He's glaring. The type of Loren Hale glare that could wither ancient gardens and set fire to cities. "No, you did not cheat on me with that *thing*." He pauses for a second and then reaches into his pocket. "Do you need to call your therapist? Because if you feel violated, Lil, then this is a whole other issue."

I frown. *Do I?* "Maybe later." Dr. Banning has a way of putting everything into perspective, and after seven years, she's been a trusted ally. "I think I could use some cold peas for my eye though. That's what you use when you get punched."

He wears this pained look like I'm hurt, not just physically. "Lil—"

"I know I didn't get punched, but it sounds cooler than having something thrown at me." I'm dealing with this my way, and it's not a bad way—it's just the Lily way. The good news: our son is with my parents right now, so he didn't get hit in the crossfire. This is what I care about most.

"Okay." Lo gives in. "Then you got punched, but I'm not calling it a penis."

"A dildo?"

He cringes. "Lets call it the *thing*. We don't need to give that shitty fuck a creative name for his weapon."

I test it out. "I was punched by the thing." *I like it.* "Sounds better."

"Thirdly." *There's a thirdly?* He pauses for a short moment, his gaze roaming my features, and then he tucks a strand of my hair behind my ear. "There is absolutely *nothing* you could do or say or *anything* that could happen that'd make me embarrassed to be your husband." He shakes his head and repeats, "Nothing."

I sniff, trying to restrain incoming tears. I put my hand to my burning eye, pain increasing. "Don't make me get all emotional."

"Well don't get so down on yourself."

"Fair enough." I feel time ticking by now, especially since people are waiting for us in his office and whoever needs to use this elevator. "Are we good?"

"Not yet." He bends down a little, and before I locate my brain, his lips are on mine. The surprise kiss jolts me, but as the shock wears off, I sink into the embrace. My hands wrap around his shoulders, and I rise to the tips of my toes, intensifying the kiss. My eager body curves against his, and our tongues skillfully tangle together.

He grips my hips, one large hand edging towards my ass.

Squeeze it again. My mind pleads.

Instead, he swiftly tugs my body further against his, the kiss deepening. A moan catches in my throat, and I tremble, heat building between us.

He breaks apart. "Now we're good." His lips are a little pinker and more swollen.

I touch mine, stinging from the quick force. *What a tease.*

I eye Lo greedily: the few brown strands hanging in his eyes, his hair shorter on the sides, his cheekbones—yes those cheekbones that I will mention from here until eternity. *You would too if you saw them.*

It's not even his appearance. It's the way that he keeps glancing over to me as he presses the elevator button. It's the way his pinky hooks with mine, just for a second, before he full-on cups my hand. It's the way he spent all this time giving me a pep talk—when I know tomorrow, I'll be there to give him one if need be.

It's the way he feels like another extremity of myself. Like a huge, overwhelming part of me.

We've been through so much, and I can see our road paved with more bumps, our fight filled with more battles—but ones we're finally equipped to face.

The elevator doors slide open, and we walk ahead.

Ready to face one more together.

[2]

June 2018
HALE CO. OFFICES
Philadelphia

Rose Cobalt

"They're late," I announce, ice dripping off each syllable. "Late arrivers must pay the consequences." I spin a pen between my fingers, seated at the head of the table in a Hale Co. conference room.

Connor is seated at the other end, the long stretch of the table separating us. His calmness proves infuriating, per usual. I make sure to send him scathing glares made of fire and brimstone.

He should be worried too. Loren is his best friend, and he's now—I check my phone—*fifteen minutes* late. It's not like Lily and Lo are always prompt, but they're usually here before Ryke.

My brother-in-law has chosen the leather chair closest to my littlest sister, both in the center of the conference table. As though to declare their neutrality between Connor and me. I would test Daisy's loyalty, but her wide-eyed baby preoccupies her attention. She rocks the little five-month-old in her arms, trying to ease Sullivan Minnie Meadows into a post-lunch nap.

I love my niece, but she was *not* invited.

Ryke peels his gaze off his daughter. "Do I even want to ask what paying the consequences fucking involves?"

"Blood sacrifice probably." Daisy wags her brows; then she tucks a yellow baby blanket tighter around Sullivan. The air conditioning blows a violent stream of cold air onto them.

The air ducts, too, recognize that babies are *not allowed* to this particular meeting. We all agreed. I dropped Jane, Charlie, and Beckett off at our parent's house. Lily did the same with Maximoff, so I don't expect to see my nephew when she arrives.

Daisy was supposed to follow suit, but she retreated at the last minute and brought her daughter here. I'm not sure if it's because she doesn't want to leave Sullivan with our mother or if she doesn't want to part with her baby.

I just want to make sure my sister is *mentally* doing fine. After what happened—I inhale a strained breath, my collarbone jutting out from my red dress. I try to block out a moment that ripped me to shreds.

I almost lost my sister.

I bear hard on my teeth and focus back on the topic at hand. "It involves *my wrath*, but depending on how late they are, blood sacrifices might need to be implemented."

Connor cups a steaming mug of coffee. "How will we decide who goes first?" he challenges. "Your sister or Loren?"

"I've had to make harder decisions in preschool." I click my pen. "My sister will be spared—of course."

He doesn't blink. Instead he sips his coffee with smugness pooling in his deep blue eyes. What does he even have to be smug about?

I click my pen more forcefully, drilling a hot glare between his eyeballs. *The war is not over, Richard. You haven't won a thing.*

His lips rise as he sets down his mug. "Your vote plus Daisy's vote against my vote and Ryke's—that's called a tie. You do know what those are, don't you?"

I flip my glossy hair off my shoulder. "Not as much as you. I *win* more than I tie." I say *win* with so much hostility that his small smile transforms into a blinding grin.

Ugh.

That didn't go as planned.

I glower and gesture to Ryke and Daisy. "And they haven't even voted yet, Richard. You can't just assume what they'd choose." My head whips to their side of the table.

Ryke is focused on someone who lingers in the hallway.

Did I mention that all of the boardrooms and offices have glass walls? A young employee loiters by a copy machine, his tie crooked and hair smoothed with too much gel. He does a pathetically awful job of pretending not to watch us.

I snap my fingers towards Ryke until I gain his attention. It takes him a second to catch up.

He raises his hands in surrender. "Fuck *no*. I'm not getting into this."

"Daisy." I lift my chin and pull back my shoulders. "Choose your next words wisely." *Sister loyalty.*

She adjusts her baby in her arms. "I don't want to sacrifice anyone. Can't we all hypothetically live?" She offers me the kindest smile. I love Daisy for being able to voice her opinions, even when they differ from mine.

Can't we all hypothetically live?

Literally, I'd fight for all of our survival.

Hypothetically and figuratively, I don't mind a few casualties.

I click my pen. "If we must."

Sullivan smacks her lips and then yawns against her mom's palm. Daisy nuzzles her forehead against her daughter's.

It's borderline nauseating.

I don't grow fuzzy feelings at the sight of cooing babies and maternal warmth. Infants are miniature devils.

Mine included.

And I love them. Including their downfalls: the snotty noses and incessant crying and inability to carry intellectual conversations. I may not appear as affectionate as any of my sisters, but I show affection in ways that don't involve using my nose to tickle a baby's nose. I'd never tell her *not* to be that way. I want her to be her. Just as I'd hope people would want me to be me.

If anyone says that my love is somehow *less* than another mother's, then fuck them. They have no clue the lengths I'd go for my little gremlins.

I watch my sister murmur a few soft words to Sullivan, the baby finally nodding off. Ryke has his arm draped over Daisy's shoulders, his focus partly on his daughter and partly on his wife. I see exhaustion in his face and hers, but more so my sister. Dark crescent moons lie beneath her eyes.

I set my pen down. "Daisy?"

"Yeah?" She keeps her voice hushed but meets my gaze.

"Connor and I would be happy to babysit anytime you need us."

Connor has his annoying finger to his annoying jaw like he's in *mock* contemplation. There's nothing to contemplate. Daisy and Ryke have been glued to Sullivan since she was born. Five months without *one* break. I understand every parent is different, but I'm worried about my sister.

Ryke runs a hand across his unshaven jaw and then swivels his chair towards Connor. "You'd be fucking happy to babysit *my* daughter?" He's disbelieving.

"Of course," Connor replies. "Your daughter is already more articulate than you are, so really, I like Sulli more than I like you." Connor sips his coffee again like he just professed the weather: *sunny with a side of fuck you.*

Ryke flips him off. The more direct approach to a *fuck you.*

They can act like they're enemies for as long as they want, but in their eyes, even I can see how much they care for one another. I've seen real hate from my husband. I've seen real hate from Ryke. What they share doesn't even come close to aversion.

Confusion furrows Daisy's brows. "...I don't know." She thinks longer. "I don't want to put more stress on you."

I scoff. "She wouldn't be any stress."

"You already have three babies."

I remember how Daisy and Ryke saw me at a lower point when I first had Charlie and Beckett. I was admittedly stressed out, and the new change scared me. I like order, but once I found a better routine and delegated more to Connor, I became invincible. In mind and body, and if I wanted to house *a hundred* children, I could do it with high heels and lipstick and a dress.

I'm the raging blizzard and the fucking wildfire. There is *nothing* that will stand in my way of what I want and what I will achieve.

I remind Daisy, "And another baby would hardly topple my world. I'm a fucking fortress." This fact makes my little sister smile. I point my matte black nail at her infant. "You dressed her in a cupcake onesie. How could she cause any stress?"

Before he pipes in, I raise my hand towards Connor, shutting him down. I already see his grin in my peripheral and the words behind his lips: *being dressed in a pale yellow cupcake-printed onesie has no relation to stress.* Blah. Blah. Blah.

I'm trying to convince my little sister of something. I'm not trying to win a Quiz Bowl right now.

Connor, thankfully, withholds his comment. Instead, he says to Daisy, "If you don't want us to watch her, I'm sure Lily and Lo—"

"No." Ryke slams the door to it first. "I'm not putting any stress on my brother."

"They've watched Jane before," Connor says before I can. Ryke has been giving Lo more credit lately, so I don't understand why he's withdrawing.

"Once we pile one fucking kid on them, it'll be two, then three. They probably only want one baby for a fucking *reason*." He exhales heavily.

I tap the table. "You look more stressed than Loren."

Ryke rolls his eyes and groans.

"And maybe they do want another child sometime soon. They've mentioned keeping that door open. We haven't heard otherwise...unless they spoke to *you* about something different." I already simmer at the sisterly betrayal, but Ryke looks at me as though I'm being overdramatic for no reason.

"No—no one said anything to me about trying for kids. I"—he groans again and combs his hand through his hair—"I..."

"I take it back," Connor says, "it's worse than talking to a five-month-old."

"Fuck you." Ryke rests his elbows on the table. "Look, truth is...it has nothing to do with my brother or with you two. Maybe Dais and I are just doing great without any of your help? You all did fine without us."

Connor and I lock eyes, understanding shared between us.

In this sudden moment, we've declared amnesty and come to eons worth of agreements. We're so aware of their role in our children's lives. We were all living together when Jane was born.

They played with her. They babysat her. They held her when she was fussy, and they found her lost lion. They brought her laughter and smiles and so much love.

It's not that we feel the need to pay it forward. We just want to be as *much* a part of their lives as they've been a part of ours.

"We did fine without you," Connor agrees with him. "But we also did better with you. Just like Lo and Lily do better with all of us, and you and Daisy do too. All of our children benefit from the love and support of family."

Translation: *you're my family, Ryke.*

I inhale the vigor of his words. Connor never had a true family. He had a mother who purposefully distanced herself from him, who refused to show him the *power* of love. Connor is acknowledging the benefit of real human connections. All the ones based on love. All the ones between us.

Ryke holds his gaze, and I think he can see the meaning behind Connor's declaration too.

Daisy is fixated on her baby, her brows still knotted in pained contemplation.

I can't bite my tongue. "Is it Mother?" At first, I even hesitated leaving Jane there for long periods of time. Lily did too. We've all had different upbringings in that house, none perfect, and we wouldn't want our children to experience what we did.

But Samantha Calloway is different as a grandmother than a mother. She's less overbearing. It helps that she has staff there to cater to the kids. She won't be overwhelmed with all four at the Villanova house, but we also don't leave them there often.

Connor and I have already started a discussion about nannies. Growing up, we've each had our fair share of bad experiences with them. So I'm still cold towards the idea, but it feels inevitable. We'll need to set boundaries so the nanny is more like a babysitter and less like a surrogate mother.

Trust is also an important factor.

Very softly, Daisy says, "It's not Mom. I'm going to leave Sulli there for a day. I will. But I'm just not...ready yet." Tears well in her tired eyes, and she pinches them, choking down a strangled sound.

Ryke rubs her shoulders and whispers in her ear.

I immediately stand at the same time as Connor—*ugh, whatever.* I normally don't go *towards* any waterworks, but this is my sister. I pad over to their side of the conference table.

Connor has already moved closer too, and we both sit on either side of Ryke and Daisy. In our shared silence, raw realizations cling to the air. We'd been right beside them on their long journey to have a child. We were their safety nets—something they could rely on if *everything* else failed.

We didn't want to have to catch them, but we watched them fight. And they did fight, so long and so hard, to bring their daughter into this world. For a while, it seemed like a real impossibility. Then it seemed like my little sister might not survive.

She wouldn't hear her daughter's first words or see her first steps or even hold her in her arms.

I don't pretend to know that grief. I couldn't possibly *feel* what she has felt, but I know my sister. I know her kindness and her love and how much she wanted that little girl in her arms.

So it's only natural she wouldn't want to break apart.

Daisy hangs her head, her tangled blonde hair hiding her watery gaze. The strands are as wild as my littlest sister. Ryke skims his thumb over Sullivan's buttoned nose, and the baby coos before falling into a content slumber.

"She's beautiful," I say in my quietest voice. My heart is *full* of this indiscernible, overpowering sentiment—because this child is so much of my sister and Ryke.

I realize I'm not making the situation any better, especially when Connor mouths to me, *what was that?*

I press my lips in an aggravated line, and then I silently huff, knowing what I need to say. "And this beautiful thing was *not* invited today."

Ryke's jaw hardens.

More calmly, Connor says, "If you let her go, just for an afternoon, she won't disappear from this world. I promise you both that."

Ryke dips his head down to look at Daisy, behind her cascade of hair. He whispers to her and then kisses her cheek. When he raises his head once more, he nods to Connor like he understands.

I'm not sure Daisy is there yet.

I put my hand on hers. "I'm *always* here for you. That won't ever change." I've expressed this sentiment many times before.

Her shoulders sink with exhaustion. She wipes at her eyes and then turns to me, her scar reddened on her cheek. "I just don't want to miss a moment. We've been given this gift, and I can't…" She growls beneath her breath as more tears fall. She rubs them away quickly before they land on her sleeping baby.

"I can't say that you won't because you will," I tell her honestly. "Maybe you'll miss that one time she snorts up food or the one time she falls on her ass, but you know the ridiculous thing about children? They do these painfully cute and stupid things *all* the time." I help brush the rest of her tears off her cheek. She nods to me again. "So you will miss that one moment, but you'll have a *million* more to make up for it."

What's not a dream: my sister has sleep problems and PTSD and depression. All I want is for her to be healthy. So does Ryke. So does Connor. So do Lily and Lo.

She just needs to let us help her.

Daisy pushes her hair out of her face. Softly, she says, "Okay."

We exchange *I love yous*, and then I'm distracted by the two guys, their chairs turned towards one another. I think Connor asks Ryke something beneath his breath. Or maybe it's the other way around. They speak in hushed tones.

I don't pretend to wonder or care what they share. Though, I sort of do. It's not often these two whisper together, not without Loren present.

I clear my throat loudly until I catch their attention. "What is it?"

Ryke and Connor glance at Daisy like they're protecting her from shrapnel and gunfire. It's absurd.

"She can handle your criticism."

"It's not fucking criticism," Ryke retorts.

I cross my arms. "I wasn't trying to be accurate. I just wanted you to talk, which was a success."

"A partial success, darling," Connor chimes in. "I hadn't said anything yet."

I gag. "Your ego is revolting."

He can't restrain his stupid grin. I find myself eyeing his lips too much, so I focus back on Ryke. "Then what were you two gossiping about?"

"Sex."

I roll my eyes. "Typical." Though I don't mention how my sisters and I talk about sex often. It's not just a guy thing.

As Sullivan stirs again, Daisy rocks her a little more. "Will you watch her this Saturday? Just for a couple hours?"

My heart swells. "I'd love to. I'll save you from all the evil cries."

Daisy mock gasps. "Did you just call my baby evil?"

"Her *cries*," I refute. "That only makes her part-evil."

Daisy breaks into a wider smile. Whatever my sisters need, I will be there faster than a fucking roadrunner.

I flinch as the door finally bursts open.

About time. Loren crests the doorway with Lily by his side. I frown deeply. Why is she shielding half her face with her hand?

Loren whispers in her ear, and they break apart to sit at the now vacant heads of the table.

"What's going on?" My voice spikes an octave. I rise in my four-inch black heels.

"Looks like Lily and I dethroned you and your husband." He swings his head to Connor. "Thanks for keeping this warm for me, love." He even takes a sip of Connor's coffee.

My husband's features are unreadable and mostly trained on Lily. He even takes out his cellphone. Ryke is seconds from pushing himself to a stance.

"This isn't about seating assignments," I retort. "But let's be clear, Connor and I always sit at the heads of the table." I snap at him to move.

Loren gives me a dry look. "Be careful, Queen Rose, you might break a talon."

I growl and then collect my thoughts. *He's distracting you, Rose.* From the real problem. My sister. Something's wrong with my sister.

"Lily?" I say. "What's wrong...?" I trail off as a male intern enters the conference room with a bag of ice. He sets it on the desk by Lily and then hurries out without a word.

I gasp as Lily drops her hand to clutch the ice.

"What the fuck?!" Ryke yells before I can.

She fumbles with the ice before pressing it to her red, swollen eye, a greenish bruise beginning to form. "I'm alright! No one freak out."

"Too fucking late," Ryke curses, already standing. Connor is on his feet too, typing quickly on his phone. Baby still in her arms, Daisy rolls on her chair over to Lily, both exchanging a few quiet words.

I whip my head to Lo. "Someone attacked her?" That's it. I march around the table, find my Chanel purse on a chair, and rummage for my cellphone.

"Whoa—everyone stop for a second." Lo has to shout louder because I'm not stopping. "Jesus Christ, *stop*, everyone!"

We all go still.

Lo isn't joking anymore, his daggered eyes flashing hot. "Did you ever think that maybe we already took care of it?"

Now I am.

"How?" Connor asks. "Did you call lawyers?"

"*Yes.*"

"Did you contact police?"

"*Yes*," he forces. "And you don't even know what happened yet."

"I got punched," Lily tells us, and I have to force myself to stay put and not walk heatedly out the door and decapitate this motherfucker. "By a...thing."

I frown, feeling Connor casually sliding closer to me. I grip the top of the chair so hard that my nails leave imprints in the leather.

"A *thing*?" I question. "What thing?" My blood simmers, picturing vile humans punching her—someone so grotesque she can't even utter his name. "I'm going to strangle him," I sneer. "Then remove his eyeballs, roast them over a fire, and *shove* them back in his mouth."

Loren cringes. "And I thought my mind was a hellhole."

Ryke pushes past the table towards the door.

I walk swiftly after him, securing my purse on my arm like a weapon. *Let's get this motherfucking asshole*—Connor blocks us at the glass door.

He's the most infuriating human.

"*Move*, Richard," I say forcefully.

"Listen to Lo. He said he took care of it."

I cross my arms. "Not to my satisfaction."

"What you find satisfying, darling, is called illegal and a fantasy."

I glare. "My nails *ripping* into his throat won't be a fantasy if you would just move."

"Are you feeding him his eyeballs or ripping out his jugular? You can't have both."

"I can. Watch me—or don't watch me, Richard. I don't care what you do as long as you don't stand in my way."

Ryke takes a step forward. Connor sets a hand on his chest and tells us both, "Let's remove murder from our list of options on how to handle this situation."

We're both angry and upset. Of course we wouldn't *murder* anyone, but we'd cause a shit storm until justice is served. In our circle, Lily is an easy target. She appears small and vulnerable, and I feel like it's partly my role to protect her. Maybe Ryke feels that way too.

And we failed.

Ryke points furiously at the window that overlooks Philadelphia, blinds snapped closed. "They can't fucking *hit* any of us."

"Security has the guy!" Lo shouts. "I told you, it's already goddamn handled!"

Ryke and I exchange a look of surrender, and we ease away from the door. I take a seat beside my sisters while the guys remain standing at the other end.

Connor pockets his cell. "You're charging him?"

Lo's jaw tenses. "With assault."

"And then we burn his balls," I add.

Lo tries hard not to smile. "Unfortunately the best we can hope for is a few weeks in jail."

"It sets a precedent," Connor says. We haven't been able to charge anyone for flour-bombings, and this'll be the first time we can swing an iron gavel. It'll make a difference, even if it's just a small one.

Closer to Lily, I inspect her eye. She drops the ice bag, letting me have a look. It's terrible. Her eyelid even threatens to swell closed.

"I'm going to kill him," I mutter. I can't help it. His hypothetical death makes me feel better.

"If it's any consolation, he didn't *actually* punch me." She squirms in her chair, red flush rising on her neck.

What?

Ryke stiffens. "What the fuck does that mean?"

Lo returns to his seat. "It means someone threw a dildo at her face."

The room falls into a heavy wave of silence for two agonizing seconds. It only breaks when I stand from my chair, and Ryke turns towards the door.

"Heyheyhey!" Lily yells at us, even gripping my wrist to stop me. "Hot-tempered triad, cease!"

I roll my eyes but sit back down.

"We need to start airing more episodes of the fucking docu-series," Ryke says roughly. "It could've prevented this."

We're the producers of *We Are Calloway*.

We control everything. We can frame the conversation how we like.

I remember the headlines after the first episode aired:

DAISY MEADOWS TELLS HER INSPIRING AND
HEARTBREAKING STORY.

She talked about the Paris riot and growing up modeling.

RYKE MEADOWS AND HIS LONELY PAST.

He talked about hiding his familial ties to protect his father's reputation.

LILY & LOREN OPEN UP:
RELATIONSHIPS & SEX ADDICTION.

They discussed, briefly, how they enabled each other as teenagers and fell deeper into their addictions.

CONNOR & ROSE: THE REAL TRUTH BEHIND
PRINCESSES OF PHILLY.

We were able to clear the air about Scott's role during the reality show. In more detail than we *ever* had before.

These were just little pieces of our overall stories, but the truthful narrative has rebuilt our humanity in the eyes of the public. People hesitate to throw vitriol and more people come to our defense, but we're only one episode in. Plenty more will help us. We just have one kink to smooth out before we continue. It's why we've gathered in this office.

To determine whether or not our children will be involved in the docu-series.

< 3 >

Ryke Meadows

"What we decide will inevitably shape the lives of our children. For better or for worse, we can't foresee, but we all have to make choices." Connor leans forward in his leather chair after his ominous fucking declaration.

Somehow, I ended up on one side of the conference table with him and my brother, and Lo sits between us. This is a couple versus couple issue, but we've split up with the girls across from us. Lily between them.

I lean partly on the table, my boot on the seat of a chair. I pick up a tabloid, more of these magazines spread out in front of everyone. Rose just poured them out of her bag as "an example of what we're dealing with"—and no one was surprised that she brought *examples* to a meeting.

I sift through a few and notice Lily and Lo photographed on nearly every fucking one.

LILY'S BABY BUMP! a few falsely say, printed a few months ago. Some aren't horrible or inaccurate.

'I'M STRONGER NOW.' LILY'S UNTOLD STORY OF ADDICTION, FAMILY, AND THE SPOTLIGHT.

I check the date and then slide the magazine over to Daisy.

She peers at the headline with her two sisters.

"That was published yesterday." It's further proof that the docu-series is helping spread truths. Daisy smiles instantly at the sight of a positive Lily article.

Lo rocks in his chair and swivels from side to side. "Here's the thing, we were all able to grow up without the media. *This*"—he gestures to the tabloids—"didn't happen until we were in our twenties."

"I was sixteen," Daisy reminds him.

Lo stops swiveling, locking eyes with my wife, a girl he knew since she was a little fucking kid. "Yeah. You were sixteen. And you were *perfectly* fine before the media came in." Guilt begins to crush his features and his fight against it, brows scrunched, cheekbones like knives.

It fucking kills every part of me.

"Lo," I start, but then Daisy speaks up for herself.

"I wasn't perfect or fine before the media. I was sad all the time… and modeling was terrible. One of my theories has already proven true, so you can't try to change it, Lo."

He stops clenching the armrest of his chair. "What theory?"

"That even if the media never focused on us, I would've still gone to Paris Fashion Week alone. There still would've been a riot. I'd still face the same trauma I do now—but it could've been worse. Because I might've never been friends with Ryke at the time." Her eyes flit to mine, pained at that idea. I feel my chest collapse. Back to Lo, she says, "And if he didn't go to Paris, I might've died that night."

Fuck that scenario.

Rose interjects, "Thank God that didn't happen."

"Let's not give God anyone's credit," Connor adds, not able to say *Ryke's* credit. I roll my eyes.

Lo sits forward, elbows on the tabloids. "You may think I forget about you, Daisy, but I don't—I haven't in a long time. I *remember* how the media harassed you."

"My friends harassed me," she says strongly. "And who knows, maybe they still would have, even without the media spreading rumors. Maybe they would've picked some other reason to come at me. I don't think we should look at my life as a standard for what our children might go through. Mom was oblivious towards my mental health, and it's not like we're going to force our kids to do something they wouldn't."

Lily nods repeatedly, more at peace with her little sister than she's ever been. Years of remorse buried. Daisy even exchanges a smile with Lily. I'm fucking proud of those two.

"Well said," Rose tells Daisy while jotting down *notes* on a legal pad.

Lo notices. "Are you planning an exam after this?"

Rose shoots him an icy glare. "I won't apologize for being organized when our children's lives are at stake."

"For fuck's sake," I mutter, "you and your husband are acting like we're betting against the fucking apocalypse."

"Maybe we are." She scratches at a line with her pen, and I see her scrawling in neat cursive: *Ryke is unconcerned.*

What kind of fucking note is that?

Lo swivels in his chair again. "Like I was saying before—we may have been raised *out* of the spotlight, but our kids will never get the chance at that sort of life. No matter if we continue the docu-series or not, they'll grow up in the public eye."

In a quiet moment, the only sound comes from the air conditioning. I watch my daughter, so fucking little and fragile, sleep contently in Daisy's arms. I hate the idea of taking something from Sulli, but I understood that bringing her into our world meant she'd instantly lose her privacy.

She'll never grow up like every other kid.

Just yesterday Daisy and I packed her stroller in my car, so we could go for a walk in a park. Not even thirty-seconds outside the neighborhood and we were tailed by paparazzi.

Going unnoticed is a battle that has no end, but we still have to decide whether or not to bring our kids on screen. Daisy and I have talked in depth about the consequences and the advantages. And I can admit it: there are too many fucking variables to sort out.

I'm not used to looking at life this way. Trying to predict the best course with the least amount of blowback. That's Connor Cobalt's thing. And maybe I do want his opinion.

No—I know I do.

That's why we're all here. To talk it out.

Hale Co. was the most convenient location. More lawyers are stopping by so we can sign an amendment for the docu-series. An amendment they'll write up. An amendment about our kids. And we don't want strangers in our houses just to sign some papers.

Who do we let in our fucking houses? People we vet for at least a week or two—like the three-person camera crew who films footage for the docu-series. We trust them because we've all personally interviewed them. Lo fucking interrogated them, and they still checked out.

As a safety precaution, we also have security cameras inside all three houses.

I pick up another false tabloid.

'I'M NOT READY FOR THIS' LOREN HALE'S REACTION TO LILY'S BABY BUMP!

I chuck the magazine, and it slides off the table. Truth is, there's a good chance Moffy will grow up and read these headlines about his parents. There's a good chance all of our kids will, and we can't stop that. We can just try to tone down whatever *Celebrity Crush* and the other tabloids want to print.

And we have with *We Are Calloway*.

"So what are you fucking saying?" I ask my brother.

Lo wears this intent, focused look. Like his thoughts have already traveled miles and miles through his head. "Moffy will never know the difference between fame and obscurity. *This* is his normal." He points an accusatory finger at the tabloids. "And if we freak out by every goddamn camera, every tabloid article, then his normal will be full of anxiety and panic. Lily and I—we don't want that for our kid. We want him to be comfortable in public and around paparazzi. We want him to embrace this life because it's the only one he's going to live."

I'd never heard my brother speak this passionately about anything other than Lily. I've never doubted his love for his son, but it fucking clings to the air between all of us right now. And there is no shying away, no hiding, no shame.

Lily raises her hand, still pressing ice to her eye with the other. "What Lo said, and we want Moffy to start getting used to being on television because whether he's in the docu-series or not, they'll most likely show him on entertainment news."

"That's true." Daisy nods. She brushes back her blonde hair before giving me a look like *they make sense.*

Lily and Lo can make all the sense in the world. It doesn't change the fact that there are two certified geniuses at this boardroom table. Two people who will *definitely* weigh in. Sooner rather than later.

Connor picks up his coffee mug. "I understand where you're coming from," he says. *Like fucking clockwork.* "But Rose and I don't feel comfortable making this kind of choice for our children, not when it'll affect the rest of their lives."

"Exactly," Rose says and underlines a few words in her notes.

Daisy's green eyes morph into more tangled confusion, drifting from our baby to our friends and family.

Lo abruptly scoots back from the table, and the look he gives Connor—I've never, in my fucking life, seen Lo cast a scathing glare with that much heat at *him*. I've been the recipient, many fucking times, but never Connor.

He pauses, coffee mug to his lips, and then he gently sets it down without a sip.

"So I'm the shitty father for making choices for my kid?" Lo asks. "Is that it, Connor?"

"I didn't say that," Connor breathes. "You're misinterpreting me."

"Now I'm an idiot?" he retorts with actual malice.

The boardroom layers with thick tension. Connor and Lo almost never argue. My eyes flit to the three girls, who whisper softly to one another and watch on, not knowing what to do.

Connor hides his reaction, blank-faced. "You know I don't think that."

"Do I?" Lo shrugs. "I don't know, Connor."

I wouldn't lie. I used to wish for this. For the day where Lo treated Connor equally like me, but justice doesn't fill me. Justice doesn't inch my lips into a self-satisfied grin. Truth is, I tense and an uncomfortable weight bears heavy on my chest.

Any jealousy I've ever had towards their friendship just fucking vanishes. Right now. I realize how different Connor and Lo's relationship is from my relationship with Lo.

I can fight with Lo.

I can push him and pull him and pick him back up.

Because I'm his *brother*.

Connor can mostly lift him, support him, catch him. He can't kick his ass into gear. I see that now. I see it more than I ever fucking have.

Impassive again, Connor shrouds all emotion, but he's not speaking either. He just stares at Lo. And Lo just *glares* at him. It kills me.

All of this fucking kills me.

Because my brother needs Connor, and whether he admits it or not, Connor needs Lo. I could go on and on. I could chart the reasons why Lo and Connor *just work* as friends. Why Lo loves Connor for who he is: the egotistical narcissist that drives me fucking nuts. Why Connor loves Lo: the alcoholic, the sober man, the sarcastic geek—all of which I proudly call my little brother.

I could go on and fucking on. I could, but I won't. What they've shared throughout *years'* worth of time is evidence enough.

I used to be pissed by the idea of being "bad cop" to Connor's "good cop" routine, but this isn't something I want to change anymore.

I cut in to protect their friendship. So it won't turn into something else.

"Fucking A," I groan. I'm doing something I'm not made to do: resolve lingering tension. "Can't we talk about this without shitting on each other?"

"Depends on Loren," Rose says. "He's usually the one taking the shits." She untwists her lipstick at this. Like she just told everyone the date and time.

I actually almost laugh. Daisy does.

Lo raises his hands, about to clap, but then he pauses. "No, you know what? That doesn't deserve a clap. Tell your husband that he's a dick."

"He's aware." Rose reapplies her lipstick.

"I am many things," Connor agrees. His attention and focus never leaves my brother. "But I'm not saying your decision makes you a bad father. I've never thought that, not behind your back, and if I planned to say it to your face, I'd be more direct."

"Then be painfully direct with me right now," Lo says. "No bullshit. I can take it."

Connor licks his lips. "You and I couldn't be more different, and that's partly why I love you—but the way I raise my children will be *vastly* different to the way that you raise yours. It doesn't make you less than me, and it doesn't make your children inferior to mine."

Lo is quiet as he ingests this.

Lily raises her hand again. "But you're a genius and possibly a telepath. Maybe even psychic, but that's still to be confirmed…" Her voice dies off as Connor's antipathy fills his blue eyes, letting all of us see. She lifts her hands in defense. "I mean, you're definitely *not* magical. Those things…don't…exist?" Lily can barely utter that last fucking sentence.

"Hey," I interject. *This is fucking ridiculous.* "He's a genius on paper but that doesn't mean his ideas are the right ones." Connor and I spent nearly all last year agreeing on our differences, and as we raise our kids different ways, I never realized how hard this might be for Lo and Lily who idolize Connor and his wisdom like he shits gold.

They only want the best for their son. They'd do literally anything for Moffy.

"But Connor always makes the right choices," Lily replies softly. *Fuck.*

"Not always," Connor admits.

Rose's expression travels from shock to a full-on fucking grin. We're all probably documenting this moment as a historic one: the day Connor Cobalt admits he's not always right.

"You're admitting this?" I ask. "Fucking really?" *Maybe he's changed.*

Unperturbed, Connor sips his coffee casually. As if the admission is commonplace. My smile fades at the sight of his grin—for fuck's sake.

"I'm admitting that on rare occasions I've picked a choice with too much risk and not enough reward. I wouldn't consider it the wrong one, just not the one with the highest benefit."

I shake my head a few times. He's still the same Connor Cobalt, but he's more tolerable for me. I don't know if it's because I've changed to fucking like him. Or if we've both just grown to meet in the middle.

Lo rubs the back of his neck, less on the offensive. "So you're going to let your three-year-old, who can't even choose matching clothes, decide her position in the media?"

Rose caps her lipstick like she's sheathing a fucking sword. "Jane has style…" She rolls her eyes and huffs. "It might be unconventional but it's hers." Rose stuffs the lipstick in her purse. "And we're not letting her make the choice until she's at least six. Even then, if she says yes, she won't be allowed to have speaking roles on the show. We'll keep letting her choose as she grows older, and if she wants more involvement in the show, then she'll get more involvement."

Lily thuds her forehead to the table and groans with Daisy.

"What's the fucking problem?" I look between them. I also notice the expression in my brother's eyes. The one that says: *I'm two seconds from sharing Lily's chair.* Just so he can hold her.

"I'm confused," Lily mumbles into the table, adjusting the ice so her face is smashed against it. She's so fucking weird.

Then again, so is Connor. So is Rose.

Everyone is a little bit fucking weird.

Daisy presses a kiss to Sulli's nose. "I'm scared we'll make the wrong choice."

We won't.

I grew up with a father I saw only on Mondays. I grew up with a mom who cared about me, but not enough and not in the way that I fucking needed. The fact that we love our daughter to put her before our reputations—that's a better start than I had. That's *right*.

I don't have to say this though.

Rose snaps her fingers, gaining her sisters' attention.

Lily peels her face off the ice and table.

"I need you two to know something. The six of us"—Rose draws a circle in the air—"we're all perceived differently in the media. We're all different people. I never thought you two would follow me. Admirable, yes. Loyal, of course. I love you both. *I'd die for you*," Rose emphasizes like a promise. "But don't choose my path because you think I'm smarter. No one knows your lives better than you do. You don't need Connor or me to tell you which direction to move, but I'll always help you stand."

Lily ponders this with more hope in her eyes. "We're followed by paparazzi more than you and Connor." Lily and Lo are the most famous, and while Connor and Rose can give their kids more of a choice, Moffy is going to be in every fucking tabloid, probably every week.

Connor chimes in, "It makes sense that you'd want Maximoff to be comfortable with the media, and if it's any consolation, I think Jane will want to be on camera with him."

Lo makes an effort to relax his gaze towards Connor. It's still daggered as fuck, but if I can see Lo trying, then so can Connor Cobalt.

Connor smiles into his next sip of coffee. "If you all didn't catch that, I agree with Rose. Just in case you needed another genius to weigh in."

Lo smirks.

"Yeah, we fucking didn't, Cobalt," I snap.

Connor raises his mug to me.

I flip him off.

Rose clears her throat at Daisy, my wife staring far past the table, almost in a trance. As Rose snaps her fingers at her sister, Daisy shakes out of the stupor. "What...?"

"What are you thinking?" Rose wonders.

Daisy slowly lifts her gaze to mine. "What if they objectify her like they objectified me, just because she's my daughter?"

My muscles tighten, jaw hardening. I was there. I was there when she tried to reclaim her body. So she could feel like her arms and her legs and her fucking hips belonged to *her* first, not second.

It tears me apart imagining Sullivan losing this piece of innocence. I wished, every fucking day, that I could've changed that for Daisy. That I could've done something more instead of just being there. Even if that might've been enough at the time.

"I was the model," Daisy says to me. "I gave them permission to photograph me, and maybe they'll think the same about her, just because she's our…" She lets out a strained breath, staring up at the ceiling like it'll give her the answer she wants.

"Hey, sweetheart." I raise my brows at her. "We can fucking protect her from that. You know how we start?"

She thinks. She's quiet. And then she nods more assuredly. "Yeah, I do. We don't let her be photographed. We don't let her be in the docuseries. It's her body, her image, and I'm not letting them latch onto her like she's a *thing* and not a person. I can't."

"We can't," I say. "I'm with you on this, Calloway." *I'm always fucking with you.* Right now, I can't imagine someone sexualizing Sulli. She's just a baby. And I'm going to have an even harder time imagining that nightmare as she gets older. As a pre-teen—*no.* It's fucking sick. It's all fucking sick.

And I don't think Janie will have the same issue. The Cobalts have filled the role of American royalty. Elegant. Classy. Janie has mostly been photographed for articles about fashion, not anything about *will she model?*

Since Scott Van Wright went to jail, Rose and Connor's sex tapes have also been synonymous with *breach of consent.* People fixate on Calloway Couture and Cobalt Inc. events and what Rose is wearing on Instagram. Not sex.

Lo spins around in his chair, his spirits higher. "And that's why I'm glad I don't have a girl."

Will she be a future sex addict? I hear the fucking condemnation.

Lily's nose crinkles. "You were the one who wanted a girl!"

"Not anymore, love. People can change their minds. I just changed mine."

I slow clap.

Connor joins in.

Lo claps for himself and flashes his usual half-smile.

Rose stands, palms on the table. "So it's set then?" she asks. That's when I notice the hoard of lawyers outside the office, waiting by the copy machine with manila folders in hand.

We all begin to nod, falling into silent agreement. Our children will be raised differently, and that's alright. I sense our strength together, our support for each other's choices.

Today, I've fallen in deeper love with these people.

No matter which direction we fucking move, we'll all still be there.

[4]

Connor Cobalt

I wait outside Jane's bedroom door with my arm propped against the wall. From inside, dishware clinks. Gently, I push the door further open, granting me a better view.

Velveteen pale pink chairs surround a tiny round table, teacups and saucers spread over floral placemats. My three-year-old daughter nimbly skips around her guests, most of which are *inanimate*. Her favorite: a stuffed lion. Seated in the most robust and ornate chair of all six.

I never played pretend like this.

Not as a child.

Never as an adult.

Yet, I feel my lips rise.

Jane pours what looks like milk in a teacup. On the other side, her squirmy eleven-month-old twin brothers babble inarticulately, but they seem to play along. Inspecting their saucers and placemats with curious yellow-green eyes.

Hair in a sleek pony, Rose bends between both boys and fills a sugar bowl with Cheerios. Fire never extinguishes from her gaze.

My grin expands tenfold.

Beckett tugs on his mother's black dress, one that just barely hides her collarbone, one that hugs her frame perfectly, like a dust jacket fit on a newly printed hardback.

Beckett asks her a question that neither of us would be able to piece apart, but Rose regards him with understanding.

"Of course. I'll take up your requests with the hostess." She kisses the top of his head, his brown hair much darker and curlier than Charlie's.

Then Rose brushes her hands together and places them on her hips, eyeing the state of the table. Every place setting is symmetrical and identical to the next.

Her gaze suddenly lifts to mine.

I don't move. I don't cower. As her glare fastens onto mine, I only grin wider. *Hello, Rose.*

Go to hell, Richard, her eyes say.

Shoulders strict and chin raised, she marches around our child's table. Even with her heels soundless on the carpet, I can still feel the hostility with each purposeful step.

She stops, grips the door like a weapon, and drills the *hottest* and *coldest* glare into me. Rose Calloway Cobalt has always been a series of contradictions.

I adore this one just as much as every other. "Rose," I say smoothly.

She bypasses the perfunctory *Richard* and snaps, "You were given *one* direction and you failed." She growls at the sight of my burgeoning grin. "I said *you failed*, Richard. Be angry."

"I'm amused," I say in a hushed voice so Jane can't hear. "And a smile usually accompanies amusement, not anger."

She huffs, her shoulders falling and eyes roaming my white button-down and composure. "Then you're amused at your daughter's loss. She wanted to surprise you with the tea party, but you've decided to go rogue and *spy* on us." Rose lets go of the door, just to cross her arms. "I'd punish you for this."

"You'd punish *me*?" I arch a brow. "Have you been reading Coballoway fan fiction?"

She rolls her eyes dramatically. Lily sent us links to fan fiction based off of *Princesses of Philly*. Willow first sent them to Daisy, then Daisy sent them to Lily, and Lily sent them to everyone.

I skimmed some, and I completely stopped reading when I crossed the title ROYAL LOVE: SCOTT VAN WRIGHT & ROSE VAN WRIGHT. In the writer's defense, this was published online long before Scott publically went to jail.

Regardless, anytime you attach "Van Wright" to my wife, it instantly becomes my least favorite fiction.

"You don't think I can punish you?" Rose burns hot and leans close, just to say with a great deal of seriousness, "I'd cut off your tongue with a dull serrated knife, and I'd finish you off in a rusty guillotine." She lifts her manicured nail at my eye. "Don't fuck with me or my babies—"

"*Our* babies," I correct her.

She skims me head-to-toe, her disdain only present to mask her love. I feel it in every glare. "I can't believe I allowed my DNA to mix with yours and create *multiple* little monsters. What was I thinking?"

Standing tall above her, I reach out, my hand curving around the crook of her waist. She relaxes at my touch, and her chest collapses. I draw Rose closer, until her legs brush my legs. In a whisper, I say, "You were thinking 'I'm undeniably, indisputably in love with the most *brilliant* and the most handsome man on Ear—"

Rose puts her palm over my lips. "I hate you." She feels my grin grow beneath her hand and she growls, dropping it.

"You love me." I study her full lips but mostly the blaze in her eyes. I'm about to express just how much I reciprocate those feelings, but then a toddler abruptly cuts off our exchange.

"Daddy? Is that you?" Jane asks. I have a major height advantage over Rose, but I angle myself out of Jane's view. In a quick second, I catch sight of her teal tutu behind Rose's slender legs, and then Rose slams the door in my face.

"He's still waiting for you," Rose tells our daughter, her voice clear through the wood. "You can introduce him. Or you can exile him from the tea party."

My lips curve up again. *You would love that option; wouldn't you, Rose?*

Jane gasps. "I can't exile, Daddy."

Did you hear that, Rose? I picture her torrid glare and the roll of her eyes.

"What about temporary banishment?" she asks Jane.

"No banishment." At three, her words are incredibly easier to understand compared to Jane at two or one, but it's not as though she enunciates "banishment" perfectly. It's partially garbled, and she only knows the word because we've used it before, just like *exile*.

Jane also adds, "Daddy's never been to a tea party."

Never one with *toys* as the guests, but Rose doesn't correct her and neither would I.

"Then you better hurry and introduce him. Even if Daddy says he'll wait forever for you, no one has the ability to stand in a hallway for eternity." Her voice is frost, but every syllable heats my body.

"Introdoozing Daddy!" she announces. "Come in, Daddy!"

I open the door with the raise of my brows, mortaring on surprise like a mask I've worn before. I sweep her pale pink room, her toddler bed, armoire and regal chandelier before landing on the tea party arrangement and her eager blue eyes.

"Tu es de toute beauté, mon cœur." *Such beauty, my heart.*

Jane's face lights, and she touches her black cat-ear headband, ensuring that it hasn't fallen. Then without pause, she grabs hold of my hand and leads me further inside. With a partial smile peeking, Rose walks to her chair beside Beckett.

She catches me staring and reverts to a glare. Rose mouths, *rusty guillotine* and mimes slashing my neck. Then she triumphantly takes a seat, crossing her ankles.

I say hushed to Rose, "I'd believe your hyperboles more if they didn't involve eighteenth-century machinery."

Rose unties her hair and combs her fingers through the strands. "Guillotines were still used *long* after the French Revolution."

She's not wrong.

Jane stops me by two empty chairs and looks up with bold blue eyes. "What's a googoniny?"

Rose tries hard not to laugh, hand pressed to her mouth, but she ends up snorting.

I can't hide my smile. "Googoniny isn't a word." What I'm about to say next would make some parents balk or flame red. "It's *guillotine*, and it's a device used for executions."

She has no clue what "execution" means, and before she asks, I take a seat in one of the free chairs.

"No!" she yells and grips my arm so I stand.

Rose is smitten at my misstep.

Matter-of-factly, Jane says, "That's Sadie's chair."

I look to Rose. "You knew this seat was taken?"

"Yes." She collects her hair on one shoulder, and I eye the base of her neck. Rose reaches over and spoons Cheerios onto Charlie and Beckett's saucers.

I squat down to Jane's height. "Sadie isn't here."

Jane puts her finger to my lips. "Uh-uh. Sadie is coming back!"

I collect her hand. "Not anytime soon, honey." I don't understand her loss. I can't comprehend it, no matter how hard I try or how many ways I explain to her *logically* why Sadie can't return. My cat nearly scratched Jane's face, too unpredictable and aggressive. What if she scratched her eye?

I won't take that risk.

I raised Sadie as a kitten, but my attachment to her is severely *less* than my attachment to these people in this very room. Call me callous. Call me unfeeling. Call me inhuman, but I raised her to be independent, to survive on her own. And I've given her a home with my therapist—this shouldn't even be an argument anymore.

Jane refuses to hear me. "She's coming back. That's her seat." She jabs her little finger at the seat. She even goes further to place her *Kitty Cats* coloring book on top, so I can't sit there. I hear her mutter, *she's coming back* once more.

I stand and wonder when a toddler will forget about a cat. If she ever will. I look to Rose, and her eyes have significantly softened. She mouths, *play along*.

I nod in agreement. We're still hoping she'll drop all talk about Sadie.

Jane tugs the heavy chair, trying to pull mine out. I help her and then sit down. All six chairs are now occupied, so I ask Jane, "Where are you sitting?"

"Imsevin!" she slurs together. I take it to mean *I'm serving*. She picks up her teapot and pours milk to the very brim of my teacup.

I don't feel silly or awkward. I never have.

I'm entertained by my daughter's delight.

When she finishes pouring, I say, "Merci." *Thank you.* I take a sip. "Mmmm. Délicieux." *Delicious.*

She smiles wider, understanding French since Rose and I make an effort to use it around our children. Then she serves her brothers. We both study Jane. We wait for her to be immersed in something else, and then—at perfect, equal timing—we train our gazes to one another.

Rose scoots her chair closer to the table, nearer to me, before whispering, "Sadie was her first friend."

I try to empathize, but I'm empty. "Who was your first friend? Besides your sisters."

Rose pretends to sip tea from an empty cup. "In preschool," she whispers, "I had a friend named Amy. She moved to Maryland just before first grade. I was *devastated*." She emphasizes the word, as though losing a friend at six is synonymous with an Armageddon.

"Hmm," I muse.

"Hmm?" Rose snaps. "What is *hmm*?"

"It's an onomatopoeia."

Rose sets her teacup down so hard, it nearly *cracks*.

"Careful, darling."

"No one invited your smartass comments to the tea party. And *hmm* isn't an onomatopoeia. Onomatopoeias have to symbolize something. Like *oink* is referencing a cow. *Hmm* means *nothing*."

"If it annoys you this much, it clearly means something."

Rose growls. "You're infuriating."

"Because I'm right, and you hate when I'm right."

Leaning even further forward, she whispers heatedly, "Because you twist things until you're right, which is not so much a gift as it is a character ink blot." She flicks invisible dust particles at me.

I adore Rose, so much so that I lean nearer too. "I think the word you're looking for is *stain*."

Jane gasps, and our heads quickly turn to our daughter. She fumbles with her teapot. Rose, sitting closer, catches the lid before it thuds to the carpet.

"Gently," Rose coaches. Her tone is still icy, but Jane doesn't regard her mother as intimidating or harsh.

Most mornings, Jane will crawl onto Rose's lap and rest her head against her mother's collar. Rose will stroke Jane's hair, and they'll flip through a Vogue magazine together. Jane likes picking out her favorite editorial pictures, and Rose will later cut them out and paste them in a scrapbook.

When Rose focuses back on me, I say quietly, "She should be over Sadie by now."

Rose narrows her eyes. "Have *you* ever lost something you've loved?"

I've lost my mother, but I didn't love Katarina Cobalt the conventional way that a son loves a mother. I've never *loved* anything as a child except my own successes. I was told not to. Rose knows this.

All I say is, "We can't bring back Sadie because a toddler demands it."

"I know," Rose agrees, "but we can't be callous about it either."

I tilt my head. "What you call *callous* I call *realistic*."

"Children aren't realistic."

"I was."

Rose asks pointedly, "And how did that work out for you?"

I set my elbow on the table. "Seeing as how I'm smarter than ninety-nine-point-nine percent of the population, I'd say it went well."

Rose raises her hand at my face. "Sideline your ego, Richard." Her gaze flits to our sons and then Jane, all three distracted by the tea party. Jane mutters softly while serving her stuffed lion. She pats his head.

"You don't sideline the most valuable player, Rose."

"You do when they award *themselves* the title of MVP."

"It's not my fault I'm the most adept at determining who should be awarded what." Before she starts referencing guillotines again, I add, "You could've been saved from feeling *devastated*. It wasn't necessary, and it only hurt you."

Rose eyes me head-to-waist since I'm partially blocked by the table. "What's the tradeoff, Connor? Not having a friend?"

"You still could've had Amy as a friend. What I'm saying is that there wasn't a need to be that invested in someone who you knew might leave."

"I was a *child*. I thought she'd stay around forever."

"Then that was your first mistake." I pick up my empty teacup and pretend to take a sip.

She pretends to take another one out of hers, eyes drilling into me. Rose presses her lips together like she's smoothing out her lipstick, and then she says, "You can't bubble wrap her emotions, Connor."

I'm not advocating to strip away their childhood the way that my mother did to me. They can fantasize about Santa Claus and the Easter Bunny. I'm even willing to play tea party with an imaginary cat and a stuffed animal.

"It's not bubble wrap," I reply. "It's just self-appreciation to the highest degree. To feel *so* important that no one comes before you, not a friendship, not a thing, nothing that could make you feel pity, rejection, remorse or *devastation*."

"No." Rose places her elbows on the table, combating me. "She will feel those things because she will *love* more than just herself. And she'll be better than you were."

I was well off, but Rose values love above all else. I never did until I fell in love with her. I know why I want to save Jane from this.

Selfishly, I don't want to see our daughter dig through these emotions, not ones that I could've helped her avoid. "You want me to watch a trainwreck?" I ask Rose.

"Multiple trainwrecks," Rose says strongly. "And when she needs you to pull her out of the wreckage—"

"I'll be there." *Remember love?* I have to remind myself of *this* feeling that overcomes me, swelling my entire chest. I watch Jane kiss her lion on the cheek.

I have to remind myself that they need love as much as I do.

Remember love.

Charlie accidentally smacks his saucer of Cheerios, flipping it over. The cereal scatters the rug, and Charlie bursts into tears, crying at the top of his lungs.

Rose and I are about to stand to console our son, but we stop almost instantly. Beckett has dropped off his chair to help collect the dry cereal. And Jane sets down her teapot in haste.

"Charlie?" Her face is full of worry. "Don't cry, Charlie." She wipes her brother's tears with her hand and then joins Beckett in picking up the Cheerios.

Rose and I pull our gazes off our young children and onto each other, face-to-face, across the tiny table. I extend my hand and tenderly clasp hers, my thumb skimming her knuckles back-and-forth. I see their love for one another, and I wouldn't want anything less.

She nods to me, reading my gaze well enough, and then she drifts into deep thought. I wish I could hear the chatter inside her head.

After a long moment, I whisper, "What are you thinking?"

"That I'd love to have another little monster with you." She rolls her eyes at herself, but my chest has already risen. "I'm insane for wanting more stress."

"More happiness," I amend.

"More children screaming."

"More children laughing."

She thinks for another second. "How can I love it all equally?" she wonders. "The *vomit* and the dirty diapers and the ridiculous things they do that end up being endearing and cute." She watches Charlie wipe away his tears with a tiny fist while Beckett and Jane fill his saucer with cereal. "I don't even think I'd want only the good moments without the horrible ones. I'd ask for it all *again*." Rose says *again* like pregnancy is tantamount to torture.

If she truly believed this—if she truly *felt* this—I'd never want her to go through it *again*. Rose's health and happiness might as well be mine.

"You love it all equally because you're entirely and unequivocally in love with them. Love isn't a weakness," I say with complete certainty.

She smiles a very rare smile, but it lasts shorter than I'd like. "It's not just about wanting a sister for Jane. Though I want another girl…sooner or later." She glows at the word *later* like she hopes for that outcome.

Once she has another girl, we've agreed to stop having children. And she clearly wants more.

"Do you have any reservations?" I ask, my hand tightening around hers. I haven't broached the topic of having more children. I never do after Rose gives birth. It's her body, her physical timeline, and I'll always be respectful of her wants and needs.

"It's been almost a year since the twins," she says. "I could probably wait another year, but I've recovered better than I thought..." Her gaze drifts to Jane who wiggles in her teal tutu, her cat headband sliding back. "Are you holding your bladder?"

Jane shakes her head and tries to fix her headband. I spot her guilt and the fib in her eyes.

So does her mother. Rose points at the bathroom. "Go now."

"I can't leave, Mommy!" she whines. "I'm hosing." She means *hosting*. My grin broadens.

Rose rotates more to face Jane. "Hostesses are allowed to excuse themselves to use the toilet, just like *every* other person. If anyone— including Mr. Lion—gives you heat about it, Mommy will disembowel them."

"What's disem-em..." Jane loses track of her thoughts, clutching her tutu, wiggling more.

"Go." Rose motions to the nearby door, right beside a white bookshelf.

Jane hurries off and closes the door behind her.

Rose captivates me to the point where she has all of my attention. My eyes, my mind, my heart.

She catches me staring and snaps, "What?" Her cheeks flush. "Stop looking at me like that, Richard."

"Je t'aime." *I love you.* I stand, walk around the table, and near my wife. Towering above her, I run my hand across the base of her neck, up to her hair.

A shallow breath expels from her lips, her head near my crotch and eyes at my belt. She strains her neck to look up at me. "I still want to continue working during every pregnancy," Rose reminds me.

I expected no less. We both enjoy our current schedule, and it won't shift.

Mondays: I'm at the Cobalt Inc. offices in Philadelphia. Rose works at home and watches our children.

Tuesdays: Rose is at the Hale Co. offices or her boutique in downtown Philadelphia. I work at home and watch our children.

Wednesdays: we both work at home together.

Thursdays: a repeat of Monday

Fridays: a repeat of Tuesday.

Eventually we'll need at least one more set of trusting hands when we both can't be home. We're both in agreement on hiring a nanny in the future.

Beckett and Charlie babble to one another, filling the silence, and my thumb skims Rose's bottom lip.

I'd take her in the next five minutes, if I could. I'd push her up against our bed and tie her hands behind her back. Spread her legs open. Fit my cock deep inside my wife, fuck her hard until she dizzied.

I wear my desire in my eyes.

She crosses her legs now. "When you were a teenager, did you ever fantasize about me?" Her neck reddens, not in embarrassment but longing.

"Sexually?" I ask.

She nods.

Just as I'm about to answer, the toilet flushes and Jane calls, "Daddy, I can't reach the sink!"

Rose swats my hand away from her face, about to rise to find the missing stepstool.

"I'll take care of her." I can just lift Jane up to the sink. Rose stays seated while I walk to the bathroom. Hand on the knob, I pause and look to Rose. "We'll continue this later, darling."

She nods tersely, but I'm not sure if she'll ask that same question again. I can't promise that I'll bring it up soon, but we have years. Many, *many* years together.

{ 5 }

August 2018
THE GOLF CLUB
South Hampton, New York

LOREN HALE

By the time we reach the seventh hole at the charity golf tournament, Maximoff is done. Boredom in his forest-green eyes, he rests his cheek against the golf cart seat, nearly slumped over.

"Same," I tell him, picking out a club from my bag, my enthusiasm worn-out.

It's not like I had much at the start.

Not like Connor, who wagered a bet with my older brother before teeing off the first hole.Not like Ryke who curses beneath his breath with each stroke, pointing his titanium driver at Connor every time our friend outperforms him.

Which is 7 times out of 10.

But no one should confuse my lack of enthusiasm for apathy.

I know it'd be easy to—because in my early twenties, my angst could fill a goddamn ocean and float a shitty fleet of naval ships—but now, things are different.

I'm different. For better or for worse.

And one look at my three-year-old son—his soft cheek on the white seat, wearing tiny orange Vans, his dark brown hair combed neatly, his little legs hanging pitifully and lips puckered in a childlike pout—it's all enough.

Regardless of what else follows.

I lean my shoulder on the golf cart and nudge his foot with my driver. Moffy lifts his head up to me.

I gape, widening my eyes. "He's alive. Jesus Christ."

His big woeful eyes might as well say, *I'm miserable, Daddy*. I thought only a sad Lily could crush my black heart, but seeing my son upset and downcast nearly obliterates it.

I try to remember that he's a three-year-old. Lily and I put cooked carrots in front of him, and he acted like we served him pig intestines. One boring day isn't the end of the world, but there's this part of me—this place belonging to my childhood with Lily—that *screams* to give this kid better than boring, better than unhappy. Better than lonely.

Better than what we had.

I take a seat beside him. He doesn't stir, but I hear his heavy sigh. I prop my foot on the golf cart dash and extend my arm across the back of the seat. "Golf isn't my favorite thing either."

Moffy mumbles, "Then why are we here?"

He asks a lot of questions, and I never thought I'd have to explain the world to anyone. Especially a toddler who digests my words like they're Holy Scripture. And he has no comprehension of sarcasm.

Through the windshield, I watch Ryke tee off first. He concentrates on his swing, and Connor stands nearby just to give him a hard time. Ryke flips him off, but most of the other teams are too far ahead of us

RITCHIE

to see. Only event photographers straggle behind, and Ryke couldn't care less if they capture him giving Connor the middle finger.

It's not like he hasn't done it before.

Gathering my thoughts, I focus back on Moffy. "We're here because we're *really* lucky—you, me, your mommy, your aunts and uncles—we all have a lot of toys and nice things, and we take time to give back." We could just write a check and not come, but showing up to an event promotes the charity too, so we do both. "Do you want to help kids who might be sick or who don't have as many toys as you?"

Moffy nods almost instantly, faster than I would have as a kid. He straightens up, the steering wheel too high and far away from his small body. He fiddles with his shoelaces. "Is-is that…why the bug people follow us? Because we have lots of toys?"

Bug people.

My stomach knots.

Bug people—it's what Jane and Moffy have started calling paparazzi, who hide behind cameras. They see the fat lenses and blinding flashes as an appendage like a nose or a mouth, unable to spot an actual face.

Connor said it was ironic. They dehumanize us, and our children are beginning to dehumanize them.

Moffy waits for my answer.

I'm stumped for a second. I've never considered myself good with kids. I never aspired to be a father—I never aspired to be much of anything. But I've tried.

I've tried damned hard to be a decent dad. No. A *great* dad. Because my kid deserves nothing less than that.

I can't tell a toddler the truth: *hey, little man, we're famous because Mommy is an heiress to a soda empire and someone told the press about her sex addiction. And it gets worse. That "someone" happens to be your uncle's mother. Surprise.*

I drop my arm onto his shoulders. "You know why they follow us?" My voice is edged like usual. I can't help that, but he listens intently, waiting. And I say, "Because they *love* you and they love your cousins and your mommy." Every goddamn word hurts.

The paparazzi tormented Daisy, caused Lily to fear leaving her house, and profited off of more false stories than true ones. But I can't have my kid soulfully, gut-wrenchingly *hating* something that I know will always be there. If he believes they do what they do out of love, then maybe he won't grow up bitter and resentful.

Usually Maximoff is loud spoken, but he mumbles under his breath again, "I wish Janie was here."

This was a gentleman's golf tournament, which meant that we couldn't bring any of the girls, not even Connor's daughter. No one was more irate than Ryke and Rose when they heard the gender stipulation. I think my left ear is still blown out from their volcanic fits of rage.

Together, with more time, I actually believe they could've changed the event rules. Those two people are damn impressive.

In a few years, I might tell my son the truth here: *hey, bud, girls weren't allowed because some white-collared prick said so.*

Right now, all I say is, "Me too, bud." I scan the flat greenery, a memory sparking and inching my lips higher. I nudge his arm with mine. "You know me and Mommy used to tag along on golf trips with our dads?"

He perks up. "Really?"

"Really. We were only a little older than you." *Christ, how young we were.* The long-ago memory with Lily gives me an idea. "Come here." I scoop Maximoff in my arms and then set him on the grass. I have to retie his shoes since he undid the laces.

Then I sift in my golf bag for another club. I find a red mini-putter for toddlers. I've let him putt all of my balls, but we're not close to the hole yet. I switch my driver with a much shorter club and then lead Moffy away from the golf cart, positioning him on the trimmed green.

"Alright, little man, that right there is your light saber." I kneel in front of my son, still taller but at a much better height for him. "You hold it like this." I grip the club like a fucking sword. "Maximoff Hale, do you want to be a Jedi Knight?"

"Yeah!" A smile envelops his face. He bounces and tries to whack my club with his, his laughter filling me whole. He's seen enough *Star Wars* cartoons to know about Jedi Knights and light sabers.

I pretend to struggle. "Jesus Christ, he's going to disarm me. Storm Troopers?!" I check over my shoulder, both Connor and Ryke watching us. "Storm Troopers," I pant like I've been running ten miles. "We've got a relentless Jedi. You better attack him." I wipe nonexistent sweat off my forehead as Moffy clanks his club against mine.

Connor grins, and Ryke cups his hands to his mouth, calling out, "Get him, Moffy!"

What a goddamn brother.

I love that guy.

Not long after, Moffy pokes me in the chest with his plastic club, and I fall off my knees to my back.

"He got me," I pant. "He got me."

Moffy jumps on my stomach, and I actually wince for real. He shouts, "Jedi Knights always win!"

I prop myself on my elbows and give him a look. "How'd you get so smart?"

"Mommy," he says proudly.

I laugh once into a smile, choked up for a second. Just overwhelmed by my love for Lily, and she's not even here.

I hold out my fist, and Moffy bumps my knuckles with his. Then I pick him up as I stand and toss him over my shoulder. Moffy giggles, and I slide him down so he's perched on my waist. Just as I carry my son to my brother, my phone rings.

I set Moffy on his feet and check my phone, stepping back. I let my cell ring to voicemail.

Ryke shakes tees out of a bag. "Want to help me put a fucking ball on the tee, little guy?"

Moffy jumps towards him and nods wildly. When Ryke crouches, he favors his right knee. A shadow of a grimace quickly passes through his hard features. He can walk without crutches, without a limp even, but sometimes pain flares in his eyes.

I don't even know the amount that stayed with him after his rock climbing accident last year. I just know that I'm selfishly glad to have my brother back—the one who wakes early every single day to run. The one who kicks his own ass as hard as he kicks mine.

The world would be a worse fucking place without that guy.

I return to my phone to check the missed caller and a new text message. Irritated lines crease my forehead. *Jesus Christ.*

Connor approaches me. "Work?"

"You mean the inner circle of hell? Yeah, that one." Daniel Perth, one of the Hale Co. board members, just texted: had a meeting with advertisers for the new organic baby shampoo. Went well. I'll send you notes.

He's not even a part of the management team. It's not his job or any of the goddamn board's to take this kind of meeting.

Connor casually fixes his already *perfect* wavy brown hair. "Is it the people or the actual job?" If he's worried about me and the stress of corporate life, he doesn't show it.

"It's always the people." I shake my head to myself.

Halway Comics is full of creative types. I work with artists and writers to fulfill their dreams of seeing their comics in print. But at Hale Co., everyone is climbing on top of each other to reach some imaginary trophy.

"I'm not against playing dirty, but the shit that the board pulls on me is petty. Like 'oh you missed that important, significant meeting? Wasn't Clarissa supposed to tell you about it?' as if the goddamn PR *intern* is supposed to keep me in the loop."

I stop myself from kicking up a chunk of the green. Chances are, Moffy will copy me.

I get what's going on at Hale Co. When my father stepped down as CEO, the board members saw me, the replacement, as a symbolic figurehead.

They didn't think I'd actually make critical decisions. They didn't think I'd actually do much of anything. Initially, they wanted to use my relationship with Rose—only to put her name on a baby clothing line. Then they wanted me to just stand there, to look pretty and say *I'm Loren Hale*. Smile. Click flash of a camera.

The minute I chose this path, I promised myself to be better than that, but I had no idea how hard they'd make it. And how much I have to remind myself not to give the fuck up—because it'd be so easy to just let them run things for me.

Sometimes I have sway, but not for things that impact the company. I'm just one voice, and they don't treat me like the voice that's running the brand.

"The board will let you in," Connor assures me, "it'll just take time."

"Like it took you so much time, love?" I flash him a half-smile.

One afternoon, Connor let me inside his boardroom while I waited for him. Cobalt Inc. owns a handful of subsidiaries, including a company that produces paints and crayons. That day, a board member joked about naming a burnt-red color *dirty whore*, and with one word—one goddamn word—Connor had the board member exiting, head hung in shame.

"Leave," he said.

That's all it took.

I've been CEO of Hale Co. for only three years. He's been the CEO of Cobalt Inc. for five, but he was respected the minute he was given the title.

I saw it.

Connor switches his club to his left hand. "I never said we're the same. It'll take *you* more time, but it never would've taken me this long."

"Of course not." I don't take the jab to heart. It's true. I rub the back of my neck and sigh heavily. "Things are so much easier for you."

I expect him to agree, but he wears this expression like I'm stepping over facts.

"I spent years preparing to take over my mother's company. It's what I *aspired* to do. I also make difficult things look easy. No one can do what I do, and it's not a fault of your own but just a testament to how skilled I am." *There's my conceited friend.* "Just so you know, when I was interim CEO, the board treated me like a child sitting at the adult table. I had to win them over too."

I wonder how he sees me.

He spent his whole life wanting to be the head of a corporation. I had no aspirations. In fact, I rejected the idea over and over. At the last minute, I fought for the position, but I had practically no competition. I'm still trying to earn my place, and I'm realizing that maybe I should have to. It's only right.

Connor taught me a lot. I'd tell him as much, but he definitely already knows.

I skim his wavy hair, still perfectly styled, and his collared shirt, all six-foot-four of him standing straight and confident. I nod, more to myself. "In short, Connor Cobalt is a god. Don't touch him."

"You can touch me, darling."

I suck in a breath. "Don't give me ideas, love. I always aim to please."

"Something we share." He grins a billion-dollar grin.

I smile with him as we head back to my brother and son. I pocket my phone, under the new belief that respect may take years, but it's years' worth fighting.

< 6 >

September 2018
LUCKY'S DINER
Philadelphia

Daisy Meadows

"Send me the link." I scrape the mustard off the top of my hamburger bun. I forgot to ask for *no mustard*, but I easily carve out a chunk of the bread.

Daisy Petunia Meadows: resident condiment banisher. Need your mustard gone? Trying to ward away that pesky horseradish sauce you just can't stand? Call Daisy. She has you covered.

I smile and adjust my earbuds. I currently sit at a secluded booth in Lucky's Diner. My laptop is wedged between the napkin dispenser and mini condiment holder. I already told Willow on Skype that she's cuddling with the ketchup and mayo.

"Okay, hold on a sec," she says. "I'll send it to you and then we can analyze." In the Skype window, Willow leans closer, her finger dancing across her own keyboard. An *X-Men: Apocalypse* poster is taped to the wall behind her.

She's in her dorm room, all the way in London.

I never questioned Willow's decision to go to college out of the country. I never stopped her or convinced her to stay. I know what's best for my best friend is what she wants, and she wanted this.

Even so, Ryke and I had a pretty deep conversation about my muddled feelings after we all said our goodbyes at the airport. It took me a minute or two, but I was able to explain them well enough.

Ryke: *She's going to come back, Dais.*

Me: *Yeah but I was her best friend, and in a year or two, I might not be anymore. And it's so stupid because people make friends all the time, but it still feels like I'm losing something.*

Ryke: *She probably will make other friends, but you're not losing anything when that fucking happens. You still have a friend.*

He was right.

She'll still *always* be my friend. No matter what happens in London or what happens in Philadelphia. We both want to keep our friendship alive, and so we have. I even brought her to Lucky's because she missed the atmosphere. When I rotated the computer to get a panoramic view of the packed diner, I basically invited other people to look at me.

I didn't have fear in my bones. I wasn't frightened. I actually even smiled. I like that I can be alone in Lucky's Diner without any of the guys or my sisters. Every day, I'm feeling better than the past.

Though, I was more amused than Price on the matter. My incredibly assertive and punctual bodyguard is all about keeping a low profile and not creating *intense* situations. He occupies a four-person table about five feet from my corner booth.

And no one has approached me because of him.

Lily came up with a theory that he has extreme powers of mental persuasion like Professor Xavier.

I check my email and open up a link to Tumblr. "Got it."

"Look at the fourth question and tell me if you think Garrison sounds off." Willow pushes up her black-framed glasses that slip down her nose.

The Tumblr user *ryumastersxx* filled out a questionnaire. Willow said that Garrison never answers them on his own accord. Usually she'll tag him first, but this time was different. It's also the beginning of their long-distance relationship, and no one, not even Willow and Garrison, are completely positive how long they'll last.

Name: Garrison
Zodiac Sign: Scorpio

I pick up my hamburger. "I found something."

"What?" She splays her hands flat like she's preparing for the news to drop.

"Your zodiacs are *very* romantically compatible." I wag my brows. *Pisces and Scorpio.* "It's even stronger than a Pisces and Virgo." Which is what I am to Ryke.

Willow smiles. "You're supposed to be finding *bad* signs."

"And leave all the good ones behind?" I give her a look and take a large messy bite of my burger. With a mouthful of bun, lettuce, and meat, I try to say, "Never" but I end up laughing as soon as she starts.

A camera phone flashes at me, but I don't pay attention to the source. Hey, at least they wanted a picture of me smiling and not one of me sullen and near tears.

Willow and I collect ourselves in the next minute, and I wash my burger down with some sips of Fizz Life. She points at her computer screen, but it looks like she's pointing right at me. "This part is so bad."

"Lemme see." I focus back on the questionnaire and sip my soda.

Average Hours of Sleep: idk used to be about 7-8? It's less, so whatever.
Last Google Search: what time is it in London?
Relationship Status: </3

I choke on my soda. He really just put a fractured heart there.

"Daisy, it's bad, right? You look freaked out."

"No, no." I control my features. "Guys are weird. They do weird things. This could just be out of angst. He misses you so much, and he's expressing that through a…" *broken heart.* "…I wouldn't worry about it. I'm not that far through, so don't stress…"

I set down my hamburger, treating this more seriously. I scroll through more of his questionnaire.

Siblings: three older brothers. Be happy they're not yours.

Love or Lust: lust doesn't hurt.

Met a Celebrity: I think I might be becoming one…

That's true.

The day that Willow became legally Willow *Hale*, the world found out she wasn't Lo's cousin but rather his sister. Celebrity news took much more interest in her life. Not to the extent of my sisters, but enough that they now pay attention to Willow's boyfriend.

Celebrity Crush wrote a short article titled: WHAT WE KNOW ABOUT GARRISON ABBEY! They don't know a lot, which made Willow happy.

"What's the consensus?" Willow asks.

"I think he really misses you, and I don't think it means that he's ready to get over you or forget you."

She nods a couple times. "I just want him to be happy…but I want him too."

"I know," I say softly.

"We had sex," she suddenly blurts out, her cheeks ashen.

"Willow Hale," I say with a gasp, smiling wide. I high-five my computer screen.

She timidly high-fives her computer screen in reply.

"Am I the first you told?"

"I meant to tell Lily, but I keep chickening out. It's just..." She sighs. "I think it turned into a goodbye because...we did it the day before I left Philadelphia. I think that's why he's so upset."

I lower my voice. "Easy fix, right? Just have sex with him again. Then it won't seem like the last time you both ever do it."

"I'm even *more* scared. How is that possible?" She smashes her face into a pillow and mumbles, "I'm so awkward."

I love Willow so much. "You're totally human, and you get to hold onto the amazing fact that you never slept with someone that makes your skin crawl." In hindsight, disgust slithers down my spine when I remember kissing Julian.

"At least now you're stronger for it," Willow reminds me. "You learned what you like."

I definitely did.

I like guys who emotionally care about me.

I like my wolf.

The diner suddenly falls hushed, which can only mean one thing.

I look up just as Ryke Meadows and Loren Hale make their way through Lucky's Diner, aimed for my corner booth.

To Willow, I say. "We have company in the form of Mr. Broody-Pants and Mr. I-Will-Butcher-All-Living-Things-With-My-Eyes. Want to see?"

Willow nods, and I spin my laptop, the screen facing the diner's entrance. Ryke and Lo both wear track pants and T-shirts, sweat stains outlining their muscles. They probably just finished running not too long ago.

I narrate, "And as the moose slowly amble through the prairie, all the antelopes perk up and admire their delectable horns and stout bodies. *Oohhh aahhh*, the antelopes whisper."

Willow is cracking up laughing, her voice only traveling through my earbuds, but as her brothers approach, they see her on the screen. Lo is the first to greet his sister.

"Look at that moose try to wave," I continue. "He lifts his hoof and gives a hearty hello to a strange technological device."

Flatly, Lo says, "You're goddamn weird." Then he slides into the booth on my left.

I gasp. "The moose can speak!" I swivel the computer towards Ryke and lift it up so it's more in line with his face. "And here stands Mr. Broody Pants. What a specimen."

Ryke playfully pushes my forehead.

My face bursts into a powerful smile.

Ryke almost smiles too, and he raises his brows at me like *what are you getting on about, Calloway?*

You.

I'm getting on about *you.*

Ryke retrains his attention onto his half-sister. "Hey, Willow," he greets before sliding in on my right side. I flip the laptop to its original position. Facing me. Not the diner.

Ryke and Lo squeeze closer to me, both entering the Skype window and able to see Willow clearly. Before they snatch my earbuds and fight over them, I unplug my headphones and increase the volume.

Lo taps into big-brother mode pretty fast. "What's new? How's school? Are the people shit?" He actually asks *five* more questions, but they all have the same heartbeat.

Are you okay, Willow?

"I'm still getting used to everything, but it's not bad." Willow shrugs and hangs her head, chewing her lip. I think she's contemplating whether or not to bring up Garrison.

"Did you guys hear that she found a comic book store there?" I lift my hamburger up to Ryke, and he kisses me before biting into it. He licks his thumb and mouths, *fucking mustard?*

So maybe "condiment banisher" isn't in my future.

Ryke loves mustard, but he knows it's not my favorite. "I didn't scrape it off?" I whisper and peek beneath the bun. *Damn.*

"It's not up to par with Superheroes & Scones," Willow says, "but it's nice to have something like it nearby." She hugs a blue pillow on her lap and picks at the fringe.

Ryke and Lo watch her for a second and then exchange this concerned look. I pass them menus, trying to distract them while Willow makes up her mind on whether or not to include them in our Garrison discussion.

"They have a special burrito today," I tell Lo. "Maybe it'll make you feel *special* afterwards, if you know what I mean." I elbow his side lightly.

An ill-humored Loren Hale flips through the menu. "Ryke, tell your wife she's confusing special burritos with special brownies."

I gasp. "There's a difference?"

Ryke taps his plastic menu to my head. Lily would call that a love-tap.

"I need advice," Willow suddenly says, instantly capturing Ryke and Lo's attention. "Maybe advice isn't the right word…maybe like a guy's perspective?"

"What happened?" Lo asks sharply, ready to protect and defend his little sister.

"Nothing bad. Well, it's confusing…Daisy?" She has these pleading eyes like *please help me explain this. I suck with words.*

I have you covered, Willow Hale.

"Garrison filled out a questionnaire on his own accord, which was a rare event, and we're both kind of questioning *what* his answers actually mean." I pop up the questionnaire in a new window for them. "So as guys, what do you think?"

Ryke leans closer and points at the screen. "What the fuck is that supposed to be?" Oh Ryke. He doesn't know that the less-than sign plus the number three is the heart symbol.

"A broken heart," I explain.

"But you're both still fucking together, right?" Ryke asks.

Willow nods. "Yeah."

"Then why the fuck…" he trails off at my wide-eyes. *Stand down, Ryke.* He's not very informed on Tumblr wit. I doubt he's even gone on Tumblr more than a few times. He would've filled this questionnaire out plainly. *Relationship Status: Married.*

The end.

Lo is really the one who'd be able to understand Garrison. His harsh glare remains strong while he reads. He finishes and says, "He's just upset that you're not around. Seems like a natural reaction if he loves you."

Willow says hurriedly, "I had sex with him the day before I left." She buries her face in her pillow and mumbles out something else.

Ryke whispers to me, "Her first time?"

I nod, and Ryke rubs his temple and jaw before turning to Lo.

Lo is frozen with his hand partially covering his mouth. They both lean against the booth and whisper, literally, behind my back.

I ask Willow, "What was that last part?"

She moves the pillow off her mouth, but not her eyes. "I think he's upset about that."

"Hey," I tell both guys, "stop, you two. She's right here, and she didn't have to tell you that, but she did and would like your advice."

They return to the screen, but Willow, no longer in frame, angled her computer camera to her *X-Men* poster.

"Were you fucking safe?" Ryke asks. His words sound coarse but his voice isn't.

"Yes." A voice comes out in the distance.

"It was consensual?" Lo asks. It looks like he's talking to the young, bald Professor Xavier.

"Yes."

I cut in to alleviate some tension, "So what do you guys think? Would this be enough to make him upset?"

"I wouldn't put a fucking broken heart thing in my relationship status." Ryke is blunt, which isn't always a good thing. "If you both knew you wouldn't see each other for a while and slept together, I would've been like, *look, this fucking girl is obviously showing me that I mean a lot to her.*"

"I would've been upset," Lo counters, "but not *at* the girl, just at the goddamn situation."

"What can I do to make him feel better?" Willow asks off-screen.

"I know this sucks but...you can't do anything, Willow. You just have to let him get used to the long-distance thing. He will after a while."

"And if he doesn't?" Willow wonders.

Lo snaps, "Then maybe he didn't love you like you thought."

"Fuck him," Ryke adds.

I interject, "Let's all remember that we like Garrison." Ryke and Lo look murderous at these plausible scenarios where Garrison breaks their sister's heart.

Willow pops her head back into the camera view. "Thanks, and I'm sorry. I didn't mean to bring up anything that'd make you guys uncomfortable."

Lo and Ryke start laughing, and Lo is the first to say, "Like that's possible."

I've heard many, many stories before I entered the picture. Back when we weren't famous. Like the time where Ryke just stood there while Lo had his hand halfway down Lily's pants. He tried to run Ryke off, but Ryke isn't easy to scare or make uncomfortable.

Before Willow and I sign off, she says to me, "Tomorrow, same time?"

"Yep. I'll be at my house with the special guest star Sullivan Minnie Meadows."

Willow smiles. "See ya."

I shut my computer while Lo orders the "special burrito" and Ryke runs his hand through my hair. I set my chin on his arm with a growing smile.

[7]

Rose Cobalt

This is a battle I plan to lose.

I take a hearty swig of sparkling water from my wine glass. Then I eye the chessboard, set on our king-sized bed, the pale blue, satin comforter beneath.

Move your rook in his line of fire, Rose. Abandon your cavalry.

Losing on purpose is fucking painful. I finish off my sparkling water with another angered gulp and avoid my husband's *sagacious* blue gaze. While bathing Charlie and Beckett this morning, he used that adjective on himself. I could fault Connor for his ego, but his self-description isn't entirely inaccurate.

He's frighteningly perceptive of his surroundings and *me* without seeming overly watchful.

Take this moment for instance. Instead of wearing my usual black negligee or chemise to bed, I chose one of his button-downs. The hem stops at my thighs, and my breasts push against the white fabric, two buttons popped. Connor has yet to mention my choice of nightwear, and I never catch him ogling me from head-to-toe. But I'm certain he's mentally jotted this down: *What is Rose up to?*

I'm not about to simply *tell* him. I'll only be spoon-feeding my infant children, thank you.

I try to take another sip of water, but my glass is empty.

My husband reaches over and drains a quarter of his sparkling water into my glass. Since I've been trying to get pregnant, Connor has kindly joined me on my "no wine" voyage. It's hell, but a hell I'd endure again and again to bring a little gremlin into the world.

Avoid his eyes.

I do.

And then he says, "You're nervous."

I glare right at his stature and composure, at his unwavering confidence. "I'm *thinking* about how to defeat you." I am thinking, but more so about how to hand him a win.

Without breaking eye contact, he takes a sip from his wine glass.

He knows.

No he doesn't. He can't know that I broke an enormous promise out of impulse. All day, I've been trying to figure out how to subtly explain what I've done, but I keep choking on my own betrayal. I'd slam a door in his face if he did what I did.

I inhale a tightened breath and finish off the sparkling water again, even the little drop that rolls slowly into my mouth. *He doesn't know.*

Both of us in the middle of the bed, my legs are splayed to the side. His elbow is propped casually on his bent knee, just dressed in gray drawstring pants.

While his abs aren't horrible to look at, I actually lose focus by the two baby monitors next to him. On the screens, I can see Jane in her toddler bed and Beckett and Charlie in their cribs, our children sound asleep by 8:00 p.m. in their rooms.

"Do we need to put a time limit on moves?" Connor asks me. "Thinking shouldn't take you this long. For other people, yes, but for you and me?" He arches a brow like I've lost a handful of brain cells in a short period of time.

I haven't. "I don't need a time stipulation, Richard."

I collect my glossy hair onto one shoulder and shift my rook. *I'm sorry for sacrificing you, but it's for the best.* After finishing, I look up, and Connor is fixated on the chessboard. His bishop can now capture my queen.

I think he's confused, but I can't be certain.

We always play with stakes, and we left this game open-ended. Winner can do anything they please, which is a higher stake than a narrowed goal. Connor could choose anything, and I'm prepared for it.

The quieter he is, the stiffer I become. I sit so straight, my neck and shoulders ache. I clutch my knees that are glued together, and my heart bangs violently.

Do what you must, Husband.

Connor slowly raises his gaze to mine. "Why would you put your queen in jeopardy?"

She deserves to be punished. I swallow that truth and just say, "That move fits my overall plan."

Connor stretches to set his wine glass on an end table behind him. "What's the capital of Norway?"

I thought he'd mentally chase me to find my true motives, but I forgot to include his dominance into the equation. His need to be in front and on top—or at the very least, right by my side. He'll make me chase him around like we're two lions wrestling in the fucking Sahara.

I have no idea why he's suddenly brought an impromptu quiz to the table, but now I'm as mentally on my toes as him. "Oslo," I reply. He knows I'd never get this fact wrong, so I can't fail on purpose here.

Try again, Richard.

"And the capital of Estonia?" he quizzes.

"Tallinn." I narrow my eyes. "C'est tout?" *Is that all?*

He knocks my queen over with his bishop. "Check."

My king is unprotected. I graze over the board quickly. "I see no way to win. Congratulations." My voice is so tight that I can hardly swallow.

"There are *two* moves you could make, and you're saying that you can't see either?"

"That's exactly what I just said," I snap and push the chessboard at him, pieces tipping over and scattering our bed. "You can gloat about it and take your win." I try to seem upset about the loss, but I've never claimed to be good at acting.

"What's the capital of the Philippines?"

Manila. "I don't know," I say hastily and then climb off the bed. "It should be enough that you've won this game. You don't have to keep testing me." As I turn and face him, I go very still.

He knows.

"You let me win. There's *no* satisfaction in that." He rights the chess pieces on the board. "The fact that you'd even think I'd believe you'd relinquish your queen is not only insulting to my intelligence but to your own. And you know every capital in less than a second."

"You can't know my knowledge of capitals." I can't believe I'm downplaying my intelligence to make a point.

I've never done this before.

Connor keeps his emotions padlocked, and I wonder if he's as dismayed as I am. I'm trying to convince him that I'm a playful house cat when I've positioned myself as a fierce lioness. I near my end table and listen to his calm response.

"At Faust, Matthew Wellington said he challenged you in capitals for a kiss."

I gag at the memory. "He *told you* that?"

"He told all of Whitman Hall that." *Whitman Hall.* The name of Connor's boarding school dormitory. There were four Halls, all titled after poets. I find myself entranced with the facts, all void of emotion so I don't crumble at my husband's feet.

You broke a promise, Rose.

I've never had to apologize for something like this, and I thought I'd begin my penance by padding his ego with a win or two. I don't intend for him to go easy on me because I wouldn't want him to. I deserve to be swept in the natural disasters I produce.

It's only fair.

I carefully sift through the drawer of my end table. "Matthew Wellington was a little weasel." I was fifteen and would *never* give my first kiss to him. I was certain I'd win that bet because, as Connor noted, I knew every capital in under a second.

If I won, I was allowed to take his Gucci sunglasses. That weekend at the Model UN conference, I wore his sunglasses every time I saw his face. Just to rub it in.

"I still have Matthew's sunglasses," I note with pride.

"You mean the sunglasses that he told everyone he *lent* you, and you were so 'infatuated' with him, you wore them all around the conference? Those sunglasses?"

I gape, my eyes scorching hot. *"What?"* Matthew wasn't just a little weasel apparently. He was also a little prick. "Did you dispel that lie?"

Connor keeps my queen between his fingers. "I called him out for twisting facts, but I still couldn't believe you'd play games with *Matthew Wellington* for a kiss."

"Because you hoped I'd play those games with you?" I question.

Connor doesn't deny this. "You hated Faust boys, and I wanted to be the one you hated most."

Translation: *I wanted to be the one always on your mind.*

I fight a mounting smile. "You succeeded."

Connor grins. "I know."

I roll my eyes dramatically and continue my search through the drawer. Now that he knows I've let him win, I can't hide my treachery any longer. I find my self-defense knife, the hilt blood-red. I quickly set it beside the chessboard, nearest Connor, and then reclaim my spot on the bed.

He hardly looks surprised or like someone who was just handed a weapon.

He picks up the knife. "Explain."

"You can stab me in the back like I've stabbed you." My nose flares, restraining an onslaught of guilt and regret.

Connor rubs his lips, but I can't tell if he's pieced anything together yet.

"I deserve punishment." There I said it. I tie my hair into a pony, ready for whatever he wants to dole out.

"We've been through this, Rose," he says so calmly. "I'd never hurt you, not even *hypothetically*."

"Not even if I cheated on you?" I test.

"You didn't." His tone is matter-of-fact. Like in no realm of possibility does that scenario exist. I can't even imagine putting a pinky toe in that direction either. I'm so tragically in love with him. To the point where breaking a *simple* promise has my stomach twisted. It's not nearly as catastrophic as infidelity.

Connor stands off the bed, knife in hand.

"Not even if I cheated on an exam?" I try again, watching him and his supreme poise.

"I'd think less of you because I know you're better than that."

"Then you must think less of me now." I cast a glare at the ceiling. *Just say it, Rose. Let your impulsive misstep out into the world.*

Connor speaks before I do. "Because you went to the doctor without me?"

He definitely knows.

Connor clasps my ankle, sliding me to the edge of the bed until my legs fall off. He stands tall above me. "Because we made a promise that we'd go together?" He kicks my ankles apart, spreading my legs wide.

I eye the knife in his hand.

Not even a second later, he places my knife back in the drawer, as though to say, *never will I harm you.* And then he returns to me.

"I wouldn't think less of you because of this." He steps nearer. "Because I know who you are. Because I know exactly why you would've broken our promise today and why you couldn't wait longer than a night to confess."

I breathe shallowly.

Connor presses his hand to my breastbone, and I follow the force of his palm. Until my back meets the soft comforter. "Because you're impetuous." He stretches my arms above my head, crossing my wrists. "Because you see our promises like vows of love and death." *I do.* "Because you feel like you broke something that's unbreakable."

I shiver, cold sweeping my arms and legs.

He fits something in my hands and closes my fingers over it. A chess piece.

My queen.

Connor hovers above my frame, his hands on either side of me, his lips only inches away from mine. My legs curve around his waist, my bare skin beginning to heat.

Very deeply and very hushed, he says, "If you were anything other than a torrid fire, you wouldn't be the woman I've admired and loved. I understand your reasons. I respect them and adore them because they belong to you."

I inhale sharply, my back arching and body rising against his. He lets out a deeper breath, skimming me for a moment, before meeting my eyes.

I clutch my queen tightly. I'd give her to him again, but not in the same way. I'd love her more beforehand.

"It drove me insane not knowing if I was pregnant," I explain. "I thought I'd just be in and out and nothing would be changed." Before going, I took two tests. One said a faint *yes* and the other said *fuck off no way.* I convinced myself that the doctor would say *you're not pregnant.*

Connor isn't surprised. Though he never really is. "I'd rather have this moment with you than have an ordinary day with anyone else, Rose."

"I won't break another promise, so don't get used to this," I say in a softer tone, much softer than my usual voice. I'm melting beneath my husband and his words and reassurance of his love for me. The *me* that can be unpredictable and fiery and full of contradictions and all the other personality traits I spent the day loathing.

As I attempt to bring my arms down, he grips my wrists together, cementing my hands where he first placed them. Heat stirs between my legs, and his dominance pours over me.

"Do you remember when you hid your pregnancy with Jane from me?"

"Yes." I could never forget my first pregnancy and how scared I'd been. I was so stubborn that I left Connor in the dark much longer than most people would—though I knew he'd figure it out. I just didn't acknowledge what was happening, and the silent battle became something more intimate between us. Something that strengthened our trust.

We might seem strange, but I can't see that event happening any other way.

"I'd never been more captivated by a person in my entire life, and that time only furthered my belief."

"What belief?"

He licks his lips. "'You have a place in my heart no one else could ever have.'"

I drill a piercing glare at him, my wrists still pinned by his hand. "And I'd believe you more if you didn't quote F. Scott Fitzgerald's *The Ice Palace.*"

His grin is blinding. "What I said was real, even if they're not my words."

"Fine."

"Just fine? You'd give up that quickly, Miss Highest Honors?"

I nearly smile at the title he uses for me, as though reminding me of who I am and why I should continue to treat myself like royalty. "I took something from you today that I can never give back." My smile vanishes completely.

Say it, Rose.

So I say it, and even supine beneath him, my words feel like mine. Like a force of nature. Like the surge that propels a tidal wave. "I'm pregnant."

He does a poor job at concealing a smile, which means he let it pass through for me to see.

"She said we probably conceived in September, so I'm not far along, but I'm pregnant. And I heard this news *alone* in a doctor's office, and all I wished was that you were beside me. I wished that you were there." My eyes flood, but I restrain tears from spilling over.

With his free hand, Connor cups my cheek, his thumb skimming my bottom lip. I search his deep blue eyes as they illuminate. "But I'm here with you now, Rose, and anything else sounds too predictable to belong to us."

Translation: *ordinary is boring, darling.*

I expel any lingering remorse. *I'm pregnant.* Internally, I might as well belong to the nauseatingly cheerful scenes in Disney films, birds chirping while I twirl and stroke my hair and sing.

Outwardly, I am Ursula.

This attracts my husband. Connor kisses me…gently. More *gently* than I ever like. My gaze narrows.

Richard.

His lips fall to my ear. "You didn't think I'd take you deep and hard, did you?"

He's going to punish me.

In the best way.

I glare. "I thought you'd be a mediocre narcissist with terrible hair. Which you are."

"Mediocre? *Terrible* hair?" His hand tightens around my wrists. *Oh God.* "You could've picked less obvious lies." His other hand disappears up the bareness of my thigh.

"It's my opinion—" I gasp as he tenderly strokes his fingers between my legs, my lacy panties obstructing his skin from my skin.

"Open your eyes, Rose."

They closed on their own accord. Just as I open them, he pulls me further onto the bed and pushes the chessboard aside. Before I hone in on the fallen pieces, he holds my face so...*softly*. I grimace, aching for his force. I'm not fragile dishware.

I could tear him limb by limb if I desired.

I don't, however. I only desire his strength to trump mine until I've melted entirely in his hands. He won't lower his body weight on me, but he's stepped off the ground, his pelvis fit above mine.

Connor captures my blistering gaze. His eyes so fixated on mine, he might as well be fucking me with them.

I pulse.

My lips part.

He whispers tender, quiet French that I struggle to understand, dizzied and lit up. I break my wrists apart to hold onto his shoulder. Swiftly, he seizes my hands once more and stretches them above my head. When I try to protest, Connor pins them, removes his other hand from my thigh, and he reaches towards the end table.

Connor purposefully *grinds* his hardened cock against my panties.

My toes curl. "Connor..."

I choke on a moan, my whole body clenching with arousal.

His erection is outlined in his drawstring pants, and I imagine him inside of me.

Hard. Deep. Rough. Not this gentle shit.

Being six-foot-four, he has the arm-span to reach the end table and open the drawer, all without moving off me. Just forward.

Grinding in.

I tilt my head back and see him collect leather handcuffs. He shuts the drawer and then locks the cuffs around my wrists. I now lose the ability to break them apart.

I try to skewer him with a single glare.

Connor only grins.

Ugh.

He leans teasingly close. His pink lips brush against mine as he whispers, "What am I?" I inhale his words as much as he breathes in my own.

"Average," I combat.

"Wrong." He puts distance between our mouths, as though to say *you get none of me.*

I grow more insolent at the idea. "Who even said I wanted to kiss you?"

"Who even said you were smart?" he rebuts with this conceited nonchalance. *He's sexy.* No he is *not.* His lips curve upward. *Yes he is.* No, Rose. I bristle at my contradictory thoughts.

Dear God,

Make it so that I can loathe all parts of my husband.

Sincerely,

Rose Calloway Cobalt.

"Princeton said I was smart. *I* say that I'm smart," I tell Connor. "And I never said that I wanted to kiss you." I lift my head and shoulders off the bed. He presses a palm between my breasts, pushing me back down.

He's reached the last button, and he slowly, too slowly, fully opens my shirt. My breasts come into view, my sensitive nipples at attention. My body begs to be manhandled, but I'm too stubborn to verbally plead.

Connor strokes my hair out of my face, and I anticipate him yanking the strands *hard.* He never does, and a frustrated sound rumbles my throat.

"Yes?" he asks, full well knowing why I made that noise. "Do you ache for something, Rose?"

"Your death."

He nearly laughs.

"And to slaughter your laugh."

He hooks my panties with his finger, and he lifts my leg, his lips trailing a hot, feather-light line from the inside of my knee to the inside of my thigh.

Bite me.

I dizzy. As he pulls my panties halfway off, he stops, his mouth partially against my thigh. "What am I?" he asks.

Give in to my husband?

Never.

I breathe, "Ordinary."

"Incorrect, Miss *Highest* Honors." He carefully, too carefully, slides my panties down my legs instead of ripping them off. I want his large hand against my throat. I want him drilling into me. All I have to do is answer correctly.

My arousal mounts, my legs in his possession. I pulse once and twice, *hungering* for his cock. He slips my panties off my ankles, and I suck in a breath.

"I *loathe* your face," I tell him. *I love his face.* Why does he have to be so handsome? His perfect abs. His wavy hair. Even his moisturized skin. It's annoying. Everything about him. Is. Infuriating.

"Such lies, darling." He tenderly kisses my knee before stretching my legs wider again. He's knelt between them, and he rolls down the band of his drawstring pants. *Dear God.*

My collarbones jut out. "Connor…" I can feel myself getting wet.

His erection emerges—long, thick and incredibly hard. Ready to fit *deep* in me. He removes his pants but takes his time to fold them, all to irritate me and prolong what I crave.

My body wants to buck up. My back wants to arch. *Do not betray me, body. Prepare for battle against thy husband.*

I buck up towards him.

Dammit.

Connor quickly places his palm on my lower abdomen, gently pushing me back down. Then he delicately, too delicately, places breathless kisses from between my breasts, over my nipples, down to my ribcage, lower and lower, spending extra time on my abdomen. And the place where our baby will grow strong.

He pauses, only to look up at me and ask, "What am I?"

My legs tremble. I jerk against the handcuffs, pleasure swelling. "You're *appalling.*"

"Réessaie." *Try again.*

"Run-of-the-mill, typical, *common*—"

Connor abruptly seizes my handcuffed wrists, and he brings my arms down in front of me. Then he laces my fingers together and extends both my middle and index fingers, pressed like I'm miming a gun. He holds my gaze, and he lifts my hands higher—up to his mouth. My muscles burn in satisfaction as he pulls.

"What am I?" His deeply whispered words stimulate me much more than the sight of his body. My veins scald and blood rushes to my clit.

The sensations escalate so quickly that I forget to spout off an answer.

"Rose," he says again. "What am I?"

"Maddening."

Connor takes my fingers into *his* mouth. His eyes still on mine. I shudder, my body quaking. I nearly come at the sight of his unrivaled confidence. My lips part, breath caught in my throat. As he skillfully sucks my fingers, he *slowly* pushes his hardened cock into me, but he never thrusts. He never rocks deeper. He just stops and torments me. Full but no friction. Full but no aggression.

My shoulders dig into the mattress, and my back arches, asking to move forward. I can't deny myself what my body craves any longer. I'm so pent up that I moan when his hand skims my breast. I breathe and cry out like I'm being lit on fire.

"*Connor.*"

He pops his mouth off my fingers. "What am I?" he asks in such a demanding tone. He kneads my hip, giving me a taste of force that he'd use all over my body.

I squeeze my eyes shut, all my soldiers abandoning this battle.

"What am I?"

"A god." He drives so hard forward that I instantly come. Clenching around his cock. He thrusts deep and hard, building me to another peak before I descend from the first. I struggle to keep my eyes open.

He kisses me with rough affection, my lips swelling beneath his. My body blazes with my mind, and he tugs my hair. Yanks until the pressure lights up every nerve. Before my eyes roll back, I peek at his ass that flexes as he drives in, so fast it's like he's running a marathon between my legs.

Connor.

He groans against my mouth. "You want to be ridden hard, Rose? You want me to *grab* every fucking inch of you?"

I mutter out a pleasured approval.

He bites the flesh of my neck, and I gasp sharply. *Connor.* He sucks my neck before wrapping his hand around my throat. I love when he chokes me, but I know he won't do it for long while I'm pregnant. He's gentler about this than usual.

He whispers in the pit of my ear, "You can feel how hard I'm fucking you." He goes deep, so deep that I arch into him and moan into his shoulder. Connor holds me against his body, cupping my ass, and pushing me closer, until he's so far in I can hardly breathe.

We both hit a staggering climax.

Even before we calm, I ask him in a tired voice to *stay in.* I'm not sure he even hears at first. I keep my cheek on his shoulder, my muscles fatigued and eyes shut. I feel him carrying me, my legs still around him, and he rests my head against my pillow, his body pressed up against mine.

I fight to stay awake.

Connor is on top of me, unlocking my handcuffs. He also, very clearly, heard my request.

"I think I just had this strange nightmare," I say with more contentment than I planned.

He sets the handcuffs aside. "What made it a nightmare?" He kisses my sore wrists, watching me intently.

"I called you a god."

His lips rise in his next kiss. "Then your nightmare is my dream."

"Not your reality?" I rebut.

He leans forward. "All my dreams are realities, darling. And your dreams are my dreams." He presses the warmest, most loving kiss to my forehead.

2019

"Fuck it."

- Ryke Meadows, We Are Calloway
(Season 1 Episode 13 — Cornfields & Butterbeer)

< *8* >

January 2019
THE MEADOWS COTTAGE
Philadelphia

Ryke Meadows

"Why the fuck did we volunteer for this?" I ask Dais, gripping the base of a silver ladder.

She stands on the second highest rung with only one foot. "Because he's one of our closest friends." Daisy rips a piece of duct tape with her teeth and adheres the string of a long blue banner to the ceiling. Our first floor is just one big fucking room, no foyer or archway to hang this across.

I grumble, "He's annoying as fuck."

My statement is interrupted by *ping ping* and *bop bop* sounds. Ten feet away, surrounded by a mound of fucking pillows in the living room area, our eleventh-month-old baby bangs on her kiddie keyboard. Nutty, our white husky, sleeps through the terrible music, curled on the foot of the stairs.

Sulli's not going to win a fucking musical award any time soon. It's not like we expected her to be musically inclined. Daisy can barely hold a tune, and I'm not that fucking great at singing either.

Though I'm a hell of a lot better than my little brother.

"But you love him," Daisy mumbles, biting another piece of tape.

"That's a strong fucking word to use between me and Connor."

She slaps the tape onto the ceiling and then glances at me with a lopsided smile. "So salty, that Ryke Meadows."

I just know that whatever we fucking do, he's going to shit on it.

So yeah, maybe I am a little fucking salty.

The tape suddenly peels off for the fifth time, and the banner falls onto Daisy's head. I reach up and clasp her thigh, so she doesn't fucking plummet.

Daisy pushes the banner off and then mock gasps, "He's touching my ass."

I raise my brows at her and then move my hand up to her round ass. "*Now* I'm touching your fucking ass." I pat her ass and squeeze.

She puts her hand to her forehead. "What will my husband think? I let another man fondle my butt?" Daisy theatrically falls *backwards* off the fucking ladder.

I anticipate it so much that I easily catch her in time. My baseball cap, that she was wearing, drops off her head and thuds to the hardwood.

In my arms, she looks up at me.

I look down at her. "Your husband is thinking he's married the craziest fucking Calloway girl."

Her lips curve upwards. "You're friends with my husband?"

I toss a piece of hair into her face, and then I fucking kiss her. My body warms at our embrace, and I feel her smile beneath my lips.

She mumbles into the kiss, "Hi, husband."

I nip her bottom lip and whisper, "Hi, wife." I abruptly toss Daisy over the couch. She lands on the cushion with a contagious smile.

Sulli laughs at the sudden sight of her mom.

Daisy sits up and leans towards Sulli. "You didn't know, peanut butter cupcake? I can *fly*." Her voice is so melodic—I could listen to her talk to our daughter every day.

I gather the blue banner and go to the nearby kitchen counter. Like I said, our first floor is all one fucking space, divided off by furniture.

"Let's just fucking tape this across the barstools."

"I like it." Daisy makes a silly face at Sulli before helping me re-tape this thing. When we're finished, the words are bold and clear in her handwriting.

Happy 30th Birthday, Connor!

"He's going to fucking hate it." This actual fact almost makes it worth it. Truth is, he will most definitely shit on everything, I most definitely do love the guy, and I also *really* fucking love when he's given a hard time. Which is rare. Because not much, if anything, flusters him.

"Very true," Daisy says. "Connor Cobalt doesn't appreciate the finer things in parties."

"And what are the finer fucking things, Calloway?"

She outstretches her arms and tosses them higher into the air. "Blindingly bright decorations! Birthday sashes! And cake! Every birthday must have cake." Daisy bows.

I want her in my fucking arms.

To hold her and kiss her and just fucking love her.

These sentiments never recede. Never end.

Daisy goes still. "You did remember the cake, right?" Rose and her sisters left that task up to my brother and me.

"It's in the fucking freezer."

Lo thought it'd be funny to give him a *vanilla* ice cream cake. Out of irony. If we had to deem anyone "vanilla" out of all of us, Connor Cobalt would be the last on the list. And you know what? I highly doubt Connor will shit on Lo's vanilla fucking cake because it's coming from Lo.

I'm not bitter. If anything, I'm glad that one part of Connor's birthday might go right because of my brother. Connor may hate celebrating his own birthday, but there's a part of all of us—even *me*—that wants him to enjoy today.

How, why, do I fucking care about him? In one breath, I want to see him struggle for once. In the other, I want him to be as happy as the rest of us—because anything else just feels wrong.

"Dada!" Sulli exclaims, in the midst of teetering towards us on two feet. She already succeeded at walking last week (we videotaped the event), but her legs still tremble beneath her with each wobbly step.

Daisy and I angle towards our daughter. There's nothing fucking cuter than this baby in a green onesie and her dark brown hair in tiny pigtails. I have thick hair, so it wasn't a surprise that hers grew in fast.

Daisy crouches and waves and cheers Sulli on.

As I stare between them, guilt gnaws at me. *Just tell your wife what fucking happened yesterday.* I can't.

I lean an elbow on the bar counter.

I can't break Daisy's heart. It's the last fucking thing I ever want to do in my lifetime. *She doesn't have to know.*

Sullivan skirts past Daisy, laughing as though she's in a race against her mom. Then our baby starts to climb up the rungs of the wooden barstool.

"Hey there," Daisy calls out. She has a hard time telling Sulli outright *no.*

So do I.

I'll get her. I pry Sulli away from her fucking adventure, holding her in my arms. When she looks at me, I make a scrunched face.

Sulli tries to mimic me, brows attempting to bunch.

This is my fucking baby. I still can't believe it, not even eleven-months in.

Daisy stands up. "Sullivan Minnie Meadows, climber extraordinaire." She nuzzles Sulli's nose with her own.

I'd never want a fucking baby with anyone but Daisy.

My wife scans the first floor. "Hey, look, we're pretty good at party-planning."

We wound gold streamers around our staircase banisters, and we blew up a few black and gold balloons. We bought most of the decorations from the New Year's Eve themed aisle, so it looks less like a birthday party. Daisy and I thought Connor would like that. We're lucky he's even going to show up. Ever since his twenty-seventh birthday party, he's let us actually celebrate with him, and he doesn't fly off to some other country anymore.

The decoration that just won't stop fucking giving: a cardboard cutout of Connor Cobalt.

I'm serious.

A life-sized version of Connor—with his conceited grin, single arched brow, tailored suit, and a photoshopped *crown* on his wavy hair—stands a few feet from the front door. It'll either severely piss him off or amuse him.

Either one is fucking fine with me.

"Ten bucks he throws himself into the trash," Daisy says.

I hold Sulli with one arm. "Fuck no. He wouldn't defile a picture of himself."

Daisy tilts her head. "I think he might show up, look around impassively, and just walk right out the door." I see a pang of disappointment behind her green eyes.

"He won't do that."

"Why not?"

"Because I know where he fucking lives," I snap. I'm not throwing him a party just so he can walk on out. No fucking way.

Daisy twists the ties of her white sweatshirt that says: *sunshine mixed with a little hurricane.* "You know, you're the only two guys that have ever understood me. Like *really* gotten to know me in a way that no one else has, and I'm not saying that I like Connor the same way that I like you. Obviously."

"I fucking hope not."

She tries to hide a smile. I wish she wouldn't hide it, even for my sake.

"You can fucking smile, sweetheart."

And so she does. "I know I don't owe him anything. The way that you said I never owed you anything for being there for me, but I just hope my friendship with him holds the same understanding both ways. If that makes sense?"

"Yeah, but the guy isn't a normal fucking guy. He views the rest of us as *food* in his animal kingdom."

Her smile stretches. "But I only want you to eat me."

Fuck. I give her the slowest once-over, and she rises and falls on the balls of her feet.

Then the door swings open.

"Which one of you crazies ordered a subscription to *Celebrity Crush*?" My sharp-jawed brother barrels into the cottage, a bright pink tabloid in hand.

"Why the fuck are you going through our mail?" I retort.

Daisy clutches my arm like she sees an incoming car crash. "Watch out, L—"

Lo collides with the cardboard Connor Cobalt and trips on top of him, simultaneously trying to upright the cutout and not fall. "Jesus… Christ," he curses.

I start to laugh with Daisy.

My brother straddles a life-sized image of Connor, and he just now registers what he ran into. He gives me a look. "Bro…what is this even doing here?"

Daisy answers, "Just in case he doesn't show up, we have this version." I never thought that was the real fucking reason, but subconsciously maybe it was always there.

Before Lo can shift the cardboard, Rose appears in the open doorway. She snorts at the sight, her hands perched on her hips, a small baby bump noticeable from her tight black dress.

"Really, Loren? You're that *starved* for time with him?"

Lo fixes the cardboard, no longer tangled with it. "You're just jealous I get the fake thing *and* the real thing."

"Jealous? *Please.*" She waves at him. "The fake Connor Cobalt is all yours." She flips her hair off her shoulder and then watches something outside behind her. "Careful over that stone, Moffy."

The toddlers usually have trouble walking up the cobblestone path.

"And you two"—Rose retrains her gaze on Dais and me—"shouldn't be padding his *ego.* It might be his birthday, but he'll carry this fact into next year." She glares at the cardboard. "I can hear it now, 'I'm so important, you all tried to replicate me.'"

"He wouldn't be wrong," Lo says.

I groan.

Rose scoffs.

Daisy smiles.

"Let's just hope it won't scare him off," Rose notes as Moffy and Jane enter the cottage.

As fast as they can—which isn't fast since they're fucking toddlers—they rush to a mini basketball hoop near the window nook. I drilled it into the wall, so both of them have something different to do when they come over. They dig in a wicker basket for bouncy balls.

Lo forces his attention away from his son. He walks towards me, but I have a feeling he just wants something in the kitchen. "Connor loves himself. I bet this'll be his favorite thing all year. Besides being friends with me." He flashes a dry smile.

Rose glares. "His favorite thing is *me.* Your friendship is in the lower third tier."

Lo wears mock surprise. "That's not what he said."

Rose rolls her eyes but also keeps watch out the door. "You're right, Loren, he loves himself, but that doesn't extend to an inferior duplication." She doesn't give anyone time to respond. "Beckett and Charlie are in the car, do you mind helping me, Daisy?"

"Sure thing." She gives a soldier's salute before leaving my side and exiting with her sister.

Sulli squirms in my arms. She'd rather be crawling around on the floor, so I set her back by her kiddie keyboard.

Lo rummages through my kitchen cupboards, opening and closing half of them.

I follow and notice the tabloid near the sink. I don't remember ordering a subscription, and I doubt Daisy would. I scowl at our address printed on the front with *my* name.

Lo slams another cupboard, a bag of chips beneath his arm, but he's now searching through the pantry.

"What the fuck are you looking for?" I ask.

"Salsa, man." Agitation sharpens his words. "You can't have chips without salsa." His daggered amber eyes meet mine for a fraction of a second. "Have I taught you nothing, big brother?"

"I don't have any."

His face falls like I killed something he loves. It's a fucking expression that nearly makes me respond with, *I'll go out and get some for you right now.*

"This party can't be called a party." Lo shuts the pantry door. "You know what it is now? A *social*—the hosts spread out things like hummus and carrots, and they expect everyone to talk long enough that they'll forget about *real* goddamn food. You brought me to a social, bro." He opens his bag of chips. "I'll never forgive you for this."

His sarcasm is so thick.

"What is that in your fucking hand?" I question. "That's real fucking food."

He crunches on a chip. "It's not real without salsa."

For fuck's sake. I open my fridge and find tomatoes, lime, some onion and…yeah, cilantro. Lo doesn't really cook, but I do.

While he eats and our children play, I start making his fucking salsa, and I have to ask him something. It's killing me. I can't keep it in any fucking longer.

I grab a cutting board, and he sits on the counter beside me. "Something happened yesterday," I say beneath my breath. I check over my shoulder, but the door is closed and the girls haven't returned yet.

It's likely they're talking in private by the car.

Lo tenses, a chip stopping midair by his mouth. He drops his hand. "Is it your leg?"

After my climbing accident, my right leg has been fucked, but physical therapy has helped. I don't have a limp anymore, but the ache has stayed. I ignore the dull throb in my knee, and it only grows if I don't stretch morning and night.

"No." I shake my head.

Lo lowers his voice. "Dad?"

"No."

My relationship with my dad is better than it has been in the past, but I won't let him watch Sullivan without me there. I never fucking will.

"Look…" I just try to come out with it. "I don't want to break her fucking heart, but something happened and—"

"Did you fucking cheat on her?" I've seen that malicious, spiteful, *I will murder you and everything you fucking love* look in my brother's eyes, all directed at me—but not in a long time.

"*No*, fuck no," I force.

His cheekbones are weapons directed at me, but he tries to relax. "You suck at this, you know?" He means delivering bad news.

I rake a hand through my hair. "I fucking know." This hasn't changed, but at least I'm *trying* to say it rather than letting these things eat at everyone.

"You're making it seem worse than I bet it is."

I start dicing the tomatoes and onion. "Yeah…" My stomach twists. "Yesterday, Sulli said her first word and Daisy was in the shower." We decided that *dada* and *mama* sound too much like noises than words, so we agreed her first one would be something else.

She was *waiting* to hear our daughter say her first word. This has been on her fucking mind.

Realization washes over my brother's sharp features. "That's it?"

"She doesn't want to fucking miss anything like that, and she missed it." I hate feeling like I took something from Daisy. I want to give her *everything* in this entire fucking world.

"What was the word?"

"Are you serious?" I glower. "That's not fucking important in all of this."

"It was '*fuck*' wasn't it?" He almost starts laughing.

I toss a dishrag at his face. "Fuck you. And yeah, so what if it was *fuck*?" A growl sticks to my throat and I dice these fucking onions more forcefully.

"Lily owes me fifty bucks, that's why," Lo retorts.

I'm not surprised they bet on my kid. We've bet on theirs for fun too. "No, Lily doesn't, not if I never fucking mention this to Daisy…" I trail off at his grimace. "What?"

"Don't lie, man. Take it from someone who is a world-renowned liar, you don't want to do it here. It might be the easier thing, but it's not goddamn better."

Yeah.

Yeah, I know.

"She'll be happy it happened at all," he tries to assure me. "You're overthinking this."

"Yeah…I probably am," I mutter. I nod to him. "Thanks. I'll fucking tell her." And then I stupidly rub my fucking eyes with my onion-juiced fingers. "*Motherfucker.*" My eyeballs scald and sting. I sprint to the fucking sink, turn on the faucet, and stick my head underneath it.

I rinse my eyes quickly and only relax when water gushes across them.

Lo pops another chip into his mouth. "I take it back. This social isn't half-bad."

I flip him off.

Hopefully we'll be saying the same exact thing when Connor arrives.

{ 9 }

Lily Hale

Why am I always in charge of making sure Connor doesn't flee his birthday party?

I text Lo.

I need an explanation because this duty seems too important for someone like me. For his 28th and 29th birthdays, Connor never actively tried to leave the country on January 3rd, but still, someone more astute and capable should be the watchdog.

Like Rose or Ryke.

I have talents. I know I do, but being responsible for a certified genius going from point A (his work) to point B (the party) is not one of them. The genius will outwit me.

I bite my nails, my nerves rocketing. No one understands how much pressure is attached to this one task. If Connor doesn't show up to his party, that's on me.

I ascend the Cobalt Inc. elevator to his office. and squeeze my hands beneath my pits to stop biting my nails. I mutter to myself, "You look like Mary Katherine Gallagher from *Superstar*." I will *not* sniff my hands like that SNL character. Nope. Not happening.

While I'm alone on this elevator, I keep muttering encouragements. "Rose insisted that he won't bail, and you believe her, don't you?" I nod. *Rose wouldn't lie to me.* "You have instructions. You know what to do, Lily Hale."

I nod more confidently.

The instructions: *Bring Connor Cobalt to Ryke and Daisy's cottage for a surprise party.*

Rose's disclaimer: *Don't fuck up.*

So she didn't say that outright, but her narrowed eyes contained too many punishments and threats. I was sweating when she just told me to get in the car. *Shit*, I'm definitely still sweating. I waft my plain black long-sleeve shirt, my black coat two sizes too big but it warms my legs. I'm not dressed properly for Cobalt Inc. since I just wear boots and leggings as bottoms, but I don't think Connor will care.

I did remember to wash my hair today, so there's that.

My phone pings just as the elevator doors whoosh open.

Because you're the best at it, love – Lo

Riiiight. I don't believe him, not even a little bit.

I step out of the elevator and then notice an incoming second text.

And he'll feel too guilty to ditch you – Lo

Would Connor feel badly about deserting someone like me? Maybe. He was my tutor before he was my friend, and even Connor Cobalt the Tutor wouldn't abandon me if I needed him.

And I do need him.

I need him to behave and follow my orders.

My nose crinkles. This'll be interesting.

I pocket my phone and search for Connor through the hallways. People busily bustle around, dressed in suits and pin skirts. All walk with purposeful strides, no one really loiters. I'd say this floor resembles the offices in *Mad Men*, but there's no smoking or alcohol and there are more male receptionists and females in their own offices.

I try to be a fly on the wall, but as I head towards Connor's corner office, eyes latch onto me. The gold nameplate on his door reads: Connor Cobalt, CEO of Cobalt Inc.

Just before I grab the knob, a man in a sleek navy suit and skinny tie slips in front of me, extending his arm to physically block me out of the way. I'm forced to take two steps back.

"Excuse me," I mutter. I straighten up and wait for him to move aside. *Channel your inner Rose Calloway Cobalt.* I silently repeat the mantra: *I am a fortress. I am a shark. No one will fuck with me.*

I clear my throat. "Excuse you." I wince at myself. Would Rose have said that? "I mean…" I shake my head. "I'm here to see Connor."

He brushes his fingers through his salt and peppered hair. "You see the glass walls?" Then he gestures to the walls right beside us like I'm dumb. Of course I see them. "See how they're frosted?" *Yes, I can't see into them.* Cobalt Inc. has electronic frost to add a little privacy.

Hale Co. offices don't have that.

I once asked Rose if she's ever had sex with Connor in his office. I'm still really proud of the moment because I didn't stammer or flush.

She said, "I'll tell you but you can't act like it's ground-breaking and you *can't* tell Loren. This is a sister thing."

"I promise." We pinky-promised. I refused her *blood pact* offer, which involves cutting our palms.

"Yes," she said, "we've had sex in his office."

I couldn't stop smiling because she did something that I haven't done yet. Though I *have* had sex in the Halway Comics office, but it's not a giant corporation like the other Fortune 500 companies.

And I've upheld our promise to this day. I plan to take it to my grave.

The man suddenly waves his hand in my face.

Oh shit. How long has he been doing that? I spaced out. Connor's frosted walls reminded me of sex. *Everything* reminds me of sex. Can he tell?

I know he can't. It's all in my head. I try to remember this.

"Did you hear what I said?" he asks.

I nod. "These are frosted walls."

"Which means that he's in a meeting."

Oh.

I didn't prepare for this. "I can wait."

He does this head-tilt thing. "How about you come to my office? I have a couch you can sit on while you wait." His gaze never deters from mine, thankfully, but this small gratitude doesn't erase his lustful expression, completely full of wrongdoings.

I'd like to say this happens far less than it does, but most people will see me and think *oh, there's that sex addict.* A select, sleazy few view this as an invitation to hit on me, believing I'll welcome their advances with wide-open legs and a bed.

The sleazy few tend to be entitled, affluent men. I thought that I'd be free of them around Connor's office, only because he said that he's strict about drug testing his employees. I realize now that my logic makes no sense. A person doesn't have to snort coke to be a corrupt asshole.

And some people with money believe they possess limitless power over others.

Even over me.

My skin crawls. "I'm okay here." I assess my surroundings, not sure where *here* is. An empty receptionist desk sits about two feet away. I sink into the robust chair, claiming this seat for now.

It's what Rose would do.

Instead of taking the hint, the man slides *onto* the sleek desk. Right in front of my chair. His ass knocks into a business card holder, and his foot almost brushes me.

I go rigid, my eyes swerving left and right.

It's official: I hate Connor's offices.

And his crotch—his crotch is eyelevel, and his fly is half open. I can't tell if that's on purpose or if he forgot to zip up after a bathroom break. *Stop looking there!*

I'm trying. I'm really trying.

I swallow hard, so uncomfortable, but I find a solution. I scoot the chair backwards. Without wheels, it screeches on the floor, but I succeed in distancing myself from him.

Take that!

"I can keep you company while we wait," he says in this sincere voice.

I hesitate for a moment, actually wondering if he's trying to be nice since I look uncomfortable or if this is just a gross pick-up line.

"That's okay." I avoid his eyes now and dig in my pocket for my phone. "I'd rather be alone."

He leans forward to whisper, "There are some men here that don't necessarily love the Calloway sisters. It's better if I stay to keep you away from their shit, and they'd definitely give you some." He tilts his head again and smiles a smug smile. "Aren't you going to say *thank you*?"

And then he tries to tap his foot to mine.

Nope. We're not playing footsie. That's not how my day is going. I have *instructions*. Connor Cobalt's sleazy employee is not a part of my instructions. And I don't want to play footsie with anyone but Loren Hale!

Rose would have his larynx ripped out by now.

My fingers whiten on the phone. "My parents never taught me those two words." I never look at him as I text. "I'm a rich brat."

I send Connor a simple text:

I'm outside your office. Waiting for you.

I don't add an SOS or help me. I don't want to disturb his meeting.

"That's funny," he says flatly. "You sure you don't want to wait in my office? It's much more comfortable. I can find something you like." His suggestive words make me sick.

I feel my face twist into a cringe.

"Come on. You won't have to deal with all these stares."

I take the bait and scan the room. A couple employees peek from their desks. Maybe they believe I'm seconds from grinding against this man. Maybe they anticipate the moment where I'll let him lead me into a bathroom.

I wouldn't.

I'm not that girl anymore. I'm not so consumed by a vice that I'd say *yes* and *yes* and never *no*. I have boundaries and rules, and here's one of my biggest:

I will not cheat on Loren Hale.

"Lily."

I jolt at that voice. His smooth tone sounds like heaven, and I spring to my feet, beyond ready to meet Connor. I approach him so fast and nearly run into his arms.

Realizing that would look terrible, I stop midway and raise my hand in a half-wave. "Hi." I peek at his frosted walls, hoping he didn't leave an important meeting because of my text.

I could've survived an hour on my own, even with Sleazebag prodding me for sex.

"I can wait until you're finished with your meeting," I add while Sleazebag slides off the desk to stand up.

Connor is blank-faced, so I'm surprised when he asks, "What meeting?"
What?

I frown. "Your walls are frosted. I thought that meant you were in a meeting."

"I always turn on the privacy glass at the end of the day." His gaze drifts to Sleazebag, and the man raises his brows accusingly at *me*. Like I made it all up.

"I told her you were available," he says.

I gape. He can't be serious? *What an asshole.*

"She wanted to talk to me a little before heading in," he continues.

My mouth just keeps dropping. *Fuck him.* And not sexually! Just to be clear, there is *nothing* sexual about this. "That's not true!" I shout out of frustration, and a hot flush rises up my neck.

"You don't have to be embarrassed about it. It's not like we did anything." His tone implies that the door is still open if I ever want to do "something" with him.

I hate how he just turned my red flush around on me. How he used it against me. I feel trapped in a corner, and I'm not even sure how I got pushed there in the first place. I'm not good at mental games unless it involves *lying* to people I love.

And that's a horrible skill. I'm ashamed I have it at all.

Sleazebag is about to say a goodbye. I see it on the tip of his tongue and the way he shifts towards the hall.

"Martin," Connor says first.

Let Sleazebag leave. The longer we endure him, the more my stomach cramps.

"If this is about the Baylor account—"

"Pack your office and be out by tomorrow."

My jaw unhinges.

Connor said that without blinking, without flinching, without his voice even elevating. He could've just said *your hair is salt and pepper* and it would've all been the same to him.

Sleazebag pales. "What?"

"I believed you were intelligent, but if you need me to reiterate, then you've just proved you're too incompetent to work here."

Sleazebag is in shock.

"You're fired," Connor says. "Do you understand me now?"

He glowers. "Because of *her*?"

"Because you thought you could lie to me. Because you have a clear problem for taking responsibility for your own actions. Because you *preyed* on someone. Any three, but mostly the third, are grounds for termination. I could fire you for much less, so take your things and leave my building. If I see your face anywhere near Cobalt Inc. again, I'll have you arrested for trespassing. Now you can stop wasting my time. I have a party to attend."

I choke on air at that last line.

The word "surprise" is in my instructions. *I'm* more surprised than Connor at this point. Surprised a Cobalt Inc. employee subtly prodded me to hook up with him. Surprised Connor just fired him. Surprised that Connor isn't surprised.

Sleazebag looks mortified, irate, and flabbergasted, all at once. He trots towards his desk with a defeated slouch, and Connor hardly pays him more attention.

He motions to me, and I follow him to the elevators.

I have to sort of *sprint* to catch up to his lengthy stride. "People are staring," I whisper.

"People always stare at me."

Of course they do.

Once inside the elevator, I ask, "Was he important?"

Connor types hurriedly on his phone like he's fixing a problem. "He wasn't in an executive position, but he was a project manager. He'll need to be replaced by tomorrow."

Guilt creeps up my throat. "You don't have to fire him because of me."

"Did you not hear me? It wasn't just because of you."

"But he'd still have a job if I didn't show up." Why am I defending Sleazebag? I know what Dr. Banning would say. My therapist would tell me that my guilt stems from my own wealth. I feel like I have no right to cut other people off at the knees, even if those people try to hurt me. I've been given too much to take away from other people. *I'm allowed to be hurt.*

I hear Dr. Banning's clear and distinct words: *he does not have the authority to hurt you. No one does.*

"Maybe not." Connor rolls up the sleeves to his button-down. It's a little warm in the elevator. "It was only a matter of time before he showed me who he really was. Martin believed we were friends, and so he thought he was invulnerable. When people are comfortable, they act more like themselves, which I foster." His blue eyes flit to mine. "Be yourself, and if your true self puts my company, my employees, and *my friends* at risk, I won't think twice about removing you from my circle."

I would applaud, but I'm too in awe. After all these years, Connor still impresses me. I can't believe he's my friend and that he's married to my sister. He seems otherworldly.

He studies my expression before saying, "If you're going to call me Superman again, don't list his mythical powers."

Like flying. I try hard not call him anything "otherworldly" but I end up blurting out, "Then you're Batman!"

If he's annoyed, I can't tell.

"Batman doesn't have unnatural powers," I start to explain.

"I know who Batman is."

"Because you're Batman."

He arches a brow.

Batman would do that. I smile at the thought and remember Connor dressing as the DC character during our Comic-Con outing six years ago.

The elevator doors slide open, and I just now realize that we're not headed to the lobby. We've stopped on the third floor. "Wait…"

Connor is already stepping out, not slowing for me. He doesn't take commands from anyone but himself…and maybe Rose, but he won't admit that the same way she wouldn't admit she listens to him.

I hurriedly follow his lengthy stride again, squeezing between the elevator doors before they close.

The third floor looks less like an executive level. Flooded with copy machines and gray cubicles, everyone is crammed tight. More people loiter around than the people upstairs, but as soon as they see Connor, they dart to their cubicles like little moles scurrying into their holes.

He doesn't break pace.

"Connor." I catch up to his side again. "Where are we going?"

"I'm bringing someone to my birthday party."

"You're not supposed to know about the party," I whisper-hiss. How did he find out? Because he's Connor Cobalt. That might be explanation enough.

He just *knows* things.

Connor has the same composed face, never changing, not even by a fraction of an inch. He must have a thousand walls hiding his emotions while he's at work. For anyone, this would be exhausting, but I think this is his normal.

He easily skirts around a water cooler. "If they truly wanted to keep the party a secret, they wouldn't have sent you to bring me."

I'm at his offices alone on his birthday. It does seem suspect. "Fair point."

Connor abruptly halts at a cubicle near an old fax machine. I crash into his back and then stumble. He just looks over his shoulder like a gnat splatted against his windshield.

I think Connor Cobalt is made of titanium.

Superman.

I frown.

Or is he Batman?

This is a real dilemma.

"You were in my way," I mumble.

He steps to the right, giving me more room to stand. I mutter a *thank you* and raise my chin like Rose. Who are we bringing to the party? I draw a blank at first, but as soon as I see him, it clicks.

Sitting fixatedly in front of a computer, a twenty-one-year-old with big bulky headphones and messy brown hair types incessantly. His fingers pound the keyboard, not even noticing the strands of hair that hang into his eyes.

"Garrison," Connor says, loud enough that anyone nearby can hear. Even hovering right in front of his cubicle, Garrison still never lifts his head. He's transfixed with whatever's on that computer.

Connor shifts, now able to wave a hand in front of the screen.

His eyes find Connor and then me, and all the while, he continues to type. Multitasking. Not my forte, but I envy those who can. So useful, it's like a superpower all in itself.

"What do you want?" Garrison snaps, his focus returning to Connor, who also happens to be his boss. Last year, Connor invested in whatever startup Garrison chose, but Garrison's choice is still a mystery to everyone. He claims he's in the "early development" stages.

"You're done for the day," Connor says. "I need you to come with us."

Garrison frowns and swings his head to me. *He's still typing.* "Is this work related?"

"Umm…" I don't know what to say. *Yes? No?* I shrug.

"Will you come with us if it isn't?" Connor asks.

"No."

Recently, we've all been a little worried about him. With Willow in London, he doesn't have a lot of friends in Philadelphia, and he never talks about his family to Lo or me. They only live one street over, but his parents aren't very social with any of us.

"Then it's work related," Connor replies. "Grab your things."

Garrison yanks his headphones to his neck. To me, he says, "Just tell me where we're going and why."

I cave.

Mostly because this is Garrison, and he worked at Superhero & Scones before he ever migrated to Cobalt Inc. Sincerity even fills his blue-green eyes, and I can't say no to it.

"Ryke's house—or cottage." We all call it a cottage; I don't know why I called it a house. "It's a surprise party for Connor."

Connor has no reaction towards the venue of his party. He *really* keeps his emotions padlocked at work.

Garrison's face scrunches up like we're both insane. "How is this a surprise birthday if you know? And why the hell do you want me to go?"

"Surprising me is so rare that everyone uses the term loosely." Then he points at the computer. "You're here at six in the morning and you leave at midnight. *Seven* days a week. While I appreciate your work ethic, as your friend, it's disconcerting."

I didn't know any of that. Garrison never kept those kind of hours at Superheroes & Scones, but that was also when Willow lived here.

Garrison inhales a tight breath, but he doesn't really exhale. "You're my boss, not my friend."

"I'm both," Connor says easily, "and since you seem to be lacking in the friend department lately, I wouldn't turn my back on one, especially friendships as valuable as mine."

I stick up for Garrison. "Having no friends isn't a bad thing."

Garrison pinches his eyes. "Can you both just shut up?" After a short moment of thought, he rolls back in his chair, grabs his backpack and slings it over his shoulder. His ripped jeans and black hoodie contrasts the suit and ties of other employees.

I doubt he cares about conforming to the proper business attire.

Garrison stands five inches shorter than Connor. "If I go, you have to stop calling me your friend. We're not, okay?" Before Connor speaks,

Garrison turns on me. "And I have friends…" He pauses and corrects himself, "One friend. She's just not here."

Connor casually checks his watch. "Most people would be on their knees to be my friend. This just illustrates your lack of judgment."

He never fails at reminding us all how special he is, even in this backhanded way, and no matter how old we are and how many years pass, I can't help but agree.

Connor Cobalt is one of a kind.

Garrison nods and says dryly, "Thanks, boss."

"Follow me." Connor motions to both of us, and now we're off to the party. At least I've succeeded on my part. I didn't fail like I thought I would've.

Garrison and I trail Connor on our way to the elevators. I don't rush to keep up with Connor anymore. I stick with Garrison's pace. As we pass a copy machine, he whispers to me, "Just so you know, you're my favorite boss."

I shouldn't take pride in that fact, since Garrison was just clearly insulted by Connor, but I hold onto it anyway.

Favorite Boss Award Goes To…

I smile wide.

I CUP THE SPEAKER of my phone by my mouth. "We're walking up to the cottage now." I trail Connor and Garrison and try not to trip on the slick stone set into the grass. Smoke plumes out of the chimney, the cottage all gray stone. It suits Ryke and Daisy the same way that the enormous, regal Cobalt estate resembles my older sister and her husband.

My house is simple and more common in comparison to theirs. Just red brick, a regular kind of yard, no fountains or tulip trees, no quaint windows or a hand-built tree house. I like simple, and I know Lo does too.

"Is he at the door?" Rose's voice echoes through my phone.

"Not yet." The white front door has half a window, but they must've taped paper over it because I can't see inside.

The blinds snap on another window, and a pair of yellow-green eyes darts from left to right until they narrow on Connor. They disappear faster than lightning.

"I saw you," I whisper-hiss.

"Shhh," she retorts.

She's shushing me? I put the speaker closer to my lips. "I fulfilled my role. I'd like some appreciation for chaperoning a *genius*." Connor is at the front door, and I think he heard me. He glances over his shoulder with this look like *do you really believe you're being quiet?*

Right.

He has superhuman hearing.

Superman.

"Thank you, Lily." Rose sounds grateful. And then she hangs up on me.

I squint at Connor as I approach. "Are you sure you don't have a bodysuit beneath your shirt?"

Garrison doesn't try to figure out what I'm saying. He apathetically leans against the stone siding.

Connor stares down at me. "If I said *no*, would you believe me?"

I think for a second. Superman wouldn't give up his secret identity, would he? "Only if you showed me. I'd need evidence."

Without hesitation, Connor begins unbuttoning his white button-down, and my whole face sears, red-hot as his bare chest comes into view. As he *strips* for me.

"Nonono," I slur, "that's okay." I'd like to have Connor's shameless attitude, but then again, he's in a league of his own. "I believe you. I believe you!"

His amused smile only makes my neck burn. "I'm glad," he says casually and leaves two of his buttons undone. Then he turns the door-knob, and we all step inside.

"SURPRISE!!"

The household says all at once. Moffy, Jane, Beckett, and Charlie are front-and-center, tossing confetti at Connor. Daisy is knelt by Sulli, helping her little baby join the other kids. Note to self: the hot-tempered triad does *not* throw confetti at parties. Rose, Lo, and Ryke are nowhere near the little bits of paper.

"Happy Birthday, Daddy!" Jane is the first to say, tossing another handful of confetti from this little pink pail.

I skirt around Connor to see his reaction.

He's smiling at all the children.

He's smiling.

Rose is too.

And then they lock eyes, and I swear the world slows for a second or two. The nerd stars are a powerful force while in orbit. I touch my cheeks, my dopey grin hurting my face.

I step forward in a daze—ohmyGod, I crash into something hard and I fall down on top of it. Is that...I shriek in horror. *I'm lying on top of Connor Cobalt!* Or a cardboard version...his smug grin is right by my lips. I have my hands on his shoulders.

Wha....is this?

Abort! Abort!

Instinct and panic overtake me. I roll off this cardboard thing about as graceful as someone unfurling a burrito. I shut my eyes tight and repeat a good mantra: *I did not lie on top of Connor Cobalt. I did not lie on top of Connor Cobalt.*

I only stop rolling when my body hits the back of the couch. I sense someone crouching over me, and I open my eyes to dimpled cheeks, a rising smile, and warm amber eyes. I don't know how it's possible, but Loren Hale has grown even more handsome with age.

When I look in the mirror, I'm still gangly Lily, a girl who could be mistaken for a fifteen-year-old, no matter how much time passes. Inside, though, I feel older. Stronger. Maybe even a tad bit wiser.

It's the insides that count the most.

Not sexually being inside, just *inside,* inside. I scrunch my nose at my thoughts.

His smile curves higher. "You alright, love?"

I shake my head. "That *thing* came out of nowhere. I was doomed from the start."

"I did the same thing," he tells me. "So it looks like I was doomed with you."

I try hard not to smile. "From the very start?"

Lo nods. "From the very start, Lily Hale." And then he lifts me in a front-piggyback. I wrap my arms around his shoulders, his lips close to my lips. I like Lo's lips *much* better than Connor's.

I'm entranced by him and only him. His hands cup my ass as he holds me around his waist, and his gaze dances around my features with this headiness that I know I share.

I abruptly kiss him, my heart racing, and before I worry that I kissed him at an inappropriate time, he reciprocates with almost as much need. One of his hands leaves my ass, and he clutches the back of my head, deepening the kiss until oxygen cages in my lungs.

I grind forward.

He slows, and my heart lurches sideways.

I can't pounce on him like a horny tiger. Not right now at least. I remember that we're in a semi-public setting, filled with friends and *children.* Maximoff is busy making "confetti angels" in the heap that covers the hardwood, Jane with him. My toddler is oblivious to my own struggle, which is how I like it.

Lo strokes my hair once, and his lips brush against my ear. "It's okay, Lil." His encouragement relaxes my shoulders, and I tell him I'm going to shift to his back.

Front-piggybacks can be dangerous territory.

He sets me down, and then I jump on his back. Now in a regular piggyback, I go to the kitchen with Lo, a fresh bowl of salsa and a bag of chips on the counter.

"Happy fucking Birthday," Ryke says as he picks up the half-crinkled cardboard cutout of Connor Cobalt.

Connor has Beckett in his arms while he appraises the cardboard version of himself.

"He loves it," I whisper to Lo, who hands me a chip. I crunch, glad he didn't put too much spicy salsa on mine.

"Nah, he seems ambivalent." Lo nods towards Rose who rocks Charlie back and forth, the little baby falling asleep against her chest. "Queen Rose looks ready to call this a birthday failure."

I squint towards my older sister. She seems her natural self. Rigid but not in a *I'm-calling-this-party-a-shit-show* kind of way. She's as likely to roll her eyes and smile as she is to glare and huff.

"Who bought the cutout?" I ask in another whisper.

"Daisy found it on some celebrity site."

I imagine fans putting a life-sized Connor Cobalt in their bedroom, right next to a Damon Salvatore or a Harry Styles. I don't think Connor would mind either.

Connor finally reacts, his million-dollar grin as rich as his clothes. He captures Ryke's gaze. "So my birthday present is *you* admitting you're my biggest fan."

Rose tries to contain a snort with her hand.

Lo actually laughs aloud, tossing another chip in his mouth.

Ryke flips them both off, and then glowers at Connor. "It's a fucking decoration."

"If you desired to look at me everyday, I'd suggest the real version, not this inferior one, but I'm sure this is the best you could do."

Ryke nods a couple times. "Me not punching you right now is your real fucking birthday present. So you better get it all out while you can, Cobalt."

Instead of giving Ryke a hard time, Connor scans the first floor: the gold and black decorations, the banner with *Happy 30th Birthday Connor!*, the balloons, all of us here together.

"I never thought I'd appreciate this day more than any other," he says, his smile lifting at the sight of Jane covered in confetti, "but I do. I am." He looks to each one of us. "Thank you."

"It was mostly Rose and Daisy," I tell him since my part was so small. Rose planned the event, and she left a lot of the details to my little sister, who volunteered to be a big role in today's execution.

Connor and Daisy exchange this friendly smile, and he nods at her in thanks.

"We ordered salmon from your favorite restaurant," Rose explains, "and we've all agreed to read passages from your favorite books before dinner." I was given *The Sound and the Fury* by William Faulkner. I reread the passage Rose highlighted *fifteen* times so I don't stumble over the words, but I still have no idea what any of it means.

Lo and Daisy said they'd trade with me. They have *Great Expectations* by Charles Dickens and *Middlemarch* by George Eliot, but I didn't want to learn their passages, only to find out they were just as confusing.

Connor grins. "I'm intrigued." He looks entranced mostly by his wife holding his son.

I whisper to Lo, "He's going to kiss her."

"They're not close enough," Lo replies, just when Connor takes two steps forward.

"Ha."

Lo munches on a chip. "He has the *I want to fuck you* look, but he's not going to do a goddamn thing until he's alone with her."

I frown. Maybe he's right. We're the two that cling to one another in public. Even if intensity brims off their shoulders like electric sparks, magnetizing Connor to Rose and Rose to Connor, they won't act on the *pull* if we're around. Not unless they forget.

And they rarely forget anything.

Rose tries to fasten a cold glare. "Today is about you, but you have one rule."

"I'm listening."

"You must contain your ego for the sake of your children. It'll asphyxiate the room."

"My ego won't hurt them, darling." He steps even closer.

She snaps in French and raises her hand at his chest.

He smoothly replies back in the same language and clasps her hand, only to kiss her knuckles. I perk up like I won a prize, but his lips never move to her lips.

"Even their sons are bored by this," Lo says. Beckett has fallen asleep in Connor's arms like Charlie has in Rose's.

I poke Lo's arm. "Hey, this is *love*. Love isn't boring."

Lo mockingly yawns. "What was that, Lil? I just woke up from a nap."

He can be so mean. I rest my chin on his shoulder, still clinging onto him tight. I instantly forget my thoughts at the sight of a tabloid...next to the bowl of salsa.

"Hey," Garrison greets Lo before sitting on the counter. They begin a short conversation, and I fixate on the headlines in view.

LILY CALLOWAY, PREGNANT AGAIN!

False, but they put an unflattering picture of me on the front. My face is all red and splotchy. I wear a gray baggy sweater that reaches my knees while exiting Superheroes & Scones, hand-in-hand with Moffy. At least they didn't say anything rude about him.

Sometimes I worry about the day where they go from LITTLE MAXIMOFF WATCHES A PHILADELPHIA 76ERS GAME! to MAXIMOFF HALE HAS A ZIT! HE'S JUST LIKE US! I can't even imagine my own awkward puberty phases put on blast. Neither can Lo.

Look away from the magazines. Look away.

I do, only to see Connor, Rose, Daisy, and Ryke in a conversation together. "I wonder if Connor's DNA is superhuman too," I mumble beneath my breath. And his eyes flit to me!

I'm *not* making this up.

Maybe he truly does have superhuman hearing. "Lo," I say softly, breaking up his short conversation with Garrison.

"Hmm?" he asks, swishing around the salsa with a chip. His other hand clutches my leg while I'm on his back.

"Do you think Connor might be Batman or Superman?"

Lo drops me.

I land on my ass, and I gape up at him. "Lo!" It's not the first time he's dropped me mid-piggyback for speaking about a DC character.

He waves his chip at me. "There are a goddamn *thousand* superheroes, and you chose two that I can't stand?"

"They make the most sense."

"They make about as much sense as calling Connor the Swamp Thing."

I pick myself off the floor. "That's just silly. Swamp Thing isn't even *close* to being Batman and Superman."

His sharp glares simultaneously says *they're all DC characters* and *you've betrayed me, love.* "Please let me know where I can find my other wife. This one in front of me is a sellout."

I touch my heart. It's like he shot an arrow through it. "I'm not a sellout. I just happen to not be an elitist about the whole Marvel versus DC thing, and I can appreciate *all* superheroes equally."

"You think they're all made *equally?*" His passion about comics brims to the surface, so alluring that I actually near him, despite his double-edged glare. "Do you want to talk Green Lantern? We can talk Green Lantern."

"Okay, okay," I immediately concede on this front. "So I have my favorites, just like you." I have my fingers in his belt loops, staring up at him.

His arms are already around me. "My best friend is *not* Batman or Superman."

"Then what is he?"

"Connor Cobalt," Lo answers without hesitation. "He's Connor fucking Cobalt, and whatever powers he has, they're all his own."

I smile. This feels more accurate than anything else. My gaze drifts to that tabloid behind Lo, and my smile quickly fades. "What is…" I snatch the tabloid before Lo realizes where my mind wandered. In the right margin, Celebrity Crush fit tiny script that says: [POLL] WHICH CALLOWAY SISTER HAS THE CUTEST BABY?

My jaw drops.

They did not pit our babies against each other.

Lo rips the tabloid out of my hands.

"They polled our babies by cuteness," I exclaim. "They can't do that."

He gives me a look. "They can do whatever they want."

"I just wish there were *some* ethical limitations," I say while he flips to the page. I try to push his hands together to stop him. "Don't! What if Moffy is ranked the ugliest." I lower my voice at that. "We'll know and we'll feel bad and it'll give him a complex."

He pauses long enough to say, "That's not going to happen. We have an *adorable* baby."

"So do Rose and Daisy."

Lo is so biased. He doesn't see it. "You don't have to look." But he's still going to.

I back away to distance myself from the tabloid. It's a bomb. He's holding a bomb. I still hate *Celebrity Crush*. At one point, I felt as compulsive towards reading them as I did towards sex.

"How'd that end up here?" I ask. Ryke hates them more than anyone. I look to Garrison but he shrugs, out of the loop with me.

Lo keeps flipping the glossy pages. "Just found out that Ryke bought Sullivan something online—a pajama set or bath robe, I can't remember. He forgot to uncheck the 30-day free subscription to *Celebrity Crush* during checkout."

Makes sense.

Lo pauses on a page, and he begins to read. When his eyes lift to mine, I ask, "Is it bad?"

"I thought you didn't want to know."

"I don't." This is a test, and I'm going to pass.

{ 10 }

January 2019
THE MEADOWS COTTAGE
Philadelphia

LOREN HALE

[P]OLL] WHICH CALLOWAY SISTER HAS THE CUTEST
BABY?

It's really dumb. They're all sisters, and so they share similar features, which means that our kids do too. It's like asking who's the prettiest sibling in a giant family. I know I'm an asshole, but this shit from *Celebrity Crush* is Grade A assholery.

Familiar bitterness slides down my throat like acid. *Let's see what we have here.*

A recent picture of Jane. Dressed in a pale yellow tutu and zebra-print sweater, she reaches for a sequined purse in the Calloway Couture boutique store, the one across the street from Superheroes & Scones. Huh. It looks like someone *in* the store snapped the photo instead of paparazzi from outside. Most likely a shopper.

I could just shut the tabloid. It wouldn't be hard to throw it out, but I keep reading. If this *one* poll about our kids gets to me, then I'm not goddamn ready for the future. Because I know it's going to be a hell of a lot crueler than this.

Moffy doesn't need a drunken, apathetic father. I know that he needs someone better. Even if I'm scared, even if I lack that same conceited optimism my friends might have, I have to persist and be aware. I *never* want to be blind to Moffy's battles or what might hurt him. I want to understand his struggle the same way my brother tried to understand mine.

I glance at Lily one more time. She drifts towards Garrison, and they chat quietly about movies. As much as I want to read about this poll, I'm grateful she doesn't. In the past, tabloids consumed Lily, and I see that pull. I know that pull.

To trade one vice with another.

I'm glad she doesn't.

I return to the article that first details the children being polled.

Jane Eleanor Cobalt, daughter of Rose and Connor Cobalt, can best be described as a mini Rose Calloway.

I shake my head at that line, and I can feel my jaw clench. I grew up with *young* Rose Calloway, horns and seven hells beneath a pleated skirt, tucked-in blouse, and crisp, ironed collar.

Jane isn't neat like Rose. She sits upright, but she'll also roll around on the floor. And she's definitely not fashionable. I don't know much about fashion, besides a brief stint as a model, but I don't need to be a designer to know that this girl is *not* stylish.

Jane is a goof. She wore striped blue and yellow stockings and a bonnet with plastic butterflies to a ballet. (We all went; it was Greg Calloway's idea of a giant family outing.)

I glaze over part of the article that says Jane is following Rose's footsteps.

Next up: a photo of my son. They chose a picture of Moffy in red Vans, jeans, a backwards baseball cap, and a Spider-Man shirt. Holding my hand and Lily's, he crosses the intersection with us. We're headed to Lucky's Diner.

Maximoff Hale, son of Lily and Loren Hale, is nothing but cool.

Lily would love that line.

Last picture: a blurry baby. A blanket partially shrouds Sulli as Ryke carries her against his chest. My brother—he does a good job at keeping his daughter out of magazines. Bitterness drips further down my throat. *Let it go.*

I do, much easier than I used to.

I remember that it's easier for him. That it'd be nearly impossible if I mimicked his steps. The result wouldn't be the same. He's just not as famous as me, and Ryke would tell me, "You're a good fucking dad, Lo."

I can't compare myself to him. Not about fatherhood, athletics, alcoholism—we may be cut from the same fucked-up cloth, but we're not shaped the same. I'm different.

I will always be different from Ryke Meadows. I love him way too much to resent him. The malicious bone in my body that attacked him, that screamed at him, that bit him until he bled—it's gone. Part of me is ashamed that I hated him *that* much when I met him, but the other part is just happy that I'm no longer living with that person inside of me.

Self-hatred is exhausting.

Ryke sits on the back of his couch. Jane and Moffy clutch his calves like koalas, and he swings his legs upwards and side-to-side while making an airplane noise. I don't think I've ever met a better person in this entire goddamn world than my older brother.

I'm proud that I know him and that my son will know him.

I look at Sulli's description in the article.

Sullivan Minnie Meadows, daughter of Daisy and Ryke Meadows, is always caught smiling.

That's true. I rarely see Sulli cry.
I skim the rest and hone in on the actual poll results.

23% Sullivan
41% Jane
36% Maximoff

No matter which way the numbers go, it's still the same shit. I roll up the magazine and ditch that for the bowl of salsa. "Little 'puff." I come up behind my wife, and she startles only for a second.

I set my chin on her shoulder, having to hunch since she's much shorter. "What are we talking about?"

"Nothing," she says too quickly and spins towards me.

I have to stand straighter, my hands full with chips and salsa. I stuff the bag underneath my arm. "Nothing?"

"That's what I said," she snaps.

"Christ, when'd you get so sassy?"

Lily crinkles her nose. *Adorable.* I stick my chip between my teeth, freeing up my hand, and I pinch her nose.

Lily pounds her fist into my arm.

I feign a wince and mumble, "Ouch, love." I tilt my head back, chip falling into my mouth.

Garrison must be irritated or trying to pick a fight with me because he says, "We were talking about *Justice League 2.*" Which isn't coming out for some time, but it still makes me grimace and glare.

People don't get it.

I have enemies, even fictional enemies. My shit list extends far beyond reality. I get what that says about me: I'm petty.

So what? I'm petty. My name is also Loren Hale.

I flash a half-smile at Garrison. "Why don't you go talk about that down the street, turn right, approach a mailbox that says *Abbey*, walk up the driveway, slam the door—goodbye." I wave curtly.

I'm also mean.

Lily is right about that.

Garrison spins an unlit cigarette between his fingers. I thought Willow said he quit. I know he won't smoke in the house, but why would he have cigarettes at all?

"You want me to go home?" he snaps and then grinds his teeth. Something's going on. I think it might just be more long-distance relationship angst.

"I want you to not speak about what-shall-not-be-named inside my brother's house, and if you can't handle that, then yeah, you can go home."

"Lo!" Lily gapes at me.

I close her mouth by pushing up her chin. I have a hard time not smiling. "Lily." I pout at her.

She pokes my chest. "You're not being nice."

"Because I'm not nice," I remind her.

She clasps my cheeks between her hands, and whatever speech she planned just leaves her eyes. They absorb my features with layers of sex and toxicity. I *want* to pull her closer, but I know I can't. It sucks. It always sucks, but I'd rather have healthy Lily every day than horny, compulsive Lily.

While holding my face, Lily is in the deepest internal battle. To make it easier for her. I reach over to the counter, setting my salsa and chips aside, then I clasp her hands in mine.

We keep some space between us, but it's hard on her and me. We both want to be all over each other. I end up wrapping my arm around her waist, and she holds onto me and then nods like *I can do this without sex.*

When I focus back on Garrison, who still sits on the counter, he opens a cupboard near his head. As he reaches for a cup, his hoodie rises, showing part of his abs and—

"What the hell?" I say mostly beneath my breath, too shocked to scream it. I raise my voice. "Garrison."

He hits his head on the cupboard as he turns towards me. "Shit," he curses, rubbing the spot. His hoodie falls back down with his arm. "What?"

I'm not the type of person to go at him, lift his hoodie up without asking, and pry deeper in his life. I've always waited for people to open up to me. I don't like poking, but this…I have to poke at this.

I don't think Lily saw.

I lower my voice so it's just between the three of us. "Where did those bruises come from?" Welts, purpled and yellowed and the size of a baseball, blemish his ribs.

His face falls, and he shakes his head. His eyes flit to Lily for a second. "Lacrosse. Drop it."

I don't believe him. I had this feeling that I let go during last year's Halloween. Something about…his brothers. The way he talks about them has *always* been off to me, but I didn't pressure Garrison to talk about it. I never have, and maybe that's on me.

Lily senses something too, especially the way that Garrison is more uncomfortable with her hearing this. Maybe she thinks whatever he says, she'll tell Willow. Even though I'm her brother, the girls share more between each other.

"Oh look—Moffy," Lily says, so obvious, so adorable. I pinch her shoulder on her way to the couch. I would've pinched her ass, but timing, place, people—all of that. I'm more aware today than other days.

Lily squints at me.

She's trying to glare. "Be nice," she reminds me.

"Yes, my Hufflepuff." I give her a partial smile, and it fades as soon as she turns her back. I rub my neck and near Garrison a bit more.

"Honestly, it's lacrosse," Garrison starts again.

"It's been Christmas break," I say, my voice edged. "When were you playing lacrosse?"

"I don't know...I just was...I was." He hangs his head, his hair falling over his eyelashes. He holds onto his bulky headphones on either side of his neck. "Let me be."

I hear myself speaking to Ryke.

Get off my back. Let me be. Leave it alone.

I'm new at being a hardass. I don't always like it, but I know sometimes people need it. I also know Garrison, and sometimes reminding him that we care helps. I hand him my bowl of salsa, and I hold the chips. I pass him one, and he stares blankly at me.

"What is this?"

"Chips and salsa. If you don't like them, we can't be friends anymore." I pop one in my mouth.

"We're friends?" he asks like he's unsure.

"Jesus Christ, do I need to make friendship bracelets for you to believe it?" This isn't the first time he's asked like that.

"Fuck you," he snaps, and I watch him hesitantly dip his chip into the salsa.

"Don't be pissy because I'm prettier. It's just a fact you're going to have to get used to."

Garrison swallows. "I thought the tall one was supposed to be the prettiest."

I always start to smile when he calls Connor *the tall one.* "Shh, we don't like to tell him the truth. It ruins his allure."

Garrison nods, his shoulders sinking forward.

I can't believe he's already twenty-one. I was so messed up at that age, and I hate that sleepless circles are beneath his eyes and that it looks like he hasn't eaten in a whole week. I wished I noticed sooner.

"So what are your brothers like; you have three, right?"

"Yeah. Mitchell, Hunter, and Davis. We're all two years apart from one another." So twenty-three, twenty-five, and twenty-seven.

I wait for him to add more, but he just stares at his hands.

"Which one's the worst?" I ask, too edged to be coy.

Garrison eyes me up and down. "I know what you're trying to do."

I could lie. I'm a *great* goddamn liar, and I have years of proof hiding an addiction and romance to prove it. But I don't, not to this guy. "Am I right?" I ask, a breath imprisoned in my chest. I gesture to his ribs. "Did one of your shitty fucking brothers do that?"

His nose flares. His throat bobs. He turns his head left and right for a way out of his own pain. I get it. I so fucking get it.

"They're just messing around," he says so quietly I almost miss the words.

I clench my teeth, my blood boiling. My instant reaction is *retaliation*. Hurt them the way they hurt him, but I breathe in, breathe out, and I settle enough to *think* first. "Can I see it again?"

Garrison glances at the living area, but everyone is seated on the couches, most of their backs turned and focus directed on the children. As his head swings to me, he lifts his hoodie, his bare skin visible.

The bruise spiders up his side, the deepest purple area around his ribs. Fractured. They're fractured—I can tell because I've had rib injuries many times. I peek at his back, more welts on his lower spine like someone kicked him. *Jesus*...a rock lodges in my throat. I never realized how responsible I felt for Garrison, not until this moment.

I've seen this guy a thousand times since he was seventeen, but somehow I never saw this.

"Let me check out your other side," I whisper, two seconds from being choked up.

He's shaking, but he shows me his left side. The bruise across his abdomen looks faded, older. Like this has happened *multiple* times. I have to tilt my head towards his lips to hear his next words.

"I'm the little brother. They just pick on me. It's what older brothers do."

I'm the little brother too, and Ryke would never do *that* to me—but I can't say that to Garrison. I hear the malicious rebuttal that I'd spout if I sat in his place, *well aren't you a goddamn lucky bastard.*

So I say, "Your ribs are fractured."

A tear rolls down his cheek. "Yeah, I know." He aggressively wipes the tear away.

"It's happened before?"

He shrugs tensely. "Whenever I see them, they like to play rough, so whatever…"

"Which brother?" I question, my eyes murderous at this point.

Garrison lifts his head, his chin quaking, and his voice cracks as he says, "All of them."

My chest collapses, and very softly, I say, "I'm not going to let them hurt you anymore."

Garrison tries to cover his face. He slides off the counter to stand, but his legs buckle, his back slipping down the cabinets until he's on the floor, forehead pressed to his bent knees.

I don't touch him because I know that touch really isn't his thing. Now it makes more sense why.

I kneel nearby, and I have to ask, "Does Willow know?"

He nods. Keeping his head down, he mumbles out, "It's not her fault…for not telling anyone. She thought it stopped. It did…for a while, but when I went back for Christmas break, they were all there…" He starts shaking again. "Forget it. Forget I said anything."

I'm really quiet as I ask, "Will you stay at my place, at least until Willow comes back?" Lily won't mind having Garrison with us for an indefinite amount of time. I know she won't.

Shock freezes him. "That's *years.*"

"So?"

He looks up at me, eyes reddened, cheeks tear-streaked. "Willow could break up with me by then."

"You'd still be a part of this family." I gesture in a circle. "I wouldn't kick you out because of it." Long before he became Willow's boyfriend, we all knew him as Garrison Abbey: the rebellious, teenage neighbor.

"I have an apartment in Philly."

"You live alone." *And I think you need someone right now.* I pause. "I'm going to be blunt like my brother. You look like shit. You're a little gaunt, and man, you smell like you've been spraying cologne instead of showering."

"I've been busy," he snaps, already defensive. "I have a job, and it's the only thing that keeps me from…"

"From what?"

He shrugs. "From feeling like a stupid loser. Like I have no purpose, alright? I have something outside of *waiting* for a girl. I have something…and I need to put time in it. I shouldn't even be *here*. I should be working—"

"Hear me out," I cut him off, just as his voice cracks. "I have this little kid who's a big pain in my ass because he keeps begging for a sibling. Every day I have to hear, 'but Jane has two brothers' and if he just saw you in the house, he'd be happy. But most importantly, you'd save my goddamn eardrums."

Garrison lets out a short laugh. "The important things."

"Damn right."

He pinches his eyes. "Stop *crying*," he says beneath his breath. *That's me.* I see and hear so much of my past torment in his aching words.

"I get it."

"Do you?" he snaps.

"Your brothers call you a pussy for crying? They tell you you're not a real man—*suck it up, Garrison. What are you, a little pussy, a little girl?* What kind of goddamn man are you?"

Surprise coats his face again, and he's about to swing his head towards my brother. Since we're on the ground the cabinets block our view.

"It wasn't my brother who told me to just *stop fucking crying*," I grit the words because I *feel* them like thick, black scars inside my lungs. Returning to that place hurts to breathe.

Garrison frowns. "Who?"

"My father." And the scary part: I really love that man.

I always will.

He stops profusely rubbing his face, letting the tears just come.

I just want to reach in and tell him something, so I scoot closer and I breathe, "You'll be okay. You won't see it today, maybe not even tomorrow, but one day, you'll wake up and you'll want to live."

"Are you sure?" His voice breaks.

"I'm goddamn sure. Look at me…" I wait for him to raise his head, his hair partially concealing his eyes, and I say deeply, "One day at a time. Can you do that with me?"

Garrison is quiet for a long moment, but then he nods repeatedly, letting this sink in. "…will you do something for me, if I move in with you?"

"Yeah."

"You don't even know what it is."

"Doesn't matter."

He deadpans, "I want you to kill someone."

I glare. "You joke, but have you met me?" Could I kill someone? I don't know—push me enough, and maybe, I think I could. It's not a talent to boast about. It's a *huge* character flaw, and I've been keenly aware that it exists inside of me.

Garrison erases the dry sarcasm this time. "Two days ago, I told my brothers that I'd never see them again. I don't know whether they believed me. They rarely take anything I say seriously, but I told them. I just don't want to talk or see them ever." His throat bobs again. "So two days ago…I also left my parent's house in a hurry and accidentally forgot one of my hard drives there."

"You want me to get it for you?"

"Yeah…but just don't…" His chest rises in a sharp inhale.

"Don't what?"

"Don't hurt them. Alright. I know it sounds stupid as fuck, but they're still my brothers. Even if I never see them again, I just don't… just *don't* do it."

Don't hurt them. Somewhere in this kitchen, I see my twenty-one-year-old spiteful self. Mad as hell. That guy would break Garrison's promise without a second thought. He'd open this cruel book of retaliation and revenge.

I can sit here and I can think, *I won't do that because* he *told me not to. Because I know it's wrong.*

I wonder how many people meet the person they once were and feel like they're staring at a stranger. I'm happy my son will never meet that man. I'm happy Lily has the husband she deserves. And I'm happy for me.

Because I finally love who I am.

"I won't," I promise Garrison, and I'm going to keep this one. "Give me your phone. I'll go get your hard drive now."

Garrison passes me his cell.

"What about your parents?" I ask him. "Do they know?"

"I've told my mom, but she just says it's *boys being boys*…and my dad likes Davis the best. They don't care about anything except making money, and ever since I got a job with Cobalt Inc., they stopped hounding me about 'doing something with my life.' If I never checked in, never returned their calls, they'd just think I was too busy for them, and they'd probably be *proud*."

"Huh," I say. "They sound like dicks."

He chokes out a laugh. "Yeah they are."

I scroll through his contacts. Garrison has a shit emoji next to the names of every brother. *Three* shit emojis next to Hunter's name.

He's the worst. I hover over his name to call him.

I think better of it and call Mitchell instead. As the phone rings, I ask, "Will they answer?"

He nods. "And miss an opportunity to pick on me?" It's the nice way of saying *to beat me up.*

I get what it's like not being able to use these specific words that turn you into a victim. Feeling like *that* word doesn't fit your situation just right.

Abuse? No, not me.

Never me. It's just this…it's not *that.* It can't be that harsh, raw thing. But it is. And then what?

I put the receiver to my ear, and the line clicks. "What's up?" Mitchell asks first. He sounds easygoing. You'd never think, *this guy beats on his little brother.*

Garrison watches me closely, his whole body tensing up.

I can't change my voice, but I don't go searching for words that'll scalp Mitchell. "This is Loren Hale, from down the street."

"Oh…oh wow, hey."

I'm his *famous* neighbor. "Garrison left his hard drive at your parent's place. He really needs it soon. Can you swing by and drop it in my mailbox?"

"Yeah, I'm on my way out tonight, so I'll drop it in your box then. Does he know where it is?"

I cup my hand over the receiver, "Where's the thing?"

"Basement table."

I put the phone back. "Basement table."

"Cool—oh yeah, I see it now…" he trails off for a long moment, maybe a full thirty seconds.

"Do you want to say something?" I ask.

He clears his throat. "Was…was he serious about the whole never speaking to us again thing? Is that why he had you call?"

Be like Ryke right now. One goddamn word response. "Yep." I literally bite my tongue.

Mitchell is quiet on the line. "Can you tell him…tell him I'm sorry, and that I think this is a good idea for him?"

Another lump lodges in my throat and I swallow every other nasty comment that chews at me. "Sure."

We both hang up, and I toss the phone to Garrison.

"What'd he say?" he asks.

"He'll drop it in my mailbox. He's sorry, and he thinks you never speaking to all of them is a good idea." I shake my head at Garrison, confusion written across my face.

"You called Mitchell, didn't you?"

"What is he—the nice one?" I know he's only two years older than Garrison.

"Mitchell could've stopped them," Garrison says. "He never did. Does that make him nice?…I don't know. I never stopped my friends from breaking into your house. I never stopped *myself* from pranking you. We're all the same. We're all *shit.*"

No.

I lean forward, and I say as clear as I can, "This guy in front of me isn't shit, and I'll still be here when you finally believe it too."

{ 11 }

February 2019
THE HALE HOUSE
Philadelphia

LOREN HALE

A little body catapults on my king-sized bed, undulating the mattress and stirring me from sleep. *Christ.* I rub my eyes. The black chandelier with candles stays motionless above the bed. It's too high for a rambunctious three-year-old to hit, but I still check to see if it swings.

"Wakey wakey! Eggs and bakey!" Moffy sings jubilantly and crawls towards me, dressed in blue and yellow Wolverine pajamas.

Lily dives *further* beneath the champagne comforter, burrowing like a frightened animal. I reach down for her, but she scoots towards the foot of the bed. *Lil.*

Moffy doesn't notice the giant lump. He wobbly stands on the mattress and starts bouncing higher and higher.

I tug his pajama shirt, and he falls to his butt.

Sitting up, I position my deep red pillow against the headboard, the red top-sheet missing. Lily must've grabbed it.

I yawn into my bicep. "Moffy, what'd we say about knocking?"

"Umm…" His brows furrow in contemplation. His dark brown hair sticks up on the side, but my bed-head is probably worse. I watch him gawk at the ceiling, searching for some words. His baby-soft face reminds me of Lily, but she put my toddler picture beside our son's as "evidence" of how much he resembles me. It was an eerie match, despite our different hair and eye colors.

"Uhh…ummm," he hums and shrugs like he lost the answer.

I give him a groggy but stern look. "We've been over this, bud."

He chews his lip for a second. "I can't remember, Daddy." With a big smile, he tries to slide beneath the bed, but I lift him back up and set him on the pillow next to me. *Oh, he remembers.* We had this conversation just yesterday.

"Knock before you enter someone else's bedroom," I explain *again*. "Then they'll invite you in. It's the polite thing to do." Listen to me, Loren Hale, teaching someone about manners.

Welcome to Earth-1610.

It's strange here.

We're not in an alternate universe, Lo! This is Earth-616, I hear Lily's retort in my head.

I might need to eat a breakfast burrito before I can process my own reality. Loren Hale: father of a cute-as-hell little boy, discipliner (but not in a shitty, Jonathan Hale way), and husband to an adorable, pinchable blanket-lump.

Moffy swiftly springs to his feet, purposefully ignoring me. He bounces and jumps and giggles.

"Stop jumping, Maximoff, and go knock." My voice is like cut glass, but Moffy's dopey grin never fades, hardly frightened by me. He practically leaps off the bed and scurries out, shutting the door behind him.

Now fully closed, I whisper to the blanket-lump, "Lil, you okay?"

She squeaks out something inaudible, and I lose time to peek beneath the champagne comforter. Moffy knocks on the door.

"Who is it?!" I call loudly. Quickly, I stretch over the side of the bed and collect my black boxer-briefs from the floor.

"Maximoff!" he replies in a shrill half-scream. "Can I come in?!"

I finish slipping on my boxer-briefs. "Yeah, little man!"

The door bursts open, and he flings himself on the mattress like a flying squirrel.

I pat his back. "Much better." As I slide to the edge of the bed, I easily pick him up and toss him onto my shoulder. He laughs hysterically, kicking his legs as though he can *steer* the direction I go.

"Do you know what today is?" I ask.

"Thoosday!" he yells out the answer.

"Yeah, but today is a different kind of special day." I set him on the suede couch next to two black armoires, all facing my bed. Our room is dimly lit and for the most part *clean* unlike the crazy raisins' place. I can't find a fucking thing when I'm there.

Moffy blinks a few times, confused. I like kids. They know less than me, and I don't know a lot about a lot of things. That's what Connor Cobalt is for.

"It's Valentine's Day," I clarify.

"Waz that?"

I could consult the internet's most accurate definition, but who gives a shit? "It's a day about love. Teachers will make you send cards to all your classmates, even the ones you literally hate, *but* it's also a day where you eat way too much chocolate and candy and"—I feign surprise, eyes widening—"heart-shaped pancakes."

"No way!" He smiles wide.

"Yeah huh." I nod towards the door. "Go watch some cartoons downstairs, and you can help me make them. I'll be there in a second."

Moffy dashes out, excited to have a task and probably remembering that he's in the middle of *Wolverine and the X-Men*.

I fix my hair with both my hands and return to the bed. The blanket-lump is silent and motionless, and it'd be funny if I didn't know that she might be sinking into a low.

Now sitting in the middle of the bed, I fling the comforter and top-sheet off Lily. She's scrunched in a ball, naked, hands covering her mortified face.

Something tugs hard inside of me. I whisper, "Lil...come on." My voice scratches my throat. I pull her onto my lap and seize a purple throw blanket, wrapping her up in it.

She sniffs, and I try to remove one of her hands, but she shakes her head back and forth. "I don't want to do today," she says so softly.

My face twists, pained, as pained as my lungs that crush together. Sex was easier when Moffy was a little baby. There was no fear that he'd sprint into our room unannounced. No fear that he'd walk in on us.

Lily and I—we'd do almost anything to keep him from accidentally seeing or hearing us having sex. We're quiet, much more than we used to be, and we've been good about sticking to a morning and night routine. For Lil, this is an accomplishment I remind her about every goddamn day.

Moffy is older now, and this is just the start to *big* changes.

Like the fact that he's barged into our bedroom for the fourth time this week. It might not seem like a lot or like a big deal, but it is. She's a sex addict, and she looks forward to sex in the morning—to sticking to this schedule. Deviating from her norm gives her anxiety, stress, and makes her want *more* than she's even allowed.

I get it.

I'm right here with her, and I understand cravings that eat at her head. That fuck with her. I get it so much, and I know just how badly Lily *doesn't* want to be upset about not having sex. Because there are a million things to be upset about, and why, out of all issues, is sex...and alcohol...why do they have to plague us? It's not worth the tears, the anguish—it's just sex. It's just whiskey.

And still, it happens.

I'm finally able to pry one of her hands away, but she keeps her eyes tightened shut like she can escape this moment and this day.

"Unfortunately, Lil," I say, "your time-travel powers haven't kicked in yet. You gotta do today. You have to do *every* day."

She sniffs again, and tears prick her eyes as she opens them. I wipe them away with my thumb. She knots the blanket, trying to stop crying, but she hiccups.

I hold her closer, my arms around her, and like she remembers just who I am, her gangly arms curve tight around me, clutching harder. She sits on my lap, and I kiss her temple before whispering, "I'm going to fuck you tonight, love. Hold onto that, okay?"

I can feel guilt shake her body. "I...don't want it." She cries into my shoulder because she wishes she didn't want it, but she does.

We cling harder to one another, and then she mumbles, "Never mind."

"Never mind, what?"

Lily lifts her head, her shoulder-length hair askew. She rubs the tears off her own face and blows out a measured breath. Then, more assured, she says, "I do want it, and that's okay." She nods to herself. "I...I want to help with the pancakes."

I kiss her gently on the lips. "Hey, Lily?"

"Yeah?"

"I'm proud of you."

She smiles a tearful smile and nods again. "Just give me a minute to get dressed?" We haven't separated from one another yet, our limbs tangled.

I clasp her small round face with both my hands. "No masturbating, love."

"I won't." Her strength cements these words as something greater than a promise. I see pure resilience flash in her green eyes, stemmed from fights fought long before today.

"I believe you," I breathe, reinforcing her armor.

This is where I have to let go.

It's hard because I'd vote to be tangled up with my best friend for absolute fucking eternity.

"You first," she says.

"You first." I comb my fingers through her hair.

She gapes like I broke a sacred rule of ours. Our only historic rule has been to love one another, and we've always succeeded at that. Maybe even too well. Then she pokes my chest. "You first."

"You first."

She squints at me. "You can't keep doing that."

"I just did, love." My lips drift to her ear. "And I'll do it again." I stick my tongue in.

"Lo!" She disentangles from me in shock, rolling off my lap.

I touch my chest. "Asshole." I point at her. "Angel."

Her lips downturn. "Angels are pure. I'm more like a sex demon... ohmygod, I'm a succubus." She cringes.

"Then you're the most adorable goddamn succubus I've ever seen." I fight not to climb on top of her.

Lily smiles and then crawls off the bed. She slowly searches for her clothes, tucking a piece of hair behind her ear. Her limbs are so awkward and thin. She looks breakable, but as our eyes meet, I see that resilience again.

I force my muscles to *move*. Out. *Go out*. I have to leave her for a bit. Just a bit. It's not out of worry that I want to stay.

It's just out of love.

LILY TAKES A QUICK shower while I descend the stairs to the living room, only in black track pants.

Maximoff sits on his yellow beanbag, entranced by *Wolverine and the X-Men* playing on the TV. Garrison is on the couch, wearing his bulky headphones. His laptop teeters on his leg while he eats a cold slice of pizza.

When he sees me pass the couch, he waves.

I nod back, happy to see that he's taking it easy and isn't already scrambling to be at work. He no longer looks like he could audition for Zombie #34 in *The Walking Dead.*

"Moffy. Pancakes." I push open the door to the kitchen, but Moffy is glued to the television. "Maximoff Hale. You want to cook or watch superheroes defeat evil?" I can't believe this is even a question.

"Superheroes," he says in a daze.

Yeah, that's definitely my kid.

I leave him be, and by the time I find the pancake batter and measuring cups, Lily enters the kitchen in gray leggings and black baggy shirt with the Superheroes & Scones logo. A giant bouquet of red roses dwarfs her small build.

I left them in the bathroom last night for her to find. I grab a vase and put it on the bar counter.

She sits on the stool, smiling this overwhelmed kind of smile. "You surprised me."

She thought I forgot, which she has reason to. We used to forget what day of the week it was. "You think those are from me?" I quip. "My heart is black, love. I don't do romance." I spread my hands on the counter, leaning towards my wife.

Lily fits the roses in a vase and then procures the tiny white card from between the stems. "Only Loren Hale would write this."

"What?"

She reads, "*These are real.*"

These are real.

I'm swept in the past, my intense, undeniable love for her all the same. In every time, in every place. "Guilty," I breathe.

Her eyes flit to my lips.

Mine hone in on hers, but I force my feet back.

I bend down to grab a mixing bowl. When I rise, Lily is off the stool and reading the directions on the back of the pancake mix.

She catches sight of the time on the oven clock. *8:04 a.m.* "You can get ready for work, and I'll make these for him."

"I took today off."

Frown-wrinkles crease her forehead. "You don't need to do that, Lo." She layers this cute sternness in her voice that doubles my attraction. I want to scoop her in my arms and kiss the fuck out of her. "I'm fine. I'm…okay. I won't do anything—"

I put my finger to her lips. "Lily. It's Valentine's Day. I've been planning to take off work all week."

She flushes. "Oh."

I place my hand on my bare chest. "World's Best Husband. I think Connor Cobalt would even agree with me on this."

Lily sets the pancake box down. "He'd definitely fight you on that title."

I feign hurt. "Connor would never fight me."

She pauses in thought and then nods assuredly. "True, but he'd have words with you. He likes words."

"I'm no genius, but I think 'having words' implies physical fighting." I measure out some of the pancake mix and pour it into the bowl.

"Only in fantasy shows…or historical…mostly medieval…" she trails off, and I watch her smooth the wrinkles in her shirt and then stand a little straighter, shoulders pulled back. She's adorable, even when she's about to begin a "serious" conversation.

I rest against the counter, waiting for it.

She seems to nod to herself again as self-encouragement, and then her round green eyes meet my sharp amber ones. "I need to talk about something serious."

There it is.

"Captain Marvel?" I ask. The new Marvel movie comes out soon, and we've both been looking forward to seeing it, especially Lil.

"No, I mean, *yes*, that's serious. But no, that's not what I need to tell you." She takes a deeper breath, and I try to prepare for the news. *Sex.* I know this is about sex. "I think we should start limiting morning sex."

I cross my arms, confused now. "We can just wake up earlier—"

"I don't want to risk it. What if he walks in on us?"

"We can start locking the door—"

"Nonono. If he has a nightmare, I want him to be able to come get us. I don't want my addiction to take anything away from him."

"He can still come get us if the door is locked."

Lily is stubborn about this. "I want to reach a place where I don't need morning sex, Lo. I can do it." It'd be easier if we could be spontaneous about sex, and occasionally, we can, but Lily feels better by boundaries and restrictions.

It doesn't mean we'll *never* have morning sex. It just means it won't be part of our everyday norm.

"If you want to try, we can try." I wouldn't stop her from this challenge.

"I want to try." Lily eyes my lips again, but they linger longer for a second and then drift to my cheekbones. She consciously tears her gaze away. Fantasizing and cravings—those come less frequent when she's had morning sex, or so she's told me.

It'll be a hard test, but what isn't?

"There's something else..." Lily crosses her ankles and then uncrosses them.

"What's that?" I abandon the pancake mix and edge closer, my hand sliding across her waist, but I don't pull her to my body.

Her gaze completely drops to my dick.

"Lily Hale, are you staring at my cock?"

Her eyes widen like *I've been caught*. "Yes," she admits, "yes, I was. You have a nice penis, even if it's in your pants."

"I know."

She slugs my arm.

I rub the spot, which hardly hurts. "Have you been working out, love?"

"I'm trying to make a serious declaration here."

"I thought it was about my nice penis."

Her neck reddens, less from embarrassment and more from arousal. "It's not...or it kind of is." She raises her hands. "Take two steps back. I can't think clearly when you're this near me."

I take two steps back like she asked. "Better?"

She nods more confidently.

I wave to her with two hands. "Lay it on me."

With a big inhale she says, "I want us to try for another baby." My lips part, and she speaks hastily before I can even process. "I know, in passing, we discussed the possibility of having another, but I'm talking about actually *trying*. Planning it and everything."

I dazedly walk backwards, my hand catching the counter for support. I'm just *confused*. She's right; we have talked about another kid, but like most things with us, we kind of put it off. We don't plan. We're not Rose and Connor. Things just happen to us.

We don't make them happen.

That's how we've lived our lives, and now that this fact is in clear focus, I only think, *that's fucking sad*. That's really sad that people have had to steer us our whole lives. That bad and good luck have dictated what happens next in our future.

"Why?" I ask. "Why now? It's weird timing, Lil. With everything that's happening as Moffy gets older." As he grows, we keep pivoting when we're so used to staying rooted in one place.

Lily comes closer on her own accord.

And then she reaches out for my hand. Slowly but carefully, she interlaces my fingers with hers, nothing sexual about the act. For a brief moment, I feel our teenage years—Lily and Lo, Lo and Lily—best friends instead of lovers. Where touch carries the depth and lifeline of every soulful and anguished emotion.

I stare at our clasped hands while she says, "We want more. We do, right?"

"Right." I've expressed as much over the years. *I can do this again,* I always say. *I'd have another.* Because my son hasn't kicked me down. When I look at him, I might as well be flying.

"Then we have to start trying and planning or else it'll never happen. We're too good at procrastinating, and we can't procrastinate on this. It's our family." She takes a breath, not finished yet. "And I decided to tell you today because I'd rather make this decision on my worst day than my best. I need to remember that there will be plenty of bad, shitty days, and those bad, shitty days can't derail my future...*our* future."

My eyes burn, my emotions flooding me at once. *Jesus Christ.* I'm going to cry, and she's not even crying. "Lily Hale." I wipe a tear that escapes. "Way to be better at Valentine's Day than me."

She bursts into a smile. "Really? Is that a yes?"

I nod a couple times. "You and me—we might not be geniuses or adventurers, but we're good together." I pause, the words just hitting me hard. "Because our worst days can become our best." I wear a half-smile. "And because the sex is great."

She's beaming. "I've decided that I'm glad I don't have time-travel powers."

"Not even to fix that time your porn played in class?" I tease.

She flushes, and it takes all her strength to shake her head. "You're there in that memory. Sitting beside me. And I don't want to miss any day with you."

I hug her to my chest. "No time-travel powers for you."

She lifts her chin up to look at me. "Teleportation is still on the table. I promise I'll take you with me."

"Where are we going?"

"Hogwarts."

"Good thinking." Priorities. Magic is always number one.

[12]

Connor Cobalt

"I don't feel well, Daddy," Jane whispers so softly I just barely catch the words. Sitting on the edge of her twin bed, I pull a stitched quilt to her neck, a thermometer in my left hand. She's warm but no fever. I wipe her runny nose with a tissue, fatigue weighing down her eyelids.

I kiss her forehead. "Je sais, mon cœur." *I know, my heart.*

She's not the only one sick on this trip.

Lo had a cold since yesterday on the private plane to Colorado. He quarantined himself in the back cabin, but the illness still seemed to spread to Jane and Daisy.

Last night, Lo deliriously and mistakenly texted me. I was sitting across from him in the living room of our rented log cabin. Bundled in blankets and empty tissues boxes, he made what Lily called a "sick nest" for no one to near.

Didn't mean to get you sick on your 23rd. Who has worse luck: you, me, or my brother? — Lo

His text was meant for Daisy. We all took off work this week to celebrate her birthday. We don't always go somewhere around February 20th, but this was a good month for us to leave work behind.

I replied to Lo: I don't believe in luck, darling.

He didn't even realize that I texted him. His phone slid from his hand, thudding to the floorboards, and he fell into a weak, tired sleep.

Jane shivers beneath her covers. I stroke her damp hair, and while cold medicine combats her symptoms, I try to ease her to sleep with history about Eleanor Roosevelt, her namesake. If I leave out a detail, she usually points out that I skipped a part, and she'll argue until I retell the history from the beginning again.

Rose said that Jane reminds her of me.

I said that Jane reminds me of her.

Rose and I determined that we're alike in many ways, and so it's no surprise that our children will be too. Lily then interjected, "You're the same nerd stars you've always been."

I watch Jane try to shut her eyes, but she forces them open as I reach the 1920s in Eleanor's history. She loves this section because of how animated and passionate Rose becomes when relaying the 19th Amendment and how Eleanor joined the League of Women Voters. Rose paints women as the superheroes they are, and she bolsters this truth until our daughter believes she is one too.

No matter how much Rose and I are the same, we're also drastically different. And I can never replace Rose in Jane's heart.

I skip one detail to see if she's listening.

Jane misses this, eyes glazed and staring at the quilt that's not hers. We're in a place that she sees as strange and foreign. This isn't the first time she's been sick, but it's the first time she's cognizant of the illness, of what it means to be sick. So for Jane, this *feels* like the true first time.

Tearfully, she says, "I want Mommy."

I lift Jane out of the bed and hold her in my arms. She cries softly against my chest. Her tears. Her illness. It's all temporary. It will eventually end, and no matter how much I *think* it, this misery she experiences for the first time in her life overcomes me.

I don't stand up. I can't bring her to Rose. I've already told her why. Rose is six-months pregnant and can't risk catching a fever. Through these circumstances, Jane lost the option to be comforted by her mother, and this frightens her, maybe even more than being sick.

Rose is always there for Jane. For everyone.

I brush Jane's tears with my thumb, her arms around my neck. For any adult, I'd be able to supply what they need, but children have wishes that drift into fantasy.

She sniffs and mutters, "Can...can you make my nose stop?"

I wipe her nose with another tissue.

"Pour toujours?" *Forever?*

My lips rise for a short moment. "You'll feel better when you close your eyes and sleep. Would you like me to stay for a while longer?"

Jane nods repeatedly, rubbing her eyes. "Please, Daddy." She coughs a little, but not as much as she did during the evening.

I tuck her back into bed, her PJs mismatched Cheetah print pants and pink plaid top. And I whisper close to her ear, "I love you."

She mumbles quietly an *I love you too* and then tries to shut her eyes. I stay seated on the edge of her bed, my hand on her arm. The darkened room is decorated in cabin décor, mostly fish-patterned items like a rug, a lamp, even the knobs on a dresser are shaped like trout.

Thirty minutes in this room and the second twin bed has been empty the entire time. Quilt rumpled to the bottom. I notice the warm glow of light beneath the bathroom door, but no sound has come from there.

Daisy is sharing a room with my daughter, so Jane wouldn't be scared alone and so Daisy wouldn't pass the cold onto Sullivan.

I don't jump to irrational conclusions.

Most likely, Daisy is awake and downstairs. It's around 5:00 a.m.—and I can't always discern whether or not my sister-in-law sleeps more than she used to. I don't live with her anymore, and Frederick is too moral to offer information about her therapy sessions.

As much as I care about Daisy's health, I have no real reason to pry. No advantages. Nothing at stake. So I haven't in a while.

Jane has finally shut her eyes, soft breaths through her parted lips, so I quietly stand. She never stirs or wakes.

I pull my navy shirt off my head, soaked in tears and mucus, and I walk to the bathroom. I plan to wash my hands before I return to Rose.

Ping.

Ping.

Ping.

Cell notifications.

Then my phone starts *buzzing* with texts.

Wonderful. Anytime there's a sudden onslaught of messages, I'm not being presented with good news. I type in my passcode and then graze over the email notifications from my publicist, a Cobalt Inc. board member, and investors.

Naomi Ando 5:04 a.m.
How would you like me to respond...

Steve Balm 5:04 a.m.
Ridiculous. I'm contacting the company lawyers...

Kent O'Neill 5:05 a.m.
Hi Mr. Cobalt,
How will this (link below) affect future investmen...

My brows slightly furrow in intrigue, not panic. I rest my arm on the bathroom door and click into a tweet:

@Lalipop2476: Connor Cobalt's hot-as-fuck father *heart eyes* #wefoundhim

I don't want to waste time thinking about Jim Elson. I send a quick reply to Naomi and then click into several texts my wife sent me from the room next door.

How is she? — **Rose**

Is she sleeping? If she needs another blanket, I have one here for her. Does she need anything more? — **Rose**

If you're deleting my texts, you'll be making a bed for yourself on the floor, Richard. — **Rose**

I begin to grin, but then I see the next text has no relation to our daughter.

Twitter has lost its mind. — **Rose**

I take her word for it and pocket my phone.

I push into the bathroom. I expect to see nothing out of the ordinary, but I didn't factor in a variable: the most likely outcome isn't always the outcome that happens.

Daisy is collapsed next to the toilet, cheek on the tiles, blonde hair splayed over her eyes, dressed in yellow cotton shorts and a long-sleeve top.

Quickly and as soundlessly as possible, I rush to Daisy's side and crouch over her while taking out my phone. I do what I would want Ryke to do if Rose were in this situation.

I dial his number.

"Daisy," I say gently. I put my hand to her forehead, my phone to my ear. She's much hotter than Jane, and I roll her onto her back. I smell vomit in the toilet, and just as I put my fingers to her neck, her eyelids flutter open. Like she's waking from a sleep.

"Connor?" She yawns and then cringes, probably at the taste in her mouth.

Ryke answers on the fourth ring. "What?" He's not as groggy as most people would be.

"Don't yell or stomp around," I say, hearing the squeak of his bed as he stands up, "but Daisy is sick in the bathroom—" He hangs up on me.

I know he's on his way because I know him, but he could've at least used his words.

Ryke acts the exact opposite of how I would most of the time, and convincing him to follow my logic is like telling a wolf to sleep in a lion's den.

There's no point in trying anymore. He does what he does. He is who he is. And I've grown to like him best that way.

"I can help you stand," I tell Daisy as she recollects her location. Her skin is pale and clammy.

"I fell asleep," she says with another yawn. "I got sick, and I just conked out. I didn't faint or anything." She tries to pick herself up, hanging onto the toilet seat.

I assist her, my hand on her waist.

"You probably shouldn't touch me," she says softly and slowly. "I accidentally... I think I gave Rose strep throat when I was seven...

you should've seen her…" She blinks and blinks. "Rose…she acted like she'd been damned with the bubonic plague. And she's pregnant now…" Daisy weakly attempts to push me away.

She looks like she's patting a couch cushion instead of swatting me.

"Unfortunately for you, I don't know how you feel." I see puke in strands of her hair that I'm positive her husband will help clean. "I lived in a boarding school as a child. I was subjected to most common pathogens, so I have a stronger immunity than most people."

Daisy smiles weakly and almost topples onto the toilet. I catch her and lift her back up. She hangs onto my shoulders for support.

"Of course you do," she says sluggishly. "You're Connor Cobalt—"

The door quietly but swiftly opens, Ryke storming through with unbridled concern. I let go of Daisy the same time she turns into her husband's arms.

Ryke holds her face and puts a hand to her forehead. "What fucking happened? Are you okay?" While she explains in an *agonizingly* slow manner, I have to squeeze past them to reach the sink.

I turn on the faucet and start lathering my hands and wrists with pine-scented soap.

Ryke flushes the toilet and puts down the lid. Daisy takes a seat, shivering and feverish, blinking like she's trying to make sense of everything. I'm certain she's not entirely coherent.

"I should've never let him…in my room. Or that house…" Daisy shudders.

Interesting.

I dry my hands with a towel and lean against the sink counter. Ryke stands above her with furrowed brows.

"Who the fuck is *him*?" Ryke growls.

"…What?" Daisy presses the heel of her palm to her temple. "What'd I say?"

I repeat it since Ryke's version will be riddled with unnecessary *fucks*. "You said you should've never let 'him' into your room or that house."

She licks her dry lips. "...the townhouse. When *Princesses of Philly* was going on...you were there." She looks up at me.

Ryke's darkened eyes set aggressively on my calm, unwavering expression.

"Relax," I tell him.

"What were you doing in her fucking room?"

"No, no," Daisy says and winces at herself. I'd guess for bringing this subject up at all. If she didn't have a fever, she probably never would have. "He interrupted...him...us."

I understand. "She's talking about Julian."

Ryke lets out a heavy breath and rakes a hand through his thick, disheveled hair. And then his eyes meet mine in apology.

I nod once. "You should've listened to me. Ninety-nine percent of your problems would go away."

He flips me off. "Ninety-nine percent of my fucking problems are you, Cobalt."

"It's strange...whenever you say fuck, I miss half of what you say. Which is every time you speak. Actually, it's not strange at all. I call it a choice."

He flips me off with both hands.

My grin widens, and I fold the hand towel and set it aside.

"Thank you." That's not Ryke. It takes me a second to realize she's speaking directly to me. "...you knew, didn't you? Back then, you knew I didn't want to do anything...with him. And so you interrupted us... on purpose."

I remember it clearly like I remember most everything. I knocked on her door, hearing her with Julian, and when I saw her reaction, which she tried to conceal, I knew she'd rather be anywhere but there. I waited until Julian left, and Daisy and I never spoke about that moment ever again.

That was five years ago.

"I did," I admit.

"Thank you," she repeats, eyes welling, maybe from exhaustion. She trembles, and Ryke rubs her arms but he looks to me.

"I never knew that."

"What would it have changed?" I don't see it affecting our relationship, which has been up and down and side-to-side and one of the more difficult things to read.

His nose flares, and he shrugs.

Daisy is so lost in thought that she just asks aloud, "Have you ever been in a bad relationship that you thought wouldn't stay with you... but it did?"

I shake my head at the same time as Ryke.

Daisy's gaze drags to the tiles. "Sometimes I feel like...the people I chose clawed into me...and it's impossible to erase the marks they made."

Ryke hugs Daisy almost immediately, and she reciprocates, burying her head in his chest. I leave them alone, just as another text buzzes.

I'm checking on Jane. – Rose

Don't. I'll be back in less than a minute. I reply, glancing at my daughter, still asleep, as I exit into the hallway.

Only one room away, I open the next door to find Rose propped up against the wooden headboard with a multitude of hand-stitched pillows. Cellphone in hand.

She reaches over and tugs on the bear lamp, illuminating the room. "Updates." She raises a manicured nail at me. "And you are so *lucky* I am *this* pregnant or else I'd already be out the fucking door."

By *this* pregnant, she means that her stomach is much rounder, her curves visible in her black silk robe. Nearing the bed, I can tell how much her back aches. The baby kicked her awake last night, so she hasn't been sleeping well.

"Richard," she snaps.

"I'm assessing you." I sit on the bed by her feet.

"Excuse me? Don't assess *me*. We have a sick daughter, and a one-year-old with gastrointestinal disruptions, also known as *intense* midnight diarrhea." *Beckett*. I smile at the way she sits straight and eases forward like she wants to cram the words inside my eardrums. "And not to mention our other one-year-old that already knows forty-words and chooses to say *wrong* more than hello." *Charlie*.

"Anything else?" I go to massage her foot.

She jerks it out of my hand, her toe pointed at my throat in threat. "I'm seconds from decapitating you."

I arch a brow. "With your toenail?"

She growls. "Richard."

"Rose."

"Are we a team?" she asks, and my grin fades.

"Of course."

"Then treat me like I'm on the motherfucking field and not sidelined because of *this*." She points at her abdomen. It was never my intention to make her feel benched. "I'm perfectly capable of hearing news and handling it with you in ways that I still can."

"You are," I agree. "I wasn't implying that you weren't." I touch her foot again, and she lets me bring it to my lap. I massage her sole, and she relaxes against her pillows. "Just so we're clear," I add, "I'm never going to act like you're not pregnant when you are."

"I wouldn't want you to," she says beneath her breath, right when I knead a knot in her foot. She inhales like *there, right there*. I apply more pressure, and her chest collapses.

When our eyes meet, she glares. "I hate you."

I smile. "Jane is fine. Both Beckett and Charlie were still sleeping when I checked on them. And your sister has a fever."

Worry crosses her face and she sits straighter. "Which sister? And what do you mean by *fine*? You couldn't have picked a more descriptive word? There are literally millions and you choose *fine*?" She crosses her arms.

"Daisy. And *fine* generally means *okay*. Acceptable. Passing. Do you need more synonyms?"

Rose narrows her eyes. "I find your diction *unacceptable* and infuriating."

"I find your response redundant and attractive."

She tries to hide a smile by rolling her eyes. "Really, Connor, does she need anything?"

I can't tell Rose that Jane called out for her. She'd stubbornly try to see our daughter, and it's not worth the argument. "She's asleep. She'll feel better in the morning."

Rose takes a moment to let this idea settle in. I kiss her ankle and then move closer, sliding my hand up the length of her leg.

Rose watches me with piercing yellow-green eyes. "Are you still *assessing* me?"

I harden by the ice in her words. "I already know all there is to know." I reach her thigh and kneel between her legs, untying the loose knot of her robe. She stubbornly knocks her knees together and anticipates me yanking them apart.

I do.

I adore the flash of *I hate you, Richard* in her flaming gaze.

Rose rubs her lips together like she's smoothing lipstick. I pull her down so she's not sitting straight up, and her heat presses against my erection.

She gasps and then glares. "That noise was *not* for you."

Blood pools in my cock. "If not me, then who?"

Rose tilts her chin. "The air."

It's hard for me to believe that between air and me, *air* is superior. Frederick would remind me that I'm not herculean, but I'm certainly better than most people and most things. Without much of a pause, I say, "Air doesn't take precedence over me."

"Oxygen is necessary to sustain life," she combats.

"Oxygen can't think. Oxygen can't solve conflicts. Oxygen is necessary for survival, but it's incomparable to *me*."

Rose mutters something about my narcissism, but I distract her as I finish untying her robe. The silk slips off her curves like water. Naked beneath, I hone in on the swell of her stomach, her shallow breath, and the fullness of her breasts.

Our gazes drift to one another, calmness flowing through us as we recognize the life we created. I will never stop loving Rose and the future we've built together.

"Say something real," she whispers.

"Je t'aime." *I love you.*

I cup her ass and bring her firmer against me. Rose clutches the quilt with two tight hands, and I place a couple pillows beneath her lower back, hoisting her body towards mine.

Be gentle, I remind myself. Even if she dislikes those two words, even if they're not my favorite either—I can't fuck her roughly, not when she's this pregnant.

I squeeze her ass and place hot kisses along her abdomen. She sucks in another breath, but she lets me do whatever I'd like to her body—and I'd like to play with my wife.

Fragile, more vulnerable, and she's still giving me permission to dominate her. This fact, combined with the changes in her body and the way her eyes burn holes right through me, stirs and grips me.

I'm entrapped.

My mind never wanders. Never diverges.

I'm fixated.

I can't think about anything but Rose.

I lower my head and kiss between her legs. She trembles, her hormones intensifying every sensation. I squeeze her ass again. Rose shudders and shuts her eyes tight. Her sex drive, in the past, has been higher during her first and second trimester and absent during the third.

I study her reaction for a moment, kissing the inside of her thigh. "Tu es à l'aise, là?" *Are you comfortable right now?* I sit up to adjust the pillows beneath Rose. She has frequent backaches, mostly due to high heels, but she'd endure nearly everything to wear a pair.

It's a paradox.

She's more comfortable in heels. And yet, they're the cause of what adds to her discomfort.

Rose blows out a hot breath from her nose. "I have to talk to you."

I have to talk to you isn't a placeholder for *don't have sex with me.* On the contrary, we talk during sex more often than we have sex in silence.

"I'm listening." I rub her thigh, and I watch her gaze flit to the outline of my cock and then back to my blue eyes. I free my cock, and her lips tic upwards before she settles back into a glare.

"You're not going to like the topic," she explains, "but it *needs* to be discussed."

"If it has anything to do with Twitter, I'm already dealing with it—"

"It's not that." She waves her hand like she's volleying that topic aside.

I press the tip of my erection against her pussy. "I could guess, but you haven't given me enough details to make an educated one."

She props herself on her elbows, as though hoping to near my face and claw it off. "You're so—" I push into her and she falls onto her back with the new fullness and pleasure. Her warmth wraps around my cock, the sensation pricking my nerves.

"What was that, darling?" I tease.

Rose raises her hand like *shut up* and then she sets her palm to her forehead. "It's about Sadie."

I rock slowly in and out, friction building sweat. "We could be talking about game theory, Nietzsche, Foucault, or evolution and you'd like to discuss my misogynistic cat who's living with my therapist?"

"Yes," she says stubbornly.

I spank the side of her ass.

She fights a smile. "I hate yo—"

I cover her mouth with my hand, her rage heating my whole body. "You *love* me, and this just might be the thousandth time I've reminded you." Knelt between her legs, I thrust excruciatingly slow, even for me. My muscles burn. "And I don't speak in hyperboles."

I drop my hand from her mouth, trailing the base of her neck, between her breasts, and I rest my palm flat on her round abdomen. I could feel small movements from our son or daughter this morning.

Rose is lost in pleasure for a moment, her breath shortening, but the fire never extinguishes from her voice. "Your ego is going to contaminate our unborn child." She presses her hand to her mouth, stifling a moan.

I grab her wrist, lifting her palm off so I can hear.

"Fuck," Rose cries out. Her shoulders dig into the mattress as she nears a peak, and she pulses around my cock.

A groan escapes my lips.

"Harder," she begs.

I squeeze her ass. "No."

"Connor…" She places her hands over her face, which she only does when she's disoriented from an orgasm—and when she's not handcuffed.

I seize both of her wrists and hold them in one hand. I don't climax with her, so when she comes down, I'm still rocking inside.

"Sadie," she pants.

I let her see my irritation and then spank her again. "My name isn't *Sadie.*"

"I'm serious, Richard." She catches her breath. "I want to bring her home." She cuts me off before I can add *we've been through this.* "The last time I saw her at Frederick's, she lazily and pathetically collapsed at my feet. She's old." I open my mouth but she says passionately, "I'll clip her nails every single morning, and I'll teach Jane not to provoke the cat or pull on her tail."

"If it was just about Jane's wrongdoing, we would've never sent the cat away. It's more than that, Rose." It's about Sadie being unpredictable and hostile.

"She's *old*, Connor." She used my middle name, which means that this subject means more to her. "It's not about Jane. It's about keeping our family together, and Sadie is a part of our family." Rose is loyal to a fault, but if she sees a change in Sadie, then it might be safer to bring her home.

I can convince myself that Sadie is fine without me, so I have no emotions towards leaving her behind, but Rose can't.

Jane can't.

I nod but then I shake my head. "I don't like giving Jane something after we repeatedly told her *no*." Our children are privileged, but I need them to understand their privilege. Spoiling them like this won't help.

"We'll remind her that Sadie isn't hers. She's her own *being* and not a toy or a reward."

It'll be difficult for Jane to understand the difference.

Rose glowers, her passion practically smoking off her skin. "Richard Connor Cobalt is afraid of a challenge."

I push deeper, and her collarbones jut out with a staggered inhale. My jaw is tight in arousal. "And Rose Calloway Cobalt is trying to incite me."

Rose jerks her hands in my hold, on the brink of another orgasm. I clutch her wrists tighter, my own climax on the horizon. Sweat beads across my chest, my abs glistening.

Her fervor stimulates me.

I come as soon as she climaxes. I carefully lean forward to kiss her lips, and I whisper, "Two weeks. We'll bring Sadie home then."

"One week," she argues.

I sense a battle in our future. One with tiles and letters and points. "Scrabble. Best out of three wins," I challenge.

Her shoulders rise with confidence. "I accept with the option of one addendum."

She could remove certain vowels or set a category like "pastoral words"—anything is possible with an open-ended addition to the game. *What will she do?*

I'm entrapped.

I'm fixated.

"One addendum," I agree to her terms.

And our love turns to rivalry.

I WON THE FIRST round. She won the next two. Her addition to the game: only use words that specify historical sites or anatomy. The categories have zero relation to each other. On the board, we had *hypothalamus* connecting to *Everest* and then *ventricle* to *Inukshuk*.

It was as nonsensical as it was entertaining.

And I blame luck for my loss. I kept blindly grabbing tiles worth one point.

Now nearly 7:00 a.m., Rose has fallen back to sleep after we both showered. Not tired, I descend the cabin's narrow staircase. Halfway down, the step creaks behind me.

I check over my shoulder.

Not surprised in the least.

Whenever we're in the same house, Ryke and I tend to cross paths in the morning. Aspen or Philadelphia, this wouldn't change.

Shirtless like me, hair astray (not like me) and jaw set hard, Ryke skips two steps at a time, barely making eye contact. Then he reaches *my* stair. No room to pass, he has to wait since I don't hurdle the steps.

"Can you let me fucking by?" Ryke asks.

"The places you have to be can't be more important than mine." I'm not descending the stairs slowly or quickly. I'm somewhere in between.

"You could've just fucking said *no*." His agitated voice is right next to my ear, and as soon as we reach the last stair, he tries to pass me.

We wedge together, stuck between the wall and the banister.

I push out in front, and he curses beneath his breath about me *always needing to go fucking first*. I'd respond, but it's mostly true. The first floor is just one spacious room containing the living room, kitchen, pool table and windows to the snowy outdoors.

Lo is asleep on the leather sofa, crumpled tissues scattered around him. Without stopping, I head to the kitchen and hear Ryke trailing me.

I check over my shoulder. "And I didn't even have to tell him to come."

Ryke hardly flinches. "I'm not in the fucking mood, Cobalt." Our paths diverge at the granite countertops. I go to the coffee pot. He goes to the refrigerator.

While I make coffee, I scrutinize him from a few feet away. It'd be a lie to say that I wasn't slightly worried. I am. Just slightly. It's not that he dismissed my banter. Ryke usually does. It's the fact that he keeps sniffling and pretending I can't see.

He yanks the fridge door open and pulls out a carton of orange juice. Then he twists off the cap...and he searches for a glass.

"I thought you preferred to avoid modern amenities."

"Why can't you just say a fucking *glass*?" He finds one and sets it on the counter.

"Because only you would say *a fucking glass*, and I'm not Ryke Meadows." I press the *start* button on the coffee machine. While it brews, I lean against the counter and watch him carefully pour the orange juice in the glass while *sniffling*.

Ryke always chugs from the container, but he wouldn't if he thought he'd get someone sick.

"You realize Vitamin C only helps prevent illness. It doesn't cure it."

"I'm not sick yet," he growls beneath his breath. Then he quickly downs the entire glass in two gulps. He begins pouring a second glass, and his brown agitated eyes flit to me. "What?"

"You're perspiring."

"I'm *not*." He wipes his arm across his damp forehead.

"Have you taken your temperature?"

Ryke swigs the second glass and then downs it. "Fuck off." He caps the carton and puts his glass in the sink.

I ease away from the counter. "You don't want to get your daughter sick, Ryke." It's why he's so concerned about *being* sick in the first place, but he's stubborn.

Ryke tenses and rubs his eye with the heel of his palm. "Alright." He steps near, only an inch shorter. "I'm going to say this fucking once, and I swear, if you grin, I will punch you."

"It sounds like a promise," I say casually, "but I haven't verified what promises from Ryke Meadows mean."

"It means you'll get fucking punched."

"We'll see." I wait for his declaration.

Ryke combs two hands through his hair. "Just touch my forehead and tell me if I feel fucking hot."

For his sake, I do my best to restrain my grin, and my best is *the* best. I'm blank-faced as I put the back of my hand to his clammy forehead. After a few seconds, I drop it. "You're warm," I confirm. "Warmer than Jane but not feverish like Daisy."

"Fuck." He sets his hands on his head and stares off.

"Just ask. I'll say yes." I'll always say *yes* if he needs me.

Ryke drifts to the sink, setting his hands on the edge as he thinks. I'm patient. I return to the coffee pot and take out a black mug from the cupboard.

"Can you look after Sullivan?" he finally asks, choking back more emotion than I thought he'd have. "Fuck." He pinches his eyes.

My chest rises in a strong breath. His emotion affects me—and it's not often that people do. "It's not a failure on your part," I tell him. "If Rose and I were contagious like you and Daisy, I'd ask you to look after my children." I get more specific. "I'd ask you *first.*"

I see surprise in his eyes, and he turns more towards me. "Yeah?"

I nod. "You're dependable, reliable." I grin. "A classic Golden Retriever."

He shakes his head. "You're so fucking…"

"Accurate, I know."

I expect him to flip me off, but he just messes up his hair again and then nods to me. "I saw Twitter this morning. Is that accurate?"

He wouldn't know the truth because I rarely talk about my father. For the past two or so hours, the world has been obsessing over a new *Celebrity Crush* article by Wendy Collins titled: WHO IS CONNOR COBALT'S FATHER?

The journalist disclosed his name (Jim Elson) but nothing else.

People on the internet took it upon themselves to dredge up information about Jim Elson, and now everyone is circulating this photo of a man from Philadelphia standing outside Citizens Bank Park.

His name: Jim Elson.

His hair: brown.

His eyes: blue.

Age: late fifties.

"You mean the photo of a man in a Philadelphia Phillies shirt?" He hears my curt tone enough to understand.

"He's not your dad."

"He's not my dad," I confirm. "He's just some man with the same name." I rest my hands on the counter behind me. "The only annoyance is that I now have to take time to placate investors and assure them that no skeleton will crawl out of my closet." *That no long-lost father will try to carve out portions of Cobalt Inc.* Thankfully Steve Balm met my father before my parent's divorce, so he knew this man wasn't the right Jim Elson.

Ryke's brows knot. "Someone just claimed to be your fucking dad, and your only annoyance is about investors? What the fuck kind of relationship did you even have?"

"None. I'm not like you."

"No kidding." He tears off a piece of paper towel from the roll to wipe his nose. He balls it in his fist when he's done. Ryke being sick makes him appear more docile than he really is.

"I was sent to boarding school when I was seven," I remind him but I add information he doesn't have. I give him more than he's ever received. "When I was twelve, my mother told me that she divorced my father. I can't tell you when it happened because I wasn't aware. I saw my mother maybe once or twice a year, if that, and my father never called me." My mother did take advantage of my birthday as a child, using the day to invite potential Cobalt Inc. investors to a party. I thought it was smart.

"Are you fucking serious?" He looks heated.

"It was mutual. Everything was mutual. I never called them. I never *longed* for them. I wasn't attached to people. I lost contact with my father before I even hit puberty, and what I know about him are just facts. That's all he is to me, and I know the lack of feelings between us are as mutual as everything else was."

Ryke contemplates this, concerned lines crossing his forehead. "You promise that's fucking it?" He wants to make sure I'm okay.

It's sweet.

"I promise." I grin. "And my promises are better than yours."

Just as he begins to roll his eyes, we hear a weak croak from the couch, "Lily?"

At the same time, Ryke and I leave the kitchen to approach a feeble Loren Hale. His hair is matted on his forehead and skin still pallid. The darkened room only brightens with the sunrise.

"Hey, beautiful," I banter.

Lo registers us above him and tries to sit up, but he weakly collapses back down. To me, he asks, "How do I get better and defeat this thing?"

"He's not a fucking doctor," Ryke cuts in.

Lo feigns contemplation. "I don't know, bro. He's *kinda* fucking close to one."

I wouldn't argue with that.

Ryke puts his hand to his little brother's forehead. "You're fucking delirious."

Lo lacks the energy to push his brother aside, so he lets Ryke take his temperature. "I'm…" He yawns. "…whatever." Lo fumbles with his cellphone, his nose reddened from using tissues all night.

"My advice," I tell him, "sleep, water, and medicine."

Lo looks to his brother. "See, he is a doctor. The physician I went to yesterday said the same thing."

Ryke tosses a pillow at Lo's head. "You're starting to sound like your wife."

Lo knocks the pillow away and glares and points at him with his phone. "Don't be a dick."

"I'm always a dick."

"So many truths," I muse.

Ryke flips me off, and then asks his brother if he needs anything. Lo is too distracted by what's on his cellphone. This time, he sits up quickly, ignoring the weight of his head and fatigued muscles.

"What the hell?" He scrolls furiously, and then his amber eyes flit to me. "Who do I need to fight?"

My lips rise, and I slip my hands into my pockets. "I appreciate the sentiment, but it's a fake photo. And even if it had been real, it'd mean nothing to me."

Lo slumps back. "If it means nothing to you, then it means nothing to me." He turns to his brother. "Can you get me a glass of milk…and toast with butter…and maybe some scrambled eggs?" If you picture Lo with puppy-dog eyes, you've forgotten what he looks like.

He will always be as sharp as glass and ice.

"Anything else, princess?" Ryke asks while he dusts Lo's dirtied tissues into a tiny bin.

Lo points at the patchwork quilt kicked to his ankles. Ryke lifts it up to his shoulders and then carries the bin to the kitchen trashcan. He never told Lo that he's sick too—he wouldn't. Because Ryke Meadows loves taking care of people.

Lo yawns again.

"Go back to sleep, darling."

"Only if you're here when I wake up," he banters.

"I'm always here." I watch him gently shut his eyes, and just as I ease away, I hear the crack of eggs and the slam of the refrigerator.

And Lo mumbles one of the greatest truths of our lives.

"I have the best brother."

< 13 >

March 2019
THE AVONDALE HOTEL
New York City

Daisy Meadows

I sprint down the hotel hall with three paper bags labeled *Ryke, Connor,* and *Loren.* Running through empty carpeted hallways with less urgency and more fun. I extend my arms as I speed ahead. *You can't catch Daisy Meadows. Look at how fast she goes!*

I veer to the door and slip my keycard in, panting a little, and with a giddy smile, I enter the Manhattan hotel room where the three guys chill out for a few minutes.

The photographer suggested leaving the "talent" in a warm hotel room while Rose, Lily, and select staff set-dress the rooftop pool area for a charity photo shoot.

My modeling days are over, but all of our husbands agreed to a wild idea.

"I come bearing gifts." I shake the paper bags and slow my speed. I've walked in on something.

Lo sits at the edge of the king-sized bed, Connor towering above. His hand tilts Lo's head backwards, and he inspects Lo's bloodshot eye.

"Did you bring the gift of sight?" Lo asks dryly. "Because my eye is burning."

I toss both of their bags on the bed. "I brought the gift of underwear. Maybe you can fashion an eye-patch."

"If I could fashion a fucking glare, it'd be on you."

Ooh. He's a whole lot less scary in Connor's care, submissive and totally banking on the smartest person he knows to make his eye better. I'm guessing some debris is irritating the surface.

"Hold still, darling." Connor examines him.

I notice Ryke doing sit-ups on the floor, and when he sets his shoulders on the carpet, I purposefully look away.

"Have you seen my husband anywhere?" I walk forward until my legs are on either side of his head. Standing right over his face. "He's full wolf. Broody. And he has a very large co—" Ryke bites my ankle. I laugh, staring down. His unshaven jaw and thick hair calls to me, but not more than those darkened, dangerous eyes.

Hello there.

"You hear that, bro?" Lo says. "The love of your life married Sasquatch."

Ryke props himself on his elbows. "How's that fucking *eye* feel?"

"How's that face feel? Gotta hurt being you."

"We're fucking *related*," Ryke snaps.

Connor tilts Lo's head towards the lamplight and says, "I assure you, Lo is better looking, and he uses more words."

Ryke groans. "Come on."

Lo tries not to blink. "At least your insides aren't ugly like mine."

Ryke groans more. "Shut the fuck up."

I'm more used to infiltrating their guy group than I used to be. Paris was the start of it all, and I know every start must have an ending. I just can't imagine one yet. I know I don't have to.

Suddenly, Ryke catches me by the waist and brings me in his arms, rolling on his side and mine. My blonde hair tangles and frizzes some, and his large hand slides through the strands. In the background, Lo and Connor discuss the state of his eye, so it's not entirely quiet.

Ryke says lowly, "Your husband must be the luckiest fucking man."

I smile. "He's definitely the kindest."

"Yeah?" Ryke can't hold out any longer. He kisses me strongly, and my body surges with tingling heat. His lean muscles wrap around my build, and I run my fingers through his thick hair and down his rough jaw, his gruff masculinity so, *so* attractive to me.

I whisper against his lips, "He's going to be so mad."

"Who?"

"My husband," I tease. "I'm kissing another man."

Ryke raises his brows at me, and then he slides his hand down the back of my jeans, cupping my bare ass. I have good days and bad where my sex drive is concerned, but lately they've been really, really good. Like now, my nerves nearly twitch in response, welcoming his advances and his coarse hands.

Ryke's lips tickle my ear as he whispers, "How'd he fucking feel about this?"

"Very, *very* jealous." I grab his wrist and push his hand deeper in my pants, and his fingers curve towards a more sensitive area. "I can't be sure, but I think he likes another part of me more than my ass."

"I know which fucking part."

I smile at the danger of his hand, creeping lower and lower. My pulse races. "Which fucking part?"

He tucks me closer to his chest, and he murmurs, "The part that makes you *come* so fucking hard."

I almost shudder in his arms. *Go for that part...right...now.*

"It's out." Connor's voice nearly startles me.

Lo stretches to a stance, and neither Ryke nor I shift out of our tangled positions on the carpet. "What was it?" I ask all of them.

Connor answers, "A piece of a contact."

I frown. "When did you start wearing contacts, Lo?"

"When I got a job that consists of staring at little words in little panels." *Halway Comics.* Lo is on his way to the bathroom, and he suddenly sees me and his brother. He shakes his head. "My eyesight didn't get fucked up enough for this."

"You and your wife are fucking worse," Ryke retorts.

"But I love my wife. I only kind of love you." Lo gives him a half-smile, but then he laughs at his own joke, much more lighthearted than he would've been in the past.

Ryke even smiles, just as Lo turns into the bathroom.

Connor collects their shopping bags to change, not even batting an eye towards us. He just disappears into the bathroom and shuts the door. I dropped Ryke's bag nearby, and he also needs to change clothes.

Rolling on top of him, I pull off his gray shirt, his dark eyes carving up and down my body. I tug his black track pants to his thighs and then playfully bite the waistband of his boxer-briefs to draw them off. I don't get far.

His muscles flex. "Fuck."

This is an urgent *stop* kind of fuck, so I stop.

"You're fucking trouble." He picks me off his lap and then stands. He must see the confusion in my eyes because he adds, "I can't get hard right now, sweetheart."

I mock gasp. "Men get erections?"

He finds a nearby thing to throw at me, which is his shopping bag.

I catch it on my lap and then toss my hands in the air theatrically. "He loves me; he really, really loves me." I fall backwards.

Ryke snatches the shopping bag, effortlessly sheds his track pants entirely, and he chucks those at my face. I smile and pull them off while he finds his "wardrobe" for the photo shoot.

I have no idea what Rose picked out for each guy. She designed a really small line of men's underwear for the summer, and all the proceeds go to charity. The marketing team said more women would buy the underwear for their significant other if Ryke, Lo, and Connor modeled them.

"I wasn't involved in the choices," I say. "I was just told to bring them to you."

Ryke holds up a pair of white briefs.

He never wears briefs. He checks the label on the shopping bag, thinking I mixed him up with his brother or Connor.

I didn't.

"What the fuck are you smiling at?" he asks, but if you saw Ryke, you'd see that a shadow of one begins to lift his lips.

"You."

He gets naked and flings his boxer-briefs at my face. My smile stretches, and on the floor, I sit up against the bed. I give him a long once-over: his lean, sculpted body only rock climbers could share. I land on his cock, and my nerves stir awake.

He has to force his gaze off *me*. Then he puts on the white briefs, tucking in his junk, and fixing the elastic band. They barely fit him.

"Do you want any modeling advice?" I ask to distract his penis.

"No." This cemented word originates from *hating* what modeling did to me. Any memories I do have contain painful sentiments he wouldn't want to dredge up.

I think about Sullivan for a second, but I try not to let it consume my focus. Frederick, my therapist, told me not to fixate on her health when I've left her in the care of family. I need to put myself first more and focus on my health too. Not just for me but for Sulli.

This is the very *first* time I've left her alone with my mom. I was only a little nervous when she kept saying, *look how gorgeous* and *look at her eyes.*

This is the first granddaughter she's had with green eyes, and I know it's insane to think she'd model off my baby. I just hear my mom, petting my hair, and saying, *your hair, look at this gorgeous hair.*

I trust that she won't take photos or post them online or even share them with her friends. Ryke told her really bluntly not to, and I seconded his declaration.

Lo and Connor emerge from the bathroom about the same time my phone buzzes in my pocket. His little brother starts laughing. Connor's grin could capsize the Titanic. It might be the combination of never seeing Ryke in white briefs and how tiny they are compared to his package. Lo and Connor were given black and navy boxer-briefs that fit them better.

Lo puts his fist to his mouth, still laughing uncontrollably.

Ryke shakes his head like his brother is the one with the issue. It's impossible to shame Ryke out of an outfit. He'll wear anything with the same amount of confidence he always exudes.

I stand up and click into my text.

Left waxing kit + shaving cream + razors for Ryke in the shower. Shave thighs, around the underwear line, legs to his ankles. Thanks! — Tiffany (event coordinator)

Lo is already snapping a photo of his brother, who has no care in the world about the briefs. Even though I'm pretty sure if Ryke shifts the wrong way, something is popping out.

"Stop!" I tell Lo.

All the guys freeze.

Ryke's brows knot. "It's alright, Dais." He clearly gave his brother permission, but that's not why I shouted.

"If you post a pic now, you'll have a 'before' and 'after' picture." Fans would definitely put them side-by-side and compare his hairless legs to the original. I doubt Ryke would personally care, but Rose would be upset if all the headlines about the photo shoot read: RYKE WAXES!

Lo swings his head to Connor while lowering his phone. "What's she talking about?"

"Ask Ryke to translate," Connor says. "That's his puppy."

Ryke gives them the middle finger.

I explain, "Tiffany left wax in the shower for Ryke."

"Why the fuck for me?" Ryke questions over Lo's second batch of laughter.

"Oh, man." Lo has to prop himself against the wall, a stitch in his side. "You better believe I'm pulling a strip off."

"It should be obvious to you," Connor tells Ryke before I can speak.

I take a seat on the edge of the bed.

Ryke outstretches his arms. "I have hairy fucking legs. Tell me why that fucking matters?" Two fucks in one rant. He's upset.

"Society hates body hair," Connor says. "Even occasionally on men."

Ryke shakes his head repeatedly. Ryke Meadows is unabashedly *Ryke Meadows* at all times, and I don't think he expected anyone to tell him to change a part of himself today.

"Welcome to modeling." I force a smile.

His hard eyes soften on me.

"I know which body parts they want you to wax, do you want me to tell you?"

Lo raises his hand. "I do." He's enjoying Ryke's slight frustration. It's a brother thing.

"No." Ryke crosses his arms. "Text Tiffany back. Tell her that I'll give them fucking permission to use Photoshop."

I send a quick text, but her reply is even faster. "She says *okay* and to go to the roof now. Robes are on the back of the door."

Connor finds them hung up, black cotton, and after they shrug them on, we leave the hotel room.

In the hallway, I walk backwards ahead of them. What a perfect photo *this* would be: all in identical robes, their strides are equal to where no one falls ahead or behind.

"Boys," I say as serious as I can, "this is the time to put your model faces on. Cry when they ask you to cry. Laugh only when asked to laugh—unless you have a nice photographer, then you can midway through. And do not, whatsoever, touch your hair."

Ryke touches his hair. He runs his hands through it and he gives me a look like *what are they going to fucking do about it?*

I love him.

"Your directions are too complex for a third of this group," Connor says. "You need to go back to basics for Ryke. Like don't piss on cement."

"Don't hump your wife," Lo adds.

Ryke rolls his eyes. "Don't fucking hump yours."

Lo feigns a wince. "Not possible."

I glance over my shoulder as we turn a corner to the elevators. "Another thing: you should all try to avoid an erection." When I photographed with a model for a swimsuit spread, he had one mid-shoot. We were tangled together, and I tried to act like it wasn't a big deal (he was really embarrassed) but the photographer yelled at him anyway.

I did tell Ryke this story once, and he just glowered at the ground, his forearms on his knees, deep in thought. The first thing he asked, *are you okay?*

Not even "were you"—just *am I* okay about it. I won't ever be able to erase these memories that flare up and make me pause. Most from modeling. Things I said. Things I did. What I let roll off my back. Hand-pats on my ass. Men slipping into dressing rooms for a second or two like they had permission when they had none.

Back then, I shoved the attached sentiments to these violations so far down. I didn't feel a thing. It's easier being numb, to have *zero* regrets, but I wouldn't trade what I feel now for feeling *nothing*. By processing these moments, I'm more apt to say *no*. I feel more empowered to walk away. To speak out about my experiences.

After my pain and healing came strength.

I'm stronger today.

"Will Rose be speaking at the shoot?" Lo asks me while we stop at the elevators.

"Yeah."

"Great, hard-on avoided." He flashes a half-smile at Connor. "You're in trouble, love."

I smile at Rose's husband. "Her voice gives you an erection?" I'm even surprised I asked Connor Cobalt this. His intense all-knowingness has a way of making *everyone* feel small and inferior.

I wait for his answer, but he just stares at me. And then he says, "I'm going to assume your question is rhetorical because you should already know the answer. Unless you're not as intelligent as I believe you are."

Burn. So my sister's voice definitely turns him on, probably among a long list of other traits. I push the elevator button a couple times since it's taking forever. "What do you think about to avoid..." *don't think about Connor Cobalt's ginormous penis.*

Too late.

I mouth to Ryke, *help.*

He shakes his head. "You got here all on your fucking own." Then he reaches for my hand, holding tight. Ryke has trouble abandoning anyone in a sinking ship, and Connor would probably call that his greatest flaw.

Connor barely even blinks. "I think about Ryke's infinitely small vocabulary."

"We know who the nerd is," Lo says.

He's probably one of the most sophisticated, yet domineering nerds I've ever seen in my life. I squeeze Ryke's hand. "Is yours still Lily?"

My older sister turns him off *that* much.

"Yeah, her and her fucking whining," Ryke clarifies.

I lean my shoulder on the elevator door. "Hey, her whine is like a cluster of koala bears, pandas and chipmunks."

"Being killed," Ryke deadpans.

I almost laugh. Lo is actually really quiet. I thought he'd say something in reply, but he stares off towards a potted plant. I'm about to ask what's up, but the elevator opens—I fall in.

Ryke still has my hand, so I don't go down.

He walks inside and pulls me to his chest. I wrap my arms around his waist. *It's safe here.*

Connor pushes the *rooftop* button, and as we rise, Lo finally speaks to Ryke. "I bet I can give you something that'll *really* turn you off."

"What?"

Lo has this rare smile peeking at his lip. He rubs the back of his neck, unsure if he's actually going to say it, but then he does, "Lily pregnant."

My mouth falls. "Is she?"

Lo nods and his smile bursts. "Yeah."

My heart swells, and I bounce on my toes.

"She wanted me to tell everyone, so don't let Rose near me with a goddamn knife for some kind of sisterly betrayal."

I'm in this happy, surprised state of shock. I never really expected Lily and Lo to have another baby. Even when they said they *could*, I didn't think they'd try. I'm not sure any of us did.

"Congratulations, darling," Connor says.

Ryke affectionately messes Lo's hair like the big brother he is, and I exchange a smile with him. Moffy will have a brother or sister, and this time no one here is worried if Lily and Lo can do this.

We all know they can.

"WHO'S THE GENIUS WHO scheduled a rooftop underwear shoot at the beginning of March?" Lo's breath smokes the air, shivering in just his black boxer-briefs.

The New York City skyline glitters behind him, the afternoon sunny. The rooftop is dressed like a summer bash: lemonade in mason jars on a nearby bar, beach towels over lounge chairs, and an inflatable swan floats in the pool.

"There are only two geniuses here," Connor says, "and I'm not to blame." His conceited aura never diminishes, his black sunglasses pushed to the top of his head, wavy hair styled totally perfect. He reclines on a lounge chair without goose bumps or reddened skin.

Connor Cobalt is impervious to frigid temperatures.

Lo can't stop shivering, sitting on a blue cooler. The camera flashes repeatedly.

Standing beside Lo, Ryke battles the cold better than his little brother, but he's as stiff as can be. The photographer has already asked him to "loosen up" three times, and Ryke shook out his arms but he's still six-foot-three-inches of stone.

Rose, next to the photographer, casts a scathing glare at Lo. "I'm the genius that wanted the *real* skyline in the photos and not a Photoshopped one."

"Your real goal is to freeze our balls off," Lo rebuts, teeth chattering.

"Secondary goal, and only for *you*, Loren."

Lo glares at the sky. "I'm officially in hell."

Rose places her hands on her hips, ignoring him and inspecting the rooftop scene. Her elegant shearling coat keeps her and her bun-in-the-oven toasty. Lily and I are hugging onto one another beneath a thin hotel blanket.

"I can't watch this for long," Lily whispers and shivers against me. Her pained eyes reflect Lo's trouble withstanding the elements. She starts typing on her phone.

How can you tell if someone has hypothermia?

She's really concerned.

"Hey, just think, Lil, if it comes to that you can use your body heat to warm him and have *epic* I'm-keeping-you-alive sex." I don't mention how I modeled dresses during winter nights colder than this. Sometimes in unheated pools.

Lily contemplates this and tugs her Wampa cap down with one hand. "I can't have I'm-keeping-you-alive sex if he's dead."

"Look alive, Loren," Rose snaps.

Lily's eyes widen like he's near death.

"He's totally alive." I point at Lo. "That's a classic Loren Hale glare, with a classic Loren Hale haircut, and a *classic* Loren Hale jawline."

He flashes a half-smile in our direction.

"Classic," I say.

Lily relaxes against my side, and I'm tall enough that I can rest my chin on her head. I might be twenty-three to her twenty-seven, but I think she'll always look younger than me.

Lo blows on his hands.

"Relax, Loren." That's the photographer.

Lo shoots him a *really* nasty look that could cut up fingers and toes. Maybe because the photographer wears a warm trench coat, winter beanie, and woolen scarf.

"Ryke, hands off," the photographer chastises.

Ryke is "adjusting" himself. "You put me in thirty-degree fucking weather *in* underwear only, and things are gonna fucking move."

"Shrinkage is a real thing?" I ask aloud.

Connor begins, "Scientifically speaking—"

"Here we fucking go," Ryke grumbles.

"—the penis and testicles move closer to the body to seek warmth when cold, all to protect sperm, which is healthiest in a set temperature range."

"The more you know," Lo says and shivers. He finds some heat just to glare at Rose again. "Think of our goddamn *sperm*."

"I'd rather drink acid."

Lo retorts, "That can be fucking arranged."

Rose leans over to the photographer. "Are there any photos where Loren doesn't look like he's going to butcher everyone's family?"

"Just yours!" Lo shouts.

"Her family is my family," Connor reminds him.

Lo sighs and then shivers again. "Jesus Christ, I'm too young to die."

Lily can't stand here any longer. As she bolts towards Lo, I give her the blanket. She's wrapped up in it, and his whole demeanor just relaxes at the sight of his wife. When I reached the roof, she already told Rose her pregnancy news, and I saw the tiniest tear-track on Rose's cheek.

A tiny one for Rose is the equivalent of a sob.

Lily wraps her arms and blanket around Lo. The photographer keeps taking pictures and tells Rose to join her husband and for me to join mine.

I hesitate because I made a promise to myself not to model anymore. *Is this the same?*

Rose is already sharing the lounge chair, drilling a glare through her husband. He only grins back.

Ryke is about to leave the photo shoot, but I go to him, making up my mind. He shakes his head at me like *Daisy, don't be fucking forced into this.*

I'm not.

"This is my decision," I tell him. I don't feel strange about it or numb. It feels right because I'm not alone here. I'm with my sisters. I'm with him.

Ryke isn't controlling, as much as the tabloids like to paint him as the "older possessive man" in my life. He's overprotective where it matters, and he *always* listens to what I want. So he backs down immediately, nodding.

Then he suddenly lifts me up on his shoulders, my legs draped over his chest.

I smile down at him.

He looks up at me.

I howl like I found my mate, and he clasps the side of my face, the one with the long, old scar. And my wolf—he kisses me.

[14]

May 2019
MANHATTAN MEDICAL HOSPITAL
New York City

Rose Cobalt

"He or she is *coming out* before midnight," I proclaim like it's ancient fact written in stone slabs. "We've made an agreement." I readjust my hospital gown, no longer suffocating at the neck. Then I hold my round stomach. Nine-months with this little monster and I'm ready for him or her to skedaddle right on out of my vagina.

It's time for you to meet the world.

Though I know, like I did with Jane and Beckett and Charlie, that I'll miss these moments where it's just me and them. Where even in the quietest closet I can whisper little nothings and little somethings and they'd kick in reply.

Connor is all logic. He'd say the fetus is just reacting to noise. I'd like to think they knew exactly what I said, and they kicked until their mother heard their voice loud and clear.

I hear you, little gremlins.

"Rose," Connor says from the chair nearest my hospital bed, "you can't make agreements with an unborn child."

I raise my hand at his grin. "I can and I did, Richard." I fix my ponytail again. Twelve hours in labor and I'm already begging for the experience to end. It has nothing to do with pain, which is mild so far. The doctor hasn't even recommended an epidural yet.

It has everything to do with being confined to a bed, in a hospital gown, with all my children out of my care and in Lily, Poppy, and Daisy's for the night. They stopped by earlier with Jane, Beckett, and Charlie, but they all left when they realized how mind-numbingly *long* this would be.

I've already reapplied my mascara and lipstick to fill the wait. I also feel more put-together and comfortable when I pamper myself. So that's why I fix my hair for the umpteenth time.

Connor and I have exhausted most of our games, including *seventeen* crossword puzzles. I've even tried sending him away so we can communicate by text, but he refuses to leave the hospital in case I go into labor.

It's admirable. I'd even give him a gold star for his loyalty, but Connor is the kind of soldier that would rip the sword out of the king's hand and knight himself. He doesn't need me to present him with any honors.

Connor leans back, his fingers to his jaw, and my gaze grows hot at his calmness. I scoot further up, sitting taller and straighter to match his poise. *Fuck slouching.* I ignore the throb in my lower back.

He holds my sweltering gaze. "You verbally communicating with our unborn child is as nonsensical as you thinking that you can end your labor anytime you like." Connor knows full well that I'd never force the baby out and jeopardize his or her health.

"Jane asked me…in so many words to make this a May baby." I point at my belly. "And I am not *losing* to the fucking universe." When midnight strikes, it'll be June 1st.

Connor arches a brow.

"You look ridiculous when you do that," I snap. He actually looks incredibly self-assured. Like he can defeat any foe. *It's attractive.* I glare at the wall.

My mind is a pool of betrayal.

"Bypassing your erroneous assessment, I need to remind you that Jane simply said and I quote, 'Mommy, do May babies look like June babies?' She's just curious because she was born in June."

"Read between the lines, Richard. She said *Mommy, I don't want this motherfucking baby born on my birthday month.*"

Connor presses his fingers to his ugly grin before dropping his hand, his smile blinding. "There's no space between her lines. She hasn't learned subtext yet. Whatever you're reading is your own motivations placed on her."

I snap my hair tie, ponytail tight and secured. "Maybe so," I admit. Jane is my first born, and I don't want her to feel like I've forgotten her with each new baby. "It doesn't change what I'm hoping for, and if fate is on my side, everything will be perfect."

I smooth out the wrinkles on the hospital sheet. He's rarely *this* quiet after I bring up a word he loathes.

"You're not going to tell me to leave fate out of this?" I question.

He stares at me intently and his lips inch up again. "Tu es absolument magnifique." *You're absolutely beautiful.*

I see how much he means every word, his love shown through his eyes. I open my mouth to respond, but the contractions escalate swiftly and sharply. I swing my head away from Connor and grimace. Then I wince, shutting my eyes tight. *Holy fuck.*

"Rose." Connor has risen from his chair, his hand on my shoulder. His other finds mine, our fingers lacing together. "Talk to me."

I hang my head towards my lap, my face scrunched as I barrel through another contraction. "Shit…" I curse. I'm not going to pretend to be verbally wholesome, not in everyday life and not when I'm pushing out a human being through my vagina.

He kisses my temple and then steps to the side like he plans to find the doctor.

I clutch his hand tight, imprisoning him next to me. "Wait," I say through clenched teeth. "I'm fine." I blow a hot breath out and then hold the bridge of my nose with pinched fingers. *Goddddd* that pain is unreasonable.

He leans his head down, until his lips graze my ear. "Tu souffres." *You're in pain.* "We've talked about this."

I don't have to put on a show of strength and fortitude in the face of my very own misery. I'm not exactly trying to—okay maybe I am.

I may be trying to appear like this isn't *excessive* pain when it's truly incredibly excessive.

You can be vulnerable in front of your husband, Rose.

I have been, many times, but there is a stubborn side of me that drags until the last second. Right now, I feel like I could ignite a thousand houses with a single blowtorch. All the while comfortably sitting in this bed. Because I literally can't move.

"Rose." His objection to my stubbornness is welcome. The force in his usually even-toned voice is too. I'm reminded that he'll unleash his own arsenal if the situation calls for it. I've already made up my mind, even as he says, "I'm going to help you."

I let go of his hand. "Fine." I watch him urgently make his way across the room, wasting no time at all. I sit up straighter. "Technically it will be the medication helping me, not you!" I call out to Connor before he leaves. "So don't let that inflate your ego…" I mutter the last line.

He's already out the door.

ALONE IN THE HOSPITAL room, I blow out measured breaths to combat the mounting pain. I place my palm on my lower abdomen. I swear the baby moves *up* as though laughing mischievously, *you think I'm coming out now? Who do you think I am?*

A Cobalt boy.

I whisper, "I know you'd like, very much, to stay right here for as long as possible—since the alternative is being in the presence of your annoyingly narcissistic father. *But* I'd very much like if you could do me one favor and come on out." My voice softens, and I rub my stomach. I can't put all the blame on Connor. Even in jest. Since I'm not the easiest to get along with. "I promise we're not that bad. Connor and I will love you with every drop of blood. We'll fight for you. Die for you. And so you know, your father doesn't love just anyone. You're already very, *very* special."

I squeeze my eyes closed with a new contraction.

Then I blow out a shaky breath. "The pain is making me say crazy things."

Connor slips through the doorway with Dr. Amora, a six-foot exceptionally intelligent woman. I relax a little at the sight of these two people.

As she checks between my legs, Connor returns to my side. My phone out of reach on the bedside table, I press my fingers to my closed eyeballs and ask, "Time check?"

"Three hours to midnight." Connor begins massaging my shoulders, kneading all the intolerable kinks.

"He's doing this on purpose," I mutter. "Babies always have ulterior motives."

"*He?*" Connor rubs the base of my neck. "Do you know something I don't?" His question sounds rhetorical. He knows I didn't cheat and discover the gender. We've been careful to use both pronouns, but maybe my slip-up has revealed my true *wants*.

I want a boy so we can have another child.

"He's refusing to come out. Therefore, he's a Cobalt boy," I explain my rationale.

Dr. Amora is busy checking my vitals, and I watch her out of the corner of my eye, her lips pressed in a thin line. *Is everything okay?*

Connor picks up his coffee with his free hand, taking a sip. He even checks his watch, and worry lines begin to crease his forehead. Whether he's worried about my mental health or physical or the baby, I'm unsure. Maybe a bit of everything.

His gaze shares time between Dr. Amora and me. "Out of the two of us, you're far more stubborn. Process of deduction, he inherited it from you."

I wave him off like he's spoken falsehoods. My energy wanes and my back aches too strongly. I sink further on the bed, Connor's hands jettisoning from my shoulder blades.

Then the doctor faces us. "You're not far enough along for an epidural yet. We'll keep waiting."

Dear God.

I glare at my stomach. "You're going to be a little thorn, aren't you?"

"TIME CHECK."

"Thirty minutes until midnight." Connor pockets his phone.

I've already been administered an epidural, finally blissful relief. I dab a towel at my damp forehead, perspiring from the now consistent contractions.

Connor remains standing, one of his hands interlaced with mine, the other busy soothing my tense shoulders and neck. Dr. Amora is here. She's been telling me to push and I've been complying like an honor student (Connor's words).

I only take a break when she instructs me to and adds, "Everything is going well."

My husband whispers, "Comment tu te sens?" *How do you feel?*

"Like I could rip out your perfectly functioning lungs and stomp on them," I say with pinpointed eyes. I squeeze his hand tight, energy seeping out of me. I don't do athletics, but my raging determination keeps me from utter exhaustion.

A smile edges his lips. "I didn't ask for a tale, darling."

"It's not a tale," I proclaim. "It's a prophecy of what will happen if you keep smiling like you're made of a billion dollars."

"I am made of a billion dollars."

Ugh.

I glower at his widened, self-righteous grin. For as much as the look boils my blood, I'd miss the day where he stopped looking at me with those lips lifted high. Those blindingly white teeth and the glimmer of love in his blue eyes.

All walls lowered.

All emotions unfolded before me.

How long it took to reach this place together.

"Time check," I whisper. I'm bed-bound, legs numb from the drugs, and the nurse already scolded me for attempting to walk—but Connor had left again and I yearned to follow.

"Let's start pushing again." Dr. Amora smiles my way. "Ready, Rose?"

I look up at Connor.

"Five minutes," he tells me.

Five fucking minutes.

That's all I have?

I nod to my doctor. "I'm ready." Shoulders pulled back, eyes focused. *You're coming out in five minutes, little monster.* This one is already playing games with us.

I begin pushing to my *highest* ability. Sweat gathers across my forehead, and Connor speaks a few encouragements in French. I only tune him out with my effort and extreme focus.

Dr. Amora is concentrated between my legs, nurses flanking her. "A few more, Rose."

I don't stop. Through gritted teeth and another push, I say, "Time check." The goal partly distracts me from the unknown. More than anything, I want my baby to be healthy, to take a great big breath as soon as he meets the world, and this goal offers me control in a situation where I have very, very little.

On the ride to hospital, Connor even said aloud, "Not all things can be altered from desire, passion, and wisdom. Some things just happen. Like love and death and *life*. Some things just are."

Some things just are.

He's accepted the things we can't control, and even as I try to, I can't pretend that I'm not scared. Because I am scared. I'm *terrified* at the thought of bringing death into the world instead of life.

"One minute," Connor answers me.

One minute.

"Take a big breath for me, Rose," Dr. Amora says, our eyes locked.

I inhale until my lungs are full, and I exhale just as well. She doesn't have to tell me to *push*. I sense that I have to—right now. With maximum effort, I push. Tears crest my eyes, gnarled cries breaching my throat. I cut off circulation in Connor's hand, gripping so damn hard that my fingers whiten.

I scream, expecting to hear a baby.

Nothing happens.

No noises but my own and the whispers of nurses.

"Is he okay?" I ask.

Connor has his arm around my shoulders, and I have the strangest urge to turn into his chest and just shield my watery, reddened gaze. *I'm fine.*

I take a staggered breath.

"Let's try to push again," Dr. Amora encourages.

Connor dips his head towards mine. "If you keep predicting the worst, the worst will come—isn't that what your fate is all about?"

"No," I snap, though I understand what he's saying.

He goes one further. "If you were down four points in Quiz Bowl, you wouldn't mentally check out because you thought you'd lose. You'd fight harder for those last four points."

I would. I channel my confidence, years of persistence in the face of adversaries of all shapes and sizes. I block out the worst. My spirits lift tenfold.

You're coming out. And you're going to be loved. And there's just no stopping that.

Connor kisses my knuckles, his strength filling me whole. We're a team. The best of the best. While this is my battle, he's here with me. He always is.

I shut my eyes, redirecting my energy. I only think about this baby. I grit my teeth as I push. *Come on. Come on. Come on.* I'm so focused, I lose track of time and place.

Then soft lovely cries pierce the air and awaken me.

Light floods my eyes, and the wiggling baby is being placed on my chest. Nurses wipe him off while my gaze clouds with tears.

Dr. Amora stands. "Congratulations on your new baby boy."

Connor strokes his thumb across our son's head, and I clasp the baby's fingers. His soft cries fade to pleasant murmurs. My body surges with warmth and powerful sentiments that burst through my icy defenses. I crumble at the sight of *our* baby. No matter how many, each one is new. Each one is different and unique, and I revel in this raw moment that strips me bare.

"He's already horrible," I mutter so only Connor can hear. "He's making me cry." So did the other three babies. I wipe beneath my eyes and look to my husband.

Connor has this profound tranquility that can only be described as the surface of a quiet lake. Weight has been added to the bottom of his lake, lifting water levels, and his blue eyes draw unbreakable lines between our child and me and him.

"What are you thinking?" I whisper.

"How breathtaking dreams are when you meet them."

I once asked Connor what quote came to mind when he looked at Jane. I asked him the same thing about Charlie and Beckett, and his response never changed.

The quote beats at my heart, and I speak every word as assuredly and soulfully as he once did. "'We can never give up longing and wishing while we are thoroughly alive.'" His chest rises, and my life with him starting at fourteen to his fifteen and lasting for *years* is all in vivid focus.

He finishes, "'There are certain things we feel to be beautiful and good, and we must hunger after them.'" Connor tries to bar some of his emotions from prevailing, but he can't remove the weight from the lake. He sees this too, and he just smiles what can only be called a gorgeous smile.

The nurses hover close to examine the baby as he rests on my chest. They nod to me and mention that his vitals look perfect, and when they distance themselves from us, Connor speaks again.

"George Eliot," he correctly names the author of the quote. "*The Mill on the Floss.*"

Eliot. I brush a finger across the baby's cheek, and he murmurs again. "Eliot," I whisper. "It suits him." George Eliot is the pen name used by Mary Ann Evans. A woman.

Connor knows this fact, and I wonder if that's why his smile only grows. "Eliot Alice," he suddenly adds. "It suits him more."

"Alice from…" I think I know, but I'm surprised he'd choose *Alice's Adventures in Wonderland* by Lewis Carroll as the namesake. Though Alice is a female character, and since George Eliot was a woman with a common man's name, Connor must like the symbolism of naming our *son* Alice in reply.

"Alice from…?" he says, wanting me to guess.

"From a story that has a smoking caterpillar and a cat that grins wider than you."

He laughs. "Alice reminds me of Lily."

I thought I was through crying, but another tear escapes. "How come?"

"They're both gentle, imaginative, can be witty in their own right, and they're prone to falling down rabbit holes."

I laugh into a smile.

Connor drowns in my expression, and I float across the temperate, soothing surface of his. Only when the nurse announces his birthday, do I remember the goal I'd set in stone.

"This little one is born 12:01 a.m. on the dot." She passes me a small cotton cap to put on Eliot's head.

My eyes widen, processing and processing…

June 1ˢᵗ.

He was born June fucking 1ˢᵗ.

I try to narrow a glare at him, but I can't do such a thing. He's too fragile to endure the heat of my eyes. *I'm so sorry, my gremlin.*

I rub small circles across his back and then look to Connor. "There's still time to name him Brutus." Before he can even reply, I whisper to Eliot, "I'd never name you that." *Forgive me.*

"You're in love," Connor states the obvious.

"You're in love," I combat.

"Two truths. What shall we do with those?"

"Have another," I declare. *Have another truth. Have another baby.*

"More love," he says, reading my subtext clearly. "I can agree to that."

Long before now, he'd never utter these words in this way. And yes, I may have lost my small goal but I see the future and I see now.

I've never felt more triumphant.

Connor & Rose Cobalt welcome the birth of their baby boy

ELIOT ALICE COBALT

June 1st, 2019

{ 15 }

November 2019

THE HALE HOUSE
Philadelphia

Lily hale

"Did you pack an axe? A machete? What do you use to kill bears again?" I ask in all seriousness.

Ryke shoves a neoprene water bottle in the side pocket of his duffel and then gives me a look like I'm weird and *waaay* off-base.

I rest my butt against the armrest of my couch. My heavy, pregnant belly likes gravity. I have this need to *sit* or *lounge* or just splat on the floor like a beached jellyfish. Everything aches in the third trimester, but my brain still constantly reroutes to Loren Hale. In my bed. On my bed.

Naked. On me.

In me.

Hormones. I love and hate them. The fact that I'm focusing on something other than Lo and sex is a huge win, even if I've replaced sex with worry.

"It's a real question," I say in the lingering silence.

Ryke zips up his duffel. "You don't kill bears."

I lower my voice. "But if they eat him…" I don't want my four-year-old to hear this hypothetical horror scenario, but he should be out of earshot since he's upstairs packing a bag with Lo. Garrison isn't around either. He flew to London for the week to see Willow.

"It won't happen, Lily," Ryke refutes. "You can trust me with him."

"It's the woods. Anything can happen in the woods." Is it just the woods though? Moffy has experienced the wilderness plenty of times. We frequent our lake house in the Smoky Mountains so often that he keeps asking when we'll return.

"It's not any different than the lake house," he brings up, "or all the other times I've spent with him while you and Lo aren't there. It's all the fucking same. So why are you flipping out now?"

"I'm not flipping out," I snap.

"Then you're being fucking weird about it."

"You always call me weird."

Ryke sighs, frustrated, realizing that he's being coarse with me, and I know he doesn't want to be. He slowly unwraps a piece of gum from his pocket but doesn't chew it.

"What are you doing?" I ask.

"Trying not to ride you hard—*fuck*." He pinches his eyes. "Not like that."

I smile because it's funnier than it used to be. "I know you said it's the same, but this feels different. This is a *camping* trip with a tent and no electricity and…" It clicks.

"And what?"

"You take a lot more chances and risks than I would with kids."

It clicks for him too. "It's about the fucking climbing wall, isn't it?"

"You put it in her *nursery*. You're the insane one!" I point at him.

He rolls his eyes at me. "It's fucking safe."

I get hives walking into Sullivan's room. Ryke built a climbing wall with footholds and handholds for his one-year-old daughter. Neon warning signs blinked in my head when I saw it yesterday. Broken arm! Broken leg! Broken toes and fingers!

Sulli ascended the wall higher than I've ever seen a baby climb anything. Daisy and Ryke were spotting her, and I was hugging the door frame. I could tell their daughter loved it, but if Moffy loved running in front of cars, I'd say *no*.

I don't know where the line is for someone like Ryke. "What if Moffy asks to run through the fire?" I step towards him, investigation mode on. "What would you do?" I poke his chest.

He stares down at me like I haven't changed in a million years.

He's right. I'm still a terrific sleuth.

"I'd say fuck no."

"Would you?"

"*Yes*, Lily." He rakes his hand through his hair. "I *care*. I'd never put them in harm's way." He rubs his jaw. "You know why I teach Sulli how to climb?"

I shake my head. Paparazzi ask him all the time: *do you want Sullivan to be a climber like you?*

His response: *fuck off.*

"Because it's a huge part of my life, and if I barred her from it out of fear, I'd be shutting out my daughter. My goal isn't to push her to become a fucking professional climber. That's her choice."

My shoulders relax only a little. "Are you hoping she'll choose climbing?"

He's rigid. "I've only ever said this to Daisy, so don't go around telling Lo and Rose and the lamp and the bathtub."

"Hey," I say, "I broke up with the bathtub long ago."

Ryke *almost* smiles, but it vanishes fast. "After what happened… no. Fuck *no*." He means the climbing accident where his friend died. "I hope she chooses something else. I'd worry about Sullivan. Every ascent where I'm not on the other end of the rope, I'd fucking worry, but like Daisy, if that's what she loved, I'd let her do it."

I must be grinning wide and uncontrollable because he looks at me weird again.

So I say what I'm thinking, "You're a worrier too."

"For fuck's sake."

"You just admitted it. No take-backs."

He sighs. "We're not the same, Lily."

That's what he said when I called him a sex addict years ago. *I know you wish I was,* he once said, *so I could join you in your little sex addicts not-anonymous club, but it's not happening.*

"You worry," I say. "I worry. Worriers United, us." I motion between our bodies.

He re-wraps his gum. "I'm not *worried* about an overnight camping trip at a little state park. I'm worried about my daughter falling from three-thousand fucking feet."

Good points.

I grow hot, and I'm not sure if it's my anxiety mounting again or just the heat in the room. I grab the nearest thing I can find—which happens to be a comic book on the couch cushion. I waft the glossy issue at my face, small gusts of air cooling me.

"Is it hot in here?" I ask. "I feel faint."

"Sit the fuck down."

"I am seated...sort of." I'm still leaning on the armrest. "I think I'm just nervous." I have to face the facts. Moffy will be attending his first-ever camping trip, and I should be thankful it's with Uncle Ryke. He's a wilderness pro.

Lo even said it was the best-case scenario since Ryke spends more time outdoors than indoors. In comparison, Lo can barely start a fire with a match. He has no patience for fire-making.

"What's the worst that can fucking happen?" Ryke pockets his gum. Before I can utter the words, he adds, "*Besides* a bear."

I slowly set the comic book back down. It's Wolverine. *Give me strength.*

"Paparazzi," I tell him. "What if paparazzi follow you and then give you hell in the woods where you can't escape? It's happened before, so it's a *rational* fear."

"Price and Declan are coming along. If something fucking happens with the media, they'll take care of it." Price is Daisy's bodyguard. Declan is Moffy's.

"What if Moffy doesn't do well? I won't be there to comfort him." Ryke isn't *me*. He's said as much.

"Look, I promised Rose that if Janie freaks out, I'd bring her to the nearest hotel. I mapped it out. Same promise extends to you about Moffy."

"Thank you." My worry starts to subside, especially at the idea of Rose, my older and wisest sister trusting Jane's life with Ryke. I bet she grilled him for a solid hour about safety.

I sink on the couch cushion, and Ryke leaves his duffel to take a seat next to me. I splay my hands on my abdomen, the baby kicking nonstop.

Ryke puts his hand on my stomach, feeling her wiggle around. He's asked many times before if he could touch. I used to freak out by our physical interactions when I was pregnant with Moffy, but I'm much better now. So I always give Ryke permission.

"Are you scared?" he asks.

I frown. "Do I look it?"

"You look a little fucking tired."

"She moves a lot and keeps me up at night sometimes." *She.* Luna Hale. I'm a little scared to have a girl, but only because of other people. I don't want them to hassle her the way they hassled Daisy. *Future sex addict*, they said about my little sister. Just because of me.

I have to believe that Luna will have an easier time than Daisy had.

I say softly, "I wish Daisy was going camping with you." My sister decided to expand a section of Camp Calloway in the "off-months"— which includes paperwork and Skype meetings.

"Me fucking too," Ryke says, "but she'll have a good weekend with Sulli."

I don't doubt it.

While we wait for Lo and Moffy to come downstairs and for Rose and Connor to drive Jane over, all I picture are *bears*. Brown bears. Grizzly bears. I'm losing my mind when a polar bear pops up.

Ryke half-interestedly flips through the Wolverine comic.

I squint at him. "Remind me why we're not going with you?"

"For one, you're fucking pregnant." He roughly turns a page, and it *tears*. Shit! He freezes.

I freeze. Lo is so possessive over the state of our comics. When I reanimate I whisper, "Stuff it in the couch cushion, he'll never find out."

Ryke checks over his shoulder before he lifts the cushion beneath his ass and slides the comic underneath.

"Lo can go with you." I pick up where we left off. "He should go with you."

"He can't even light a fucking fire with a match, and he kicked a canteen into a bush the last time we went camping together. I love my brother, but he'd be more trouble than help. I bet you anything he doesn't even want to fucking go."

"He'd rather stay at home?" I thought he'd rather go with Moffy.

Ryke clears his throat like he's hiding a secret. "Yeah." *What a lying liar.*

I fasten the best glare I have, and it must do the job because he cracks under the pressure of Lily Investigator Hale.

"Look, I'm the fun fucking uncle who gets to take his niece and nephew on a camping trip. And it just so happens that it gives you and Lo all weekend to fuck each other as much as you want."

My jaw unhinges. "That's the reason *this*"—I wave my arms around—"is going on?"

"Why can't you just fucking say *camping trip*?"

"Ryke," I snap.

"Part of the reason. There are multiple fucking reasons, Lily."

I cross my arms the best I can over my large belly. "I don't want to fuck him."

"Bullshit." It's one of the firmest *bullshits* I've heard all year.

I let out a long, heavy sigh. With my hormones raging, it'll be nice to have more alone time with Lo. I just don't like the whole orchestration for sex. I constantly have to remind myself that this doesn't make me a bad mom.

Most people would like alone time, not just sex addicts. *Right?* Right. Right?

I'm confusing myself.

"Thanks then," I tell him, "for giving us the weekend."

"I'm the fun fucking uncle. It's what I'm here for."

The door blows open. "MOFFY!" Four-year-old Jane shouts as she enters the living room from the foyer. "CAMPING TIME!"

I stand with Ryke.

Jane, in a pale pink coat, searches the room with eager eyes.

"He's upstairs," I tell Jane.

"Thank you, Aunt Lily!" She darts up the stairs, falling on the second one, before hastily picking herself up and shouting, "MOFFY!"

As soon as Rose sees us by the couch, she reroutes her course towards Ryke. Connor right behind her.

"Do you have everything?" Rose's fiery yellow-green eyes wield a million threats.

Ryke returns to his duffel and casually stuffs his hands in his pockets. I resume my leaning-against-couch position.

"Yeah." He taps his duffel with his boot as proof.

Connor gently sets a pink princess bag down beside the black duffel. He seems calmer than I imagined he'd be. He is sending his only daughter off into the woods with Ryke Meadows, but I've never been good at reading through Connor's poker face.

"Are you concerned?" I ask him. "At all?"

He barely blinks. "That it may rain, yes. There's a fifty-five percent chance." Obviously he's not worried about the possibility of bears or cameramen lurking behind trees.

That's all you, Lily.

Rose is even subdued. No verbal threats about Ryke's balls and penis. I cringe. *Stop thinking about his dick.*

Rose and Ryke did have a conversation yesterday about the camping trip. He was over her house, fixing a fence, and maybe that's when he made the promise to bring Jane to a hotel if she freaks out.

Footsteps patter down the staircase. Lo enters the living room with Moffy and Jane on his heels. He dumps Moffy's Black Widow bag on top of the princess one.

Moffy pushes his little Ray-Ban sunglasses to his head. Then he struggles to zip up his leather jacket. Lately, he dresses more and more like Ryke.

Lo kneels in front of Moffy and tries to help zip him up. Moffy exhales loudly and peeks at Ryke, trying to impress the person he's emulating. His admiration for his uncle shouldn't be awkward, but the media fixates on three-way rumors between Lo, me, and Ryke.

His closeness with his uncle might prompt a tabloid to spread worse rumors. Lo said that *Celebrity Crush* tried once. A journalist speculated that Moffy was really Ryke's son. Connor squashed the article before it went public, thankfully, but when Lo told me, his voice was raw and hoarse.

"It's not my feelings," he said, "it's about *his*. The doubt, Lil—I don't want him to doubt this."

I hugged onto Lo, and he gripped onto me.

We reaffirmed that we wouldn't ruin our relationships because the media sucks. We'd never actively separate Moffy from Ryke. He loves his uncle, and that should be one of the best things in the universe. It *is*.

I just worry. I'm a worrier. *It's been decided.*

And I worry that if Moffy hears about my dirty closet, he'll find me gross. He'll find reasons to hate me. I'll lose a close-knit relationship with my son because he soaked up the media's perceptions of who I am.

I've been in the news long enough to have a sense of how I'm perceived. Alone, not beside Loren Hale, it's not-so-good—but it's not as bad as it was.

Most popular tweet from the past: Lily Calloway is a cheating, dirty whore. Ew. Think about how gross her vagina is.

I wish people would stop thinking about my vagina. Because then I think about my son thinking about my vagina, and I want to bury myself in blankets and never come out.

The good news: every tabloid and news outlet stopped calling me a nympho after *We Are Calloway* aired since I explained *why* it's so hurtful. It's not like they grew a moral backbone and listened to my plea. Fans go after *Celebrity Crush* with pitchforks if they criticize Daisy's PTSD and depression, and they attacked the tabloid for using the term nympho so much that they retracted their article.

Connor said that consumers dictate what industries produce, and I never really understood that until recently.

Lo stands after he finishes zipping up Moffy. "I packed an extra jacket for him if he gets cold."

"Perfect." Ryke slings his black duffel on his shoulder and easily picks up the other two bags with each hand.

Moffy already tears away from Lo and rushes to Ryke. "Are we ready? Can we go?" His enthusiasm lights up his face.

"Yeah, let's head out. Janie?"

Jane pulls on a glittery leopard-print baseball hat. "Au revoir." She says *goodbye* in French, waves to her mom and dad, and then she leads the parade out the door.

Moffy catches up to Ryke's side. "I can carry my bag."

His brows rise. "You can?"

Moffy nods repeatedly.

"Take fucking hold, little guy." He lets Moffy grip a strap.

I drift towards Lo, who watches our son with crossed arms. *This is hard.* Moffy is only four, but he already asks to do things that older kids do. What if he forgets about us?

Lo hugs me to his side.

I whisper, "I think this is what it must feel like for a Hufflepuff and Slytherin to have a Gryffindor baby." Why is this making me so emotional? I dab at my eyes. They're dry. *Still.* "I'm sad."

"Lil." Lo squeezes me. "We don't know what house he's in. He's not *eleven* yet."

This is true.

"And we already agreed. We'd be happy if he ended up in Gryffindor."

This is even truer.

Moffy and Ryke disappear in the foyer, but I don't hear the door slam shut. *Something's wrong.* Just then, Moffy sprints into the living room, eyes on us.

He hugs Lo's legs. "Bye, Daddy."

Then mine. "Bye, Mommy." We barely have time to reciprocate before he races back to the foyer. The door shuts this time.

He didn't forget about us.

I smile, in a slight daze.

CONNOR AND LO LEFT to watch the car depart from the driveway. So I return to my spot on the couch cushion. I think I'm the only reason Rose stayed in the living room.

"This was a bad idea," I tell my sister as she sits beside me.

"You need this."

I frown, not liking that *I'm* the first thing that came to mind.

Maybe she sees this because she adds, "Did you see their faces? They'll have more fun than we would among dirt and bugs." She pauses. "I'm sure she'll come home with a million bug bites. Which reminds me…" She whips out her cell and starts typing a note. "*Buy calamine lotion.*"

"I can do just night sex," I remind Rose. "Up until the third trimester, I've been acing my schedule."

Rose pulls her hair into a pony. "You practically fuck him with your eyes whenever he's in the room."

"I'm that obvious?" I worry.

"Yes." She procures her lipstick from her purse and uncaps the tube. "There's no shame in taking personal time. You need it. I need it sometimes. And you should take it, especially since you'll have to go without sex for a while when Luna arrives."

The six-week "no sex" after giving birth rule. It's doomsday all over again, but I succeeded after giving birth to Moffy. If I can do it once, surely I can do it twice.

Rose isn't showing off much of a baby bump in her blue dress, not too far along. I still can't believe she's pregnant again. Then I can. She's determined to have a girl, and so she conceived right when she was able to have sex following Eliot's birth. *Six weeks and then pregnant again.*

Insane.

Daisy would say that our older sister loves the insanity of it all. Cobalt chaos is a real thing now, and Connor and Rose thrive on every second.

"It's already penciled in, darling. Lunch tomorrow," Connor says, walking in the living room with Lo by his side.

"Tell your assistant *tacos.* I'm not your wife. I hate sushi."

Rose can't have raw fish when she's pregnant, but she'll still eat vegetarian rolls.

"That was an oversight on his part," Connor says. "I wouldn't forget your preferences."

Rose secures her purse on her elbow, rising like a queen. "Time to leave." She sets a blazing glare on Lo. "Loren, please remind my sister that this situation isn't just for her benefit."

I stare at my hands.

"This isn't just sex, Lil. I want a date night with my wife."

The rush of guilt escapes my body, freeing me.

As Rose and Connor leave, my sister's voice fades. "Please tell me you unthawed the chicken fingers before we left." They feed their children what their children prefer. *Celebrity Crush* still speculates that Rose and Connor serve fancy five-course meals every night.

Not true.

"Who do you think you married?" he asks.

"A narcissist, not a chef."

I imagine his blinding grin before the door shuts.

The room blankets with silence. I crane my neck over the couch, just to sweep his sharpened features.

Every day I wonder when Loren Hale the boy turned into Loren Hale the man, and I wonder how I could've resisted him for so long. It's not just about his jawline and cheekbones. It's how he sees me. In one look. In one stare.

Worthy.

Beautiful.

You're far from trash, Lily Hale.

His perception of me defeats all the ugly ones that exist. It reinforces what I believe about myself.

Worthy.

Beautiful.

You're far from trash, Lily Hale.

I drink in his love. Desire pools between my legs. *His hands on your hips, down your thighs.* Yes. Yes. I practically pulse when my thoughts descend to his dick.

All of it.

In me.

Now.

I freeze, really pulsating, and I concentrate on the present. I am *not* up against Loren Hale, as much as I'd love to be. He's still standing on the other side of the couch.

He stares at me so knowingly that my cheeks immediately flush. I remember what Rose said about me eye-fucking him. Have I been?

I'm so obvious.

Tension builds in the overwhelming silence. My neck aches, so I focus on the blank television and pat my knees. "So..." *Lo's cock.*

I press my thighs together, lost for a second. I shake out my arms to keep from drifting in a fantasy. Why do I feel so awkward? I've known him all my life. I wake up next to my best friend. I sleep next to my best friend.

The proof lasts for centuries.

I don't check him out. I just drum my fingers on my knees. "Date night?" *That's why this is weird.* When do we ever call them date nights? "What are we going to do?"

"Watch the *Rogue Cut*." He takes a seat beside me.

Four words catapult my spirits. The *Rogue Cut* is a special edition of *X-Men: Days of Future Past.* We always put off finishing the bonus scenes in favor of shows and new movies, plus cartoons for Moffy.

I angle towards Lo. "OhmyGod, what if there's a secret Magneto scene?" I scrunch my nose. "Oh no. Do you think they made Rogue and Magneto hook up like in the comics?" I place a hand over my heart. "My shipper heart can't handle it, Lo. That is *literally* my least favorite pairing. Ever."

"That's Earth-295," he reminds me. "It'd be a stretch to include it here." I open my mouth to counter, but he adds, "*But* if it does happen, I'll be fast-forwarding that shit."

I let out a big sigh of relief. "Thank you."

"Anytime, love. Fast-forwarded shit is my favorite kind of shit." His dry smile dimples his cheeks.

My body throbs. *Focus. On. The. Movie.* I chant.

I relax against the couch while he turns it on. Fifteen minutes through the extended edition, his legs are kicked up on the coffee table, our sides touch, and his arm is curved around my shoulders.

I sit stiffly, knowing if I cuddle against Lo, my hands will wander to his jeans. I'll unzip him and then rush for an orgasm. *Slow*, I often remind myself.

Twenty minutes pass.

I squirm. *Lily!*

Sex seems better than superheroes. Which is a thought that's played out plenty of times before. But Lo dubbed this date night, and what if he's hoping I'll wait patiently until the movie ends?

I'm not ruining date night.

Not with sex.

I risk a peek at Lo. The movie hypnotizes him more than me. His brows scrunch as Magneto appears on screen, and he rewinds the scene by ten seconds just to listen again. This is why it takes us forever when we watch director's commentary.

I eye his crotch.

What if I sit on him? Backwards…

Anal.

My doctor advised against anal while I'm this pregnant. I still think about it though.

Anal. Why does a word that sounds so ugly have to feel so good? My thoughts are so weird, and yet, I'm okay with this. *Embrace your weirdness.* I nod confidently at the idea.

Lo pauses the movie. "Are you doing okay?" His amber eyes flit from my head to waist to hands, evaluating my state of being.

"Great. Why?"

"You nodded to yourself." He cups my cheek, and I do this thing—I nestle towards his palm. *More. More. Closer.*

He can't hear my chant, but he must see it in my eyes. *Date night.*

Who knew "date night" would be a chant against sex? It is though. For me, it is. I clasp his wrist like I'm going to peel his hand away. I end up freezing, his large palm so warm against my cheek.

You nodded to yourself, I remember him saying.

"So?" How is nodding bad? I'm a nodder. A confident, self-proclaimed nodder. I frown. Is a nodder even a thing? I need Connor Cobalt to tell me if it's a real word—but not right now. I *do not* need Connor Cobalt in regards to sex.

Lo flips the remote in his free hand. "You only do that when you're boosting yourself up over something."

I clear my throat. "I'm reminding myself that anal may sound like an ugly word and I can still like it and that's okay." I nod again. Fuck it, I'm a nodder—whether that's a word or not.

Lo laughs into a smile.

I realize I'm still imprisoning his palm against my face. "This is yours…" I give Lo his hand back.

His smile fades to the point where he looks wounded.

"Unless…can I have it?"

He leans forward like he plans to kiss me, but then he teases, inching a breath backwards. I gasp, needy.

"Lily Hale," he says my name in a sexy whisper. *So close.* Kiss me. Kiss me. *Kiss me.* "You can have more than just my hand."

Yes.

I try to kiss him, but he teases again, his lips bypassing mine.

Against my ear, he murmurs, "Slowly."

I ache and throb. He rotates more towards me, his knee on the cushion. His hand takes a perilous journey through the sleeve of my muscle shirt.

He skims the skin beside my breast. *Closer. Closer.*

"Lo," I breathe, even more needy. I try to kiss him again.

He turns his head, and my lips touch his jaw.

"You're the biggest tease," I complain.

Lo smiles like he could tease me a thousand more years. "What about now, love?" His thumb brushes my nipple, his full hand cupping my breast. He flicks the sensitive bud, and I jolt, my lips parting, nerves lighting up.

I whip my head to the side, my legs shaking. Then I notice the movie paused on the screen. *Date night.*

"Lo…" I wince at myself.

"Lily?" Alarm spikes his voice. He rests his palm on my pregnant belly, scared for the baby, then his other hand touches my cheek. Scared for me.

"ImfineImfine," I say so quickly. "But date night?" I don't want to be the reason we cut the movie short.

His shoulders lower, relaxing. "Can I tell you a secret?" His voice deepens to a whisper again. Then he gently guides my back to the couch, so I lie lengthwise.

As he remains above me, I fixate on Lo, his hand back beneath my muscle shirt. "Does it involve cocks?"

He squeezes my small breast. "One cock."

I'm wet. "Your cock?"

He grabs my hand. "This cock." He unbuttons and unzips his jeans before stuffing my hand down his pants *and* boxer-briefs.

He's so hard.

My eyes grow big. I didn't think he'd be hard right now. I thought he was in movie-mode.

Lo says, "I want *this* night with you. Because *I* want to fuck you, not just because you want to fuck me or because of the six-week *no-sex* period after Luna arrives."

My pulse quickens. I open my mouth to speak, but words escape me. In my silence, he removes my hand from his pants, and then he wedges a pillow beneath my lower back, my legs already split apart for him.

Come closer. Kiss me. Fill me.

I blink a couple times. What if I'm interpreting him wrong? What if he's not suggesting sex right now? "Wait…what does this mean?"

Lo hovers over me. "Lily Hale." His eyes never leaving mine, he plants a burning kiss to my collarbone. Another on my neck. I try to buck forward, but the weight of my stomach keeps me grounded. "I…"

He pulls my shirt off, my breasts in view. "Want…" His lips skim my nipples. I shiver. *Oh my God.* "To…" His tongue laps the stiff flesh. "Fuck…"

Inside me. Come inside me.

His hand dives down my leggings and panties. He cups my heat. "You…" He pushes two fingers inside of me.

I gasp, my head rocking back, my muscles tightening. *Yesyesyes.* He pulses his fingers, and my toes curl. "OhmyGod." I dizzy.

His lips catch mine. I sink against his affection that deepens, that originates from the pit of his soul. We kiss like we've been told this will be our last. We show each other why it couldn't be the end. Even if other people said it should be.

He breaks apart, just to pull off my leggings and panties with one hand, his lips right against mine, our eyes glued to one another. In my ragged breath, I ask, "Are you hornier than me? That's not…"

"Not *what?*" His edged voice makes me quake in *want.*

By the time I respond, we're both naked. "Not…possible." I writhe as his fingers find the most pleasurable spot. He pulses them faster, over and over, and my back arches.

I cry upwards, my fingers digging into his shoulders. "Yesyesyes!"

Lips back to my ear, he whispers, "You're about to feel how horny I am, love."

Oh my…my hands skim his abs as his hardness nears me. "Closer," I beg.

"How close?" he teases, waiting and waiting.

Sweat coats my skin. "All the way…in."

Lo has one protective hand on my abdomen. As though reminding himself to take this easy for our baby. Then he fills me so full.

It sets me on edge. I tense up, and the way he stares at me does me in. Our eyes connect while he rocks against me, his muscles flexing.

"Closer, closer," I keep begging, even if he's as close as he can go. I want to be completely consumed by Loren Hale.

A grunt in his throat, he moves slower but deeper. I feel each shift inside of me. I want to sit on him. I want to blow him. I want to do a thousand different things to him, and I want him to do a thousand different things to me.

My world rotates at the next thrust. "Lo…"

His fingers graze my nipple. He pinches. I shudder and moan, hugging onto him.

"*Lo.*"

His hand runs down my leg, towards my thigh.

"I want to sit on you," I suddenly blurt out. I also tell him four more positions that are impossible pregnant. "…and come in my mouth."

I'm high-maintenance in bed. He told me so last week. In a loving kind of way.

Lo kisses me on the lips while he rocks forward. I clutch his sides, still full of him. We're one. We've always been one.

And when our bodies meld, the need feels beyond *need* and more like survival. We're surviving this world together.

I reach a peak and only look at Lo, my body shaking in euphoria.

His amber eyes flood with profound, deep-seated love, and I'm anchored to him.

8:47 P.M.

Lo rejected most of my positions, but he let me blow him. He knelt on the couch while I sat up, and I took him in my mouth. His expression is one of the best parts. Infatuation and *lust* coats his eyes, and he'll hold my hair out of my face. When he comes, his whole jaw tenses. He'll tilt his head back, and his glare murders the ceiling before his eyes roll.

Lo climaxing turns me on, and he knows it. So he had to help me again.

"No more," he reminds me.

"I know." I tuck my towel out around my pregnant frame. We just took a shower, and I must have this horny look while I think about our sex-capades. It's much easier to fall into compulsions when I'm pregnant. I'm not allowed to seek hundreds of orgasms.

My phone suddenly buzzes on the bathroom counter. I waddle because the floor is slippery. Lo uses his towel to dry his hair before his body, but I'm not complaining. I like a naked Loren Hale.

"Who is it?" he asks just as I grab the phone. Lo comes up behind me, the screen illuminated.

My heart twists. The notifications say *Ryke* and then the partial text. I quickly click in. We haven't heard anything besides the occasional *we're here* and *everything's fine* since he left for the camping trip.

My worry mounts for a brief second.

Then I let out a breath.

He sent a photo. Ryke, Jane, and Moffy sit around a campfire and roast marshmallows. They both have huge goofy smiles. *Priceless.*

Ryke, who even has a hard time lifting his lips, smiles too. I bet one of the bodyguards snapped the photo for them.

"He looks happy," Lo says, a smile to his voice.

"Your brother or our son?" I wonder.

"Both."

I click off the phone and spin towards him. "I'm glad we did this." I nod. "We chose well." Moffy spending quality time with his uncle. Lo and I having quality time alone.

It's all positive.

And it has nothing to do with sex, even if the sex is *so good.*

Lo's hand falls to my abdomen. "Luna," he says her name much more gently than he says most. "Are you going to be into camping? Or are you going to be scared of bears like Mommy?"

I slug his shoulder.

"It's a good fear," I defend.

"The best fear there ever was." Then he kisses the outside of my lips, *teasing*.

I grow serious in a quick second. "Are you worried?" I've admitted that having a girl would be more frightening than having a boy. Lo even said that raising a girl would be different, maybe even tougher beneath the limelight.

"I'm not scared of any goddamn bears," he quips, but he knows what I'm really asking.

"Lo—"

"I'm going to protect her," he says strongly and certainly. I must still look concerned because he repeats it. "I'm *going* to protect her, Lil. And you know what, she might not even need me." He cups my cheeks. "If she has even a fraction of your strength, she'll be okay."

He kisses my lips, cementing this truth.

Lily & Loren Hale welcome the birth of their baby girl

LUNA HALE

November 30th, 2019

{ 16 }

December 2019

THE LAKE HOUSE
Smokey Mountains

LOREN HALE

"This is all your goddamn fault," I tell my brother as I zip my snow jacket higher. We hike through the dense woods in search of a fir or spruce tree to replace the last one. Temperatures dropped overnight, and my breath smokes the six a.m. air.

Ryke hikes ahead of me. "You think I fucking knew the tree had bugs in it?" That's right. My brother had one job. One goddamn job and he blew it. He picked a Christmas tree that had a *nest* of spiders in it. We set up the tree, decorated the thing, and two days later, spiders started crawling on presents.

We're lucky none traveled to the kid's bedrooms.

On top of that horror show, I still hear Rose's laugh in my right ear. Last year, the girls found, chopped, and wheeled an eight-foot spruce tree home, all on their own. This year was our turn, and I get it. This was a shit display, but I've been over tree hunting before it even started.

Connor scrolls through his phone and successfully avoids colliding into trunks while simultaneously landscaping the area for a fir. The guy can multitask better than some people can take a shit.

Sam and Garrison bring up the rear.

I yawn into my arm, falling behind even them. "Goddammit, why'd we wake up this early?" The sky is a dim blue color, the sun rising but still hidden.

Sam stuffs his fists in his dark red snow jacket. "Shouldn't you be used to the morning by now?"

Right. Samuel Stokes is the one who told me I'd be a "morning person" after I had *one* kid. Well, now I have two, and my feelings are the same. I wake up early to run with my brother; I yawn for five straight minutes while stretching. I wake up early to feed my kids; I yawn for ten straight minutes while wandering up and down the hallway.

"No, Sammy," I say. "I prefer a warm bed, next to my wife, and not out here with you, freezing my balls off." I wear a half-smile that feels as brittle as the air.

Ryke finally shortens his stride so this trek isn't as miserable. Don't get me wrong, it's still fucking miserable. *I want to be with Lily*, I keep thinking. If I say it out loud, my older brother will tell me to stop complaining.

"Does your leg hurt in the rain?" Sam asks Ryke. "Because of the titanium."

My brother has an eight-inch plate in his femur, eleven screws, and a rod and pins in his tibia. He acts like he was never hurt, but I helped him rehabilitate his leg, so I know his body isn't what it used to be. I lost my brother for a while, but stubborn Ryke Meadows is back now. I hold onto that every goddamn day.

The Ryke who gives up is not someone I ever want to meet again.

The elevation increases as Ryke hikes up the snowy trail. He shakes his head towards Sam. "No. In the cold, my leg is fucking stiff and might cramp, but it doesn't ache any more or less than usual."

Connor's grip tightens on his phone, his annoyance so apparent on his face that I don't even question its existence.

"Did the artist fuck-up their oil painting of you? I told them not to forget your crown." I put my hand on his shoulder. "Let me at 'em."

"That's what our dog is for, darling." Connor smiles.

Ryke hears and throws his middle finger backwards at us.

We both laugh.

I never really pry or ask for more details about Connor's phone, but he waves his cell towards me, trusting me enough to explain.

"Social media is a wasp's nest. I have no problem stepping on it once and a while. I *willingly* take those steps, but when people throw the nest in my face out of idiocy and fallacy, it's the equivalent of twisting a screwdriver in my eardrum." He scrolls on his phone. "I'm in the process of yanking out the screwdriver."

I rub my gloved hands together for warmth. "What kind of social media?"

He reads, "At *Connor Cobalt.*" It's a tweet. "*We know you planted the evidence against Scott Van Wright.*" Evidence…he means the tapes of Daisy giving a blow job to her old boyfriend. She was underage, so it was considered child pornography, and it's what essentially got Scott Van Wright's ass thrown in jail three years ago. He was the one who filmed it during *Princesses of Philly* and then kept the footage to watch later—without any of us knowing, including Daisy.

Ryke screeches to a halt. "What the *fuck?*" He swings back towards Connor, and we all come to a stop in an open clearing, evergreens jutting to the sky all around us.

"I'm not finished," Connor says like he cut him off mid-fuck. "*You deserve to go to jail, not SVW.* Hashtag *criminal.* Hashtag *jealous.*" He slips his phone in his pocket. "All morning, I've been sent hundreds of notifications like that one. Each time my assistant blocks them, the person creates a new account."

Connor would never waste time blocking people himself. Unsurprisingly, he has employees for that.

"That's fucking bullshit," Ryke curses. "Scott deserves *life* in prison for what he did to Daisy, for what he did to Rose." *Child pornography. Sex tapes.*

My jaw locks, and my blood heats. I don't know how Lily and I escaped that sick fuck. *Luck*—we were lucky. Daisy got swept under. Ryke—he's still torn up about it.

"People see what they want to see," Connor says, "and some people liked *Scott* with Rose during the reality show. Their taste was questionable from the start."

It's almost unfathomable the things Connor must've heard…maybe even seen, just to find justice in relation to Scott. We're all thankful of Connor. For being in our lives. For what he did. But none of us truly realize what he mentally went through back then. No one does except him.

Garrison leans against a tree and smokes a cigarette. "I've seen the VanWrighties whole conspiracy theory shit on Tumblr. It's in *depth*."

"VanWrighties?" Sam frowns.

"Sammy," I say. "Where have you been?" This was a *Princesses of Philly* era. Forever ago.

"Staying away from you," he rebuts.

I clap. "Looks like we have something in common. Miracles do happen."

Sam actually smiles.

Garrison blows out smoke. "VanWrighties are the fanatics obsessed with Scott Van Wright. They chose the name."

Ryke gestures for Connor's phone.

Before he hands the cell over, he says, "If you piss on it, it's still mine."

He growls in annoyance. "Fuck you." And he rips the phone out of Connor's hand.

Ryke scowls at the cell. "What the fuck...? Are these people for real?"

"There are real living humans on the other end, yes."

Ryke reads, "Hashtag *Free SVW*. *I hope Conner, Loren and Ryke poo-poo in their pants tonight.*"

I burst out laughing with all the guys, even Ryke. He tosses the cell back to Connor. It's easier to let these events roll off. They're too frequent to waste energy on.

"They also spelled your fucking name wrong," he mentions to Connor, trying to annoy him.

I swing my head to Connor. "They put an *e* instead of an *o* at the end of your name again? I'll fuck-em up."

"My name is everywhere. It says more about their spelling skills than anything about me."

"Conceited and perfect." I touch my heart. "When can I have one of you?"

Connor grins. "You already have me."

Sam rubs his reddened ears and then lifts up his jacket hood. "What exactly happened?" he asks us. "I know the news said Scott had tapes of Daisy with her ex-boyfriend, all when she was underage—but they never said how you knew they existed."

I interject first, "Because the news doesn't know he found the info first, *Sammy*. That doesn't leave here." I draw a circle in the air around all of us. The girls also know, but the media only learned that Daisy called the police and reported the crime. Not that Connor had any help in convicting Scott Van Wright of child pornography.

He never asked for recognition. Never wanted *thanks* or anything. Connor did what he did, and he left it at that.

"It doesn't matter how I knew about the tapes," Connor tells Sam.

"It does to VanWrighties." Garrison sucks on his cigarette.

Ryke glowers. "Can we stop fucking calling them that?"

"I didn't make up the name, dude. I don't even believe their theories. They've been deluded into thinking they know all of you, and they feel entitled to pry since you let them in."

"Fuck *Princesses of Philly*," Ryke swears.

"Their theories are speculative," Connor says. "It's no more accurate than the tabloids that claim Ben Affleck is half-alien and the real Brad Pitt is frozen in an iceberg."

Garrison nearly chokes on his cigarette. "You read *The Outer Star Magazine?*" That tabloid is garbage.

"His wife pointed it out in the grocery checkout." Connor, of course, has his eyes on me.

"My wife is adorable. I know you're jealous, but she's just cuter."

"Impossible." Connor grins.

Garrison stomps on his cigarette butt. "You know, if you let me look at the Twitter accounts, I can find their IP address and send them a virus. It might just be a few people."

Connor arches a brow. "No. You're employed by Cobalt Inc. which means that you can't commit a crime while working beneath me."

Garrison kicks up snow and dirt. "What happens if I do?"

"I'd fire you." Connor tightens his gloves and scans the woods for a tree. I'm here for moral support at this point. I yawn into my arm again.

Connor heads towards a nearby fir. "We should pick a tree around here. If we hike any further, it'll just take us longer to carry back."

Garrison blows smoke up at the sky again. We invited him to Christmas way before Willow even said she could come this year. He still lives at my house, and he asked me to tell everyone about his brothers. So now they know why he hasn't spoken to them or his parents since he moved into my place.

He started smoking again, too, but he only smokes outside, so we're trying not to gang up on him about it.

"Who has the tape measure?" Connor asks beside the green fir. Queen Rose wants an eight-footer.

Ryke digs in his jacket pocket for one.

"You don't need that," Garrison says. "Just let him stand in front of the trees." He nods to Connor.

Connor looks almost bored. "I'm six-four. That'd be inaccurate."

Garrison shrugs. "Close enough."

"No it's not," Connor says, "and I'm investing in you, which means you should be beyond elementary math."

Garrison rolls his eyes.

Ryke points his axe towards the fir tree. "It looks around seven feet."

Rose will be happy that the girls found a taller tree last year, and Connor must be okay with that ending because he nods to Ryke. My brother starts swinging, chipping at the base of the fir.

I yawn again. *Jesus Christ.* I blame having a new baby. Lily *just* had Luna in November. I want to be with them, but I have to suck it up. All the sisters like spending time together without us, and I can't always be around Lil.

Connor sidles next to me. "How's the six-week *no sex* going?"

My expectations: me being hornier than Lily.

My reality: me being hornier than Lily.

With a little kid and a baby, she's too tired to even think about sex. She won't have sex to combat stress either, so it's made her resilience sky-high. When I'm not with her or the kids—when I'm at work—I think about sex. I miss fucking my wife, but if a sex addict can grow the courage to shut-it-down for six weeks, I can too.

"Great," I tell Connor with a dry smile. Then I add more seriously, "It's not as terrible as last time."

"Because we all had to suffer," Sam chimes in.

"What does that mean?" Garrison's face contorts. "You don't...I mean..." He tugs down his black beanie. "I thought Lily was monogamous."

"What?" Sam's eyes pop out. Garrison is implying that they all had to abstain from sleeping with Lily too.

Connor laughs into a billion-dollar grin. "Clarity is key, my friends."

Sam's distress is the best part of this. I nod to Garrison. "Lily is monogamous, but when Maximoff was born, the sisters made a pact that they wouldn't have sex when she couldn't."

"Fucking...insane." Ryke grunts as he swings the axe hard, the tree crashing down.

"Just be glad it didn't happen this time, bro."

Garrison stomps on his second cigarette. "You all are weird as hell."

I gape at my brother-in-law, the one with the self-righteous Captain America complex. "Look at that, Sammy, you were included in our circle of weirdness."

Sam smiles. "But I'm the normal one."

"Normality is relative," Connor says. "To someone somewhere, you're as strange as the rest of us."

2020

"Being away is difficult, but the hardest part is the physical act of leaving."

- Willow Hale, We Are Calloway

(Season 2 Episode 06 — Probabilities & Whatevers)

‹ 17 ›

Daisy Meadows

I stare at the breathtaking views of New York City from Frederick's office, my fingers on the glass like I could step right off and fly. Weightless—but then maybe I'd fall.

I back away and drift towards the figurines on a bookcase, a porcelain ballerina next to a swan. Frederick watches from his leather chair, adjacent to a matching couch. I spend most of my time wandering around instead of sitting down, but he never seems to mind. I don't think Frederick has many patients besides Connor and me.

Just a theory.

"Did you ever think Connor would be famous?" I wonder, my fingers skimming the bookshelf as I amble past.

"Not in the same sense that he is now," Frederick says truthfully. "I thought he'd be revered among people in his profession, not the entire world." He only ever answers these opinionated-based questions about Connor, never anything about his personal history or topics they discuss in his sessions.

I've grown to understand what I can and can't ask. I also like when the focus shifts off of me for a while.

Anyway, Frederick has to know what happened yesterday. It was all over the news.

I never slept last night. Not one hour. Pressure refuses to leave my chest. I want to sink to the floor but then I want to run through every door and *never* come back.

"What kept you up at night?" he asks me the first hard question.

"I wasn't scared." It had nothing to do with PTSD, which hasn't plagued me in a long while. I drift and drift, examining his nameplate on his desk. "People, the media—they can't hurt me anymore, but she's just a baby. And then she'll be a kid. Then a teenager. Like I was. Sometimes I wonder if I'm meant to watch her go through *every*thing I went through."

"What happened yesterday isn't a prelude to your worst fears for Sullivan."

I face Frederick from across the room. "We didn't want the tabloids to have tons of photos of her. I knew eventually she'd have some, but not like this—and not because of *me*."

I took Sulli to her swim lesson, and I don't know who was hiding and where they were, but they captured *ten* photos. She went from having blurry, crappy images online to being in high-res, picking a wedgie. And in the span of two hours, she became an internet meme. All before she turns two next month.

SULLIVAN MINNIE MEADOWS FIRST HIGH-RES BABY PICTURES! People photoshopped…well, it doesn't matter does it? People can be creative without realizing a real person is on the other side of the picture.

#RaisyBaby is still trending, and so are all the jokes attached.

"It's not your fault," Frederick says, "but you've heard that already. Haven't you?"

I think about my support system. Ryke, he didn't blame me. Not a single time. He was more upset that I was upset. Rose, Lily, Lo, Connor, and even Garrison all came over last night to be there. Willow also dropped in via Skype.

I nod, my eyes glassing. I walk towards a potted fern.

"Your daughter will have the same support system, Daisy. She has people her own age in the same boat all around her."

Moffy. Jane. Beckett. Charlie. Eliot. Luna.

"She's not destined to be you," he continues. "She's going to be Sullivan Minnie Meadows, and she'll experience the world in a different way and in a different time."

I draw closer to the center of the room, facing him again. "Rose told me it's always been easier when the tabloids focused on her and not Jane, but I never really understood the feeling until now." I rock on my feet and set my hands on my head. "I'd give *anything* to have them yell at me."

We Are Calloway helps, every day, with the venom and violence directed towards us, but like all things, there'll always be cynics. Thankfully nothing like the flour-bombers era.

"What would they yell?" Frederick asks.

I see what he's doing. Every weighted word on my chest screams to be released.

"Daisy Calloway is *too stupid to live.*" I stare at him strongly, hearing all the voices I've heard. All the ones I squashed before. All the ones I could stomp out again. "An annoying brat. Attention seeker!" I shout it. "She never acts her age! How could Ryke love someone like that? WHAT AN IDIOT!!" I yell so loud that something heavy explodes inside of me, obliterating. Less cumbersome.

What if she can't fight back like this? What if she's sad and lonely? What if she cries herself to sleep? What if she *can't* sleep?

Frederick must read the questions in my eyes because he rises to his feet, power in his stance. When he becomes this wise yet unrelenting figure—just by posture alone—I can see why Connor chose him as his therapist. Why he's known him for so long.

Frederick tells me, "No one would ever wish your experiences on another person, and we all hope she won't have them, but if she's ever sad, Daisy, she has a mother who has experienced pain beyond some human comprehension and who has continued to persevere. A mother who has the ability to empathize with lows that appear for no reason at all. Lows that some will never understand. *You* understand them."

I take a deep inhale like my ribs have been blocking airflow to my lungs. And just now, I breathe.

"The greatest medicine on Earth isn't a pill. It's *compassion*. The ability to make someone feel less alone. Someone very close has been this for you."

This is where I start crying. "Ryke." I rub my watery eyes. Sometimes the world looks bleak. Like every road is barricaded. Like pounding through walls to reach a happy future takes too much effort. Like it's not in the cards for me. Then I remember it's not impossible.

This is temporary.

This feeling will go away soon. *Just wait.*

The walls will dissolve. *Just wait.*

The sun will rise again.

Just wait.

We can wait in the arms of the people we love. That's what I'll tell Sulli. It's what I'll do when she's upset.

"She'll be okay," I breathe, coming to this simple but freeing realization. *She will be okay.*

Frederick sinks back in his chair, and I drift towards the couch. I end up lying down, hanging my shoulders and head over the back. I wipe off the wet streaks on my face.

"My sister would totally call you magic."

"Lily?" he asks, but he already knows she's the truest believer of us all.

"Do you ever bring up magic with Connor just to annoy him?" Suddenly, the door cracks open, and I stare at the incomer upside-down. "Speak of the genius."

Connor arches a brow. "Why am I not surprised?"

"Because you never are," I answer with the wag of *my* brows. I think he's referring to us discussing him and me being upside-down.

"She's one of the smart ones," Connor says, shutting the door behind him and walking further into Frederick's office, closer to the couch. "But not smarter than me."

Frederick checks his watch. "You're an hour early, Connor."

"I don't have to check my watch to know I'm only fifty-two minutes early. You're not playing your best game, Rick."

"Or maybe I'm just not playing the same game."

Connor eyes our therapist with more agitation than he lets most people see in a week. "Then tell me why I'm here."

Is this what it's like between them? I've never really been with Frederick and Connor at the same time. Frederick assesses Connor as fast as Connor assesses him.

"I'd rather not discuss your motivations in front of another patient, especially one that's a part of your family."

"Hey there, brother-in-law," I say with a weak smile.

Connor pockets his cellphone in his slacks. He says nothing in response to either of us yet. He just waits for me to move my feet off the leather cushion. Ryke would've just picked up my legs. Lo would've said *move your goddamn body.* Connor—he just stares at me like it's expected. Like the couch is his.

The floor is his.

The air, the water, all of life's necessities. *His.*

And for some crazy reason, I don't question it. I just scrunch towards half the couch, sitting up more, and he takes a seat beside me.

"Does that always work?" I ask, knowing he'll understand what I mean.

"Only if you're me." He rests his elbow on the leather armrest, his fingers casually to his temple. "Daisy, would you mind if I joined your session?"

My curiosity piques. "Not at all."

Frederick sighs in slight annoyance, but this seems like the kind of invite you'd never reject.

"You do joint sessions all the time," Connor says. "You shouldn't be disgruntled by this one."

"You purposefully showed up early to crash her session. That calls for a stronger emotion than discontent, but this isn't about my feelings. If she's agreeing to this, then we'll do it, but Daisy, I don't think this is a good idea."

"It's okay. I feel better."

Connor studies the dried tears on my face.

Frederick reluctantly rises off the chair, grabs a second folder from a filing cabinet, and returns to his seat. He flips through the papers, a few falling to his lap. He tries to stuff them back inside.

Connor watches intently, and a smile snakes across his face. "Did I catch you off guard, Rick? Do you need more time to prep?"

Our therapist lets out a tight breath. "Why don't we start with a commonality between the two of you?" He plants his gaze on Connor. "Scott Van Wright."

Boom.

I haven't heard that name in our sessions in a couple years. The whole "Scott Van Wright illegally filmed you blowing your previous boyfriend, lied about destroying the tapes and then continued to watch them" was a segment of my life that I've snipped away and filed under *Super Shitty Shit.*

I'm curious to see how Connor handles this topic, though. Since his privacy was also invaded by Scott. Only difference: his sex tapes were blasted out to the entire world. Mine aren't online because it's child pornography. Scott never uploaded it.

But there's something else that strings us together, I know this.

Connor was the one who discovered the tapes of me. They were in Scott's house, and Connor somehow befriended Scott in a way that only Connor Cobalt could do. He found the tapes. I'm not sure if he watched them. I never asked.

My suspicions point to *no*, since Pennsylvania law prohibits even *watching* child pornography (I was seventeen in the videos), and Connor is sitting here and not in jail. Though, I wouldn't have pressed charges if he did. I'd understand if it was something that had to happen to catch Scott in the act.

"We have many commonalities," Connor counters with barely a blink. "Why choose this one?"

Frederick leans back in a comfortable position, no longer stressed that we're here together. "You both have been violated by Scott—"

Connor doesn't wait for him to finish. He grimaces strongly and says, "*Violated* is a grossly exaggerated term to describe what Scott did. He *pissed* on my front yard. He's the equivalent of a rodent scurrying from a nearby tree and urinating on my property. That's it, Rick."

My eyes slowly grow. I'm watching an unfiltered version of Connor, something only seen in a director's cut edition, and I shouldn't really be privy to it.

My brother-in-law glances at me, as if reminding himself of my existence, but he doesn't sweat it or bat an eye. "That word, I'm sure, belongs to Daisy. Let's talk about that."

I smile. "But I'd rather talk about rodents urinating on lawns."

Frederick cuts in, "Daisy, what do you think about the word *violated*? Do you think it pertains to you?"

So we're going here? I take a deeper breath. "Yes," I say. "Because what Scott did was awful and unconsented." My skin crawls just picturing Scott and his friends watching me on tapes that I never knew existed.

"*Awful* is too kind," Connor says.

Frederick shifts his papers again. "What words would you use?"

"Heinous, flagrant, egregious, despicable—but even better, he deserves none of *my* time pondering his actions or what he is. I've spent too much on him already."

Frederick pauses. "You won. He's in jail. You don't lose just because you *feel* from the events, even after they've ended."

Connor looks to me. "This is Rick's way of telling me to *cope* with sentiments I can't understand. He forgets that I'm not like everyone else." He turns back to Frederick. "I'm not wounded. I'm *irritated* by the constant need to discuss what's dead. It helps most people, like Daisy, but I'm not most people."

I can't tell who's right. Maybe they both are. Maybe Connor struggles to reach the bottom of his emotions, ones he truly thinks don't exist within him. Maybe it's Frederick's job to pull them out.

"You're human," Frederick tells him. "It's human to be affected by trauma long after the trauma ends."

Connor rubs his lips, his agitation more than apparent. "I willingly did what I did. I skewered a rat on my lawn and made him eat himself. I feel *justified*. We should really be discussing last night's events." Before Frederick can speak, Connor asks me, "Did you sleep well?"

"The best I ever could." I know he can catch the lie in my smile. I pick at a tear in the leather couch cushion.

"How many hours?" Connor asks again. "Were you frightened?"

I wonder if Rose's concern sent Connor here, wanting more answers about my health. I don't want to worry her or him, so I stray from seriousness, my eyes widening in mock horror. "Fifteen hours of sleep. It was *insanity*. You should've been there, total party in my bed." I smile at that funny innuendo.

"Is she always like this?" Connor asks Frederick like my runaround antics would be exhausting after a while.

Frederick wears a kind-hearted smile. "Sometimes."

I swing my legs from side to side, unable to rest my chin on my knee. "Why are you so interested in what happens beneath my sheets, Connor?"

He just stares blankly at me. "It's like chasing a puppy that runs after its own tail."

I smile again. "I'm the puppy?"

"Obviously." He checks his phone like someone texts him. *Definitely Rose.* "You were crying?" he asks before setting his deep blue gaze on me again.

"I imagined a life without chocolate."

"And unsurprisingly, I don't believe you."

"You don't believe that a world without chocolate is absolutely, entirely *devastating?*"

Connor's brows furrow like I'm a fool if I think I'm *fooling* him. "I believe that you like sprinting in pointless circles." Another text lights up his phone. My sister's concern suddenly yanks at my heart.

"I didn't sleep at all," I finally answer.

Connor contains his emotion. I can't read him.

So I add, "But tell Rose that I plan on taking a nap when I get home, and that I already feel better."

"I will." He texts Rose in front of me, not shocked that I figured out why he's here.

Frederick taps the armrest. "Let's reroute to Scott Van Wright."

Connor sets down his phone. "I'm beginning to think you have a fondness for rats and swine."

Frederick actually smiles. "Daisy, do you have any questions for Connor about what happened? Anything you want to express?"

I think there is something. "You never told me if you saw any of the footage. You had to confirm the tapes were of me. You couldn't just leave without knowing for certain. So...how?"

Connor's gaze is cemented on Frederick, Frederick's cemented on his. Whatever passes between them in the brief silence, I guess could only be described as *understanding*. An understanding that this topic would be broached sooner or later. That this moment would come to fruition.

"Tell her," Frederick urges with a slow nod.

Connor doesn't balk, not once. He slowly but surely rotates to face me. Calmly, he says, "Five seconds. I tried leaving sooner, but I did see you half-dressed." He pauses. "I didn't see you giving head, if that's what you're asking."

"That's what I always thought, and I really, *really* appreciate it. What you did…"

"Don't." Connor's deep blue eyes never dart away from mine. "Don't appreciate me, Daisy. Because it wasn't for you. I manipulated a man and used your evidence to further a ploy that benefited me and my family."

He can paint the selfish portrait, but that picture is only half-complete.

"Maybe your intentions were never to help me, but you did. And it's not the only thing you did." It's more than just interrupting Julian and me during *Princesses of Philly*. "How many photographs have you bought? The ones that photographers took of me backstage when I modeled?" I'm not sure if there's more than just the one from Paris, but I remember that one like a deep, visceral scar in my body. Photographers captured pictures of me *naked* backstage at a Paris fashion show.

I never knew what happened to them.

They never leaked online. In time, I realized that Connor Cobalt is the *only* one who had the resources to buy them. To stop them.

To help me.

I believe he did it because he loves Rose, and Rose loves me. What power their love truly has.

Connor observes me for a second, his features harder to interpret. Then he turns to our therapist. "You see, I'm not as self-serving as you believe me to be."

"As you believe yourself to be," Frederick corrects.

I drop my feet to the floor and stand up again, hating to sit this long. I start wandering towards the bookshelf.

"Both of you know that Scott's sentence will be ending soon, maybe even earlier if he gets out on good terms. How are you going to handle it?"

Connor calls out, "Daisy." He wants me to go first?

I thumb through hardbacks on a middle shelf. "I wish he could rot away forever, but he did his time. Now he'll be on the sex offender's registry." I look over my shoulder at them. "I think that has to be enough." It has to. Because I can't be worried Scott will appear again and hurt us. That fear has no room in my world.

"Her answer is mature," Frederick tells Connor. "I'm guessing yours will be more verbose."

Connor arches a brow. "Guessing? Aren't you supposed to be a professional? I don't pay you to *guess*."

"You tell me," Frederick says, a smile playing at his lips. He picks up his coffee like this is normal. I smile too, realizing it's normal for Connor to insult everyone.

Even his own therapist.

"He might be set free in time because of our judicial system, but he'll be imprisoned emotionally and mentally. I will always see him as what he fucking is. Swine, a rat-snake, someone not worth my time. I'm mostly annoyed by ignorance, by people who think it's acceptable to directly send me messages about events that did not and will not ever happen. People who believe he's virtuous." Connor shakes his head. "I won't scream and open their eyes and make them hear and see. If they can't understand reality, then so be it. They're *gnats* to me."

The air is thick.

Connor sits forward to add one more statement, "He will *never* come within eyesight of my family or Daisy's family or Lily's. I'd stomp him down before he reached within fifty miles of us. It's not an illusion. It's a fact."

I realize that Connor may never ascribe the word "violated" to himself, but I think Scott Van Wright definitely violated him at one point in time. His hostility, that I never see, makes me believe that Scott crossed a boundary with Connor that others never do.

I touch the ballerina figurine again. "I'm glad it's over." He's gone. We're all safe, and as we deal with the leftover emotions, we can move forward and forge stronger paths. I walk much lighter towards the couch again.

This might be one of the best sessions I've had.

"It shouldn't surprise you that it's over," Connor says, his grin growing. "I always win in the end."

I laugh into a bright smile.

It might be conceited but it's very, *very* true.

Sweet Disposition by the Temper Trap starts playing, the ringtone set for Ryke. He's usually really careful about not interrupting my sessions. One time, he spent a whole hour searching for our motorcycle helmets, which I stuffed in a suitcase. My idea of cleaning is to just wedge things in other things until more space appears.

Ryke could've texted or called me, but he actually waited until I arrived home. He considers very few events more important than my therapy sessions, so my stomach tangles as I dig in my jean shorts for my phone. In seconds, I place it to my ear. "Is everything okay?"

Connor and Frederick are eerily quiet, not even pretending not to listen into my call. I face the bookshelf and wait for the tormenting pause to pass.

I can sense Ryke hesitating on the line, his breath cut short. Then he says, "Yeah, it's fucking fine. Call me when you get home."

"You're not home?" I frown and then make a fast choice. On a chair by the door, I grab my backpack and my helmet. For Christmas, Ryke gifted me a lime-green Kawasaki Ninja supersport motorcycle, which can reach nearly a hundred-and-ninety miles an hour. It's even faster than my old Ducati, the bike that I gave to the EMT who basically saved my life.

That was almost two years ago now.

Ryke growls at himself like he really, *really* didn't want to interrupt me—hating that he did.

"Ryke, it's okay. I was done." I sling my backpack straps on, and in my peripheral, I see Connor stand up. I shift my phone to my other ear. "Is it Sulli?" Fear spikes my voice.

"It's not fucking serious, but...*fuck*." Just by the tone of his voice, I can tell that he's upset. *It's Sulli.* It has to be about our daughter, who'll turn two next month.

"Just tell me where I need to go." I have my hand on the doorknob.

Another long pause before he says, "The ER."

Color drains from my face. "As in *emergency room?*" My hand slips, and my helmet clatters to the floor.

"What the fuck was that?" he asks as I pick it up.

"My helmet." I have no time to ask what happened—he speaks again, as though remembering I rode my bike to New York City.

"Don't fucking ride upset. Last thing I fucking want is my wife and my daughter in the hospital." He suggests calling my father's private driver as an alternative, but he doesn't realize that Connor Cobalt is ten feet behind me.

I rotate my helmet in my hands, restless, my lungs in my throat. I'd rather ride my bike, not just to reach the hospital faster but because my body screams to *move*. To lunge. To speed ahead.

"Daisy?"

I listen to my husband's wish, and before I even ask Connor, he says, "I already called my driver. He's waiting."

"Thank you." I focus on my phone call and tell Ryke that Connor is here to see Frederick. "He'll bring me to the hospital," I finish.

Ryke lets out an audible breath like *thank fucking God*. In the background, I suddenly hear Sulli crying. No more lingering, I *run* out the door.

WITH MY BACKPACK ON and helmet in hand, I say goodbye to Connor and rush into the waiting room of the ER.

"Is that Daisy Calloway?" I overhear a flurry of whispers, the waiting room crammed and loud with crying babies, sniffing patients, and a television playing GBA News.

I bypass most of the people to reach a chair, tucked in the corner between a magazine stand and potted plant. Ryke tries to calm Sullivan by combing his fingers through her dark brown hair, her cheeks tear-streaked and splotchy. Sitting on her dad's lap, she hugs her white stuffed starfish, her chin quaking either from pain or the new hospital surroundings.

Ryke sees me halfway across the room, relief loosening his shoulders, and he whispers to Sullivan, "Who's that?"

She follows his finger to find me, and she tearfully shouts, "Mommy!"

Before she tries to spring off his lap, I'm here. I kneel, my hand on Ryke's knee in comfort, and I gasp at Sulli. "I hear you've been on a *big* adventure." I try to hide away all my worry and fear. A piece of toilet paper is stuffed up her nostril and soaked with blood.

"It...it hurts..." Sulli tries to sniff, and she starts *wailing* at the discomfort in her nose. Ryke told me what happened over the phone. *It's not life-threatening,* I remind myself throughout her piercing cries. It still sucks watching my daughter in pain. It still sucks being stuck in the crowded emergency room, unable to know *when* a doctor will see us.

It still sucks catching people snapping our pictures during a moment I'd rather not document.

I playfully use the corner of her starfish to dry Sulli's chubby cheeks. "Hug Starfish with *all* your might, and she'll make you feel better."

Sulli squeezes the stuffed creature like it's her life force, her wails dying and muffled in the soft animal. Ryke picks out a seashell clip that has fallen down a strand of hair, his hard eyes meeting mine. I never take my hand off his kneecap.

"You should fucking sit." He's about to stand up and give me the seat. Such a Ryke Meadows thing to do, but I shake my head, so he stops. Sulli is comfortable on his lap, nestled in the crook of his arm and his chest.

"I'm good here." I set my helmet aside and take off my backpack, staying knelt.

While Sulli calms, Ryke reaches out and massages the top of my head in a *hello*. I smile at him, but his lips never upturn. Guilt hardens his jaw and darkens his features, and not long after, he rakes both of his hands through his thick hair.

"It could've been worse," I say quietly. Ryke and I don't always sit still, and the times where we do go hiking, camping, snowboarding, surfing, and even off-roading, we bring our baby with us. Two years with Sulli, and we try to tone down the *risk* in our choices, but it's difficult to cut out *everything*. Admittedly, we both struggle with what's *too dangerous* because we love bringing her along on our experiences.

We like having a third companion, and it seems more selfish to leave her home and bar her from sharing these moments with us.

So I add softly to Ryke, "I think most people expected Sulli to break an arm rock climbing." The mini rock wall in her room is so much safer than it looks.

The truth of the matter: a random *bead* from a broken keychain caused Sulli more harm than any of our daring adventures. She stuffed the thing up her nose when Ryke wasn't looking. He said he tried plucking it out with a tweezers, but it's lodged in there.

Ryke takes a deep breath, pinching his eyes. "A fucking bead."

"A fucking bead indeed," I say so lightly that his lips tic up, and he drops his hand. He soaks in my green eyes, my mouth, my blonde hair and long, long legs. My white tank top says: *Feed Me* with a giant flower graphic.

"How do you fucking feel?" he questions, even though he already asked this morning. I answered earlier, *I'm seeing Frederick today.*

Now I say, "Better."

Ryke holds Sulli even closer to his chest, our daughter relaxing into her starfish. With his free hand, he ruffles my hair and pushes my cheek. My face brightens tenfold, and I clasp his wrist before he drifts away.

"I need practice," I say, layering on as *much* seriousness as I can.

He lets me have his hand. "For what?"

I lower my voice. "*Kissing.*"

His brows rise at me. "Someone tell you you're a bad fucking kisser, Calloway?"

"I just know that I'm definitely not up to par with my husband. He's *so* good with his tongue." Ryke's dark expression never alters, and my smile only grows. "I can kiss you to see if you're as good as him, but I need to practice first."

"Ask your husband if you need fucking practice."

"Do I need practice?" I ask Ryke.

"*No.*"

I mock gasp. "Yes?" I pretend to hear him wrong and then make out sloppily with his palm.

When I lick his skin, he starts laughing and then reclaims his hand, just to push my forehead, but then he clasps my shoulder, so I don't sway far from him.

I laugh at the sight of his laughter, and then Sullivan, our two-year-old sad baby, starts giggling up at us, sharing in our merriment. Bloody nose and all.

Ryke and I exchange an identical expression that just screams *I fucking love you.*

Five whole hours pass by.

Ryke is no longer seated, his leg too cramped in one position. I'm not seated, too restless. We're standing around the same area, still waiting for a doctor to call us, and Sullivan sits on her dad's shoulders, hands on his head.

We distract Sulli from her constant nosebleed by interviewing the "mermaid under the sea" for Shell Time TV, a game I concocted on the fly a few months ago. It's helped Sulli grow comfortable at the mere sight of cameramen, especially the crew for *We Are Calloway*. She thinks they work for Shell Time.

And until very, *very* recently, she's been mostly hidden from paparazzi. I remember everything Frederick told me today. *The wedgie photos aren't a prelude to a horrible future.*

She'll be okay.

I call up to Sulli, "What's your favorite thing to do?" I needed something to do with my hands, so I'm currently crafting an intricate tree out of green scrapbook paper. I always bring the paper to my therapy sessions, so luckily I had some with me.

"Wuhaa…" She takes a few breaths as she discovers the right word. "Whaa..water!"

"Water," I say with surprise. "You like to swim?"

She nods vigorously, tugging at her dad's thick hair.

Ryke watches me most of all, his hands on our daughter's ankles. I sway back and forth while he's as still as a mountain. He asks her, "Sing us a song, Sul?"

"Hubba bubba boooo…" she sings so horribly, but it's somehow cuter. "Doody doooo…starfishy and meeeee…"

My smile fades when I notice Ryke staring threateningly at someone to the right. I follow his gaze. Between an old lady in a wheelchair and a teenager doubled-over in pain sits a familiar pot-bellied man in jeans and a plain tee. He raises his phone at us, recording. At his feet lies a camera bag with probably a Canon inside.

Paparazzi.

We can't really shield Sulli in the hospital. I've succumbed to the fact that there *will* be photographs of our daughter out in the world.

She's not alone. Moffy and Jane share these same experiences with Sulli. My unease starts to wane, remembering she'll have others to confide in.

Sulli quiets while Ryke and I acknowledge the cameraman's existence, and before she hones in on her nose, I say, "Keep singing, peanut butter cupcake."

She mumbles out lyrics that she creates on the spot.

I edge closer to Ryke, and his hand slides to my waist. I whisper, "When I told Connor what happened to Sulli, he actually proposed something on the ride here. I totally forgot about it, but…I think we should all consider it."

"What the fuck is it?"

I crease my green paper, appearing more tree-like. "A concierge physician."

Realization hits his eyes. If we had a trusted doctor who made house calls, we wouldn't need to wait in the emergency room for hours on end. We wouldn't fear people and cameramen invading our privacy.

Ryke nods. "It's a good fucking idea."

I smile. "I said that to Connor, but without the *fuck* and he told me, *I know. I only give out good ideas. The bad ones come from all of you.*"

Ryke rolls his eyes. "Typical fucking Cobalt."

"Poopy poo," Sulli singsongs up above. "Fucky fuck…"

I can't help but laugh, and Ryke sighs like he's *tried* really hard to sway her away from *fucks* but it's an impossible task. I actually love that it was her first word—because she's so a part of Ryke. When he told me that I missed that first-word milestone, I wasn't upset. I was happy to hear that she started speaking, and hey, I was able to hear her *second* word.

Coconut.

Ryke suddenly lifts Sulli off his shoulders and mimes tossing her in the air. Normally, he actually would, but she still has that bead up her nose.

Sullivan stretches out her arms and legs to take flight.

"Meadows!" a nurse calls.

"That's me!" Sulli shouts.

I gasp. "You don't say."

Ryke tucks her protectively against his side, and he combs her flyaway hair out of her eyes. Sulli tries to rub noses with me, forgetting that hers hurts. I kiss her soft cheek and then gather all of our things: backpack, helmet, and a couple water bottles. Three minutes later, we've been ushered into a hospital room, and now we wait for the doctor.

Ryke sets Sulli on the crinkled paper, and she stretches her arms for one of us, frightened of this new room. I hop up beside her, and she crawls onto my lap. I hug her against my chest, and Ryke stands stiffly close by us.

Sulli plays with the tree I crafted, and I yawn into my arm. "What's the time?" I ask Ryke.

"Almost eight p.m." He studies my state of being, concern bunching his brows.

"So after this, Poppy said she could bring me back to New York."

He shakes his head once like *I don't fucking follow.*

"I need to pick up my bike," I explain. "I can't just leave it in a parking garage overnight." It's *expensive*, and Ryke knows this since he bought it.

"Fuck that. You haven't slept in *forty* hours, Dais. You should be passed out by now…" His voice dies down as Sullivan looks up at him.

I don't fact-check him about the forty-hours thing. It could be ten hours less than that, and he'd still repeat that declaration. Ryke wanted me to go home and take a nap, but I wanted to be here when Sulli saw the doctor. She missed one of her naps too, so she'll crash sooner or later.

"Let me get your fucking bike."

I cover Sulli's ears for this next part. "I know you want me to sleep, but I'm…" My tired eyes well. *I'm afraid.*

"Dais…" Ryke holds my cheek, the one with the long, old scar.

"What if I sleepwalk and you're not there?" Sleep deprivation has triggered sleepwalking for me in the past, and the more hours I collect wide-awake, the more likely a strange symptom will follow. I'd rather go to sleep with Ryke next to me, just in case something happens.

Ryke's large hand cocoons my face, warming my skin. "Then I'll go where you go."

An exhausted tear rolls down my cheek and his hand. I've been blocking most out with false energy, grasping to lingering adrenaline.

"Price," Ryke suddenly tells me. "He has a motorcycle license. He's ridden *your* fucking bike before. He'll get it from the parking garage." My bodyguard, the one my dad hired. This isn't the first time I'm thankful for him.

The doctor raps lightly on the door and then slips inside. "This little one have something in her nose?" he says kindly.

Sullivan nods. "A fucking bead."

I laugh, and Ryke is nearly smiling. The doctor looks more amused than horrified. He holds out his hand to us. "I'm Dr. Clarke."

We shake, and he explains the procedure: *look up her nose, see what's there, try to use a bulb to suction it out. If that doesn't work, sedation and a forceps to pluck it out.*

Ryke is even more rigid at the word *sedation.* "Is that necessary?"

"Yes but it shouldn't come to that." As Dr. Clarke tells Sulli about the procedure, he uses a gentle baby-voice and lets her stay on my lap. He removes the bloodied tissue and peers up her nostril with a medical instrument.

I tell her how amazing she is, and not even ten minutes later, Dr. Clarke suctions out the bead with a rubber bulb. Sulli is crying all over again.

"It's out! Ta-da!" I tell Sulli jubilantly. "All done."

She rubs her eyes, uncertain.

"Sweetie." Ryke waves a lemon sucker at our daughter, and her green eyes grow to orbs. She clutches the sucker and mumbles a *thank you, Daddy.*

"What's this?" Dr. Clarke checks out Sulli's yellow-stained fingers. I asked the same thing to Ryke, but he wouldn't tell me. When I asked Sulli, she said, "It's a secret!"

I think it's marker.

Dr. Clarke believes the same. "Marker?"

Ryke nods once and leaves it at that.

On our way out, Ryke carries Sulli, and I undergo a yawning fit. All the way to his car. By the time we finish buckling Sulli in her car seat, and I've settled in the passenger seat, shutting the door to the Land Cruiser, I'm on my millionth yawn.

Ryke turns the ignition, his dark concern all over me, even as he drives onto the highway.

"I have this theory," I yawn again, "that yawning is really your body's way of exercising your jaw. It's basically shouting, *exercise time…*" I yawn. "…*Daisy*." My jaw hurts.

Ryke is quiet, and I glance over my shoulder, Sulli totally conked out, drooling on her car seat.

I yawn. *Stoooop yawning*. I rub my aching jaw. "Maybe my body is preparing me for a blow job."

He glowers. "That's not fucking funny."

"It is because I wouldn't give you one." I bring my feet onto the leather seat, and he relaxes at my words, knowing I won't try to convince him just for the hell of it.

For one, I've never been able to take all of Ryke in my mouth. He's just way too big. For another, I've never liked giving blow jobs, and Ryke is anti-anything-Daisy-Meadows-hates.

Ryke glances between the road and me. "Lean back and fucking sleep. You don't have to stay awake right now."

"I'd rather wait until we're at home." My feet drop to the floor.

His hard eyes glued to the street, he reaches for one of my legs, stretching it over his lap. I turn, my back against the door, and I stretch the other one across Ryke.

It's not a suggestion. It may appear flirty, my foot may graze his crotch, but the new position allows me more room and greater extension of my body in the car. I like it. He knows I like it.

I've fought sleep and sleep has fought me so many times that I easily remain awake throughout the car ride. After parking, Ryke unbuckles Sulli and carries our sleeping daughter in his arms. My heart has an extra beat watching them together, and I unlock the front door, flipping on the lights to our cottage.

Coconut greets us by the door, tail wagging excitedly. She first looks up at Sulli, as though ensuring she's okay. I whisper that she is, and Coconut nudges my cheek with her nose.

"I missed you too, Coconut." I scratch her neck and kiss her. Then I pat her belly and run with her towards the backdoor. I let her out to pee, the stairs creaking as Ryke brings Sulli to bed. And then I see something.

In the kitchen close by. I leave the backdoor open, drifting towards the counter beside the oven. *Ryke.* I instantly start crying, my fingers to my lips.

He baked a chocolate cake. *Yellow* icing spells out:

we fucking love you.

I remember what Frederick said about people having *compassion* for other people. Ryke knew I was upset, and he meant to comfort me. I picture Sulli on the counter, helping with yellow icing, staining her fingers. I bet she found the beaded keychain in a kitchen bowl—where we store knickknacks and other junk.

Dazedly, I wipe at my wet cheeks. Coconut bounds back inside, and I shut the door, put a slice of cake in a bowl, and trek upstairs. My white husky follows at my heels. I check on Sulli, fast asleep (no Ryke), and then I slip into my bedroom.

Ryke situates cable-knit blankets onto a hammock, strung in our wide window nook. Our rustic bedframe is made out of wooden logs, bark and all, but when I have trouble sleeping, which is rare these days, I usually migrate to the hammock.

The moonlight illuminates the nook, almost like it could exist outside under the stars. I wander closer, eating cake. Coconut hops onto the bed, lying down at the foot, paws beneath her chin. She's alert and watchful.

I know what I want to tell Ryke, but I can't break the sweet quiet. The serenity he's created tonight warms me like a sun that sweeps the dock of a lake. I sidle next to my husband, my hands occupied by spoon and bowl. *Cake comes first.*

He watches me eat a *giant* spoonful, and a smile peeks at his lips. His fingers descend to my shorts. He unbuttons and unzips me. I step out of them. Watching him. *I love watching Ryke Meadows.* His hands disappear beneath my tank top.

He unclips my bra. It's a rusty skill since I don't wear them often, but he succeeds. I pass him the bowl, needing to pull my tank top and my bra off my arms. Now just in cotton panties, he returns my bowl to me, and he unbuttons his jeans and takes off his shirt.

In seconds, he's left in dark green boxer-briefs.

Ryke Meadows is thirty.

I'm twenty-three, and I fawn over his broody demeanor, his caring personality, and his compassion before I do his supremely defined muscles and rock climber body.

My wolf.

I climb onto the hammock, stretching out, and he climbs right beside me. I drape my arm and leg across his chest, pressed against him, the blankets enveloping me. I rest my head on his shoulder, able to finish my cake in a couple more bites. I offer only a spoonful to Ryke since he's not crazy about super sweet foods, but he'll eat pretty much anything.

The hammock brings security, but no more so than my husband. Tucked together, protected. Bowl set aside, he pulls the blankets up to my shoulders. Exhaustion tries to tug my eyelids closed.

I look up at him.

He looks down at me.

And I whisper, "I fucking love you too."

His heart pounds against my heart. He kisses me with that *skilled* tongue, and slowly, safely, I begin to drift to sleep with love all around me.

[18]

Rose Cobalt

I'd like to return to when I was just ten, and there was this loathsome neighbor boy who tagged along on all family trips. We were left in the care of our nannies one week in England while our fathers dealt with business and my mother vacationed with her friends.

It stormed all seven days. We stayed indoors and played hide-and-go-seek in this old manor. The neighbor boy drew closer to my closest sister. His laughter became hers. Her smile became his.

I wanted to preserve our sisterhood, but he wedged himself in our lives.

He could never be a Calloway sister.

He was just the loathsome neighbor boy. He'd be gone in a year or two years or three.

Couldn't he see?

I held more animosity towards him than I realized. I even tried to forget the day I hid inside a wardrobe between musty overcoats and old laced shawls. I waited quietly for someone else to be found. It wasn't long until I heard slow footsteps.

Then the wardrobe door creaked and swung open. I scrunched my legs to my chest, but the seeker pushed clothes aside.

The neighbor boy found me.

I stared right at Loren Hale.

And I waited for him to claim victory and laugh at my loss. As our eyes latched, as he saw my hate, he wore remorse like he understood how much my sisters meant to me and how much he'd take away. Lily would become his best friend over me. In time.

His gaze dropped.

He shut the wardrobe door and let me stay hidden. He kept searching.

I'd like to return to when I was just ten and tell myself that this loathsome neighbor boy would always be a part of our lives.

Loren Hale would always be one of us.

Maybe not a Calloway sister, but the closest thing to one.

"Take a seat, Mr. Hale, Mrs. Cobalt."

"No," we say in unison to one of the fourteen Hale Co. board members. Loren and I stand side-by-side at the head of the conference table, a red megaphone in his hand. We've practiced how this unnecessary meeting will pan out, and neither of us will shelve our battle armor and weapons for this fight.

It means too much to me, and I've learned in the past three years that it's meant equally to Loren.

Loren stares down the fourteen shareholders. "I'd never manage the board. It's not part of my job description, I get that, but you can't manage *management*."

Of course I understand what we're dealing with here. I don't have to be the CEO of Hale Co. to understand the corporate hierarchy.

The CEO oversees management: the Chief Marketing Officer, Chief Operations Officer, Chief Financial Officer, Chief Communications Officer, etc.

The board of directors is an entirely separate entity, full of shareholders who *should* be in favor of the company's best interests, not their own. Seeing as how Jonathan Hale opened the door and invited in these *rotten* shareholders, Hale Co. is in need of house cleaning, but you can't just dismiss a director.

You have to put up with them.

Loren has done his best, and I can see in his angered amber eyes that he's about to do even better.

Daniel Perth rises at the other end of the table, unfurling file folder after file folder as evidence to our three-year revamp of this company.

I'm proud of *every* single folder.

After he dredges up more, the towering stack hiding the man beside him, Daniel says, "*These* are all the women you've hired to this company."

I smile triumphantly.

Loren says, "I'm the CEO, and this is part of management. I have the authority to hire and fire anyone I *goddamn* want."

The board lets out disgruntled noises. The four women who serve on the board stay quiet.

I snap, "What's the issue? They were all qualified—"

"Caitlin Brown," Daniel cuts me off, shaking a folder like it's his sole piece of evidence. "She has *no* experience to work in the marketing division, yet Theo Balentine hired her and seven more."

Loren promoted Theo to Chief Marketing Officer just last year. He went from Mark's assistant to taking Mark's job, and he agreed to help us in our mission.

"Todd Wentworth," I rebut. "He has *no* experience for an entry-level position in sales, and yet *he* was hired five years ago." I list off ten more names until the men around the table grow red-faced with agitation. "Hale Co. has been hiring white males based on potential, not experience, and just as Loren starts diversifying this company with more women and women of color, you start throwing tantrums."

Someone on the board—I should name his name but my rage has stabbed holes into it—pipes up with, "We're trying to stop the company from turning into a sorority."

I see red, gritting my teeth with widened *hostile* eyes. I turn my face away from the board and growl to Loren, "I'm going to bludgeon him slowly and set his ugly hair on fire." *Violence is not the answer, Rose.* My hyperboles still feel good. I know I can't give these men a reason to generalize women as *unpredictable* and *unruly* and whatever else they want to attach to me, to then attach to them.

Loren doesn't have time to respond to my fury.

Daniel Perth adds, "We're trying to direct you to a more profitable avenue. We don't like huge risks."

Loren turns on his megaphone and uses it wisely. "Bullshit." His loud voice booms through the conference room. "Can you hear me now?"

I raise my chin while his glare slaughters their intolerance.

"Let me explain then." Daniel is still on the offensive, but so are we. "You've used company money to add in a *daycare* for the children of… *twenty* female employees. Not to mention, you hired dozens of women who could potentially need maternity leave."

At this, the *entire* board, including the four women, stare right at my baby bump, incredibly visible in my high-collared black dress.

My due date is next month.

"If they were men, they'd need paternity leave," I rebut.

Daniel shakes his head. "Not as long."

It can't be about money. Why do I know this? Before Loren Hale became CEO, women were being paid *significantly* less than men who were in the same positions. Theoretically, they would've hired *more* women in the past to keep costs down.

But they didn't.

Loren says out of the megaphone, "Everyone we hired is driven and motivated to do a damn good job, regardless of gender or race—"

"This isn't the time for change—"

"Cut me off again, Millard, and we're going to have a bigger problem than this goddamn meeting," Loren says with the *utmost* confidence. He can hold his own in front of these men.

I talked with Connor about this meeting on the phone, about an hour before it started. I was in the bathroom, and he told me, "I believe Lo can do even more than we all think."

The Loren Hale today is a stark difference than the one years ago. It's his self-confidence that will annihilate their contempt. I can't restrain my smile.

I whisper to Loren, "Slay them."

Loren speaks into his megaphone. "Anyone else?" Everyone is quiet for a second, and then he spins to me. "Rose?"

My turn.

I take one step forward and brush my hair off my shoulder. "The company's job is to reach out to the market. Our market is mostly female. More *women* buy Hale Co.'s baby products than men. I was tired of seeing men being hired as interns, and I brought this fact up to the CEO three years ago. He made sure that in ten years' time, this company will look less like a WASP all-boys boarding school and more like the world it serves. If you're upset with this, then…" I think about what Connor would say. "…then maybe you should *reflect* on your own choices and try to understand this one."

That was fairly calm for me.

I let out a breath, knowing it's not over here.

I have enough privilege to reach executive levels in companies, regardless of my knowledge and aptitude. I can use my power at Hale Co. to change the demographic of their employees, but I can't use it to close the gap of inequality in other jobs around the world. Not in *this* way.

It's a start somewhere.

Every day, I know how fortunate I am. To be able to work at home and split time with a husband who can do the same. I wanted to hire women who didn't have the same luxuries I do. Who needed the benefits of daycare in order to work in a billion-dollar company. They shouldn't miss out on these opportunities for that reason.

Daniel sits in his leather chair and cups his hands together. He's in his early forties, an aquiline nose and no-nonsense eyes like most of the board. I've heard Lily call his brown hair "fluffy" which to me just means that he combed out his natural curls.

"I've always been blunt with you," Daniel tells Loren. "We didn't call this meeting for shits and giggles."

"And you think I did?" Loren says so spitefully. A chill snakes down my neck. "You want to cut out all the bullshit, Daniel, here's the goddamn truth. You think I didn't hire *the best* for the job, but I did. Yes, you have a right to question management. But you don't have a right to tell me who to hire. So really, me even letting you have this meeting was *kind* on my part."

Slay them.

Lo sets his megaphone on the table. "I'm the CEO of Hale Co. and I'm not asking you to start treating me like it. I'm *telling* you to. There's been miscommunication between the board and management since I've been here. It'd serve the company's best interest for every director to instate me as chairman of the board."

My jaw nearly unhinges.

Loren Hale just went rogue.

The fourteen shareholders look caught off guard as they mutter between one another. So Lo takes a moment to whisper to me, "What, Queen Rose? You didn't think I had it in me?"

I narrow my eyes at him. *Why didn't you tell me?* I don't have time to ask though because the shareholders quiet down.

To any of the doubters, Lo adds, "The president of the board is supposed to be the face of the company. I'm already the face of Hale

Co., so whatever differences we've had, you know this makes the most sense. I'll have an easier time working with you. You'll have an easier time working with me."

"Let's take a vote," Daniel says, here and now.

It all happens so fast that my neck stiffens and eyes continue to grow. I'm scared that they'll reject Loren. If he's afraid too, I can't tell.

"All in favor of instating Loren Hale as the chairman of the board instead of Earl Pennington, raise your hand." Earl is an older gentleman who's apparently been there since Jonathan started the company. He pushes up his spectacles, and he's the first to raise his hand.

All thirteen follow suit.

Most everything is a fog until Loren and I exit the boardroom together. Before I congratulate him, I say with frost, "Why didn't you tell me?" We stop by his office door. I'm about to add *we're a team, Loren*, but the sentiment lingers beneath the way he stares at me and the way I stare back at him.

"Because Rose," he says, "I wanted to see the look on your face when they all raised their hands." He wasn't scared then. He believed in himself the whole time.

"And how did I look?" I bristle as I try to recall my features.

"Weepy." He feigns confusion. "I didn't know dragons could cry."

I scoff. "I did not *cry*." I pat my eye, just to see if there are leftover tears…my eyelashes are wet.

Loren touches his chest. "I would cry over me too." He flashes a dry half-smile. "It's something you have in common with your sister."

"I *revoke* your congratulations."

"What congratulations?" He lets out a short laugh, and I realize I never congratulated him aloud. "Christ, Rose, you have to lay off the demon blood. Drinking that shit makes you weird."

It's so easy to hate Loren Hale.

And it can be just as easy to love him.

He smiles an actual smile this time, nothing half-assed or full of scorn.

Loren might not have been a Calloway sister, but he's been more of a brother to me than any other man in my life.

[19]

April 2020
THE COBALT ESTATE
Philadelphia

Connor Cobalt

"You really want to play with fate like this, Rose?"

My wife is seated at the other end of our long mahogany dining table, a spiral-bound notebook in her clutch. On a rare Tuesday, we're both home together by noon. Rose didn't want her water to break in the Hale Co. building where people might tip the media, and she's too close to her due date to take the risk.

"We already play with fate every day. What's once more?"

"I believe that fate likes Mommy best of all."

That's clearly not me.

The dreamy and assured voice comes from our four-year-old daughter, hoisted on a booster seat near the middle of the table. Rose helped Jane dress this morning into a pastel green tutu and a zebra-print shirt.

Our daughter even picked out her favorite cat-ear headband, one coated with gold glitter.

I remember when she couldn't even speak, and now here we are.

"Fate has good taste then," I tell Jane, "but fate would have better taste if it liked *you* most of all."

Jane smiles big and looks across the table. "I want fate to love Charlie and Beckett too." Her two-year-old brothers are in their own booster seats, eating mac-and-cheese with their spoons. Beckett picks out the peas. "And Eliot," Jane notes like she would never forget her other brother.

I hold the eleven-month baby in my arms. Eliot naps against my shoulder, wearing a blue onesie with a tiny crown stitched on front. Gifted by Daisy.

"It's decided," Rose decrees, "fate loves us all. With this, we should begin the ceremony."

I adore her formality. My lips rise as Rose stands from her chair.

"Jane, when you're ready, just set down your spoon, and we'll begin."

Jane scoops up a noodle. "Before we start, I…I think we should tell Charlie and Beckett…" Her noodle drops on her lap. "Oopsie noody come here." She retrieves the noodle from her tutu, and Rose has trouble not smiling.

She completely and hopelessly loves our daughter.

My grin stretches. I completely and hopelessly love them.

Rose catches me staring, and I don't pretend I wasn't. As her eyes narrow, I hear her ice-cold voice. *Richard.*

I reply through my gaze, *Rose.*

"Sadie!" Jane calls out in glee. She almost slips off her booster seat to chase the orange tabby cat that prances beneath the table.

"No, Jane," I tell her before Rose can. "Wait for Sadie to come to you, honey."

Jane nods, remembering, and she sits still on her booster seat, but her eyes widen big and dart every which way the cat goes.

Sadie rubs up against my ankles, purring softly. We brought her home over a year ago, and she's been mostly content. She has temperamental days, but I can't fault her for them. I scoot my chair back so I can lean down and scratch behind her ears.

"What were you saying about Charlie and Beckett?" Rose asks Jane.

"Oh well..." Jane tries to tear her gaze off Sadie beneath the table. "The Name Ceremony is all about names and...and I...I think Charlie and Beckett should know theirs."

She means the meaning behind their names. Jane likes hearing about her namesakes, and she often asks about Charlie and Beckett's, so it's no surprise she'd want to share this information with them.

Rose raises her wine glass, filled with sparkling water, and she clinks her knife to the side.

Beckett giggles, "Mommy!" and he kicks his legs in delight.

Rose nods to him in acknowledgement and then proclaims to the table, "Jane Eleanor is asking for a preamble to today's ceremony. Are we all in favor?"

"I am," I announce.

Rose places her hands on her hips, staring me down. "You just want to delay fate," she concludes.

"If I truly wanted to delay the Name Ceremony, I'd find another way besides adding in a preamble that continues the topic of *names*." I've zeroed in on my wife, the world shrinking to just us in a quick, sudden moment.

Rose cringes. "I see you have a twitch in your eye, Richard."

"You've forgotten what a *wink* is, darling?" I did wink at her, just to see her eyes flame, even for the briefest, most torrid second.

"I don't forget anything. You're just terrible at winking."

"Impossible." I grin, especially as her gaze drifts to my lips like she'd love to simultaneously kill me and kiss me. "I'm skilled in everything. It's more likely you're just not adept at spotting a good wink from a bad one. Don't take it to heart. You can't win them all. Not when I can."

Rose gags at my narcissism. "I suggest a *new* preamble. We silence all those named Richard Connor Cobalt."

"No, Mommy." Jane shakes her head vigorously. "Freedom of speech."

Rose looks too proud of Jane to be upset at losing the battle.

Jane licks the mac-and-cheese sauce off her thumb. "What's a pre-amble?"

Rose answers as she walks over to the dining hutch. "It's an intro-duction."

"Like an opening statement to a statute," I add.

Jane mouths all of our words as though processing each one. Rose procures a cloth napkin and slams the doors closed. I study her for a moment, as she lingers with her hands on the drawer. Then Eliot stretches against my chest. I stroke my thumb in circles across his back, and he falls back to sleep.

"Rose?" I call out, my voice even-tempered. I don't want to frighten or excite Jane over the possibility of Rose going into labor.

Rose pulls her hair into a ponytail and then returns to the table, eyes ablaze. "I'm fine."

I don't believe her fully.

Her nose flares like she's restraining pain. With a tight collar, she slides the cloth napkin to Jane. "This is for you, my little gremlin."

Jane nods with a *merci*, and I adjust Eliot on my side, about to ask Rose what's wrong. She must sense this because she shakes her head at me. Then she picks her phone off the dining table.

In seconds, mine buzzes.

Not a contraction. — Rose

Then another text.

Holster your concern, Richard. We have a ceremony ahead of us. — Rose

With my free hand, I respond: the ceremony can wait if you're in pain.

I watch her glare at my message and type feverishly. I anticipate her text more than I would any other.

"So we'll begin," Rose declares just as she sets her phone down.

Read my lips. — Rose

My eyes flit up.

And she mouths, *patience, Richard.*

Patience? I nearly laugh at the idea of Rose telling *me* to be patient. I'd remind her that she's the impatient one between us, but she clinks her glass again.

"Jane, would you like to tell Beckett his namesake?"

Jane nods enthusiastically and sits straighter. "Beckett Joyce Cobalt," she recites theatrically. "You were named after Samuel Beckett, a play...a play-something or other."

"Playwright," Rose coaches.

"A playwatt," Jane nods.

Beckett is more concentrated on not eating his peas, but Charlie is listening to Jane with an expression that Lily recently dubbed "the who farted" look.

"And this playwatt is famous for something or other named *Waiting for* Gouda."

I put my fingers to my mouth, my grin blinding.

Rose presses her lips together to keep from laughing. She slips into her chair, and we both silently push the responsibility of correcting her at one another until I'm the first to concede.

"Godot," I correct, swallowing my humor. "Gouda is a cheese."

Rose snorts into her own cloth napkin.

"Something amusing, darling?" I tease.

Rose takes a deep breath, collecting herself, and unties her ponytail—just to flip her hair over a shoulder as though to say *fuck you, Richard.*

I nearly harden.

"Continue on, Jane," Rose says, "You're doing a perfect job."

"Beckett," Jane proudly announces, "your middle name is from a writer called James Joyce."

I always pick out their middle names. Rose chooses their first. Most disagreements between us are settled by a bet or a game. With a win or a loss. This, we just knew. I value middle names. I go by mine. Rose values first names. She goes by hers.

"And Charlie." Jane tries to stand on her booster seat.

"Jane," both Rose and I say sternly for her safety, and her bottom thuds to the seat.

"Charlie," Jane begins again like nothing went wrong, "Mommy was antipating"—she means *anticipating.* I'd correct her, but she speaks too quickly—"a girl. You were meant to be *Charlotte* after Charlotte Brontë."

Rose decided to alter the name to *Charlie* once she saw that they were twin boys.

Jane stumbles over her words as she tries to recall the reasoning behind Charlie's middle name. She looks to me for help.

I seize the expression tight. My mother never wanted me to exchange that look with her, not even when I was a child. *If you're a big boy, you'll figure this out on your own.*

I did, of course. I thrived without parents, but this expression, this exchange with my daughter, holds an incredible amount of value to me. I'm necessary in my children's lives. It's not a weakness on their part.

Can you help me?

Always.

I will always help them.

"Charlie Keating Cobalt," I say to my oldest son.

"That's me," Charlie says in a much clearer tone than most two-year-olds.

"And do you know why you were named Keating?"

He shakes his head.

"You're named after the poet John Keats." Since Rose decided to alter Charlotte to Charlie, I followed suit and altered Keats to Keating. To this day, I remember the *rare* smile that spread across her face when I called him Charlie Keating.

It was like she took a step to the side, and I willingly stepped with her.

"Right." Jane nods as though she hadn't forgotten. "And so it shall be." She taps her spoon against her purple plastic cup, mimicking her mother.

Rose rises to her feet. "And now the Name Ceremony shall begin. Jane Eleanor Cobalt, will you accept the honor of naming your brother?" We haven't checked the gender, but Rose is positive we're having another boy.

Without any scientific indication, I can't be as sure.

"I will." Jane reaches for the notebook and nearly topples her cup.

Boy or girl, I've had a middle name in mind, but I won't say what until Rose chooses the first name. She's written twenty names in the notebook, and Jane is supposed to point to her favorite.

Why is this more like chance? Jane can't read.

And so, Rose believes she's letting "fate" guide her to the perfect name. I believe she's letting our daughter *randomly* decide.

Jane spends barely a second with the notebook before pointing to a name. "This one!"

Rose steps hurriedly to Jane, wide-eyed. "Are you sure you don't need a minute longer?"

"This is what happens when you leave important events to fate," I tell my wife.

Rose shoots me a hot glare, but I sense the words beneath, *we're leaving the greatest event of our lives to fate, Richard. Remember?*

Of course I remember. I remember every day that this baby could be our last. I remember every day that I'd love one or two or even three more children. I remember that we made an agreement not to have more after Jane has a sister, and I won't break what I promised.

I remember it all.

"I'm sure," Jane tells her mother. "This is it!"

Rose peers over Jane's head, reading the name, and the corners of her mouth curve upwards. "His name is Tom."

Named after *The Adventures of Tom Sawyer* by Mark Twain.

And I say, "Tom Carraway Cobalt."

Rose tries hard to restrain a pleased smile. Nick Carraway is a character from *The Great Gatsby* by F. Scott Fitzgerald.

"You love it," I say the obvious.

"It's okay." She twists her hair on one shoulder, completely downplaying how much she loves the name. I love that compliments don't come easily.

I'm about to reply, but Rose and I both watch Jane slip beneath the table. I duck with Rose to see where our daughter is going. Sadie is curled in a ball, napping, and Jane strokes her soft fur and whispers, "You're the prettiest kitty, Sadie. The prettiest I've ever seen."

Sadie stretches her paws and rolls to let Jane pet her belly.

"Told you so," Rose says to me. I could comment on her kindergarten retort, but I let it pass this time.

"I never said she wouldn't warm up to Jane."

"You said Sadie wasn't capable of loving anyone else but you."

I truly thought she wasn't. "Pets change," I realize.

Just like people.

8:08 P.M.

Jane screams bloody murder from upstairs. I'm already off the couch, alarm rushing through me like fissured ice. Eliot, who'd been attempting to walk for the first time, tries to follow. He falls to his bottom and wails like the world is coming to a sudden end.

"Go!" Rose calls after me. She lifts her body off the couch as fast as she's able. "I'll meet you."

I leave Eliot with Rose, and quickly, I run through the archway and into the foyer.

"DADDY! MOMMY!" Jane screams and screams.

"JANE!" I sprint up the marble staircase. I can't draw irrational conclusions. I can't anticipate what's wrong before I see the facts. Even so, my blood is cold and my breath is locked in my throat.

"DADDY! DADDY!"

"JANE!" I reach the second floor in seconds, running down the long hallway. Her screams tunnel out of her bedroom. Jane decorated her door with construction paper and pink glitter to spell out her name *Jane Eleanor* across the front.

As soon as I slip inside the darkened room, lit only by a tiny nightlight, Jane—tear-streaked and grief-stricken—darts past her toddler bed and tea party table and then clings to my leg.

"Daddy," she sobs.

I set my hand on her head, canvassing her body and her room hurriedly. "Are you hurt—what's wrong?" I squat to her height.

She flings her arms around my shoulders, blubbering into my chest. I tenderly clutch the back of her head. In one breath, I crave to comfort my daughter. In the other, I remain vigilant and alert about the origins of her fear.

An illogical thought creeps into my head. *Paparazzi broke into her room.* It happened to Daisy, but that was before we moved into a gated neighborhood. That was before I fucked over Scott Van Wright.

Nothing like that can happen to my children. Not in this house.

Not with me here.

Jane sobs harder, her voice turning hoarse.

"Shhh," I whisper in a soothing tone. "Mon cœur." *My heart.*

I examine Jane, just to be certain she's not physically hurt. Her teal cat-print nightgown isn't torn. She didn't limp and she hasn't favored any of her limbs. I lift her brown hair off her shoulder and gently press her neck and along her spine. She doesn't flinch.

She's simply inconsolable.

Emotional. This is emotional pain.

Jane mumbles a few words that I can't piece apart. My need for information heightens, and I lift her, using a hand to keep her propped against my side. She hugs me even stronger.

I step further into her bedroom.

Jane goes hysterical. "Nonono!" she screams.

"Shhhh." I stroke the side of her hair and then whisper softly, "What's wrong, Jane?" I can't see anything out of place. Her pastel pink sheets and blankets are twisted and kicked to the edge of her bed, but Jane wiggles in her sleep—so this isn't abnormal.

Jane raises her head and rubs her little fist against her cheeks.

I brush her tears away with my thumb. "Are you frightened?"

"Yes."

"About what?"

She points to the double doors of her closet, partially opened. Enough for a body to squeeze through.

"Connor…? What is it…?" Rose pants and blows out a measured breath, just arriving. She rests her hand on her round abdomen and sets down Eliot who squirms against her side. Beckett and Charlie linger inquisitively by her legs.

I have four children, five including the impending one, and a wife as strong-willed and courageous as any person comes. I'd do anything to sustain this life with them. To keep them feeling safe and protected.

Love is power, and I can't tell you why. It transcends every word I can conjure. In these catalytic moments, love surges through me like battalions made of fire and water. Made of ivory and rose.

I awaken and I know.

I come second.

I will always put them first.

Quickly, I go to Rose beside the door. "Something's in the closet." Before I even suggest it, Rose is already speaking,

"Boys, stay in the hallway." She ushers Beckett and Charlie back, and then her eyes flame against mine. "Is it a squirrel?"

"It might be."

Rose rubs Jane's back and whispers something in her ear.

Jane nods and sniffs loudly.

I pry my daughter off my chest and set her beside her brothers, my heart remaining with them and with her…I watch Rose clasp the doorknob.

She inhales, hesitant for a second. "It's most likely a rat or a roach…"

"That's a possibility too." I can't be sure what it is until I at least *hear* it.

"Do you need a baseball bat?" she asks, her voice higher-pitched in concern for my safety. "Pepper spray, a knife—"

I kiss her on the lips and murmur against them, "Je t'aime." *I love you.*

Rose is frozen for a moment, but then she reciprocates. Warmth floods me, and when we tear apart, she says, "If you need backup, I'll be in there in less than a second."

I know she would. "I'll keep this in mind, darling." I clutch the other knob, on the other side of the door. The last thing Rose sees is my mounting grin.

The last thing I see is her sweltering glare.

And we shut one another out. The door *clicks* closed, and I focus my attention on Jane's closet. *What's wrong, Jane?*

The irrational side still believes a person has broken into her room.

The rational side is telling that side to stay fucking quiet.

I'm confident about my approach to the closet. I'm empty-handed, but the situation calls for less than my fists. I flick on the closet lights and then clasp both door handles. Swiftly, I pull them apart. Jane's dresses and shirts and skirts are hung neatly throughout the walk-in.

I see it.

Instantly, I see.

I bottle my sentiments. Regardless, I'm not entirely sure what I feel at the moment. I just stoically approach the large woolen pillow that Jane keeps tucked by the floor-length mirror, towards the back.

Then I set a knee on the floor and find myself sitting next to this white pillow, a ball of orange fur in the center. I rub my lips, my tabby cat curled up and lifeless beside me. I've met death one other time in my life, and the emotions I grapple with still warp me, confuse me—bear against me.

Once upon a time, as the way most tales are told, I found this abandoned kitten. Sadie has been with me through years and years' worth of time, but here, right here, the tale ends.

I whisper, "Adieu." *Farewell.*

In the mirror, I catch sight of my features. If my eyes weren't reddened, you'd think nothing was different, that nothing had changed.

Jane must've found the cat like this.

Sadie was fifteen and weak enough that she was ready to go—and she chose Jane's closet because, like people, animals seek comfort at the sight of their end.

She sought comfort near Jane.

I stand and by the time I swing the door open, Rose is already halfway doing the same. She nearly falls towards me, but I clasp her hip and hold her close. Our children are seated patiently, huddled around Jane as she flips through a photo-book of countries and their capitals. She still silently cries, and her brothers try to cheer her up by pointing to the book.

"Look, Jane," Beckett says until he catches her attention.

"Connor?" Rose stands rigid and alarmed. "Tell me I just need to call an exterminator or buy a rat trap—"

"Sadie is dead," I whisper.

Her mouth falls. "What?"

"She's not moving. I think she must've felt that she was going to go." I swallow this strange lump in my throat.

Rose touches her lips, eyes widened in shock. "…in Jane's closet?"

I nod. "I'll carry the cat out."

Rose holds onto my bicep, partially for support, I can tell. "She deserves more than a shoebox burial. She's a Cobalt." Rose fights tears and raises her chin to combat any waterworks.

"I agree," I say softly, "but we still have an issue."

Rose follows my gaze to our daughter, and with one knowing exchange, Rose and I take a seat in front of our four children. I help my wife ease down, and she lets out another long breath.

I don't ask if she's okay. Her glare says *don't talk about it, Richard* and I only listen because she leans her weight against me. I wrap my arm around her waist.

"Jane," Rose says, "what do you think you saw in your closet?"

Jane wipes her nose with the back of her hand. "Sadie…she's not well. She won't move." Jane bursts into tears again.

I bring her onto my lap, and she calms a little. The boys aren't at a developmental age where they'll be able to understand what this means, so they take more interest in the way we speak and the picture book.

"Will you make her better?" Jane croaks.

Rose looks pained, but I can say it all. I can speak as bluntly and as honestly as they need to hear. I wouldn't sugarcoat life for a teenager or a one-year-old. So I don't start now.

"No," I say.

Jane's chin trembles and her sadness flares into tearful anger. "Why not?!"

"She can't be healed, Jane," I say. "Sadie has died."

Jane looks heartbroken, but she argues, "She can return again."

"Once something or someone has died, it can never return."

"Liar!" Jane wails like she never has before, tears splotching her cheeks. "You're lying!"

Rose distracts the boys by sliding between them, lifting Eliot on her stomach.

My voice never changes octaves. "I would never lie to you, Jane, and if you don't see this now, you will in time."

Jane exhaustedly falls against my chest. Sobbing, she cries, "...I don't want Sadie to die."

In a hushed voice, Rose asks, "How much did you love Sadie, Jane?"

"So terribly much," she mumbles into my chest.

Rose says, "Sadie felt *all* of your love. She lived with more *affection* because of your kindness and your heart."

Our daughter's big tearful eyes drift between her mother and me.

"You can be sad because she's gone," I whisper, "but you can also be happy because she existed."

"You," Rose says, "Jane Eleanor Cobalt had the honor of meeting Sadie Cobalt while she was still here." Jane begins to nod, as though she had the good fortune to see Sadie when others didn't. I tuck a piece of hair behind Jane's ear.

"When you grow older," Rose continues, "what will you tell all of your brothers about Sadie?"

Another tear rolls down Jane's cheek. "How sweet she was."

Rose and I exchange a look, and I nearly grin. I could call Sadie many things, but *sweet* would be far, far down the list.

Rose mouths, *don't correct her.*

I mouth back, *I won't.* I adore her opinion, no matter if it differs from mine. Beckett yawns, then Charlie. I say to them, "C'est l'heure d'aller au lit, mes chéris." *Time for bed, my darlings.*

Jane flinches at the idea of returning to her bed, in her room, where Sadie is dead.

Rose is the first to say, "You'll be sleeping in our bed, little gremlin."

Jane relaxes at the thought. I stand up and set Jane on her feet. I clasp Rose's hand and her waist, helping her rise.

Standing, Rose swats her hair out of her face and then plants her hands on her hips. Color suddenly drains from her cheeks and horror flits in her eyes.

Then I notice water gushing between her legs.

"No," Rose mutters.

Her word doesn't match the reality.

The world is very much saying *yes.*

Yes, Rose is giving birth the same day Sadie died.

We're prepared. We always are, but the next ten minutes is still mayhem with four kids under four, a dead cat in a closet, and Rose obsessing over the dirtied hallway.

"Call my sisters," is her first command.

I already called Lo, who then looped Ryke into the conversation. Lo and Lily are coming over to take Jane for the night while Ryke and Daisy take our younger children.

Before Rose tugs towels out of the hall closet, just to wipe the floorboards, I catch her face between my hands and say, "This is happening, Rose." The edges of her OCD are flaring up.

Rose lets out a breath. "We have time to spare."

"Not to clean. I promise, the house will be spotless when we return."

Her shoulders begin to loosen. "Are you ready?"

I grin. "I always am."

She rolls her eyes.

"Ensemble," I tell her. *Together.*

Rose nearly rises twenty-feet tall. She holds onto my arms as she says, "Ensemble."

Connor & Rose Cobalt welcome the birth of their baby boy

TOM CARRAWAY COBALT

April 21st, 2020

2021

"When you meet me, you're
not going to love me,
but maybe in time...
hell no, you still won't."

- Loren Hale, We Are Calloway

(Season 3 Episode 03 — Ice & Stone)

{ 20 }

March 2021
SUPERHEROES & SCONES
Philadelphia

Lily Hale

I successfully park my BMW on the street of Superheroes & Scones, but unfortunately, I couldn't find an open spot near the store. I'm horrible at math and not-so-good at predicting my own life, but I'm thinking I have a five-minute walk in my future.

"Little Luna, little Luna, *beep beep*," Moffy singsongs and taps her nose at *beep beep*. Their innocence flutters my heart. I have to always take a breath and remember that Lo and I created something pure together.

Moffy is already five and taking the role as big brother to heart. He asked if he could help me with Luna while I unbuckle the one-and-a-half-year-old from her car seat. He's up on the leather seat, putting Luna's mini-Wampa cap on her head. The one that used to be his. He wanted her to have "his favorite hat" (his words).

Lo turned to me that day and said, "You and me—we raise superheroes."

I'm smiling like a dopey fool just thinking about that moment. But it's a smile I clutch close.

"Moffy!" Luna beams. She tries to imitate her brother by tapping his nose. She pokes his cheek.

He laughs, and I lift her out of the car seat and onto my hip. Just as Moffy climbs out of the BMW, two cameras flash in quick succession, the lens pointed at us.

"Whaa…" I stare wide-eyed.

"LILY CALLOWAY, LOOK HERE!"

"HOW ARE YOU DOING, LILY?"

"LUNA HALE, YOU'RE SO BIG NOW! LOOK HERE."

My stomach nosedives. I'm one of those sitcom characters where their face reads: *Noooooooo…*

This is when I wish for Garth. My bodyguard was luckier and found a closer parking spot. I think he's waiting at the front of Superheroes & Scones already.

Moffy clutches onto my hand when I reach for him.

One baby in arm, one five-year-old in hand, and a longer walk than I like to take in my house, let alone a public street.

Don't freak out. I chant. *Don't freak out.*

If I freak out about being trailed for five-minutes by paparazzi, Moffy will freak out. I'm withholding my inner-freak for him.

Sexual freak. That freak too. He will *not* be seeing Lily Sex Freak Hale. Nope. Never. Goodbye.

I shut the door, lock the car, and all the while the paparazzi shout questions. I wave sheepishly to them as I head down the street lined with shops. Around evening on a weekday, people are out for early dinner, so they ogle and gawk.

Some stop and pull out their phones.

Two paparazzi become four, then five.

All within thirty-seconds.

My arm strength is puny, but I'd hold Luna longer than Kate Winslet let Leonardo DiCaprio share a door in *Titanic*. The thought puffs out my chest like I'm invincible.

Luna whips her head up and down the street. Aware of the onlookers. "Luna, over here!" Different cameramen repeat her name and confuse her.

"Don't be scared, Luna," Moffy tells his sister during our trek. "They won't hurt you."

"What your big brother said." I nod resolutely.

Luna nods like me. She has chubby baby cheeks that Lo smothers with kisses. I wrap Luna more securely and warmly in my arms and kiss her cheek with a whisper of, "I love you, Luna."

She kisses her palm and then puts her hand over my...eye.

I smile, but it fades as three paparazzi start walking backwards just to videotape us from the front.

"Hey, Maximoff," a college-aged cameraman greets, much younger than the other paparazzi. He's shared info about his personal life with us. Like dropping out of Penn State to make a living filming the Calloway sisters, their men and children. Like how he prefers cargo board shorts and tying his long brown hair in a bun.

Out of all the paparazzi, he's the least threatening and never aggressive.

Every kid, from all of our families, loves him.

"Robby!" Moffy smiles and lets go of my hand for a second. *Don't freak out.* Moffy knows not to talk to strangers and paparazzi when we're not with him and to stay close when we are, but his guard drops around Robby.

Moffy bumps fists with him.

I'm shier and more introverted than a five and one-year-old. This is my weird universe.

"Have you been up to anything cool, Maximoff?" Robby asks as he walks backwards, camera in hand. Lo and I have repeatedly taught Moffy that anything he says *will* be uploaded online or aired on entertainment television. He might only be five, but he does understand that he's different.

He sees that we're the *only* people being followed, especially in a city that's not known for celebrity sightings, tour buses, and camera crews. To them, it feels like they're the only ones being treated differently.

"Daddy showed me how to skateboard yesterday." Moffy smiles big, and I catch up to him and clasp his hand again.

"Don't let go, Moffy. Okay?"

"Sorry, Mommy." He hugs my side like I'm the one in need of consoling. *Don't freak out.* He still lets me baby him. *Remember that time where you wiped his shirt after he spilt orange juice?* Yes. Yes, I do. That was yesterday.

I nod.

"So awesome, dude," Robby says and then swerves the camera up to me. "Anything new, Lily?"

I shake my head. "Not really."

Like he's mentioning the sunshine, Moffy says, "Mommy had to wear big girl pads because she didn't feel good."

OhmyGod. My neck roasts. I started my period—which I try to avoid 85% of the time—and I failed my mission to find a tampon. I did find pads deep within a cupboard, and Moffy asked what I was doing. I just said, "Mommy doesn't feel that great right now."

Don't freak out.

Rose would say that there should be *zero* shame in periods. I blow out an awkward breath and then blurt, "I'm not pregnant."

I just announced that to a flurry of cameras. *Why?* Why did I just say that? I wince at myself.

Moffy looks up at me. "What does that have to do with big girl pads?"

I whisper like we're sharing a secret. "Later."

He nods like he's in the loop.

"Maximoff, look here!"

Moffy ignores that cameraman.

Robby says, "You have a joke for me today, Maximoff?"

Superheroes & Scones is in view! We're in the home stretch. Safety awaits. I didn't have to abort the mission. We're alive.

Moffy jumps over a crack in the sidewalk, tugging me forward. "What do you call a woman with four legs?"

"I don't know? What do you call her?"

"Doggy style!" Moffy shouts.

I'm dead.

My heart is in my throat. "Saybye," I say so fast and steer Moffy away from the curb and closer to the storefronts.

He just said doggy style.

Does he know what that is?

What if he knows what that is?! Luna says, "Mommy, red." She pats my cheeks with both hands. *Shit.* I'm a burnt tomato.

"Bye, Robby!" Moffy waves.

The long line of people stretching outside Superheroes & Scones suddenly *screams* at the sight of us. I imagine Banshee, an X-Men, sounds just like this. Both Maximoff and Luna immediately cover their ears with their hands.

Garth—burly, bald and beautiful Garth is waiting at the glass door. He holds it open, and we slip inside. Customers aren't as loud, but they quickly whip out their phones to catch a picture.

"Break room," I tell Moffy.

He skips ahead of me. The break room is semi-full, and I tell everyone *hi* in under a second. Then I direct Moffy into the storage room, no employees in sight.

He hops on a cardboard box, sitting next to an old Magneto cutout that used to be in the window. My puny arm starts to give out, so I put Luna in a box of Iron Man plushies. She hugs one and starts giggling.

I call Lo and press the *speaker button* while it dials.

"Why are you so red?" Moffy asks. "Are you sick?" He tries to reach up and touch my forehead.

"I'm not sick." I sit in front of him, phone ringing, Luna in a box of plushies beside me. "I flush for a lot of different reasons, but none are bad." *Don't be worried about me.* It's my job to worry about *him.* I brush his dark brown hair off his forehead. He needs a haircut soon. "Moffy…?"

"Yeah, Mommy."

"I'm okay. I'm your mommy, and I worry about you so much. But you never have to worry about me. Your job is to play, be the big brother to Luna, read comic books and run around the yard. The last thing you need to do is worry about me."

His face falls. "But I love you."

I wipe the corners of my eyes.

"Don't cry, Mommy!" He rubs my face with all of his fingers.

I just realize that the phone stopped ringing. "Lily?"

My heart sinks. "Lo?"

I hear papers rustle, drawers slamming, and maybe the jingling of keys. "Where are you?"

He heard a lot. "Nonono, you don't have to leave work."

"Daddy, Mommy's crying."

"It's okay, bud. Where are you at?"

"Superheroes—"

"I'm not crying anymore. I shed one tear!" I tell Lo. I also put my hand in the Luna box. She grabs hold of my fingers with a giggle.

"You could tell me you were flying with Peter Pan, and I'd still leave to come find you."

I frown at that scenario. "That doesn't make any sense, Lo. You're my Peter Pan.

"Maybe not in an alternate universe."

"I don't like this." I hold the phone closer to Moffy's lips. "Our son told the paparazzi a joke today. Moffy, want to tell Daddy?" Please let him share in my mortification. I don't want to be alone here. Though, I know I will be the only burnt tomato.

Moffy leans towards the speaker. "What do you call a woman with four legs?"

I hear a soft, *Bye, Mr. Hale* in the background. "What?"

"Doggy style!" Moffy shouts just like last time.

I hear a *bang*. "Christ."

"What happened?"

"This wall came out of nowhere." He walked into the wall.

I smile.

"Mommy's smiling!" Moffy narrates.

Lo asks, "Where'd you hear that joke from?"

"Jordan." A boy down the street. "Isn't it funny? It's like Coconut. She's a girl and she's a dog."

My shoulders lower, and I exhale. He has no idea it's about sex. If there's a magical wizard watching out for me, thank you for this one. I really needed that. I'm not ready for a huge sex conversation. Moffy didn't realize that all girls have vaginas until Luna was born, and I wasn't there when he told Lo, "Mommy's not the only one with a vagina."

I kind of wish I was present because it would've been a good prep course for the big leagues: *the* sex talk.

I tell Moffy, "How about we keep that joke just between all of us?"

"Like a secret?"

"Yep."

Moffy nods in understanding just as the storage door opens. Garrison Abbey slips inside, black shirt and black jeans. Since he no longer works at Superheroes & Scones, his sudden appearance seems less like a coincidence.

"Lo," I say into the phone, "you didn't tell Garrison, did you?"

"Tell me what?" Garrison stands by an old, dusty comic stand.

Moffy leaps off the box and runs towards Garrison. "Uncle Garrison!" He gives Garrison a cool secret handshake.

"Never mind," I say to Garrison about the same time Lo says, "What?"

I realize Lo wouldn't send Garrison, out of everyone, to check up on me. We check up on Garrison—it's how it's always been. And we told Moffy to start calling him *uncle* about the minute Garrison moved in with us. There was a chance he'd never be with Willow long-term, but we knew Garrison would always be a part of our family, no matter what.

"I have to go," I tell Lo.

"I'll see you soon, love." After quick *I love yous* we hang up on one another.

Garrison walks closer to me, Moffy trying to mimic him step-for-step like Garrison is his best friend. "I need your help on something." It's why he's here.

I tickle the Luna box, and she tugs my finger with another giggle. "What can I do?"

Garrison sips his Lightning Bolt! energy drink and gestures to the cardboard boxes labeled *The Fourth Degree*. Freshly plastic-wrapped comics in each, all extras to replenish shelves or too obscure to take up shelf space.

"I need every comic that has Sorin-X. There are too many issues and spin-offs now. Honestly, I just don't have time to go through all of them."

I don't ask why he needs them yet. I pick myself off the floor. "Moffy, there's a little Luna in a box—"

"I got her, Mommy." He goes to the Luna box and plays with his sister. I was in full-on *make this sound fun and not like a babysitting chore* mode, but he squashed that instantly. To him, I think babysitting *is* fun.

I pat the dust off my leggings. My baggy *Star Wars* T-shirt hangs to my thighs. "They're all in here." I guide Garrison to *The Fourth Degree* labeled boxes. "Lo will be here soon, and he might be more help. He's read every issue about a million times."

We rip open two boxes and start flipping through the comics, setting aside the ones with Sorin-X. The ones without the comic book character, I try to gingerly slip them back into their plastic covers.

"Are you going to read these?" I wonder.

Garrison places another comic on the pile. "What else would I be doing with them?"

"I don't know." I try to narrow my eyes at him and piece apart his motives. "You don't really read comics, not like Willow." I point out another fact, "You had no clue who Cypher was when you started working here."

"Yeah, and none of the employees ever let me forget it." His lips begin to rise like he misses those days where he worked at Superheroes & Scones. Willow was here back then, and I think she's the soul of his nostalgia. "I've read New Mutants, by the way."

My giddy smile spreads across my face. "Because of Willow?" *Young love.* I witnessed their beginning—and much, much more. I don't think I'll ever have to witness their end.

It's not so much a prediction as it is a fact now.

"Yeah, because of Willow." He tries to shake a comic back into the plastic.

"Which brings everything to Twitter," I tell him. "*Gillow Engagement* has been trending all day, did you see?" I remember reading the headlines of articles: WILLOW HALE GETS ENGAGED! CHECK OUT LOREN HALE'S NEW BROTHER-IN-LAW INSIDE!!

He proposed to her in London, and even though they'd mentioned marriage to one another before, he looked so nervous at dinner. She had no idea we were in the restaurant, and after he dropped to one knee and she said *yes*, we surprised her by appearing.

There was an abundance of tears and smiles.

Now that he's back in Philly, Willow stayed at college in London, so they're still split apart while she's studying and he's working. None of us questioned their engagement. Daisy said that when Garrison talks about Willow and when Willow talks about Garrison, they look like they're smiling up at the moon.

Rose called them love-struck in London.

I think they've been love-struck since the first moment they met. Long-distance did nothing but strengthen them.

They're planning to marry around the time she graduates, but they're keeping this fact secret from the media. It was too hard to conceal the engagement news with all of us together in London.

I also tell Garrison, "Connor said you both made GBA Entertainment News last night too." I thought Connor only watched CNN and Bloomberg TV, so it's possible he just cruised through the channel and caught the Willow and Garrison segment in passing.

"He watches entertainment news?" Garrison says with cinched brows.

"That was my reaction."

Garrison flips through a comic. "You also forgot about *Garlow Engagement* and *Wilson Engagement*."

All three have been trending. It's been years and no one can decide their ship name. Willow said she doesn't want to choose a side with the fans, so she supports all three. Garrison isn't into ship names like us, but we look past his flaws.

When they had no relation to us, they used to be out of the tabloids completely. Now they've made television news, magazine headlines, and even Twitter trends.

"Does all of this bother you?" I wonder. "You and Willow never talk to us about the media presence."

He shrugs. "Being around you guys, it just comes with the territory, and we both kind of gradually stepped into it." He tilts a comic upside-down, his brown hair hanging in his eyes.

In all the years I've known him, he's never changed his hairstyle. He did ditch the hoodies though, about the same time he moved into our house and stopped seeing his brothers.

"Lily...can I ask you something?" He peeks over at Moffy to make sure he's not listening. Moffy climbed into the plushies box with Luna and chatters away, even if she can't speak much yet.

I smile at them and then nod to Garrison. "Sure."

"I just..." he trails off and then shakes his head. "Forget it. It's stupid." He chucks a comic aside.

"I bet it's not." I sidle closer.

He stares down at the comic. "The airport—I don't want to be mobbed like that when I go to London alone."

Paparazzi and fans encased us after our flight to Philadelphia landed, coming home from the engagement. With all the children with us— Ryke, Lo, and Connor went into dire protection mode. I'd never seen them all so focused and intent. No yelling. Just intense *protect the babies* and shove forward.

I think that might've been Garrison's first time in a situation that overcrowded, most of the attention directed on *him* rather than us.

"I just...I don't want to be touched like that again."

A breath locks in my lungs. Fans put their hands on my shoulders and arms, even with bodyguards trying to block them, so I'm sure something similar happened to him.

I ask, "Are you scared to go back to the airport?"

He shrugs and then nods.

"I can ride to the airport with you when you need to go, and there's this thing we can do." Sometimes we do it, sometimes we don't, but I don't think we've ever offered the option to Garrison when he's alone. "We can drive right up to the private plane and bypass the normal airport entrance."

"We can do that?" He frowns.

"We've done it before. The airport gives us permission because we cause a lot of disruption. It's safer for us and for everyone else."

"But it's just me...I don't usually fly in a private plane."

"Yeah but you can take our planes alone. We don't mind. We'd want you to."

Garrison is already shaking his head. "It's too much for just me."

"Then I'll send Garth with you. He's the best." Garrison already has a bodyguard but two are better than one. "If it's only you, the crowds won't be as bad. I know they won't."

He nods.

"Have you told Willow?"

"*No*," he forces like *you don't tell her either.* "If she knew, she'd start flying to Philly to see me instead of the other way around." He licks his dry lips. "Willow gets anxiety when she's stuck in the middle of crowds. I know she'd brave it out for me, but…"

"You want to brave this out for her," I realize.

He nods more firmly. "Yeah."

Moffy must've heard that last part because he shouts, "I think you're brave, Uncle Garrison!"

Garrison smiles weakly and says to me, "Your kid is funny."

"Or maybe he's right."

Garrison lets out a breath like it's been sitting on his chest. "So I can take Garth when I fly to London?"

"Without a doubt, no take-backs. Cross my heart." I remember to make an *x* motion over my heart, and I also add, "He's pretty much the family bodyguard, and you're our family."

Garrison smiles more. "Thanks. I appreciate everything, you know?"

I nod again. I know he does. We see it in his eyes all the time. Years ago, he was just a teenager, knocking on the door of Superheroes & Scones and asking for a job that Lo once offered. He almost turned around, but I let him in.

We both let him in our lives, and the good person we saw beneath the layers of hatred and self-loathing emerged.

"So really," I say as we resume our Sorin-X search, "what are you doing with all of these?"

"I guess I have to ask about it anyway, but you have to promise not to tell the tall one. He's literally throwing hundreds of thousands of dollars at my face. I'm scared shitless he'll shut the entire thing down and fire me if he finds out."

It's about what he's been secretly working on for three years at Cobalt Inc. No one really knows what the project is, and Connor gave him five years to execute it, which he said is realistic for someone working alone.

"Cross my heart." I catch myself making a cross-symbol with my finger instead of an *x*. I stop midway and just drop my hand. I was doing so well.

Before he spills the news, the storage door cracks open.

Moffy whispers to Luna, "Shhh." Hidden in the cardboard box, Moffy yanks down a flap.

Lo pockets his keys as he enters, and we instantly lock eyes, the magnetic pull drawing me to my best friend, and Lo urgently reaches me.

"Lily," he breathes, his hands on my cheeks.

"I'm okay..." He has the prettiest pink lips. *Focus.* My mind wanders to nefarious places, and I hang onto his belt loops. "We're okay."

Lo kisses me lightly but only for a second.

My body warms. I push against him. Melded. My chest up along his. I cling to him like a tree, but he's holding me back.

While he stares down at me, I steal another kiss. I feel a smile on his lips, but he's the one who breaks apart. He scans the area, nods to Garrison, and then asks quickly, "Where are our kids?" His edged voice carries a severe amount of panic.

Then the box giggles and laughs.

His alarm depletes, but Loren Hale is not nice. I know what he's going to do before he does it.

"Moffy?! Luna?!" He layers on fake fear and panic. "Lily, go call 9-1-1 right n—"

"No!" Moffy shrieks with tears in his eyes. He pops out of the box and bolts to Lo as fast as he can. "I'm right here! I'm right here!" He hugs onto Lo's legs, and Lo crouches down to hug him tight, acting relieved to find him so quickly.

I lift Luna out of her box, and she keeps one of the plushies clutched to her chest.

I whisper to Lo, "You just wanted that hug."

Lo smiles like that was his evil plan all along. Then he assesses Moffy. "Are you in one piece? Are you okay? Did the aliens get you?"

"What aliens?"

Lo lets out a choked laugh. "You didn't hear about the alien invasion last night? What were you—*sleeping?*"

"Yeah, I like sleep."

"No way, me *too*."

Moffy holds his dad's hand as Lo rises to a stance beside me. "If you were sleeping and I was sleeping, then who was awake to see the aliens?"

"Crazy Uncle Ryke and Aunt Daisy," Lo says without a beat.

I break into their conversation since Garrison still needs help finding comics. "We're trying to separate all the ones with Sorin-X. He said…" I trail off because Garrison is shaking his head at me like *stop talking*. "What?"

I'm not good with these kinds of cues.

Moffy runs off towards a bucket of Tilly Stayzor action figures, a very popular female character in *The Fourth Degree* universe.

"I did have something to ask you," Garrison says to Lo. I think he plans to bring up the airport subject, but then he suddenly takes an abrupt detour. "Will you be my best man at my wedding?"

Lo looks floored.

Garrison says, "You've been more of a brother to me than my brothers. I probably wouldn't be *here* if it weren't for you…and you." He looks to me.

I wipe my tears.

Lo's amber eyes glass. "Of course I'd be your best man."

Willow asked Daisy to be her maid of honor the day she got engaged. Garrison might've been worried Lo would say no. He overthinks a lot.

"Thanks," Garrison says. "Do you think the tall one and the angry one will want to be groomsmen?"

"Connor, without a doubt, and Ryke goes with the flow." Lo laughs. "Christ, if you put him in the back row, he wouldn't even care or take it to heart."

"Okay good." Garrison lets out another long breath.

Lo picks up a comic from our stack. "What's all this for?"

I say, "I don't know, Garrison was just about to tell..." Okay he's doing the *shake the head* signal again. How do I abort a conversation now that it's begun? Daisy is better at social transitions than me. I just flounder with my mouth half-open. "Uhhh..."

Lo says to Garrison, "Is this about your video game?"

Garrison's face falls. "What?"

Lo wears a half-smile.

Garrison chokes out, "How'd you know?"

"You're working for *Connor Cobalt*, man. The guy probably has fifteen brains and seven pairs of eyes. You might not know what he's thinking, but he knows what you are." Lo touches his chest. "And he's my best friend. He told me you're working on a game based on a comic book character."

Sorin-X, I realize. He's creating an entire video game from scratch—without a team behind him.

Whoa.

Garrison rocks backwards, disbelieving. "And he didn't give a shit? I thought he'd pull the plug on the project."

"He actually likes the idea. So do I."

Garrison gawks. "What?"

"*I* own the video game rights to *The Fourth Degree* series, and Belinda and Jackson told me they'd rather eat their left arms than see a thousand people turning the game into a money-making soulless franchise."

Belinda and Jackson Howell are a young brother-sister duo and the artist and writer of *The Fourth Degree* universe.

Garrison collects his thoughts fast. "I have most of the technical shit coded, but I'm at the point where storyline is important. That's why I was looking through the comics, but eventually I'd need Belinda and Jackson for the art. I can only code, and what I'm making is classic, indie. I think the game style fits what the comic intended to be."

Lo fought for *The Fourth Degree*—but he never thought it'd become the next *X-Men* or *Justice League* since Halway Comics lacks resources and name recognition like Marvel and DC.

It's happening though. The popularity has been rising exponentially, right in sight of the comic titans.

All because Lo said *yes* to Belinda and Jackson after reading their submission. When every other big comic publishers told them *no,* he helped turn their potential and their dream into success and reality.

"I've been mentioning the video game to Belinda and Jackson for a full year," Lo says, "and they're interested. I know they'd work with you. I'll give you their numbers."

Garrison is speechless.

I struggle keeping Luna on the crook of my hip, and Lo takes her from me. He kisses her cheeks so fast that she starts giggling.

I think about all the ventures we've ever made now that Garrison is beginning his. *Halway Comics. Superheroes & Scones.* All three of us used to lack ambition, not because we didn't love something, but because we never believed we could be better than the people around us. Why try when someone else will just step right over you?

It seemed like too much work.

Now we've all discovered ambition and pride—but not without believing in ourselves first. That we could beat our own sad expectations.

And we did.

"Mommy's bleeding!" Moffy shouts.

"What, where?" I spin around, so confused.

"Your butt."

Ohmygod. I can't feel my face. I bled through my underwear and leggings. Lo grabs onto Moffy's shoulder before he tries to touch my butt.

Garrison acts interested in the comics to give me privacy.

"Is it bad?" I ask Lo, about to find a pair of extra pants in one of these boxes. We might've been shipped in some Thor pajama bottoms. The God of Thunder will get me through this.

Lo checks out my ass. "It's just a spot." He has this face that screams *it's a bloody mess back there, love.* He even reaches for me, like he wants to hug me to make it better.

It's not better. Paparazzi took pictures of my backside, which includes my ass. *My bloody ass.* I wince at myself and then point at him, so close to calling him a lying liar.

Luna distracts me when she kisses his jawline.

I melt.

Moffy tugs on his dad's shirt. "Mommy's hurt! We have to help her."

"She's not hurt, Mof. This happens to girls every month."

Pants. Pants. Thor, where are you? Further in the back, I peek into a few plastic containers, only to find shields and swords.

"No, that's not fair!" Moffy shouts. "I don't want Luna and Janie to bleed from their butts."

I knock into a metal shelf and rub my forehead. Lo and Garrison stifle their laughter, but I can see their smiles through the shelves.

Instead of explaining periods in-depth, Lo just says, "It's not happening any time soon, bud, and it doesn't hurt them."

"You promise?"

I watch through the shelves like a peeping Tom, but I can't turn around.

"You think I'd let anything bad happen to your little sister?"

"No," Moffy says without a pause, "because you make all the monsters go away."

I rub at my watery gaze.

Loren Hale is not the monster in his son's eyes.

He's the hero.

[21]

September 2021
ARRAPIA CAFÉ
Philadelphia

Rose Cobalt

"This is beyond ridiculous." I slide the *Celebrity Crush* tabloid to Ryke. The headline in neon pink reads: ROSE CALLOWAY BABY CRAZY!! PREGNANT WITH SIXTH CHILD!

My scowling brother-in-law lowers his massive burger and then wipes his calloused hands on the *tablecloth* of all things.

I bite my tongue but not for long. "A napkin is next to you," I snap.

His brows knot. He didn't even realize he spread beef grease on decorative linen. Also, he doesn't care. "Do you want me to read the fucking magazine or wash my hands?"

I huff. "Read."

Ryke flips through the tabloid, his scowl never changing shape.

I grow impatient. "The headline alone is ridiculous. Calling *me* baby crazy is like calling the sun a flaming ball of shit."

Ryke ignores me as he reads.

This is the *last* time I invite him out to lunch. At least not without one of my sisters or Connor or Loren present. When we're alone together, I feel like I'm arguing with myself. Or a caveman. Or both.

I tug at the hem of my blue dress, the chair creaking. The lighting in the café is more suited for dinnertime: too dim, the blinds nearly shut closed. It creates a *mood* that I'd rather share with no one. Not even Connor.

Okay, *maybe* Connor.

Maybe even more than *maybe*. But I'd never tell him so.

"It's fucking stupid," Ryke states after a prolonged minute of silence. He shuts the tabloid and tosses it aside.

My eyes narrow. "It took you *that* long to come to that assessment. What were you doing? Fact-checking them?"

He glares, but it's minor in comparison to the ones his little brother doles out. "For fuck's sake, Rose, I was actually reading what they wrote. And if you did too, you'd know that they just mostly talk about how you're pregnant...which you are."

I'm only fifteen weeks along, but it was far enough that we discussed it on our latest episode of *We Are Calloway*. I wanted to leak the information before a tabloid did, and I succeeded on that front. I realize these tabloids are expected, but I never really prepared myself for the "baby crazy" moniker.

Especially since I still very much dislike babies that aren't my own.

Though the criticism is nothing new. I have warring voices from tabloids, fans, and random people that'd just like to comment on my life.

How can she have so many children and still go to work? That's so selfish.

How can she be considered career-driven and independent with that many children? She's a sell-out.

My values haven't changed with motherhood. I still work because I'm passionate about fashion. I still have children because I *love* my little gremlins, and I have the resources to have more while juggling my career and family, so I do.

Independence has nothing to do with whether or not someone chooses to be single or to be married, to have children or to not have children. Independence by definition is about self-governing. About *choosing* for yourself. About making *your own* decisions.

All of my decisions belong to me.

I chose this life. I love this life, and fuck everyone who wants to choose for me.

I swirl my straw in my water, annoyed by the white rose centerpiece. It's wilted, for one. For another, it's intimate, and I actually believe the hostess is a fan of Ryke and me...*together.* I grimace, almost losing brain cells at the thought of his name attached to mine.

What'd Lily call our ungodly ship name? RoRy?

I recoil.

We should've also paid the restaurant to leave the surrounding tables vacant, but since it's so early in the afternoon, on a weekday no less, neither of us bothered.

Two teenage girls occupy the adjacent table: a redhead with excellent cat-eye eyeliner and a blonde with a gorgeous deep blue statement necklace. The redhead tries to stealthily snap a photo of us, but it's extremely obvious.

Ryke dunks his fry into mustard. He'd never say *you're quiet, Rose.* I doubt he even realizes we've been sitting in utter silence.

I lower my voice, very hushed. "I've tried talking to Daisy."

Ryke rests his forearms on the table, his attention successfully mine. I see the question in his dark gaze: *About what?*

I scoot my chair closer to the table, so I can speak even lower. "About trying surrogacy after my baby arrives." The talk didn't go as planned. "Daisy brushed me off." I sigh heavily. "She said we should wait to even have the discussion until after I give birth." My gaze descends to my half-eaten avocado on rye.

If she's interested—and my intuition says she is—I want to fulfill my promise. The doctor was able to extract her remaining eggs during her surgery. We can go this route, but I worry she'll reject my offer out of guilt. Like she'd be restraining me from growing my own family. I've told her it's not like that, but I'm not sure she truly believes me.

Before I even had Jane, Connor professed (multiple times) that he wanted *eight* children, and this fact might be stuck in my sister's head as some sort of "Coballoway" finish line.

"I think she's right," Ryke suddenly says.

"*Why?*" Anger laces my voice. I point my black-matte nail at him. "Aren't you the one who tells her to scream off rooftops? To voice her opinions until she's blue in the face?"

"Yeah, and she's telling you her fucking opinion. She wants to wait to have the discussion until after your baby is born. The end." Ryke pops another fry in his mouth like the situation is as easy as that.

My gaze pierces his ratty hair and then his unconcerned eyeballs. "Where were you born?"

He expels an aggravated breath. "If this is bait to an insult—"

"Simple Town?" I cross my arms. "With simple answers to problems?"

He slouches back in his chair, on the verge of a partial eye roll. "You've been spending too much fucking time with my little brother." He waves in my general direction. "Sometimes I wonder if you've been body-fucking-snatched by him."

I gag. "*Please.* I have an automatic *destroy and castrate* function if anyone named Loren Hale tries to get inside of me." I pause at the string of words I just used. *God.* "This is why I don't do lunch with you. I say things like that."

Ryke hardly cares that I talked about his brother inside of me—*Stop, Rose.*

I'm stopping.

My own mind is trying to vacuum itself.

"You invited me," Ryke reminds me.

This is completely true. I prefer sharing people's company during lunch and staying a part of their lives somehow. I wouldn't let this change when Lily went to a different college than me, when she retreated into her addiction, and I won't let this change when we're all building families of our own.

I take a large sip of water. When I set my glass down, I ask, "Why can't we have the discussion now?"

"Because it's fucking pointless." He uses the napkin to wipe his hands this time. "If you have a boy, then you'll want to try for a girl again." *But if I have a girl, then they're more likely to go along with the idea of surrogacy.*

My lungs tighten at the realization. Why didn't she tell me this? Why didn't I guess it? She must've avoided the details to spare my feelings. Even though Daisy has come a long way from tiptoeing around everyone, she's still one of the kindest people I know.

I'm sure she's even framed my response. I say it to Ryke anyway. "If she's ready, I want to be her surrogate, even if my baby is a boy."

"It's not that fucking *simple.*"

And so the issue circles back to the beginning. They *both* refuse to stop us from growing our family. "Okay," I concede. "We'll wait to discuss this until after my sixth child is born."

"Thank you." His eyes drift to my cell. "Did you put your fucking phone on silent?"

"What?" My phone screen is lit up with a caller, but it's not buzzing or ringing. It's possible Beckett or Eliot unknowingly messed with the settings. As soon as I read the caller ID, my pulse quickens.

Dalton Elementary

Jane.

She started kindergarten with Maximoff last month. Dropping my daughter off at pre-K was difficult, but leaving her at the doors of Dalton Elementary left my stomach viciously twisted. I sent my child into a savage land where her wit, smarts, and social skills will be forged and tested. I'm one-hundred percent certain that I gave her all the tools she'd need to outlast, but it's not like with my sisters. I'm not *in* school with her. I can't ask her if she's okay at her cubby or locker.

I can't carry her books if she doesn't feel well. I can't give her enemy a scathing glare in the hallway. I can't be there.

This is new for me.

I feel like I'm in the audience of a play that could go horribly wrong. And my daughter is the lead.

She skipped towards the building, Rose. She didn't even hesitate.

She's a lion for God's sake.

She's fine.

I put the phone to my ear. "This is Rose Cobalt. Is everything okay?"

Ryke immediately straightens, brows furrowed in concern. He flags down one of our bodyguards across the café.

"Hello, Mrs. Cobalt." A sweet (nauseating) voice echoes through the receiver. "This is vice-principal Morgan-Stuart. I need you and your husband to come to the school."

"What for?" I'm already gathering my Chanel purse and a tube of lipstick I left on the table. Ryke fishes out bills from his wallet. I'll pay him back for my share.

The vice-principal says, "We're sending Jane home for the day. I'd rather we discuss the issue in person."

I hold back a curse, and I put a palm over the receiver to tell Ryke, "It's Jane."

I barely get her name out before he pushes ahead of me, clearing a path while our bodyguards follow. My heels clap on the tile, walking briskly through the dim café.

People stare. Two cameras flash—no, *four*.

I ignore them.

"Is she okay?" My voice drips with ice, wishing Morgan-Stuart just began with *Jane is fine.*

"It's nothing like that."

"Nothing like *what?*" I'm picturing Jane with a broken arm, bloodied nose—

"She's fine," she clarifies, but it hardly tames my temper.

"Then what?"

"Like I said, I'd rather talk in person. She'll be waiting in the office until you arrive." She hangs up on me.

She hangs up on me.

"That fucking—"

We step outside, and my voice dies at the sudden cacophony by the curb: honking traffic, paparazzi screaming our names.

"RYKE! ROSE!"

I'm swarmed by cameras. Ryke checks on me with a glance over his shoulder. I motion for him to leave me be. My bodyguard is already flanking my side. Ryke nods and sprints to his Land Cruiser straight ahead.

"WHERE'S DAISY AND CONNOR?"

"HOW'S THE BABY?"

"WHAT DID YOU EAT IN THE CAFÉ?"

So predictable. They always ask about our meals.

By the time I climb into the passenger seat, Ryke slams the driver's door closed. He twists the key in the ignition, and his car rumbles to life.

"Let's go." I physically snap my finger, as though willing him to miraculously send me there. "Dalton Elementary."

"I'm fucking trying." He cranes his neck over the seat, paparazzi blocking the Land Cruiser and caging us in. "Unless you'd like me to run one of these motherfuckers over."

"That will do."

Ryke rolls down the window, about to yell at the cameramen, but a gaggle of young fans *rush* to him and stick their hands into the car. I stiffen as they grab at his arm and squeal like they touched some form of royalty.

Personally, I'd crown Connor before Ryke—and I can already picture his smugness. *You think of me as a king, Rose.*

I want to put my hand over his face, and he's not even here.

"Rose! Rose!" they begin to shriek and reach for me.

I stay still and wear a curt smile. I'm not the warm one or the nice one—I'm just *me*, and I almost feel sorry that these girls aren't graced with a Lily or Daisy or Poppy type.

"Hey, girls," Ryke says, and a girl with a blue streak in her hair starts crying, overwhelmed by him. "We're in a fucking rush, and the last thing I want to do is hurt any of you by pulling out."

"You can pull out of me!" a brazen girl blurts.

"You can pull out of me too!" another one pipes in.

"Fuck," Ryke grumbles under his breath.

I could laugh, but I'd rather coach Ryke through this moment out of solidarity. Before I can direct the girls to the sidewalk, Ryke is clarifying himself.

"Pulling out onto the fucking *street*." He tenses. "Please back up."

"Okay, we will."

"I love you so much!"

"Have my babies!!"

All these exclamations blend together as the girls retreat to a safe place on the sidewalk. The paparazzi continue to bombard our car.

"Hey!" Ryke yells at the nearest cameraman, the lens directed at Ryke. His exchange with the girls will most likely be on GBA Entertainment News tonight. "Move the fuck out of my way! Unless you want a tire on your motherfucking foot!"

They shrink backwards, probably just thankful Ryke gave them more "newsworthy" footage. He drives into a line of traffic, deserting the paparazzi and café.

While he rolls up his window, I ask, "When you're alone with my sister, do fans grab Daisy like they grab you?"

"No." Ryke runs a hand through his thick hair. "At least not since she described what her friends and paparazzi did to her on *We Are Calloway*."

"Good." I pause. "But if *you* need to talk to someone about being touched without permission—"

"I have a fucking therapist and his name isn't Rose Calloway."

My eyes flash hot. "That's assuming I would've offered myself, which I wouldn't have. I'm not a professional." I twist my hair on my shoulder, remembering that Ryke started seeing a therapist after Adam Sully died.

I lean over to check his speedometer. "Can you not drive faster?"

"Yeah, let me play bumper cars with the line of fucking traffic."

"Let's."

"No," he says like I'm "fucking" crazy.

His grip tightens on the steering wheel. "Is Janie okay?" Worry darkens his features.

"The vice-principal said she was fine, but she wouldn't offer me anymore details." I hold my purse close to my chest and cast a heated glare out the windshield. "If she's doing this to trick Connor and me into taking photographs in her office, I'm going to raise hell."

"I will lose my fucking shit before you."

Unlikely.

I raise my phone to my lips. "Call Richard," I say into the speaker. If I put my cell to my ear, I may just throw it out the window—for no good reason other than the enjoyment of throwing something.

When the line clicks, I start speaking before he can. "Jane's school called. We need to go in and have a conversation with the vice-principal. I don't know why. All they said was that she's okay, but the administration would rather 'talk in person'—as if seeing my face will be better. The *only* thing they'll be seeing is literal *fire* coming out of my eyes and burning them to ash."

"Are you driving?" he asks.

I gape. "That's the first thing you're asking, Richard?" My voice escalates. "Our daughter's second month in kindergarten and she's being called to the office—an office that's withholding information from us—and you're asking if I'm *driving?*"

"Yes because I'd prefer to have my wife in one piece."

I hear the sound of shuffling papers like he's preparing to leave our house. "You can't leave the other kids alone."

"Clearly I wouldn't," he says. "I'm calling Diana and Adalene." *Our nannies.*

After an *extensive* interview process and background check, we hired these two women, both with a great deal of previous infant care experience. We only call them when we need them.

He'll most likely leave once the nannies arrive to our house.

"Are you driving?" Connor asks again.

Ryke says, "I am."

"Wonderful." His dry tone is noted. "Don't speed. I'll be there as soon as I can, Rose. Try not to overreact. It shouldn't be too serious or else they'd let us know." His even-tempered voice does soothe part of my worry, but I don't like how he's more focused on *me* than on Jane.

"Where are your loyalties, Richard?" I test.

"With my family."

I see what he did there. "Fine." Before I hang up, I snap, "And I'm *hardly* overreacting." I hit the *end call* button before he rebuts.

"Why did I have children with him?" I slip my phone into my purse. "He's insufferable."

Ryke rakes his hand through his hair again.

I glare. "What are you doing? Keep both hands on the wheel."

"Fucking A." He grabs the steering wheel. "It pains me to say this, but *he's right*. You need to calm down."

I scoff. "He never told me to calm down. He said not to overreact."

"Same fucking thing."

I flip him off.

He shoots me the finger in reply.

Maybe *his* presence is frustrating me more—or maybe I'm just naturally overwhelmed with the unknown. I want answers. I like answers. I pride myself on finding them, but the vice-principal has given me a worksheet with censored and redacted questions. How am I supposed to fill this thing out without information?

Patience, I hear Connor.

I roll my eyes. Patience. It's clearly not my forte.

Now I'm relying on Ryke Meadows to take me from point A to point B. He turns on the stereo and switches on a song. I can't name the artist, but the string instruments sound like an indie or folk band.

We bump along the road, and I count the dreadful seconds that pass agonizingly slow.

The city landscape morphs into a more pastoral setting: robust trees, greenery, and lush land. Dalton Elementary comes into view, with its historic, steeple clock tower jutting from the shingled roof. The faded red brick building has two white columns by the entrance and a flagpole in the green turf.

I hastily jump out of the car before Ryke slows into the parking spot.

"I'll wait right here," Ryke says.

I leave my door ajar for a second. "Why?"

"I don't want to get in the fucking way and make things worse." He fixes his rearview mirror, which is disturbing seeing as how he's adjusting it *after* we've parked.

I shift my weight, hesitating. "I need you to come with me…at least until Connor arrives."

Now he asks, "Why?"

"Because…" I pause. "I'm really pissed, and I'm afraid of what I might say to the vice-principal. The last thing I need to do is accidentally get my daughter expelled on her second month of kindergarten."

Can they even expel her for my behavior? I blink a couple times. *That's a frightening prospect.* Even worse, I'm actually worried something like that might happen. What does that say about me?

My temper.

I unleash all my claws and my razor-sharp teeth when it comes to my sisters, my children—my family. I won't back down, even when I should.

Lily is right.

I'm one of those piercing corners on the hot-tempered triad. I eye my brother-in-law, his aggression palpable in his brooding eyes.

So is Ryke.

But I'm hoping he can maintain a level-head this once. For me. Maybe it'll be possible.

Maybe.

Ryke wavers. "I may say some fucking shit, Rose."

"Better the foul-mouthed uncle than the witch mother." I know it's what they'll call me, and since I have *many* more young children who'll eventually attend Dalton Elementary, I can't set every bridge on fire. For their sake.

Ryke takes the keys out of the ignition. "You're not a witch. By Lo's fucking definition, I'd be a witch with you." Outspoken. Hot-headed.

"You're not a woman. You wouldn't be called one," I remind him, my eyes cold.

His gaze nearly softens.

I add, "Let's not forget that I've called Lo names too. We tease each other. It's what we do."

Ryke nods. "I'm thinking more about what my daughter is going to have to fucking deal with."

"If she's anything like me, you can expect at least *one* person to call her a bitch." I tap my nail to the frame of the door. "Are you coming with me?"

He's already climbing out of the car. "Let's go."

Together, we walk along the cement path to the double doors. I hope fate has good fortune in store for us. I hope that one side of the hot-tempered triad can cool off for just *one* meeting.

Is that even achievable?

"SHE DID WHAT?"

"Maybe you should sit down," Mrs. Morgan-Stuart suggests for the fifth time. I've abandoned one of two wooden chairs that face her sleek oak desk. Ryke stands beside me like a loyal soldier, and I combat the vice-principal's hot and heavy judgment with a scathing glare.

She treats me like a sixteen-year-old who was sent to the principal's office, and to be precise, that situation *never* happened. I prided myself on being a model student.

"I'm not sitting down until you explain why *that* warrants a parent phone call." I swear, if they punish her for this, I will create the mother of all fucking storms.

"She *kissed* a boy," Mrs. Morgan-Stuart repeats.

My daughter's first kiss was in kindergarten. Of course it was.

"And?" Ryke asks, his muscles as strained as mine.

"And it was in front of the jungle gym where other children could see. It was highly inappropriate for someone her age."

"She's a child," I say. "Children are curious, and it couldn't have been anything more than a simple peck on the lips."

"Regardless…it was still out in the open where other children could see and get ideas."

I stifle this maddened noise that scratches my throat. "It was a small kiss. You're acting like she masturbated in public."

Mrs. Morgan-Stuart flushes red. "Mrs. Cobalt," she scolds and avoids meeting Ryke's gaze. Her embarrassment is unmistakable.

"Masturbation isn't a swear word," I rebut. "I won't apologize for saying something we all do."

Mrs. Morgan-Stuart is about the shade that Lily turns when she's mortified. "I think it's best if we wait for your husband. Mr. Meadows… you should leave."

"She's my niece," Ryke refutes, the three words beyond stilted, as though he's trying very hard not to include a *fuck*. I watch him mechanically take a seat in the chair and raise his hands like he comes in peace. Then he nods to me like *let's go fucking easy on her.*

If we must.

I settle in the chair next to Ryke. "My husband is on the way. I'd like to discuss this now." *I need more details.* "Did the boy kiss her back, did he run away, what else happened?" If it was an unsolicited kiss, it changes the narrative.

"He kissed her back."

My shoulders slacken.

"According to the students, Jane and Wesley kissed a few more times on the cheek before the teacher intervened. We've given her entire class a stern speech about appropriate behavior between classmates, but the children are all very animated about the situation. We think it's best that Jane go home today."

Smoke gushes out of my ears. I swear to all that is righteous. "You're *suspending* her over a peck on the lips?"

"Just for the day. Jane being in the school is a distraction to the other students."

I rise out of my seat, and if Connor had been beside me, he would've tugged me down. Instead, Ryke is rising *with* me. I can't think about the negative result of recruiting Ryke as a teammate.

I breathe fire. "The administration created *more* of an uproar by acting like kissing is the plague."

"Mrs. Co—"

"She did *nothing* that'd warrant suspension."

"Is Wesley being suspended for the day?" Ryke questions, still carefully choosing his words.

I fume silently, watching Mrs. Morgan-Stuart waste time by shifting papers in a beige folder. "Is he?" I snap.

"Wesley wasn't the one who initiated the kiss."

Ryke mutters under his breath, "You've got to be fucking kidding me."

"This is insane!" I shout. "What kind of place is this? I didn't send my daughter to the Academy of *Kiss-and-Be-Punished*." I'm seconds from pacing.

Ryke rubs his unshaven jaw aggressively and then drops his hand. "Look," he says to Mrs. Morgan-Stuart, "this is kindergarten. Why not just tell them *don't do it again* and call it a fucking day?"

She looks disgusted. "Please, watch your language."

The slip-up was bound to happen.

Ryke turns his head, and I think he's worried about the future when his own daughter enters kindergarten. He's holding back with his niece, careful not to step on my toes, but if this had been Sullivan, rest assured, he'd be as volatile as me.

"Dalton has values that will be upheld," the vice-principal says. "We'd appreciate if you talked to Jane thoroughly about what's inappropriate for school grounds."

"I will," I say, "and do you know what will be on my list? Drugs, bullying, stealing, cheating, *murder*. Not a kindergarten kiss."

"Please," she tries to reason with me. Am I being unreasonable? "Maybe take a good look at what goes on in your house…or places your children visit."

She went there.

Subtly, she pokes at the sex tapes of me and my husband, and the fact that my little sister is a sex addict who lives down the street. As if we're all *so* deviant.

This is ridiculous.

"This is fucking ridiculous," Ryke growls beneath his breath.

Thank you.

"It'd be wise to play by the school's rules. This display is hardly putting good will towards the future of *both* your children."

I go very still.

Ryke and I just made an utter, shitty mess of things.

[22]

September 2021
DALTON ELEMENTARY
Philadelphia

Connor Cobalt

I walk down the quiet hallway of Dalton Elementary. A little girl with a worried pout waits slumped on a plastic blue chair—right outside the principal's office. She accessorized her plaid, private school uniform with green pom-pom hair clips and fuzzy pink and yellow socks.

Incredibly mismatched.

The corners of my lips rise high.

Jane Eleanor Cobalt is in pursuit of finding her own identity, and I'm grateful to be a witness.

As I approach, Jane picks herself out of her slumped state, relief in her blue eyes.

The twenty-something teacher's assistant stands and greets me. "Hi, Mr. Cobalt. Your wife is in the office speaking with vice-principal Morgan-Stuart. I can let them know you're here."

"Actually, I'd like to talk to my daughter for a minute first."

"Sure, yes. Of course." She searches left and right for what to do, and then she decides to head to the nearest bathroom out of earshot.

Since the administration wouldn't tell Rose what happened, I assume they view Jane as being in the wrong. I don't believe she would've hurt anyone. Jane apologizes to her stuffed animals when she drops them. She even gives them medicine.

Literally, she spooned fruit punch on her lion.

Rose hand-washed him until the cherry-red stains disappeared, and then I made certain the *real* children's medicine was still locked in our cabinet out of Jane's reach.

I squat in front of my daughter, light freckles scattering the tops of her cheeks and nose.

She scoots to the edge of her chair. "I'm so sorry, Daddy. I didn't know…I didn't think it was wrong. Princesses do it all the time." She lets out a breath. "For as long as I live, I'll never, *ever* kiss another person." Tears flood her eyes.

She kissed someone?

Surprise jumps my brows. *She kissed someone.* I expected a variety of things, but this never crossed my mind. I don't know what I feel. On one hand, she's a curious child. On the other, she's my six-year-old daughter, and every year I fight this irreparable need that says, *spare her heartbreak and misery. You have the power to do so, Connor. Do it now.*

I hear Rose, *they will feel more than you ever did, Richard.*

They've already begun.

"Mon cœur." *My heart.* I brush my thumb across her cheeks, just as her tears overflow. "Parlons." *Let's talk.*

Jane sniffs and nods in agreement. "Parlons." *Let's talk.*

I rest my knee on the floor but remain here, closer to Jane's height and not towering over her little frame. "Who was this someone?"

"Wethley." She slurs his name. I know of a Wesley in the same class as Jane.

"Why'd you kiss Wesley?"

Very softly, she says, "Because of Jane and Rochester."

I shake my head once. "I don't follow." Then I do remember. *The boy*. His name is coincidentally Wesley Prescott Rochester. And Jane is a little passionate about her namesakes.

My daughter explains, "Jane Eyre falls in love with Mr. Rochester, and so I kissed Wethley so our love would begin...and then Miss Turner yelled at me and dragged me into the classroom by my wrist." Her chin trembles. "I'm so very sorry. I didn't know..." She rubs her eyes.

Repeatedly, I replay the part where the teacher dragged her by the wrist. My jaw muscles tic, my teeth bearing down harder. I try to remember that Jane embellishes her stories like her mother. Not entirely inaccurate just hyperbolic.

I waste no time.

I gently roll up the sleeve of her buttoned blouse and check her wrist. Front and back. No bruise or reddened skin. I try to ease myself with this knowledge. *She's physically fine.*

Calmly, I tell her, "Kissing another person isn't bad, but love doesn't work that way, Jane. You can't kiss everyone with the name Rochester and expect to fall in love." I sense her disappointment before I see it.

"Mommy said that some people are fated to be together. Fate guided me to Wethley."

I nearly cringe at the talk of *fate*, especially in conjunction with Jane and *love*. "Mommy also believes in ghosts. It's all just mere coincidence and partially fictitious."

Jane pouts and crosses her arms.

She reminds me so much of Rose here. Even with the talk of *fate*, I feel my grin rise. The precious moments in life, I hold very close.

"My advice," I say, "don't seek love from other people. Just love who you are enough that it won't matter whether or not you find your Rochester." Rose would explain this to Jane all the same.

"Can I love you?" Jane wonders.

My own mother would've told her *no*.

I smile by her words. And I say, "Bien sûr, mon cœur." *Of course, my heart.* I kiss her cheek and then lift her into my arms as I stand. I put her on the ground in front of the office door. "Ready?"

"Oui." *Yes.*

When we head inside the office, the sight doesn't surprise me. Rose and Ryke, red-faced with ire, stand side-by-side like two crackling fireworks prepared to blow. What's mildly irritating? Ryke here. Next to Rose. He's where I'm meant to be.

"Rose...*Ryke*," I greet first, their murderous eyes swinging from me to Mrs. Morgan-Stuart who looks relieved by my entrance.

She shouldn't be.

The vice-principal hasn't realized yet that I will always be loyal to my wife.

Does her relief shock me? No. Since I can remember, this has always been a common expression when I enter the room. They might as well be muttering, *thank god Connor is here.*

I'm god in every scenario.

Jane hides behind my legs, scared of the vice-principal. I keep a comforting hand on her shoulders.

"Jane just explained to me what happened." My gaze drifts to Ryke.

Ryke raises his hands in defense. "I didn't do anything you wouldn't fucking do."

"Our actions are never similar. I use the toilet. You use the woods," I say in front of the vice-principal. It's why Ryke lets out a short, flabbergasted laugh like I'm the biggest prick in the world. He doesn't care what people think, but he'd never insult another person in front of others like he believes I do.

I just tell the truth.

Also a truth: I would've never roused Rose in this situation like he did.

He outstretches his arms. "You want me to fucking leave? I'll leave. Rose was the one that asked me to come here."

I already know why. Rose wanted another voice, maybe even in case she grew too volatile.

She wanted *me*.

But Ryke is dependable. He's here when Rose needed someone, and I value that attribute. I value *him*. "I'd like you to stay, my friend," I tell him.

He only nods once before Rose bursts forth.

"They're suspending Jane today," Rose says heatedly, hands on her hips, "*and* they're refusing to suspend Wesley."

I see. I take a few calm steps towards Mrs. Morgan-Stuart, and Jane rushes to her mother's side, whispering quietly to her.

The vice-principal rises to her feet. "I was telling your wife that we have a code of conduct here at Dalton Elementary, and we can't overlook what Jane has done."

"I see," I say calmly.

She even offers me a thankful smile. "Then we'll see Jane tomorrow."

"Yes, you will." I run my fingers across the edge of her desk. "And when we bring her home today, we'll teach her about sexism within this school system. So thank you for giving us the opportunity to remind our daughter that life is full of inequities."

Rose brims with pride, and when she catches me staring she doesn't hide the sight. *I love him* is written all over her features.

The vice-principal looks microscopically small.

I also have that affect on people.

Before I leave, I say, "My daughter can use words to express her sentiments, and I'd expect Dalton's faculty to do the same. Next time a teacher physically drags one of my children, you'll see me under different circumstances and with far less passivity."

Rose, beside me, whispers heatedly, "They *what?*"

The vice-principal gapes. "That...we don't tolerate *that.* I promise you."

We have *many* more children left to attend this school. Jane is just the first, but I was prepared for the students and the faculty to *see* them differently.

I even understood that could translate into being *treated* differently. I'd stand in this office with thousands of words to aid them, to help them—to lift them to their feet. I have no doubts in my own ability to protect my children, so I fear nothing.

They should fear me.

The last thing I say to the vice-principal leaves her ashen and mute.

"Only my promises can be trusted," I tell her, "so your words are meaningless to me."

< 23 >

October 2021
EDDIE'S HOUSE
Costa Rica

Daisy Meadows

Eddie is one of Ryke's oldest climbing friends and often travels to Venezuela, Peru, and Chile to scale new rock faces. Whenever Eddie leaves his home for a week or so, he invites Ryke and me to stay at his empty property. A house lodged in skyscraping trees and located in a remote part of Costa Rica—we accept without a moment's pause.

No electricity.

An outhouse.

A well for water.

Our trips here, I always pretend that Ryke and I are stranded in the rainforest together like *Blue Lagoon* or *Swiss Family Robinson*.

This time we have company.

A naked three-year-old presses her itty-bitty fingers to a floor-length window. She gasps with wonder and awe, nose to the glass. I smile wide, knelt behind her as I dry her sopping wet hair. I clasp a cotton towel around the dark brown strands, beads of water rolling along her tanned skin.

Palm fronds pat the window, no blinds or curtains, but Ryke unknowingly captivates our daughter. Right outside, Ryke balances on the deck railing and clutches a rope, one tethered to a tree about ten or fifteen feet from safety. No pool, no lake, just the rainforest to swing towards.

I whisper close to Sulli's little ear, "Do you want to see, Daddy?"

She nods like I offered the world's greatest chocolate bar.

I drop her towel, lifting the softest naked baby in my arms, and nuzzle her nose with a quiet declaration, "I love him too." I unlatch the door. Ryke childproofed every exit the first moment we arrived. We're *high* up in the trees, and we both kept picturing Sulli running off the deck in glee and *falling* to…well, it wouldn't be a happy ending.

As I slip barefoot outside, I keep Sulli tucked against my hip. Ryke turns to us, and I whistle suggestively at his six-foot-three build and dark, dangerous eyes that say, *I fucking see and fucking hear you, Calloway.*

I wag only my right brow.

He almost smiles, but his hard gaze descends to my topless body, breasts exposed, only wearing neon-green cotton panties. He raises his brows at my feet, which are currently very friendly with the grimy deck. "Didn't you just have a fucking bath?"

"I prefer being dirty with you."

Now he smiles.

"Can I touch?" Sulli asks, reaching towards the rope. Her inquisitive green eyes swing between her dad and me. Ryke makes a *come hither* motion with his fingers.

I edge closer, not about to drop our totally clean baby on the deck. Having Sulli around has changed our dynamic more than we even thought.

Little things: we never used the claw-foot tub before. We always took cold showers on the deck together. Now with a toddler in our midst, Ryke spent an hour gathering four pails of water from the well, heating the liquid on the wood-burning stove, and filling up a bath.

Bigger things: I'm not teetering on the railing next to Ryke. Where I would be if I didn't have Sulli in my arms. But I'm not barred from this action either. I swung on the rope yesterday while Ryke had Sulli in *his* arms.

In this gentle, quiet moment, we both let Sulli inspect the rope. We did consider strapping Sulli to Ryke's chest and letting her swing that way, but we decided not to test it after the wind shook the branches and I had trouble returning to the railing.

"What's this fucking called, Sul?" Ryke asks.

"Rope." She hugs a portion to her chest, as though cuddling with her stuffed starfish. "Can I swing? *Pleeeease.*" She peers up at Ryke with big pleading doe eyes. He has yet to say *no* to this innocent, earnest expression.

He mumbles beneath his breath, "Fuck." He rakes his hand through his thick hair.

I sway side-to-side, Sulli swaying with me. Ryke meets my gaze, not uncertain. He *knows* we can't allow her to swing, but he scowls, hating that we have to tell Sullivan *no* to something she might love.

I whisper to him, "Hey, at least she asked." We didn't teach Sulli to ask *is it okay if I do this?* but she does more often than she springs towards things.

"*Pleeease,*" she pleads again, gripping the rope in a toddler stronghold.

I kiss her chubby cheek, struggling to say *no* as much as Ryke, but some events can't be given approval. Regardless, we're here in Costa Rica with a daughter we thought we might never have. No matter what happens, no matter where we go, we're living an *awfully* big adventure.

I begin to smile at Ryke, our eyes never drifting, and I murmur, "The danger of it all."

Towering over me, his dark features break, light streaming through. He messes my hair, the evening sun shining between palm fronds and bathing his bare chest. I watch Ryke carve out this moment, soaking in my features and his daughter's, almost disbelieving that this is his life. That we're all together. That we're here with him.

"Please?" Sulli asks pitifully this time, her brown hair frizzing.

Ryke bends and kisses Sulli's head. "When you're fucking older."

She looks to me for a different answer, but Ryke and I are almost always on the same page when it comes to Sulli. "You're too little to hold on for long, and you'll slide *alllll the way* down." Really, she would fall over twenty-feet, but we try not to instill fear or scare her with talk of *death*.

Sulli frowns. "How old?"

I stretch my free arm out wide. "Really, *really* old."

As though promising us, she says with such conviction, "I'm really, *really* old now."

"Yeah?" Ryke hangs onto the rope, still standing on the railing. He scratches his ankle with his right foot, acting like he's grounded when he's *definitely* not. "How fucking old are you?"

"Seven." She's three.

I mock gasp. "You're seven?"

"I'm old like you and Daddy." Sulli reaches an arm towards Ryke, but sensing the risk, he refuses to take her from my clutch. Thunder rumbles, dark clouds starting to blanket the sky.

"We're all seven then?" I distract Sulli, prying the rope out of her fingers. I let the excess hang off so Ryke can swing. He mouths to me, *bed?*

I feign confusion and mouth, *sex?*

Another change: he would physically push me or maybe playfully kick me if I didn't have Sulli in my arms. He stops himself and just says, "Cute, Calloway."

Birds chirp over the echoing thunder, a resplendent quetzal nest nearby. Sulli spent two hours just oohing and awing over their lime-green tail feathers, gorgeous red breast, and constant chirruping yesterday. I think the noise eases her mind away from the rope too.

She rests her cheek on my chest, twisting a strand of my blonde hair around her finger. "Daddy is eight. You're twenty-somety-two-ey. I'm seven."

I walk backwards to the door, eyeing Ryke all the way. "Did you hear? Our daughter is already seven."

"Fuck that." Ryke grips the rope. "I'm not aging up my three-year-old."

I'm not aging up my three-year-old. It's more than just a declaration. It's how we've lived thus far.

We intake all these moments like they could be our very last. The last time we hold a toddler. The last time she tugs at my hair. The last time she asks us to swing. We take nothing for granted.

She might even be our one-and-only. We agreed not to open the door to surrogacy until Rose is *certain* she's ready, and we're not in any hurry to have another baby.

Rose thinks I'm selfless, but she'd put me before herself in this situation. *I'm your sister*, she'd say, but she doesn't have to make this sacrifice for me. Rose deserves whatever size family she envisions, and I won't restrain her from those dreams.

"Who's three?" Sulli asks.

"You are, silly." I plant a slobbery, playful kiss against her cheek, and she laughs, kicking her feet. I gently shut the door behind me, and then let Sulli down. Coconut patters closer to us, tail wagging.

Coconut *loves* Sullivan as though she's the soul of my happiness. She protects the baby, nudges Sulli's cheek with a wet nose, just until Sulli laughs and hangs onto Coconut's soft white fur.

While we were packing for Costa Rica, Sulli asked, "Is Coconut coming?"

"Do you want Nutty to fucking come along?" Ryke wondered.

Sulli nodded. "She's my best friend."

Sulli kisses the top of Coconut's head, as she's seen me do a thousand times before. The white husky is most content when we're all content, but her ears stay perked and alert. As though keeping us safe is her primary job.

I pat Sulli's bare butt. "Hop onto bed with Coconut." I'll put her in PJs soon. The tiny house is just one room: claw-foot tub, wood-burning stove, wooden bed, little kitchen and four-person round table.

Sulli jumps onto the fluffy white bedding, and she calls after the dog. Coconut follows and lies next to the toddler.

While I clean my feet with a towel, I watch Ryke through the windows. Grasping the rope with only one hand, he steps off the railing. He swings out about fifteen feet, palm fronds brushing his body. I take a large inhale, practically feeling oxygen rush through me as he slices through air.

The rope goes stagnant, and he ascends towards the knot, nearly disappearing in the foliage. Then he shimmies across a thick branch like a monkey bar—until he drops back on the deck.

Crazy.

People attribute that word to me, but it fits Ryke just as much, if not more.

I also lack his incredible upper-body strength, so when I swung yesterday, he had to pull me back to the deck with a broom.

About fifteen minutes later, I finish helping Sulli dress for bed, and I cuddle her beneath an airy white comforter and feather-light pillows. I draw soothing circles along her arm while she scrutinizes a strand of my hair and my features up close.

"Why do people sleep?" Sulli wonders with a soft yawn, fighting slumber that wants to pull her away.

Sleep.

It's been a foe and a friend, and these days, I welcome sleep. I *need* sleep, just as she does. "Because it replenishes your energy. So when you wake up, you're ready to play and go to school—"

She makes a grossed-out face at *school*. We haven't put her in pre-K yet because she recoils at the idea of being stuck inside. *Are there pools? Is there outside? Where will I be all day?*

We told her about recess, but she still thinks school is about *work*. Regardless of whether she wants to go or not, school is a requirement, and she has to go at some point.

She talks hushed, rain starting to patter against the windows. "If I don't sleep, can I skip school?"

I murmur, "No. You'll just be really, *really* tired at school."

Coconut perks as Ryke slips inside, a towel wrapped low around his waist. I steal a second to admire his body, one that sleeps pressed up against me every night. I bet he took a shower outside, but the rain drenched him again.

When he catches me staring, his brows rise at mine, and I mime a howl, a true mating call. He flips me off, a smile playing at his lips, as loving of a *fuck you* as Ryke can go.

I concentrate on talking Sulli to sleep while he pulls on boxer-briefs. "You don't want to sleep?"

Sulli says softly, "I want to stay up with you."

She's scared of missing out. "Sleep is one of the greatest things in the world. Guess why."

Sulli thinks hard, fingers to her lips, then she shakes her head. "Nothing's good about sleeping."

"Yes so," I breathe. "When you sleep, you *dream*. Amazing things happen in dreams, Sulli. You can *fly* and swim forever, and eat all the candy that ever existed. Great, wondrous things happen in your dreams, so every time you shut your eyes, think about all the places you'll go. All the creatures you'll meet."

Sulli's green eyes flit up and down my face. "Will you be in my dreams?"

"Sometimes," I whisper.

"What about Daddy?"

"What about me?" Ryke climbs on the bed, lying on the other side of our daughter. Coconut at our feet. He props his head on his hand and stares down at us.

"She wants to know if you'll be in her dreams."

He must've heard my response because he says, "Sometimes."

Sulli looks thoughtful. Squished between us, she reaches to my cheek and touches my long scar. I sense Ryke watching Sulli inspect me. It's not the first time she's traced the scar, but it's the first time keenness and questioning blinks in her eyes while she outlines the shape.

The only sound is the pitter-patter of rain and our gentle breaths. Sulli then puts her finger to the scar on Ryke's brow. *From the Paris riot.*

Then her little hand falls to his abs, tracking the thick scar between his ribcage, cutting long and veering to one side. *From his transplant surgery.*

Sulli peers to Ryke, then to me, and she whispers, "You need Band-Aids?"

"No," Ryke says with the shake of his head. "These are really fucking old, sweetie."

Seven years have passed since Paris.

Sulli studies my cheek once more. "How'd you get that booboo?" She rolls towards Ryke and points up. "And that booboo? And what's this?" She tenderly skims his transplant scar, not wanting to hurt him.

Ryke stretches his arm around Sulli and me, his palm on my shoulder in comfort. I've thought about what I'd tell her before, but all the words flit away. I look to Ryke for help because I just keep thinking about a two-by-four, nail attached, ripping through my face.

"We were in a fucking accident." His tone is tender, despite cursing. He gestures from my cheek scar to his small brow scar.

Sulli's face scrunches at the word *accident*. "What's that?"

I explain, "It's an unlucky event, but we're better now."

"You were unlucky?"

"Very. But guess what?" I nuzzle close.

"What?" she whispers.

"You've brought us *all* the luck in the world." I kiss her nose. "So there'll be no more accidents."

Sulli sits up and plants her little hand on my cheek. She kisses my scar, like she's seen her dad do before. "Mommy," she says softly. A moment passes as she gathers her thoughts, but we hold gazes, our eyes the same green hue. "You're the most beautiful mermaid in the whole wide sea."

Tears well. I've expressed that sentiment to *her* before. "That's you, Sul."

"No, it's you." Sullivan stares at my scar as if I wouldn't be *me* without it, and then she looks to Ryke for confirmation.

"You're both fucking beautiful." He sits up against the headboard, his knee bent. He messes Sulli's hair until her smile overtakes her face.

I whisper wistfully to Sulli, "Sleep, dream." *Peace.*

Ryke and I pull the covers up to her shoulders. She's not ready to sleep, but we watch her, waiting, and she shuts her eyes this time. I replay everything she said, all her love towards us overwhelming me, and I look up to my husband.

He tucks a piece of Sulli's hair behind her ear, but his hard eyes rest on me.

"I'm alive," I whisper, "for these kinds of moments." In Costa Rica, so long ago, he proclaimed this beneath a waterfall.

You're alive, Daisy Calloway, for these kinds of moments.

Ryke pinches his eyes for a second, and when he drops his hand, emotion surfacing, his overcome smile fills me whole. I rub my face, my own tearful smile bursting through. I've never been so happy. I've never loved this much, but my bones vibrate with *life*—with every morsel of breath we breathe. With all the joy we scream.

I encapsulate this quiet day, this time, this second, tucking it gently away for safekeeping. I never want to lose this feeling, but if it happens to wane, I'll remember that I can meet it all again. As long as I'm living. *Just wait.*

❀ ❀ ❀

SULLIVAN FINALLY FALLS ASLEEP, and Ryke and I slide off the bed, careful not to wake our daughter. I tiptoe past Coconut, and Ryke gestures with his head to the door. I follow, both of us quietly exiting and latching the door shut so Sulli can't leave.

Rain still drizzles. Ryke sets his palm on my lower back and leads me to a wooden picnic table, dry because of a roof overhang on the deck. The trek seems slow with anticipation, tension winding between us in the silence. I grow hot as his gaze drips down the length of my body, mostly pinned to my constantly moving hands. I twist the elastic band of my panties.

I eat him up just as hungrily, eyes grazing his abs and the bulge in his boxer-briefs.

Sulli is almost always with us, so sneaking in sex here and there has become an expedition. Ryke has a knack for pulling me into the shower with him. I have a knack for pulling him into the pantry, right up against the chocolate syrup and granola cereal boxes.

Ryke *loves* having sex outdoors, so whenever I'm feeling up to it and the timing's right, we just *go*. I watch him watch me, and he hooks his finger in my panties, staring down. Lips close. The back of my legs hits the side of the picnic table, stopping. We attack one another at the same time, my hands all over his shoulders, his ribs, along his phoenix tattoo, down his biceps.

He kisses me, breaking apart my lips with his tongue, wrestling, never choking. Skillful, natural movements that latch my body to his and his body to mine.

Ryke cups my ass beneath my panties, his other hand rising up to my breast. He kneads, his thumb flicking my hardened nipple. My high-pitched cry tingles against his lips. He's strong like stone, tall like every mountain, and dark like lone wolves.

The way his hands explore my body, I feel *loved*. Cared for. Like every inch is precious to him. Like he'd never do me harm, never take advantage, and always, *always* listen to what my body says. What *I* say.

Ryke tugs off my panties, and I step out. I run my hands over his unshaven jaw, through his thick hair, and he nuzzles my face up until I lift my lips, able to kiss him stronger, heartier. His muscles flex against me, and I can't help but smile.

I pull our lips apart, just enough to whisper, "Can I watch you?"

Ryke's arousal darkens his features even more, which makes my insides flutter. *The thrill of it all.*

He's so turned on, the outline of his erection visible in his boxer-briefs.

He cups my heat, so lightly, as though protecting me from the elements. His rough jaw skims mine, his lips veering to my ear as he whispers, "You want to watch me touch myself, Calloway? Is that what you fucking want?"

My heart pounds *hard*. "Definitely, yes."

His fingers skim my clit, and I shudder. He lets go and then climbs onto the picnic table. There are *so* many windows in the tiny house. No matter where we go on the deck, the bed is in view. *She's sleeping*, I just keep telling myself. I do *not* want Sullivan to see us.

I take a few steps backwards, towards the railing. Rain wets my hair and rolls down my arms and stomach. Ryke rests his soles on the bench, his ass on the actual table, and he removes his boxer-briefs. My breath shallows, and I dazedly lean against the railing, my body quivering just at the sight.

I'm aroused today, my blood pumping hot.

Ryke notices, but he listens to my request. He lets me watch him spit in his palm and then grasp his shaft. He rests his other hand on the table, slightly leaned backwards too. He masturbates, up-and-down, up-and-down, his eyes always on me.

I touch myself, my hands to my breasts, then lower.

His head tilts back. "Fuck," he grunts. Then he rocks forward, his hand moving faster along his cock. My pulse speeds, sweat building faster than the rain can wash away.

His gaze flits from his erection to me. "Come here, sweetheart."

My hands fall to my sides, and I approach him. He knows how to get me off better than sometimes I even do. Swiftly, he uses both of his hands to clutch my hips and he lifts me to the table. I'm standing. He pushes on the small of my back until I'm in line with his head. While he's sitting at a slight angle, he has the perfect height to kiss me between the legs.

The sensation nearly buckles my knees. I clutch his hair, and he clutches my ass, his tongue doing *wonders* to me. I cry, open-mouthed and out of breath. I watch how his right hand returns to his cock. *Oh God.*

His tongue does something—I cry so loud that I cover my mouth with my hand. *Holy shit.*

"I can't…" I'm blinded. *Ahhhh…oh my God!!*

One of the faster times that I've come, he effortlessly changes positions, transitioning me to my back on the table. Before I even blink. Before I've even descended from this mountain. His fingers stroke my heat, building me. *Building me.*

I buck up, legs wrestling beneath him. He has one knee on the table, hovered above me, and he jacks off. *Oh…* I can't close my mouth.

I stare him up and down, dying in pleasure. "Ryke," I cry. His masculinity thunders above me, and I'd watch this beautiful storm morning, noon, and night.

Dear God, give him to me always.

I ache for him to fill me, and my back keeps arching to reciprocate all the nerve-splitting sensations. I rake my nails down his arms. He teases my clit.

I light up, eyes rolling back. *Fuck. Fuck.*

"Dais," he groans, his ass flexing as he rocks forward, craving to be inside me. He spits in his palm again, no lube. We didn't bring out lube.

"Am I wet?" I ask in a short breath, practically panting. I can't catch my breath like him. My shoulders grind into the stiff wooden table.

"Yeah. Don't fucking worry about that, Dais." I see his glistening fingers, even though he never put them inside of me. He rubs his erection only two times more, not coming yet. Then he lifts me in his arms, setting me on the deck, and he kisses me with such hunger that my body pulls into his. I walk backwards while he walks forwards.

My spine hits the railing.

He hikes one of my legs around his waist, his cock pressed against me. I dizzy, and he pauses for a moment so I can take a few strong inhales. He watches me closely, his brows rising at me, my own eyes glazed.

"Holy..." *shit.* I pant.

Rain pelts his shoulders and soaks his hair. "How do those fucking orgasms feel, Calloway?"

I smile. "Very, *very* euphoric." He's still the only one who can make me come, and I'd *never* try with anyone else. "Tell my husband thanks?"

His body up against mine, he says, "I'd rather give you another one and push my fucking cock inside of you."

Oh my God.

I pulse, but my gaze drifts towards the window. If Sulli wakes up, she'd see his ass and one of my legs wrapped around him.

"Hey," Ryke says lowly, his hand suddenly on my cheek. His brows furrow. "What's fucking wrong?"

I hold onto his waist. "Sulli...windows..."

"Don't fucking think about it."

I hope that his body will distract me, but not even the constant sight of his erection keeps me from peeking over his shoulder. Towards the window.

Ryke spins me around, and I clutch the railing while he stands behind me. He spreads my legs open a little wider with his foot. We don't fuck in this position often, so he has to help angle me. Pulling my hips backwards, stretching out my torso so I'm not standing straight up.

I crane my neck over my shoulder, but only to look at him. Ryke pushes his erection right up against my opening, and I tighten in expectancy, body thrumming.

He's about to fuck me from behind, *not* in the ass. A moan catches my throat even before he pushes in, our gazes locking. I find the breath to say, "What an animal, that Ryke Meadows."

Ryke literally has my hips in his grasp, his expression just a thousand times *I'm going to fuck you, sweetheart.*

This primal position builds heat all around us, though I have a difficult time watching us unless he videotapes the act. Which we don't do anymore.

I strain my neck as much as possible, wanting to see. He slowly, inch-by-inch, fills me with his cock. I gasp, a cry stuck. I grip the railing harder, and my head falls. He thrusts against my ass, the friction wild. I tremble, and not long, he brings me up, clasping my face. He kisses me while he fucks me from behind.

I can barely stand straight, light bursting in my brain.

Fifteen minutes in, the fullness brushes against every nerve. I'm melted in his arms, and he holds me against his chest and drives deeper. I cry and cry, all sounds of pleasure, and he grunts into my neck, "Fuck...Dais. *Fuck.*"

And then…

Knock. Knock.

"Daddy! Mommy!"

Knock Knock.

I freeze, just hitting a climax that sputters out faster than the other two. I glance over my shoulder, our three-year-old at the door with her stuffed starfish, lightly rapping the door. She stares *right at us.*

"Ryke…" I have no clue what to do. Sulli can see his naked body up against mine like we're two animals mating on National Geographic.

Ryke is already looking over his shoulder, then back to me. "Hey, she won't remember any of this, Calloway. Fucking relax."

I must look horrified.

He tries to cheer me up by messing my hair, but it's too damp to ruffle. I just fixate on his words: *she won't remember any of this.* She's too young. It eases my shoulders. Ryke gently pulls out of me, and I relocate the rest of my senses.

"I'll see what she wants."

Before I go, Ryke kisses my lips and asks, "You feel okay?"

He means physically after sex. "I just had five million orgasms. I think I'm better than okay."

"Five fucking million?"

"I know you're jealous of my husband, but he's just *that* good at sex." I wag my brows, migrating away from him, and he looks like all he wants is to pull me back into his arms.

I slip into the house and crouch down to Sulli, Ryke pulling on his boxer-briefs much farther away from us. "Hey there. Why aren't you in bed?"

She rubs her tired eyes with a fist. "I saw that you were gone, and… and I got scared." She peeks curiously behind me. "What were you and Daddy…" She yawns and forgets *that* question. I could find a way to answer, but I'm glad I don't have to.

I nudge her arm with mine. "You know who will *always* protect you, even while you're sleeping, even when Daddy and I aren't around?"

"Who?" she asks.

"Coconut."

Sulli spins around and stands on her tiptoes, peering up at the white husky. She lies content at the foot of the bed, observing us, constantly alert, a smile in her big blue eyes as though to say *I love you all too.*

Without another word, Sulli braves this foreign place and crawls back into bed, hanging onto the familiar animal. Coconut welcomes her with a lick to the cheek.

I know life is different with a baby. The little things and the bigger things, but I smile at every new moment, every crazy second. I wouldn't trade a thing.

{ 24 }

October 2021

DALTON ELEMENTARY
Philadelphia

LOREN HALE

Career Day.

Moffy needed to bring one of us to school, just to speak about our job field in front of his classmates and other parents. In prep school, I plagiarized papers, refused to do presentations (even if they were worth half of my grade), and I cheated on exams by slipping answers up the sleeve of my shirt.

I'm not exactly the person you want to show off to your teacher or the person you want *speaking* in a room full of children. Lily and public speaking—they don't go well together either. She trips over her words and starts sweating.

To see who'd attend Career Day, we did the mature thing and played rock-paper-scissors.

I lost.

So I'm sitting in the tiniest plastic chair, a line of them pushed against the wall for parents. We all wait our turn.

If you told me at twenty—ten goddamn years ago—that I'd be here, today, giving a speech to my six-year-old's kindergarten class, I'd have laughed at you. Then I would've reminded you that I'd *never* have a child and subject them to a life of pain and misery.

To a life with me.

My old self is sitting apathetically in the back of the classroom, wishing this day would end. While I sit up at the front and wish today would last just a little longer.

Paper ghosts dangle from the ceiling. Painted pumpkins taped to the windows. A bowl of candy corn sits on the teacher's desk. It just reminds me that my thirtieth birthday and Halloween will be here soon.

I'm sandwiched between a doctor in blue scrubs and a stockbroker in a suit. I wear jeans and a black V-neck shirt. This might be a private school, all the parents upper-class, but it's clear that I'm the odd one out.

It has nothing to do with my goddamn clothes and everything to do with being famous. They've seen my face on magazines, television, and the internet.

I hold onto the fact that the children might not recognize me. Unless their parents let them on the internet without parental controls. Or watch reality TV—which would be doubtful. Our docu-series is uncensored on cable.

Ryke is no longer bleeped every four words.

I scan the desks. Two kids stare at me hardcore. Either they haven't been taught it's rude or they don't give a shit. Maybe their parents subscribe to tabloids and they've seen my face in the pages.

I flash the driest half-smile, my features cutting like blades with that one action.

Their eyes bulge and they sink lower in their chairs.

Don't pick on my kid, I'm thinking. He has to deal with enough, and I know what it feels like to have guys running after you in the hallways.

I feel the heat of a parent's glare beside me. They've all been sizing me up and down since I walked in the goddamn room. For Christ's sake, they've been watching *me* instead of the parent who speaks. I'm more uncomfortable because these aren't strangers.

They're the parents of Moffy's peers, maybe even his friends.

I'll never say this to Rose…but I wish she could be here. She's stuck in another room down the hall. There are only four kindergarten classes at Dalton, and Jane and Moffy were unluckily split up.

"So when you're older and you need your teeth nice and straight," an orthodontist explains, "you'll come to me." He smiles wide, showing off his pearly whites. Everyone claps, and my nerves shift.

"Thank you, Dr. Ellis. That was very informative." The teacher checks her list.

I fear mostly that I'll do or say something to worsen Moffy's situation. With Jonathan Hale as my dad, I learned to antagonize the people that hurt me, some that even tried to help me. Cut them up. Spit them out. I'd rather Moffy try to make friends than enemies, and I'm an influence on which way he goes.

I get it.

I crack some of my knuckles, and my nervous energy piles up at the teacher's incoming words.

"Next is Maximoff's father. Everyone give Mr. Hale a nice welcome." She claps and the kindergarteners follow suit.

I slowly rise.

Moffy is already out of his chair before the teacher even says, "Maximoff, come and introduce your father to the class." He wears a charcoal gray Sorin-X shirt and a Rylin Water's wristband, all superheroes from *The Fourth Degree*.

As soon as he stops by my side, his bright face smothers every dark emotion inside of me. He has the biggest overpowering smile, three of his top teeth missing, and his eyes shine with some sort of pride. Of me. *Jesus.* My son is proud of me.

I'm not sure what for, but it almost rocks me back.

"This is my daddy." Moffy motions to me with his thumb. "He's got *two* jobs." He holds up two fingers. "He owns Hale Co. and Halway Comics. The baby stuff is alright but the comics are soooo cool, and my mommy owns this café and comic book store where all the comics go. She's awesome."

Lily is going to freak out when I tell her this. That just made today worth every goddamn thing.

Moffy tilts his head up to me. "Alright, Daddy, it's your turn."

He hugs my side, I squeeze back, and then he returns to his seat.

Tone down your voice. It's all I think right now.

Tone down my edged, *I'm-going-to-kill-you* voice. So I clear my throat once before I smile—a half-smile. Great.

I look to Moffy, and his lively smile never vanishes.

I can do this.

"Like Moffy said," I tell the class, "the baby stuff is alright. The really neat thing is working with comics for a living." My voice is harsh but not terrible. *I can do this.* "For my job, artists and writers submit comics they want to see in print. I have to choose which ones my publishing company will pick up. From there, I have a team that specializes in marketing, editing, design and merchandise. Like making action figures and posters."

A little girl with brown pigtails raises her hand.

I point at her. "What's up?"

"Do you have any girl superheroes?" she wonders.

"We do." I nod. "In *The Fourth Degree* comics, there's Tilly Stayzor, a fan favorite, but my personal favorite is Rylin Waters. She has the power of—"

"Electricity!" a little redheaded boy exclaims. He leans towards the girl. "Ohmygosh, it's so cool. You need to see it, Mindy. She's on *The Fourth Degree: You and Me* cartoon!"

The first season just aired.

"He's right," I say. "Rylin Waters can manipulate electricity, but if she pushes her powers too far, she can also short-circuit and lose her memory." I gesture to Moffy who has the bag of action figures.

He climbs out of his chair and sets Rylin Waters on Mindy's desk.

"We brought some action figures for everyone from the line. That's Rylin," I tell the little girl. She's awed for a moment, and then I help Moffy pass out the rest.

"So that's about it," I tell the class. "I get to play with toys all day."

Another hand in the air. I hold my breath for a second, always expecting a bomb to drop, but I nod for them to speak.

"What about your other job?" the redhead asks. "Hale Co.? What's that?"

"It's a company that produces baby products. If you have baby oil or diapers or pacifiers in your home and notice an HC on the label, that's Hale Co."

Another hand. *Christ.* "What do you do there?"

"I'm the CEO," I say. "Which means, I run the entire company."

Lots of child-like *ooohs* while the parent section is far from impressed. I'm not looking for their approval, but the guy that I'd been sitting next to—the stockbroker—yeah, he rolls his eyes.

"Like I said," I proclaim, "the comics are more fun."

"Aren't you an actor?" a blonde girl asks. "I've seen you on my TV."

"It's not acting," Moffy cuts in. "It's *real*."

"What Moffy said." I turn to the teacher, hoping she'll end this now. *Princesses of Philly* was so fucking long ago, and to this day, networks still air reruns, which blows my mind. We didn't even make it to the end of the season. I can name a hundred better television shows to play on loop.

The teacher must take note of my sharpened glare. "Class, let's give Mr. Hale a round of applause." She thanks me while the kindergarteners clap again.

I return to my seat, my heart thrashing in my ribcage. My nerves just catch back up with me, even though it ended.

The stockbroker leans in towards me and whispers, "You did a great job. Didn't look conceited or anything."

His sarcasm is too thick to ignore.

But I almost laugh. Not dryly. A real fucking laugh. Because I've never been called conceited. Not one day in my life. Entitled, yeah. Arrogant, pompous—no.

This might be one of the few times I don't seek out the last word. I don't even want it. Moffy chats softly with a girl beside him. Still talking about my presentation, he points towards me and grins from ear-to-ear.

I smile back.

He's the *only* one I ever needed to impress.

[25]

November 2021
MADAME DAPHNE'S SCHOOL OF BALLET
New York City

Connor Cobalt

"Now for the butterfly," the ballet teacher says, seated on the floor among the circle of young children.

They try to imitate Madame Daphne: feet together, heel-to-heel. The six-year-olds have an easier time, but the five and four-year-olds seem to struggle.

I've already watched them do the leapfrog and spread peanut butter and jelly with their feet. Metaphorical peanut butter and jelly, obviously. The childish names for these moves grate on me. I understand that it's pre-ballet, but I'd rather Madame Daphne use the correct terminology: dégagé, tendu, rond de jambe.

It might take them longer to comprehend the action with the word, but it's better than teaching them how to do the *peanut butter and jelly*.

Jane is the only six-year-old with her feet not pressed together. She spreads out her legs, her pastel turquoise tutu less dainty than the other girls. Jane picked it out, content with her lack of conformity. Much more than Beckett.

Just four, he tries to be precise in his foot placement, fixated on the instructor and her movements.

Jane has already attempted two somersaults of her own fruition. Beckett shrunk when the instructor scolded her the second time, as though he was in trouble by extension of his sister. He wasn't, but each sibling affects the other in varying degrees.

"She's going to get in trouble again," Charlie tells me, his words very clear for four, but his tone is clipped. Almost deadpanned. He's seated beside me on the long row of chairs, mostly filled with mothers.

I study Charlie and his frustrated but concentrated gaze. I shared that familiar look as a child. *Maddened.* I was maddened with, at, and by the world. His IQ is just shy of mine, and the more acutely aware he becomes of his surroundings, of *people*, of intentions and meanings and humanity, I draw closer to him.

There will be a breakdown.

I'm prepared for one with Charlie. I'm not sure when it will happen, but it will come.

My phone buzzes. I check the text.

Iron Man. Batman. Thor. – **Rose**

The corners of my mouth rise at the Fuck, Marry, Kill question. I'm able to concentrate on both the class and the message without missing a moment.

I text: Are you asking for Lily or for yourself?

Rose and Lily are eating lunch at our house with the rest of the children while Ryke, Daisy, Sullivan, and Lo go hiking for the day. Ryke has an expensive backpack-carrier for Sullivan since she'd never be able to hike at her age.

Both, but it doesn't go against our rules. You're still required to answer, and answer truthfully, Richard. — Rose

"This is stupid," Charlie says softly, but his focus is on his twin brother and his older sister. He can see, as well as I do, how nervous Beckett becomes by Jane disregarding the instructed moves in favor of her own.

"He's okay, Charlie," I whisper.

Charlie crosses his arms and sinks in his chair.

Rose and I agreed that our children could choose their hobbies, even "trial runs" to potentially see what they liked. If they're in the hobby or sport for longer than a couple weeks, they have to provide a good reason for quitting. We want our children to finish tasks, not take an easy way out. With their level of privilege, this is extremely important to us.

Today is just the first day of pre-ballet class, and only Jane and Beckett hopped on the idea. Charlie declined but said he wanted to watch, not with the hope of eventually joining. I think he came to support his twin brother.

I find time to text Rose a response.

Marry. Fuck. Kill.

Marry Iron Man. Fuck Batman. Kill Thor.

Thor is ridiculous, and I don't mean the Norse mythology. I mean the one played by an actor on a movie screen.

Rose is quick.

Of course you would marry Iron Man. He's as egotistical as you are. — Rose

Another text.

Lily said you're Batman, so you just fucked yourself, Richard. — Rose

I rub my lips, my grin escalating tenfold. I reply: I have good taste.

I have better taste — Rose

I type fast. You did choose me, so I think we can agree that we both have equally great taste when it comes to sex.

A pause before my phone buzzes.

Fine. We're equals. It's cemented. — Rose

Out of the corner of my eye, I notice Jane holding her feet and rocking.

"There she goes," Charlie narrates.

Sure enough, Jane tumbles over her head and onto her bottom, a laugh widening her smile.

"Jane!" Madame Daphne scolds. "This isn't gymnastics. We're doing butterflies right now." She snaps her fingers. "Back in the circle."

Slowly, Jane scoots beside her brother. Beckett remains entirely rigid, certain pieces of his hair curlier, others just a little wavy, and he's only one of two boys in the class. When we arrived, he never batted an eye at the fact.

Beckett suddenly looks to Charlie.

Charlie looks to me.

If they both choose ballet again, we'll put Beckett in a different class from Jane. I want him to feel comfortable, but sometimes that comes from within.

"Il va bien," I tell Charlie. *He's fine.*

Beckett is enjoying the class, despite his sister's nonchalance. Twice, he asked Madame Daphne, "Like this?" Just to ensure he's doing the move correctly. When she praises his technique, he smiles.

Charlie lets out a puff of breath and scans the ballet room filled with floor-length mirrors and windows that overlook Manhattan.

My phone vibrates in my palm again.

I did something. — Rose

I stiffen.

I have to commit to this. I promised I would. — Rose

I'm as intrigued as I am confused. *Details, darling.* I press send.

Charlie's demeanor suddenly changes beside me. He straightens and scoots closer to my chair. "Daddy…" His voice spikes just enough for me to catch his worry. My phone buzzes, but I can't respond or look at the text.

I immediately follow his gaze to one of the mirrors. In the reflection, a woman cups her phone like she's recording, but she's not angled on the circle of children. The lens is pointed towards the mirror, directly at my reflection and Charlie's.

I'm tall enough that I can see over each head of every woman. I stare directly at the one with a brunette bob and pearl earrings. Only four chairs away. She notices quickly and drops her phone to her lap. When she senses my gaze still on her, she swivels her head. "What?"

I don't know if she plans to profit off us either financially or by social media notoriety or simply to just show her friends and family the footage. I have an issue, mostly, with the fact that my children haven't consented to being filmed.

"Do you mind if my security team looks at your video footage before you leave?" My tone is extremely casual. I even offer a smile. "It's just precaution. They won't bite." *They will delete anything involving Charlie.*

"Sure. Would I be able to get a picture with you before you leave?"

"Just of me, yes."

She tries to relax her giddy smile before facing the children.

I text a member of my security team who waits outside with a few bodyguards, and I watch Charlie close his eyes in boredom.

I rub his shoulders and scroll through my missed messages.

I gave Lo permission to name our baby. (Only the first name, of course.) – Rose

I'm actually surprised, so much so that my grin overtakes my face.

He wrote down the name and gave it to Lily in an envelope. I can't take back this promise. I'm about to open the envelope. I swear if he named him "Loren" I will stab Lo in the eye. – Rose

She included "knife" emoticons. I have to wait for her next text, but I think about how she said "he named *him*"—as in a boy.

We asked to see the gender of our baby this time. This will be our sixth child, and even I hoped for a girl. Not because I don't want any more children. I do want more, but I know what it would mean to Ryke and Daisy for *them* to have another.

They're both too selfless to ask about surrogacy. They're both too kind to press Rose about the option. They only warmed up to the idea when they thought Rose might have a girl.

Then we all learned that there will be another Cobalt boy.

And they slammed the door shut to surrogacy faster and more forceful than I even expected.

Here I was *wishing* for an outcome for someone else. I wished my family ended so that theirs could grow. I rarely wish for anyone but me, and my wish didn't come true.

Rose is still adamant about trying surrogacy, but we're going to have a harder time convincing Ryke and Daisy now. Ryke is known to be stubborn. It's like dragging a sitting dog by the leash. I'm not entirely sure he'll budge.

I only worry about Rose's health, but if she's okay, if the doctors say *yes,* then I don't see a reason not to try.

My phone vibrates. Rose sent a picture of the note in Lo's handwriting:

Ben
* Named for Ben Obi-Wan Kenobi who mentors Luke Skywalker
* He reminds me of Connor
* I could've made him Obi-Wan, Queen Rose, so put away your talons
* This means a lot, so. . .thanks

Ben.
My grin can't be restrained at this point.
Another vibration.

He can live another day. — Rose

She loves the name too.

I never thought my choices would contain so much *feeling* but with each middle name, I only see fractions of logic. *This name is melodically pleasant.* And so on. And so forth. Most, I chose out of nostalgia, out of something heartfelt and visceral that can't be described with numbers or bare facts.

I choose Pirrip, as in Philip Pirrip, from *Great Expectations* by Charles Dickens.

I choose Pirrip as Ben's middle name because I saw Rose reading that very novel when we were sixteen. She won't remember because she never saw me. I passed her in the conference room lobby during Model UN. She sat straight as a board on the edge of the hotel's lobby fountain, the book opened on her lap.

I wanted to stop and talk to her, but I was with three Faust boys. We pushed onward, and my head turned.

I had never looked back in that way before, but for the very first time, I did. I looked back, and I only looked back at her.

2022

"I spread wildfires
everywhere I go.
It's a symptomatic quality
of being me."

- Rose Calloway Cobalt, We Are Calloway

(Season 4 Episode 09 — Nerd Stars & Raisins)

Connor & Rose Cobalt welcome the birth of their baby boy

BEN PIRRIP COBALT

March 29th, 2022

{ 26 }

June 2022
THE HALE HOUSE
Philadelphia

LOREN HALE

Beneath my champagne-colored comforter and red sheets, I grasp Lily's wiry frame to my hard body. On our sides. Coated in sweat. Sheets stick to us from last night's four-hour fuck. Now morning, we kiss one another desperately. Urgently.

Our legs tangle. Starved for one another, I part Lily's lips with mine. I pull her *closer* before she mumbles out the word. Her legs vibrate against me—*Christ*. My blood heats, and I deepen the kiss, my tongue slipping against hers.

She clings to my body like she needs to burrow further into my fucking soul. I'm lit up. Our skin-on-skin might as well be sparkplug-to-battery. Every second Lily shakes against me, my cock *begs* to fill her silent request.

Inside me.

Inside me.

I can practically hear her. I kiss her raw lips. *I'll take care of you, love.*

No one understands her sex addiction better than Lily and me. We fucked all last night because we wanted to. Not because she spiraled out of control and fed into compulsions. Not because she needed to medicate stress with sex.

Because she's reached this strong place where she can mentally stop before fixating on orgasm after orgasm. Because this isn't an everyday expectation or *need.*

It's a want.

A goddamn head-splitting, mind-blowing *want.*

I have Lily tucked against my chest, her leg hiked around my waist. I clutch the back of her head and kiss her even more fully. She trembles again.

Jesus Christ. I harden against her body, and she writhes. My muscles coil, taut and searing. Our lips break apart for the first time. My forehead on hers, desire swims in her big green eyes, and my sharp gaze bores through Lily.

Inside me. Inside me. I see the words all over her adorable fucking face.

"You want something, love?" I tease, our lips brushing as I speak.

"Closer," she begs in a soft whine that grips my cock. Blood rushes out of my head, dizzied.

Still lying side-by-side, I slowly push my erection inside of Lily. She inhales, and her head begins to tilt backwards as she mentally, physically, and emotionally succumbs to this insane pleasure. No trouble getting off.

I thrust with a staggered, unpredictable rhythm that leaves Lily incapacitated. I fuck my best friend who gives herself to me with the simple request of *make me feel good.*

No problem, Lil.

Lips a breath apart, I close the distance, kissing her deep before rolling on top. I stretch her right leg over my shoulder, the other around my waist. I go from quick, deep thrusts to suddenly short and slow.

She lets out a noise that sounds close to a whimper. "Closer."

I push so far inside of Lily and just stop.

She quivers, pulsating against my dick. *Goddammit.* I lean forward, one of my elbows on the mattress. I breathe heavily, and my eyes and hand rake her body. I thumb her hardened nipple before descending to her abdomen and splay my palm on the tiniest bump, almost unnoticeable.

Lily is about eleven-weeks pregnant.

We decided to start trying for another baby at the beginning of the year. We knew we could handle it, and we both wanted another. It took some months, but we're thankful it happened.

I shift my hand lower and lower, and then I rub her clit.

Her back arches with a sudden gasp. I put my hand on her cheek, holding her head upright. I grind against Lily, my blood blazing. She shudders at the movement again.

Her eyes flutter closed.

"Lily Hale," I whisper.

She forces her eyes open, but she's gone. Lost. Sex is on another plane of existence. Her heartbeat races against mine. She clenches around my cock.

A groan scratches my throat. "Goddammit," I curse, my jaw unhinging then locked tight. I grit my teeth hard, my eyes rolling.

Goddammit. My nerves are on fire. I toss the comforter over us, heat gathering. The smell of Lil almost rams me towards a climax. I almost just come right there. My muscles contract.

I hold her round face while I rock faster and harder.

Just now, the door clicks open. "Daddy, Mommy, can I go swimming please, please, *please?*"

"Moffy!" I yell, pissed. Lily and I are entirely beneath the covers, so I'm not sure what he can see. This is the first time he's walked in on us *while* we're having sex.

Lily blinks over and over, her cute come-face morphing into horror.

"What are you doing under there?" Moffy asks, walking closer.

Before she rips off my dick, I pull out and then climb off my wife. I just peek my head from the comforter. My ice cold glare shrinks my son backwards. He's already in orange swim trunks, goggles around his neck.

He'll be seven in a month. He *knows* to knock.

"Moffy," I say sharply. "How many times have we told you to knock before you enter someone's room?"

His chin quivers. "I...I was just asking a question. I didn't think you'd be mad."

My heart stings, but he *has* to listen to us. If he thinks there's no punishment at the end of this, then he'll do it again. And next time, we may not be under the goddamn covers.

"Go wait in the hallway." My voice is like shrapnel. "Close the door on your way out."

Moffy retreats, worry sparking in his green eyes. Because I usually tell him to try again and knock this time. Once the door clicks closed, I lift up the covers. Lily lies on her stomach towards the other side of the bed. Right near the edge.

Like she planned to reach for her clothes on the floor. Something kept her from diving over. Probably sex. The thought. The want. Still inside of her. She can't even *speak* right now.

I'm goddamn hard, ready to burst. I don't waste time. I come up behind Lily while she's flat on her stomach, and I raise her hips slightly and slide inside.

Surprise and want jolts her, and she looks back at me, lips parted. Heady and *gone* again. Pressure squeezes my cock, and my chest rises and falls as quickly as I thrust. I grip the crook of her hip and her tiny ass. Friction builds, and I end this faster than I ever would. My pace like lightning.

She comes with a muffled cry into the mattress.

I choke on a groan, and I don't linger inside of Lily. I pull out, find a pair of boxer-briefs and black sweat pants. I tug both on. Then I turn to Lily and wipe the sweaty hair off her forehead. She's still making sense of where she is while sluggishly fighting with the armholes of her baggy shirt.

"I'm going to go deal with our kid," I tell her.

She finds the energy to kneel and tries to stick her head in her shirt. "It's…not his fault, Lo."

I lower my voice so Moffy can't overhear us. "It *is* his fault. He knows better. We've told him a million goddamn times."

She fits her head in and pulls the black shirt (my shirt) down. "We shouldn't have had sex—"

"*We're* the parents." I point at my chest. "I'm allowed to fuck my wife. You're allowed to fuck me and not feel guilty about it." For Christ's sake, we were doing so well for a minute there. It's all circular. Addiction. Shame.

Lily hesitates, doubtful and uncertain.

I clasp her face between my hands and say strongly, "I would've slept with you this morning, even if you weren't an addict. Would you still feel guilty if he walked in then?"

She thinks for a second. "Yes…because he should always come before sex." She cringes at the word *come*. "Not like that. Notlikethat."

I comb her hair back again. "It's *not* about sex. It's about the fact that he didn't listen to us."

Her brows crinkle, not seeing this from the same lens as me. "It *is* about sex."

I let go of her and step back. I lick my lips, thinking. I can't see away around this, so I make up my mind. "I'm grounding him."

Lily springs from the bed, her black shirt falling to her thighs. "Don't, Lo!"

I'm already walking to the door, and she tries to drag me backwards by the waist, but I end up dragging her forwards. When I reach the door, I spin around on Lily.

She crosses her arms, her seriousness tensing the room and me.

I have my hand on the knob. "I'm doing this, Lil."

"Then we're in a fight." She nods resolutely.

My stomach twists. I can't remember the last time we fought. "Lily…"

Tears well in her eyes. "I don't want to punish him for this."

"We have to."

She shakes her head repeatedly. "We'll lock the door next time."

"It doesn't change the fact that he didn't listen to us." Our kids can't walk all over us. Not when there are things in *our* lives that are so goddamn dangerous.

Alcohol. I will slam my foot down on the idea, on the concept, on the cold reality. They won't be able to say, *But Dad, the kid next-door drinks; can I have just one beer?*

No.

No. I'm not a pushover, and they have to see the threat of disobeying us. They have to think in the back of their mind, *my parents will ground me for this.* Maybe then, they'll hesitate enough to stop.

Lily shakes her head one more time.

I swallow hard. "I guess we're in a fight." Every word is a punch in the gut. I open the door and go outside. Moffy at least waited in the hallway like I asked. He sits by his bedroom door, snapping the elastic of his goggles. As soon as he sees me, he picks himself up.

"I won't ever do it again," Moffy says quickly. "Can I just go swimming? Please?"

It's summer, no school for our children, and a bunch of us have to meet up with Garrison and my sister around noon. While we do that, the plan is to bring all the kids to the Cobalt's for a "painting party" thing. Cobalt Inc.'s subsidiary company, ColorPalace, overproduced their neon line of finger-paints. Great for our kids who can now play with the extras, but shit for Cobalt Inc.

I tower above his pleading eyes. I don't want him to feel powerless. Like I can dictate which way he turns and where he goes. I don't want to be my father. I rebelled against *every* demand he cast towards me. I hated it. I hated all of it, and I can't even imagine a world where I do that to Moffy. Where he feels so emotionally trapped that his solution is to shit on everything.

But I can't let him live without boundaries. I had that too. I drank in excess at eleven. I stayed out late. I made excuses and lies.

There has to be a balance between being overbearing and being too lenient.

I squat down to him. "What'd you do wrong?" I start out.

He holds my gaze better than adults can, but his voice is meek. "I didn't knock."

"When you do something wrong," I begin, watching his voice flood with sadness, "you have to be grounded."

Moffy blinks back tears. "Like timeout?"

"Kind of, but it lasts much longer."

"Nooo." His chin quakes again.

My chest caves. "You can still paint today with your cousins and sister, but for two days, no swimming, no cartoons, no comic books—"

Moffy bursts into tears. "Mommy!" he wails and tries to race to my bedroom, but I grab onto his shoulders and spin him towards me. "I want Mommy!" He rubs his cheeks with his fists and hiccups.

I have fifteen arrows in my heart, and I have to keep shooting more right in. "She knows you're getting grounded, bud."

He pushes off me and sobs like I've sentenced him to death.

"It's only two days, Moffy."

And then he cries, "I hate you!"

My eyes burn. *I hate you* rings in my ears. "You can hate me for two days, Maximoff, but I'll love you for a thousand more." I wipe his tears with my thumb, and he sniffs, calming down for a minute. "It may seem unfair, but we're your parents—and if there's anyone in this world you need to listen to and trust, who will always have your back, it's *us*. We just need you to respect us when we tell you something.

The same way that we respect you when you ask us questions. What do we do?"

He thinks for a moment. Then he says softly, "You listen to me, and you always answer back." He rubs his nose with his arm. "What if Luna watches cartoons? Can I watch with her?"

"No. That's not how being grounded works."

Moffy cries again, "Can I see Mommy?"

"In a minute." I stand back up and tell him he can go eat cereal before we leave for his aunt and uncle's place. He trudges away, still in tears.

I slip into my bedroom, the mattress empty, and the shower pipes groan in the walls. When I enter the bathroom, Lily steps into the shower. Our eyes meet for a second. Hers are bloodshot like she's been crying more.

She hesitates about opening the misted door wider for me or shutting it closed.

"Are we still fighting?" I ask, approaching with the intent to wrap my arms around Lily and pull her close.

"I don't want to," she says, eyeing my lips, "but I have to."

"Love—"

"You didn't listen to *me*," she notes. "I know I think in different ways, but I didn't ever want to punish him for that."

I can't take it back. I would've still done it, no matter what. "But I did it. So now what?"

Lily hones in on my abs, but then she tears her gaze off me and yanks the shower door. It sticks on her, and she struggles to shut it while water pours onto her head. Literally, she lets out a groan to pry the thing closed.

I smile and then push the shower door shut for Lily, closing myself out.

"Thank you!" she yells over the water. "And we're still fighting!"

I realize that.

❤ ❤ ❤

CONNOR AND I RIDE up a graffiti-decorated elevator. Mechanical light bulbs strung with metal chain above us. I've been here a couple other times, so the metal and concrete style isn't as jarring as the first. This industrial factory in Philly was converted into premium lofts about a year ago.

The doorman at the building's entrance says enough about the cost of this place. It's not mine. Not Connor's. This place belongs to my little sister.

Willow graduated from college, and she had a small garden wedding on May 31st. She left with Garrison to Hawaii right after, and they haven't been back in Philly for that long. In that short time, they've been trying to move into their new loft, but Willow has been worried that cameramen can see inside.

The window is partially tinted, but my sister doesn't want to live with the curtains closed for the rest of her life. I don't want that for her either, and this transition can't be easy since she's been in London for four years. Away from the media.

Away from us.

She probably forgot what this whole circus is really like.

So far, no one has posted snapshots of the loft from outside. But it wouldn't be the first time someone stored a ton and then dumped them all online at once.

We're here to help test the visibility of the window from the street. The whole "plan" isn't going very well at the present moment.

Connor speaks to a cluster-fuck of a group call. "Listen—"

"Rose, put your sunglasses back on! Someone will notice you," Lily whisper-hisses. I almost smile, but then I remember we're in a fight. My muscles tense up.

"Stop flailing, Lily," Rose rebuts.

Daisy whispers, "Breaker, breaker. The hummingbird and the sparrow are currently hiding behind a bush. Someone is onto us." I remember that Daisy paired off with Willow, and Lily is only with Rose.

Before I can even process what they're saying, the three Calloway sisters start talking over one another.

And then this. "Hey," Ryke cuts in, "why the fuck am I in this call?"

I lean towards Connor's cell. "Because you were *supposed* to come with us, bro." He ditched at the last minute to stay with the kids at the Cobalt estate, painting right now with their grandparents and Poppy. We planned to be back early, but Sullivan stared pitifully up at Ryke and said, "Will you stay with me, Daddy?" She even pouted and added, "Pleaseeeee."

My older brother can't resist his four-year-old.

"Fuck off." Ryke hangs up.

"Avoid paparazzi," Connor reminds the girls.

"Thank you, Richard, like we hadn't realized that was part of the plan from the start." Rose grumbles, "I'm not wearing the ugliest hat I own for nothing."

The elevator comes to a halt on the fifteenth floor. Connor tells Rose, "I'd advise you to speak softer. I know it's hard for you, but you're on a *city street*. Unless you're lost, then we have a much larger problem."

Rose growls. "I hate you."

"You love me." He grins as the elevator opens to a distressed metal door.

"How do I evict you from this call?" Rose asks because she wouldn't hang up on Daisy, even if it meant she'd hang up on him.

I unlock the door with my set of keys.

With one hand, Connor yanks it open, the metal screeching as it slides. "You can't get rid of me, darling."

"So you're like herpes," she rebuts. I don't even have time to feel that burn because Connor is quick.

"More like air. I'm necessary in your life. Not detrimental. And you enjoy fighting against the one person who helps you."

I laugh, feeling the heat off that one. I walk further into the loft while they bicker.

Boxes are stacked in the large open space and most say **Abbeys — kitchen** or **Abbeys — living room**. Connor and I go straight towards the massive window.

I can practically feel Rose's glare. "Your ego *asphyxiates* me."

"It stimulates you."

They could do this all damn day with each other, and it'd probably end with Connor fucking Rose. I don't fixate on that.

I haven't heard Lily on the line in a while. "Lil, you okay?" I ask into his phone, just as we stop by the window.

"…I'm not supposed to talk to you."

"Who said?"

"Me."

I sigh heavily, my aggravation and frustration constricting my shoulders. This fight can't last long. Right?

"We're on the move again," Daisy whispers.

The loft window overlooks a street of eclectic shops and a miniature park. Rose and Lily are supposed to move far left towards the shops while Willow and Daisy are towards the park. I scan them from the fifteenth floor, but most people look like specs in the distance.

The girls are quiet while they focus on reaching their positions that we mapped out.

Connor cups his hand around his phone's speaker. He's not in a suit today, just a blue shirt and workout shorts, but he looks like a god in any fucking attire. It's never been about his clothes. His confident, *I'm better than you* demeanor draws my gaze to him—while also shrinking me. And I'm six-two.

"What happened with Lily?" he asks me in the calmest, most comforting tone.

I imagine Rose questioning Lily right now too. Connor and Rose have been there for us from the start. I mean, Christ—the four of us, we *lived* together first. Because they were trying to help us cope with staying sober while keeping our relationship upright.

One is hard enough. Both, together, seemed impossible.

But Lily and I—we made it.

It doesn't mean we don't have bad days, and today just happens to be our first fight in…I don't know how long.

Years, probably.

"Moffy walked in on us," I explain. "We were beneath the covers, so he didn't see anything, but I grounded him for not knocking. Lily didn't want to." It's all I need to say. Connor could put a picture together with even less pieces. "I'm not my father. I know I'm not."

Moffy doesn't get how nice I am in comparison.

My dad would've dragged me by the neck into my bedroom, called me a fucking idiot, chewed me out until I pissed my pants, and then slammed the door in my face.

Connor studies me for a second, understanding *why* Lily and I are at odds. It has to do with both of us feeling justified in our actions. Both of us being confident and resilient in our stances. We've never had that before.

Then he says, "Even I disagree with Rose on minor issues like the best route to drive our children to school. Though, we settle our arguments with trivia."

I laugh. "You're such a nerd."

He smiles, not denying the fact. "I just don't want you to believe you're not doing your best. You can't be me, of course, but your best is somewhere below—but not on the bottom."

I feign confusion. "I thought I was your bottom, love."

"You're many things to me." His smooth tone just melts the tension in the air like a drug.

I look at my best friend who could give wisdom to a fucking tree if he wanted to, but he wouldn't. He collects time like the rarest commodity, and to this day, he doesn't spend it on just anyone or anything. So I say, "I'm lucky you spend so much time on me, aren't I?"

"No." Connor shakes his head. "It's not luck, Lo."

He doesn't have to say it. I know he won't spell it out. But I understand.

It's his love for me.

That's why he chooses me. Maybe that's why I choose him and Lily and all these other people around me. It's love.

That's what it's always been.

Connor takes his hand off the phone's speakers, and Daisy shouts, "Camera at the ready!"

"I'm in position," Lily chimes in. "...a non-sexual position. Like a standing doing nothing kind of position."

My smile hurts my face. Then I remember we're in a fight, and my smile fades again. The girls are pretending to be paparazzi on the street and directing the camera lenses up at the fifteenth floor. At us. We can't see them.

I lift up the corner of Connor's shirt. "Can you see Connor's nipple?"

Connor says to me, "If you wanted me undressed, all you had to do was ask, darling."

"Will you strip for me?"

Just like that, he pulls his shirt off his head. Sculpted abs and arms, lean muscle, not bulky because he prefers to wear slim, well-fitted suits. Ryke and I always joke about the day where he accidentally packs too much muscle and rips his tux.

That day has never happened. Connor seriously knows his body like Michelangelo knew art.

My phone vibrates in my short's pocket. I check the group text, sent to Willow, Ryke, and me.

Lunch this Saturday. You may bring your wives and husband. Children not allowed. This is an adult lunch. — **Dad**

We do Sunday luncheons with Lily's parents about once a month, not every week, but it's not a surprise that my dad would want all of his kids together on Saturday. It wouldn't be the first time he asked.

It's not even the first time he's banned the children from attending. His topics of interest range from business to personal life to things that put all of us on edge. And even if the children were allowed, Ryke wouldn't let Sulli go.

She sees her grandfather way less than Moffy, but I won't let Moffy be alone with him for longer than a minute or two. Still, he likes his grandfather, so he'll be bummed about not going.

"You bringing your husband to lunch, Willow?" I ask over the phone.

In the short pause, I can practically feel her smile at the word *husband*.

Willow says, "Maybe, I don't know."

It's about our dad. Jonathan Hale is warming up to Garrison, but Garrison doesn't like Jonathan. Not ever since our dad criticized his proposal to Willow, all because she was still in college at the time. He sounded like Greg Calloway, overprotective about the entanglement of relationships and future, but maybe it has something to do with Willow being a girl.

Too soon.

Too young.

Too rushed.

Too eager.

Jonathan said.

Garrison called him a gutless fish.

I was shocked. Ryke was shocked. My dad doesn't back down. He would verbally attack until someone bled out.

Jonathan called him a cunt.

Ryke lost it. I tried to shift things off Garrison, especially because of his past history with his brothers. I couldn't do much. Everything escalated between my dad and him. Then Garrison just shut down. He avoids conflict at a certain point.

So he walked out of the lunch and wouldn't talk about it again. Only to me, he later confessed that he didn't know what to do. He wants to respect Jonathan because he's Willow's dad, but he can't stand him.

I had to go into a lengthy explanation about Lily and me. How my dad tried to push a marriage on us for the betterment of our reputation and those around us. So as much as I love Jonathan Hale, he shouldn't have the power to guilt anyone into anything. Not into a marriage and not out of one.

I think he'll come around and stop antagonizing Garrison. Having a daughter is new for him, and he really shouldn't be picking out pages from the Greg Calloway handbook.

"Move around." Rose's frosty tone echoes from the speakers. "We're taking pictures now."

I picture Daisy wagging her brows as she suggests, "You can pretend to make-out."

"What?" Lily says. "Who?"

"Connor and Lo," she clarifies. "We need to see if Garrison and Willow getting it on will be caught on camera."

Jesus Christ. "That's my *sister*," I snap. Then I cringe at Connor and give him a look like *help me wipe that from my brain.*

"Oops, sorry." She whispers, "Sorry, Willow."

Connor grins at me. "I'll make it better."

I nod. "Pretend make-out with me, love?"

"Just like we did last night?" he quips.

"Just like that."

Then he grips the hem of my black shirt and lifts my V-neck over my head. I comb strands of my light brown hair back. We're both worth billions of dollars, but he looks it head-to-toe, inside and out.

His amusement curves his lips.

It's infectious.

I try hard to fake disappointment. "I remember you doing more to me last night."

"You want more, darling?" His face is all humor.

I touch my heart. "I'm all yours."

Connor puts a hand to my chest. With more force than I expected, he shoves me back—my shoulders hit the window with a *thump*. My own smile matches his. I'm not even a little surprised we're pretending to mess around.

We've always been too comfortable around one another to give a shit. We might confuse other people, but what other people think about us has never mattered to me. We both know we're just friends. Our wives know we're just friends. So we can joke around with one another and still be the same.

Connor presses his hand against the glass, right beside my jaw. He acts like he's going to kiss me, and then his lips diverge past my cheek.

I let out a short, dry laugh. "And Lily calls me a tease."

His conceited grin could light the goddamn world. "Can you see anything?" he asks the girls, his phone tight in his fist.

"I see—is that a hand?" Daisy asks.

"My hand," Connor answers. He takes it off the window and then plants his palm on my shoulder, pushing me. "Down."

I drop to my knees, realizing the girls need to determine whether or not his face is visible—and I was blocking him. I have no clue what to do with my hands in this situation. My face is near his crotch.

Connor shakes his head at me like I'm his worst pretend lay.

"Dammit," Rose curses.

Connor grips my hair. "If you can see this, we have an issue." He tilts my head back, jerking my chin and face up so that my eyes meet his.

"Goddamn you're aggressive, love."

"If you want softer, you're with the wrong man."

A truth I've always known, and I didn't have to pretend make-out with him to find out.

Lily inhales. "Is Lo giving you a blow job?"

Connor releases his grip, and I cock my head towards the phone in his hand. "A pretend blow job, love."

"Ohmygod."

My pretends with Lily are real. They always have been.

I stand up. "Lily Hale," I say towards the phone. I think about all the things I could say, but I end up with this one, "I love you."

Her voice is a lot more subdued. "I love you just as much."

I relax. "Is this the end of our fight?"

"Yeah."

"Maybe I should give more pretend blow jobs," I say to her.

"Ohmygod. Is my face hot?" she asks her older sister.

"Nice nipples, boys," Daisy says.

Connor picks up his shirt and passes me mine. "They can see through the window," he states what we all now know.

I put my shirt on. "Can we get someone to tint the windows more?"

"One of my subsidiary companies focuses on tinting," he reminds me. "I'll see what they can do."

"There you go," I say to the girls on the line. "Connor Cobalt saves the day again."

In our world, it's a common ending.

‹ 27 ›

July 2022
THE MEADOWS COTTAGE
Philadelphia

Ryke Meadows

"When does rain stop? What is rain made of?" Sulli lies on a mound of pillows she calls Mermaid Rock and kicks her feet like she's splashing water. "What if it rains *forever*? What would happen then?"

At four, she has dark brown hair, wild and long, inquisitive green eyes, and tanned skin from the time we spend outdoors, especially in the fucking summer. Rain thrashes against the windowpanes, and Sulli knows it's the reason why we aren't in the backyard.

I'm on the living room floor with my daughter, the two of us awake at an early fucking hour. Around 5:00 a.m. in Philly.

"Rain is water that comes from the fucking clouds," I say after I eat a big spoonful of cereal, "and too much creates a flood."

Sullivan doesn't ask me to define a flood. She places her hands beneath her chin and scrunches her nose at my half-eaten bowl of granola cereal. She spits it out whenever I let her try some—but it's not the only food she hates.

Vegetables? Fucking *never*.

Meat? Not yesterday or a fucking year from that.

Fruit? Mostly melons and tangerines.

She only ate a fucking *waffle* after Daisy put whipped cream and caramel on top.

Sullivan kicks her legs again, dressed in a green mermaid skirt and a tiny bikini top. When I woke, I peeked into her room and found her hastily tugging on her skirt. Like she was running out of fucking time.

"Hey, sweetie." I bent down and helped pull up her shiny green skirt, and then I fumbled with the strands of the bikini top.

"I'm gonna be late." She sprinted around me, worry in her eyes.

"Sulli!" I ran after her and muttered, "Fucking A."

"Mommy! Mommy!" she shouted, swinging her head for any sign of Daisy. "It's mermaid day!"

I picked her up before she reached the banister. She wiggled against me and outstretched her arms towards the air as though she could fly right to her mom. It nearly broke my fucking heart, but I just remembered, *she knows her mom.*

She has one.

In some different kind of world, she'd never meet Daisy, and her life wouldn't contain the same breathtaking light.

I threw Sulli over my shoulder to distract her, brought her back into her room, and plopped her down on her wicker swing. I grabbed hold of the fucking sides so she wouldn't dash off.

"Mommy's not fucking back yet," I reminded Sulli. I told our daughter that she'd be gone for three days. It's been *one*.

Her chin trembled. "Why?"

"She's checking on all the fucking kids at camp." Daisy isn't the camp director. She's the owner, so she's not there full-time in the summer. But during the two-week and month-long sessions for campers, Daisy will attend their Spirit Days, which are really a kid's last three days at Camp Calloway. It's filled with more celebration and activities, including hanging out with Daisy, a world-famous celebrity.

Sulli began crying. "But she's my fairy godmother…"

Dais and Sulli play dress-up when our daughter wants. If I ever join them, I'm the fucking pirate who says bad words. I didn't think Sullivan would declare today as mermaid day, but she misses Dais. There's a gaping hole in our lives when she's not around.

Sulli blubbers out, "I thought she'd be back. Can you tell her to come home soon? Please, Daddy. Will she come home?"

When Sulli cries, my heart caves. My world fucking caves. *I* cave.

How do I cheer up my fucking daughter?

Simple.

I became the fairy fucking godmother.

In less than a minute, her tears stopped, she led me to her trunk of trinkets, and she passed me Daisy's pink tutu outfit and purple paper wand.

It's what I wear now. I squeezed the fuck into my wife's leotard, thankful she's tall or else there would've been *no* way this would've worked.

Sulli called me the grumpy fairy, like there are seven of us. Now we're eating breakfast in the quiet cottage on the living room floor. Sullivan nibbles on a tangerine slice and rattles off more questions.

"What is water made of?"

"Molecules." I say before eating another spoonful of cereal.

"Why are molecules cold?"

"Ask your fucking uncle."

"Why does Uncle Connor know everything?"

"Because he's a fucking know-it-all." I wipe my mouth with my arm, my brows scrunching as Sulli rolls onto her back.

She peeks beneath the waistband of her mermaid skirt. "Daddy?" Concern spikes her voice. I'm about to scoot closer and pull her off the mound of pillows, but she asks, "Where did my hair go down there?"

Fucking fuck.

Before I changed into this fairy outfit, I thought she'd been staring at the trail of hair that runs from my belly button and disappears beneath the band of my track pants.

"You're too fucking young to have hair down there."

She pouts sadly and keeps staring beneath her skirt. "Will it come soon?"

"No." *Fuck no.* I'm not ready for her to go from *four* to fucking *puberty* yet. I seriously feel like she was just born yesterday. Truth is, I can't imagine seeing her as anything other than my *little* girl.

I sip the milk from my bowl, set it aside, and text Dais:

how do you feel?

Right when I press send, my phone beeps with an incoming message.

Ryke... – Lo

I cancelled on the gym this morning with my brother and Connor because Sulli was upset. That one text skyrockets my nerves.

What's wrong? I send it. A second beep.

Groovy :) – Daisy

I'd smile more if my little brother didn't just send me a random ass text. Third beep.

Can you come to the gym? – Lo

Something's wrong.

I don't think twice. I just act. "Want to go for a fucking ride, Sulli?" I'm already lifting her off the pillows.

Sulli nods rapidly and spits out her tangerine.

I practically storm out the fucking door.

I ONLY REMEMBER I'M in a fucking leotard and tutu when I park my Land Cruiser at the gym. Four cameramen are waiting by the curb.

"Fuck," I curse, unbuckling. I turn to the backseat, searching for a pair of pants.

Sullivan waits patiently in her car seat, not afraid of the paparazzi because of Daisy's Shell Time TV game, but she's not friendly towards them either. *Don't fucking talk to strangers*, we've repeated to Sulli a thousand fucking times.

Ropes. Carabineers. A fucking climbing helmet but no change of clothes. "Fuck it." I open my door to intense hollering and camera flashes.

I'm on an *ignore* and *fuck off* setting. I open the passenger door and start unbuckling Sulli, her hands pressed over her ears because of this:

"RYKE!"

"TURN AROUND, RYKE!"

"RYKE, RIGHT HERE!! OVER HERE!"

"SULLIVAN! OVER HERE!!"

"LET'S SEE YOU SMILE, SULLIVAN!" More paparazzi start pulling up in the half-filled parking lot.

I lift Sulli out of the seat. I'd like to carry her inside, but she asks softly, "Can I walk, Daddy?" I put her down on her feet, and she takes my hand.

At this point, the pink leotard rides up my fucking ass, but it's not even on my list of concerns. One cameraman almost cuts in front of us.

"Back *the fuck* up," I curse and another cameraman grabs that guy's shirt, pulling him out of our way.

"He's new!" someone shouts, disassociating with that other guy.

That's it. I pick Sulli up in my arms.

"Daddy." She wiggles to be set down.

"Just until we go in, Sul." Two seconds later, I'm pushing open the doors. The gym is sort of fucking empty, but everyone still looks towards us. Even if I didn't wear this costume, I'd still be stared at.

"W*ooow*." Sulli gawks at the rows of equipment. From ellipticals to treadmills to stair climbers. She's never been in a gym like this one before.

Like I promised, I put her down and then guide her towards the weight benches in the back. I find my little brother on one, Connor spotting.

I scan both of them quickly, but they seem…fine.

"Hey!" I shout angrily.

Lo turns his head, wide-eyed with a *what the actual fuck* expression— his arms give out. My lungs plummet until Connor seizes the bar, right before it can hit Lo's chest.

I let out a tight fucking breath.

Lo sits up and motions to me, then to himself, then to Sulli, back to me. He bursts into a smile. "Is it my birthday? Because it's either Halloween or you forgot to tell me you've become a part-time ballerina."

"He's my grumpy fairy godmother," Sulli explains, smiling up at me.

"Only one-third accurate," Connor says, wiping his hands on a towel.

"Two-thirds goddamn classic." Lo takes a photo of me.

I don't mind.

"Uncle Connor?" Sulli walks closer to him but then notices a shiny barbell and heads that way. Still, she asks, "Why are molocooles wet?" She forgets how to say *molecules*, and he doesn't have to answer because she tries to pick up the fucking barbell.

I'm already pulling her back a foot or two.

She looks at me like *can I touch?*

I crouch, pick up the weight, and let her look at it. At this, I focus on my little brother. "What's going on with you?"

"With me?" Lo pockets his phone and uncaps his water bottle. "You're the one who showed up in a tutu. Were paparazzi still outside?"

"I don't fucking care." I don't care about the tabloids or my costume. I care about my little brother. "What's wrong? You texted *me*." My jaw hardens.

His face falls. "Christ…you ran over here, didn't you?" Guilt eats at him for a quick second, and he rubs the back of his neck.

"I'd fucking do it again. You okay?"

"Yeah. I just wanted you here, not *need*. Just want." He watches Sulli put her ear to the barbell like she does conch shells. "Do I need to start putting SOS in my texts so you can tell when I'm dying?"

I groan, "No. I only need one Lily in my fucking life."

Connor banters, "SOS I can't find the remote."

Lo laughs because that was an actual fucking group text Lily sent when we all lived together. "SOS Ryke has a leotard wedgie."

"Like father, like daughter," Connor muses, referring to Sulli's famous wedgie picture.

I shake my head. "Fuck you and fuck you too."

Sulli pats the barbell. "Fuck me!"

Fucking fuck.

"Ohh, shit." Lo winces.

Connor lets nothing pass his features. I rub my temple and say strongly, "Hey, Sulli. Don't ever say that again. That's fucking *bad*."

It's hard because I can't tell when I curse until five seconds later, and even then, I have to *think* about it. Sullivan frowns, not understanding.

Lo proclaims, "I will go batshit crazy if Luna says that."

"Not fucking helping." I run my hand over my face once and then figure this out. "Every time you say bad words, you have to eat another veggie."

"No." Her lips downturn. "Daddy…"

I hear my brother whisper to Connor, "He's a sucker for this."

"Give him a minute."

"One vegetable," I say. "That's it, sweetie." It's my fucking fault she curses, and she acts like I'm subjecting her to criminal punishment.

"Okay," she says so fucking sadly. I almost tell her *never mind, we'll let this one pass,* but then I glance at my brother and he mouths, *law, lay it down*—and he mimes a gavel.

So I kiss the top of her head and stand up.

Lo starts slow clapping. "Progress."

Connor joins the slow-clap. "*Minimal* progress."

I have to bite my tongue from calling them *prick* and *major prick.* "You're lucky Sulli's here."

Connor, who usually pisses all over the word *luck,* lets it slide this time.

"Damn right," my little brother says, "or else we would've missed this." Lo never motions to my costume.

His words burrow much deeper than right here and right now.

DAY TWO WITHOUT DAISY, and I miss her like fucking crazy. I wake up around 5:00 a.m. again, my blankets not rumpled, not fucking entangled like someone kicked and rolled and turned. The bed never squeaks.

I don't see her fucking smile or hear Nutty scuttle around while checking each and every door. The white husky stays with Dais at Camp Calloway. The thought slowly hardens my jaw.

I'm jealous of a fucking dog.

I scratch at my disheveled hair, the dark room quiet and fucking lonely.

Truth is, before we had Sulli, Daisy and I could be apart and communicate fine through text, maybe a two-minute phone call here and there—but we never *needed* to be together at all times like my brother and Lily. I feel the change in us.

No one will ever be like Lily and Lo, but for fuck's sake—I *miss* Daisy like I haven't seen her in a year, and it's been two fucking days. I rub my face, trying to snap out of it, but I'm certain that once I see Sulli, Daisy's absence will slam at me all over again.

Sitting on the edge of the bed, feet on the floor, I grab my phone off the fucking nightstand. Green paper lanterns sway overhead with the hum of the ceiling fan. I click on my first contact and press *FaceTime*. So the screen isn't pitch-black, I flip on fucking lights and then return to my same spot.

Daisy answers on the second ring, and I instantly meet sunny, green eyes amid dimly-lit surroundings. She moves back-and-forth, her hair in a messy fucking bun, and the longer I search her features, the greater her smile expands. Frogs croak softly and birds chirp in the fucking background, the sun not yet risen, but wherever she is outside, a lamp must illuminate her.

"Hey there," she whispers, resting her cheek on her hand, grasping rope?

She's swinging, I realize.

I picture her alone in the quiet, gentle fucking morning, swinging beside the lake. Racks of kayaks nearby, campers still sleeping while she's wide awake.

She can't restrain her smile. "You've missed me?"

More than you fucking know. I wear the answer all over my face. "How'd you fucking sleep?" I rest my forearms on my thighs, bent forward as I peer at my phone.

"Mmm," she practically fucking moans. "The best I've had."

My brows rise, disbelieving that it's the fucking *best* ever. "That so, Calloway?"

She laughs, not able to pretend for long. "The best for not being at home with you. I slept for a good six hours. I only woke up a couple times." Daisy adjusts her phone and chucks something. She rotates the camera.

Nutty bounds towards the lake, paws splashing water, and then the husky enthusiastically brings a stick back to Daisy.

My relationship with Dais was never founded on words, so when dead-silence arrives over a call, it's not tense or strained. It's fucking peaceful.

I'd rather share the quiet with Daisy than sit in silence alone.

Her swing creaks, and she faces the camera again. Very softly, she says, "I miss you too."

"Yeah?"

"Oh yeah." She picks at the rope. Back-and-forth, back-and-forth, always fucking moving. "Every mountain reminds me of you."

My lips almost lift. "You're speaking to fucking mountains now, sweetheart?"

She laughs, which instantly makes me fucking smile. "Only the mountains you've touched. Those are my favorites."

I watch Daisy peruse my features, and the *I miss you* she spoke about suddenly translates to her eyes. "Anything new? Is Sulli okay?"

"I'll see if she's still sleeping. She'll want to fucking see you." I stand at this, and I recall yesterday. The gym. The fucking paparazzi. "Have you been online?"

Daisy chucks another stick. "No. Spirit Days are always jam-packed, so I haven't even been on the internet." She pauses. "Why did something happen?"

Before worry creeps in, I say, "It's just a fucking picture of me. Lo keeps texting me the photos with heart emoticons." I slip into the hallway, and register *another* smile that pulls my lips. I couldn't care less about what *Celebrity Crush* prints, unless it hurts Daisy or any of the Calloway sisters.

This was fucking harmless.

Daisy must search the internet, her hand to her rising lips. When her eyes start glassing, I stop in the middle of the hall.

"Dais?"

She's smiling. "You dressed up for her?"

My heart fucking radiates because of my wife. "I fucking tried."

Daisy laughs, wiping tears that fall. "I know people always remind Lo of this, and for Connor, it's just known, but Ryke..." Daisy smiles into another heartfelt laugh. "You're an *amazing* dad."

I'd be lying if I said it didn't *hit* me like a thousand tons. I promised myself that I wouldn't be like Jonathan Hale, and I broke the mold faster than my brother could. I had no *good* father figure, nothing to emulate, but I knew what I never wanted to fucking be. What I'd never do to my daughter.

I'd be there *every day*, not just on Mondays.

I'd love her more than I loved money. More than I loved my reputation. More than I loved myself.

I'd dig for fucking happiness and hand it to Sulli.

Daisy's smile is infectious. I end up laughing lightly and shaking my head—grateful for my wife, my daughter, and this fucking life.

"Daddy?" Sulli's bedroom door begins to open.

Daisy swings faster, her excitement shining at the sound of our daughter.

Quietly, I tell Daisy, "I wasn't the only one who really fucking missed you."

Daisy mock gasps. "Is it the moon? Did the stars miss me? Or was it the sky?"

"It was this fucking tiny one." I rotate the camera onto the bedroom door, just as Sulli emerges, half-dressed in the same fucking mermaid outfit.

I squat. "Want to say hi to Mommy?" I face the screen to our four-year-old.

Sulli gasps, but a real fucking gasp, and she races towards the phone. "Mommy!"

Daisy smiles. "The most beautiful mermaid in the whole wide sea."

It's 5:00 a.m.—and we're all together again.

{ 28 }

December 2022
HALE CO. ELEVATOR
Philadelphia

Lily Hale

I'm in a nightmare.

If I could rank a scenario as "nightmarish" this, *right here*, would be mounted at the top.

"Press the button again!" I yell at Ryke. I've already repeatedly pushed the elevator button, but maybe it's operator-error. Maybe Ryke has the magic touch.

Not a sexual touch! Just a touch that makes a Hale Co. elevator *go* when it's come to an abrupt, terrifying *stop*.

"I've pressed it fifteen fucking times already," Ryke snaps. He listens to my demand anyway and pushes the red *call help* button. Nothing happens. No chimes, no beeps, no intercom system.

It's broken.

Our only way out is broken. We're trapped about ten floors beneath our destination: a Hale Co. Christmas party.

I pace in the small, confined space. No mirrors, just maroon wallpaper, dim lighting and soft Christmas music from the corner speakers. "Here Comes Santa Claus" is the current anthem to my nightmare.

I bite my nails while Ryke crouches by the maintenance box below all the buttons. He tries to pry it open with his fingertips. If those fingertips can scale rock, surely they can save us. Right?

My swollen ankles hurt. I lean against the wall for support, my hand splayed on my large baby bump. The extra weight drags my body down. *Stay upright.* I motivate myself. I'm due at any time. In fact, I almost stayed at home and ditched the party for pajamas and television with Moffy and Luna.

At the last minute, I decided to go and support Lo. And…the Christmas cookies. He enticed me with a photo of frosted sugar cookies, and I caved.

So, naturally, I hitched a ride with the Always-Late Ryke Meadows.

If I would've known that attending the party would result in being stuck in an elevator with the Always-Late Ryke Meadows while I'm Very Pregnant Lily Hale, I would've stayed in my PJs. And pretended I was eating sugar cookies.

I anxiously pick at the fuzz off my ugly Christmas sweater (the party theme). The red wool stops at my thighs, and white pompoms are hot glued over every inch. Ryke wears a green sweater with a reindeer pooping ornaments and glitter. Gold stitching says: *Merry Fucking Christmas.*

Daisy bought it for him.

I pull out my phone. "Check your service again." I raise my phone to the ceiling. No bars. No signal.

"Lily," Ryke growls my name. "Sit the fuck down." His magic fingers fail at opening the screwed-in maintenance box. *Magic fingers?* I start picturing his fingers in not-so-wholesome places.

Then I start picturing his fingers on my *sister.*

Cringing, I cover my face with a hand. I didn't mean to think it, I swear.

I take a breath and focus on my cellphone. "If I sit down then that's me giving into the idea that we'll be here for longer than five minutes." I raise my phone. "Maybe if you boost me up, we'll find signal."

"*No,*" Ryke argues. "You're nine-months fucking pregnant. I'm not boosting you anywhere."

"Shhhh!" I whisper-hiss and stretch out my arms. "Did you hear that?"

Ryke goes quiet but returns to a phone box that he's already checked out four times.

I listen and hear soft chatter. "HELP!" I scream. "HELP!! WE'RE STUCK!!" *Please every wizard in every land, please get me out of here.*

Ryke puts the phone to his ear and presses another button. His features significantly darken. "What's the fucking point of having this if it doesn't fucking work?"

I blow out a steady breath, sliding down the wall. I can't hold myself up any longer. This is me, literally sinking in defeat.

Ryke doesn't see me halfway to the floor as he says, "Sit the fuck down, Calloway. We're not going anywhere."

Shit.

TWO HOURS.

We've been stuck in this elevator for two brutal hours and counting. I slouch against the wall and struggle to unlace my boots. My ankles need to breathe.

Ryke scoots in front of me and starts untying them.

I think I mutter out a thanks, hot and exhausted from doing nothing but sitting in fear. Every so often, we'll start shouting for help, but no one has heard us. I've forbidden him from crawling into the elevator shaft. The first time he proposed the idea, I played out the brutal scenario where he's crushed to death.

He told me that I was being fucking overdramatic, but he relented for a while. Then he tried again and again and on the fourth try, he succeeded in opening the ceiling hatch.

Then I screamed so horrifically that he stopped.

He hasn't tried after that.

Ryke dying hurts to think about. I felt it once, and I don't care to relive that day in Peru. There'd be a bottomless void that can't be filled by just anyone.

I blow out controlled breaths, and he yanks off my left boot and works on the right. I wiggle my toes. All intact. Ryke stares at my belly for a long moment.

I'm so pregnant—it's not good.

I've been tightlipped about the pain that started about an hour back, which feels a whole lot like contractions. Denial is a natural mode for me, but then I start thinking about losing this baby. Sweat gathers on my neck.

I can't lose him.

As he unties my right boot, I ask, "Hypothetically, if we're stuck here for eternity, do you think you could help deliver Xander?"

Ryke glares. "We're not going to be here for eternity."

"But if we are."

"We aren't."

"But *if we are,*" I say like I've trumped him—and then I blow out another breath.

He yanks off my second boot. "If we are, then we need to think about other fucking things too. Like food. Water."

"Sex," I blurt out and cringe with him. "Nononono! Not with *you.* I just mean." What did I mean? I waft some air onto my face with my hands. "Whenever anyone starts listing off necessary things to survive, sex always comes to mind. Not with you, just to be clear. Just in…general." I wave around the elevator as though it contains all the generalness of the world.

He rubs his face with his hands as if trying to wake up. Then he groans like he can't believe we're having this conversation at all. "Fucking A."

Pain shoots up, and I grit down and shift some. "But seriously…" *I'm afraid.* "If we're here for the next twenty-four-hours, could you… help or…"

He raises his head from his hand-fort, and concern engulfs his face beyond anything I imagined. "Are you having fucking contractions right now?"

"I don't know," I mutter. "Maybe."

Ryke rakes his hands through his hair. "What's *maybe*? Like really fucking intense or…?"

"I don't know," I repeat.

"How could you not know?!" Ryke yells, mostly out of panic. "This is your third kid."

I touch my hand to my chest. "I'm still not an expert like Rose."

"For fuck's sake." Ryke motions to me. "You're just as smart as her. Three babies or six or *none*. It's all just fucking…" he trails off as he watches fright invade me. "Are you crying?"

"No." I wipe beneath my eyes, a tear on my finger. "Rose wouldn't cry."

"You're not Rose," he says harshly. "And you don't have to fucking be her. She wouldn't want you to be anyone other than you."

I nod. He's right. I just thought having a little extra Rose strength wouldn't hurt, but maybe all Xander needs is my strength.

I wince at another sharp pain, and I tighten my eyes shut.

Ryke slides even closer and starts asking a thousand questions. *Where does it fucking hurt? What can I do to fucking help? Do you need to lie down? Do you want my fucking sweater as a pillow?*

I wave my hand at him to stop. He quiets, and I whisper, "Just…talk about something else. Distract me?" My anxiety and fear could be to blame. *Relax, relax, relax,* I chant.

I open one eye.

Ryke flips his phone in his palm. "If you hate his fucking name, you can always pick another one."

My other eye pops open. "What? No." I didn't think he'd bring up *this*. "Lo and I love the name Xander." After we learned we were having a boy, we began brainstorming names from our favorite comic book characters. Months passed with too many options and more indecision. It wasn't as easy as Maximoff and Luna.

So we gave our long list of potential baby names to Ryke and told him to pick one.

He handed back the list, and he circled a name but crossed off a portion of the letters.

A̶l̶e̶xander Summers

Also known as Havok from *X-Men* and the brother to Scott Summers. His choice made Lo choke up, especially when Ryke said that he researched every name before he picked this one.

He only needed to choose a first name since we haven't given our children middle ones—out of the pure fact that we want them to go by their first name. And not a second one.

"Good, I'm…" Ryke starts. "…Lily? *Fuck.*"

I must be pale because he puts his hand to my forehead. I speak quickly, "I can't have this baby today. It's Christmas *Eve*." This tacky Christmas sweater party is a late-night adult-only event. All the children are in bed and together at the Cobalt estate. It's like a giant slumber party for them, and Poppy opted out of joining the adults, so she's there in case anyone wakes up and needs a parent.

I ramble on, "Tomorrow is Christmas, and I'm supposed to watch Maximoff and Luna open presents. Daisy will film everyone and narrate—I'll miss the narration! I can't miss it." I blow out a shaky breath.

"Hey, you can replay the video at any fucking time."

My hands on my abdomen, I say to Xander, "Don't come out yet. *Please*." I swear he just nosedives down, down, *down*. I grab hold of something to squeeze, which happens to be Ryke's wrist. "I just wanted a sugar cookie!"

I doubt Lo would've brought me home any extra, and if he did, there would've been a great possibility that he would've eaten it in front of me. He's a cookie tease too.

Ryke tries opening his internet again, but nothing will load. *Out of service.* Everything is out of service except my body, which keeps trucking along. I bite down and scream through my teeth, the next sharp pain comes quick and severe.

His jaw hardens, and so do his eyes, his panic bottled unlike mine. "Hey, Lily." He takes off his sweater, balls up the soft wool, and stuffs the makeshift pillow behind my lower back while I slouch against the wall. "Whatever happens here, it doesn't fucking change us. You're my friend, and I love you. Alright?"

Tears well, and I nod over and over. I know what this means.

Ryke has to look between my legs.

I don't recoil or balk or turn red. I'm not flooded with embarrassment. Just overcome with pain and determination. This isn't just about me. It's about Xander, and I need help.

I squeeze Ryke's wrist at the next contraction, and he slides my hand into his calloused palm. I try to focus on the roughness and hardness of his hand—*a rock climber hand.* The thought nearly drifts me away from the pain. I breathe out measured breaths.

Just as I start to shimmy my leggings down my thighs, not wearing underwear today.

Ryke helps me a little, and I stop halfway at an incoming contraction—and then something else.

I wince. *Oh my God.*

Wetness trickles between my legs, soaking part of my leggings.

"*Fuck,*" he curses. Reality just smacked both of us in the face.

My water broke.

I'm going into labor.

In this elevator. Without Lo. Without a hospital. No doctors, no pain medication, or anyone to ensure that Xander is healthy and alive at the end.

"Nonono," I repeat, knocking my head back against the wall. I stare at the ceiling. "Lo," I cry. "I need Lo." I scream towards the elevator hatch. "LO!!" I can't do this without Lo. I don't know how to do this without him. "LO!!!" My wail breaks in half.

Ryke clasps my face. "Lily, Lily, shhh, it's going to be alright."

"I need Lo. I can't do this without Lo." Hot tears cascade down my cheeks. "Lo," I croak. *Lo please find me.*

He always finds me.

"Lily fucking focus." Ryke grips my cheeks harder, and my eyes fall to him. "You got through three fucking months without him. I was there with *you*. Remember that?"

I nod tearfully. When Lo went to rehab. We were all so much younger. I rub at my eyes but then I clutch my chest. My heart is rupturing into a thousand shards. "I don't want to do this without him."

"But you're going to fucking need to."

The emotional turmoil trumps every ounce of pain. The contractions descend beneath agony that burns through me.

My knees are already bent, my legs already spread. Ryke pulls the leggings off my ankles. *Star Wars* calf-high holiday socks and my ugly sweater still on. Ten floors above us, people are laughing, clinking eggnog, and rosy-cheeked with Christmas cheer.

Ryke peeks between my legs. I don't watch.

"You have to start timing your fucking contractions." He messes with his stopwatch on his wrist. "Tell me when the next one comes."

I shake my head dazedly and then nod. Tears slick on my cheeks. I mumble out responses, sickness rising in my throat. My love for Lo overwhelms me in ways most would chastise. *It's too much. It's too toxic. Stop it.*

He's a part of me.

He's in my soul.

It's always been this way.

His absence tears and *tears* my insides. Any other moment. I'd give up three months with him again, just to have him here *right now* for this birth. I'd cash in all Christmas miracles. I tell that to Ryke, I think, because I hear something about a fucking Christmas miracle—but I lose track of the details.

I try to reroute my head. *Baby. Being born.*

It'll be okay.

It'll be okay.

Even if he's not here?

It'll be okay.

I want him here.

It'll be okay.

I cry. I wipe my nose. I've lost sight of my contractions, and I try to tell Ryke that, but he says not to worry.

Maybe I'm truly delusional—but I swear the ceiling hatch opens. Some blonde man I've never seen sticks his head in, assessing the area.

"LO!" I scream. It's all I think to say.

Then the blonde man disappears.

And then. "LILY!!"

It's Lo, his voice near. I listen to rustling up above, and then his sharp features come into view, his head in the hatch opening. His longer hair on top falls towards his eyes.

I burst into more tears, overcome at the sight of him. He's here. *He's here.*

Or maybe I'm just imagining it all. Is this a fantasy where I make-believe he's in my arms? It wouldn't be the first time I confused pretend with reality. My heart aches.

I watch him disappear.

No. "No," I choke. *Come back.*

I hear urgent chatter, and then he drops down the ceiling hatch. His feet land on the floor, his black ugly sweater rising on his waist, red and green threads stitched like a DJ elf spinning records.

He wastes no time, his knees beside me, his hands on my cheeks. "I'm here. I'm here, Lil," he repeats. I hone in on his amber eyes that contain a million *I love yous* and a thousand more concerns.

"Is this real?" I blink and my tears slip along his hands.

Lo nods. "This is real, love."

He kisses me, a desperate *irresistible* kiss that soothes my emotions. When he breaks apart, I wince, the pain below slamming towards me like a car crash. As much as it hurts, I'd take it over the other pain. I would. Any day.

"When did her water break?" Lo asks, sliding over towards my legs.

Ryke checks his watch and shifts towards my side by the wall. "About an hour ago."

What? I wince again, my hand now in Lo's. "That's wrong."

"You've been fucking out of it, Lily."

I retreated in my head. It's what I'm good at, unfortunately.

Lo places his free hand on my kneecap, and he peeks between my legs. I'm too lightheaded to read his reaction. "How has she been?" he asks him.

"Out of it," he repeats.

"An ambulance is coming, and maintenance is working on restarting the elevator," he explains. "I couldn't get a hold of either of you—and I thought…" He glares at the ceiling, his eyes flooding, upset and angry. "I called every goddamn hospital nearby. Then we found your car in the parking lot, and I knew you didn't get in a wreck."

Ryke stands up. "You saw that the elevator was fucking stuck?"

"Connor did. We found someone who knew how to get into the elevator shaft, and maintenance has been trying to restart it for the past two hours—"

I scream at the contraction and squeeze the life out of Lo's hand. *Ohmy*…I almost puke from the pain, nausea building in my throat. Lo strokes my cheek and whispers something that I can't make out in my state. I dazedly nod.

Ryke goes to the open hatch. He jumps, grabs hold of the edge, and pulls his body up with one hand. I have no energy to spare to freak out. Plus, he returns in a quick second. "I hear sirens." Though it's a distant sound.

An ambulance is coming. Or is it in my head?

I try to relax at the first thought.

Lo and Ryke lock gazes, and they exchange a look of gratitude for one another. For Ryke taking care of me. For Lo coming to the rescue.

"She needs you," Ryke tells him.

Lo stares back at me, and I stare at Lo. Our history blankets me with warm security, and I drown into those amber eyes. He cups both of my cheeks again.

"You and me," he says.

"Lily and Lo," I breathe.

"Lo and Lily." He wipes his own fallen tear and he nods. "We're going to be okay."

I murmur, "I believe it."

The next events happen quickly, rushed between never-ending contractions, my screams, and an incoming baby. The elevator groans to a start. When we reach a new floor, the doors open to paramedics, and I'm hurriedly put on a stretcher.

My sisters appear. So does Connor.

I can hardly think while they assess and then move urgently, all to bring to me to the hospital. I never let go of Lo's hand.

Outside, as snow flutters in the pitch-black Christmas Eve night, the paramedics open the ambulance doors and I'm wheeled towards safety. My hands on my knees, gritting my teeth.

Rose shouts at Xander to stay inside my uterus.

Connor coaches me to breathe.

Ryke talks to an EMT.

Daisy sets a reindeer-shaped sugar cookie on my belly. *Thank you, Daisy. It's what I really wanted.*

And Lo is right beside me, clutching my hand, telling me that this is real. That no matter what happens, he'll be here.

By the time the world catches up with me, I'm in the hospital, the clock strikes an hour past midnight.

And a Christmas miracle cries softly in my arms.

Lily & Loren Hale welcome the birth of their baby boy

XANDER HALE

December 25th, 2022

2023

"I married someone much braver than me."

- Garrison Abbey, We Are Calloway

(Season 5 Episode 12 — Street Fighter & Diamonds)

< **29** >

March 2023

THE MEADOWS COTTAGE
Philadelphia

Daisy Meadows

"Are you sure?" I ask Rose for the twentieth time. Rose has a great track record when it comes to decision-making. She's resolute, firm and unbending. I see that each time I ask, *are you sure?*

"I want to do this for you. Let me." Rose clasps my hand, both of us sitting together on the window nook. Connor and Ryke are quiet on the couch, watching us.

Rose had her last child about a year ago. Ben Pirrip Cobalt. He naps in a nearby playpen next to Tom and Eliot. I can hear laughter from outside, today a rare warm day.

I glance out the window. In the cul-de-sac, Moffy rides his bike in a circle while Janie, in a pale blue skirt and cheetah sweater, stands on the back pegs, her hands on his shoulders. They'll both be eight in the summer.

Coconut circles Sulli, not to catch her attention exactly. The white husky protects the five-year-old, ears perked and alert. Sullivan has one of Moffy's skateboards, but she's still learning how to use it. She keeps tripping into the grass, but like her dad, she never gives up.

Today is all about Ryke and me making babies, but not in the traditional sense.

Sullivan has cousins as close as brothers and sisters. She'd be fine as an only child, so that's not really why I'd want another baby.

I was in surgery and close to dying after I gave birth. There was a greater chance that I'd never wake up and see the next day. I *wasn't* supposed to live, and in the moments where Ryke was told that he might lose me—where he knew he could become a single father in an *instant*—he thought about the chance where I'd see him again.

He thought about me and what I'd want.

Ryke made sure the doctor preserved my remaining eggs. In what he calls one of the two hardest moments of his life, he did this for me.

Through my body's twenty-some years of ups and downs and a risky birth, I was left with eggs on a laboratory dish. Combined with Ryke's sperm, they became embryos, all frozen until we need them. I feel sick at the thought of wasting something that *feels* like the last pieces of a certain part of me—something that Ryke made sure to keep safe.

We might not have physically had sex to make those embryos, but so much love went into that creation. I want to try and see if surrogacy will work, but for however daring I may seem, I'm terrified often. And parts of this terrify me.

"I can't be the sole decider in this," I tell Rose. "I just can't. It's a *huge* deal, and it's going to affect all of us." I look at Ryke. Then Connor.

Rose does too.

Connor sets down his coffee mug and then leans back. "Ryke and I have concerns."

Rose's back arches, preparing for battle. "You've been talking? Together?"

"Yeah," Ryke says. "We fucking do that sometimes."

Connor stretches his arm over the couch. "Though it can be mildly annoying when he just stops speaking like someone cut off his tongue."

"Not everyone has to fill every fucking pause."

"Concerns?" I interject to steer this sinking ship to land. "You've both been talking about concerns that involve...us?" I motion between the four of us.

They're quiet again, their gazes intrusive and intense and practically burning through Rose and me.

"Okay, so just my sister and me," I realize. Rose squeezes my hand in support. I silently hear her war chants: *we shall prevail over our foes.*

Which just may be our husbands in this scenario.

"Darling," Connor begins.

"Don't *darling* me," Rose snaps. "We don't need coddling from *either* of you. We're trying to make a fucking baby, not be babied."

"Hey, I didn't say a fucking thing," Ryke growls.

This went astray real fast. "Let's regroup here." They all respect my voice so much, and I don't have any sort of problem saying what I want to say. So I just speak. "I think it's important that we listen to everyone's point-of-views on the issue because it *really* involves us all. I don't want to infer what you guys are thinking, so just let loose." I wave to them like I'm bowing, but I can't really bow while I sit.

Ryke nods to Connor to be the one to talk. Ryke isn't much of a talker, but that's already been established.

"Here's what we know," Connor says calmly, his new approach easing Rose more than before. "There are only two embryos. If they fail, it's over."

Part one of why Daisy Meadows is terrified. I had more eggs, but not all of them successfully created an embryo with Ryke's sperm. Only two did.

We have two small chances.

"And?" Rose crosses her ankles, in a black Calloway Couture dress that hugs her frame beautifully.

Connor says a word in French and stops himself, his eyes flitting to me. I'm the only one who can't speak the language, so he respectfully keeps it in English. "We're concerned about the possibility where this fails and you're both emotionally distraught in the end."

Rose glares. "Then stop thinking about us being emotionally *distraught*." My sister is defensive because she wants this to work as much as I do, and bad realities hurt.

"My *main* concern is with you, Rose." His severity grips every word. "Grief is a realistic outcome, and will you be able to meet it?"

"*Yes*," she says strongly. "This is complicated. I see that as much as all of you. She's my *littlest* sister, and of course if this fails, I'll feel partially responsible. It's my body that'll reject the embryo, but I want to help."

I turn to Rose. "Please don't blame yourself if something goes wrong. *Please*."

"I will," Rose says icily. "And you have to accept that."

Part two of why Daisy Meadows is terrified.

Silence blankets the room. I'm the one who ends up breaking it. "We can put it off until you and Connor have a girl…" It's taken many, *many* months for them to change our minds about this timeline. Rose even tried to bribe me with chocolate cake. It was a valiant effort, but her genuine tears did the ultimate trick. I *felt* how badly she wanted to do this now and not wait.

Rose shoots Connor the worst kind of look, like he returned a hurdle to their track.

"Daisy." Connor draws my attention to his calm exterior. "Rose and I aren't going to try for another child until we do surrogacy."

"Do you even want to attempt it?" I motion between Ryke and Connor. "You both seem so upset." If you could see their faces, you'd know *they're* the distraught ones.

Just to do something with my hands, I start twisting my hair in a high, messy bun on my head. Both men exude a type of masculinity that makes them feel larger than the room. Every time I hone in on this, I remember how much younger I am in comparison. To take my mind off the age differences, I focus on Ryke's unkempt hair and unshaven face, polarizing Connor's smoothness.

But their distraught features never change shape. They are upset. They don't even say differently.

Ryke rubs his jaw and then drops his hand. "Because we fucking love each of you, and we know *exactly* how you'll be if this fucking fails."

Because we're sisters. But that's why Rose and why I want to do it in the first place. I couldn't think of a better birth mom for our baby. I'd be the baby's biological mom still, and I like that our child will know that her aunt carried her for nine months.

The downside is disappointment and heartache if everything goes wrong. I worry about Rose's health, but she always combats with, "I'm thirty-three. I'm not dead yet."

I think about everything and ask the men, "But you two—you're both okay in the event that everything goes *right*, right?"

"Why wouldn't we be?" Connor asks, though there's no confusion in his face.

"This bonds all of us in a way. Rose and I want that, but do you two?"

Rose wears this expression like *oh, the tables have turned.* We're definitely on the offensive now. Rose pushes it one step further.

Bluntly, she says, "Ryke's baby is growing in my body, and you *both* have to watch. So if you're not able to handle this, speak now."

I wait for Connor's *I can handle anything* arrogance, but he's pokerfaced and silent.

Ryke shakes his head. "It's not our fucking place to say whether we do or we don't. Either way, it shouldn't be a deciding factor."

I rock back in shock. "So you *do* have issues with this?"

Rose is even surprised. "Connor?" I hear the vulnerability in her voice when she says his middle name right now instead of *Richard*.

"I can view nearly everything from a scientific standpoint, but emotions are variables and this has many more than I'm used to."

I feel like they're both speaking around something. "Can you just come out and say it?"

"Look," Ryke says. "We're good friends, but when I think about Connor, I'm not filled with warm fucking feelings." They can grate on one another.

Connor, more clearly, tells us, "It's about sex."

"What?" Rose swings her head towards both men.

My eyes widen at this realization. Oh. It's just been proven. Their friendship chips away at their maturity. Which is usually at one-hundred percent *unflinching, unabashed, we can do anything* kind of levels.

It's plummeted to something strange. I want to make a joke about this theory being proven, but I'm a little speechless.

When Rose is pregnant with our baby (aka Ryke's baby), she'll still have sex with Connor. This whole thing is new territory, sure, but the only reason Connor and Ryke are taking short pauses at the idea is because of their complicated friendship. Otherwise, I think this would be smooth sailing.

To Rose, Connor says, "I can't tell you my emotions about it because I'm not sure exactly what I feel."

Ryke leans forward, closer to us, his forearms on his knees. "Connor and I talked it out, and we both don't want it to sway the fucking decision one way or the other."

"We agreed on something," Connor says. "It's rare, so let's leave it at that."

Rose is as rigid as can be. "You both made this weird."

"It was fucking weird to begin with," Ryke says.

"It's funny if you think about it," I chime in with a growing smile. It must be contagious because their lips slowly inch upwards. Now that we surfaced the buried concerns, we exchange more certainty than before.

"Let's vote," Rose says. "I'm *for* surrogacy as soon as possible." Her piercing yellow-green eyes set on me.

I don't hesitate. "For."

We look between the men.

"For," Connor says easily.

Ryke nods. "Fo—" *BEEEEEEEP!!*

The loudest honk outside jars all of us to our feet. Coconut barks outside, an alarmed, deep throaty noise that means *bad things are happening.*

Oh God.

The children are in the cul-de-sac.

Only a quick glance out of the window, I see the kids stare at something incoming. Sulli—she's in the middle of the street unlike Jane and Moffy, who've ridden their bike to the grass.

My lungs ram in my throat, and in seconds, we all rush out the door.

< 30 >

March 2023
THE MEADOWS COTTAGE
Philadelphia

Ryke Meadows

I run down our front yard, Daisy right behind me. "SULLI!" I shout, my veins beating out of my fucking neck. Sulli kneels on the pavement like she just tripped off her skateboard. Our white husky stands in front of her, growling at the massive tractor-trailer that drives down our fucking street. Headed for the end of the cul-de-sac. Straight towards my five-year-old daughter.

The horn blares.

Right before I reach the mailbox, Moffy drops his bike, preparing to run out into the street to grab her.

"STAY BACK!" I scream at him. He freezes in place just as my shoes meet asphalt. I pick Sulli up in my arms and sprint to the yard, Nutty trailing close behind. We fall onto the grass at the loud *crunch*, and our dog licks Sulli, like making certain she's cognizant and not sitting in fear.

The driver just crushed the fucking skateboard beneath the tires.

You've got to be fucking kidding me. My nose flares. That could've been my fucking daughter. How did this tractor-trailer even get through the *fucking* gates?

Jane holds onto the bike and stares wide-eyed at the scene. "Merde." *Shit.*

I frown deeper.

It's the first time I've ever heard her curse in French, and by Rose and Connor's quick exchange, I'd fucking bet it's theirs too.

"Sulli?" I climb to my feet and then help my daughter stand. She's in a state of fucking shock. Nutty nudges Sulli until she responds with a pat to the dog's head. Then Daisy wraps her long arms around Sullivan, and our daughter relaxes at her mom's embrace and hugs back.

I grab Moffy's baseball hat that fell off when he was about to sprint into the street. "You alright?" I put my hand on his shoulder. "Moffy?"

He looks as shaken as the other two, and I'm just as fucking concerned about him as everyone else. This is my brother's oldest kid. Same jawline, currently the same haircut. He's the one who had a seventh birthday and held Eliot by the candles. Asking him to blow them out. The one who served a slice of his own birthday cake to every kid before he cut his own. The one who could make the rowdiest children settle down and the quietest ones speak up.

He's the fucking leader of this pack.

"No one ever comes down here," Moffy says, dazed until he looks to me. "I wouldn't have left her in the street. I wouldn't have. I *promise.*"

"Hey." I shake my head. "It's not your fucking responsibility." *Stop carrying that weight.*

He beats himself up over it. The driver climbs out of the tractor-trailer with a clipboard, and that's when I *really* examine the trailer portion of the vehicle.

The blood just rushes out of my head.

"Uncle Ryke?" Moffy frowns.

Connor, who normally has to be involved in everything, never approaches the driver.

He knows it's for me.

Rose knows it's for me.

Daisy's eyes start to flood with tears, and Nutty sticks closest to her.

"Mommy, what's wrong?" Sullivan asks.

Daisy is too choked to answer. She gives Sulli a weak smile and then kisses her nose.

I mechanically meet the driver at the base of the fucking driveway. "This has to be a fucking mistake." I forget to chew him out about nearly running over my daughter. My head pounds, and my skin has turned ashen white.

"You're Ryke Meadows," he states, not asks, grinding coarsely on a piece of gum. He unclips an envelope, hands it to me. My name scrawled over the front.

Ryke

I can't place the handwriting with anyone I know.

"I just need you to sign off here, and I'll unload the Jeep."

The Jeep.

The forest-green Jeep that I've ridden in hundreds of fucking times towards cliffs, quarries, the shittiest climbs and the greatest ones.

I can barely think. I don't know what else to do. So I sign my name on the line and then watch as he fucking unloads my history.

An arm curves around my waist. My muscles unbind by Daisy's presence, and I find some words. "I can't take Sully's Jeep." What the fuck am I supposed to do with it? How can I ride in it?

Sulli slips between us. "I have a Jeep?"

It fucking guts me for a second.

I pinch my eyes—I just can't hold it in anymore. *What the fuck am I going to do?* Daisy wavers, unsure of what to say since we agreed not to bring up Adam Sully until our daughter was older. She'll ask what happened to him, and death can be petrifying for five-year-olds.

He died really fucking young.

"Daddy?" The fear in her voice splinters down my spine.

Eyes burning, I drop my hand to her head. She peers up at me, tearful and confused. Daisy whispers in her ear and rubs her arm.

"Hey, Sul," I say in the softest tone I can muster.

"Hey, Daddy."

I wipe my eyes, and then I tell her, "You're named after one of the greatest guys I've ever fucking known. He was a rock climber. That's his Jeep."

Awe brightens her green eyes.

"Adam Sully," I tell her his name, and just as the Jeep reaches the pavement, I rip open the envelope. A letter inside.

Ryke,
We're moving this week. We don't have space for his Jeep anymore, and we can't bring ourselves to sell it. He'd want you to have it. Take care.
Barbra Sully

He'd want me to have it.

I turn to Daisy. "I'm keeping the Jeep."

She smiles. "He always said he had the better car than you."

I laugh because it never felt fucking true until now. This Jeep has more value than any other material possession I own. And I'll take care of it. *Yeah.* I think he would want me to.

❀ ❀ ❀

"QUICKDRAWS, HONEY, BANANAS, CHOCOLATE-covered espresso beans," Daisy reads a receipt, one of *many* stuffed in the fucking glove compartment of Sully's Jeep. I parked in the garage, still behind the wheel while Daisy sits cross-legged in the passenger's seat.

I sift through his old CDs on the visor: *Oasis, No Doubt, Héroes del Silencio,* a band he introduced me to when we were eight or nine. We learned Spanish around the same fucking time.

No one cleaned his shit out, so after *years'* worth of time, it stands like a relic of my long-lost friend.

"For fuck's sake, Sully." I find *dried fruit* beneath his car mat, moldy like it'd been stuck there a long time while he was still alive.

Daisy passes me a few receipts. We spend the next thirty minutes just fucking remembering him. I break a smile at a few National Park maps, areas off-the-beaten path circled with a dull pen. He wrote my name beside the ones he wanted to bring me to.

When Sully fucking called me to climb, I went. All these places with my name—I've been there with him. I catch Daisy's eyes clouding, and I reach out, my hand on the back of her head. She leans into me, and I hold my wife. I'm not even fucking thinking anymore.

I just exist in this moment, as tranquil as I'd be on a crag. Scaling *thousands* of fucking feet towards the sky. I look down at Dais, and her eyes flit up to me.

"Every day that I grow older is a fucking blessing," I say lowly, my voice hushed in this Jeep. Next to the sun of my life. "But every day that I grow older with *you* is fucking priceless." I watch her chest rise high. "I've been so fucking lucky."

Lucky to be with Daisy.

Lucky to be alive.

Lucky to hold my daughter.

Lucky that we have *two* chances to have another baby when we could've easily had none.

When we mention surrogacy to one another, we talk about not being able to squander this gift we've been given. We talk about how we live our lives taking one fucking risk after the other. This'll be the same. And I fucking worry about Daisy and Rose—but today, I've been reminded of something.

"Whatever happens, Daisy, this—all of *this*…" *Look at my life. Look at how long I've lived. Look at the sun right next to me.* "It's fucking priceless."

She has to sit up, her eyes glassing more. She smiles with a short laugh, but both fade too fast. She rubs the corners of her eyes and tries to give me a smile. It's weak. I can tell that she wants to share my sentiments, but she struggles to.

In this second at least.

"Hey." I pull Daisy onto my lap, and she buries her face in the crook of my arm. "I don't need fucking pompoms and confetti." I kiss her head. "If you're sad, you can be fucking sad."

Daisy rests her chin on my chest, and I toss a strand of hair in her face. The sun has set somewhere between the surrogacy talk with Rose and Connor, our daughter almost getting crushed by a fucking tractor-trailer, and digging through the contents of this Jeep.

I see the *I'm sorry* on her lips, but she doesn't utter the words. Instead she says softly, "I'm just as lucky to be growing old with you." Her smile lasts a fraction longer, and I hang onto every fucking second. When depression leeches onto Dais, she usually tells me, *I feel heavy.* What I suggest next might not help completely, but it's enough to shorten the wait.

"Run with me, Calloway?"

She nods, and not a moment later, we're out of the Jeep—and I throw Daisy across my shoulder. Breath ejects from her lungs, and she swings her head back to me, light bursting in her eyes.

I raise my brows at her.

"This must be that 'can't-eat, can't-sleep, reach-for-the-stars, over-the-fence, World Series kind of stuff.'" She quotes *It Takes Two* often.

"No," I deadpan.

"Just *no?*"

"Fuck no."

Her lips pull upward. "Then what is this?"

"It's so much more than that."

She gasps. "It's chocolate."

I drop her down my back and grab her ankle, stopping Dais before her head meets the floor. She's safe and out of breath.

When I pick her back up, when she's upright in my arms, I fucking tell her, "It's us at one-hundred-and-fifty miles per hour without brakes."

Daisy says as softly but more tearfully, "I really fucking love you."

"You going to be saying that after I run your fucking ass, Calloway?"

"Oh yeah. I might even add another *fuck*."

"You really fucking *fucking* love me?"

She smiles, the biggest one so far. "Fucking fucking *fucking* yes."

[31]

April 2023
HALE CO. OFFICES
Philadelphia

Rose Cobalt

I vaguely concentrate on my work.

Do not fuck this up for your littlest sister. She deserves everything. She deserves the entire world.

Every waking minute, I try to *annihilate* self-doubt that muddles my thoughts in a pool of *you will fail, Rose Calloway Cobalt.*

You will fail miserably and excruciatingly.

Shut up.

My eyes narrow at the uncomfortable stabbing insecurity. Pressure mounts on my breastbone. I let out a tight breath and stiffly sip my ice water. I have reason to be concerned. I'm waiting for the results—whether or not the first embryo took.

There are only *two chances.*

I hone in on that word: *chance.*

I can't study harder. I can't prepare. I was told to just *hope* for the best—that my body would either accept or reject the embryo. And that will be that.

This is just a semblance of what Daisy must've experienced when she first tried to conceive. I never *felt* the painful uncertainty and lack of control, not until I stepped into this position, side-by-side with her.

I might be older, but in this process, she's my confidant. My coach. *My* role model. I want to do right by my sister, and all the risk is on me, the outcome is on me—*do not fuck this up.*

I pound on the spacebar, completely forgetting what I planned to type out. My phone rings beside the stapler and cup of black pens. I inhale sharply, thinking it's the doctor. I check the caller ID.

Connor Cobalt

It's his day to stay home with our six children. I put the cell to my ear, my anxiety never leaving. "Richard."

No response, but the line isn't silent. Little children shout *shrilly* over one another—it is the most deranged, inhuman noise in this world. And I hear it *daily*. To say it's been a madhouse would be an understatement.

We have three boys under three, two five-year-olds, and our only daughter is seven.

When Connor takes *four* seconds longer to respond, I stand from my chair and start hurriedly gathering my things.

"Connor?" I try again.

"Rose…" His voice is level, but I feel an undercurrent beneath my name.

Purse on my arm like extra arsenal, I leave my office, keys in hand. Just before I tell him I'm on my way, he speaks again.

"Rose, I need you." At first, I think it's gravely serious, but then he adds, "If you can spare the time, darling."

"My time is yours," I tell him, no hesitation. "I'll be there soon." I don't ask what's happened. I reaffirm that I'll be home, and we hang up.

On my drive to the gated neighborhood, I sit pin-straight, both hands tightened on the wheel. I honk at four of the *slowest* drivers who've ever graced a fucking highway. The click-click of the blinker barely calms my violent pulse.

After going through security, I enter the neighborhood, and it's not long before I park by my water fountain, too stressed and high-strung to even reach the garage.

I walk quickly, locking my Escalade, and then head inside the front door. I scan the foyer, regal marble staircase and glittering chandelier. Chatter and footsteps *all* originate upstairs, so I climb.

"Connor!" I shout.

I reach the hallway, and my head whips towards every empty room. I aim for the ajar door at the end: *the children's playroom.*

"That's not fair!" Beckett screams shrilly.

"We didn't do anything, Daddy," Charlie pipes in, less emotional than his twin brother, but his voice only adds to the volume.

I enter the mayhem and barely have time to scan the playroom. I notice Connor knelt in front of Beckett, one-year-old Ben also crying and kicking his feet near a stuffed teddy bear.

Each head-splitting wail slices a knife through my chest. These are *our* monsters, and while tears are acceptable, I want to eradicate the source of their pain.

If only children didn't cry over things like one broken crayon with an entire *unbroken* pack clearly in front of them.

In an even-tempered voice, Connor tells Charlie, "Why did this mess start?" The way he asks, I know Connor already has the answer, but he wants Charlie to use his mind and words.

Charlie stays defiantly quiet.

My husband shifts his eyes for a fraction of a second towards me, and he lets me see his irritations, scratching his deep blues. On any other day, I might take pride in his demise, but I don't care about outwitting Connor when *our* children are the source of his rare frustrations.

Connor visibly exhales as he *gives* Charlie the answer, "This mess started because you didn't share your book."

Charlie plants his hands on his hips and declares, "Correlation does not equal causation." At five, he's saying things like this. I question whether he actually understands the meaning or if he just overheard Connor using the phrase.

Connor opens his mouth to *speak*—what he does best, even if his words are rooted in narcissism and conceit.

He's cut off.

Beckett stomps his foot, tears surging forth. "Eliot pushed Charlie! Why are we in trouble?!"

Connor blinks for a second longer than usual, the noise puncturing his eardrums and mine. "Because you pushed him back. We don't fight with our hands."

"Then Charlie shouldn't be in trouble."

Connor's voice slowly rises. "More than just you two are in trouble, I assure you."

Ben lets out a deadly wail, slamming his fists into the carpeted floor. I walk further inside, my left heel at a strange tilt. *I'm* standing at a fucking tilt. I remove my black heels, the left one about to break.

I let out a strained breath.

I quickly sweep the playroom and tune out the screams. Four bookshelves of children's novels, two window nooks, light-blue painted walls, and a wooden trunk of toys.

Lettered blocks scatter the carpet, and Jane cries softly by her—*no.* One of the boys *smashed* her dollhouse. Beckett would be the first to help her fix her toys, I'm sure, but he's too concerned with Charlie being punished.

Three-year-old Eliot screams, "Mommy!" He bounds over to me and grabs the hem of my black skirt, two-year-old Tom trying and helplessly racing after his brother. Eliot tugs me towards the toy trunk as though to say *play with me.*

He's a little menace. I wouldn't be surprised if he turned out to be the culprit of the demolished dollhouse. As I walk past my husband, Connor turns his head *fully* to me for the very first time.

My jaw drops.

A welt surfaces underneath his left eye, bruise forming. His eye reddened, pained by whatever impaled him. I'm not given time to process.

Jane lets out an angry, *shrill* scream. "I hate this! There are too many boys!" *I know, my gremlin.*

I'd like to think this is a one in a million occurrence, but it's not. The chaos of our children is our daily routine. That *crayon box* sob session? That's a real anecdote. I showed Tom all the crayons he could play with, and he still wailed over that fucking broken one.

This might be typical, but Connor usually multitasks better and smoother than this. I start to wonder if something else threw him off today.

I want to help clear his mind, so I start to tell Jane, "We'll fix it—"

Eliot yanks at my skirt, my white blouse no longer tucked in. I squat to pry his little fingers off my skirt. He pouts.

Jane cries softly, "It's ruined."

Connor rises to his feet as he tells Beckett, "You can't push your little brother, not even to defend Charlie. You know *many* words; use them."

Beckett screams.

Connor shuts his eyes for an even longer moment, and then his gaze finds mine. "It's impossible to reason with the unreasonable." He wouldn't try if they weren't his children.

As he holds my gaze, I realize that he seeks a social exchange that doesn't end in high-pitched wails and irrationalities.

I open my mouth to reply, but this time, I'm cut off. Tom tries to crawl up my body. He clutches my blouse at the collar, tugging hard while I wrestle his little devious hands off the fabric. I feel my smile form. *Why am I smiling at you?*

I try to glare.

It's more difficult.

"Jane," Connor says to our daughter. "Tom will help you clean up."

"No, I won't!" Tom says gleefully while popping buttons off my blouse—Eliot chases after them.

"Eliot, no!" I shout and glance towards Connor, his welt turning purple. *What hit him in the face? Who is to blame? Which child needs disciplined first?* I am ready to join his ranks, but I can't do so without the proper information.

Connor is just as preoccupied. Ben cries to him, "Daddy!"

Charlie speaks, but not over Beckett's emotional screams, face splotched red.

Eliot hops towards the loose and scattered buttons.

"Eliot Alice Cobalt!" I yell, my finger pointed at the three-year-old. He freezes. "Do *not* put a button in your mouth."

"Charlie, Beckett," Connor says deeply, his grave tone close to a *shout*. "*Stop*. Think about the reason I've given you, and you'll find greater meaning. I'm not explaining anything else." He picks up Ben, calming our youngest child.

Tom begs to be held, so I lift the little gremlin in my arms—and he yanks at my blouse again, my blue-laced bra visible. He tries to wrench my diamond earrings.

"No, Tom."

"But Mommy!" he shouts.

Dear God.

"My point," Connor tells me.

In a tense breath, I refute, "*But Mommy* could lead to an insightful argument. Give him a moment, Richard. He needs longer than you."

Connor's lip tics upwards, feeling the beginning of a dialogue between us. "The moment will pass soon."

"Tom destroyed my dollhouse!" Jane cries as though I've betrayed her—I'm conversing with the wrongdoer.

Tom grins and shakes his head. "No, I didn't."

Dear fucking God.

"And there the moment goes." Connor sidles next to me, his hand brushing my waist. I'm physically more rigid than him, shoulders in an uncomfortable bind. Connor tells me, "He's escaped timeout three times already."

"I did not!" Tom shouts, still *grinning*.

I ask my husband, "Have we birthed a liar?"

"He is something." Connor then tells Tom, "And I clearly can count better than you."

"No, you can't," Tom says matter-of-factly.

Connor tilts his head towards our two-year-old. I try to read more of Connor's features, but my focus zooms onto his bruise. "One day you might count better than me, Tom, but right now, you're two and creating more chaos in a minute than I ever created in my lifetime. What would you call that?"

Tom ponders this for less than a second. "No, you can't!"

Connor's irritations flare mildly again, and he fixes the unkempt strands of his hair, not styled to perfection. To Tom, he says, "I've never been amused by absurdities, and you're just reminding me why."

Tom swings his head to me, maybe expecting me to combat with Connor. I don't. "*Timeout* in the rocking chair."

"No!"

"I hate that word," I snap and put him in a tiny rocking chair that faces the wall. "If you move, you'll just be here for another five minutes."

Tom huffs, but we let Eliot sit near and keep his brother company. His own punishment will come soon enough.

Connor didn't call me to calm them. I'm not that type of force. *He* soothed Ben; our boy's cheek is pressed to Connor's shoulder, tears dried.

I have other uses. I'm an extra set of hands and another voice our children respect. I've contained Eliot and Tom—though they're talkative and *rowdy* in the corner. At least they're not flying across the playroom like little winged devils.

Connor's hand slides up my arm, and I face my husband. Without heels, I feel naked. I clear a lump in my throat, today's stressful events catching up with me.

Connor almost imperceptibly studies my body, my features—my pierced gaze. My collar is tight, spine erect and rigid. I even tuck a piece of hair behind my ear, wishing I had a tie to pull the strands into a tight pony.

"What did you need from me? Is there something more?" I whisper to Connor.

His hand skims my stiff neck, and his lips drift to my ear, "We can talk later, darling."

"I'm here to help you," I rebut. "You're not here to help *me*."

"Stop laughing!" Jane yells at Tom and Eliot, the boys giggling merrily. "You don't deserve to laugh, you toad!"

I have to snap, "Jane, don't call your brother a toad."

Tears well, her mouth agape as though I betrayed her in favor of Tom once again. *Not happening.*

"And Tom," I quickly add, "silence in that corner *now*." Eliot and Tom immediately grow quiet.

Jane rubs her tears with her cheetah-print sweater. "There are too many boys."

Connor is *so* off his game because he tells her, "Women make up twenty-five percent of this family, Jane."

I scoff. "That's not even *half*, Richard."

He stays quiet, even recognizing that the statistic could be better. He blinks a few times, as though trying to clear his mind and bring his intellect into utmost focus.

"Boys aren't so bad," I tell Jane, my voice stilted. I do believe this, even if it's a chore to say. "Tom can be a little demon, but he also helped you paint your kitten mural yesterday, didn't he?"

Jane sighs heavily. "I suppose."

Connor rests his hand on the base of my neck, my pulse thumping in my veins. He searches my gaze once more, the room dissolving into subdued chatter. The storm hasn't settled, but the roar isn't blistering.

"What happened?" I ask beneath my breath, and I reach up to his eye.

Connor clasps my hand before I can touch, authority *always* in his stance. "After Beckett shoved Eliot, Eliot threw toy blocks at him. I was a casualty of war."

My lip quirks. "Obviously."

He absorbs my smile, and his grin truly appears, maybe for the first time since I've arrived. "You take pleasure in my wound?"

"Yes," I say without a beat. "A three-year-old chinked your armor."

His grin only grows. "But I've won the war."

I roll my eyes, about to pick up the blocks, but Connor seizes my arm just as I shift slightly. My chest collapses at his soulful expression, clear and decipherable, one that says, *talk a little longer.*

I need you, Rose.

I swallow, and his breath heavies like he can't imagine me spinning around. Like he can't imagine me leaving for work. Like he'd rather go through this day with me and *only* me.

He peruses my unoiled posture, Ben falling asleep on his chest. "And you?"

"And me, nothing." I could easily leave his grasp, but I don't want to. I like the strength of his firm hand on my arm. I like knowing I have the power to say *no*, and he'd listen in an instant.

His brow arches, eyeing my demeanor more outwardly so *I* see that he sees my anxiety. "Your body says otherwise." He's aware the news will fall today, and maybe that also prodded him to call me, to ask me to return home, so I wouldn't battle these sentiments alone.

"Then stop *staring* at my body. I can pluck out your eyeballs if you can't restrain yourself."

"Rose—"

"I'm here to help *you*," I remind him. "This isn't about me."

"We're on the same team, Rose," he says, forcing this truth. "You can try to argue, but you won't win."

Translation: *I will aid you on the battlefield until death do us part.*

I begin to surrender, letting his hand slide to my cheek. He kisses my forehead, and I ask him, "Is there something more with you?"

"My father called."

I freeze. "What?"

Connor hardly reacts, but Jim Elson has had *no* relationship with Connor, not after his mother was granted full custody of their son in their divorce. And Connor and Jim were distant before that instant.

I remember that Katarina Cobalt gave their son *her* last name from the very first moment he was born—breaking common tradition.

Connor says that his father never cared to have any claim over him, and it was fine—he never wanted to be claimed by anyone. "Our lack of feelings are mutual," he'll always say.

So now...why now? I glare, ready to unleash fiery hell upon his father. "Should I break out my knives? A match? Lighter fluid?"

"Hypothetical *arson* this early in the morning," he says with a rising grin, like he's not surprised I'm weaving exaggerations already.

My eyes narrow. "I wasn't trying to surprise you. I'm trying to plan a flaming ball of destruction."

"Focus your energy on someone worthwhile. Jim Elson is no one. He called to ask me about lawyers. Someone discovered him online, and he wants to protect himself from being publically profiled. It's a task I never wanted to add to my list."

Connor can easily shove those responsibilities onto other people, but needing to use his resources to help Jim Elson would be grating for him. He'd only do it to put the situation to bed and avoid exacerbating the issues.

"RETURN THAT, YOU THIEF!" Jane shouts, in a tug-o-war with three-year-old Eliot for her stuffed lion.

They all start yelling over one another, and Beckett solves the issue before we can, yanking the stuffed lion towards Jane.

Eliot falls on his ass, but he rolls over and acts like nothing happened. Tom is supine on the carpet, acting like he's *dead*.

He does this.

He's not dead. He's grinning.

My tense breath is like daggers in my ribs, and Connor kisses my forehead once more, our children out of hand, but his attention partially on me. "They're terrible," I mutter. *I love them all.* It lifts my carriage—and then my phone rings.

I smooth my lips together, eyeing my purse in the center of the room. I can't even recall setting it down. I'd rather ignore the call and stand opposite Connor, but without heels, I'm much shorter than his six-foot-four height. I want to be at equal footing in all ways.

Maybe we are. His hair unkempt, his eye bruised. My blouse astray, skirt crooked. His father's phone call. My impending one.

Our vulnerabilities at the forefront in the same moments.

At the same time.

Connor starts, "I can answer—"

"I have it." I leave him, and he follows, setting Ben on a bouncer. I dig through my Chanel handbag and find my cellphone.

My throat constricts, and I rise uneasily. "The doctor is calling."

Connor edges close, until I have to crane my neck to meet his eyes. I don't feel shrunken. His power and fortitude transfers through my veins, and his hand glides up my arm, resting on my breastbone. My raging heartbeat *pounds* against his palm.

I'm frightened by the worst, and he can see and *feel* just how severely.

"'Nothing will come of nothing,'" Connor whispers a quote from Shakespeare's *King Lear* and adds his own words at the end. "You've at least tried to do more than nothing."

I'm on the second to last cellphone ring. "And what if nothing comes from something?"

"What if," he says like the phrase has stalked him in the past.

I answer the phone, and I'm dazed by the doctor's words. I listen, trying to ingest every syllable, but the result bludgeons me. "I understand," I say strictly before ending the call and dropping my phone to my purse.

The embryo did not take.

I'm not pregnant with my sister's child. I only have *one* more chance to get this right.

One chance.

I can't prepare. I can't do anything but wait.

Connor clutches my cheek, forceful. Commanding. "Rose." He murmurs French softly in my ear, but I can hardly process. I'm supposed to be here helping *him*. I think I must express this aggressively, my palms on his chest, fisting his dark blue shirt.

"We're a *team*, Rose," he repeats again.

"Then we must both be losing." My eyes sear as blistering tears build.

He shakes his head. "This is not our worst."

This is not our worst.

Eliot suddenly bounds over to us and chants, "Kiss, kiss, kiss!"

My nose flares, chest collapsing and rising so heavily. Connor has me pressed close, my arms locked as tight as my unbending body, never loosening my fierce grip on his shirt.

"Kiss! Kiss!"

Connor's fingers slide assuredly from my cheek towards the back of my head. He leans down and tilts my chin up. His lips nearly brush mine as he murmurs, "I hear your heart."

Tears slip from the creases of my eyes—and before I turn my head away from him, away from our children, he shields our faces with his cupped hand.

I murmur just as softly, "And what sound is my heart making?"

His words dive deep into me. "It beats—it beats." He whispers against my lips, "It *beats* in equal time with mine." He kisses me, raw and smooth sentiments cutting and flowing through us.

We never leave for our closet, to the darkest, dimmest depths. We kiss in the open, with nothing but his hand as the sole barrier between our children and us.

He breathes assuredness and self-belief, filling me completely.

This is not our worst.

< 32 >

July 2023
SUGAR LOAF BLUFF
Winona, Minnesota

Ryke Meadows

Daisy steps on and off a small boulder at the base of a limestone rock pinnacle called Sugar Loaf Bluff. I tie a figure-8 knot at the end of my rope, wondering what she's thinking. We've been in Minnesota all week because of me.

I had a fucking Ziff commercial shoot for a summer campaign. The new drink tastes better than anything they've made in the past eight years. The label just has a Z and the new brand name: *Ascend*. For the shoot, I trad climbed a tough route. This forty-five foot peak at Sugar Loaf is nothing in fucking comparison to yesterday's grit and grind.

Daisy spins on the rock, catching me staring, and mock gasps. "You look just like my husband."

I crack a smile.

She shares it, but they fade together. An undercurrent has been swelling beneath us all week. The first embryo failed, and the test results for the second one should be coming in soon. We go moment-by-moment, and we've been reminding each other everything I once said in Sully's Jeep.

We're lucky. No matter what fucking happens.

Daisy drops off the boulder, and I near her first, cupping her face with one hand. My thumb brushes her long scar. We've never been able to hide what we've been through.

We wear it all.

I kiss her cheek, and I feel her smile return.

She whispers, "There's a peanut butter cupcake behind you."

I look over my shoulder, just as Sulli finishes buckling her harness. You can see it in her fucking eyes—she cuts *no* corners, focused and determined to get it right.

"Done!" she tells me proudly. Yesterday, she watched me climb and Daisy said she told a production assistant, *that's my daddy.*

I part from Daisy to bend down to our five-year-old. "What's the next step?" I quiz her and set the rope aside.

"Re-check my work. I make sure all the buckles are double-backed."

"What happens if they aren't?"

"I fall."

I hold her by the waist and tug on her harness, tight enough. "Where are the fucking buckles?"

She points to three places: her waist, the left leg and the right leg.

I check each one and then ensure her leg loops aren't twisted. "What next?"

Sulli has this keen concentration that pinpoints her eyes. She's not flighty like Daisy. Even now she remains focused and stationary while Daisy wanders around us. But she lacks a certain fucking darkness like me. She's innocent and light.

"Leg loops?" she questions.

I nod. "And then?"

Sulli stares at the blue sky for answers. "Um." She touches her lips. "Ropes?"

"You check your partner's fucking harness and vice versa. Their life is as much yours."

Sullivan motions to me. "But you're only wearing a chalk bag?"

I finish checking her and stand up. "I'm going to wear a fucking harness and belay you." She's five. She can't climb all forty-five feet, but she can try to ascend a small portion of the route. I chose Sugar Loaf today because it's a good sport climb for Sullivan.

And a great free-solo climb for me.

It'll be the first time I free-solo in six long fucking years.

As I bend for the rope, handing it to Sulli, my right knee throbs but dully. Nearly in the back corners of my mind. It hurts no more than yesterday and the day before that. It reminds me of Adam Sully more than it reminds me of our worst day together. I hang onto *him*. He's what I fucking loved, and I didn't even realize how strongly, how powerfully I identified rock climbing with him—and how much it'd all change once he was gone.

During the trad climb for the commercial, I decided that I'd free-solo at the end of this trip. It's a feeling. A *yearning* desire to push myself where I'd been.

It's back.

I fucking feel it again, and I'm not letting go.

I squat back in front of Sulli. Daisy veers towards us, her phone in her hand, but I tell our daughter, "I'm going to fucking climb first. Alone."

Sulli nods.

Daisy tears her gaze off the cell to add, "What he can do, only highly-skilled professional rock climbers do. So don't be scared. He's *this* strong." Daisy playfully squeezes my muscle and then tries to push my arm upwards but acts like it's a thousand fucking tons.

She pants, pretending to be out of breath.

I push her forehead and she drifts, anticipating my response and playing up my strength for Sulli.

Our daughter tries to puff out her chest. "I'm not scared."

Daisy wraps her arms around her, and Sulli is the first to brush noses with Daisy.

I fucking love them.

Then a Beyoncé song interrupts the moment. *Fucking A.* Rose is calling. Daisy hesitates to answer her cell. "I can call her back after you climb."

If it's bad news, would I be able to climb today? No. I wouldn't. I couldn't. I'd be fucking worried about Dais, and I'd want to be on the ground with her.

"Here." I motion to the cell.

She hands it to me, letting me decide. I answer. I have to fucking answer. "Hey, Rose."

"I have to make this quick because my arch nemesis wanted the results by noon." She obviously means Connor. "Is Daisy there?"

"Right here." Daisy speaks into the receiver.

"You'll want to buy a cake."

Daisy eats cake for sad and fucking happy occasions, so this isn't helping. "What kind of cake?" Daisy draws out the inevitable.

"Fuck that. Just fucking tell us."

"It worked." I can hear Rose's smile in her voice before I feel mine spread. *She's pregnant.* "...why is there silence? I need *something.*"

I put the speaker closer to my mouth. "Dais is crying. Thanks, Rose." *Fuck.* I'm crying. I wipe my eyes, kiss Daisy's cheek, and she crouches to Sulli's height and hugs her. Sullivan doesn't know all the details yet, but she knows we're happy.

So she smiles with us.

"Talk later." Rose hangs up.

I mess Daisy's hair and whisper, "I'm going, sweetheart."

She nods and looks up at me. "We'll be here. In Winona, Minnesota." She wags her brows. I push her face affectionately, and she bites my finger.

Winona, Minnesota.

And here, I stand. No rope. No harness. I dip my hands into chalk and near the rock pinnacle. I grip the rough surface with two fingers. Weightless.

My body and my will keep me fucking alive. I lift myself off the ground, quickly reaching for the next handhold, placing my feet. I rise. I climb.

And I hear the soulful call of the mountains.

Hello again, old friend.

{ 33 }

September 2023
THE HALE HOUSE
Philadelphia

LOREN HALE

"Are you sure you want to babysit?" I ask Maria.

She casually leans against the door frame of the kitchen pantry. Three-year-old Luna has physically attached herself to her older cousin's ankle. Luna stares up at Maria with beady amber eyes, half-giggling like she's invisible to Maria. And Maria, my fifteen-year-old niece, just stands there like this is the most normal thing in the entire world.

"It's not too late to back out," I add and shove a tray of fish sticks into the oven. "If you have important shit to do, we can call someone else."

"Like what?" she asks, arms crossed, more "chill" than even her mother, Poppy. And I really didn't think that was fucking possible. "Homework? I dropped out of Dalton Academy this year, remember?"

I slam the oven door closed harder than I intended. "You didn't *drop out*." I already hear her dad in my head. Samuel Stokes couldn't shut up about the whole ordeal.

My daughter is choosing acting over a traditional education.

You'd think Captain America would be upset over the choice, but Sammy was over-the-moon. Like actually proud. I forgot that Sam had been into art growing up, kind of like Poppy, but he ditched his dreams for her. And he ultimately ended up working at Fizzle, her father's company.

He's happy she chose her passion.

Maria makes a face at Luna and shakes her long brown hair at the toddler.

Luna giggles but never speaks, still acting like she's invisible. My lips curve up. My kid is cute. Example A: she's in a dinosaur bathrobe and penguin slippers. Example B: she's my kid.

"I kind of did drop out," Maria says to me.

I give her a look. "What, do you want to be a dropout? You switched to *homeschool*. Last time I checked, the word *school* still implies an education."

Maria shrugs. "It's the same difference."

My eyes narrow. "Take it from someone who *has* dropped out of higher education. It's not the same. In one you learn…things, the other you don't." I stop myself from saying "learn *shit*" in front of my three-year-old. I set the timer on the oven and turn my full-attention to Maria. "What I'm trying to say is that you're fifteen, and you started a career. Lil and I wouldn't be pissed if you stopped babysitting for us."

Maria lets out a laugh. "I was in a couple indie films, Uncle Lo. I'm not a big-time actress or anything. Plus, there are a lot of family dramas that deal with children. This is good experience for me." She pauses and finally speaks to Luna, widening her eyes for my daughter. "Where'd you come from Lunalien?"

Luna gasps like she can't believe she's been found. "Outer space!"

"You have the antennas and everything."

Luna wears a sparkly green headband with bulb antennas. Moffy called her a dinoalienguin this morning because of her wardrobe combination.

My small smile stretches. That's my little girl. *Christ.* I love her more than I love most things. More than I love most fucking people. Moffy, Luna, and Xander fill this deep place in my heart that only Lily could ever reach.

"Let me guess." Maria focuses back on me while Luna disappears into the pantry. "You'd rather stay here. Your dad is really scary, you know. Luncheons always suck when he shows up, so I can't imagine dinner with him is pleasant. Like…" She shudders. "*No.*"

"It's plesant-ish," I say dryly. Not even surprised she has a bad taste in her mouth from Jonathan over the years.

Lily pushes into the kitchen, Xander on the crook of her hip. In a deeper sleep than usual, his cheek rests on Lil's arm, drooling too. While Rose, Connor, Ryke, and Daisy have been dealing with their fertility stuff, the media has leeched onto us, almost cannibalizing our newborn for nine-months and counting.

It hasn't slowed down. It won't. His birth made international news. Not because he almost became an "elevator baby"—and really, Jane's birth was *way* more insane since Connor delivered her himself in a goddamn limo. It's not even because he was born on Christmas day.

It's because Ryke and Lily were the two stuck in that elevator.

[BREAKING NEWS] LILY CALLOWAY GOES INTO LABOR WITH ONLY RYKE IN ATTENDANCE!

Versions of this landed on every major tabloid and entertainment news site. It's technically accurate. He was the only one there at the beginning, so we have no room to complain.

They just twist the fucking facts. Making it seem like Ryke has closer ties to my wife than I do. That he cares for her beyond the role of a friend and brother-in-law. It's dumb as fuck, and it's not affecting anyone but Xander right now.

Journalists seek after him like a piece of celebrity meat. His life is newsworthy because his birth was literally *everywhere*. We can't say the same for the other kids. Not like this.

Every new article they post, more people click into, which prompts them to keep writing more and more and *more* about him.

WHAT'S XANDER LOOK LIKE NOW?
WHO IS HOLDING XANDER?
WHERE DO THEY TAKE XANDER?
IS HE HAPPY IN SO-AND-SO'S ARMS?

Moffy didn't even have this kind of specific attention when he was first born.

When we go out, we can't stop the cameras from hoarding around Xander. We can't stop them from screaming his name. He cries every time we leave the house. He's not even a year old yet, and this is just terrible. The only thing we can do is hold Xander close and tell him we won't let anything or anyone hurt him.

Sometimes it just doesn't feel like enough.

Maria cups her hands to her mouth. "Roll call!"

"Maximoff!" I hear from upstairs.

My daughter pops her head out of the pantry. "Luna!"

"Xander." Lily speaks for our baby, wipes up his drool with the sleeve of her shirt, and then sets him in Maria's outstretched arms.

Maria cradles the baby and rocks him back and forth. "You should hear the Cobalt boys do roll call. They're awful at it. They all insist on using their full names and then correcting each other. Beckett still believes he was born before Charlie."

Lily beams at the fact that our kids do something better than Connor and Rose's. I bet it's chaos at the Cobalt estate, but Connor, who's never frazzled, probably views the hurricane like scattered showers.

Maria only babysits over there when Connor and Rose need a third set of hands. They already have two nannies on-call. Mostly, Maria helps out with our kids—and Sullivan, on rare occasions.

"Looks like I have things covered here," Maria says in a hushed voice now that Xander is in her arms. "You two go to the pits of hell or whatever my mom calls Jonathan's house."

"Satan's lair is actually across the street." I flash a dry smile.

"Satan has great heels," Maria says, knowing I'm referring to Rose.

I give her another look. "You're such a disappointment, Maria Stokes. I thought for sure you would've taken after *me*." I never believed this. Maria has revered Rose since as long as I can remember. "I have the better looks, the better comebacks—"

"But not the better wardrobe." Maria smiles. "Rose is queen, Uncle Lo. I hate to break it to you, but she's way more badass than you."

I feign a wince. "My ears are bleeding."

Luna races over to me. "Daddy! Mr. Zebra Cake will make you feel better." She has the whole box of Little Debbie desserts beneath her armpit.

I hold out my hand. "Thank you, love."

Luna dumps every plastic-wrapped zebra cake onto my hand. Lily grins from ear-to-ear, and my own smile expands. I grab a cake and then come up behind Lily. I drape my arms over her shoulders and rest my chin on her head.

"Let's go, my love." I guide my wife towards the door, my steps short as she takes small ones.

Lily looks up at me, fixated on my lips for a second.

Instead of kissing her, I lower my head and stick my tongue in her ear.

"Lo!" She slugs my arm.

"Right, I forgot." I still don't kiss Lily. I turn slightly back towards Maria. "No boys!"

Maria groans. "Uncle Lo." Her brows rise. "I'm fifteen, just dropped out—I mean, *switched* to homeschooling—and forty-year-olds were my co-stars in my last two movies. I have no love life."

"Good."

She gives me a smile at that. "Have fun with the real Satan."

My dad. Maria has no problem calling him that because we've all labeled him worse things in front of her. On our way to the door, I kiss Lily's cheek. I watch her stifle a needy expression, but she licks her lips and spins around to hook her finger in my belt loop.

We reach the foyer, and I swiftly lift her in a front-piggyback. Her legs wrap around my waist, her hands on my neck. She unconsciously grinds against me. I swallow a knot in my throat, my blood heating.

I hug her against my chest. "You. Me. Car. Now."

Then I really, *really* fucking kiss Lily Hale.

Forgetting about where we're headed, just for one more moment.

"I SHOULD BE IN there with her." Garrison paces in my father's den, twirling a cigarette between his fingers. He quit smoking about a month before he married Willow, which was a year ago. So Ryke has been snatching each one—there he goes. My older brother steals the unlit cigarette from Garrison and tosses it into a trash bin.

Garrison is too anxious to care.

I lean against my dad's desk, a ship-in-a-bottle in hand. "Willow wanted to do this herself."

Ryke glowers at the door to the hallway, not liking where Willow is either. Down the hall, turn right, then left, and you'd reach the fine dining room of the Hale mansion. That's where she is. With him.

I point the ship-in-a-bottle at Ryke. "You," I snap. He barely rotates to me. "Dad's not going to do anything to his own daugh…" I trail off at the glare my brother burns through my face. It could almost rival mine—almost, but not quite.

I hear the message: *just like Dad didn't do a fucking thing to you?*

He crosses his arms.

Garrison tenses more.

When did I become the one that has to alleviate fucking tension? *When Connor Cobalt chooses his pregnant wife over dinner with the real devil.*

"Daisy and Lily are with her," I tell them both. That's the best I can do for positivity right now. "Don't make me try to act like a candy gram to cheer you two up. I can only take so much pain."

We'd be with the girls, but they banished us to the den. Lily pulled out the "hot-tempered triad" card, and we both relented. It's not our news to share. It's Willow and Garrison's. He'd be with her, but he thinks Jonathan will flip out if they drop the news while he's in the room.

That's how much bad blood there is between them right now.

Connor said that Garrison is in the "most unenviable position" of being Jonathan Hale's *only* son-in-law. He treats his daughter-in-laws like *daughters*, but that same respect for his son-in-law just doesn't translate for some reason.

My dad has never treated women and men the same. So we're not surprised.

Garrison knocks over a vase with his foot. He paces towards the dark wooden cabinets.

Before he goes slapping all the books and knickknacks, I say, "The maid will just pick that up."

Garrison stops. Thinks. Then he paces towards the leather couch. He stops again and yanks at a string to his black jacket. His wardrobe has been an easy attack for my dad, and it's been played to death already.

Do you go into work like that?

Do you even own a suit?

Ryke hates the insults the most. Mostly because he wears track pants and T-shirts to dinners and lunch, and our dad never gets onto him for it.

It's just what Connor said. Being Jonathan Hale's son-in-law is different and the most unenviable position.

No one has said a goddamn thing yet, and the air is still thick. I never claimed to be Connor Cobalt. Now I point the ship-in-the-bottle at the leather furniture. "I lost my virginity on that couch."

I can touch the memory a million times without drowning.

Garrison wakes up from his rambling thoughts, his face scrunched at me like *what the hell.* "You lost your virginity on a *couch?* What happened— your demented father guarded your bedroom door on prom night?"

"Uh, no. I was fourteen." I set the bottle back on the desk and meet Ryke's gaze. We're both thinking about it. Our children losing their virginity at *fourteen.*

Ryke shakes his head at me. "Not fucking happening. That's *way* too fucking young."

Garrison says, "You know you're old *when.*"

I must be ancient then. "Fourteen, fifteen, sixteen—hell, twenty-seven, I'd like my children to be celibate until…hmm, *forever.*" I wear another half-smile. I can't think about Moffy losing his virginity in only *six* years. And I'll bust a vein in my neck if I even contemplate Luna in bed with anyone other than a stuffed animal.

"I'm fucking okay with that," my brother agrees.

Garrison plops down on the leather chair. He rubs his face with his hands, and I realize my virginity story is off his mind now.

Ryke and I exchange concern, and then my brother throws a hacky sack at Garrison—I honestly…I don't ask where that hacky sack came from.

Garrison looks up as the hacky sack pelts his arm. "What?"

"You and Willow are fucking adults." Ryke doesn't add that they're married, which wouldn't really matter to Jonathan. He doesn't even add that they're both well-off. Garrison with his job at Cobalt Inc. and Willow by opening a Superheroes & Scones in London. The store is still in the early phases, but she's in charge of that branch, flying back to London every now and then. This wouldn't matter to my dad either. It's not about money.

It's just personal.

"Like he cares," Garrison snaps.

Ryke jabs a finger towards the door. "He has no fucking reason to be upset that she's pregnant."

And there it is.

Willow is pregnant.

She's not the seventeen-year-old lost girl waiting for me at Superheroes & Scones. She's twenty-five and knows what she wants out of life. When Willow told me, she just said, "Garrison and I don't ever want to go backwards, back to *before*." She meant to the time before they met each other. "We want a family together…" She pushed up her glasses. "Someone that's *ours*."

It made sense.

It *makes* sense.

Living in Philly, stable careers—they saw a clearer future together and all the things they wanted next. So they tried for a baby.

Garrison rubs his eyes aggressively with the heel of his palm. Like he's trying to wake up from the nightmare of Jonathan Hale. "If he wants to talk to me, I think it should be alone." He pushes his brown hair off his forehead. "Honestly, I don't need you two flocking me. I'm not a fucking kid."

At twenty-five, Ryke free-solo climbed the Yosemite Triple Crown, started dating Daisy, and had it out with Greg Calloway. At twenty-five, I already had Moffy, just squashed a neighborhood feud that involved Garrison, and threw a Halloween party in my backyard.

I get it.

He's an adult, but there's a part of me that will always see him like the little brother I never had.

"But I know my dad," I rebut. "It's better if we're there."

Ryke nods in agreement.

Garrison lets out a heavy breath. "I don't like him. I won't *ever* like him, but I'd rather him see me as a man than some scared little boy bringing his two sons as some kind of shitty backup."

Ryke rolls his eyes.

Mine just keep narrowing, seriousness weighing on my chest and shoulders and head. We both want to protect Garrison, more than he even understands. Our relationship with our dad is toxic. I see that. I get it. And I can take all the verbal attacks. I can take *everything*. But I can't take pulling Garrison into another toxic relationship—not when he ripped himself from the one with his brothers.

Garrison's blue-green eyes fix on mine. "I can handle it."

Silence heavies the den.

"You can probably handle it," I say, the first to break the quiet. "It doesn't mean you should have to."

His glare grows hotter. "I need to do this." I hear the endnote: *for Willow.*

"You don't." My edged voice cuts my throat raw. I stand off the desk. "You're *never* going to be a man in his eyes. It has nothing to do with you, and everything to do with him."

I feel Ryke focused on me. Like a burning lamp. Intense. Observant. Even hesitant. I spend most of my time defending our dad. Ryke is the one that shakes me. Tells me what happened. Tries to open my eyes.

I have truths that I haven't really said out loud. Not in a while. Maybe not at all.

Garrison drops his gaze. "Yeah, Willow has told me some stuff… but she said that he's always nice to her."

Because sobriety changed him. Because she's a girl. Because Ryke and I would stop talking to him if he so much as insulted her.

"She doesn't know everything," I tell him, "but he's a lot better now than he was." My mind reels and speeds through all the years. All the progress he's made.

He's not as terrible as he once was. Despite nagging on Garrison, he's always supported Ryke's rock climbing. He's always supported my love of comics.

I continue, "There are still some things that make him tick. I think you remind him of me when I was in prep school." *Apathetic.* Even though he has a job. *Sarcastic. Dead to the world.* Garrison exudes this lazy vibe. Like he'd rather be anywhere but with you.

Knowing Garrison Abbey, I'd never in a million years label him as lazy. He's smart as hell and spends more time coding than I do reading comics. And I read a fucking ton of comic books.

Garrison goes quiet again and stares at his hands. I see him start to shake his head, still stuck on the idea of seeing my dad alone. I've seen how they are together, how my dad spins backwards into someone we all hate. I can't let this happen.

I lick my dry lips. "What I'm trying to say…" I take a pause. *Say it. Say it.* My jaw sharpens, and I shift my weight from one foot to the other, standing in the center of the den.

Say it.

From the chair, Garrison looks up at me.

Say it. "My dad verbally abused me for most of my life, and I'd rather break my knees than put you in that crossfire. So if you want at him, you're going to have to go through me."

Ryke lets out an audible breath. He's stunned because I said the actual word. In the past, I've agreed to the statement. I've nodded along. But I doubt I've ever said it like this.

My features sharpen towards Ryke. "What, big brother?" My eyes burn and start glassing at the sight of his cloudy ones.

His chest rises and falls heavily. Then he nods at me, so much in that one action. Apologies, pride for me, love—a lot of love.

I nod back.

I still remember the day Ryke made me pull my car into a gas station. There, he said: *"Our dad abuses you. He's verbally abusive, and he's fucked with your head."*

I told him, *I know.* A part of me had always known. No one had really used that word with me before Ryke.

I've come to terms with my past. I can talk about what happened. I can even admit that my love for my father never bled away. Despite everything. He could gut me with a knife, and I'd still love him. After years of therapy, I understand that it's partly my own insecurity.

Of feeling like I'm unlovable.

Feeling like he might be the only person who could ever love me.

And wanting, desperately, for someone to love him. Believing we're the same. He has to feel a similar pain too, and he wants that pain to go away.

There's no hate in my heart for my dad. Ryke carries all of it for me, but I wouldn't wish my relationship with Jonathan Hale onto Garrison. Or anyone else.

Garrison has no real time to respond.

My blood ices over the minute the door swings open. My dad steps inside, shutting the door behind him. His hair has grayed, more salt than pepper.

I'm still standing with my brother, but Garrison rises off the chair as soon as my dad walks further into the den.

"You." My dad points at Garrison. "We need to talk."

"You can fucking talk here," Ryke pipes in first. My brother feels responsible for not just Garrison but for me too.

"Actually." Garrison zips up his jacket and slips his phone in his jean's pocket. "I'm out."

My dad physically stands in front of the door. "Don't be a little coward. I barely even said a fucking word to you."

Ryke and I fill the distance between Garrison and my dad, so they're not standing close.

"Little coward? That's a nice one," Garrison says dryly.

My dad rolls his eyes, but I can tell he's trying more than usual. He stuffs his hands into his pockets. "Just sit down."

Garrison contemplates this. "I'm trying not to make this worse for my girl, so the minute you come at me, I'm done." He sits.

My dad nods. "That's fair." He leans his shoulder on the door. "Since we're family, I'll give you this courtesy."

"Oh now we're family. I must've missed that abrupt step-up from the shit on the bottom of your shoe."

My dad lets out a short laugh. "This is why you have no friends—"

"Fuck you," Ryke curses.

"Dad." I shake my head at him. That's what my dad used to tell *me* when I was younger. Garrison isn't me. I swear remorse flits in my dad's eyes.

Garrison cuts in, "It's whatever. What do you want to say to me?"

"Congratulations," my dad says in a much more light-hearted tone. "I would've started with that but you attacked first."

"For fuck's sake," Ryke mutters like our dad is insane. I get him though.

"So you're…okay with this?" Garrison frowns.

"If Willow is happy, then I'm happy. And she's the happiest I've seen her." There aren't any handshakes or offers to smoke a cigar. Because he adds, "I thought you'd be different from Loren on this account." He's referring to Moffy. "What happened to the box of condoms I gave you?"

My brows shoot up. *My dad gave Garrison condoms.* I almost laugh.

Garrison cringes. "First of all, the pregnancy wasn't an accident. Second, I threw that shit away. I can buy my own."

"Wasteful, but maybe I would've done the same."

Garrison looks repulsed at the comparison between him and Jonathan. He stands again, but not on the offensive or defensive. He's neutral. My dad is neutral. Garrison asks, "Is that it?"

"You're not my favorite," he reminds him.

Garrison shrugs. "You're not mine either." He goes towards the door. I follow with Ryke too, but Jonathan Hale still blocks the exit.

"That's not it."

Garrison stops.

My dad captures his gaze as he says, "If you walk out on my daughter and her baby, I will find you and bleed you for all you're worth." He pauses. "And then I will find a way to make sure you never procreate again. Understood?"

Of all the things he's ever said, this is pretty mild.

Garrison snaps, "*Our* baby. It's not only hers."

My dad casually steps aside. "Is something wrong with your left eardrum? Did you not hear the rest?"

"About bleeding me, cutting off my dick—yeah, I heard all that."

He nods. "Awesome. I'd feel the same way if someone broke her heart. I love Willow, and I'm not going anywhere, so you'll just have to deal with me being your least favorite."

My dad walks to a beverage cart, just water and lemons on the silver tray. "I never fucking said you were my least favorite." He picks up a pitcher of water. "Just not my favorite."

"Who's your least favorite?" Garrison has to ask.

My dad just fills up a crystal glass. "You three should return to your wives. They're outside gossiping, I'm sure."

Ryke grumbles something about sexism before pushing out the door. I follow behind with Garrison. *Neutral.* That's where they left the state of things.

In my dad's world, that's enough to be considered family.

As we walk down the dim hallway of a mansion that doesn't feel like home anymore, Garrison asks me, "Who's his least favorite?"

"Connor Cobalt."

Garrison nods once and doesn't ask why. He's heard about their history. Even though my dad apologized to Connor, he's still not a fan of Connor Cobalt. Why? *Simple.*

Jonathan Hale hates to be bested, and only one man has ever really beaten him. And only one man probably ever will.

[34]

November 2023
THE ABBEY LOFT
Philadelphia

Connor Cobalt

I wash dishes with Ryke after Thanksgiving dinner. The dishwasher broke before we could start the first load, so we dry them by hand. I don't have to follow his gaze to know where his eyes land.

"The more you stare at her, the more she won't sit down." I pass him a plate to dry, but he's too distracted by a twenty-week pregnant Rose. My annoyance slowly creeps towards the surface, and I shove most down. "In layman's terms, which you clearly need, *bottle your fucking concern.*"

I flip the plate in front of his face.

He snaps out of it and rips the dish from my hand. "I did five minutes ago, and she's still fucking standing." We have the same goal. Make sure Rose is comfortable. The issue: Ryke can't grasp the interworking of Rose's mind, not even as I attempt to coach him.

I'm the best tutor, so the failure is all his.

"You can't treat her any differently than you usually do." Dishware clinks together as I set more dirtied bowls in the sink basin.

"I'm usually fucking concerned."

"I assure you, not like this." We're all treating this baby like it's our first one. The only advantage is that I understand Ryke. I understand Rose. I understand them all better than they understand each other. I also understand Daisy, who has been the shining light of Rose's pregnancy. They both nearly glow when they're together.

Ryke holds my gaze. "Just fucking look at her and tell me she's not in pain."

"She's been standing beside her empty chair since dinner ended. Her feet hurt. Her back hurts. She hates you but not more than she hates me, and she wishes we'd both stop discussing her body. I know Rose," I tell him. "I don't have to blatantly stare at her to understand. You've confused me with you."

His jaw hardens. "I don't blatantly fucking *stare*."

"Yes you do." I've seen him stare for longer than she'd allow most people.

Ryke rubs his unshaven jaw. "This is fucking hard for me," he admits.

"That's obvious."

He glowers.

"Yes?" I begin to smile.

"You could've just fucking said *me too*."

I arch a brow. "So you'd like me to lie to you."

He groans and throws a dishtowel at the sink faucet. We both never signed up for a marriage with one another, but here we are: washing dishes together, having a baby in some fashion *together*, and bickering like we've known each other for far too long.

Which we have.

"You're making it hard on yourself," I tell him. "Take a breath. Relax. Maybe try yoga, I hear that helps for expecting mothers."

"Fucking hilarious." He does relax at my words. He understands. Rose is the one pregnant, and if something were wrong, she'd tell him. She wouldn't outwardly alert me because she wouldn't have to. I'd know *immediately*, and I wouldn't be anywhere but by her side.

I check my watch. I've distracted him for long enough. "She's sitting now."

He tries to subtly check, and I see his shoulders drop. "Thank fucking God."

"Or you could thank someone who actually helped." *Me.*

Ryke stays quiet just to piss me off, but I don't grant him the satisfaction.

"Oh crap!" Moffy shouts, followed by more guys groaning in defeat. Behind us, two flat-screen televisions are side-by-side, two teams on beanbags. Girls vs. Guys.

Jane and Moffy have the only two game controllers, pounding the buttons quickly.

Sorin-X from *The Fourth Degree* comics is on each of their screens, both playing the identical game and tracking how far they go into the storyline. It's the game Garrison created. The one I invested my resources and time in. It launched at the beginning of November to record sales, and the reviews validated his talent.

AN ORIGINAL MASTERPIECE . . .

GAMING HAS NEVER SEEN AN ADVENTURE QUITE AS FASCINATING AS THIS ONE . . .

YOU'LL NEVER WANT IT TO END . . .

He coded the game, which means that the functionality, the storyline, the gameplay all originate from his mind first. I don't think anyone was prouder than Lo.

"A-B-pull-backwards," Charlie coaches Moffy, trying to help him move along in the game. I'm no more surprised Charlie memorized special moves than I am at Tom's disinterest. My three-year-old looks like he jumped on the beanbag, face-first, and just never moved from there.

Rose stands up, a few three-ring binders in hand.

A timer buzzes. "Switch," Garrison calls to both teams.

Moffy passes the controller to his dad. Then Jane tries to pass hers to Lily, and she hot-potatoes the controller, not expecting to be asked to play.

Ryke and I both dry our hands on dishtowels as Rose slides towards us, one of her hands perched on her lower back. With each pregnancy, her body becomes sore sooner than the last. The cause is a combination of her heels and forcing her back straight with the extra weight.

I don't approach her yet, but she stops between the island counter and the sink. "Does this look even? I polled the girls, but the results are *extremely* biased." More people placate Rose when she's pregnant.

She raises the black binder and shows us the title scrawled across the front.

The Evolution of Tom Carraway Cobalt's Style

"Carraway is crooked, darling."

Her eyes flame at her work.

Ryke gestures to the binder. "It looks fucking straight to me."

I cut in, "If you don't trust me over Ryke then we have a bigger issue than an off-kilter title."

Rose skims the title again. "I trust me more than both of you combined…is this smudged?" This time, she just asks me.

"No."

Rose's piercing eyes flit to my lips. Her nose flares, less fight in her eyes and more softness, like hot magma. Not sparking fire, not blistering flames. Just molten lava. Her rare melting expression *consumes* me.

I cock my head. She shifts sideways like she means to return to her chair, but she lingers here. Rose is unquestionably *overly* aroused.

I wait for a moment or two longer, and she turns to me and asks, "Is this ugly?" She has the binder opened to the second page. She called Tom her fashion soul mate until he went from a plain black wardrobe to a black wardrobe with gothic elements: ghosts, skull-and-crossbones, headstones.

He's three and severely influenced by his older brother, though Rose will rebut that Eliot refuses to wear prints like Tom, and he likes deep red, green, and purple before black.

I hear the faucet behind me, Ryke continuing the dishes.

"The entire page?" I question.

"The way the three-rings jut out. Should I go with a different binding?" She flips it back towards herself, her gaze darting from me to the binder. Tension spindles between us.

"No."

She inhales shallowly and steps towards me, but then shifts away.

I come up behind her, sliding my hand along the base of her bare neck, my other hand skating across her collarbone. I whisper in her ear, "You want my advice, Miss Highest Honors?" She's hot to the touch. "Then I advise you to walk to the bathroom, keep your legs together, and wait inside."

Rigid, unbending—I scan the length of her legs, one of my hands descending to her ass. "Dépêche-toi, chérie." *Hurry, darling.*

She sets her binder on the counter, and instead of glaring, she keeps her back towards me, heels clapping against the floor. Rose heads to the bathroom.

I roll up the sleeves of my button-down higher, and I put her binder on a barstool, safe from the dirtied counters.

"Is she alright?" Ryke asks me, his concern unable to retreat.

"She's better than you are."

Ryke flips me off.

I tell him that I'm checking on Rose before I leave. I slip down a very short hallway, the whole kitchen and living area still visible from here. I knock. "It's Connor, darling."

I hear the lock click.

I open the door and then lock it back. The minimal bathroom has a tub, toilet, and concrete sink, industrial-styled like the rest of the loft.

Rose grips the sink behind her, neck elongated as though her own vulnerability frightens her. I reach her in seconds, towering above her frame. My hands drift tenderly along her shoulders and waist.

I kiss her forehead and whisper, "Vous êtes en sécurité avec moi." *You're safe with me.*

She clutches fiercely onto my biceps, and then she covers her face with one hand, as though trying to hide how submissive she is. She's not trying to impale me with her eyes. She's not spouting off death threats and resisting on purpose.

I tear her hand away and then stroke her hair. "Relax," I murmur in my smoothest tone. "I'd never hurt you, Rose." I always keep reassuring her when she feels this way.

Her breath shallows again, and I guide her head to my shoulder. While she calms, I slip my hand beneath her dress and hook my fingers in her panties. I rip them off. She shudders and lifts her head up a fraction.

I run my fingers between her legs.

She's soaked.

Rose is unmoving, her joints locked tight.

"Vous êtes en sécurité avec moi." I massage her head and then I kiss her hard. She *whimpers* against my mouth. Her neck flushes at the noise she made.

I harden instantly, my cock begging to be inside of my wife.

I adore all of Rose, this moment as much as the enflaming, raging ones.

Effortlessly, I lift Rose to the concrete sink counter, my cock at perfect height with her pelvis. And now she isn't straining in her heels. I still have a clear height advantage, needing to stare down. She doesn't combat me.

Rose grips the waistband of my slacks with white knuckles, legs spread wide open. I have to rip her hands off, just so I can remove my pants. I set her palms on my shoulders. I step out of my slacks, and then she tries to bury her face in her arm.

"Rose, Rose," I whisper. "I'd never hurt you." I lift up her head.

She tightens her eyes closed.

"Breathe, darling."

She tries.

I kiss the base of her neck while I free my erection. Her nails dig into my shoulders, her forehead pressed to my chest. My blood stirs. My lips trail up to her ear, and I whisper the same truths. *I'd never hurt you. You're safe with me, Rose.*

I cup her face and grip my shaft. I'd like to fuck her hard until she collapses against me, but she's pregnant.

Not with your baby.

The single thought tries to gnaw at my unyielding logic.

Not with your baby.

With Ryke's.

Here's another truth: I'm possessive when it comes to my things. So is Rose. But I don't like sharing. She does. It's why she's carrying her sister's baby and why the situation fucks with my mind.

I choose not to hesitate. By the time my lips skim hers in a deep breath, my hand clutching the back of her head, I drive my erection into Rose.

She comes immediately.

I shield her staggered moan beneath my palm. I rock deeper in, building her to another climax before she finishes the first one.

"Connor," Rose breathes, a tinge of fear in her voice. She's putty *and* she's pregnant.

"Shhh." I kiss her forehead once more. "Vous êtes en sécurité avec moi. Vous êtes en sécurité avec moi."

Rose gives herself completely to me, and I honor that trust to the fullest degree. I hold her waist and grip her hair. I take care of her needs. Soft and slow as she quivers. Deeper when she clings tighter to me.

I whisper rapidly in her ear, my unwavering declaration arousing her. While she arouses *me*. Rose clenches around my cock so frequently that my head lightens, blinding.

I hit a peak with Rose, and while I gently milk the rest of my climax, I hold her against me, her body collapsed in exhaustion and submission. Cheek to my shoulder.

I comb her hair off her face and tuck the strands behind her ear.

Tiredly, she whispers, "Je t'aime." *I love you.* As her eyes flit up to me, a spark returns to those yellow-green orbs.

I grin.

Je t'aime.

{ 35 }

December 2023

DALTON ELEMENTARY
Philadelphia

Lily Hale

"Moms and Dads, I think it's about time. Let's begin our December meeting." Maggie Hollybaum clutches a wooden clipboard like it's a second appendage. Hair in perfect blonde curls, pearl earrings clipped tight, a yellow monogrammed purse perched on the teacher's desk—I wonder how she looks so clean and *neat*.

I can't even keep stains off my clothes. Right now, I think I have peanut butter on the collar of my shirt.

At least…I hope it's peanut butter. *Please let it be peanut butter.*

I don't check.

We all quiet down while Maggie scans her clipboard.

As the head of the PTA, I initially thought Maggie would be the most stuck-up, judgmental parent of them all. I was prepared for her disdain to rain down on me. Then she made a fart joke to Daisy and laughed when her own son picked his nose.

I like Maggie, but it's not to say the rest of the PTA like me.

I currently sit in the back row of the elementary classroom. I feel like I've stepped into some fucked-up time machine.

Maggie clicks her tongue in thought. "Okay, here we go. Annie and Summer have already agreed to head the annual ornament painting festival. We still need someone to organize the cookie fundraiser." Her finger runs down the roster of parents.

One desk over, Daisy whispers to me, "Don't look her in the eyes."

Connor sits on my other side. He halfheartedly followed us to the back row of desks. Apparently his inner honor student withers away the longer he's in the "apathetic" row. Personally, I love Apathetic Row.

At least when it comes to school.

I try to follow my little sister's instructions and stare at the surface of my desk. I squint at a faint marker doodle. Did someone draw a dick and balls? *Noooo.* This is just my dirty mind. It could be a weirdly shaped hot dog?

I whisper to Connor, "Is this a dick doodle?" I point at my desk. I'm glad he doesn't question why I asked him. Ryke definitely would've, and I'd have to explain that since he has a penis, he'd be a better judge than me. Even though I've seen my fair share.

Connor examines the doodle in about one second flat. "Yes but it's crooked."

"Lily Hale."

I jump at my name, my neck roasting. *They didn't hear you talk about a dick doodle.* For some reason, I rest my arm across my desk, covering up the crooked penis like I'm the one who drew it.

"Yeah?" I look to Maggie.

"You're not signed up for anything."

"Really?" I stare at the ceiling. "I could've sworn I signed up for that…thing." Lo and I made an agreement not to be swept up into too many activities. We already have *enough* on our plate that we don't need to add ornament painting to it.

"How about you head the holiday cookie fundraiser?" Maggie suggests nicely. It nearly sways me to say *yes*.

Then Frank Kale, the only other man here besides Connor, interjects, "You shouldn't give that much responsibility to someone like her."

He's the second worst person in the PTA. Moffy tried Little League for one season (he likes swimming more), and we all saw Frank scream at the coach to make his son pitcher. The coach asked his son if he wanted to be pitcher. To which the boy said, *not really*. Frank dragged his son by the arm and took him off the team.

Lo called him a helicopter dad.

Ryke called him a fucking prick.

Connor called him Frank Kale.

His whole persona makes us all cringe. So Connor ended up being the most accurate. Like right now, I cringe at Frank and wish he'd turn his judgy eyes onto the whiteboard.

Before I can respond, Maggie sticks up for me. "Lily helped with the Easter Egg hunt last year. There were no issues, Frank."

"Because Rose handled that event, not her."

"I helped." I stick up for myself. Though the truth: the cookie fundraiser might be too much responsibility for just me. So the heart of what Frank said is correct. I hate that it is, but it is. I have a baby that's about to turn one. A bouncy four-year-old. And an eight-year-old with a crazy swim practice schedule.

I love cookies, but I don't know where to squeeze in an *entire* cookie fundraiser between all of that and Superheroes & Scones.

I suck at multitasking. I'd willingly give myself an F. So there.

Then Justine whatever-her-last-name-is physically swivels in her seat to cast a snide comment my way. "Where are you even going to bake the cookies?"

She is the absolute worst. To my face, Justine said, "I don't mean to be rude, but you probably shouldn't have children." It hurt, and it hurts worse when she tries to spread lies to her gaggle of friends. *They don't keep a clean household.*

Kids shouldn't hear sex. Or see it.

She's disgusting. We should have her children kicked out of the school.

They've tried and failed. I have a secret weapon called Rose Calloway Cobalt and Connor Cobalt. No one can defeat nerd stars.

Connor speaks before I find words to reply. "*Bake* implies *kitchen*, which most commonly implies *house*. It's simple language skills."

Justine purses her lips, brown hair in perfect waves from a curling iron no doubt.

"I haven't signed up for anything either," Daisy says to the PTA-filled classroom. She tries to spin the spotlight on herself and off me. Rose and Connor never signed up for an event this year too, but they haven't been called out. I'm just an easy target sometimes.

Frank tightens his silver-plated Rolex watch in front of Connor. "Then you should do the fundraiser instead of her."

"I have a name," I mention softly. My shyness escalates to eighty-percent functionality. I'm just happy I'm not hiding beneath my desk.

"I can do it with Lily," Daisy says.

"The three of us can," Connor notes.

I relax at the sound of teamwork. I truly love the concept, especially when the guys are better bakers than us (especially Ryke), and it's likely they'll just take over. That's my idea of *excellent* teamwork.

"But at which house?" Justine asks.

"Mine?" Is this a trick question?

Justine bristles. I failed the mommy mind game. She whips towards me. "I don't think any cookies should be touching your counters."

"Justine," Daisy says, beating everyone to speak. "We're doing the cookies at my sister's house. And you can go to hell."

My eyes pop out. *Whaaa…?*

Daisy crosses her arms and acts like the protective older sister, the role reversal something that happens between us. But never has she come to my defense by telling a mom to go to hell. It's so unlike Daisy.

Even Justine gapes in shock, unsure of how to respond. Whispers float around the room.

I smile at Daisy.

She smiles back.

Hushed, I tell her, "I feel like I could throw out some middle fingers in a weird champion-like dance." I *feel* it, but executing it takes a different kind of courage.

Daisy wags her brows. "Let's totally do that outside."

We smile more.

2024

"I never understood how much
I had lost my voice until I
started using it."

- Daisy Meadows, We Are Calloway

(Season 6 Episode 07 — Motorcycles & Crosswords)

{ 36 }

Lily hale

I carry a sleeping four-year-old Luna up the flight of stairs. Proud of my arm strength. *Good job, arms.* Green glitter is tangled in Luna's brown hair. I'm sure she'll fuss when we both try to pick it out in the morning. She still wears a pair of 2024 sunglasses and New Year's Eve stickers all over her alien-printed PJs.

When I reach her room, I gently rest Luna on the mattress and slide off the sunglasses. I pull up her white comforter and tuck her into bed.

Luna's room is an explosion of personality: alien-stuffed plushies, plastic blowup chairs (green, of course), multi-colored carpet, and a lava lamp. Sometimes I just catch her watching the colors and glow-in-the-dark stars on the ceiling.

"Night, Luna," I whisper and kiss her head before tiptoeing to the hall. I shut the door closed.

I yawn when I enter my dimly-lit bedroom. "Luna's passed out." I plop on the bed with my arms and legs splayed.

This is what a pancake must feel like.

Lo sheds his shirt. "Moffy too. He'll be upset he didn't make it to midnight this year."

"We can tell him he didn't miss anything exciting." I roll on my stomach and reach for the baby monitor by the clock. Xander is fast asleep in his crib. He turned one on Christmas. It was the start of us trying to make his birthday memorable, despite having to share it with a holiday.

Lo pulls off his socks. "So my sister told me the name of her baby tonight."

I perk up and set the monitor back. "What's her name?" The Abbey baby isn't due yet, but we all know she's having a girl. "Is it based on a video game character? Is it Zelda?" I kneel on the mattress, my thoughts wild at all the possibilities. They're into pop culture like us, so the options are endless. My eyes grow big. "Are they naming her Hermione?! I might die."

"Don't die, love." Lo drops his pants, the bulge in his boxer-briefs calling out to me.

"…it'd be a happy death," I say dazedly. *His cock. In me.* "…I'd die out of…love."

Lo crawls onto the bed, and I try to shimmy down towards him, so he can crawl *on top* of me. I even wiggle out of my pants, now down to my panties and muscle shirt. He sees the needy suggestion in my eyes, but he's not taking the bait yet.

Focus off his cock.

It's so hard.

I flush at the double meaning.

"Are you going to give me any hints?" I wonder.

"Vada Lauren Abbey," he tells me the name. "Vada for—"

"*My Girl*," I finish. The lead character of that 90s film is named Vada. Garrison reblogs a lot of *My Girl* gifs and makes them for Willow, but both Lo and I first saw that movie when we were about eight or nine. It fits them better than all of my suggestions, even Hermione. "And Lauren, as in—"

"Me," he finishes this time.

My eyes well. "Lo."

"Yeah, I know." He nods. "It's a horrible middle name." His sarcasm is so apparent, especially as his smile grows, overwhelmed by being a namesake.

I wipe a fallen tear. "Is it spelled the same?"

"She asked me if she should do the L-O-R-E-N version, and I told her to go traditional. I figure I have thirty-three years of bad karma stored up in that name. Best way to dodge it is by going L-A-U-R-E-N."

I nod. "Smart thinking." As the topic of conversation fades, my mind reroutes to what's knelt in front of me.

Loren Hale in black boxer-briefs. Loren Hale with cheekbones that cut like ice. Loren Hale with a six-pack and muscular thighs. Why his thighs turn me on, my nefarious brain cannot compute. It just sees them and his biceps and those cheekbones and chants, *closer, closer, closer.*

Lo leans forward, finally, and his hands fall onto either side of my head. He hovers above me. I try to tug him down so his weight adds pressure against my body.

He never lowers.

So I ask, "Lo, are we going to have New Year's Day sex?" I'm honed in on his rising lips and the dimples in his cheeks. I sense him studying my body for a second, but I can tell he's horny (maybe not as much as me) by his hardness and the flex of his muscles.

Then his lips dip down to mine but veer off to the base of my neck. "Yes," he says into a kiss. *Yes!*

My pulse hammers, skin tingling by my neck. I lie flat on our bed but I've already split my legs around his body. I've already grabbed onto his shoulders. If I could do a pull-up, I'd already be against him.

Reasons to work out.

It's so enticing, but not as enticing as *not* working out.

"The first sex in 2024," I muse. "This is a big deal. Give me a second. I have to think how we're going to do this." I squeeze my eyes shut because his body, his face, his eyebrows and hair are *all* distracting. "Anal? Or maybe on top? OhmyGod, maybe we should do it standing up? No, on the floor! No, in the bathtub!"

My mind actually races between positions, so fast that I bite my thumb nail. I've opened my eyes, but I stare off into a faraway sex land called Lily Hale's Dirty Mind.

"Lil, calm down."

"Huh."

He pinches my cheek.

"Hey!" I rub my cheek. *So mean.*

"Calm down," he repeats, his face blanketed with seriousness.

"I am calm. Calm but excited." I try a pull-up on his body. Nope, not happening. I wait for the *thud* on the mattress, but I quickly realize that I never lifted myself off the bed to begin with. *Weakling*, that's me.

"If it's a big deal for you, then I'll make it the best sex of the goddamn year, but I want you to enjoy it without being compulsive, yeah?"

I'm about to wholeheartedly agree, but his movements distract me. His left hand has left the mattress, and his fingers lightly skim the sliver of skin above my cotton panties. I follow his carnal gaze, and my travel leads me to my white muscle shirt, the fabric askew. My boob is exposed, nipple hardened.

I spend so much time ogling him that I forget what I even look like. And how much he's attracted to me. Which I can see is a whole lot.

My hand drops off his shoulder and onto my hipbone. I stop myself from inching lower. *Don't be compulsive.* I think about his previous declaration.

"Can we scratch the *best sex of the year*?" I ask. "Because if that's true then all the rest of the sex this year will be not-the-best, and I won't have anything to look forward to."

His amber eyes abruptly tear off my nipple and set daggered onto my face. "Lily Hale, are you telling me you wouldn't look forward to fucking me?"

Now that he phrases it like that…

"Absolutely not. Scratch everything I just said. I'm not picky. Best sex. Okay sex. Awesome sex. Any kind of sex is what I look forward to—as long as it's with you." I try to nod resolutely, but it's harder lying down.

"Okay sex?" He frowns and nearly sits up. *No, come back!* I tug at the band of his boxer-briefs, and he lowers to his previous position. *Yes!* "When have we had okay sex?"

"When something interrupts us and I don't come."

His jaw tightens, but then he nods like he gets it. "Tonight, I promise not to let anything interrupt your orgasm." He holds out his pinky finger. Loren Hale initiating a pinky-promise.

My heart sputters, and without pause, I hook my pinky with his.

Lo kisses me urgently, deeply. My lips swell beneath his, a moan tickling my throat. His hand slides beneath my muscle shirt, kneading the soft flesh of my breast.

I run my hands over his arms, his abs. His cut muscles are the product of many workouts that help him combat stress better than a bottle of bourbon. I kiss him just as vehemently, my legs tightening around his waist. He's still too far away.

Lo disconnects from my mouth. "Lil." His voice is low and hoarse. "You. Naked. Now." He lifts my muscle shirt over my head while my dazed mind has already imagined him inside of me.

"You…aren't naked?" I try to tug at his boxer-briefs.

He groans as he attempts to pull my panties off my legs. I won't disentangle from his waist. We're a hot mess, but my mission is his cock, not undressing myself.

Lo pries my gangly legs off his waist.

I make a noise that may be a whine, but it's an *I want you* whine and *come back to me!* plea.

Lo handles my body like someone nurturing and stimulating an animal in heat. His narrowed eyes flit to the ceiling, very briefly, to contain his own arousal. I could pounce on him and fuck him, and as I squirm for Lo and only Lo, the muscle in his jaw tenses.

He quickly pulls my panties off my ankles, and I clutch his lean build. I want to be a koala clung onto the Loren Hale tree, but so much space still separates his body from mine.

He's knelt between my legs.

My breath hitches, my skin hot and beginning to glisten with just my thoughts. I unsuccessfully removed his boxer-briefs. He pulls *up* the black fabric, air and that article of clothing separating us. Without panties, I'm exposed and empty. I need his hardness, the pressure right up against me.

"Lo," I moan in desperation.

Sex might be more complicated for him than me. I'm on *reach orgasm* mode while he's on *focus on Lily's health, don't come before Lily, nurture and protect and then fuck her good* mode.

Anyone else could easily take advantage of my addiction, but he doesn't. Lo would never propel me to a bad place just because I'm willing to do anything in bed. I need restrictions. I need slow.

I need him.

Lo seizes my hips that rock upwards. "Easy, love." He pushes my abdomen down, and then his hand drifts between my legs. I tingle and clench, even before he slips two fingers inside.

I shudder so fast, and he deserts me just as quickly. "Lo," I whimper. I don't realize my hands are sliding down my thighs until he grips my wrists.

He kisses the edge of my lips and whispers, "Take a breath."

Fuck. Fuck. I want to fuck. I inhale a short breath, my head slightly leveling. In the middle of the bed, he stays on his knees.

I sit up. "Please," I beg. I just need his skin on my skin. I wrap my arms around his frame, tucking my body against Lo.

He does something out of the ordinary.

Lo slowly lies backwards, his shoulders meeting the champagne comforter.

I splay my palms on his chest, lifting myself up just a little in realization. I'm on top of Loren Hale. I'm straddling his waist.

I rarely ever end up on top or in control because I take it too far.

My lips part while my whole body shakes. Lo watches me. His amber eyes bore through my soul. He also lies here for my pleasure, but my brain only sees this body that can offer me the *best* orgasm of my life.

I can't just stay motionless. Not in this position. I dig against the hardness in his boxer-briefs, grinding only twice before my otherworldly orgasm throttles my mind. "OhmyGod," I gasp. My fingers scrap his chest, and I bury my cry into the crook of his arm.

Yesyesyes.

I've barely calmed before my hand dives down his boxer-briefs, about to pull out his cock for my own use.

He seizes my wrists again.

"Lo…*more*," I beg, grinding. I'm grinding again.

He then grabs onto my hips. "Lily." His low, hoarse voice reveals his growing *need* too. "You can't steer this ship, love." If I want to be on top, he has to push into me and he has to be the one to move me. The rules blink in and out.

I reach for my clit.

"Hands," he forces and then sits up suddenly.

I raise my hands to his face, my pulse bursting. I'm on his lap. His dick is halfway out of his boxer-briefs. I barely intake his sharp concern. Too needy. Too horny.

"Look at me," he says.

I try to focus on his eyes.

When I do, he tells me, "Arms above your head. Repeat it, Lil."

"Arms…above me."

He stretches my arms upwards so I understand. "Let me take care of you."

I nod and keep my arms hoisted.

He lies back again, shoulders on the comforter. I do as he asked, but my elbows definitely bend, mostly due to my poor arm-strength than me not listening.

Lo rocks *his* pelvis up and back-and-forth against me. I clench, so wet against him that I soak his boxer-briefs. Lo understands that the longer foreplay lasts, the longer I can bask in the journey instead of being disappointed by the end of the destination.

My own body revolts against this concept, just seeking the high, the rush, the climax, but I appreciate what Lo does for me. My compulsive self feels strained and teased, but in the end, it's so much better and healthier for me this way.

My arms droop, but I clutch onto his thighs inside of mine. My head tilts back and my eyes shut, trembling at all the heightened sensations. "Yes," I murmur.

He sits up, his mouth against my breasts, taking my nipple between his lips. He kisses with eagerness that thrums my bones. When he lies back again, he pushes his bulge against me until the pressure blinds my senses.

My toes curl and a noise tickles my throat. I hold onto his arms like I'm falling off a cliff.

He stops moving and waits for me to come down.

I pant at the second orgasm, and his cock isn't even in me yet. My body just kind of splats against his chest, no strength left.

"I'm sorry," I whisper, blood rushing back to my head, unable to pick myself up. I was a little compulsive. "I thought I could wait until you were in me." He hasn't come yet, but he can easily if I just kiss his cock and look up at him.

He holds me to his chest, and in seconds, I'm on my back and he's on top. He hoists his body weight off me. "There's no limit on orgasms.

You can take as many as you want." Meaning I can still feel him inside of me tonight.

We usually have sex until he comes or when we both decide that it's enough. It varies every night, but I've been doing really well. We set boundaries together, and he makes sure I don't cross any promises I've made to myself in the heat of the moment. Which is why he told me to raise my arms.

Loren Hale used to be synonymous with the word *selfish*. Every time we're in bed together, I'm reminded of his selflessness. He always puts my needs high above his, and every night I settle down in his arms, I feel lucky to have him.

"Lil." His voice cracks. "Why are you crying?" He rubs my tears with his thumb, concern and hurt crossing his beautiful face.

"I don't deserve you," I say softly, our legs tangled together.

His glare could murder a family of geese, but the familiar sight is more than comforting. "Then we're two undeserving individuals because I sure as hell don't deserve you, Lily Hale. *You* help me every day stay sane and sober. I couldn't live this life alone." His thumb skims my wet cheeks. "And you know what?"

"What?" I whisper.

"The world went and fucked itself because the two most undeserving people got more than they deserved."

I laugh and rub my eyes. My gaze drifts to his hard-on. I'm not always an equal opportunity girl in bed, and Lo knows this. I've already surrendered to my faults.

"Does that hurt?" I wonder.

"Like hell." He takes off his boxer-briefs, so erect that I tighten at the sight.

"I can blow you," I offer.

He's already breaking open my legs with his knees. "I'd rather be inside you."

Third orgasm, here I come.

His arm stretches towards one of the nightstands. Birth control has made me feel too bloated and too nauseous recently, so I stopped with the pills a couple months ago. I've been searching new forms of birth control in the meantime, and we've been vigilant about condoms.

Lo opens the drawer but then hesitates and shuts it. No condom.

I frown. "Are we out?"

He shakes his head and kisses my cheek. "Let's not use it," he whispers.

My heart thumps. "What?"

"Let's not use it, Lil," he repeats.

"I heard that, but I don't...understand...?" Is he saying what I think he's saying?

Lo puts his hands on either side of my head and stares right into me. "One more kid," he says. "Just one more and then we'll be done. I can get a vasectomy and you can do whatever you need to do." His gaze never drifts off mine. "What do you think?"

I think this is crazy.

We carefully planned out Luna and Xander's births. We gave ourselves *time* between each of our children. We never talked about a fourth. Maybe because there was a silent agreement that four is a big number.

Bigger than we'd ever imagined.

Bigger than us.

But is it?

"Four," I mutter, expecting chills but only warmth bathes me. What do we expect for ourselves?

No children.

Unhappiness.

Loneliness.

Frequent misery.

No self-worth.

Loveless lives.

No. I think. *No.*

Loren Hale is on top of me, *telling me* that we should expect more for ourselves. "We can do this," he says strongly. "I know we can."

I smile. "I know we can too."

He leans in for a kiss, but he teases, stopping a breath away. "We have the perfect name if it's a boy or girl."

"What?"

"Keller for a boy," he breathes. "Kinney for a girl."

I smile wider into my tears. Julian Keller and Laura Kinney from *X-Men* comics. Hellion and X-23. His two favorite characters in all of Marvel. Characters that I love immensely out of his love for them. Why we didn't think of these names for our third baby—maybe because we knew these characters are the most precious to us. And our story wasn't closed yet.

One more.

"Yes," I agree to our future, to everything.

His body and lips press against mine with new desperate vigor. He pulls me up into his chest, stretches my leg around his waist, and he's in me. Thrusting deep like this is where he was always supposed to go.

I cling to Lo.

Our eyes, our bodies, and our souls—they never abandon each other.

‹ 37 ›

March 2024
MANHATTAN MEDICAL HOSPITAL
New York City

Daisy Meadows

I've had many theories, but the theory I have today overwhelms all others.

I have a theory that, together, sisters can do extraordinary, miraculous things. People will underestimate us, undervalue us, maybe even forget us, but together, *together*—we succeed.

About an hour ago, Rose scooted over on her hospital bed, urging me to be beside her, and I am. We lie towards one another, a delicate, precious baby cradled in my arms. Rose post-thirteen-hour-labor is one of the most emotional Roses there ever could be. Tears have been running down our cheeks, and we're quiet, listening to Winona breathe softly.

Rose gently sweeps her finger across the newborn's nose. "She looks just like you, Daisy."

I rub the heel of my palm over my wet face. I tilt my head towards Rose. She tilts hers towards me. And I say, "Thank you."

Tears cascade harder. For us both. Rose tries to wipe mine with her thumb, and then she kisses my cheek. I love my sisters more than life itself, and what Rose did for me digs to the *very* core of love. It exists entirely and soulfully within Winona.

I'll never forget being by Rose's side during the labor. Holding her hand. How Ryke and Connor were with us. I'll never forget how much we all cared. We picked out the middle name *Briar* because we wanted to honor Rose—she cried the day we told her, but not as much as we cry now.

Rose brushes my tears away before she finishes drying her face with the corner of the sheet. "Ryke was fated to be surrounded by women."

I laugh and rub my nose with the back of my hand. "He'd say *thank fucking God*."

Connor and Ryke hear me, just now slipping inside the room, coffee cups in their hands. Their eyes on Winona.

"Why would I fucking say that?" Ryke asks.

I repeat what Rose said, "You were fated to be surrounded by women."

Ryke smiles one of the most beautiful smiles he's ever worn, and he says, "I fucking prefer it that way." He was hoping for another girl.

Rose extends a hand towards Connor, and he places a coffee cup in it. Then his free one slides on her shoulder as he tells us, "This has less to do with fate and more to do with chromosomes."

"Booo," I say, my thumb down.

"What my sister said." Rose sits up and sips her coffee, a hot glare planted on Connor. She never loses her edge, not even after labor. Rose is made of something stronger than the rest of us.

She speaks in hushed French with Connor, both at ease.

I sit up more too, Winona swaddled and content in my arms. Everyone has already held her, even Lily and Lo, who left early. All the kids are having a sleepover at their aunt and uncle's so they're excited about today, just maybe not for the same reason as us.

I kiss Winona's cheek and pass her to Ryke.

He sets his coffee on a chair's armrest before cradling our baby. I melt at his affectionate, soft expression. He whispers to her in Spanish, and then rocks her back and forth. She nestles towards his chest.

I peek over at the stiff hospital couch. Sullivan, already six-years-old, is conked out, a thin blanket pulled to her shoulders (thank you, Ryke).

"Should we wake her?" I whisper to him.

He glances at Sullivan and grimaces at the thought of disturbing her sleep. It's our fault she sleeps strange hours, and more our fault that she forces herself awake. "I don't want to miss anything!" she always exclaims. So when she does *actually* sleep this heavy, we try not to jostle her awake, but she hasn't met her little sister yet.

"Let's give it another five fucking minutes," Ryke suggests, taking a seat in the chair beside me. Connor is already sitting in the one by Rose.

My older sister asks her husband, "What quote comes to mind now?" She takes another relaxed sip from her coffee.

Connor begins to smile, eyes dancing to each and every one of us. "'Happiness, knowledge, not in another place but this place, not for another hour but this hour.'"

Rose identifies the quote, "Walt Whitman from 'A Song of Occupations'."

Connor says an affirmation in French.

"I fucking have one." Ryke suddenly captures Connor's attention. And to Connor, Ryke says, "'I have learned that to be with those I like is enough.'"

Connor raises his coffee to Ryke, the most tender smile on his lips. "Walt Whitman."

"Walt Whitman." Ryke nods.

On Connor's thirtieth birthday, we discussed poets and playwrights and authors. As we recited his favorite portions from his favorite books,

Connor said that he'd always been drawn to Faulkner. He could quote nearly any line off the top of his head like he lived and breathed the words since he was a child.

That day Connor asked Ryke and I to read a few poems.

They were all Walt Whitman, and he said that Whitman fit with us like Faulkner did with him.

Sullivan stirs, so Ryke brings the newborn over to the couch. "Hey, Sulli," he says softly.

She rubs her eyes and quickly sits up. "Did I miss it?"

"No, sweetie." He takes a seat beside her. "This is your new sister."

I wrap my arm around Rose. She may hate hugs, but she holds onto my arm this time. Her eyes fight to hold back stronger sentiments as she watches Sulli and her new sister. Rose whispers to me, "That's me and you."

We're about six years apart, like Sullivan and Winona. Two generations of sisters. I rest my chin on Rose's shoulder, and she places her hand to my head lovingly.

Sullivan stares in awe at the baby and she says, "I love you, Nona."

Ryke & Daisy Meadows welcome the birth of their baby girl

WINONA BRIAR MEADOWS

March 24th, 2024

{ 38 }

April 2024
THE HALE HOUSE
Philadelphia

Lily Hale

"You don't need those, Lil." Lo tries to pry the diagrams from my hands, but I tug the printouts back.

"What if he asks for pictures," I whisper, standing a foot from Moffy's bedroom door. "I need to be prepared."

Lo straightens out his twisted arrowhead necklace, all casual and at ease while nerves swarm me. "If he asks for pictures, then we'll tell him we'll buy a book. It's better than these." He suddenly yanks the papers, and the printouts escape my fingertips. He scans them. "Huh." He flashes the black-outlined, fuzzy diagrams at my face, pointing at the copyright in the corner.

1982.

So I chose the first thing I saw in haste. "Sex organs were the same in the eighties…right?" What if we're all mutating? What if penises are genetically *better* in the future? My mind races.

Lo waves his hand in my face. "No spacing out, love."

Right.

I have to be one-hundred percent cognizant during this talk. I hop like a warm-up, then stop and realize I'm two-seconds from a jumping jack.

I have to give *the* sex talk to my eight-year-old son. Not run a marathon. Although, this kind of feels like there's a finish line at the end.

I always knew Moffy would ask one of us about sex. Hell, I thought it'd be sooner than now. I just didn't think he'd ask me over Lo.

But he did.

This morning before his 6:00 a.m. swim practice, he stood halfway out the door and paused for a moment. I thought he forgot his breakfast, so I brought him his half-eaten peanut butter banana toast. Ryke's Land Cruiser sat idle on the curb, waiting for Moffy. Ryke and Daisy bring Sullivan and Maximoff to early-morning practices while we do after-school ones.

Moffy took his toast with less interest and eyed my small baby bump. I'm around thirteen-weeks pregnant. Out of seemingly nowhere, he asked, "You have to have sex to have a baby, right?"

It caught me off guard, but I nodded. He's asked small questions throughout the years like *why do girls have vaginas?* and Lo did most of the answering while I nodded in agreement. I realize today that I must've done a decent job because he didn't feel like I'm the closed-off, awkward parent. He felt comfortable enough to ask *me*.

"Do you want to know more?" I wondered and managed to keep my cool.

"Yeah."

I told him we'd talk about it later tonight because he had swim practice. And I secretly needed time to figure out the right way to go about this.

Well, it's later tonight.

Lo balls up all my printouts.

I stare at the closed bedroom door. When I tried practicing a speech earlier, Lo cut me off and told me to just be natural. No practice needed. Now I regret not rehearsing a speech, but I also think he has a point. I don't want sex to seem like this big monster, and the more I make it into a huge deal, the worse it'll be. I've done well so far; I can't mess it up now.

My other giant worry: I screw this up and Moffy will *never* ask me questions again.

"You sure you want to do this?" Lo stares at my crinkled eyebrows, all concentration and a little bit anxiety. He's already offered to talk to Moffy, but our son asked me. I want to be the one to tell him.

"I'm sure." I nod to myself.

Confidence slowly but surely travels through my veins. I pull back my shoulders and remember that I can think and talk about sex without being overcome with shame. I've experienced healthy sex. I have it every day. I can do this.

I'm strong.

Just in my own way.

I don't look to Lo for any more reassurance. One hand on the knob, I knock with the other. "Moffy?" I call out. "Can I come in?"

"Yeah!"

I slip into his dark room, his five-foot lamp bathing the area in a warm orange glow. Lo stays out in the hall. He told me that he'll eavesdrop, but he understands that this is something I need to do on my own.

Spider-Man framed posters are hung above his wooden dresser, a Wolverine decal over his closet door. It's the only art in his room. When he turned seven, he asked if he could paint his walls black, and he wanted a special bed for his birthday.

So when I shut the door and pass his dresser, the Batmobile bed is the focus of the whole space. Lo can barely spend two minutes in Moffy's room before he walks out. It's a surprise that he let the Batmobile bed into the house at all, but Lo loves Moffy more than he hates Batman.

In the middle of the floor, Moffy sits on a round orange rug, papers scattered in front of him. He uses a textbook as a writing surface and scribbles his homework on notebook paper.

"Why don't you work on the desk?" I ask him.

He shrugs. "I like it better down here."

That's as good a reason as any, I suppose. I sink to the floor.

He lets out a long groan, focused on the scattered papers.

"What's wrong?" I ask.

"I hate Janie's math notes," he complains. "They're so hard to read."

I crane my neck and notice all the doodles in the margins of her notes. Hearts. Stars. Stick figure cats sipping milk and prancing on rooftops. Her messy scrawl contrasts Moffy's neat handwriting. They've been trading notes since they started second grade.

Jane makes better grades in math and science, but she dislikes the reading portion. According to Moffy, Jane doesn't like the books they assign. So he helps her with the reading and writing. I thought it'd been going well.

Yesterday he told us that he can't wait for third grade. Apparently that's where all the big kids are. With a summer birthday, we could've chosen to start him early instead of late. I don't regret our decision. He might be the oldest in his class, but he's also excelling. It's more than I can say for Lo and me at eight-years-old. Or really…ever.

School was not our thing.

"Maybe you should ask Jane to write more legibly," I suggest.

He nods. "I'll try." He outstretches one of his legs, his textbook slipping off his lap. Moffy doesn't notice, his green eyes planted on mine. "Did you get the books on the list yet?"

"Soon."

He just gave me his summer reading list this morning. Instead of choosing the required three books, he wants to read every single one.

Ten books. I never thought we'd have a child who likes reading outside of graphic novels and the occasional fantasy book.

Then again, I never thought we'd have a baby that grew up to love Batman.

Moffy has been full of surprises.

Just as he takes out a calculator from his backpack, I say, "Hey, Moffy. Do you remember what you asked me this morning?"

"About sex?" His voice is nonchalant. He starts typing on his calculator.

"Yeah, sex." I don't stammer, which boosts my confidence even more. I sit cross-legged and hold onto my knees. "Do you know what it is?"

"I think so…it's how babies are made."

"Right." I go along with this. "And remember how we told you how a baby is made. When a man's sperm goes inside a woman, it joins with an egg and the baby grows in the woman's uterus."

I think I may actually buy him a book for visuals. A *recent* book. Just in case we've all evolved.

Moffy sets down his pencil, brows scrunched in deep contemplation. "Yeah…but how is that sex? I'm just confused. Whitney Rivenfell says two people can do it without making babies. Why would they want to do that?" He shakes his head. "And how exactly does the sperm get inside?"

Calmly, I answer the second question. It seems the easiest. "Sperm comes out of a penis, and so when the man puts his penis into a woman's vagina, the sperm releases." *Nailed it.* Continuing on, "And as for Whitney's assessment, two people can have sex without making babies. She's right about that."

"*He,*" Moffy corrects. "Whitney's a boy, Mom."

First strike, but it had nothing to do with the sex conversation. I'll take it.

He keeps talking before I can explain further, "So that's what you and Dad do?" His face twists. "Does it hurt you? Are you okay?"

Uhhh…I didn't think *the sex talk* would take this detour. "It doesn't hurt, Moffy…well for some girls, it does their first time. But that's not really part of what I want to say…" I trail off, lost for a second. I try to recollect my dispersed thoughts, but his compassion for family members pushes this conversation in another direction.

"So…Janie, Sulli and Luna…" He stares off, confused and concerned about the girls he knows.

"Sex isn't something to be scared of, but none of you should be having sex until you're much older," I tell him, words rushing towards me all of a sudden.

Moffy stares off in thought.

So I just continue, "It can feel good for grown-ups, which is why people do it outside of making babies. When you get older soon, you might even have urges to experiment with yourself…and that's okay, but it's something you only do in private."

Lo and I played "doctor" when we were nine, and we both had a concept of what sex was—we just wanted to see how it felt.

Moffy frowns. "How old were you when you started?"

Don't freak out. "Having sex?"

"Yeah."

I lost my virginity when I was *thirteen*.

But not to Lo.

I'd do anything to keep them from having sex that soon, so I say, "*Old*." I worry that he might ask this to someone else. I add, "Personal sex questions like that stay private between couples, so it's better not to ask other people that one. Does that make sense?"

"Yeah." He nods and then asks about Winona and surrogacy again. I explain the whole process so he understands that Rose and Ryke did *not* have sex, and Winona is biologically Ryke and Daisy's daughter. I watch clarity sweep his face, and he nods more confidently.

"Do you know what a condom is?" I ask next.

"Not really."

"It protects your partner." I think about an STD talk, but maybe I'll leave that for another time, so I just mention how condoms prevent pregnancies. "It's like a plastic glove that wraps around the penis so sperm can't enter a woman. Make sense?"

He thinks about this for a long second. "I dunno. The whole thing seems painful and gross."

"Well it's a grown-up thing," I reinforce this notion. "You don't have to worry about it until you're much *much* older, and maybe then it won't seem so gross."

Moffy relaxes more, happy that it's not something he has to concern himself with right now.

"Anymore questions?" I wonder.

"Yeah." He looks down at his paper. "If Benji has twelve apples and Mary has three-hundred-and-forty-five, how many apples do they have in all?"

This I can handle. Hell, after today, I can handle anything.

After I finish helping Moffy with his homework, I step into the hall. It's barren, empty of Loren Hale. I check the next couple of rooms, only to find him in Luna's.

He lies on the carpet with our four-year-old daughter, staring up at the glow-in-the-dark stars on the ceiling and goopy shapes and colors from the lava lamp.

"And on my planet Thebula, all the *waters has glitters*. No one can drown," she tells him, kicking her feet up on her plastic green chair.

"Glitter?" he asks. "Does that mean you'll be all glittery when you get out of the pool?"

"Uh-huh." She nods. "And *brover* won't be able to drown."

My heart lurches. She saw a trailer on television where a boy drowned. Some thriller movie coming out for the summer, and now she's worried about Moffy since he spends most of his time in the pool.

Lo turns his head towards our daughter. Flyaway pieces of her light brown hair touch her round face. She has a red cape tied around her neck, already bathed and in star-printed PJs.

Lo brushes a strand of hair off her forehead. "Moffy isn't going to drown, Luna. He took swim classes so he won't."

"Butbut," she slurs her words. "What happens if the swim *classes* fail?"

"They won't, you wanna know why?" Lo props himself on his elbow, head on his hand, his eyes on our daughter. Lo never thought he could be gentle, not even with his own kids, but he was wrong. He might not have the softest voice, but his innocence surfaces—innocence that we both lost at a young age. He finds and gives it all to them.

"Why?" Luna asks.

"Because Moffy is the best swimmer in the entire neighborhood. He's so good that I think it's his secret superpower, but *shhh*." He puts his finger to his lips. "You can't tell him about his superpower or else it might go away. That's why we call it a…" He feigns surprise.

"A what?"

"A secret!" He tickles Luna. She giggles and rolls from side to side.

I'm smiling so wide, even as Lo glances at the door for the first time. Seeing me. He nods for me to come further inside. I skip on over, only to rest down on the other side of Luna.

"Mommy!" she exclaims. "I was telling Daddy about my planet Thebula. I think that's where I'm from." She's adamant that she was not born on Earth. That Lo and I had her on another planet and then she returned to this world on a spaceship, bringing her with us. Her imagination is the highlight of my day.

"Thebula," I muse. "It sounds familiar."

She inhales a large breath of air. "Really?"

I nod and she springs to her feet and runs over to her little work desk by a strange looking plant she waters every day.

"Whatcha doing?" I ask Luna.

"Drawing it for you!"

I'm glowing as Lo places his fingers to my chin, slowly drawing my face towards his. He kisses the corner of my lips, both of us lying on the fuzzy rug.

"When did you leave?" I ask, scooting closer and closer. Until our legs and arms tangle.

"When you started talking about Benji and Mary and apples." His amber eyes fill with something soul-deep. "I always believed in you, Lily, but that was…extraordinary."

"I didn't blush. Not once." Pride swells up, something so foreign that I hold onto it tight.

"You're amazing." He kisses me once more. This time right on the lips—where the sentiment of his words sings through me.

[39]

Rose Cobalt

I closed the boutique.

Just for the day. Interior designers left about five minutes ago after canvassing the space and snapping photographs, all for Calloway Couture's retail expansion into New York City, San Francisco, and Chicago.

The boutique is quiet, and so I sit behind the cash register and sketch a lace bustier. I spend most of my time creating baby clothes and dresses, but I've been drawing some haute couture gowns and thinking about fabrics. They're incredibly unaffordable for the everyday woman, which is not what Calloway Couture is about, but I've felt compelled towards the designs, more inspired to go down this path.

My five-year plan is to create a fall fashion line of them. I'm constantly busy, even with all my gremlins in school, but a five-year timeframe should be achievable.

I check the clock. Ben, just two, is in pre-pre-K for another hour and then I have to pick him up from school. I tap my pencil to my sketchbook and skim the racks of clothes, the ottoman cushions, the twinkling chandeliers. This one store will become many. My clothes are being worn by thousands, and I'd return to myself at twenty-three and I'd just say, *breathe*.

I worried so much about my fashion line. Would it survive the media fallout? Would my dream last? It took a lot of time, more work than I sometimes thought capable, but Calloway Couture survived with me.

Outside of my store, paparazzi start sprinting to the curb. Their cameras and bodies angled towards the street. A black limousine parks.

I instantly know who's inside.

Connor Cobalt emerges like the celebrity he probably always envisioned inside his head. Though now he has literal cameras flashing in his face. He acts as though it's all background to his world, his wavy hair perfect and the sleeves of his button-down rolled up his forearms.

His confidence is his most alluring accessory, and I find myself pressed against the checkout desk to near him. *Honestly, Rose. He's not as amazing as you.*

I flip my hair off my shoulder.

Domineering and poised, Connor heads for my store, and cameramen part like the Red Sea. Connor unlocks the door with his set of keys, a small white shopping bag in his hand. He shuts and locks the store behind him.

The paparazzi can't catch much through the tinted glass, so they don't linger for long.

"You cheated," I say as he approaches me.

"So you've reminded me seventeen times now." He places the shopping bag beside the register, a tempting distance. I try not to eye it for long.

Stay firm, Rose.

"And yet you still lack remorse."

His amusement lifts his lips. "I didn't personally cheat."

"You can't blame Eliot and Tom. They were on your team. Your entire *team* cheated." We played Pictionary last night. Jane, Charlie, and Ben were on my team, and Beckett, Eliot, and Tom were on Connor's. The two four-year-olds kept flipping the sand-timer over during their rounds to give themselves extra seconds.

Connor says they thought it was a toy, but children have their motives. They're devious little things.

He rests casually against *my* checkout counter. "We gave your team extra time in the final round, and yet *you* still lost."

I glare and raise my hand at his face. "Your voice just shriveled the last of my eggs. I'm barren and frigid." I point at the door. "The exit is that way." I do the thing that annoys him most.

I ignore him.

And I resume sketching.

"I bought you something. I didn't mean for it to be a peace offering, but it can if it satisfies you."

I struggle to bite my tongue. I don't even last a full thirty-seconds. "You're *terrible* at admitting defeat."

"Because I'm not capable of feeling defeated."

It's easy to forget that he's not just a narcissist in a loose sense. I smooth my lips together, my glare investigating his calm, relaxed exterior. "I reject your peace offering."

Why is he grinning?

I rise to my feet. "I said *rejection*, Richard. I just rejected you."

"Rose."

I quickly cover his mouth with my hand. "Can you not say my name like you're fucking the syllable?" I feel his smile beneath my palm. *Ugh.*

He clasps my wrist and tears my hand off his face. "I said your name how I always say it. *Rose.*"

"You have a death wish." His strong grip on my wrist stimulates my sensitive nerves that only scream, *more, harder, deeper.*

He walks around the checkout counter, so nothing, not even the register, separates us. "How do you plan to kill me?"

I raise my chin. "With a pickaxe in each eye." I can't stand his smile, and yet, I want it to stay. I reach out with my free hand to cover his mouth.

He seizes my other wrist. *God, yes.*

Then he tugs me towards his body, so abruptly that a sharp breath escapes my lips. I keep my piercing glare on his deep blues, his eyes as smooth as water and silk.

He towers above me, but I lift my head as much as I can and say, "Then I'd set you on fire."

His lips hover close to whisper, "Tu l'as déjà fait."

You already have.

Before I think properly, he hoists me up, my legs around his waist, dress riding up to my thighs. His defined muscles cut sharper in his biceps, even through his white button-down. He carries me towards a dressing room, veiled by a black curtain.

My collarbone juts out, my oxygen tight in my lungs. Connor kisses the bone before noticing the necklace I wear. I feel his breath stagger.

His liquid gaze looks to me in complete and utter *knowing.* He catches the diamond pendant, pear-shaped like a water droplet, between his teeth.

I pulse.

This necklace is the first piece of jewelry he ever bought me. I was in college. We'd just started *officially* dating. I kept it in a safe deposit box so I wouldn't lose it, but I thought about it today and checked it out so I could wear it.

All of a sudden, my back hits the dressing room wall, the black curtain yanked closed. My legs are still parted around his waist, and he seizes my wrists again, this time with one hand. He elevates them above my head, stretching and pinning them there.

"I hate you," I argue in the shallowest breath.

"Tu m'aimes." *You love me.*

He drops the necklace, and his lips find mine. The aggressive, forceful kiss contains aching need and desire. When he nips my lip, his mouth trails to the pit of my ear. "*Rose.*"

Good God.

I melt but tense against him. It's such an oxymoron. I know he loves those. Our faces are so close, and his free hand starts ripping off my panties.

"I'm going to claw your face off," I pant, more breathy than I intend.

He cups my jaw, then drifts to my throat. *Choke me.* He squeezes much harder than he's been able to in the past since I'm not pregnant.

"You know what I heard you just say, Rose?" He kisses me and then murmurs, "I heard you say that you *love* my mind, my body…my cock." Connor removes his hand to slip his two fingers inside of me. *In and out.* I shudder. He rams his body against mine, and I jolt with pleasure.

Connor cages me to the wall with his six-foot-four build. My nerves electrify, and I grow so wet that I moan when he grips my hair and pulls. I feel utterly and completely in his possession.

He kisses me once more, my lips stinging by the force. His hand returns to my wrists, and his fingers between my legs never leave. Against my mouth, he asks, "How much pain?"

"None," I whisper.

He's not asking how much pain I want. He's asking if I'm in any.

I gave birth to Winona *four* weeks ago, and the rules are *six weeks, no sex.* My mind is a pool of betrayal. 100% horny and undone. I'm leaning towards breaking all the rules in favor of sex.

Traitor.

Rose Calloway Cobalt doesn't break rules. I follow them.

Do it, Rose. Let his cock drive so hard inside of you.

There aren't any security cameras inside the Calloway Couture dressing rooms. Everything says *yes* except this one stipulation.

Fuck it.

I consent to this with a nod. Horny Rose wins today. Connor barely pauses, unzipping my dress and pulling it off my head. He lets me have control of my hands, only to unbutton his shirt. He unclips my bra, and I'm entirely bare as he steps out of his slacks and pulls off his boxer-briefs, while still tucked up against me.

His erection, so hard, thick and long, wastes no time outside of me. He thrusts in. I'm so full, no space separating us, and he rocks his hips to ram deeper. One hand on my ass, the other imprisoning my wrists.

I try to force out new words, "I'm...going to ki—"

"Kiss me?" he teases.

I glare but gasp, my head hitting the wall. He runs his thumb down my lips.

"*Kill*," I moan.

He pushes *in* so hard. My toes curl.

"Go ahead," he taunts, his words against my ear, "try to kill me, Rose." His deep, ragged breath is the equivalent of his fingers stroking my clit.

I can't kill him.

I love him. Still, I try to escape from the wall to fuck with him, but he only fucks *me* faster. I lose it at this. His pleasure erupts in his eyes and parted lips, and mine coats my entire body.

I constrict and clench against him. My moan dies in my throat, but I can't shut my mouth. He breathes hot against my neck, coming hard while I twitch around his cock, full of intense pleasure.

It takes a full five minutes for Horny Rose to get the fuck out.

And then I realize what just happened.

I broke the six-week, no-sex rule.

I broke the rule when Lily never even did.

WE'RE BOTH CLOTHED AGAIN. I lie on the bench in the dressing room where my betrayal occurred. I have my legs raised against Connor's chest and shoulder while he straddles the bench. He has the little shopping bag, and I wave my hand for him.

"Pass it here."

"You rejected my peace offering. Did you forget already?"

I glare. "So you just brought the bag in here to show me what I missed?" I'm about to fling my legs off him, but he hooks them with one arm, keeping them in place. It's actually *more* than that. He lifts them higher and forward, so his semen will move towards my eggs faster.

I'm serious.

He came inside of me, and we're not squandering the opportunity to have another girl. *Please, God. Give me a girl.* I've been able to get pregnant fairly easily, but I still like over-preparing and putting in extra effort.

Connor already called me an excellent pupil, but I made sure to note that I'm not *his* pupil. We're equals. And I am fucking excellent.

"Do you want what's in the bag, Rose?" he asks.

"The bag can go to hell. I'll take what's in it." I hold out my hand.

He smiles, and he reveals a garment. A black...lacy bustier, almost similar to the one I was sketching. *It's beautiful.* I hold it up, my head still on the bench. It's soft and the perfect shape for my body. Years ago, I would've shuddered in distaste at the idea of a man picking out lingerie for me.

Connor knows me so well, and the gift is never an overt suggestion. It's simply: *I saw this and knew it's something you'd buy yourself.*

"And?"

"It's hideous."

He gestures for me to give it back to him.

"You can't have it back." I clutch it to my chest. "You already gifted it to me."

"You must love hideous things," he banters.

"I do love you," I snap back.

He runs his hand down the length of my legs, drinking me in. My hot words should sear him dead, but they only pool love in his eyes. I could set Connor on fire a million times over, and he'd never burn to ash. I suppose that's why we're made for one another.

He can withstand every single inexhaustible part of me.

Willow & Garrison Abbey welcome the birth of their baby girl

VADA LAUREN ABBEY

May 11th, 2024

[40]

August 2024
THE COBALT ESTATE
Philadelphia

Connor Cobalt

It's 7:00 p.m., and after baths and story time with everyone in Tom's room, Rose and I make rounds and tuck our six children into bed, each with their own rooms. I have to tell one of them something tonight, and to be truthful, I'm uncertain how he'll handle it.

I pass Rose in the hallway, her hand on the door frame to Ben's bedroom. "Tonight?" she asks.

"Tonight." I nod. We've been putting off telling him because he won't like it, but school starts soon. We can't wait any longer.

"Just one of us should be in there," Rose whispers. "I don't want him to feel…"

"Picked on?"

"Yes."

"I'll do it."

Rose tightens her ponytail. "Beckett gave Ben his tooth to put under his pillow, so who's dealing with that tonight?"

My jaw tics at the subtle mention of the fictional Tooth Fairy. I have played into the charade for years, which has been the equivalent of chewing gravel. It's been tolerable because all of our children treat Santa Claus, the Easter Bunny, and yes, the Tooth Fairy, as fables, not real creatures.

Everyone but Ben.

He believes he can actually meet the Tooth Fairy.

It makes the pretense a little more grating. I'd rather be upfront and explain to him that it's not real, but I made a promise that I wouldn't extinguish this childhood *magic*.

I haven't, and I wouldn't begin now.

Though I have to mention this, so I lower my voice. "It's not Ben's tooth. The Tooth Fairy shouldn't reward selflessness."

Rose glares. "You'd rather the Tooth Fairy promote greed?"

"We're paying our children for their *teeth*. If anything, we're teaching them they can sell their body for money. It's linear to prostitution, but it's acceptable because everyone does it, isn't it?"

She scoffs. "*You* took it there."

"Society took it there. I simply *think* about what everything means. It shouldn't be a hard concept, using your brain, but so many people forget to do it. It's why I'm better than them."

Rose raises her hand to my face to shut down my narcissism. I'm not close enough, but I imagine kissing her palm. She whispers, "It doesn't change the fact that one of us will be slipping money under Ben's pillow tonight. You or me?"

"You, darling." I willingly hand her this task.

Rose glances at the door that I need to head through. She tenses. "I'll see you soon?"

"Yes."

A moment later, Rose slips into Ben's room. I keep walking to a different door, a different room. When I go inside, my five-year-old son is already beneath his green covers but wide-awake. He asked for a portrait of a raven for his fifth birthday, and the dark oil painting hangs above his dresser.

As soon as Eliot sees me, he sits up and pulls *three* old hardbacks from underneath his pillow. "One more story. Just one."

"One more, but it can't be long."

Eliot smiles. He loves stories more than he loves physical books. It seems, at a glance, that there's no difference between the two, but there is. His lamp casts a warm glow over his bed, and I take a seat next to him. He quickly pushes the hardbacks on my lap.

"Which book?" I hold them together and show him the spines.

Eliot has my brown hair color, the strands falling straight. He always has an impish look in his eyes, as though he's seconds from a dramatic entrance and exit with folly swept frenziedly in between.

He takes a very long time examining the spines. "This one." He points at *Edgar Allan Poe: Complete Tales and Poems.*

"What is that one?" I ask him.

"Poe." He memorized the color of the book and remembered the title that was spoken to him before. He isn't reading the words. It's currently his favorite, which is why he asked for the painting of a raven. Rose is itching to give him Shakespeare, but we both think he'll be overwhelmed by the words right now.

I set the other two books aside and open this one to the table of contents. "Which story?"

Eliot looks up at me. "Can you read *The Black Cat* again?"

I smile at his choice. He likes gothic tales, and while some parents would chastise *me* for letting a five-year-old read Edgar Allan Poe, I purposefully brush off societal constraints like ages. I always have. Every person is different.

So are my children.

I wouldn't force Poe on a child that could barely sleep at night. Eliot isn't frightened by the insanity and murder in tales. He sees them as what they are. *Stories.* At the very end of *Little Snow White* by the Brothers Grimm, the queen is forced to put on burning shoes and dance until she dies.

He'd rather hear the original versions than censored ones, and if asked, I'm certain he'd be able to recite a portion of *Little Snow White*.

In German.

"Find it in the table of contents," I tell him, "and we'll read it together."

Eliot pouts. "But I want you to read it." He crosses his arms and leans back away from me, already upset.

"Why don't you want to read it with me?"

He kicks at his covers. "You're better at it." His speech is clear. He doesn't stumble over words, but his handwriting is nearly illegible. He had trouble holding a pencil until I helped him switch to his left hand. We had three teacher-parent meetings in kindergarten because he refused to read aloud during group story time.

At one point, he chucked the book and started crying.

The teacher said that he has no patience, lacks focus, and she called him "too lazy to try"—she only sees Eliot as unruly. He's loud-spoken, not shy, and he's unwilling to follow reading instructions.

It's not because he doesn't want to. It's because it's difficult for him, and I can't understand what it's like. I can't imagine being road-blocked in an area of learning, but he is. He shouldn't be disciplined. He should be taught to use his strengths, so school isn't challenging to the point of being unbearable.

We have tutors outside of school for all our children, in case they need extra help, but if knowledge bores them, if they'd rather be outside, Rose and I aren't authoritarians on the matter. We don't shove them in their seats for hours on end. Facts, history, books—these interested us, but if they don't interest them, we wouldn't push.

I turn the open book towards my son. "Then I'll read it, but can you at least pick out *The Black Cat* from the table of contents?"

Eliot concentrates, but then he gives up, defeat in his eyes. "You can read something new."

"Eliot," I start to tell him.

Then he sighs and just points. "This one." *The Devil in the Belfry.*

I put my finger beneath the "the" and ask, "What does this word say?"

"I don't know." Frustrated tears fill his eyes. "I don't know!"

I immediately set the book aside and hold Eliot in my arms.

He cries into my chest, and I rub his back. "It's okay, Eliot," I whisper.

"All the other kids can read more than me," he cries. "It's not fair." When we read out loud, we make sure he follows the words in the book, but it's still really difficult for him to *visually* process them. It'll take time.

"Just because you can't read as fast as the other children, it doesn't mean you're not smart."

He rubs his cheeks with his fist.

I wipe the rest of his tears with my thumb. "You just learn in a different way, and your way will make you *incredibly* gifted."

He starts crying again, this time just overwhelmed at that word. *Gifted.* None of the teachers call him smart, and he's often compared to his brothers and sister who excelled before him. I once asked him what he sees on a page. He said, "Words all around." Eliot made a scrambled motion with his hands. If the letters look different in the same book every time, he'd struggle picking out *The Black Cat* from the list of tales.

Rose and I want him tested for dyslexia, but the administration says he's too young. Children develop motor skills around this age, and they said that they couldn't conclude whether he has a learning disorder yet.

They think we're jumping to conclusions since our other children surpassed common milestones far faster. "It's likely he's just more normal than your other kids," the principal said.

We're not upset that our son isn't up to par with our other children. And I don't want to fix him so he can become "normal" or whatever *normal* may mean to the administration. I want Eliot to learn at a rate that doesn't cause him to cry or feel inferior to the students around him. So he's not anxious at being called on in class or so frustrated he'd throw his books.

To do this, he needs to focus on his strengths and not be forced to learn the same way as everyone else.

Eliot sniffs, calming down, and then he asks, "How will I learn to read?"

"Here." I touch his ears. "These are your gift when your eyes fail you."

If he struggles visually processing words, then he'll have an easier time learning through sound. Rose and I have already started talking to Dalton Elementary about allowing Eliot to use audiobooks for the first grade curriculum.

I believe almost everyone has value. People have gifts and attributes that I lack, some that I admire. I respect people at their best. Eliot at his best may not involve penmanship, the same way my best isn't among comic books or rock climbing. For Eliot to find his best, he needs the right tools to learn.

Rose and I will fight to give him every last one.

I start tucking Eliot into bed. "Every night, you'll put on headphones and listen to books being read to you. You'll need to follow along on the page the best you can." We'll probably give him an index card to block off the other line of words, if it helps.

He might never understand how words look on paper the way that I do. The way that you do. But it doesn't mean he can't read. It doesn't make him unintelligent. It doesn't mean he can't love stories just as much, if not more, than everyone else.

"Will you still read to me?" he asks.

I nod. "There's one more thing." Sitting next to him, I open up the book and turn to *The Black Cat.* I meet his impish eyes. "Mommy and I decided that it's better if you stay in kindergarten for one more year. It'll give you more time to learn the way that's best for you."

His mouth falls. "But...?"

"You'll be in the same grade as Tom—"

"Really?" His face brightens. Eliot and Tom are as close in age as they are in friendship.

"Only if you agree to use this extra time to your benefit. Otherwise, you'll go to first grade."

"I will, I will! Can I tell Tom now? Does he know?" He nearly springs out of the bed.

"Tomorrow, you can tell him." I grin at the sight of his own smile. I tuck the covers back around his small frame and then position the book on my bent legs, angling the pages towards him.

Rose told me earlier, *"The teachers will hate us more than they already do."* I didn't disagree. Eliot and Tom together might be mayhem, but he needs more time. It's easier to grant him extra when he's this young and when his birthday is in June.

"*The Black Cat* by Edgar Allan Poe," I begin, my voice smooth and tranquil. Jane says I make her fall asleep. She prefers Rose reading.

I also prefer Rose's hostile, icy tone, but maybe not over my own.

"'For the most wild, yet most homely narrative which I am about to pen, I neither expect nor solicit belief.'" I look at Eliot while I read the next line from memory, and he too, remembers it, mouthing all the words, "'Mad indeed would I be...'"

I smile as his lips move.

His memory matches mine. And I never forget anything.

Lily & Loren Hale welcome the birth of their baby girl

KINNEY HALE

October 3rd, 2024

{ 41 }

December 2024
THE MALL
Philadelphia

Lily Hale

In hindsight, we probably should've delegated all Christmas shopping to assistants or even bodyguards. (They can do double-duty and run errands for us). But the thought of not picking out my children's gifts made me sad.

This'll also be Kinney's first Christmas and Xander's second birthday. I won't half-ass these two monumental moments.

One positive upside of shopping in this particular mall: no paparazzi. They're barred from entering.

One downside: people still approach continuously for autographs and selfies. I like greeting fans and taking pictures. Seeing their happiness by even a simple wave makes my heart swell. Though I saw two fans whispering about how I brushed them off. I felt bad. It's not intentional.

I'm just frazzled, and the pressure to shop combined with not alienating people who love us—it's a lot.

Two hours into the shopping extravaganza and I only bought Moffy one gift. A Batman Lego set that he begged us for last month. I also included a Spider-Man one so Lo won't feel like we're turning into DC parents.

"I think I've taken more photos today than the entire year," I express, collapsing onto an iron chair adjacent to Rose's. Roasted Beans Café has open seating and views of the mall's second floor. Little potted plants mark off the café's territory, and Rose chose a table in the very corner, shopping bags piled on one of the four chairs.

Five bodyguards surround Rose. They shoo people away from her area with authoritative looks. I last saw Poppy and Daisy disappear into a sporting goods store to find gifts for their husbands.

Rose cuts her spinach and goat cheese toast with a fork and knife. As though this is any other day. I suppose it is. Crowds gathered just on the other side of the potted plants. Phones point directly at Rose to see her food choice and her pregnant belly. She looks exceptionally regal today, a glittery statement necklace, form-fitting black dress (Calloway Couture), and deep blue matte nails.

Our bodyguards watch the crowds, but they don't block their view of us. We always tell them not to worry about that. We don't mind the pictures, especially when they're of us *without* our kids.

"I told you to stay in this protective *circle*." Rose gestures around the table with her knife. If icy looks could kill, I'd be buried. "It's the safe zone."

Just as Rose finishes her declaration, two teenage girls try to pass the hostess podium, phones in their clutch. They plead for selfies with us, but Garth is telling them *no*.

I feel bad, but I have to remember that I spent the past two hours taking photographs. I can't spend my entire life taking them.

"Rose," a college-aged girl with dark brown hair calls. She squeezes past Garth and the two teenagers. The other bodyguards let her through. She looks winded like she hustled to the café with all her might. "I found the polka-dot tights for Jane, but I couldn't find any pink glitter hair clips."

Rose jots a note in her little spiral-bound pad beside her plate. "I'll make those clips then." She rips off a bottom piece of paper and hands it to her assistant. "Here's more of the list, and I'll need you to run to a craft store if the mall doesn't have one."

She reads the list quickly.

Rose eyes her for a short second. "Hope?"

"Yeah?"

"The last item on the list is serious. You can't skip it."

Hope skims the list and then relaxes. "I won't. Thank you, Rose. I'll have the rest to you soon." She skirts away.

Rose sips her water and cuts another piece of toast.

Yes, Rose Calloway Cobalt gave her shopping duties to another person. For someone who not only loves to shop but struggles with delegation, I never thought the day would arrive. The fact that she's thirty-two-weeks pregnant swayed her decision. Plus in Rose's mind, missing out on a sisterly excursion is comparable to abandoning Daisy, Poppy, and me in a sinking raft.

"What was that last item?" I ask.

"For Hope to take a break and eat lunch. I had to remind her yesterday that I wouldn't fire someone over a simple mistake. Do I look like a drill sergeant?" She grips her knife, her yellow-green eyes pierced and cold like the rest of her features.

"Uh..." *Is this a trick question?* "Yes?"

Rose rolls her eyes. "Well, I don't act it, even if I look it." This is true. She gives more gifts to her assistants and bodyguards than I remember to give Superhero & Scones employees, and she's an advocate for vacation time for her staff when they need it.

I just now notice a bowl of chips and dip behind a toy store bag. I put the bag on another chair and dunk a chip into the chunky blue cheese. "The protective circle has chips. I like it." I munch.

Rose cranes her neck and zones in on my *one* shopping bag. "Make a list. We can send someone to shop for you."

"No." I shake my head. "I'm going to make a second pass. Maybe bring two more bodyguards with me to keep the fans engaged with other things." This plan actually sounds decent. I dunk two chips at one time.

I miss Lo.

He'd appreciate the chips with me but definitely not the blue cheese dip.

And he'd order tacos. I remember that he's with Connor, Ryke, Willow, and Garrison and all the kids. They planned to play in the snow and then watch Christmas movies at the Cobalt estate.

Rose's knife clanks against the plate like she dropped the utensil. I watch her hands rest on her lower abdomen. She blows out a long breath.

My eyes grow. "Are you okay?"

"The little monster won't stop moving." She swallows hard, her neck stiff. Then her glare ignites me. "*Stop* looking at me like that."

"Like what?" Blue chees dribbles down my chin and onto my baggy sweater. *Shit.* I wipe it up with a napkin.

"I'm fine." She waves like she's brushing off all the worry in the atmosphere. "Fate might want this baby out a little early, and I can handle whatever comes my way."

I choke on a chip and pat my chest. "Early like *now?*"

"No, not now. I'm *fine.*"

I only believe Rose because I've seen her combat contractions. She'd be more rigid than right now, and her collarbone would protrude. "Are you nervous you'll have another boy?"

This is Rose's seventh pregnancy and her seventh child, though she technically birthed eight children. One just happens to belong to Ryke and Daisy. I think mentally she might be done after this baby, boy or girl. She's thirty-five, and she's told us that she doesn't want to spend the rest of her thirties birthing babies. Lo said that Connor worries about the strain on Rose's back, so he's ready for this to be the last one too.

But if she has a boy, I wonder if she'll feel like fate is telling her to have an eighth baby.

"No, I'm not *nervous*," Rose snaps like I shouldn't apply that word to her. "If it's a boy, Connor and I agreed to make a pros and cons list and then go from there."

I bet *fate* would weigh a lot on Rose's side of things, but *Rose's health* for Connor just might be the ultimate trump card in determining what happens.

If they have a girl, this all becomes irrelevant anyway.

I dip my napkin in my water glass. Rose gives me a look. Whatever. I rub at the stain on my black sweater. I think I just made the white spot more noticeable. Does it look like jizz?

My cheeks redden. *No one thinks Loren Hale's cum is on your sweater.*

I do.

I'm thinking it.

I point at the spot and ask Rose, "What do you think?" *Cum or not cum?*

"I think you should make a list," Rose replies with an icy, villainess smile. Then she digs in her Chanel purse and tosses me a stain-removal pen. Very un-villain-like. *I love you, Rose.* "And you can keep me company."

It's tempting. "You could've baited me with the stain-removal pen."

"I'd rather you stayed with me because you want to be with *me* and not my cleaning products."

Oh. "I love you both."

She almost smiles and then rolls her eyes at the way I touch the removal pen to the sweater. "You're doing that incorrectly. Come here."

I stand up and go to Rose's side. She rises with me and efficiently scrubs at the stain, able to defeat it in a few seconds.

I have a better view of the mall's second floor and notice a sign beside a pet store. *ADOPT TODAY! LAST CALL SHELTER DOGS & CATS LOOKING FOR LOVING HOMES!*

Kittens are in the window front while dogs stay confined in a little gated area outside the store, two employees in Pet Paradise shirts.

Rose has already tucked the stain-removal pen in her purse, and now she's smiling at her phone.

Connor texted her, I infer, and then a puppy steals all my attention. He—I think he's a *he*—walk-hops in a circle inside the gate, his big floppy ears flapping with his goofy stride. Then he literally face-plants on the hard floor.

I wince, but the little pup picks himself up, shakes his head, and continues his happy walk-hop around all the other dogs. Not a care in the world.

The puppy tugs all the strings connected to my heart. Fans suddenly start gasping, their phones spinning to the right. That's when Daisy appears on the other side of the plants. She chucks her bags onto our pile and hikes over the plants to our side.

"Hey, big sis," she says to me since Rose is engrossed in her phone.

"What does *last call* mean?" I ask Daisy.

She follows my gaze to Pet Paradise. "Ohh," she says sadly. "Whoever isn't adopted might be put down this week or even as soon as tomorrow."

"What?" My face falls. I'm not a pet person, which I know isn't an excuse, but I never knew this actually happens.

I've never wanted an animal as much as I want this puppy.

"What are you staring at...?" Rose trails off and then connects all the dots really fast. She must spot desire shining through my eyes. She does have six children, so I'm sure she sees this look often. "Lily—"

"I'll be right back." I rush out of the café, Garth following behind me. It isn't until I reach the fence that I realize Rose and Daisy have left Roasted Beans too and joined me.

The two Pet Paradise employees perk up at our arrival. The younger girl looks like she might faint. She has her hands to her mouth and freezes in place.

The older girl greets us, "Do you want to hold a puppy?"

Daisy gasps with a big smile. "You read my mind."

The frozen employee unthaws at Daisy's bright demeanor, her hands dropping to her side to reveal a giddy smile of her own. "Hi." She waves at Daisy.

"Hey there." Daisy asks, "Which one needs hugs?"

With her phone to her ear, Rose stands in front of the kitten window. Felines curled in little glass cubicles, some stretching awake.

While the younger employee lets Daisy into the golden retriever gate, I ask the older employee about the floppy-eared puppy. "Can I see this one?"

Crowds have congested the entire Pet Paradise area, and some fans even ask, "Are you looking for a pet?"

Yes. Yes, I am.

The employee lets the floppy-eared dog out of the gate, slipping a loose leash around his neck. "This little guy is a ten-month-old basset hound." She pats his belly.

I bend down, and the puppy immediately licks my elbow and cheek. I crumble with love.

"He only has today left to be adopted. The shelter is overcrowded this year, so all these animals need good homes."

Poppy slips through the crowds, a shopping bag hooked on her arm. "What's going on?"

"Lily wants a dog, and I'm giving free hugs." Daisy smiles, petting all the golden retrievers while they jump on her lap.

Poppy's maternal guidance bears down on me like a raincloud. "Lily, you can't get a dog. You have a two-month-old at home."

"So?" Daisy and I say in unison. She gives me a nod like we're part of the same club. Maybe the Dog Lovers United. I've never been a part of this club before, but suddenly, it feels like the right one to join.

"I found the fierce one," Rose says into her phone. In a glass cubicle, a black kitten with big yellow eyes stares fixatedly at Rose. Then she slinks closer and paws the glass right in front of Rose's face. Rose snorts at the cat and then speaks to her phone. "If we do this, you have to remind her not to bring home strays."

Jane.

She tries to corral stray kittens in the street and lure them to her house. Connor calls it inventive, but overall, Rose and Connor always tell her *no* to letting them inside. Most of the cats have flees and are extremely feral.

Think Sadie times a thousand.

Connor must say something else, and Rose agrees in French and then shuts off her phone. She says to the kitten, "You can eat a million birds, just not *the* bird. If you have any disagreements, tell me now."

The kitten meows and rubs her cheek against the glass like *scratch me.* For a moment, I think: *Rose Calloway Cobalt can communicate with felines.*

Proof! *Proof!*

Rose is Catwoman to Connor's Batman.

This is a historic moment. Let me digest.

"What do you mean by bird?" Poppy asks, the eldest of us. She also has no pets, but I think she's mostly concerned about the hoopla behind us and all the craziness we let into our lives.

"Ben has wanted a bird." Rose grips the door handle of Pet Paradise but pauses at Poppy's confusion. "What?"

"You're about to buy a bird *and* a cat right now?"

It's an impulsive buy for Rose, but she's done way more impulsive things in our lives. "I called Connor, we agreed on the purchase. I'd rather have a motherfucking *bird* than a snake."

"Who asked for a snake?" Daisy wonders.

"Who do you think?"

"Eliot," we all say.

"And he's not getting it." Rose yanks the door open. "I'll meet you back here in a second."

"Wait," I call out before she disappears inside the store. "Sisterly advice?"

Those magic words lift up her lips. She sees me pet the basset hound. I know my four kids will love him as much as me.

"You can handle a dog," Rose tells me so strongly. "The better question is if your annoying husband can."

"Ooooh!" the crowds shout at Rose's insult.

Rose only wears satisfaction as she enters the store.

My brows crinkle. *Lo.* I definitely have to ask him before I make this decision. I hurriedly take out my phone, snap a picture of the basset hound, and text Lo.

Puppy????????

Daisy steps out of the gate and says to Poppy and me, "I think I'm going to stick around and make sure all these dogs get adopted today. I might be able to attract more people over here." *Might* is an understatement.

There are *tons* of people around Pet Paradise because we're here. My little sister has a big heart that might not be noticed by all, but I feel Daisy's kindness every time we're together.

My phone vibrates.

:) – Lo

A smiley face! I'll take it.

"WHAT THE FUCK, LIL?" Lo whispers heatedly, our bodies partially turned away from Luna, Moffy, and Xander across the living room. They play with the basset hound by the sofa, the dog licking their faces when they attack-hug him.

Cuteness levels in the Hale household just shot through the roof.

Which is why it's so hard to surrender to Lo's anger. "You texted me a smiley face. I thought that was a yes!"

Moffy glances over at us, and we both quickly angle more towards the kitchen door. Lo whispers back, "How was I supposed to know you were asking to get a goddamn dog? We"—he gestures from his chest to my chest—"don't do *animals*. That's not the Lo and Lily thing."

"*Lily and Lo* thing," I correct in a small voice.

He tilts his head and then cups my cheeks. "Lily Hale, we have *no* clue how to take care of a dog."

"We didn't know how to take care of a baby and now we have *four*," I say proudly. "Didn't just yesterday, you said, 'you and me'"—I gesture from his chest to my chest—"'we can do anything.' Huh, *huh*?" I poke his abs.

He pinches my cheek.

I squint.

He almost smiles, but his sharp glare shadows the sliver of one. "You realize I said *we can do anything* in relation to fixing the toaster."

"And that was a proud moment. We didn't have to buy a new one, and we were able to save ourselves from cold Pop-Tarts."

"That was a pretty great moment," Lo says in a way that I hold my breath for the punch line. "It was so great I realize we should break the toaster every fucking day and fix it." He mockingly opens the kitchen door for me. "You want to start, love?"

I realize I should've told him more clearly. "I'm sorry." Guilt knots my stomach. "I'm really sorry, Lo. I should've actually called you like Rose called Connor. I fucked up."

"No," he immediately says. "It's okay." The guilt in my face reflects on his, and he wraps his arms around my shoulders and draws me to his chest.

I hold onto his waist. "I know a dog is an everyday chore, but it's not unfeeling. It gives as much love as it receives." His eyes sink downwards, so I add the truth, "I'll find a new owner for the dog today. Rose will help." She always does. "It'll be like he was never here."

Lo sets his chin on my head, and he watches our children chase the basset hound around the couch. He face-plants into the floorboards, and they all help him up and then he hop-skips after them. When he nears Kinney's little rocker, she squeals in delight.

I look up at Lo.

He's smiling.

Not a shadow of one. Not a partial one. A clear, whole smile.

His eyes drop to mine, and his acceptance washes me with light. "We know nothing about dogs," he reminds me.

"Daisy already gave me some pointers, and she's bringing over puppy food and some of Coconut's old things tonight."

Lo smiles again when the basset hound collapses on the rug, panting with his tongue hung out of his mouth. Luna rubs his belly, teary-eyed with happiness. Pleasing children is really easy. I gave Xander a lime popsicle yesterday, and he acted like I conjured a rainbow out of the sky, just for him.

"What a dork," Lo says about the dog. "Looks like he's going to fit right in with all of us."

I beam. "Are you sure?"

He kisses my cheek, his arms still around me, mine still around him. "I'm sure, Lily."

Moffy springs up from the ground, out of breath from laughing, but he darts over to us. "We came up with his name!"

We angle towards our nine-year-old son. "Let's hear it," Lo says.

Moffy grins. "Gotham."

You should see Lo's face. He looks dismayed and perturbed. Sometimes I think Moffy gravitates towards DC comics just to see Lo's *what-is-the-world-coming-to* expression that pops up solely for moments like these.

Moffy is already laughing again.

"This better be your biggest joke all year," Lo says.

"No, really, that's his name." He calls out over his shoulder, "Right, Luna?"

Luna nods rapidly. "Gotham!" She giggles when he licks her cheek.

"Jesus Christ," Lo says beneath his breath.

"It's a great name, Moffy," I tell him.

"No it's not," Lo says flatly.

"Lo," I whisper.

Lo turns to me. "I'm not calling our dog Gotham." He looks personally offended by this, and as soon as Moffy can see, his smile starts fading.

Our son starts, "We can change it—"

"No!" I shout. "You chose it. Right, Lo?" I lower my voice so only he can hear. "It doesn't mean anything. Moffy just loves Batman."

Lo tries to accept this. Then he says to Moffy, "If you want to call him Gotham, you can call him Gotham."

"Are you sure?"

"Yeah, but don't expect me to call him that."

Moffy begins smiling again. "What will you call him then?"

"Ham," Lo says in all seriousness.

Moffy bursts out laughing and keeps nodding like *that's perfect*.

"Ham?" My brows crinkle up at Lo. "I don't think that's an upgrade."

Lo hugs me closer to his chest. "Oh it's a fucking upgrade."

In his Marvel-loving mind, I'm sure it is.

2025

"I give my time to the people who are most important to me. Odds are that person isn't you."

- Connor Cobalt, We Are Calloway

(Season 7 Episode 10 — Hamlet & Hogwarts)

[42]

Rose Cobalt

I breeze through memories and land on one day.

Over thirteen years ago, I hurried across Princeton's campus, my umbrella catching the afternoon rain. All my exam and paper due dates rattled in my head on loop, and I walked faster. Heels against wet pavement. The Princeton library in view.

Up the stairs, through the door, I shook out my black umbrella and stiffly checked my phone, hoping for a reply.

Connor Cobalt was the top contact in my messages, but he didn't respond to the ones I previously sent.

I inhaled a strained breath.

I *hated* that I sent him five texts. *Five.* All in quick succession. It would've been better if he responded, but it'd been two hours, and he was utterly silent.

We'd started dating not long ago, and it couldn't have been worse timing.

Lily had just told me that she was a sex addict.

Thanksgiving was approaching, hence all the college due dates raising their swords at my armor. The last thing I wanted was to be consumed by Connor Cobalt and *dating*. It was a betrayal to my sister and my studies.

This was my senior year. *Don't lose focus now, Rose.*

Just to ensure that I hadn't sent anything humiliating, I glanced over my texts and walked further into the library.

The last one he'd sent: let me take you to lunch – **Connor**

I'd replied with five frenzied messages.

Text #1: You can eat alone. I don't have time for food and drink and dates. My sister is my number one priority, and she needs me. Do you know what I did last night? I spent five hours researching sex addiction and contacting professionals in the field. And I'm no closer to helping her than I was the day before.

Text #2: I will not go to lunch with you.

Text #3: I have a French paper worth fifteen-percent of my grade due tomorrow. I haven't even read Franz Fanon's "Les damnés de la terre" yet, and now I'll have to skim the book. (I never skim.)

Text #4: I don't even have study materials for my Strategy and Information final tomorrow. My economics professor decided to "up the final to November" to alleviate the stress on the first week of December. I loathe him. I'm not alleviated. It's worth fifty-percent of my grade, and now I have less time to study. His logic is ridiculous. He also added extra reading supplements and teased us about specific questions from these textbooks. Which means I have to take time and go to the library. I'd withdraw, but withdrawing admits defeat. I will not be defeated by a professor.

Text #5: disregard all previous texts except the second one.

I still couldn't believe I told him that I actually considered withdrawing from an upper-level econ course. He'd never admit that to me.

You should've never started dating him, I kept thinking.

Rereading the texts only rusted my joints, my neck strict and shoulders rigid. I slipped my phone in my Chanel bag and strutted past the checkout and returns. The library smelled like old hardback bindings and worn pages. I entered the common area of the first floor, ceilings vaulted, bookshelves lining a couple walls. Wooden tables and chairs were scattered in the middle.

I needed to log onto the library's database and figure out where my books were shelved. They most likely weren't on the first floor. I stopped by a short bookshelf and scanned the library for a free computer, people quietly studying.

My narrowed yellow-green eyes flitted this way and that. And then they froze. Right on serene deep blues, six-foot-four feet of arrogance and intellect, and a perpetually assured grin.

Connor Cobalt leaned against a wooden table, skyscraping bookshelves back-dropped his stoic frame. I'll never forget how he stood out among an ancient, grandiose library. I'll never forget how he appeared taller and more omnipotent than the towering hardbacks behind him.

I took a heartier breath and strutted towards Connor. When college exams and the texts made me feel frazzled, my wardrobe flooded me with confidence. Black skirt, sheer tights, booties with five-inch heels, a blazer over a loose white blouse, topped with a sleek pony and a Chanel handbag—I was ready for battle.

As I neared, Connor stepped from the table, his wardrobe equally put-together: navy slacks, leather belt, expensive loafers, an Oxford collar button-down and tie beneath a gray sweater.

He had always dressed better than most men, but I wouldn't dare compliment him.

I spoke hurriedly and hushed. "Did you slip and fall and forget that your allegiances are to Penn, not Princeton?"

He almost laughed like I couldn't see what was right in front of me. "Richard—"

"My allegiance is to you, Rose."

My heart skipped a beat, too stunned to move. He calmly took my wet umbrella and placed it in a chair. That was when I noticed the textbooks across the table. I passed him and picked up a few, my eyes widening in more realizations.

These were the four books I needed. "How…?"

Connor leaned his ass on the table again, mostly—I realized—to be at the same height as me. I was angled towards him, a black textbook in my hand called *Game of Strategy*. His fingers skimmed my wrist, my skin on fire like never before.

Then he flipped open the book, letting me hold it. Highlights, notes scrawled carefully in the margins, he turned to the very first page with a name in the upper corner.

Connor Cobalt.

This was his copy.

"The course isn't called Strategy and Information at Penn, but I realized it was just advanced Game Theory. I've already taken those courses, and I assumed the reading material would be identical."

He was right.

And he saved me at least forty-five minutes of hunting through the library. "Thank you," I said under my breath, still outright dazed. He'd been my rival since I was a teenager, and I'd yet to fully understand what it meant to have him as a teammate.

We'd been on a handful of dates before this, mostly fueled by quick wit and my glares. He'd been extremely supportive of my Calloway Couture runway show, but today was different. I didn't ask Connor to collect these books. I didn't ask him to meet me at the library.

I blinked out of my stupor, unable to look at him directly. I set the book down. "Don't you have somewhere to be?" It sounded more hostile than I really meant.

"Yes," he said, "and I'm already here."

I swallowed as my iron walls lowered for him. They had never lowered for anyone before. "I have a French paper due first, and I need to wait for a computer."

He stood straighter. "You can use my laptop. I'll buy you a coffee, and when you finish your paper, we can go through the game theory textbooks."

Before he moved, I said, "I don't need Connor Cobalt the Tutor. I'm perfectly capable of studying on my own." My lungs burned hot. I could barely breathe. I could barely meet his eyes without being overwhelmed by sentiments I'd never met in my life.

Very deeply, he replied, "I'm not Connor Cobalt the Tutor right now."

I hesitated to ask. *Rose Calloway does not cower.* I lifted my chin, locked eyes with his, and questioned, "Then who are you giving me?" He changed for people. It was a fact we both acknowledged and understood.

Connor waited to answer, tension jutting out my collarbone. Tension constricting muscles in his arms. "You have Connor Cobalt the Boyfriend."

Boyfriend.

In a hushed voice, I asked, "And how much of him is real?" How fake was he being with me?

Connor began to smile. "Terribly real, darling."

Darling.

It was the first time he called me *darling.*

At that, he walked away and only looked over his shoulder to remind me, "I'm buying you coffee. I'll be right back."

Slowly and incredibly dazed, I sunk into my chair and removed my blazer. I found his laptop and just clicked straight into a blank document. I wouldn't snoop. I valued my privacy too much to be hypocritical and destroy his.

I tried to focus on my notes. *FRE 371: World Literatures in French.* I had pages and pages, and I began skimming the Frantz Fanon text. By the time Connor returned with two steaming cups of coffee, I'd written a thousand words.

I told him I was halfway through, and he spent that time reading over my *ECO 418: Strategy and Information* notes. He only distracted me once. When he leaned forward in his chair and slipped a pencil behind his ear.

I glanced over and watched his calculated eyes graze over my handwriting. I could barely admit it then, but I can now: it turned me on. Even his fingers lightly gliding over my notes *turned me on.*

After a full minute, he caught me staring. In French, he asked, "Fini?" *Finished?*

"Presque." *Almost.*

I typed out the last line, emailed myself the paper and then pushed his laptop aside. He slid his chair closer beside mine, our arms brushing. Connor pulled all the reading material towards us, and we began to talk about sequential bargaining under asymmetric information and applications for perfect Bayesian equilibrium.

Two hours flew by. My pencil broke while I wrote out a complicated formula to an equation. He slipped his pencil out from his ear and held it to me.

I lost all thoughts. My heart sped rapidly, and my chest collapsed in a shallow breath. I pushed my notebook to him before he noticed. "Can you finish the line? I'll find a pen."

He lingered for a second and then accepted my request. Connor finished the formula, and I dug in my handbag for a pen.

What the hell is going on? my iron walls seemed to shriek. This was unlike me. Letting him stay. Letting him help. Letting him near.

I didn't want to push him away. I wanted Connor right here next to me.

I found my pen. I placed it on the table, and his arm extended over the back of my chair. He started talking about the equation, but I couldn't think straight.

"Rose?"

I glanced at him, just slightly.

He studied me with noticeable affection behind his blue eyes.

"Continue," I told him, my voice stilted.

"No."

My eyes flamed. "No?"

His hand encased my cheek and jaw, large and assured. My pulse beat my veins alive. His other hand rested on the outside of my thigh, climbing towards my ass.

I held onto his shoulder. Our lifetimes of combatting one another seemed to flip over like a spinning coin that fell to one side.

His lips an inch from mine, he whispered something, not a quote. Not in French. Connor Cobalt murmured, "What's inside this feeling that screams at me?" His eyes spoke of battles and wins and years positioned right across from me. "Devotion." He neared. "*Fealty.*"

His lips touched mine.

Our very first kiss. My rigid body stayed erect, but I heated like a thousand burning stars. He deepened the kiss, in control so I wouldn't have to think.

I was thinking.

I thought about how my mind sparked and blistered. I thought about how his hands commanded the moment as much as his lips. I thought about how he held me like I'd always been in his possession, as he'd always been in mine.

What's inside this feeling that screams at me?

Devotion.

Fealty.

It's what I remember as I scream in a hospital. As I squeeze my husband's hand. He towers beside me—as invincible as the day he leaned against that library table.

"Push, one more," the doctor encourages.

I push with everything inside my soul. I scream so horrifically, my throat scorched and raw. Then I hear the shrill cry pitch the air. *That cry.* It eases me like morphine, and I thud against the hospital bed. Connor dries my forehead with a towel, and we both watch the nurses clean our baby, the doctor assures us of good health.

Then the nurse places the newborn on my chest. I don't hear the nurse's next few words. Tears well and burn. Seven children and this one affects me all the same.

"Rose, darling." Connor lifts my chin, and I meet his glassy blues, his grin terribly gorgeous. "We have a girl."

"What?" *A girl.*

I didn't hear the nurse. I didn't remember to look.

Connor kisses my forehead and then he kisses hers and whispers soft French. A rare tear slides down his cheek.

When he looks back at me, I say quietly, "What's this feeling that screams inside of me?"

His glassy eyes carry their own extraordinary grin. Sparkling like cut diamonds. "*Love*," he tells me with such certainty.

His single tear dries faster than the waterfall my ducts let through. Connor brushes beneath my eyes with his thumb, and we watch our daughter coo peacefully.

I stroke her soft, tiny arm.

Years.

I wanted another girl for *years*. There was even a possibility that we wouldn't try again after our seventh child, but we had her.

I smile. "Fate was kind to us after all."

"Chromosomes," Connor says. "Science. Not fate, darling."

I shoot him a glare, my energy rising a little, even after intense labor. I rub my eyes once more and hone in on our newborn's thin hair.

"She has red hair?" No one on my side of the family has red hair, but Connor's mother did. "I thought your mother dyed her hair."

"She did dye it a deeper red. Naturally, her hue was more orange."

My lips inch upwards at our baby.

I feel her heart patter against my chest, her little mouth opening in a breath. "Audrey," I say the name I've had picked out for years. After Audrey Hepburn.

Tears fall again.

I'm a tsunami today. More water than rage.

Connor pulls his chair close and sits beside me. "Audrey Virginia Cobalt." After Virginia Woolf.

I sweep up more tears with my fingertips. "Ugh. Audrey, I'm so sorry, little gremlin." I wipe my nose with a tissue that Connor hands me. "This is *not* a good representation of me."

"On the contrary." Connor captures my gaze; his unrestrained emotion could power the world. "This is a good representation of both of us."

Vulnerable and in love.

So in love.

He laces his hand with mine.

I see Richard Connor Cobalt in nearly every frame of my life, and as his lips upturn with arrogant satisfaction, I know the greatest pieces of us have always remained the same.

"Mommy!"

The door whips open, and an excited two-year-old bounds forth, Jane clasps onto his shoulders, tugging him to her legs.

"Stay very still, Pippy," Jane whispers to him, the nickname a play off of his middle name *Pirrip.*

Ben stands at attention as the rest of our children slip into the hospital room. Seven-year-old twins: Charlie and Beckett. Five-year old Eliot. Four-year-old Tom.

Audrey on my chest.

Seven children.

Seven healthy, beautiful little gremlins.

Lily hangs by the door since she brought all of them to the hospital. Tears cloud her eyes, a smile illuminating her round face. She catches my gaze and mouths *see you later.* She gives me time alone with my family, and I nod in reply, the movement stiff.

I'd like all my sisters here, emotionally, but she closes the door to one sentiment just to make room for a thousand more.

"Come closer," I tell our children.

Connor stands and gestures all of them towards his side. They collect in front of his legs by the hospital bed. I sit up a little more, and I look to each of them as I say their names, "Jane, Charlie, Beckett, Eliot, Tom, and Ben."

They radiate, and the room teems with power and vivacity.

"We'd like you all to meet your new sister. Audrey Virgina Cobalt." I have the baby in my arms to show them.

Jane's hands fly to her mouth, tears brimming. "A sister?"

Over the years, she's seen me with her aunts, the support and love we share for one another. Over the years, she's waited, like us, to see if we'd have a girl.

"Yes, a sister."

Jane cries into a smile.

Connor sees our daughter and has to shift his head, angling his body more towards me. Away from our children. The sheer emotion on his face—I'll never forget that either.

While the children speak softly to Audrey, I say to Connor, "We did it."

"We did all of it," he clarifies.

This room.

This love.

Our future.

Our dynasty.

His hand strokes my cheek. I hold onto that hand, and his fingers thread mine.

Connor & Rose Cobalt welcome the birth of their baby girl

AUDREY VIRGINIA COBALT

January 27th, 2025

< 43 >

May 2025
PHILLY AQUATIC CLUB
Philadelphia

Daisy Meadows

At a crammed indoor pool, parents cheer for the 9 & older swimmers at a competitive meet. Lily and I are squeezed in between our husbands on the packed bleachers, all of us trying to ignore the onslaught of shouts, but hey, at least they're not at *us* for once.

"Come on, Sydney!"

"Go, Michelle!"

"You got this, Jenn!"

Moffy and Sulli aren't in this female 100-meter backstroke race. For one, Sulli is only seven and a part of the 8 & under category, which will race in about ten minutes. Moffy will be up first since he's already nine.

Lily bites her nails. "OhmyGod, I see him. Does he look nervous, Lo?"

As I crane my neck Moffy stands totally chill by the blue-tiled wall. Swim cap on, ready to go, he just adjusts his goggles a bit.

Lo feigns fright and clutches Lily's shoulder. "Christ, I think he's about to *hyperventilate*. Oh wait...that's just you." He flashes a half-smile at his wife.

Lily gapes and almost goes to slug his arm, but she sees little baby Kinney in a gray woven wrap on his chest, sleeping peacefully.

Two-thumbs up for earplugs. I just wished one-year-old Winona liked them as much as Kinney. She picked hers out three times already, and she wiggles on Ryke's lap, much squirmier than Sullivan ever was.

"You need CPR, love?" Lo teases, clutching the back of her head.

Lily tries hard not to smile. "Lo..." She kisses him before he even has a chance to kiss her.

I search the crowds for Sullivan and pick at the fray on my jean shorts. "I hope she's not stressing." *Wherever she is.* Ryke hears me over the mix of disappointed and delighted cheers from parents. His hard, darkened eyes fall down to mine.

I never had ambition and drive like Sulli. Ryke did. He still *does*. Every day he climbs, he sets new heights to reach. Sulli takes after him, and he can relate to her competitive spirit more than me. Once upon a time, Ryke was the *captain* of a collegiate track team.

"She's going to fucking stress because it means something to her, but she's also having fun, Dais." He knows I'm worried that she's not enjoying the sport. He always tells me not to mistake her frustration for hate. Overcoming challenges and roadblocks is part of the allure in sports.

I lift the brim of my green baseball cap higher, seeing more of him. "How much fun? Like *scream off the rooftops of the world* fun or *howl at the moon* kinda fun?"

Ryke taps the brim down, covering my eyes. A total flirt.

I smile wide, my world dark beneath the hat. "So *that* kind of fun?"

He leans close, lifting the hat, and says, "If you're implying what I think you're fucking implying, *no.*"

"You don't want someone to tap her baseball cap?" We've always been physical with one another, but it's not always sexual, even when it appears to be.

He spins my baseball hat backwards. "I don't want someone to fucking tap her anything. She's a baby."

"She's seven." I don't restrain my smile.

Ryke tosses the only thing he can at me—a half-bitten chocolate turtle that I tried to share with him earlier. I try to catch the snack in my mouth, but it thuds to the bleacher.

I put my hand to my forehead. "The disaster." The wasted chocolate at my feet.

It's a sad sight, indeed.

Suddenly, the bleacher vibrates underneath us. Nine-year-old Jane drums her feet in excitement, smiling big, her brown hair in a low, loose pony.

She sits between Lily and me, a Tupperware container of chocolate turtles on her lap. She always brings her favorite snack to meets, and she savors every single bite. I'm really the only other one who appreciates the chocolate pecan dessert.

As seen by Ryke who barely bit into it. He'll also be the first to start any food fight.

A chocolate turtle drops out of Jane's hand and into the container. "There he is!" She points and searches for the two pompoms she fashioned with their favorite colors.

Orange for Moffy.

Turquoise for Sulli.

Finding them by her feet, she waves the pompoms as the boys start gearing up for the 200-meter individual medley. Moffy's best stroke is the butterfly—which apparently most kids hate—and Sulli's is freestyle, but they both like the medley the most.

The referee blows a whistle over the intercom, signally for the competitors in the heat to remove all clothing except for swimwear. I'm more relaxed at these events than Lo, Ryke, and Lily. The two brothers suddenly go deathly still. Their jaws lock as the swimmers take their positions at the sound of a *long* whistle.

Moffy false started at the biggest meet last year, and he cried on the ride home. So the beginning is a big deal.

"Is that a Hale kid?" I hear the loud voices about two rows behind us, only because others join in and talk about him.

"Maximoff. He's the oldest one!"

Two little girls, right below us, point at Moffy. "He's so cute."

"I can't believe he's right there!"

Jane sets her snack container down and then springs to a stance with her pompoms. I can't tell whether or not she notices the chatter. "Destroy and conquer, Moffy!"

"Quiet in the stands," the referee tells everyone. The bleachers fall semi-hushed, most still whispering. Jane shakes the orange pompom like maracas.

Moffy puts one foot at the front of his starting platform. *This is it.*

"Take your mark."

Beep.

He's in the water with the other swimmers. Lo and Ryke exhale, and we all start cheering. He stays beneath the water for a while before surfacing and kicking.

"He's in the lead!" Jane shouts. Her next exclamation is in French. Lily beams, reminded that Moffy understands the foreign language like the Cobalts.

Moffy slows down during the backstroke, falling behind.

Jane still cheers like he's number one.

Lane three tags the edge.

Moffy is lane five, and when he reaches the finish, he pulls up his goggles and checks his time.

2:46.12 – 2nd

"Is he upset?" Lily asks Lo.

It's all we care about at these meets, not whether they win or lose but just how they *are*. Happy or sad. Angry or distraught.

Lo shakes his head. "I don't think so."

Moffy climbs out of the pool, wiping water off his face, and he hears Jane whistle loudly by putting her fingers in her mouth. She asked me to teach her last year. I join in and Moffy waves big at us, his smile returning.

"Good job, Mof!" Lo shouts.

He gives a thumbs-up to his dad and then to Lily who claps with such vigor, her pride overwhelming her round face. She wipes the corners of her eyes, tearing up.

"There's Sulli," Ryke tells me.

I spot her waiting at the back of a long line. Moffy does too. Towel in hand, he approaches his cousin, and they start talking.

Jane places her pompoms aside, her posture straight, ankles crossed. I notice how she stares off towards the pool, and then she quickly swings her head to Lo and Lily. "Did he mention it to you? He was desperately upset last night. I, for one, told him that he should tell you." She takes a short pause. "Did he tell you?"

Uh-oh.

We all tense. Our pasts are riddled with some bad, just plain mortifying and *never speak of it again!* events. Unfortunately for us, Google can surface 88% of these. Parental-blockers help, but kids gossip at school.

Rose and Connor warned us about this. They said that there'd be a time where all of our children stop opening up to us, and we won't know *how much* they really know. We've been in big arguments with the resident geniuses. The four of us are firmly against them for once.

Wait until they're older, we say.

Tell them everything now, Rose and Connor rebut.

Once we unleash every bad event, the kids will talk to each other, so Rose and Connor aren't telling their children without a unanimous agreement between us all. They're still trying to convince us, but now maybe this'll bite us in the ass.

Lo planned to give his son the "no alcohol" talk when he turned ten. (Lo started drinking hard liquor by eleven.) Ryke wants to give Sulli a similar talk around that age too, but all of our kids are still really young.

Lily is wide-eyed, a dozen *ohmygods* written along her eyes.

With sharp cheekbones, Lo asks, "What happened?"

Jane's shoulders drop. "So he didn't tell you." Her worried blue eyes flit across the bleachers. I rub my legs, up and down, totally confused. I need way more puzzle pieces to fit together this picture.

And I'm not the only one.

Lo turns more towards his niece. "*No*, he didn't say a thing."

"He might not speak to me for the rest of the week, but I'm willing to undergo best friend silence for this." Jane prepares herself with a deep inhale and then she softens her voice so no outsiders can hear. "He has a rash on his penis."

Half of us sort of relax. We just dodged a bigger catastrophe.

Lo leans toward her, his face twisting in a series of emotions. "Did he show *you?*"

"No," she says quickly, eyes popping. "*No.* He described the malady. I searched Web M.D., and I concluded, off very little knowledge mind you, that it's irritant dermatitis." She checks over her shoulder for eavesdroppers, then back to us. "From chlorine in the pool."

Now the other half—Lo and Lily—begin to relax.

Jane rises to her feet. "I should tell him that I betrayed our friendship for the benefit of his health." She's so verbose, but so are the rest of the Cobalts.

I still have this theory that Connor reads them the dictionary every night.

Lily agrees with me.

None of us have a chance to respond to Jane. She's already stepping over people to leave the bleachers.

"I almost puked." Lily touches her clammy cheeks. "Why'd she have to start off with *desperately upset?*"

"Because she's Rose's spawn." Lo rotates his taut shoulders, eyes narrowed towards Moffy and Sulli. His son pats my daughter's shoulders in a *good luck* fashion and then heads towards Jane. "Why wouldn't he tell me that?"

"Maybe he didn't want to worry you," I say.

Ryke adds, "Or he thought it'd go away before he fucking had to."

"Or the nerd stars are right," Lily says softly.

We all look at her, knowing she means Connor and Rose.

"Fuck that," Ryke snaps.

"They're not little anymore," Lily whispers. "It's *happening.* They're keeping things from us, and one day, they'll find out…"

About her sex addiction.

Lo glances at Kinney, wrapped to his chest. I look to little Winona who tries to pick her nose. None of us want to rip away their innocence before we should. I grew up too fast. So did Lily, and both of our husbands watched it happen.

"Come on, let's fucking wait," Ryke says. "It's too *early.* My kid is just a kid." He motions to Sulli who's in line for the next heat.

We all quietly contemplate our decision to shelter these events and facts. Then Lo's phone buzzes.

All the older kids share one cellphone when we go out, just to promote the buddy system. So I notice Moffy with his phone, Jane close by.

Friendship intact.

Lo eases even more. "Moffy just texted. He said that he planned to tell me if it didn't go away tomorrow."

"See," Ryke says. "You three, stay fucking strong." He gestures to us. Ryke is the same age as Rose, and nearly the same age as Connor. The rest of us are younger, and it's easier to back down against them. But we won't today.

"She's up." I cheer and clap as she reaches the platform. "Go, Sulli!" Since Jane is missing, I wave the pompoms.

"Take your mark."

Beep.

Sulli is in the water, staying under for longer than the other girls. She breaches the surface, good technique on her butterfly stroke, which pushes her ahead.

"GO, SULLI!" Ryke shouts.

She laps the other girls by the time she reaches the breaststroke. When she wins, it's no surprise, but she quickly takes off her goggles and checks her time, fingers to her lips in contemplation.

It's today, of all days, that I see how much my daughter races against herself.

2:40.13 – 1st and she beat the boys from the same event, but I remember all her records. *2:40* flat is her lowest, and if I peer close enough, I detect the gears in her brain rewinding. Trying to figure out *where* she gained extra time. Where she should've shaved more off.

This race might as well be a "what can I do better?"

Ryke kicks my ankles off the bleacher. No longer stationary, my legs now swing.

I smile, loving him.

He reminds me, "I'd be the same fucking way at her age." He said that he stopped fixating on his record-breaking times for climbing when he grew older. He just enjoyed the experience.

And her diligence and persistence—it's good. She might not celebrate a competition win, but I have to remember that she'll celebrate her own personal victories.

The referee calls out the winner. *Lane four.*

Loudly, a man grumbles behind us, "They let Bigfoot go against a bunch of little girls, of course she *won*." I tense, and his disdain immediately turns Lo and Ryke around.

"What?" the man snaps. His glare can't match Lo's.

"You want to talk Bigfoot?" Lo starts. "I can talk Bigfoot all goddamn day, and it's *not* that girl." His eyes flash hot.

The man crosses his arms, his snooty wife examining us with an upturned nose. "She beat the boys because she's taller than all of them."

She's the same height as Moffy right now, but he's older.

"She's seven fucking years old," Ryke sneers.

"She looks *twelve*."

Ryke doesn't understand the attacks. He didn't grow up as The Giraffe, the tallest girl in the grade, towering above all the boys.

I did.

"She's not twelve," I interject, twenty-times less hostile than Lo and Ryke. "She's just tall for her age. I'm five-eleven and my husband is six-three. She's genetically *tall*." Can't he leave it at that? Children are often labeled as cruel and unthinking, but adults can be just as vicious.

"It's not fair to the other kids," he tells us. "You should pull that Bigfoot out of the meets."

Ryke is about to stand up in defense, his nose flaring, and Lo is the one to plant a hand on his shoulder, keeping him down. Connor is usually that person, but Lo can be too on occasion. Especially when Connor Cobalt is missing in action.

Which only happens when he has more important things to do.

You should pull that Bigfoot out of meets.

People suck. A foul taste fills my mouth, and I feel myself cringe. Lily is gaping like he's insane to argue about the height of a child. I don't want to ruin Sulli's meet by fighting with another parent. We just need to leave this situation.

So I stand up. Lily stands up. Lo and Ryke stand up, our young babies in arm.

Just as we leave, Ryke turns around and tells him, "Sullivan beat your fucking kid because she wakes up at four-thirty every morning to practice. That's it."

He huffs like *yeah right.*

We don't waste time convincing him of anything more. We just put distance between him and us.

"YOU'VE GOT TO BE fucking kidding me," Ryke mutters under his breath. We just entered The Fixings, a little burger joint in Philadelphia, and the "Bigfoot" douchebag is seated at a long twelve-person table towards the back, beneath the flat-screen televisions that play baseball and tennis.

Where we have to go.

"What?" Sulli asks, catching Ryke's words. After the meet, she dressed in sweat pants and a loose-fitted tee, her wet brown hair tied in a high bun. Ryke adjusts her swim bag on his shoulder, and Winona wiggles in my arms, pouting at me to set her down.

I brush my nose with hers, and she kicks her legs and tells me, "Down."

I have to tune her out while I listen to Ryke.

"Do you know that fucking man?"

Sulli follows his harsh gaze. "He's Courtney's dad, I think." We've never seen that guy before, so we didn't think he was part of the same swim club. Four of the girls from the Philly Aquatic Club wanted to meet for dinner, and another parent made reservations for twelve and invited us.

I don't want to make eye contact yet, but I stare long enough to take in his suit and tie, brown parted hair, and entitled attitude. He never drops by practices with his wife, but it's not like we're overly friendly with the other parents. We don't do much small talk, and we try to keep to ourselves.

"Don't fucking talk to him," he tells Sullivan.

She never questions the request. There are many more people she shouldn't talk to than there are people she should. Sulli touches Winona's tiny hand as she squirms in my arms. "Is this okay?" She means having dinner in a public place.

Sometimes we have to dip out early if crowds are bad, but usually that's if we're with Lily and Lo.

Price and Ryke's bodyguard have already claimed a table nearby, and no one's really aware that they're *with* us. They blend in well, just wearing shorts and plain gray shirts.

"It's totally okay. We want to celebrate how you want to celebrate."

Ryke adds, "If you're fucking stressed or feel unsafe, we can leave at any time, Sul."

She nods, keeping this fact close, and then she's the one to head to the table first. Sitting at the end with all the seven and eight-year-old girls.

As we trail Sulli, Winona shrieks to be let down, tears building. I try to coo and make her cries shush, but she's not giving up.

Ryke must feel my frustration because he picks Winona out of my arms and tells her, "You're fucking trouble."

Winona sniffs but stops screaming. I have this theory that she prefers being in his arms because he's taller than me, so she's up high. Ryke only agreed when we were in our bedroom last week. He raised her in the air—she stopped crying—and then he dropped her to his side—and she wailed.

I love the way Winona rests her chin on his shoulder and stares out at the great big world. We take seats in the middle, *away* from Courtney's dad. Neither of us acknowledges him, and we try to focus on our baby while the table fills with parents and kids.

I undo one of her droopy pigtails, letting half her light brown hair hang free.

Ryke's muscles coil. I bet he's replaying what that guy said.

"Hey," I whisper.

He stares down at me, beyond brooding, but he's the first to say, "I'm not talking to that fucker."

What if he talks to you? It's a possibility, but I try to think positive thoughts and smile at Winona. "A getaway baby is trying to crawl over your shoulder."

Ryke effortlessly slides Winona back down to his chest. She plops on his lap with a frown. "No fun."

"I'm fucking fun," Ryke refutes.

"No."

Ryke blows a raspberry on her cheek, and Winona shrieks with laughter, more piercing than Sulli's. I hide behind a plastic menu, and when I pop out with cross-eyes, Winona screams with glee. "Mommy!"

I hide behind the menu again, but this time, I hear that male voice from earlier.

"Our girls stand no damn chance against her. She's taking medals away from them."

I lower the menu with a weak gasp at Winona. She still giggles like I performed the funniest trick. Ryke is texting, and my legs bounce so much that Winona scoots over to my lap so she can go up and down with them.

I hold onto my one-year-old and risk a glance at the man. He sits at the end of the table, close to another thirty-something father, and he barely makes an effort to whisper.

"Maybe she'll slip and fall." And then his eyes swerve to mine, but he wears no remorse or guilt in what he just said. "We were talking about the Riley Park Club. Beast of a girl on that team. You know the one?" The way they say *beast*, it's not an endearing term.

"No." My voice is stilted. *No confrontations.*

It's easier for me than for Ryke. He taps out words on his cellphone, venting to someone.

"The beast is four inches shorter than *your* girl."

Ryke looks up.

Both men shift in their chairs, sitting *straighter*.

The waitress thankfully comes around, and tension spools as we all go quiet. "Can I take your orders?" The big menus dwarf the little girls, but they all try to pick out what they want. Sulli's brows bunch, fingers to her lips.

I whisper to Ryke, "She doesn't know what she wants." I hold the menu out to him, and we both scan the items for something our daughter would actually eat.

Salad? It's a vegetable, so *no way*.

Burgers? Maybe if they trash everything but the bun.

Chicken fingers? She'll take one bite and spit it out.

"Maybe they have a breakfast menu?" Sulli likes most breakfast foods, but mainly waffles, pancakes, French toast, and donuts, all packed with whipped cream and syrup. At home, we try to find creative ways for her to include vegetables and healthy food in her meals, but we still give her children's vitamins because we don't think she gets enough with what she eats.

Ryke turns the menu around, but it just lists out desserts: hot fudge brownie, banana split, and milkshakes.

"What would you like?" the young waitress asks Sulli, her smile bursting with her next words, "Can you sign this?" She holds out her notebook with scribbled orders.

"Uh…" Sulli dazedly looks to Ryke and me for approval. I can tell she's still stuck in thought about what to eat.

"We can sign it," I suggest and wave the girl over with a friendly smile.

"Oh my God. Thank you!" She skips over to us, which gives Sulli more time to decide her food choice.

"Just our names?" I wonder, feeling the two douchebag men smirking like we're Hollywood trash. We're all east coast natives, but it wouldn't be the first time people act as though we're not even from Philadelphia.

"Yes, that'd be *amazing*." She has her hands to her mouth in shock.

I scrawl my name and then Ryke quickly signs his initials. Winona perks up like she wants to write her name out too—which would really be misshapen lines—but I clasp her fingers with mine and bounce her on my legs, distracting her in an instant.

I ask the waitress, "Do you guys do breakfast?"

"Not really, but I can ask the cook if he'll try."

The man coughs into his hand, "Princess." Some people never grow up.

"That's okay." We can always stop at Lucky's Diner and pick something up on the way home if she's still hungry.

The waitress returns to Sullivan. "Do you know what you want?"

She shuts her menu. "I think I'm good with water."

The "Bigfoot" douchebag mutters to his friend, "Good, maybe she'll faint next meet."

Ryke passes me his phone that buzzes, and he rises, all six-foot-three of him towering above. "I need to fucking talk to you. Outside."

I try to focus on Sulli so she doesn't see the hostile exchange between the men. "Did you see the back of the menu?"

Sulli flips the menu over. "Oh wait." The waitress stops from moving onto the shorter blonde girl. "Can I get the strawberry milkshake, fries, and fudge brownie?"

I'd smile, but this idiot guy laughs, "Outside? Really?" He acts like he's too cool for a conversation with Ryke.

His wife nudges him though. "Kenneth."

Kenneth. He has a name.

"Fine. Let's go *outside*," he says like it's a silly concept. Paparazzi are currently on the curb outside, about five or six cameramen, but it's not like Ryke can speak to him privately anywhere else. The burger joint is pretty crowded, and he'd rather throw out curses and threats outside than in front of Sulli.

Maybe she'll faint next meet.

I'm concerned about her safety, but we'll just send Price to practices with her from now on. I know Ryke will want someone there when we can't be.

Ryke leads the man outside, and his phone buzzes in my hand. A text conversation in full-blaze. Winona looks at the device with me.

I read the newest text.

Don't do anything I wouldn't do – Lo

Lo would probably butcher him with insults, ones that'd be on every entertainment news site. Ryke doesn't fight that way.

The phone vibrates again.

Better advice, don't punch him. – Connor

"What can I get you?" The waitress jolts me for a second, and I blink a couple times, clearing cobwebs.

I glance at the front window, street lamps and camera flashes the only light.

Ryke stands opposite Kenneth, and even though I can't hear him speak, the threat is clear in his dark, dangerous features, practically ripping through his stone exterior.

"Daisy Calloway?" she asks. I'm too used to the first-name-and-last-name attachment to flinch—or even the casual use of my maiden name.

"Actually…" I see the shadowed road we're all headed down. Ryke's fists clench as he *yells* over this other guy. Ryke fights with his body, rarely words. "Can you cancel her order? We have to leave."

"Huh?" Winona gawks up at me. I lift her on my side, and she tries to wiggle out.

"No, Nona," I whisper. "Shhh." I pick up Sulli's bag and apologize to the parent who invited us. Sulli scrapes back her chair, knowing we need to go.

Price rises, and Ryke's bodyguard, Quinn, suddenly appears from the kitchen door, nodding to Price. I slip Ryke's phone in my short's pocket, feeling the concentrated gazes of *everyone* in this diner. I pull Sulli closer to me, and she takes her swim bag off my arm.

"Can you help him?" I ask Price.

"He wanted me to stay with you and the girls." Price takes out his car keys while we linger by his table. "We're going to leave through the kitchen and out the back. Quinn is pulling the car around." I swing my head, noticing that Quinn is gone again.

Okay then.

The camera flashes suddenly go off like fireworks. I make sure Sulli and Winona aren't watching, faced towards the kitchen door.

Ryke and Kenneth fume much closer to one another. Kenneth points a finger and then he abruptly launches his fist towards Ryke's jaw. Ryke ducks and then knees Kenneth in the gut. So hard that the man *falls* to the sidewalk.

Ryke never says another thing. He just leaves, storms back inside to us—and Price directs all of us towards the back. We slip into the busy kitchen, the cooks watching as we hurry through to the backdoor.

"What happened?" Sulli asks her dad over the sizzle of burgers.

"Stay away from that fucking man." Ryke pulls Sulli very, very close, so protective that it almost scares me. What'd he say to him? Ryke sees my fear, and he sets his hand on my head like *don't worry.*

My phone starts beeping while Ryke's vibrates in my pocket again.

I don't answer either of them yet. I wait until we're all in Ryke's Land Cruiser, Quinn behind the wheel, Price in the passenger's seat, the four of us in the back.

As soon as the tires bump along the road, Winona falls asleep in her car seat.

"Sorry, Sul," I tell her softly.

Just as quietly, she says, "I didn't like it there anyway." She slouches. "Can Dad make pancakes?" I smile at her request.

"Yeah," Ryke says. "Anything else?"

"Captain Crunch cereal." She'll put it *on* the pancake like a topping. I take out the phones. Ryke's new texts stare back at me.

At least he punched first, bro. – Lo

Small achievements. – **Connor**

My sisters and Willow started a text thread with me.

OMG!!!!!! Did you all see the video? Ryke called him a dirty motherfucker — Lily

I'd stab his eyes out with my heels. Ryke should've taken a fork to his skull. — Rose

What's going on?? — Willow

Check out Celebrity Crush and GBA Entertainment News. Do you want a link? — Lily

Media is fast, but I knew it'd be online the minute Ryke stepped outside.

Found it. Omg. — Willow

Daisy, did the man really wish that Sullivan would faint?
— Poppy

You think Ryke just concocted this for laughs? Why the hell would he say, 'You wished my seven-year-old would faint—not to mention slip and fucking fall.' Of course it's real. — Rose

I'm just looking at all sides. — Poppy

Rose sent our sister devil and knife emojis. I relax at the exchange. What Ryke did was smart, even calculated. He aired threats that the man made in public, on record, almost as a safety net for our daughter. If someone tried to hurt her, Kenneth would be the first suspect.

He might even be banned from the Philly Aquatic Club after this.

I return Ryke's phone to him, and he searches my gaze, as though wondering where my head lies. I whisper, "We're okay." *We're all okay.*

He nods strongly. "We're really fucking okay."

{ 44 }

September 2025
DALTON ELEMENTARY
Philadelphia

Lily Hale

Luna has been in kindergarten for only two months, and the teacher asked us specifically to come in for a parent-teacher conference. While we wait for Ms. Jacobs in the little classroom, I begin to sweat.

I try to slyly sniff my armpit, just to confirm that I don't stink.

"Lil," Lo says. "You don't smell. He lounges in the tiny plastic chair like he's slacking off in fourth period biology.

It's not an accurate depiction of today.

We're in the front of the classroom, not the back. We're at a round kindergarten table, not a desk. And we're waiting for bad news, not for the bell to ring.

Why else would we be the only parents called for a conference?

"I'm sweating," I mumble and tug at my T-shirt for ventilation.

"This whole thing is probably nothing." His voice strains, so I know he doesn't fully believe that. He wraps his arm along my shoulders, and my gangly arm slips around his waist.

The door creaks open, and Lo gives me a tight squeeze like *we got this.* Ms. Jacobs smiles warmly. "Hi, Loren. Hi, Lily."

Moffy had Ms. Jacobs for kindergarten, so we're on a first-name basis. Brown curly hair, sympathetic eyes and an equally tender voice, she's been one of my favorite teachers at Dalton Elementary. I was really excited when Luna was placed in her class.

Now I don't know what to think.

"Hi," I say while Lo remains quiet. He no longer slouches, but he squeezes me again, mostly for my benefit.

My face must contain tons of dread because Ms. Jacobs splays her hands like *stay calm.*

"Everything is fine with Luna. I just have a few things I'd like to discuss before we move further into the school year." Ms. Jacobs takes a seat at the round table while my worry mounts.

I catch myself biting my nail, and I stop.

She slides a couple drawings and writing worksheets over to us. "The good news is that Luna is really excelling with her writing skills." I read the sentence she scribbled in the large notebook guidelines.

My name is Luna Hale. I was born on planet Thebula.

My cheeks hurt, smiling way too hard. Lo's amber eyes even lighten.

"She's also on track in math."

"Then what's the problem?" Lo questions cuttingly, that light snuffing out.

Ms. Jacobs clears her throat, not used to Lo. "By this time, the children start building friendships with their classmates. Sometimes the shy students take a little longer, but Luna isn't quiet or shy and approaching her classmates hasn't been an issue."

My stomach knots and rewraps and knots all over again. Lo's strong grip around my frame feels more like a lifeline between us.

"I want to caution again that there's no reason to be upset. Many kids struggle in different areas early on, and kindergarten is really the time to see those weak points and try to strengthen them."

Lo and I have been dealt enough shitty hands to know that a pile of shit is about to fall on our daughter.

"So what's her weak point?" Lo snaps.

Ms. Jacobs stays fixed on me, unable to meet the harshness of Loren Hale's eyes. "Luna isn't making any friends. She's left out of group activities unless I make the other girls include her."

My face falls.

Lo's jaw muscle constricts.

"How is she doing at home?" Ms. Jacobs asks. "Do you regularly set up play dates? Does she have any friends in the neighborhood?"

"It's complicated," Lo says tersely.

It's not an excuse, even if it feels like one. We've tried really hard to set up play dates for Luna, but some parents in the neighborhood don't like us. It's just a simple fact.

Moffy was uninvited to three birthday parties because the parents either don't trust us or they just don't want their children to associate with that "reality TV" kid. Moffy shrugs it off, like most things. But Luna never even had the chance to have a sleepover at another girl's house.

No one asked yet, and I always thought that might change when she grew older and started making school friends.

"She has friends," I say the truth. "Her cousins. She hangs out with Eliot and Tom a lot. They're in the same grade."

"Eliot and Tom Cobalt." Ms. Jacobs nods curtly, as though their names bring arthritis and back aches. Separately, they're more manageable. Together, they're definitely a handful. "The whole administration knows who they are, and they're currently in Ms. Nalah's class. But I think it's better for Luna to make friends with girls her own age and kids that aren't related to her."

"It's easier said than done," Lo replies. "In order for our kids to even go to someone's house, the parents have to sign a non-disclosure agreement. Most parents don't want to deal with that shit."

Our children are too young to understand, and all we want is to protect them. To make sure other people don't exploit them. The NDA's are a formality, but it's a giant safeguard that we can't skip.

"I know your situation must be more difficult," Ms. Jacob says, "but Luna doesn't need to jump through any hoops to make friends at school."

I wrack my brain. "I…I don't know why they're not including her. Is it because she's on *We Are Calloway*?"

"No. At least, I don't think so. I believe most parents won't let their child watch the docu-series. It's on a premium cable channel."

Lo and I both nod. It's like letting a child watch *Game of Thrones* but without the incest and sex and murders. *Bad example.*

Ms. Jacobs suddenly stares at the table and then lets out a soft sigh. "This is really hard for me to say, but I want you both to know that kids this age, they can be judgmental."

I'm not even breathing at this point.

"Some of the other girls…and boys have taken to calling Luna names behind her back. Whispering. That sort of—"

"What kind of names?" Lo cuts in, his eyes reddening, no longer blinking.

I teeter between anger and pain, both sentiments coiling around my lungs and yanking tight.

"Weirdo. Creep."

Each word stabs my heart.

Lo swings his head towards the door, glaring and forcing down every brutal emotion that suddenly impales us both.

Creep. It rings in my ears. I try to swallow a lump down, but it won't budge. Lo and I haven't let go of one another. I rub my eyes with the heel of my palm. I just never wanted her life to be harder. We both wanted *easy, painless,* and *happy* for our daughter.

"She's just a little different than the other girls her age," Ms. Jacob says, "which isn't all bad. As far as I can tell, she understands social cues, but she's not at an age where she fully grasps shame yet."

I immediately start crying at the word *shame*. She'll be ashamed of what she likes soon, is that it? Other kids will make her feel guilty for saying the wrong thing and in the wrong way. She'll be pressured to be more like them and less like herself.

I wipe my tears fast with Lo's shirt.

He tucks me closer to his chest.

"I'm so sorry." Ms. Jacob slides over a box of tissues. I take about five—or ten. I rub my nose, and she continues, "I want to give you some examples, if that's okay?"

Lo and I both nod again.

"Luna will talk in different voices sometimes, and the times she talks normally, she'll discuss things like imaginary planets and someone called FinFarley Hunter." FinFarley Hunter is a comic book for children, a line that Halway Comics published a couple years ago. It's kind of like a spin on Nancy Drew, and so far it's stayed very niche.

"That's just the kind of stuff she's into," Lo says, his face twisted. "I'm not going to tell her to abandon the shit she likes because other people don't get it. It's not her fault. It's *theirs*."

"I understand, but maybe try to get her involved in a mainstream activity or interest that'll make it easier for her to connect with other girls."

It seems like the right thing to do, but a tiny voice in the back of my head whispers, *why does she have to like what other kids like just to make friends?* Why?

Lo rubs the back of his neck. "We're not going to force her into something, but we'll…introduce other stuff and see if she likes it."

It's not like we haven't already. She tried soccer and huffed and puffed and then quit.

I sniff and nod at Lo. I know we have to keep trying, especially if it'll make her school life easier.

Lo asks, "If things—if they get worse, what would happen if we switched her to Ms. Nalah's class?"

"I don't recommend it. Not this year. The entire kindergarten class shares a recess. They all know each other, and they'll ask Luna why she was moved out of my class. Just wait, please. It's still early, which was why I wanted to chat now instead of later in the year."

We say our thanks and then finish up the conversation. When Lo and I climb into his Audi, we just sit there for a while, not able to start the car. Not able to drive home. Our bodyguards wait in the SUV behind us, probably questioning the hold-up.

Tears prick my eyes again. "We weren't ever called weirdos..." I just see her future unless something changes, and it contains more heartache than we ever pictured. "You were an asshole. I was...shy." Luna's not shy. She's outspoken and loud. Her opinions and imagination fill a room and don't fit into a certain mold. She's different, but why is that so bad?

"She'll be okay." Lo nods to himself like he has to believe this statement. He turns the key, the Audi blinking to life.

I repeat his words. Over and over.

{ 45 }

November 2025
MANHATTAN MEDICAL HOSPITAL
New York City

LOREN HALE

I *run* down the hospital hallway. Chest on fire. Legs numb. My body rages so far ahead of my brain. Ahead of my emotions.

Ahead of me.

I only slow when I reach the hospital door. Ajar, but no noise filters into the hallway. *Go in there, Lo.*

Walk the fuck in there, Lo.

Why did you stop, Lo?!

Fear chokes me by the throat. I tug the collar of my crew neck. *Move your goddamn feet.* I stop waiting around for this *feeling* to disappear.

I step carefully and slowly inside. It feels like I'm walking on glass, cutting deep in my soles. Slicing open my feet. As soon as the hospital bed comes into view, I stop walking.

Stop moving.

Stop looking at him. But I can't tear my gaze away from the scene in front of me.

My father lies on the firm mattress, sheet-white, eyes sunken. He stares hauntingly at the ceiling, his lips the same pallid color of his skin.

He already looks dead.

I choke on a strangled noise, caught between grief and anger.

His head tilts limply towards me. I'm not comforted by the sight. He's still alive but just barely. Jonathan Hale teeters between life and death.

I lick my dry lips. All I want to do is grab ahold of him, wrench him back to me, to this life, and to this world.

I still need you. I want to scream at myself for thinking this goddamn thing. *I still need you, Dad.* Did I ever really need him? Somewhere inside me, I truly believe I did, and I can't let go of that.

My eyes cloud. In front of him, I instinctively shield my face with my hand. I wait for him to say it, *"Stop fucking crying, Loren."*

I still hear it in my head. I always *hear it.* Even when he's different. Even when I know I'm different.

I still hear it.

"Come here, Loren." His coarse tone slices me up, but I hold onto the familiarity.

My throat is swollen closed. I swallow hard and manage to step forward. Pain radiates up my shins and legs and arms. Just at the single movement. My body screams for me to stop. So I stop.

I don't go after the pain. I don't ask for it. I don't *want* it.

I don't even believe I deserve it.

I point an accusatory finger at my dad. The man who's dying right in front of me. "Why didn't you tell *me?* You said you were on a fucking vacation—to Hawaii?" I nearly spit. Grief and anger rattles my bones. I'm his son. I'm the *one* that gives a shit whether he lives or dies.

And he didn't tell me.

I should've known it was all bullshit. He gave me too many details about the resort, about his "lady friend" he planned to fuck all weekend. It seemed too elaborate to be the truth.

Maybe I just wanted to believe the story. He sounded happy. My dad on some getaway trip. To relax. To suntan. To have a goddamn fling.

"A lie," he says, as though it's nothing. He points to the stiff chair by his stiff bed. "Sit."

I grimace. "Jesus Christ, Dad. Don't say it like it's fucking nothing. You lied. Okay? You *lied* to me." I jab my finger towards the floor. "The nurses said you've been here for a whole week." Rage pushes me forward. "Why didn't you call me?!"

I breathe heavily, already knowing the answer before the question escapes. He's Jonathan Hale. He protected me from the knowledge of being a bastard. He protected me from an ugly rumor about him molesting me. And he protected me again.

From the torment of watching him slowly die.

"Sit." He points to the chair again, the gesture tugging his IV cords and shifting the metal stand.

I make it to the chair. I collapse on the seat. I just might sink all the way to the ground through the floorboards and down, down, *down* to the dirt in the fucking Earth.

I have to hunch forward, forearms on my thighs. It hurts to look at him. Hurts to be here. But I stay and I try to look.

I'm scared if I don't, he'll disappear. My chest caves at the sight of him. I blink, and tears fall. "Dammit," I curse, glaring at the ceiling.

Why is this happening?

"Loren." He says my name with frailty I've never heard. "Will you call your brother and sister? I want them here."

I knew he would. "They're on their way." My leg jostles and my shoulders sway from side to side, pent up with *so much*...

My amber eyes rise to him again.

He never reaches for my hand. Never pulls me closer. He's never been that kind of father. But his presence is so large it fills the room. His spirit is bigger than his body.

I don't have to ask what happened. I spoke to the doctors over the phone. At his request, they called me first. For the past couple of years, he's been suffering from chronic liver rejection. It's common for liver transplant recipients to have some type of rejection, but *chronic*—it means this has been happening for a long period of time.

He was only admitted to the hospital when his liver started shutting down.

He's too low on the transplant list. No donors in sight. Ryke already donated once, and he can't again.

What the hell has he been going through for two years? He knew he'd die. He knew that all hope was shot. I'm so goddamn angry he never said a thing. He went through this alone.

I can't wash the malice out of my harsh eyes. "You should've told me." *I'm your son.*

He laughs briefly like I'm just a kid.

I'm thirty-five. I'm not just a kid.

But I am his.

"I should've told you…" He lets out another weak laugh and shakes his head. "And have you tiptoe around me? You want to put me out to pasture like cattle—fine. You have the chance now." He extends one of his arms. "Bury me."

I cringe. "Jesus *Christ*. Stop it." My eyes flood. "You're going to be okay."

His dry smile fades. "You've never been a dreamer, Loren. Don't start now."

His words should piss me off. I should be enraged, but they remind me that he knows who I am. He raised me. He was there for me. For a really long time, it had been just me and him. I can't forget the fact that he chose *me*. I was the bastard, but he never flung me out like trash.

There is love so deeply rooted between us. Beneath all the dark and the black and the tar that bleeds our souls. There is love. It exists, and I realize I'm about to lose it forever.

Don't go, I want to tell him.

I hear his reply in my head, *you think I want to?*

"There must be some way to get you another transplant." I fight for him.

His sharp, withering glare tries to destroy me. I don't let it. My own cutting look rivals his, and I think, *I learned from the best.*

"Don't be ridiculous. You saw the list. Even if I could find one, it'd be unlikely my body would accept it. Say goodbye. It's why you're here." His lip twitches. "Do what everyone does when confronted by someone on their deathbed."

"What's that?" My words sour in my mouth. My other leg starts jostling. *Stopstopstop.* I can't.

My dad rolls his eyes, annoyed that I haven't caught on. "Shower me with praises. Tell me how great a father I was. Yada, yada, yada."

I open my mouth to speak, but my throat closes again. It hurts. Being here. Sitting here. My brain is a thousand tons of get-me-out-of-here. My gaze lowers to the sheets of his bed.

Dammit.

Dammit.

I wipe at the tears that roll down. "You were…" I struggle. I'm *struggling.* More than I can even express—I'm drowning right now. I shift in my chair. I clench the armrests, my knuckles whitening.

Slowly, I lift my head and meet his sunken eyes.

In a single look, we share a thousand truths. He wasn't a good father, but he was the only one I had.

"You were alright."

The corner of his lip rises. "Just alright." It's not a question. He knows his faults. I don't wait for an apology. Not for all the harm he caused me, for the verbal abuse that paved the way for harsher, crueler things in my future. I don't wait for one because like he said—I've never been a dreamer.

Did I ever imagine Jonathan Hale apologizing as he dies on a hospital bed? No. Never. Not once.

I don't expect it.

I don't even care for it.

I don't even *want* one the way my brother did. The way my brother asked. The way my brother got his.

I'd rather have this man in front of me. The one so painfully flawed. The one filled with endless amounts of love. I'd rather face the end with him.

"Honestly, Loren." His voice slices me up again. How many more times will I hear him say my name? I glare at the ceiling, tears flowing backwards, dripping out of the corners of my eyes. He finishes with, "You're better than I was. I want you to know that."

My body runs cold. "Everyone at Hale Co. still loves you—"

"I wasn't talking about the goddamn company," he cuts me off, and the quiet abruptly cloaks us. I have to sit here and repeat his words over and over in my head for them to make sense.

You're better than I was.

You're better than I was.

You're better than I was.

No matter how many times they play out, I still can't believe *that's* what he chooses to tell me. My father never admits defeat, rarely puts others above himself. He only ever wanted me to embrace my potential, but he never saw my potential as anything more than a flickering ember, ready to die out at the slightest gust of wind.

"Loren," he says my name again. Is *this* the last time I'll hear it? I keep my glare on the ceiling, tears still dripping out the corners.

"You're a better father," he tells me. *Stop crying.* "A better husband." *Stop fucking crying.* "A better man."

I drop my gaze, not covering my face. I cry in front of the man who always told me to *goddamn stop.* I'm hunched like if I try, I might be able to hug myself. Pain obliterates me from top to bottom, engulfing all that I was. All that I am.

"Loren."

"Stop," I choke. "Just stop." I set a glare on him.

He sets one on me. "I won't *stop* because you can't control your tears." There it is. In my fucked up reality, I'm almost glad to hear it. One last time. My older brother would think it was sick, but I can't help it.

I rub my eyes with the back of my sleeve. When I look at him, he canvasses me like he's remembering me for the final time.

"I've always loved you, son." *I know.* He never let me forget it. "It was a decent ride. The whiskey could've been better towards the end."

I can't laugh at the joke.

He stayed sober. My dad stayed sober for a long time. For me. For Ryke. For Willow. For himself.

"Will you remember?" he asks, fear creasing his eyes for the first time.

"Remember what?"

"That I loved you."

I realize he's worried about his legacy. That maybe in time Jonathan Hale won't be remembered as the man who fought to bring his three children together—but rather as the old drunk who shouted slurs and spiteful things.

I'm not sure what'll happen in the future. How I'll describe him to my children as they get older, but I know I won't leave out the fact that he loved us. And he tried. *God, he tried.*

I nod a few times. "I'll remember." I rub the back of my neck. "You know..." It's inside of me. I've said it before. *It hurts.* "You know...I love you too."

He stares at the wall this time, away from me, as though repeating those words in his head. I wonder if he thinks that he doesn't deserve my love. I know my brother feels that way.

If so, my dad never tells me.

We're silent the rest of the time, and my tears dry.

"Dad?" Ryke emerges in the doorway, Willow beside him. He's stoic, his gaze locking on me longer than our father.

I wrench my body up from the chair. I step back, giving Ryke and Willow time with him. Ryke stays put, letting Willow go first.

I'm a million pounds.

I'm sinking.

I go to leave, but Ryke catches my shoulder. Then he shuts the door, locking my escape. I barely hear him mention that he talked to the doctors. They said our dad wouldn't make it through the night. I blink and look for an out. I tug my collar.

Leave, my brain screams.

Bottle. Booze.

Leave.

"Hey," Ryke grits in my ear, shaking me by the shoulders.

I swat his hands away and glower like he's the enemy. *I'm the villain.* I hate myself more right now than I have in goddamn years.

Stop.

Fight.

"Lily," Ryke tells me, reminding me. I let out a deeper breath. As I calm down some, Ryke releases his grip on my shoulders. "I'm going to stay. I think we both fucking should."

Despite the past, Ryke made more peace with Jonathan than I ever thought he would. And now he wants to stay.

And watch him die.

I shake my head, my eyes cast down to the floor. My dad knew I couldn't handle it. It's why he waited until the last minute, and even now, I choke.

"I can't..." The air is too thin. The walls too tight. I'm uncomfortable in my clothes. In my body. I could fucking puke.

How did I live with this feeling for so long back then? I feel like I'm dying.

I was dying. Every goddamn day.

I need a drink.

Stop.

Fight.

Lily.

"Hey." Ryke cups my face, my eyes returning to his. "I can't even fucking imagine what it's like for you, but if you leave, you'll regret it."

My *many* regrets are layered beneath my skin. Imprinted in my bones. Regrets that will never leave me. That will always haunt me, but ones that I have to face and accept.

Most deal with drinking and every shit decision that hurt Lily. Even though we're together now, every day that goes by I regret not being the man she needed. Not being able to help my best friend. Days and nights fogged by booze. Drinking.

Drinking.

Dying.

I regret how long it took for me to wake up.

I'm awake now. I can't forget how the haze is gone.

I'm awake. I'm alive.

Slowly, painfully, I walk back towards his hospital bed. I pull out another chair. I sit there.

And I watch my father die.

< 46 >

November 2025

EDEN CROSS CEMETERY
Philadelphia

Ryke Meadows

My father's funeral ended about ten minutes ago.

I stayed behind, alone. Facing a pile of fucking dirt. The headstone he picked out towers above all the others. It's fucking *huge*. I roll my eyes at it—and at the empty plots surrounding it. The ones he bought for his children, for our families.

I shake my head over and over. I spent so much time suppressing my feelings that I haven't come to terms with his death like I should've days ago. Connor told me he'd look out for Lo, and then he bluntly added, "You can cry."

I glowered, but I never had to tell him why I couldn't cry. He knows. It's not just overwhelming concern for my little brother. It's that I hated my father for so long, even when we'd been at peace towards the end. I just keep thinking, *why should he get my fucking tears?*

I'll remember the last words I said to my father for the rest of my life. "Thank you for fucking pushing me to meet Lo." My brother and my sister—they're the only good things he ever gave me.

The last thing he said to me, "You've always been stubborn."

I rake my two hands through my thick hair. I skim the new dirt, the engraved headstone—rich, every way I turn.

What I say next, I have to say to my father six-feet-under. Because I never would've said it to his fucking face. I rub my jaw. Then I go still.

My pulse slows. The wind howls around me.

Quietly, I say, "I loved you in the fucking end."

I don't cry for him. I don't fucking need to, but I needed to say this.

I HIKE UP A mountain, leaves orange and yellow. All around me.

All around my family.

While the world goes fucking insane with my father's death—camera crews positioned outside of the neighborhood gates twenty-four-fucking-seven like royalty passed—I just leave that circus and find better solace.

Daisy, Sulli, and I hike in the Smoky Mountains, planning to camp at a remote site that we've been to a few times before. I carry Winona in a backpack baby-carrier, built for long treks. When Sullivan was a baby, she'd sit patiently and ooh and awe at every fucking tree.

Every baby is not even close to being the same.

One-year-old Winona kicks my back and has already tried to unbuckle herself by rattling the straps. Daisy keeps an eye on her while our seven-year-old races out ahead of us. Sulli's determined to push her pace to the limit.

Winona knees my spine.

"Fuck," I curse.

Daisy smiles. "Need to trade?" She wears a dark green pack with our camping gear.

"Depends, Calloway."

"On what?"

"Whether or not you plan to fall fucking down." She usually skips around, not paying attention, and she's face-planted on the dirt *four* times already. Her hands are cut up, but if you saw Daisy, so carefree, you'd hardly notice.

"Me? I don't fall."

"Then what happened ten minutes ago?"

"I gracefully lied down."

She makes me fucking smile, and I smack the rim of her baseball cap, shielding her eyes. She's made me laugh four times today—and *fuck*, after everything, that funeral…I shake my head in thought.

There's nowhere I'd rather be than in the woods, on a mountain, with Daisy Meadows.

With Sullivan Meadows.

With Winona Meadows.

With my fucking girls. My family.

Daisy calls out, "Go right, Sulli! Follow the red stakes." We marked out a trail about five or six years ago. Sulli veers to the right, a little red-faced and sweaty as the elevation increases. We can't always include Sulli in everything. A lot is still too dangerous. Like riding a motorcycle. Like jumping off fucking cliffs in foreign countries. When we do say *yes, you can*, she goes after the task like it's her only chance.

So she hikes like this is the first and last time she'll feel her soles on this mountain.

Daisy spins her hat backwards while Winona babbles incoherent fucking things. My wife elbows my side and screws open her water bottle. "Guess what?"

"What?" Every step higher, I feel fucking stronger.

"You have a little animal on your back."

Winona giggles like she's up to no good.

"That so?" I crane my head, meeting Winona's big brown eyes, flecked with hazel.

She kicks her feet and shrieks happily, "Daddy!"

She's fucking cute. I reach behind me and tenderly rub her head. She holds onto my finger for a minute or two before letting go. Daisy watches us with the most loving smile while sipping her water bottle.

"Hey, sweetheart?" I wait for her eyes to land on mine. "We made that fucking baby."

"I thought she looked a lot like you." She smiles into another sip of water. "I wasn't sure for a while there."

"Yeah?" I take the bait. Winona has my eyes, but she looks a lot more like Dais. "There were other men who could've been her dad?"

"Tons," she jokes. "About a billion."

"You fucked a billion men, Calloway?" We didn't have sex to have Winona, but I'm being about as serious as Dais is right now.

"A billion and one *men*."

I don't crack a smile, which only makes hers grow. I scan her in a long once-over and then raise my brows up at Daisy. "Bullshit."

She smiles. "I thought for sure she was Fred's."

"Fuck Fred." Then I grab the water bottle out of her hand, which spills over her mouth.

She chokes on a laugh, water dripping down her chin. She doesn't care to wipe it up. "So aggressive."

"Such a fucking tease."

She laughs more full-bellied. I almost smile and then I hug her closer to my side. I kiss Daisy's head, glad to have her right here.

About twenty minutes later, Sulli already ahead of us, we reach the precipice of a mountain, a fire pit already made out of stone. Sulli stands on a secure boulder, face awed as though she's never seen the horizon.

Daisy and I approach on either side of our daughter, the world vast and landscaped by orange, red and yellow trees. Two birds glide through

the bright blue fucking sky. I breathe like this is untouched air, pure—
absolved of pain, of death.

Here, I connect to every living thing. To who I am. Where I am.
What I am.

"Wow," Sulli breathes. She saw what death looks like today: a coffin.
Buried. Gone.

Right now, the size of this world reflects in her huge green eyes.
Overwhelming her. I begin to smile at my daughter, as she looks grateful
for this view. To be here.

To be fucking alive.

Wow.

{ 47 }

December 2025
THE HALE HOUSE
Philadelphia

LOREN HALE

On the couch, Lily glances at me throughout the movie. *Toy Story* plays on our flat-screen, our toddler watching from his red bean-bag and nibbling pretzels while one-year-old Kinney has conked out on Lily's lap. By this time, I'd pick up Kinney and hold her as she sleeps.

I don't.

I can't blame Lily for being concerned.

I've also been fidgeting and shifting. Uncomfortable. On this couch. In my skin. I've stood up and disappeared in the bathroom about seven times. Just to splash water on my face. Usually, we're tangled together when we watch movies. Usually, I have my arms around her hips. I've wedged more space between us, which draws worried lines across her forehead.

Most days I feel like I can move mountains. Recently I feel like the mountain has fallen on top of me.

My dad's death is still fresh. Less than a month since the funeral. Yesterday, I told my brother I couldn't go through our dad's mansion. I can't pack his shit up. I can't be the one to sell the home I grew up in—I selfishly wish he took all of that when he died. It'd be easier.

Ryke just said, "I'll take care of it. You don't have to think about a fucking thing, alright?"

"Alright."

But I am thinking. Every day, my mind won't stop. With what's happening tonight, I should be relaxed. Happy, even. Moffy, now ten, was invited to a sleepover, and his six-year-old sister finally got an invite too. Different friends in the neighborhood. Different houses. Both sets of parents signed the non-disclosure agreements with barely a bat of an eye.

Luna practically bounced out the door, overly excited to attend her first sleepover. Even though her interests still don't line-up with other girls. Even though she still likes to make beeping noises like she's R2-D2 and BB-8.

I should be happy.

I know I should.

But I can't shake a feeling that yanks my shoulders. That literally keeps my brain on a repetitive, circular track. Thinking and thinking about the *one* goddamn thing that could shut down a terrible ache inside my ribs.

I rub my burning eyes.

Antabuse, I remember. I'm on Antabuse. It's been years since I've taken the drug that causes physical illness if I drink alcohol. After my dad's funeral, I filled my prescription and started up again. I'm *terrified* of the moment where I convince myself it's worth it.

The moment where I forget the people I love. Just in a split second. That's all it'd take. If I'm shoved further down, I feel like I might do it.

I've already sat outside a liquor store. Yesterday. The day I called my brother, and he assured me that he'd take care of everything. Then I felt guilty that I shoved these responsibilities on him. I called Lily, and she just spoke softly about Hellion and X-23. I relaxed enough to turn my car around.

Paparazzi tailed me right then. I was lucky they didn't catch a photo of me in the parking lot. I don't want my kids to think I chose alcohol over them. Everything is just tearing me up inside.

Just driving there, I feel like I betrayed my family and myself. Guilt should stop me from taking a sip, but I reroute to these thoughts: *what's the point, why not just cross that line and actually do it—then I'll get something out of it. Then I'll stop feeling like shit for a moment. Maybe then I'll just be numb.*

I look to Lily, about to tell her that I'm leaving the house for a minute. She sees something in my eyes because she says, "Can you hold Kinney?" Lily is about to pass our sleeping daughter to me, but I stand up before she can.

I whisper, "I'm going to go out, just for like ten minutes."

Lily searches my features, and I do everything to block out the truth. Not long after, she whispers firmly, "No. You need to stay here."

"I'm fine, Lily." Anger laces my voice. "I just want some fresh air. Maybe I'll go to Ryke's."

Lily rises and sets Kinney in a bouncer next to Xander's beanbag. "I can call Ryke to come here. I think you should stay."

Ham perks up from his spot next to my youngest son, his dog tags jingling. The basset hound's big orb-like eyes practically beg me to take him for a walk. Beside him, Xander leans over his beanbag, looking upside-down at me. His brown hair hangs with his head. "Daddy? Where you going?"

My stomach tosses. My muscles bind, and acid scorches my throat. "To Uncle Ryke's, little guy."

He mumbles out words that sound like *can I go with you?*

"No, I won't be long." I walk around the couch and enter the foyer, out of sight from the living room. Lily suddenly darts around me, skids to the door and splays out her arms on either side.

She's so much smaller than me and weighs just barely over a hundred pounds—but to see her try to physically stop me wrenches my insides and scalds my brain.

I love Lily more than I love myself right now.

"Lily Calloway," I say her maiden name, which feels weird on my lips. I haven't said *Lily Calloway* in a long time, but it hurts more when I remind myself that she's connected to me. My wife. My best friend. My first and only love.

My soul mate. If I hurt, she hurts.

"Loren Hale," she counters, trying to remain tough. She pushes out her chest like she can truly keep me from walking out that door.

I step closer and motion to her. "You think this is really going to stop me?"

"Yes," she says, chin high. "Because you're better than this."

You're better than I was. My father's words dagger my chest. I glare up at the ceiling and shake my head, my eyes glassing almost instantly. "Right now, I'm not."

He was wrong. I can't shake these urges and these cravings. No matter if I have one kid, two, three, four or none. I'm still an addict. I'm *always* going to feel like this. There's no escape.

I want to leave this skin.

"You are," she says strongly. "This is a horrible day, night, week, month…maybe even year." Her chest rises and falls with heavy breaths. "But there'll be good days. You just have to get through this part, Lo. Okay?"

We've unconsciously drifted closer to one another. I'm fragmented, and when I pull her in my arms, when I tuck her to my chest, when she holds on so tight, when her warmth blankets me—I'm whole. Like this is where I belong.

Cravings don't magically end with her embrace, but she reinforces my defenses, my belief in myself. It's not really a girl who fixes me. It's an army of people who I love and who love me.

It's a phone call to my brother. It's Connor's reminder that I'm doing my best. It's Lily being the other half of my heart.

I stare down at my best friend. Her eyes carry the same pain as mine. We share our feelings like we share everything else. I fight this agony.

I'm barely able to say, "I don't think I can take a horrible year, Lil."

She holds me tighter.

I clasp her cheek, my thumb catching a tear.

"One year is a blip in our lifetime, Lo," she whispers. "You've been through worse. You can take a horrible year. I know you can."

I nod a couple times, letting her words sink in. Maybe one year will feel shorter than I think.

"There'll be good," she suddenly adds. "You might not see it now, but there'll be good in the year. We'll see our sons and daughters smile." My chest rises. "We'll hear Luna tell us stories—"

I kiss Lily. A kiss that blisters my entire soul. *I'm alive. I'm awake.* I hold her face and deepen the kiss until she pulls further against my body. Breathing life into me.

I want to keep my eyes wide open for the little things. A smile. A laugh.

A story.

I don't want to close my eyes and wait for the year to end.

We only break apart when someone knocks on the door. Then my phone starts ringing in the pocket of my jeans. We both struggle to let go, but when we finally disentangle, she heads to the door and I check the caller ID on my phone.

Shit.

It's Hannah Yankton. The mother who lives one street over on Cider Creek Pass. She's hosting the sleepover. The one Luna is at right now.

Just as I answer the call, Lily swings open the door. My brother in track pants and a gray Camp Calloway shirt suddenly crosses the threshold. My features sharpen at the sight of his dark concern for me, but I love him. I love that he's here, and I'm glad Lily called him without me knowing.

Hannah greets, "Hi, Loren?"

"Is everything okay?" I watch Lily's worry rise. She tugs at the hem of her long-sleeved shirt. My older brother walks further in the house, peeks in the living room. I hear him greet Xander before returning to the foyer.

"Um…" Hannah falters a little. *This isn't good.* "I'm calling because… um, Luna needs to be picked up. She wants to go home early…can you or Lily swing by to come get her?"

WIND BITES MY EXPOSED skin, my soles hard against the street while I run. I left without grabbing a jacket, but the Yankton's house is on the adjacent street. Not far. So I just ran out. Less than a minute and my legs grind like steel and iron. At the corner of Whisper Ridge and Cider Creek, I slow to a walk. Dragging.

Go, Lo.

The sooner I move, the sooner I can take Luna home. My heavy breath smokes the air, and I glance at my older brother. He's kept my pace, skidding to a walk with me.

Lily didn't follow us, not since Ryke did, someone who will *definitely* make sure I won't take a sudden detour. He can actually physically stop me if it comes to that.

But it won't.

I *won't* choose alcohol over my daughter. She needs me, and that has to be enough tonight.

Ryke reaches down and massages his right thigh.

"Cramp?" I ask.

He nods. "It's fucking cold."

Winter is worse on his leg, and he didn't stretch prior to running. "I can help you stretch later."

"Gym after this?" He blows on his hands. His offer sandpapers some of the grit in my bones.

"Yeah." *This.* What is *this?* It might be cold, but my body runs hot, boiling at different scenarios. I pick up my pace, but my stride shortens to a weak jog. I end up walking really goddamn fast down Cider Creek.

Ryke's shoe comes untied. He's able to tie it *and* keep up with me, not falling behind. It's not because I'm slow. It's because my brother strengthens his body every day, hurdling over an accident that once dragged him down.

Him, here, reminds me that we can all stand back up again.

I can do this.

And I run. He's right by my side, and when I reach Hannah's mailbox, I slow again.

"What do you think fucking happened?" Ryke asks as we jog up the cobblestone to an oak-finished front door. The house is large, white siding, several ten-foot white columns and a manicured yard. I step onto the red welcome mat. On the front porch, three rocking chairs creak with each gust of wind.

The place is nice. Friendly, even.

"Maybe she got scared." I knock on the door and then ring the bell. "It's her first sleepover." At a place other than Aunt Rose and Aunt Daisy's, at least.

Ryke beats the door with his fist.

Then a second later, it swings open, a petite thirty-something brunette on the other side. "Hi." Hannah squeezes into the doorway, containing the warmth inside and the cold outside. "Luna is just grabbing her things."

She never steps aside. I realize very quickly that I'm not invited in. It wouldn't be the first time.

"What happened?" I ask.

Hannah shivers, her cheeks flushing. I'm not sure if it's the cold or something else. My defenses catapult, but I try to take Connor's sage advice: *don't overreact. Get the facts first.* It's much harder than he makes it seem.

"I'm so sorry," she tells me quickly. "I didn't know that Jeffra and the other girls planned to do something...like that. If I knew that she wasn't really friends with Luna at school, I wouldn't have let Jeffra invite her."

All the blood rushes out of my head. Ryke's nose flares, and just as I open my mouth to ask for more details—to start from the goddamn beginning—my daughter appears in the doorway.

She tries to open the oak door more so she can slip by Hannah.

Ryke helps and pushes the door, warmth rushing out and cold rushing in.

As soon as we fully see her, time stands still for a moment.

"Daddy," Luna calls out to me, tears brimming. "Can we go home?"

I don't have to ask Hannah what the other girls did anymore. I see it. On Luna's forehead. In permanent marker. They scrawled a word.

WEIRDO

Fire fills me. Something that overpowers hatred. This paternal urgency races through my veins—this resolve to protect my daughter from this shit. To take her far, far away from here.

I barely hear Hannah talk while I move fast with my brother. I bend down to Luna, who drags her alien-shaped backpack and rolled-up sleeping bag, dressed only in purple PJs, no shoes. Luna throws her arms around my neck.

"I'm...I'm *so* sorry," Hannah stammers. "I've had a talk with all the girls. Really. This is just a huge mistake, and my daughter will definitely be punished."

I rub Luna's back and pass her backpack to my brother. He unzips it and digs for her shoes and coat. He passes me one sneaker. Luna is too upset to put them on herself, though her tears haven't fallen yet. I fit her foot into the shoe. Ryke hands me the other, and I put that one on.

When he finds her puffy white coat, Ryke squats down and helps pull her arms into the holes. I stand up while he distracts Luna from me. So I can speak to this mother.

I lean towards Hannah and say lowly, "If *any* of this ends up online, you'll be sued for all you're worth."

Color drains from her face. "It won't."

I don't say another word to her. Ryke zips up Luna's coat, and then I pick up my daughter, carrying her on my side. My brother grabs her backpack and sleeping bag. We're out of there in less than two minutes, and when we reach the curb, I feel something wet soak my shirt.

I glance down, her crotch stained.

Luna sniffs. "I fell asleep first, and so they put my hand in water. They said they always do that." Her glassy amber eyes look right up at me. "I didn't know the sleepover rules."

We're a block away, and I set her down and kneel on the asphalt, close to her height. "There aren't any sleepover rules, Luna. Anyone who pulls pranks like that isn't a friend. They're not good people."

She rubs at her forehead, knowing what's there. "It won't come off."

Ryke's jaw is hard as a rock, and he has to walk past us for a moment, cursing beneath his breath.

I take Luna's small hand, stopping her from touching her forehead. I hold it. "It's permanent marker," I say, not candy-coating this shit. "You'll have to wait and it'll fade." Each word comes out calm, but I could wrap my arms around my daughter and cry with her.

Luna's lip trembles. "I can't remove it?"

"It'll disappear in a day or two, that's it." I squeeze her hand. "Luna, I need you to know something."

She raises her big eyes to mine, and for the first time, she cries. Tears slide down her soft cheeks, and I brush them with my thumb. "I love you," I tell her strongly. "Your mom loves you. Your brothers and sister love you. Your aunts, uncles, and cousins all love you." I cup her cheeks. "You're *so* goddamn loved."

"You said a bad word, Daddy," she says, snot dripping. I wipe her nose with the bottom of my shirt. "And you forgot something."

"What did I forget?" I ask.

"I don't have any friends that love me." The way she says it—like it's what matters most—breaks my fucking heart.

"Luna Hale," I reply. "Let me tell you the secret of the universe."

She rubs her eyes with her fist, but the tears just keep flowing. "The entire universe?"

"The entire universe," I affirm. "Your worth isn't dictated by the number of friends you have. You can have *zero* friends and still be the most amazing, *spectacular* person in the whole galaxy. You want to know why?"

"Why?" Her voice is meek, but the waterworks have ended.

"Because the love friends give you isn't even comparable to the love you give yourself. Do you love who you are, Luna Hale?"

She nods vigorously. "Yes."

"Then you're the queen of your own galaxy." I stand up, and she grabs onto my hand as we walk ahead.

Ryke falls in and nods to Luna. "Hey, sweetie."

"Uncle Ryke, I'm not a weirdo." She reaches up to rub her forehead again.

"So what if you are?" Ryke says. "Weirdos are fucking cool."

"Really?" she asks, frowning. She doesn't chide him for cursing since all our kids know that *Uncle Ryke is allowed to say bad words.*

"Yeah, really." He messes her hair and then fits her Wampa cap on her head. It must've been in her backpack. "And to add to what your dad told you. Friends come and fucking go. Family is forever."

We walk maybe one more block and a car rolls down the lamp-lit street. Rose's Escalade rolls to a stop, and I look to my older brother. He's the only one who could've told someone what happened.

He shrugs like it's nothing. "I sent a group text. I had to...fucking release." I can imagine the kind of words in that text thread.

The window slides down, revealing Rose Calloway Cobalt in all her 10:00 p.m. glory. Hair twisted in a pony, dressed in a black silk robe. She flicks off her headlights since Luna is squinting, and Rose leans towards the window, piercing yellow-green eyes landing on me.

"I have two boys in my car that want to have a sleepover at your house. They're also *grounded*, so they can't watch television." She says that last line loudly, and we can all hear laughter from the SUV. Her eyes narrow at me again. "I'm serious. Don't let them watch TV."

"Moffy's at a sleepover," I say, though she probably already knows that. "So if it's Charlie and Beckett—"

"It's not." She turns in her seat and tells her children, "You can climb out. Behave at Uncle Loren's."

Five-year-old Tom exits the car first, his golden brown hair combed back. My muscles frost, my body solidifying like ice. I can't believe what I'm seeing.

A word is written on his forehead in black marker.

WEIRDO

He sets his black duffel on the ground while his older brother jumps out of the car. "Thanks for driving us, Mom!" Six-year-old Eliot calls out and spins around, the same word on his forehead.

My softened eyes flit to Rose.

She shakes her head, but she's grinning. "Not my idea. They overheard Connor and me. We were talking about it, and then I caught them in the bathroom like this." These are Rose's sons. There is no question about it.

Solidarity.

For my daughter to have that. *Christ.* I internally shake my head, whiplashed. We speak of moving mountains, but sometimes people can completely rotate the world, just so someone else can land upright on their feet.

I nod to Rose in thanks, and she rolls up her window. We wait for her to reverse her SUV and drive back towards her house. Then we begin walking towards mine again.

I take Eliot and Tom's bags, slinging them on my shoulder.

Luna is laughing. "Why'd you go and do that?" She points at Tom's forehead.

Tom sticks his hands in his coat pockets. "Because if they're gonna call *you* a weirdo, then that means we're weirdos."

"Definitely," Eliot agrees.

As we head home, I *feel* all the sentiments Lily told me earlier tonight. Our bad days have the ability to become better. It may be a horrible month. A horrible year. But there *will* be good days, good moments, great seconds.

I vow to never forget that.

2026

"You're all incredibly boring."

- Charlie Keating Cobalt, We Are Calloway

(Season 8 Episode 12 – Hot-Tempered Triad &

Older Kids Club)

< 48 >

June 2026
CAMP CALLOWAY
Pocono Mountains

Daisy Meadows

"Look at that land crab go! Such pretty pinchers and shell, she crawls and she crawls," I narrate Winona's adventure while I sift through papers on a desk. Inside the director's office of Camp Calloway, my two-year-old hops from one colorful beanbag to the next. About seven spread out.

It's very kid-friendly in here.

"Oops, she falls!" I say as Winona splats on a yellow beanbag.

Sullivan, eight-years-old, pretends to be sleeping in the middle of the beanbags, and then she suddenly uncurls and rises to her knees.

I gasp. "A wave is coming!"

Winona shrieks.

Sulli smiles wide and raises her arms like she's about to consume her little sister. "Woosh woosh," Sulli plays along.

"Waves sweep little land crabs away. Go! Go! Go, Winona, go!"

Winona shrieks again, laughter stuck beneath the squeal. She hops to the red beanbag. My face brightens. I have a hard time concentrating on the legal papers. The camp director needs my signature on about ten before I leave.

My lawyers drew them up, so it's not a blind transaction.

Winona splats on the blue beanbag, her brown hair much lighter than her older sister's. Set free and loose. As wild as Sulli's. I'd record this event, but Ryke has the video camera. He's somewhere outside. About an hour ago, he videotaped Sulli climbing out of the car.

It's her very first time at camp.

…and soon we'll drive away without her. I tuck a strand of hair behind my ear. I built this camp. I know she's safe here, but I've never been away from Sulli for longer than four days.

While Sulli descends upon her sister, Winona shouts something that sounds like *I'm just a land crab!* She dubbed herself the Mightiest Land Crab in All the Land this morning. She bit Ryke's arm when he picked her up, and then she pinched his cheek. "My crab claws!" she told him.

I couldn't stop laughing, so he smacked the rim of my baseball cap over my eyes. Which only made me laugh more. Then I spun the green cap backwards.

I still wear it now.

Ryke and I mostly watch Nat Geo and Discovery Channel, so Winona's knowledge skews towards animals and nature. Last week she told us she was a panther, and she hid behind the living room furniture and spent a whole hour stalking Ryke.

Who was sitting in the same place as he ate granola cereal.

I call out, "There goes the wave!"

Sulli lifts up Winona's white shirt and blows a raspberry on her belly.

Winona laughs, "Sulli!"

Sulli tickles her sister's sides. "Gotcha, squirt."

I uncap a pen with my teeth and sign the top paper, rocking on my feet. Winona's laughter fades, and I hear Sulli tell her that she'll be right back. So I look up.

My daughter unzips her turquoise duffel, a matching sleeping bag rolled up nearby. Sulli wears this deep contemplative look. One that surfaces nearly every day. She re-zips her duffel and then scratches at her head, then near her hairline. That right there—the head-scratch—tells me that she's nervous. She scratches just below her swim cap during "the most important" meets.

I haven't signed another paper yet. However I feel about leaving Sulli here for a whole month might not even compare to how she feels.

I spit my pen cap out. "Guess what, Sulli?"

Sulli faces me and then walks closer. "What?"

"I have your cabin assignment." I sift through the papers for her camp welcome letter. I meant to give it to her when we exit the office, but maybe this'll take her mind off potential homesickness. Bam! I find the letter. I wave it at her and she snatches the envelope.

She unfurls the letter and reads quickly.

Winona is busy rolling on every beanbag.

Sulli's shoulders sag, just slightly. "I thought I was going to be in the Yellow Daisy cabin?"

"Yellow Daisy is for ten-year-olds. You'll be there in a couple years. Right now, you're starting out in the Red Poppy cabin."

Sullivan refolds the letter.

I scoot around the desk and then nudge her elbow with mine. "What's up?"

"I don't know…" She glances out the window and tugs at her loose-fitted tank top. Campers move into their wooden cabins and hug their parents goodbye. Some are weepy first-timers. Others are jubilant camp veterans. The excited ones race off towards the mess hall where the Welcome Bash will begin.

I always thought that'd be Sulli, and I think she thought it'd be her too. For years, she's talked about being old enough to *finally* attend Camp Calloway.

Her long brown hair hangs in tangled waves. "Are you sure you can't stay?" she asks. "Can't you be a counselor this year?" She hops up on the desk.

I sit beside her, our legs swinging. She knows I'm the owner, not a counselor or director. "The counselors here are totally amazing, so hey, you'll hardly know I'm not here."

Sulli lifts her feet to the desk, her long, long legs tucked towards her chest. She touches her colorful ankle bracelets, as though ensuring they're still there. We made tons this year already.

Sulli sets her chin on her knee and tilts her head towards me. "I already miss you and Nona and Dad, and you're right here."

Tears brim in both our eyes. We brush noses, and I whisper, "I'll be back for Spirit Days. I know it's far away, but there's so much about camp that you'll love."

"Like what?" she says just as quietly.

"Horseback riding. You've *never* been horseback riding, and you feel free, Sulli. You'll play *huge* games of capture the flag that'll have your heart racing. Zip-lining, the beautiful lake, rock climbing. And then you'll grow close to the girls in your cabin. You'll stay up late at night telling stories. You might even go prank the boys' cabins, just because you can."

She laughs softly into a smile.

"You'll probably hate the showers, but so will the other girls. You'll laugh and bond and realize that you're all equally homesick but at least you're homesick together."

Camp Calloway is as old as Sullivan Minnie Meadows. I never attended camp when I was her age, but throughout eight years, I've seen enough campers and their experiences to empathize and feel everything I say.

Sullivan drops her legs and swings them, a little more cheerful. "I wish Jane was here."

I rub her back.

Jane was sick at the last minute. She tried very hard to come anyway. According to Rose, Jane packed her bag and sat in the car, waiting to go. They would've brought her too, but she had a hundred-and-one degree fever.

"Moffy is here," I remind Sulli, though I know it's not the same in her mind. Cabins are segregated between boys and girls. Some activities are too. So she won't see Moffy all the time.

Sullivan takes a deep, hearty breath and glances at the window again. "We're allowed to swim in the lake, right?" This is the tenth time she's asked, worried the answer may change.

I reaffirm that there's definitely swimming, and then I say, "So I have this theory."

Sulli immediately smiles. "Can I guess?"

Theatrical, I wave her on. "My peanut butter cupcake."

"Your theory is that I'll make at least one lasting friend. If not this year, then next year, and if not next year, then the year after, and if not then, well…maybe I already have that kind of friend."

She came up with this all on her own. It's a theory with a positive outcome no matter what happens. We're both smiling, and we're both in tears again.

"That's a brilliant theory if I ever heard one," I say.

She laughs.

I laugh.

We hop off the desk together, and I hug my daughter.

"I love you so much, Mom."

"I love you just as much." We nuzzle noses again, and then when we break apart, she's lighter on her feet. She picks up her bag.

"I can help. Do you need me to carry your duffel? I can walk you to the cabin?"

"No. I think I want to do this on my own." She slings the duffel and tucks her sleeping bag beneath her arm. "Will you come say goodbye?"

I gasp. "You think I wouldn't?"

She smiles. "No, I know you would." I want to make sure she's settled with her bunk and take some photos before we leave.

Sullivan clasps the door and waves to her little sister. "See you, squirt."

Winona rolls off her beanbag. "Bye!" She has no clue Sulli won't be around for a whole month, or else she'd be crying and grabbing onto Sulli's legs. Ryke already prepared for a tantrum on the ride home. He bought two chocolate bars for me. Because chocolate is the cure to most things.

Cake is the cure to everything.

"Sulli," I say before she goes. "You may see your dad out there." I *think* he most likely went to test the rock wall, confirming that all the anchors are secure. He usually does this every summer, and some years, he'll fill in as the climbing instructor for a week or during Spirit Days. "Just to warn you, he'll want a hug before you leave and he may cry."

Sulli smiles again.

"Oh and he may not want to leave you, so you'll have to try and convince him to come home with me."

She laughs. "It won't be hard. Dad loves you like...so much."

I love him like *so much* too.

And then she's out the door. I watch her through the door's window, walking to the Red Poppy cabin alone and brave. So brave. Because every camper probably knows who she is before she even introduces herself. In the same breath, she has no idea who they are.

It's unequal footing, but if there's anyone who has the endurance and will to pull themselves higher—it's Sullivan Minnie Meadows.

Just like her dad.

OUTSIDE, I SIT ON the wooden steps of the director's office, Winona between my legs. She picks at my ankle bracelets and tries to unknot one. I wait for Ryke so we can say goodbye to Sulli.

Loren Hale leans against an oak tree only about fifteen feet away, his attention cast towards the White Rose cabins. Pretty far from here. I catch sight of Moffy's shirt: a Vic Whistler logo from *The Fourth Degree* comics on the back. He talks with two other boys by those cabins.

I say aloud, "Accurate depiction of saying goodbye: *hey, Daisy, this is going to suck as bad as you suck*—"

"Whoa," Lo cuts in, his gaze cemented on me. He points towards his black crew neck shirt. "Not your husband."

I mock gasp. "You're not? You look a lot like him."

Lo flashes a dry smile and then says to Winona, "Your mom thinks she's *really* funny."

"Because she is!" Winona shouts.

I smile, and Lo feigns hurt. "Winona, you just pierced my heart."

Winona tugs at my ankle bracelet and mumbles, "That's because I'm a crab."

Lo gives me a look like this child is one-hundred percent mine. "I thought I had a monkey for a niece?"

"Oh no, she's a crab now."

"Goddamn."

Winona hears curse words too often to even flinch at that one.

Lo straightens off the tree, and he must remember the heart of what I said before. "The first time is the worst because you're not sure if they like it or not, but Moffy couldn't wait to come back. For a kid that isn't very trusting of anyone, he was *excited* to go to a place populated by his peers. That's something, Daisy. What you created, it's good. It's really goddamn good."

I brighten with my features. "Thanks, Lo. That means a lot."

"Hold onto it because I only give one compliment a year and you just hit your limit."

I act like I grab the compliment out of the air and pocket it in my *bra*. I pat my chest. "Safe keeping." I'd literally do this with only Lo or

Ryke—Ryke because he understands my humor the best. Lo because of his *what the hell* reactions.

He grimaces. "Now I have to bleach my brain when I get home."

I wince. "Sounds painful."

"Not as painful as other things..." His gaze and voice drifts towards the lake. Ryke said that November had been the worst month for his little brother, but he persevered.

Jonathan Hale left his house specifically to Lo. He was the one who grew up in those four walls, who had memories in each room. Ryke said that Lo wanted to part ways with the home—that it was a past he could revisit but ultimately one he knew he had to leave behind.

In March, Lo found the strength to walk through his father's house.

In April, he sold it.

The rest of Jonathan's other assets were split between his three children, per his request.

If you saw Lo now, you wouldn't find a weight on his shoulders. You wouldn't see burden or torment behind his amber eyes. He stares towards the lake like he's met the pain he mentioned, but today and tomorrow, all he feels is free.

He only turns when Ryke emerges on the dirt path, caring a *huge* tree trunk. About eight-feet long.

"What the hell are you doing?" Lo shakes his head in disbelief. "Did you stumble into a time warp and come out as a lumberjack? Bring back my brother." He teasingly shoves Ryke's shoulder.

Ryke almost smiles and sets the tree trunk on the ground. Bark flakes off.

"Look at the size of that log." I wag my brows at my husband. "What is it, eight, nine, ten-inches?" I zero in on his crotch.

Ryke raises his brows at me. "Hey, Calloway?"

"Yeah?"

"Wrong log."

I feel my smile pull my scar. "But it's my favorite."

Lo scrunches his nose, his head swinging between Ryke and me. "I'm still in earshot, raisins. Wait until I've left before this begins." Then he points to the log. "Seriously, bro, what the fuck?"

"It was rotting," Ryke says. "I didn't want it to fucking fall on anyone." Lo can act like his brother is crazy, but when it comes to safety of little kids, he can be even more cautious.

"My brother," Lo declares and then tilts his head to me. "You've married this person, you realize that?"

I look to Ryke while he looks to me. His darkened features conceal a million dangerous adventures. Ones that we've taken together. Where we're anything but alone. His lips begin to lift higher and higher. I pick up our wiggly two-year-old in my arms, and his smile touches his eyes.

You've married this person, you realize that?

It's a familiar question from Lo but with a new twist. Usually he asks Ryke if he realized who he married. I grin right at Lo because he knows me and loves me for reasons beyond bringing his brother happiness. He loves me for me.

"What?" Lo asks me like I'm the strangest person in the world. I just grin more, and he throws up his hands. "You know what, don't tell me. You're probably grinning because the *sun* is in the sky." He nods to his older brother. "You know who you married, right?"

Never leaving me, Ryke says, "That I fucking do."

[49]

July 2026
THE LAKE HOUSE
Smokey Mountains

Rose Cobalt

" I declare this a sworn pact between Calloway sisters and our honorary sister, Willow Hale." I raise a sharp knife, and my three sisters and Willow exchange wary glances. We've gathered in the kitchen, a baby monitor close by and our youngest four girls in a living room playpen together.

Our husbands and the rest of the children play outside since yesterday's rainstorm confined everyone indoors. We'll join them in a second, but first, we have to finish this pact. Last night, we all collectively shared a similar mode of feeling, and it only seems right to solidify this promise together.

Poppy's maroon bohemian dress flows to her ankles and hides her bathing suit. We're all in cover-ups, mine sheer and black. I already set my floppy hat aside. Now we stand in a circle between the kitchen counters.

Lily raises her hand. "Can't we just spit on it?"

I glare. "There's a reason why it's called a *blood* oath and not a *spit* oath."

"I'm game." Daisy smiles wide, her blonde hair tangled and still wet after jumping in the lake. Water collects at her bare feet. My littlest sister turned thirty in February, but Lily still looks five years younger.

Willow pushes up her glasses. "Is this safe?"

"Probably not." Poppy never raises her voice, not even when combatting me.

I give my oldest sister a cold look. "It's sterile. I have matches, and we'll clean the blade after someone uses it." They hesitate, so I add, "Calloway sisters don't welch." Coconut barks in the background, pawing at the sliding glass door to come in.

We all turn our heads. Outside, Ryke scratches Coconut affectionately by her ears and then whistles for her to move further onto the deck. Then he notices us through the glass. His *what the fuck* expression drifts away with him.

"We've welched plenty of times on your blood oaths," Lily notes, but that fact crinkles her brows like maybe they've been terrible sisters. Maybe in all the years I asked, they should at least give into this *one* moment to solidify something between us through blade and blood. "Okay...I'll do it."

Willow nods, bravery in her eyes. "Me too."

"Why not?" Poppy smiles and looks to me. I press my lips together to keep from grinning eagerly. Bells are ringing. Confetti is falling. All the annoying sentimental things that I usually can't stand—even *birds* with their brutally irritating chirps—I hear them and I only think, *I love my sisters.*

"I'll go first." Without flinching, I knick both of my palms with the kitchen knife, sliced deep enough that blood shows in the cut.

I clean off the knife, sterilize, then pass it to Daisy.

She's been rocking excitedly on her feet, and she raises the knife in the air. "Rejoice!" Then she cuts her palms without trouble. Poppy goes next, and when it's Willow's turn, she winces a little. Daisy cheers her on until she finishes.

Last is Lily.

I clean off the knife. "You've given birth. You can survive a cut."

Lily places her hand on her heart. "I'm not a warrior. I'm the village person who hides in their hut and waits for help." I don't think she always believes this. Maybe just in the face of these daring tasks opposite people like Daisy and me, she forgets all that she's ever done.

My hands hover over her shoulders. "Lily. You're a *fucking* warrior. You slay enemies left and right. You stomp on critics and you've risen from ash." I narrow my eyes at her. "Say it."

I'm much taller than her in heels, so she has to look up. "I'm a warrior?"

Dear God. "Say it like it's true."

"I'm a fucking warrior." She nods slowly. "Yeah…" She nods *faster*.

"Yeah!" Daisy raises her fist in the air.

"Yeah!" Lily shouts like she gets it. "I'm a fucking warrior. Take that. Ha!" She tries to do a side-kick, but she whacks a cabinet. "Ow."

Daisy laughs and gives her a thumbs-up.

"Hold out your hands," I tell Lily.

She focuses and splays out her palms for me. I knick her skin less than I did mine, but enough that blood appears. She keeps her eyes tightened closed the entire time.

"Done." I set the knife aside.

Lily opens one eye and relaxes at the sight of a small cut.

"What are you crazies doing?" Lo has cracked the sliding glass door, and our husbands are gathered on the porch, acting like they're *not* watching and just grilling hamburgers and hot dogs for lunch.

They're painfully obvious.

"Go away, Loren!" I call.

Lo waits for one of my sisters to explain, but no one is betraying this circle of sisterly secrecy and trust. "Don't let her sacrifice you for a year's worth of heels!"

That's it.

I break ranks to shut up the naysayer.

"Go, Rose!" Daisy starts clapping.

My heels click-clack against the floorboards, and I *yank* the sliding door out of Loren's grasp and shut it. His sharpened glare battles my piercing one, and I flick the lock before he can claim victory.

He flashes a half-smile, and his next words are muffled through the glass, "Harm my little 'puff, and see what's up, Angelica."

"I'd sooner rip out *your* heart than I would yank a hair off my sister's head." Then I spin around and enter the circle.

All my sisters are smiling.

"What?"

"You're badass," Daisy is the first to say.

"So are you." I'm quick to encourage her.

"Not in that way." Daisy smiles. "I'm really glad you're my sister."

My eyes are burning. *Tears* are coming and we haven't even finished this.

Lily nods in agreement. "We'd all be worse off without you."

"You'd be fine," I say.

"No…I don't think we would've." Lily awkwardly tries to lean her weight on the counter, but it's too far away. "You're our Emma Frost."

I'm not entirely sure what that means. I know of the comic book character, but I don't know much about her except that she means a lot to Lily.

That's enough for my heart to grow. "Enough with the sappiness. We have an oath to finish." I clasp hands with Lily, then she clasps Poppy, who grabs hold of Willow, to Daisy, and finally Daisy and I close the circle.

"We're here today, to make a promise," I say. "We promise to *always* be there for one another, to support each other's choices, to be the tides that wash away negativity and foes." I look around at all the girls, and they nod, remembering how we all stayed up until three in the morning, just talking. We might have families of our own, but when we can be together, it's like no time has passed at all. "However long we live, however hard life becomes, we'll never lose sight of this sisterhood."

We raise our clasped hands, and my sisters and Willow make a *second* and *third* and so forth motions, and as I stare between them, I'm truly grateful for these women in my life.

They're each so different from me, but I wouldn't want them to be the same. I love them for all their oddities and for all their strengths.

WE JOINED OUR HUSBANDS on the deck outside and they will not shut up about our bandaged palms.

"I fucking hope you all used Neosporin," Ryke says while flipping a burger on the grill. Daisy sits on the railing of the deck and shucks corn, Coconut lounging beneath her with constant tail wags, content.

Connor helps grill, a perfect distance away to avoid grease splatter on his bare chest.

Ryke is a messy cook. And I can't believe he's the one bringing up *Neosporin*. As though he's a model for *cleanliness*.

Lo sips a Fizz Life, sitting on the deck's picnic table next to Lily. Both are physically clingy. Even in the heat, they're hugging onto each other like it's more unnatural if they separate.

"Does it hurt, love?" Lo keeps asking Lily, grimacing at her palm that is *barely* cut. Down below towards the grass, their dog, Gotham, is chasing butterflies, his ears flapping.

Sam passes Poppy a margarita. "How did Rose rope you into this?"

"You think *I* persuaded her?" I cut in, busy trying to re-knot a string to my sheer cover-up. "I can't even convince Poppy to get a bikini wax with me."

"I like it all natural." Poppy waves towards her vagina.

Lo says, "Things I didn't think I'd ever know: Poppy has a bush." He gives her a half-smile.

Poppy combats him with a replica of his half-smile.

"Poppy, when'd you get so feisty?"

She sips her margarita. "I've always been this way. You just never notice."

After I finish tying my cover-up, I catch Connor *grinning* at me. I muster the hottest glare, and then reroute my gaze to torment him a little more.

Garrison and Willow sit close together on a patio couch beneath a tan umbrella. Their two-year-old daughter, brown pigtails and blue-green eyes hidden behind toddler sunglasses, sucks on a banana-flavored popsicle between her parents. Vada is more cooperative than *every* baby I've ever had. She will hum theme songs to video games and minds her own business on international flights.

I don't think their baby is human. Vada is obviously some sort of deity. Like a Greek goddess. Like Athena—only I'd think Athena would have better sense than to transform into a little two-year-old.

Willow helps Vada hold the popsicle stick, and Garrison watches his wife and daughter with fondness. He whispers something to Willow, and then he kisses her cheek before kissing her lips.

I whip my head back to Connor. His attention is on the grill, not me, and I try to stifle my disappointment. *You did the same to him.* I did, but most commonly, he's the one who chases after me.

My focus diverges anyway.

Splashes escalate from down below, and I can even hear combined exclamations from Moffy and Jane, the eleven-year-olds.

"Go, Sulli!" Jane shouts. "Overthrow our adversaries!"

"You got this, Beckett!" Moffy cheers. "Come on! Come on!"

In the shallow parts of the lake, Jane has Sullivan on her shoulders while Moffy has Beckett on his. The two eight-year-olds wrestle, attempting to knock one another off in a classic game called *chicken*.

We all fall hushed on the deck, observing the children for a moment. I nearly smile, sensing the years that have passed, seeing what our futures have become. This morning Connor said to me, "The lake house puts our lives in vivid perspective." I didn't quite grasp the full meaning until now.

Without background noise—the tabloids, cameramen, and our jobs—we're left strong together, with simple moments that drum ferociously through us all.

Jane takes one hand off Sullivan's leg and tries to push Moffy.

He dodges Jane and laughs, "What was that, Janie? Can't get me!"

"Don't be so sure, Moffy! Just you...ohhh...no." Jane starts falling backwards with Sullivan, but Sullivan careens her weight forward and clasps Beckett's shoulders, keeping them in the game.

I can't pick an allegiance to either team. Jane and Beckett are my children, and my heart is with them both equally.

"Jesus Christ." Lo grabs his megaphone and switches it on. "MOVE AWAY FROM THE DOCK!" They're not close enough that they'd hit their heads. I never thought Loren Hale would be the most anal, but I did think he would be as overprotective as he is.

I quickly scan the backyard for all my gremlins. Eliot, Tom, and Luna are on the hammocks, strung between maple trees by the water. Three-year-old Xander and my four-year-old Ben play with Legos on the hill, right beside the red Adirondack chairs and an incredibly silly basset hound, leaping after air particles now.

I swing my head left and right. "Where's Charlie?"

Connor sets down the spatula, his phone already in his hand. He calls our son, putting the speaker to his ear. My back arches, prepared to stomp around the entire house in search for our son. It wouldn't be the first time. Yesterday, I found Charlie on the *roof* of all places. I truly wondered if he was my child until he pompously jabbered about physics and scientific theories like he discovered them himself.

He is a Cobalt, through and through.

"He's not answering," Connor tells me, incredibly calm since this is a common event. It's why we've given Charlie his own cellphone.

"CHARLIE!" I shout at the top of my lungs.

"There goes my left eardrum," Lo says with edge.

I point my nail at him. "You used *that*." The megaphone.

"My voice doesn't sound like cats are being slaughtered."

I produce a hostile glare, and right when I go to rip the megaphone from Lo's hands—about to use it myself—the sliding glass door opens.

Charlie, who looks more and more like Connor every day, barely acknowledges us before skipping down the steps and heading towards the dock. I love him so entirely, like all my children, that my hatred towards his disappearing acts diminishes to just a handful of worry.

"Is he okay?" Daisy asks, passing shucked corn to Ryke for him to grill.

"He's mentally bored," Connor says. "I'll play chess with him later."

Charlie sits at the edge of the dock. Maria, now eighteen, tans on a yellow inner-tube nearby, her Ray Bans blocking the sun. When I sweep all the children again, my jaw unhinges, and I take *off* down the steps.

He did not.

Oh yes he did.

"Ben Pirrip!" I shout, my heels sinking into the damp grass. I get stuck on the way to my four-year-old who has walked off the quilt, left Xander and the Legos, and found himself a *giant* sinking hole of mud.

I do what I never do.

I abandon my heels.

I free myself and go barefoot across the hill to this terribly *disgusting* muddy area near the tree line. "What are you doing?" I have never birthed a child more unpredictable than this one.

Ben rolls in the mud, giggles, and tries to remove all his clothes. I sense Connor reaching my side about the same time that our youngest boy frees himself of his pants.

"Are you sure he's ours?" I ask Connor without tearing my gaze off Ben. His big blue eyes shimmer with an inordinate amount of light, the rest of him covered in mud.

I *feel* Connor's blinding grin. "Most assuredly, he's ours."

"I'll get the hose."

Connor is the one who grabs the wiggling four-year-old, and he brings him towards the side of the house while I pull out the hose and twist the faucet. When Connor places Ben on the grass, our son tries to spring up and escape back towards the mud.

By the way, Ben is completely nude.

That's my boy.

I snort at Connor. Ben put his little hands on Connor, who just wears navy swim trunks. So two muddy handprints decorate my husband's chest.

Connor arches his brow. "Yes, darling?"

"Our son has marked his territory. You're it." I wield the green hose like a weapon, and Connor eyes the nozzle, then me, his eyes sparking with intrigue.

Ben smiles. "Let's go play!"

"Not in the mud," Connor says easily.

Ben pulls at the grass, even his lips caked in mud. "Don't I get a choice?"

Connor kneels in front of Ben. "Your choices: if we wash you now, you'll be able to play with Xander; or if you return to the mud, you'll *never* be allowed inside ever again."

"The mud!" Ben doesn't miss a beat.

Connor shuts his eyes tight. This is the first child that *always* chooses the option with the worst personal benefit, and Connor has painstakingly tried to tell Ben to do what's best for him.

"Ben goes with his heart," I remind Connor.

"His heart chooses wrong."

Our son tries to spring towards the mud, but Connor seizes him again.

"If you stay outdoors forever, you'll miss Wednesday night dinners." For the past four years, our children started counting down to those dinners. The most common question has become: *is it Wednesday yet?*

Ben hesitates.

"You'll never see Pip-Squeak."

"I'll take him with me!"

"He's an indoor bird."

Ben, a little mud monster, gawks at Connor. "Thatsnotfair." He slurs the words together.

"Every choice has benefits and costs, some greater and some smaller than others. It's up to you to use *this*"—he touches Ben's head to illustrate his brain—"to determine which is better for you."

Ben plops on the grass, saddened. I'd feel worse if he didn't look like a tiny creature from the bottom of the lake.

Matter-of-factly, I tell him, "Being clean is more fun than being dirty."

"Mommy," he groans and scoffs like I'm *so wrong*.

I'll show him. I squirt him just a little, water spraying his body.

He instantly smiles.

"What about now?" I challenge. I spray him lightly once more.

Ben picks himself up and outstretches his arms while sticking out his tongue. As though I am Mother fucking Nature commanding a rain shower for my son. I smile in satisfaction.

Maybe I am.

Connor returns to my side while I hose down our four-year-old. Ben begins to hop and dance in the wet puddle, but at least he's cleaner than before.

Swiftly, I change direction of the hose and squirt off Connor's chest and hands. I expect him to flinch, but he practically expected my action. Motionless, stoic.

He begins to grin.

"Richard." I squirt that grin off too.

And he laughs, his face glistening. "Rose."

Rose.

I'll never stop loving and hating the way he says my name.

‹ 50 ›

July 2026
THE LAKE HOUSE
Smokey Mountains

Ryke Meadows

I pull my shirt off my head. 10:00 p.m. at the lake house. Everyone is quiet, and if they are fucking rowdy, I can't hear from our bedroom. Even Nutty is out of it, the white husky fast asleep at the foot of the wooden bed.

I just checked on our two-year-old in the nursery—where all the little girls sleep.

Winona recently transitioned out of the fucking crib and has grown the habit of hopping on her "big girl" bed. Making the act of sleep time more difficult than it needs to be.

In a month or two, I hope the fucking novelty of the bed wares off so she can sleep earlier.

On *our* bed, Daisy splays her arms wide. In constant motion, she moves them up and down like she's making a snow angel within the bear-patterned quilt. "I have a theory," she says.

I unbutton my jeans. "Yeah?"

Daisy mock gasps. "*Fuck* yeah."

I toss a stitched pillow at her head.

She rolls on her side, facing me with a lopsided smile. "It's actually two theories. One is wrong. One is right. It's yet to be proven which."

"Let's hear it, Calloway." My attention is hers. I stop unzipping my jeans for a fucking second.

She sits up on the heels of her feet, wearing a thin white tank top that says *Shell Yeah* with two waves beneath. Her yellow cotton shorts ride up her fucking ass. Last year, she chopped her blonde hair in uneven layers but let the strands grow past her chest.

Daisy has always been beautiful, but for reasons beyond looks. She brightens at the simplicity of tonight. The fact that we're alone in this room. The fact that I listen to all of her fucking theories. The fact that when she rises to her feet, standing on the mattress, I only edge closer.

"First theory." In her dramatic pause, she watches me as I watch her. My muscles flex, and my cock begins to harden.

"The lake house has magical sleeping properties that produce *erotic* dreams."

I raise my brows at Dais. "I missed the part where you moaned out the words *lake house* when you orgasmed in your fucking sleep last night."

Her smile stretches. "Second theory—"

I yank her ankle out from under her. She thuds onto her back and radiates with happiness. I climb on top of my wife and nuzzle her cheek. She lets out a throaty noise, her hands dipping down the back of my jeans. I hold Daisy's jaw and kiss her hungrily, our tongues tangled. I pull her up against me, and she inhales until she can't breathe.

I break apart so she can catch her breath. "Second theory?" I ask.

She pants, "Second…theory." Her hand playfully descends towards the crack of my ass.

I don't flinch. "You fucking exploring, Calloway?"

"Do you like it?" She wags her brows.

I grind my body forward, putting pressure between her legs, and she cries out. I nod to Dais. "I like that fucking sound more."

Daisy removes her hand, just to hold onto my shoulder. "I have this theory…" She bucks her hips, and my muscles strain, my erection pushing against my jeans. "…that having sex with someone before sleep produces really, *really*…erotic…dreams."

That can be fucking tested.

I lift her in my arms so fast that she gasps against my shoulder. I carry Daisy to the circular rug, our luggage and clothes scattered all around the fucking room. I kick a toddler scooter aside. *Winona's.*

When I set Daisy's back on the rug, I already start quickly undressing her. Tank top off. Small, cute fucking breasts exposed. Her hands feverishly roam my abs, my biceps—my hair. I nip her lip and slip off her cotton shorts. Then I hook my fingers in her cotton panties, sliding them down her long, slender legs.

Her big green eyes travel across my hard jawline.

She's physically so much fucking younger than me. I'm physically so much fucking older than her. That's never changing. Neither is me *caring* about her body, her heart—her whole self.

I knead her breast with my fingers before replacing my hand with my mouth, kissing. Then I suck her hardened nipple, my tongue flicking every nerve. She trembles—*fuck me.*

Again, I pull Daisy's entire body up against my fucking body. She lets out a high-pitched noise, and my large hand races to her mouth, muffling the sounds.

Daisy tries to tug off my jeans. I help her shed them and my boxer-briefs.

Both buck-naked on the rug.

I stretch her legs over my fucking shoulders.

"Guess what?" I say lowly. I slide two of my fingers into *my* mouth, hovering partially above Dias, not lowering my full fucking weight on her.

"What?" she pants beneath my palm.

I pull my fingers out. "I'm going to *fuck* your theory right…here." I push my two long fingers inside of Daisy and pump them, my thumb toying with her clit. Her pleasured cries vibrate against my hand. *Fuck*, a groan rumbles my throat. All the blood wells in my fucking erection.

Her breath shortens, body shakes.

Fucking…my muscles sear, sweat building as fast for me as for my wife. Daisy watches my fingers, how they disappear *deep* inside of her body. Her reaction fucking kills me in the most visceral, primal way. My muscles answer with *fuck her like she wants to be fucked. Kiss her like she wants to be kissed. Love her like she deserves to be fucking loved.*

I hold her body like it's the most precious fucking thing in this world.

When her eyes begin to roll back, I swiftly stand and lift Daisy to my shoulders. The extra weight is nothing to me. Not when I've gripped *my weight* with only a fucking finger on a sliver of rock.

I lean her back against the wall, her body more at an angle. I eat out Daisy Meadows.

I could fucking explode. *Fuck me.* Sweat really coats my bare skin, my mouth against her heat. I look up at Dais, and she's *fixated* on my right hand.

I rub my shaft because it gets her off every time. My nerves well, the pressure fucking *fuck*—I grunt, gripping my cock harder. Pumping faster while my tongue does what it does best.

Daisy moans into my left hand, her toes curling, lips so fucking parted. Her back arches, spine curving towards me. Shuddering.

Daisy responds to every orgasm like it's her first fucking one. I still remember that day, that moment, that fucking time.

I even recall the first time we had sex. In a tent. *I'm fucking you, sweetheart.* Right now. I slide her down my waist, pinning her back against the wall. She rests her forehead on my shoulder, honing in on my long erection. Daisy tries to split her legs open wider, so I stretch them upwards, her ankles towards my neck.

I know she envisions my cock rammed inside her, even before I slip in. She clutches my sides, her hand over my phoenix tattoo, breathing shallow fucking breaths.

Slowly, I push in and gauge her reaction every inch of the way. I search for signs of pain, but it's been so fucking long since she's felt any. My nose flares at the tightness and sudden warmth wrapped around my cock.

She trembles, lit up, crying in pleasure against my hand.

I start rocking, and I fuck the wildest girl I've ever known.

Daisy watches our bodies join together, her skin glistening. Her hands fall to my ass, feeling me flex against her tall, lean build. We've fucked against more trees than we have walls, but this works just as well.

I follow her gaze to our pelvises, and I push deeper, letting her take in more of me. She makes the throatiest noise against my hand, like that pleasure ascended from bottom to top. My veins protrude in my arms, my teeth clenched as my arousal fucking heightens.

Fuck.

Fuck.

This is a girl I never thought I'd be with—not like this. Not nine-inches deep between her legs. Not warm metal on my ring finger. Not two little girls with our features.

I thought for fucking sure I'd be alone.

I thrust with purpose, knowing what it'd lead to—she comes with a sharp inhale, pulsating around my erection.

"*Fuck.*" I come, pushing hard into Dais.

Not long after, exhaustion sinks her shoulders, her eyelids, and I pull out and carry Daisy in my arms to our bed. Eyes closed, she sleepily whispers one last thing.

"Say that again."

I don't say *fuck*. I lean down, my mouth against her ear, and I tell my wife, "I fucking love you, sweetheart."

She glows like a million suns.

I'M NOT THAT FUCKING tired, so I check my email on my cellphone. Daisy has already rolled onto my chest, off my chest, and now back onto my fucking chest. Her legs are tangled with mine, arm across my abdomen and head nestled towards my shoulder.

I don't shift enough that I'd wake her.

I squint at the bright light of the screen and click into an email from *Celebrity WorldWide Entertainment*. I have no fucking idea what this could be, but the subject line reads, **congratulations**. That entrainment site isn't as salacious as *Celebrity Crush*.

I know because *Celebrity WorldWide Entertainment* rarely posts negative articles about anyone. Most of their time is spent marketing fucking movie franchises and actors in whatever television shows Lily and Lo watch.

I read the first line of the email.

Dear Ryke Meadows,

Congratulations, Celebrity WorldWide Entertainment has picked you as this year's Sexiest Man WorldWide!

"What the fuck," I mutter, skimming the rest of the email that basically says *you're welcome* and *this is a huge honor*. I don't keep up with this shit—so I'm just really fucking confused.

Why me?

I rub my mouth and then group-text my brother, my sister, Lily, Connor, Rose, and Garrison.

I type out: did any of you fucking get this email?

I remember how to take screenshots on my phone, thanks to Daisy showing me, and I send them the image and message.

Not a second later, my phone buzzes so rapidly and loudly that I have to mute it. "For fuck's sake," I mumble.

Sexy motherfucker — **Lo**

Clearly I wasn't in contention — **Connor**

There's only one Sexiest Man WorldWide of the year. It's a big deal — **Willow**

Remove your ego from the thread, Richard. You weren't the chosen one. — **Rose**

I'm the only qualified one to judge this contest, and guess who I'd choose, darling? — **Connor**

Are they really flirting in the fucking group text? I can't shut them out, and here comes Lily…

IS THIS REAL?!?!?! — **Lily**

I don't even have time to text back. Someone else does.

Clearly — **Connor**

It wasn't that clear. — **Rose**

This is a mess — **Garrison**
Garrison leaves the group a notification pops up in the text thread. I'd do the same fucking thing, but I'm not sure how.

How is Ryke Sexiest Man WorldWide before Loren Hale????
– Lily

I believe you meant me – Connor

I can't take it anymore. I just ignore it, but I can't even use the fucking internet without text messages popping up every two seconds. I gently lift Daisy's arm and legs off me, really fucking careful not to wake my wife. I want her to sleep as many hours as she can.

I want her to fucking *dream*.

I've seen her do both more than I ever thought I would.

She stirs, just enough to roll onto her side and fall into a deeper slumber. I stand, scrolling through rapid-fire texts between Connor and Rose. I pull on track pants before I step into the hallway.

FTFY Lily – Willow

My sister photoshopped an image for Lily that says: LOREN HALE SEXIEST MAN WORLDWIDE!

My brows scrunch at that acronym, not understanding. Down the hall, I reach Lily and Lo's door first. I rap my knuckles and then open.

Lily and Lo are beneath the covers, the room so fucking dark, I only make out their faces. Lit by their cellphone screens.

"Stop fucking texting."

"Congratulations," Lily says before registering what I said. "Wait… you texted *us*."

"Yeah, well I changed my fucking mind."

"He can do that now, Lil," Lo says. "He's the Sexiest Man WorldWide. He's got eight-pack powers. His abs can kill." My brother just starts laughing so fucking loud that I flip him off. I'm not sure he can see.

Before I shut the door, I ask, "What's FTFY?"

"Fixed That For You," Lily answers, nose pressed to her cellphone screen.

I glance at my phone, but the only people left in the thread are Rose and Connor. Fucking flirting. I don't read the messages. I shut my brother's door and cross the hallway to Connor's.

I knock once and open.

I freeze.

Fuck.

Rose is handcuffed in a black nightgown, no more than a slip, cupping her cellphone, and Connor straddles his wife, his phone in one hand, other hand on her fucking *hip.*

Before I can even blink, they see me. Rose's eyes flame like she could castrate me.

I immediately turn my back for her privacy. "Stop fucking texting." I'd like to leave it at that, but Connor never would let me.

"No," he says the word with severe finality. "Shut the door. Hopefully you can manage that simple task."

I flip him off without facing their bed, but I don't leave. "I'm fucking serious."

"So am I."

"I will put your balls in acid," Rose threatens, less hostile because— believe it or fucking not—they're still *texting.* While in the same fucking room.

"Fuck this." I power off my phone and shut their door.

Only halfway down the hall, what just happened slaps me across the face. *I walked in on Rose and Connor about to have sex.* We all lived together, and I avoided that accident.

I mean, fuck.

We rarely even catch those two making out. And the strangest fucking thing? After tonight, I'm pretty sure their foreplay isn't the typical kind of foreplay.

I'm pretty sure their foreplay is *words.*

[51]

Connor Cobalt

"Charlie!" I race after my eight-year-old son, who just stormed out of the principal's office at ten a.m., backpack slung over his shoulder. He indignantly and *resentfully* pushes through the double doors, not slowing, and the moment I'd seen coming for years has finally arrived today.

The front of the school is quiet except for the American flag dinging the pole. I quickly read his body language, angled diagonally like he plans to step off the path and cross the grass—opposite the parking lot. Charlie goes where he wants to go, and usually it's nowhere at all.

"Charlie, *stop*," I say vehemently, my voice trembling with more emotion than I typically show.

It forces his feet to a complete and sudden halt. He stands directly in the center of the path, breathing heavily, still dressed in his prep school uniform: navy slacks, button-down, Dalton emblem and tie. I left work just to pick him up after the principal called.

I walk closer, only a few feet away.

And then he swings around. "Why didn't you tell me?!" His reddened face pumps with fury. "Why didn't you tell me it'd be like *this?!*" He grabs at his short brown hair, as though trying to reach for his brain and say *take it back. I don't want it anymore.*

"Because you wouldn't have wanted me to spoon-feed you. You would've rather drawn the conclusion yourself in time."

He angrily chucks his backpack onto the grass. He usually has no trouble using words, but I know besides his own family, no one has been listening to him today, yesterday, and most days before that. He's been treated like his age. The principal patronized him five minutes ago, and that's what pushed him to rush out.

"You can talk to me. I'll always listen."

Charlie stares at the bright blue sky, quiet for a long moment. And then he says, "It takes them *forever*. To think, to solve the stupidest problem, to see what's right in front of them."

"People don't think like you," I say. "They can't. They won't—"

"They should!" he screams, vexed and irate. He points heatedly at the building behind me. "Annabelle hangs out with girls that hate her, but she *actually* believes they're her friends. Mr. Crowder takes an extra five minutes calling attendance because he won't say the first name only. And these *dumb* guys make fun of Beckett for going to ballet class after school."

He takes one step near me. I stare calmly down at him.

"I'm surrounded by stupid people in a stupid world and everyone does *stupid* things, and it's slow. It's *so* slow." He cringes in distaste, his face pained. "I'm stuck here, aren't I, Dad?"

"What do you think?" I ask first.

"I think that if I left *here*." He motions to the school. "People would never take me seriously. *Oh, look at cute little Charlie Keating pretending to be so smart and old.*" He lets out a short laugh, and his eyes flood with tears but he restrains that emotion.

"The world is frustrating," I tell him. "When you know every answer and everyone else takes a thousand times longer than you, you just want to bang your head on the desk. You want to walk out. You want to help them solve the equation, but even if you did, they still would *never* be as fast as you."

His lips part at the realization that *I know* exactly what he feels.

"You can't make people think like you. You're it, Charlie. The world will never go at your speed."

He winces. "No, Dad."

"Some people are illogical, irrational, and *emotional*, but people have to be free to fail, to fall, and yes, to do stupid things. I know it's irritating. I know you want, so badly, to tell people which way to turn because you see *that* way is in their best interest, but you can't."

"Why not?"

"Because society doesn't work like that. You can walk backwards while everyone walks forwards, but you can't force everyone to walk backwards with you."

I never used my intelligence to stop crime, to save the world, to help people—I used it for my own benefit: self-knowledge, self-growth. Esteem and power.

I'm immoral. I'm selfish and egotistical. But if you had the mind and the eyes that illuminated every facet of the world, that had the ideas and solutions to fix micro and macro problems—how maddening would it be to watch people do illogical, emotional things to their determent and others, knowing you hold all the tools but in the end, you're *powerless* to stop them.

If I took that route, I would've gone insane. If Charlie takes that route, he will too.

We can't *fix* what's wrong with the entire world. I simply live by their rules and step outside when it suits me. When I need to feel free.

And I use my intelligence for *me*.

Charlie fights tears and shakes his head repeatedly. "If no one listens, if no one cares, if I can't make them go my speed—what's even the point?"

"You can do anything. You can be anything. There'll be constraints everywhere you turn, but there'll be *none* inside your mind, Charlie. You don't need to bang your head on the desk because they can't keep up. Think about ways in which you can go faster. *Only* look at you."

I'm teaching my son how to be self-centered, so the slothful world he's stuck inside won't drive him mad.

Charlie understands, more realizations washing his face.

I notice a van in the far distance, driving through the opened school gates.

Paparazzi.

I pick up Charlie's backpack. "You have to skip third and fourth grade."

Charlie must've known I would propose this because he's not surprised at all. "You didn't skip."

"You're not me."

He eyes me skeptically. "Weren't you bored?"

"Every day, but I didn't want to miss out on experiences that other people had. I wanted to relate to them. So I could blend in. It was useful, and I liked gaining useful skills. It was a self-interest."

He thinks about this for a long moment.

The paparazzi van drives closer.

Charlie is so quiet as he processes a future that he tries to pave out. "I don't want to leave him..." His chest collapses at the thought. If he skips grades, he'll no longer be in the same classes as Beckett. He'll go to high school and college before his twin brother.

Rose and I offered homeschool to Charlie once, but he rejected the idea. *I want to stay in school with Beckett,* he said. "Homeschooling is an option—"

"No." Charlie frowns deeply. "I want to be in the same school." He pauses. "I'm scared to leave him…"

"He knows how school is for you, Charlie."

Beckett has asked us to *do something* twice before because he feels his brother's frustration, his irritation, how upset and mad he becomes by the end of the day. He senses all of that pain, and he just wants him to feel okay.

"I can be like you," Charlie tells me. "I can just…stay in third grade and think about myself."

"You're not me," I repeat. "If you were, every time someone patronized you, you would've thought, *I'm better than you*, and moved on." I was six when I realized what he's realizing now, and I had no family that needed or wanted to be loved.

He does.

Charlie sees the incoming paparazzi van.

I put my hand on his shoulder, directing him towards the curb where my limo is parked. A cameraman jumps out of the van and starts asking questions. He stays about five feet away from us.

"What are you doing out of school, Charlie?" the cameraman asks.

Charlie unknots his tie. "Ruminating."

I grin.

The truth: he told one of his teacher's a more efficient way to teach 3rd grade math that would benefit the whole class. He argued his point until the teacher told him that it didn't matter what he said because he was the student, "the child"—so Charlie walked out of class.

The teacher found him sitting alone in the empty cafeteria, reading a book from home, and he was then escorted to the principal's office.

The rest is just history.

Charlie ignores the camera. He's used to its presence, and he must not be concerned whether his next question is aired.

"You see more benefits in skipping to fifth grade when you didn't even do it?" he asks me.

"For you, yes."

He hesitates. "Why?"

"Do you want to blend in or do you want to walk backwards?" He knows that a sea of people will *always* walk forwards, but he can choose to move with them or against them. Where do his self-interests lie? To learn to be fake or to learn to be real.

His eyes are no longer filled with tears. He holds this powerful understanding that pushes his carriage outward, pulls his shoulders back, lifts his head to greater heights. And he says, "Walk backwards."

"That's why."

You're not like me.

2027

"I believe the human brain is capable of great and terrible things. We're dreadfully complicated creatures."

- Jane Eleanor Cobalt, We Are Calloway

(Season 9 Episode 01 — Tacos & Pastels)

< 52 >

Ryke Meadows

I'm fucking used to being surrounded by girls.

Just not these two.

By the Cobalt's fireplace, Janie and Maria are in a fit of laughter over I don't fucking know what. They both wear long black robes, hiding gowns beneath. I sit on the living room chair, phone cupped in my hand, waiting for Connor to arrive from work.

I need his fucking passcodes to his storage unit, just to grab a shotgun that we share. And yeah—we share a couple guns. My little brother, who *hates* guns, revolted at the idea of me buying another one for safety.

"Just use *bear spray*," he countered.

I didn't tell him that a cougar had attacked me on my hike to a rock wall. Alone in a desert, over a hundred miles from civilization and other fucking people. I only escaped because I threw my pack at the animal and then grabbed my knife. In any other circumstance, I could've been mauled to death.

Only Daisy and Connor knew the extent of what happened. To ease my brother's anti-gun stance, Connor bought the shotgun with me, plus another Glock.

Lo views Connor as the most levelheaded, intelligent human being on this fucking planet, so he trusted his judgment and stopped arguing. I'm at a place with Connor where he actively chooses to side with me over Lo. It makes my life fucking easier. Except he won't divulge his passcodes over text, email, or phone, so I have to wait for him.

And he has reason to be cautious. Daisy, Lily, and even Rose have had their email hacked about three or four times, even when they change their passwords weekly. Tomorrow I'm leaving to climb alone in a desert again, and I want the fucking shotgun.

Maria speaks in between laughter. "And then he said, 'Eighteen is the new twenty-five'—and I was like, 'no, eighteen is still eighteen. Twenty-five is still twenty-five. And idiocy is still you.'"

I tense at this story since Maria's eighteen. Janie is just eleven. I remember where they're going tomorrow, and it suddenly puts me on fucking edge.

"And what'd he do?" Janie asks, her laughter fading.

Maria says like it's nothing, "He called me a bitch and then walked away."

My jaw hardens. "Is this the fucking actor you're dating?"

Maria and Janie spin towards me, humor coating their faces again. Maria Stokes is nominated for a Critic's Choice Award, and out of all people, she chose Janie as her plus-one. They fly out to California tomorrow, but I know why they're in robes now. Maria asked if she could wear something from Calloway Couture for the red carpet. Rose calls them "haute couture gowns"—a fashion line that she unveiled in a December runway show.

It earned more praise than I think Rose even imagined. A model wore her dress on the cover of Vogue. I've seen Connor look proud of his wife, but when she stepped out on the runway as the designer acknowledging the audience, his pride for Rose was overwhelming and unmistakable.

"Uncle Ryke," Maria tells me, "you should talk to Uncle Lo more or at least ask him why you're always the *last* one to get information."

I roll my eyes. That's not completely fucking accurate all the time, but she can think I'm out of the loop if she wants. I motion to Janie. "I could text your mom, and she'll just come down here and fucking tell me what's up."

I've already texted Rose: where the fuck are you?

In my home office, making a couple adjustments. I'll be down soon. — Rose

Her home office upstairs has a sewing machine, so I figure she's fixing something for their dresses.

She also sent one more text.

And Ryke? Do NOT let them convince you to make coffee. They've already had more caffeine than they're allowed. — Rose

All the girls, in every family, come to me first if they want something. Because nine times out of ten, I give in. I can't fucking help it.

In my fucking defense, they asked for coffee before I received that text, so I made them a pot. Their mugs sit on the fireplace mantel.

Maria raises her hands. "No need to text Aunt Rose. I have all the details." She shrugs. "So that story wasn't about the same actor you're thinking of. I'm not dating him or anyone. The one you *are* thinking of—he's seriously just a friend."

I can't remember his fucking name, but he's twenty-one and just became *really* fucking famous for playing Sorin-X in *The Fourth Degree* movie.

Janie rises on the tips of her toes. "I'm dreadfully biased, but I think I'm a better date than her other options."

Maria hooks her arms with her cousin. "No contest."

The ceiling rattles with a flurry of fucking footsteps. The Cobalt boys must be on the second floor. I vaguely hear Janie suggest taking photos of their outfits but *no social media*. Maria agrees and they both slip off their robes, dressed in Calloway Couture gowns.

"That's what you're fucking wearing?" I ask Janie, my brows scrunch hard.

"Yes, isn't it magnificent?" Janie twirls but trips all over the fucking fabric, too long. The deep red gown plunges in the back, half sequined with long draping sleeves.

She's *eleven*.

Not eighteen like Maria, who wears a black long-sleeve gown, embroidered and sequined as fucking intricately as Janie's dress. Look, Janie doesn't even resemble herself, not only because it's too old for her frame but because it's not her fucking style.

I shake my head a couple times. *Isn't it magnificent?* "Fuck no," I say flatly.

Maria laughs.

Janie smiles kindly. "Mom said she'd hem the gown before tomorrow. I know it appears long."

It appears more than just fucking long. "Has your dad seen the fucking gown yet?"

"No, but he won't mind...will he?"

His first-born. His daughter. The baby he delivered in the back of a fucking limo. Without question, he'll care.

[53]

January 2027
THE COBALT ESTATE
Philadelphia

Connor Cobalt

"This is yours." I pass a small slip of paper with my storage pass-codes to Ryke. He met me by the front door, which means he's ready to leave my house quickly.

Ryke nods once in appreciation and steps around me, hand on the door frame. He hesitates.

"Yes?" I arch a brow.

"You'll see it in a fucking second."

Wonderful. It's vague enough that it could imply anything. I don't jump to irrational conclusions. I just file his comment away and say in Italian, "Fai attenzione, amico mio."

Be careful, my friend.

He nods again. "It's an easy fucking climb."

"It's the hike to the climb that carries more risks."

He raises the slip of paper between his fingers. "Which is why I fucking have this."

"Paper is a useless weapon against an animal," I quip. "You should already know this since you commune with them."

Ryke glowers. "You're such a fucking smartass."

"I don't disagree." I begin to smile.

"At this…" Ryke flips me off and then shuts the front door on his way out.

As I head further into the house, I unknot my tie and roll up the cuffs of my black button-down. I hear footsteps from upstairs, children racing back and forth, and the boisterous sound of my sons chatting to one another.

My grin expands at one thought.

My life is never boring.

I crest the archway to the living room, and my stride slows. I shove my emotions aside and just pick apart the facts. Maria and Jane planned to try on their gowns today, so Rose can make minimal alterations before the award's ceremony. Rose also has a surprise in store for Jane, one that'll change our daughter's mind about the red dress she wears now.

It's foolish to be anything other than impassive, I remind myself. Her current gown is temporary, so my feelings should be even more fleeting.

I rub my lips once and then unclip my watch.

"What do you think?" Jane asks, twirling in a circle. She trips on the excess fabric, and Maria catches her with a laugh.

I think the gown suits a grown woman. Instead of chastising Jane and wailing on like a hyena about appropriate attire, I simply ask, "What are your intentions with this gown?" I near the girls, walking past the couch.

Jane adjusts the excess fabric. "Well, I hope to display a Calloway Couture garment for Mom."

I pocket my watch. "She'd prefer you wore a dress in your own style. Try again."

Jane smiles in thought, and she sways back and forth, hands clasped in front of her. "And what if my intentions are altruistic? What if I prefer to support Calloway Couture?"

Maria drinks from her mug of coffee, staring merrily back and forth between Jane and me.

"Then you'd sacrifice your personal self in favor of someone else. What does that sound like to you?" I question.

Jane looks to the ceiling. "Dispiriting, I suppose, but the benefit for Calloway Couture outweighs the personal cost."

I almost think I hear her incorrectly. I blink once, twice, trying to subdue the emotion that flickers in my eyes and scratches at my brain. "No," I tell her definitively. "You're not beholden to our companies, Jane. Unless your dream is to be a fashion designer or take over Cobalt Inc., your job is to follow your own passions, *never* to protect ours."

Jane sways once more, deep red fabric cascading. "Then I'm changing my intentions."

Better. "What are they now?"

She lifts her chin, and her brown hair falls further out of her messy pony. "I intend to look my best."

"For what purpose?"

Maria smiles in her mug like she's witnessed this back-and-forth before. Rose and I challenge our children to think about their actions, and I'd much rather broaden their minds than send them stomping to their rooms.

"With the purpose of…" Deviousness twinkles in Jane's eyes, and she says, "*Love.*"

I'm not entirely surprised, but the word tenses my shoulders by just a fraction, which is *far* more than usual. "Love," I repeat, letting her response sink in. I feel my jaw clench.

Maria cups her mug. "Do you have an eye on a boy, Jane? Or maybe a girl?"

"I'm not attracted to girls in that way, but I appreciate the inclusion, Maria." Jane picks up her mug and they clink theirs together.

Ryke always talks about not being ready to watch his daughters grow up, and like most aspects between us, we differ on certain levels. I *want* to see who my children will grow to become. I just can't fathom the idea of my sons or daughters being manipulated by another person or being hurt by their own choices—when I can't and won't choose for them.

It's a possibility that Jane will date a boy that I find inferior to her. It might even be inevitable, especially if she's choosing to wear a dress just to attract *someone else*. In this regard, I'd rather all my children stay young forever. I'd rather dream up an impossibility than meet a worse reality. One that I can't control. One that I can't truly change. I just have to wait and watch.

Remember love.

I love my children like extensions of myself, so seeing them fumble is like seeing myself fumble. But there is also power in love.

Every day, I remember.

"So you intend to look your best for the purpose of love." I lean against the armrest of the couch. "Is love a specific person?"

Jane sets her mug back on the mantel. "Oui." *Yes.*

Maria guesses, "Is it Ian Eastwick?" The boy who drew a penis on the back of Jane's math notebook.

My muscles start to strain. My eyes start to reflexively narrow. I arch another brow when Jane catches sight of my displeasure.

"No, it's not Ian Eastwick," Jane says and then she smiles at me. As though she's constructed a riddle that I can't solve.

In less than a second, I know. "Love is you."

Jane grins and claps quickly. "Well done." To Maria, she says, "I wish to dress my best because of the love I have for myself. Not for a boy, but for me." She fans out the draped fabric on her sleeves. "If I never fall in love, I wouldn't bat an eye."

I'm most surprised by this conclusion.

"And why is that?" I ask.

"Because I'm full of the love I have for my siblings, the love that I have for you, for Mom, for myself and the love you all give me in return.

I won't spend my life agonizing over the idea of falling in love. I don't need it any more than I need an appendix."

I had no siblings to love and no parents who supplied love. Her upbringing vastly contrasts mine. Love surrounds her, and I see that she embraces it fully. Except for the idea of love from a significant other, as if love is quantifiable and she has hit her maximum threshold.

In one breath, I am proud of her independence and the fact that her mode of thinking will save her from immense heartache. In another, I can only hope that she's open to love if it comes. When it appeared in my life, it was a struggle to accept it, to hold it, to return it.

Jane is not me, and I see that she could be someone far better.

My grin is nothing but earnest. "Mon cœur," I murmur. *My heart.*

Jane touches her heart, expressing the same sentiment. "Did I surprise you?" she wonders.

"Marginally."

She brightens, knowing that's more surprised than I usually am.

"Speaking of surprises." I straighten up as I hear Rose's heels against the hardwood. She passes beneath the archway with a garment on a hanger, jewelry box also in hand. Inside, I know, are Cobalt Diamonds in the form of two glittering bracelets.

Jane's mouth falls at the hung garment. "What is that?" Then tears fill her eyes. "Mom?" Her hands fly to her lips.

Rose holds a pastel blue tulle skirt and a sweater with *thousands* of hand-stitched sequins that create a cheetah-print. In her other hand, she has chunky cheetah-sequined heels with pastel pink buckles.

Rose made everything for Jane.

"Did you know?" Jane asks Maria.

Maria smiles. "What can I say? I'm the best secret-keeper."

Not better than me.

Jane reaches for the tulle skirt, and Rose brushes away our daughter's tears with an affectionate hand. Very quietly, Rose tells both girls, "*Never* sacrifice your personal style. Don't be anyone but you."

Jane sniffs and hugs the heels that Rose gives her. "I won't." She whispers a few tender endearments in French.

Rose swings her head to me. I read the accomplishment in her gaze: *it worked.*

I knew it would.

Last night, Rose talked about what would happen if Jane wore the red gown. I believed the event would never come to pass. Jane would always wear something else. So in bed, not even five minutes after Rose came down from an orgasm, her mind rerouted to *this*, "I'll bring sheers with me on the red carpet. I will *stab* the motherfucking people who start sexualizing her."

She's eleven, and we both know the concept of women in media is much different than men in media. We're all living, breathing proof.

"She won't wear that dress," I reminded Rose for the tenth time. "I'll also schedule you an appointment with an otolaryngologist."

Rose glared. "I can *hear* you. I just don't think the same as you."

"You don't think that I'd convince her to wear something else? Or in the very least, that *you'd* convince her?"

Rose bristled at my tone, about to roll on her side away from me.

I clasped her arm, still hovered over her body. "Rose."

She froze and then rose on her elbows as though to say, *I'm just as* everything *as you are.* "Would you bathe in pig's blood for me?"

"Yes."

"For them?"

"Yes." I never hesitated.

Her doubt towards herself and me flitted away.

I'd do anything to ensure the safety and well-being of my family. Including, at the very last effort, physically barring my daughter from leaving the house in that dress.

The reason why I'm so much better than everyone else:

To win, I only ever need words.

[54]

March 2027
THE COBALT ESTATE
Philadelphia

Rose Cobalt

I zip around Ben's bedroom that's decorated with finger-paint artwork: handprints directly *on* the walls. We gave him the ColorPalace paint, but we didn't give him the idea to forgo paper and canvas.

That is all Ben.

We told him if he ever wants to change his walls in the future, he'll have to paint over the sloppy artwork he created. I made sure to use words like *daunting* and *long hours* and *aching work*.

Ben smiled and said, "Cool."

Now I hurry around his bedroom in search of a fucking *bird*. "Pip-Squeak," I say seriously, "do *not* do this to me, not during his birthday party." I find myself cleaning up as I move, fluffing his blue pillows and organizing the crayons on his desk.

I reconvene by standing in the center of the bedroom and raise my finger. "We're on the same team Pip-Squeak. *Come.*"

Nothing.

I growl. "Lady Macbeth, if you ate this bird during his birthday party, I will kill you." *Don't think about it, Rose.*

The gray cockatiel, bright orange patches on his cheeks, has been in our family for over two years. In that time, he's learned to sing the The *Adams Family* theme song from Eliot and Tom, survived a playful black cat named Lady Macbeth, and bonded with his owner who's turning five on Monday.

Since Winona turned three on Wednesday, Ben offered to do a joint pirate-themed party for Saturday. Growing up, I balked at the idea of sharing my birthday with *anyone*. It was the one day that I never had to share.

Ben was adamant about a joint party.

Today is Saturday.

Children have already invaded my backyard and the street like locusts. He invited his whole grade. Endless chatter and commotion travel into the empty house.

We don't let anyone inside, not even to pee.

There are port-a-potties on the street.

I'm not risking anything missing from my children's bedrooms and put on eBay. Or pictures taken of their closets, just to be sold to *Celebrity Crush*. Their school friends can piss in a high-quality rented toilet. Some are wearing diapers, so they can shit in those.

"Mom, did you find him…?" Beckett trails off, noticing my finger raised without a bird perched on the tip. I've already tried waving around bird treats. Pip-Squeak can't be bribed. I respect his loyalty.

But where the fuck is he?

I lower my arm. "We'll find him." I'm an iron fortress, and my nine-year-old son will *not* see my uncertainty. "Let's check your room." I go to the doorway.

"I already did." Beckett and Ben have similar hair, wavy with a few curlier strands, and people believe they look more alike than Beckett does to his own twin.

It's not their hair that unites them. Beckett is the only brother searching for the bird because Pip-Squeak grew fond of him. Unless he's defending Charlie, he's the most even-tempered and the calmest of *all* my children. He can move his arms like billowing silk. He dances so gracefully that at nine he's begun classes for twelve-year-olds.

Your hands are too tight. Softer, Rose, the ballet instructor would chastise me as a little girl. I was stiff. Unbending.

Beckett is the surface of a rippling lake. Water. Just like his father.

"We'll look in your room again." I have a hunch that the bird flew over there. Either that or Pip-Squeak is very much dead.

Beckett trails after me, "He'll cry. Tom stepped on a caterpillar yesterday, and Ben wept by the oak tree." My heartstrings tug.

"I'm *finding* this bird if it's the last thing I do," I say with so much conviction.

Beckett nods, his doubt receding. We both slip into his bedroom. Gray and white bedding, dark wooden furniture. Much, *much* neater than every room down this hallway (except mine). Though the way he positioned his books at a slight tilt on the fourth and fifth shelf looks off.

I cluck my tongue, my eyes flaming. "Pip-Squeak, reveal your feathery ass or we'll serve you to Lady Macbeth."

Beckett whistles and peeks beneath his bed. "I taught you *happy birthday* to sing to Ben, not to hide. Where'd you go?"

I keep my finger raised in case Pip-Squeak decides to join the party, and I fix some of Beckett's books, pushing them upright. Also I put two of his pencils into a holder.

Beckett whistles again as he stands. The sound dies midway and he shouts, "Mom!"

I freeze in the middle of the room. Beckett rarely raises his voice. He rushes to his bookshelf and meticulously angles the novels I pushed up. Then he scans the room, sees the pencils out of place, and sets two side-by-side in the center of the desk.

My blazing eyes simmer a little.

He can't look at me as he says, "Why do you need to touch my things *every time* you enter my room?" Beckett clutches the frame of his desk chair.

For years we've known that he has OCD. He knows that he has it. Charlie knows.

"I'm sorry," I tell him. *I'm sorry you have to experience this. I'm sorry my OCD tries to trump yours.* "I won't touch."

"That's what you said before."

"I'm trying, Beckett." My chest is tight. Sometimes it's harder with so many children. Jane's room is *always* messy. I might as well be living with Daisy again. I just have to shut her door and block out the disaster.

I like things arranged a certain way. Orderly and in their proper places. When I was younger, I had nightly bathroom rituals that would take two-hours to complete. I manage to *not* obsess about the way I brush my teeth and how many times I wash my hands.

Now I just worry that his OCD will become a much greater enemy like mine did. First slow, then fast, and before he knows it, he'll waste *hours* obsessing.

"Beckett, if we need to schedule another therapy—"

"I'm fine." Beckett faces me. "It's only my room." He's frightened we'll forbid him from dancing.

So I have to say, "Need I remind you, I was in ballet classes all throughout prep school? It *breeds* perfectionism like this pretty little monster."

Ballet is about perfect technique, perfect form, perfect timing. He can be OCD and be a ballet dancer. Connor even believes it'll make him a better one, but if his health plummets, my claws will come out.

I'll try to annihilate everything that hurts him.

Even ballet.

Beckett stands stick-straight. "I know, but I promise, it's not any worse than it was." His honesty rings truthful.

"My gremlin," I say in a quieter tone. I reach out for his hand.

He takes hold, his eyes sad. "Will this be easier one day?"

I squeeze. "Yes."

He squeezes back, and like fate has spoken, Pip-Squeak lands on Beckett's shoulder. I'm about to chew out the bird, but then he begins singing happy birthday. To the wrong boy.

Beckett and I share a smile.

And he squeezes my hand again.

{ 55 }

July 2027
DISNEYLAND
California

Lily Hale

Before we split into three groups (at least one parent in each), we gave all of our children a stern talking to about our Disneyland adventure.

Rose: "Remember the buddy-system. Do *not* wander off alone." We all looked right at Charlie.

Daisy: "Have fun!"

Me: "Do not eat a hamburger before riding Gadget's Go Coaster. Lo will second this." I learned that the hard way.

Lo: "She puked on her feet when she was ten." All the kids laughed. "No talking to strangers."

Ryke: "And if you need anything, tell whichever fucking parent is with you."

Connor: "Use your brains. You all have them."

I'm not so worried about their safety. We have an incredible team of bodyguards with us, some of which are *very* familiar with Disneyland, so we opted for this park instead of Disney World. We've even been taking secret tunnels to avoid tons of attention, but it doesn't eliminate it all. I just hope our kids can experience the magic of the park the way that Lo and I did when we were younger.

But it's definitely different growing up famous.

"Oh my God, there's Xander Hale!" someone screams.

"Lily Calloway!"

"XANDER!"

Splash Mountain in front of us, my four-year-old boy hugs my leg in a death-grip. Hiding. It's loud. Not just with people calling our names but with the general park chatter and excited squeals as the log ride descends the watery mountain. We're not in line for Splash Mountain, but we're waiting for the big kids with Ryke and Lo to ride down.

My bodyguard stands very close, blocking people from approaching.

"XANDER!!!"

I lift Xander in my arms. At four, he's starting to be really heavy for me. Then he buries his face in my shoulder, and I think, *I can carry him for light years! My arms are steel. I am titanium.*

I hold him tighter. "You're okay. I'm right here." We never put Xander on the docu-series. It'd just terrify him more. We also hoped he'd be in the media less, but *Celebrity Crush* has started running articles about Xander's physical appearance.

[PHOTOS] XANDER HALE: MOST PHOTOGENIC BABY!
XANDER HALE: FUTURE MODEL
10 REASONS WHY XANDER HALE IS CUTEST
BABY ON EARTH!!

Luna spotted that *Celebrity Crush* headline in a grocery checkout and said it was inaccurate. Xander is from planet Thebula 2.

I'm biased, but I can see why they'd peg him as photogenic. His intense, bold amber eyes contain more emotion than most. If we were all on Animal Planet, he'd be the cuddly cub that mesmerizes the viewer by sheer expressiveness.

He's captivating when he doesn't mean to be, and I try my best to make him comfortable so he won't miss out on the magic. He was supposed to be in the second group of kids with Eliot, Luna, Tom, and Ben, but he wouldn't release his death-grip on me.

I selfishly love having someone hug me this tight. I hug right back and try to ignore the ache in my arms. *Steel arms, stay with me.*

Xander is slipping.

SOS!!

I adjust him and pant a little. His gray tank, a *Star Wars* logo across, bunches up towards his belly button. I somehow maneuver him to my left side and then tug down the hem to his jean shorts.

I could pat myself on the back if my arms weren't so busy.

When Xander peeks from my shoulder, I take full advantage of the opportunity. I ask him over the surrounding noises, "Are you hungry?" He was painfully shy this morning at breakfast. He hardly ate his strawberry waffle, and as a former shy child, I can relate to letting my food go to waste but still wanting to eat.

Xander nods.

"Me too." I set him down, my wimpy arm muscles throbbing and shrieking in thanks. I crouch next to Xander and dig in Ryke's backpack. I stuffed all my snacks in the front pocket. Gold Fish, a few smashed Ding Dongs—ah-ha! I snatch the plastic baggie of cheese puffs.

He takes a handful, then I do, and we both eat cheese puffs together. We're on the lookout for Moffy on the log ride, and Xander pays more attention to Splash Mountain and his snack than the cacophony around him.

I can only smile.

Parenting success.

"Did you see me?!" Moffy jubilantly rushes up to us, combing a hand through his dark brown hair. He just turned twelve last week. I hone in on his orange *The Fourth Degree* shirt, slightly *wet*. Oh shit. I missed him descending Splash Mountain.

Parenting fail.

I make up a half-truth. "A little bit. It was hard to see."

"It was so awesome!" Moffy explains the thrill of the ride, especially to Xander who's too young to go on it. By the end, I realize that Moffy is the only one here—besides his bodyguard Declan.

"Where's everyone else?"

"They're coming. We got on an earlier boat." He squats to his little brother's height, and Xander shares a cheese puff with him. Moffy crunches on it and asks, "I saw Goofy walk past, you want to go take a picture with me?"

Xander's gaze drops and he shakes his head.

"What about an autograph?" Moffy wonders, knowing how his brother dislikes photos. He even finds ways to hide behind his older siblings in group pictures.

Xander wavers, unsure. He hasn't clung onto me since I whipped out the snack food, so this is good progress.

"Come on, Summers," Moffy says with an easy smile. "You have to fill up that autograph book. What happens if Ben has more than you, huh? You can't let that happen."

Summers.

Every time Moffy calls him that, my chest swells with love. He's the only one who uses that nickname with Xander, since his namesake is Alexander Summers.

His soulful amber eyes rise up to Moffy. "Will you stay with me?"

"I'm your sidekick, Summers. I wouldn't leave you for the world." Moffy extends his hand.

Xander grabs hold, and they both stand together.

"Can I take him alone?" Moffy asks me. "I mean with Declan and Xander's bodyguard. But..." *Not with me.* Before an incoming arrow pierces my heart, I remind myself that I bring attention wherever I go. He'll have an easier time avoiding crowds without me, and I like that Moffy wants to hang out with his little brother.

Hesitating, I teeter from one foot to the other like I have to pee. Moffy may be twelve now, but Xander is only four. What if something happens? This seems like a decision Lo and I should both make together.

"Maybe you should wait..." I trail off, seeing Lo in the distance with the older kids and Ryke, all a little wet from the ride. For probably the eleventh time today, I count heads quickly.

Sullivan.

Beckett.

Jane.

Where's Charlie?

I crane my neck. I lean sideways. My pulse begins to quicken, and that's when both Ryke and Lo start frenziedly scanning the area around them. Realizing Charlie isn't with the group.

"Charlie?!" Ryke shouts, drawing more attention to us.

I wait for the nine-year-old to pop out from behind a bench or a cluster of Mickey-shaped balloons. Nothing happens. I see phones pointed at us. I hear people call *our* names, but I don't spot the oldest Cobalt boy.

Xander hides behind Moffy's legs.

My bodyguard contacts the fleet with his earpiece. "We're missing one."

We're missing one.

We just lost my sister's child.

{ 56 }

July 2027
DISNEYLAND
California

LOREN HALE

With my cell gripped tight against my ear, I stand in the middle of the park's offices. Ryke and Lily talk to the park coordinators in a backroom, and at the front, Jane, Sullivan, Beckett, Moffy, and Xander sit on plastic chairs by the wall.

"He wandered off," I say, practically hysterical over the fucking phone. "I don't know where the hell he could be, Connor. He won't answer when we call."

This isn't the first time Charlie Keating Cobalt strayed from the pack, but it's the first time in goddamn Disneyland. I overheard his *very* long conversation with his parents before we arrived, and the general gist was to stay with the motherfucking group.

I run my hand across my neck.

It'll be my fault if something happens to Charlie. I'm the one who convinced him to ride Splash Mountain when all he really wanted was to chill at the hotel.

"Lo, calm down," Connor says, his voice serene.

My face sharpens. "Are you serious? You're telling *me* to calm down? How are *you* calm right now?"

"Because I know and understand my son. He most likely found the ride pointless, and he might've slipped out at the last minute. He's either at the hotel or he'll find you."

He'll find *me*? "He's *nine*, Connor." I exhale a jagged breath. "You're supposed to be the smart one."

"His age is meaningless, and I am the smart one, which means my opinion holds the most weight." He whispers to someone else, voices muffled, and then he focuses on our call again. "Lo?"

"Still here," I snap. "Is Rose on her way to the hotel?"

"Yes. Call me if he finds you." He says it like there's *no way* I'll locate Charlie before he locates me. After his reasoning sinks in, I no longer argue. Charlie is intelligent, maybe a notch below his father, and if anyone knows that boy, it's Connor Cobalt.

"Are you looking for him?" I ask.

"I have my bodyguards working with security, and I'm working on tracing his phone." It'd be easier if Garrison were here. He's good with electronics, but for the whole month, he went to London with Willow and their daughter. "But I choose not to panic."

"Rose doesn't carry the same philosophy." Lily said her older sister turned into Xena: Warrior Princess over the phone, throwing out things like *battalions, combat, blades* and *death*.

"Neither do you," Connor says easily. "Neither does Ryke. I believe there's a name for this." I hear the smile in his voice.

Hot-Tempered Triad.

That's the damn name.

I let out a deep breath, my shoulders relaxed. Connor eases the alarm in my gut. He's always been able to make uncomfortable situations more comfortable with just his voice and some words. Our lives would be drastically more difficult without him.

After we hang up, I think about what happened. I think about the future where we're not around the kids while they go to high school—while they go to college. I think about this, and I storm towards the row of older children.

Sulli and Beckett sit on the carpet, doing crunches side-by-side in quick spurts. No one counts. They're not competing against one another. These crazy nine-year-olds think training for swimming and ballet is *fun*. And we're at *Disneyland*.

My face scrunches like they're from another planet. I can't even comment because I've seen it all before. Push-ups, pull-ups, sit-ups at random hours and random places—I've seen it from my own brother.

It's a different breed of person.

It's not me.

Jane drew a tic-tac-toe board on her hand and plays with Moffy and Xander, but my oldest son registers my looming presence, features serrated like a knife. He lowers the blue magic marker, not nervous or scared. I'm not trying to frighten Moffy.

Sulli and Beckett stop mid-crunch, eyes on me.

"You four." I motion to all of them.

"There are five of us, Dad," Moffy says coolly, smiling. His little brother is perched on his knee with a bag of cheese puffs.

"Xander isn't part of this speech." My youngest son looks up at me, reflective amber eyes that carry *pure* innocence, his gray *Star Wars* tank stained with orange cheese dust. "You've been an excellent Disneylander, Xander." I only use the word *Disneylander* because I heard Lil use it, and it reminds me of her.

Xander starts to smile at the compliment.

Moffy frowns. "So that means we did something wrong?"

Jane raises her hand, but she speaks before I even focus on her. "Uncle Loren," she says my full name like every Cobalt kid. "I propose that we not be punished for my brother's personality."

Moffy nods in agreement. "We can't look out for *Charlie*. I've tried, Dad, but it's not possible."

I never have the chance to ask why.

Beckett speaks from the floor, sitting straight with one bent knee. "Charlie doesn't want us to keep him in the group."

Moffy adds, "He wants to do his own thing."

Jesus Christ. "All of you—you have to look out for one another. This is just the start to the kind of chaotic places you'll go. And I get that Charlie likes to go off on his own, but you four need to stay in touch. At *least* get info on where he might be headed. If he won't tell us, he should tell all of you." I look to Beckett, the only tame yellow-green eyes I've ever seen.

He shakes his head, dark brown hair swaying with him. His expression just says, *I'm sorry, but you're not right.* "The whole point of being alone is so that you won't be followed and found. And if he did tell me, I would be the first to tell you, which is precisely why he wouldn't tell me."

Connor said something about that over the phone. Beckett is as concerned about Charlie's safety as the rest of us. Maybe even more.

Sulli elbows Beckett's arm and says, "Rep of push-ups?"

Beckett nods fast, and they change positions, doing meticulous push-ups. Lowered all the way to the floor before rising back up.

Jane splays her hands on her legs, hair falling out of a pony. "Maybe we should check the Matterhorn. I heard him mentioning that ride."

I also remember Moffy saying how he wanted to ride the Matterhorn before the day ended. I might not be Connor or even smart like my brother, but I'm *not* an idiot. She doesn't really think her brother is there. Or else she would've mentioned Matterhorn from the moment Charlie went missing.

Jane stands.

I set a cold glare on the twelve-year-old.

Slowly, she returns to her seat. "He'll find us. I'm sure of it," Jane says confidently. "In the meantime, can't we do something more?"

"You're right. Let's go. We can ride some rides, pretend you brother isn't *lost* in a theme park where millions of people *know him*, and he doesn't know a goddamn soul. Do you want some cotton candy with that?"

Jane's shoulders just plummet, and Moffy nods to me like he understands. I don't want them to think they're like everyone else. Because they're not.

They never fucking will be. The minute they forget there are people who could easily do them harm—who think about them while they stand unaware, vulnerable—that's when everything will go to shit.

"We're not leaving this room until..." I trail off as the door opens.

With a slowly falling mouth, Sulli mutters, "What the ever loving fuck." That's a new one—that I've *never* heard my brother say—but it's accurate.

In walks a clean-cut, well-dressed nine-year-old, his eyes hidden behind black-as-night sunglasses, and when he lifts them to his brown hair, he casually takes in his surroundings. As though he expected all of this.

"Did I miss the party?" He lifts a gift shop bag. "I brought presents." Charlie meets the ice in my eyes. Unaffected, he says like I'm not understanding, "That was a joke. I didn't actually think there would be a party."

To stop myself from spouting off something *mean*, I think about the good things.

He's safe.

He found us.

Connor was right.

This isn't my child. I don't have to lecture him, give him some speech he won't listen to, or punish him. That's the king and queen's job. So I gesture to Charlie. "You must've forgotten who your parents are—unless you just wanted to see your funeral."

"My metaphorical funeral," Charlie muses as he takes a seat next to Jane. "Will you cry for me, Uncle Loren? I'd cry for me." From the way he speaks, fluidly, his voice like silk but *filled* with humor—the rest of the kids laugh.

I'm on edge.

"I'd weep for you, Charlie," Jane says as Moffy draws an X on her hand.

Charlie kicks his foot on another chair, lounging, and he doesn't have a single *clue* how high-strung Rose was from the moment he disappeared. How much Lily felt guilty for his journey to—where the hell did he go?

I cross my arms while Charlie pulls down his sunglasses and then rummages in his gift store bag. "For you."

I'm unsure of who he's talking to until he removes a Mickey Mouse hat and reaches out towards…my youngest son.

Xander is stitched on the back.

I swallow something down, maybe my anger.

My four-year-old clutches the hat, his lips upturning at the gift. Moffy helps his little brother fit on the mouse ears, the hat flattening his brown hair.

Coming from Connor Cobalt, I might question the complete sincerity—he obviously would have other motives. To appease us, calm tempers, but I'm almost positive that's not *Charlie's* intention.

I've seen him grab Winona's hand before she crossed the street.

I've seen him help Xander secure his kneepads before he tried Moffy's skateboard.

He's kind with no expectations of receiving anything in return.

And he couldn't care less if we stayed pissed, if we all hated him.

I test it. "Am I going to hear an apology?" I question sharply. It'd be hypocritical for me to ask for one. I don't need any *I'm sorrys* when I handed those out like turds growing up.

Charlie thinks for a moment before saying, "'I exist as I am, that is enough.'"

Off my confusion and *what the fucking hell*, Beckett says, "He quoted Walt Whitman."

My head throbs. I press the heel of my palm to my temple. Then I think about what could've happened. All over again. How he left. How he was my responsibility. The room goes silent, my jaw clenched, amber eyes daggered.

Moffy covers his little brother's ears with his hands, and then he whispers towards Charlie, "Dude, you're fucked." All our kids hear curse words, but they know not to say them at school—and I get it. I'm not with them, they might be saying *fuck this* and *fuck that* in fifth grade without my knowledge.

But Sulli is the only one who gets in trouble for swearing at Dalton Elementary, so the rest of them have a better time hiding it—or they just don't curse.

Moffy also likes to reinforce the lenient *don't swear* rule for his siblings, which is why he just "earmuffed" his little brother. He picked that up from Lily.

Charlie doesn't remove his sunglasses, but his face is angled towards me. *He was your responsibility.* I know.

I'd never forgive myself if something happened to Rose's son.

"Charlie." His name sounds like a goddamn curse on my lips. I exhale a tight breath, shifting my weight to my other foot. *He's nine.* Connor might say it's meaningless, but it means *something* to me. I'm in a position of authority, and I don't want to make him feel small—but I can't treat him like he's as tall as me.

He fucked up.

"Don't be like me," I say curtly.

It must surprise him because he sits up. "How was I like you?"

"Uncaring about your own life." Before he refutes, *I care*, I snap back, "You must not care about whether you live or die—because there are people who'd hurt you. Who'd want to lure you to places you'd never want to go."

"I'm smarter than that, Uncle Loren."

My face twists. It doesn't matter how smart he is. He's a nine-year-old boy, and that fact isn't changing until he grows older. "Oh, so you can overpower two, three men? Maybe even women. All older than you. With what?"

"My words."

"They gag you, they blindfold you—then what?" The kids are eerily quiet, but I'm not sugarcoating their reality. They're getting older. They're *meeting* the world too fast. I nod to Charlie. "*I'm smarter than that.* Tell that to every person with hands larger than yours. As they grab you. See if they care."

Charlie goes rigid, shaking his head once, then twice. He stares at the ceiling. "I hate irrational people."

But they exist. And how many times have we met them?

Christ.

I take another breath, feeling the massive cement block I unloaded on them. *Disneyland.* We're in Disneyland. This is what happens when you bring a known villain to the party.

Kidding.

I'm not the villain, but I'm the kind of hero who forgets an overly happy theme song for the credits. I'm too bitter to be that sweet.

IN A PIGGYBACK, I carry Lily out of the Star Tours 3-D motion simulator, my big brother and the older kids skipping ahead, talking about the attraction. We dropped Charlie off with his parents, and Xander asked softly if he could stay with Ben and Luna for a while.

After letting him go, Lil looked crestfallen in the most magical place in the world. I told her she was a sopping jellyfish that washed ashore my beach.

"You're not too happy yourself," she said and poked my forehead where my scowl formed.

"Have you forgotten me already, love? This is my normal face." I gestured to my glare and then gave her a dry half-smile.

Lily eyed my lips. "I have not...forgotten."

Then I whispered beside her ear, "Have you forgotten that you and me—we know what happiness feels like?" Her green eyes welled with *years* of victories. Victories that we've shared. Obstacles that we've hurdled.

So we're not with our youngest kids for a couple hours at Disneyland.

It's not even close to being the worst thing in our world.

Lily nodded firmly.

Now we exit the *Star Wars* simulator together, Lily riding piggyback, and we sing the theme song that we know and love. Not even a second through, and Moffy and Jane join in. Jane pumps her fist in the air like a sword.

Beckett and Sulli are talking down the hallway, disinterested. Some people quickly snap pictures of them, but they don't pay attention. I try not to either.

"Duuh duuh da da da," we sing.

Lily is so off-key that Ryke, nearby, keeps shaking his head like he has a migraine.

"Hey," I snap in the middle of our song. "Don't rag on my 'puff."

"I didn't say a fucking thing."

Moffy's laughter and smile slowly die down, his gaze pinging questioningly to me, to his mom, to Ryke. I'm just messing with my older brother, but the look in my son's eyes—it practically stops my fucking heart.

He's quiet.

The rest of the day. When Jane asks what's wrong, he just shakes his head. Lily and I don't pressure him to open up yet.

Lily has been biting her fingernails to the beds, but she's the one who tells me, "We just have to take what comes." She turns only a bit red. "Not like *coming*, coming. The normal type of come."

I almost smile, but my stomach never unknots. It's not until dinner-time. It's not until we order room service at the hotel so everyone can chill out, relax, without the fear of cameras and giant crowds. It's not until everyone congregates in the Cobalt's suite with burgers and fries— it's not until this moment that Moffy separates from the pack.

He dazedly opens the door, almost in a trance. I follow at a distance. Lily, Ryke, Connor, Rose, and Daisy all see me leave into the hotel hallway with him. By the time I shut the door, Moffy has stopped halfway down, clutching the archway frame to the *vending* area.

His hand touches his eyes. And I know my son is crying.

He disappears inside the vending enclave, and I follow, rounding the corner. Rock in my throat. Moffy is slumped by the ice and Fizzle machines. He looks up, and his reddened face shatters, crying harder. Guttural sobs that pull his body forward.

I instantly sit next to him, before he even tries to stand. He attempts to wipe at his face, but he just sobs into his palms, cheeks soaked with tears.

I hug my kid tight. He's just twelve.

He's just goddamn twelve, and he tries hard to act like he's twenty-two. We include him in a lot. When Ryke, Connor, and I go out to eat, we'll invite Maximoff. He likes feeling older. Like he's one of the grown-ups, but he's not.

It's a weird balance because I need him to stay a kid. He deserves that. But the universe might be saying *Maximoff Hale, you have to grow up now.*

I don't push my son to talk. I just tell him, "You can cry, Mof. Whatever it is, you can cry."

Moffy takes short inhales and leans back, his head thudding against the black and gold Fizzle machine. Silent tears draw tracks down his cheeks. My arm rests across his shoulders, and he holds one of my hands strongly—like he doesn't want me to leave.

Lily thinks that every day our oldest son looks more and more like me. But there's no malice in his sharp jawline. There's no spite in his daggered gaze. He has my features but his soul is clean.

Moffy stares up at the ceiling, tears flowing with each blink.

My eyes burn, and I swallow that rock. He usually doesn't take this long to open up with me. He's comfortable talking about almost anything.

Not much fazes Moffy.

We hear the ding of the elevator and a few kids fighting while parents scold them. Their door shuts, and the hallway goes quiet again.

I stare down at my son. "I can listen," I whisper.

More silent tears cascade. Then, very shakily, he says, "I have to ask you something." His voice cracks, but he musters the courage to look me right in the eyes.

Most people can't stare at me for longer than a second, and he holds my gaze, his face broken. Pained.

And he asks, "Am I your son or am I Uncle Ryke's?" I open my mouth, but he speaks again, fast. "And I don't mean in the *metaphorical* sense. I mean, biologically."

"Biologically, metaphorically, spiritually—any which way you turn it," I tell him, my voice clear and proud and full of never-ending love, "you're *mine*." I take my hand off his shoulder, touching my chest. "You're *my* son. I don't know what you've read online, but it's a load of shit. Your mom and Uncle Ryke were never together."

When I was younger, I thought I could protect him from this. I wished he'd never experience doubt. As I grew older, I knew it'd come. I *knew* it would, so it doesn't hurt the way that it would've years ago. I was just hoping he'd meet these rumors when he was sixteen, seventeen.

Not twelve.

Moffy searches my features like he's trying to find *me* in him.

"I look just like you, bud."

"Not our hair color."

"You have your grandfather's dark hair. So what?" I shrug, shoulders taut. "It's Ryke's hair color? So what, Moffy, you're still *mine*." I gesture from him to me. From me to him. "You're *my* son, and I love you."

His chin quivers, and I hug him to my chest. He cries into my shoulder. I know it hurts. It's people doubting the truth. I've felt that. When people claimed my dad molested me.

That pain drove me to relapse.

And maybe it's our fault for putting it off. For a long time, Connor and Rose have pled with all of us to tell the children about our histories. Lily's sex addiction. False rumors. The most we did was talk about alcohol addiction, but the rest, we just kept saying *let's wait.*

They're too young.

Maybe Connor and Rose were right after all. Maybe there's never a perfect time. Maybe we can't blame ourselves for not knowing when to surface adult issues with kids. Is it too early? Is it too late? There's no known calendar for this shit.

We just do what we can, the best we can, when we can. And we hope that's enough.

Moffy dries some of his tears and lifts his head up to me, my hands on his shoulders. Ready to pull him to my chest if he needs me too again.

The ice machine groans nearby, cutting through the silence.

"Where'd you hear the rumors?" I ask quietly.

"A Tumblr site." His face contorts, wincing, but he's stopped crying. "They compare me with you and him."

I haven't seen the photos, but I'm sure Moffy is placed side-by-side next to my brother and me. My gaze roams the small vending area where we sit, but my mind travels somewhere else. "You shouldn't be on Tumblr."

We have celebrity gossip sites blocked on parent control. Just like Tumblr *and* Twitter. So we can keep our kids from seeing shit said about them.

Protect their mental health.

Moffy is older, and he has more access to these things than our other kids—but *not* Tumblr. His throat bobs. "A guy showed me at school."

I tense. "A friend?"

"Not really." Moffy pauses. "I mean…I thought he was alright until then, but he's just like the rest of them." I hear the endnote.

Untrustworthy.

Moffy scrutinizes my hair for a second. My muscles bind and sear. Is he taking note of the color? How it doesn't match his? Then he touches his hair, almost the same cut as mine. Slightly shorter on the sides. Longer on top.

His chest collapses. "How could you let me dress like him?"

I'm confused. "What?" My voice is sharp.

"As a kid, I always dressed like Uncle Ryke. Right in front of you…I did that *to you*…"

"No, bud." I shake my head heatedly. "You didn't hurt me. I *love* my brother. I love that you admire your uncle. For Christ's sake, *I* admire him. He's a goddamn superhero."

"You're a goddamn superhero," Moffy says strongly.

It brings tears to my eyes. "Moffy, your uncle, my brother…" I choke on my words. I don't want him to hate Ryke. I never thought this would happen. I thought it'd spin the other way. I thought he'd hate *me*, doubt me. Instead, he believes me beyond everything else.

"If I wear sunscreen all the time, will I look more like you?"

Yes. I can't say it. His plan starts churning in his eyes. Knowing I'm not as tan as Ryke because I don't spend hours outside like him. I see these ideas feverishly crawl into my son's eyes.

I can wear sunscreen.

I can dye my hair to light brown.

"Don't do it, Moffy."

"I don't want to look like him!" he yells, gripping his shirt like his heart is breaking.

"Because of other people? Don't let them drown you. Don't let them change you, Mof. Would you want Luna to change who she is because people say things?"

He's hauntingly still, and one tear rolls down his cheek. He shakes his head, eyes flitting up to me.

I clasp his shoulder again. "I need you to know something."

Moffy breathes heavily, but he nods like *go on*.

And I tell my son, "My brother saved my life. I wouldn't be sober if it weren't for him. I might not even be here. Your mom might not be here. We wouldn't have had you. *He* helped me become a better person."

Moffy relaxes at every syllable, every word, trying hard not to villainize the person that we all love. If he should hate anything, he should despise the media and what it tries to do to us. He rests his back against the Fizzle machine.

I follow suit next to him, our arms brushing. "You know what—I might be a superhero, but there is no question, Ryke Meadows is one too. And he's standing right by my side, heaven and hell."

Moffy seems older. In this one moment. Life aged him, and he turns his head to me, more at peace with all this knowledge that would capsize most people. It would've crushed me.

I remember the day he turned eleven. He took a Harry Potter quiz, and he was sorted into a wizarding house.

Maximoff Hale is a Hufflepuff.

And he's so goddamn strong.

I can feel one unspoken question billowing in the air. "You have another question." I don't ask it. He nods, but before he can speak, I say, "You want to know if your mom is a sex addict. If that's a lie too?"

His brows pinch. "Is she?" he wonders. I think he realizes that he can't find the truth online or from other people. Only we have the real story, and most of it is documented on *We Are Calloway*. A show we haven't let any of the kids watch. "Some people at school…they mention it. I didn't want to upset Mom, and I thought, maybe it was just another rumor."

He was ten when I told him about my history with alcoholism. I explained addiction, dependency, abusing liquor, and how his grandfather had been sick too. But how do you explain sex addiction to a child?

"You know how I'm addicted to alcohol," I start out slowly. Moffy stares straight ahead, lost in thought, and I finish, "Well, your mom is addicted to sex. That part is true."

Moffy is still in a daze.

"Moffy," I call out, trying to keep my voice level. "I don't want this to affect your view of your mom." My insides compress and explode, anguished at the thought—Lily. *Lily.* She'd be devastated and wrecked if he treated her differently.

Just because of her addiction.

"She's still your mom. She *loves* you like you're a part of her goddamn soul. *Nothing* has changed. It's just something that she deals with like I deal with alcohol."

He doesn't say a word. *Goddammit.*

"Moffy."

"You're my dad?" he asks again.

Don't fucking cry.

"I'm your dad," I say forcefully. "Your mom and I have a monogamous relationship. That means she's not *with* anyone else but me. She doesn't have sex with anyone else."

Moffy is confused. "Then how is she a sex addict?" He grinds his teeth and scratches at his arm. He looks hollowed out.

I think he wanted this to be a lie. So he could tell his friends to *fuck off.* To get over themselves and stop spreading rumors.

"This isn't something to be ashamed of. Your mom's not ashamed. Okay? It's a part of her. The *same* way my addiction is a part of me." He can't love me and hate Lily. I might as well be sawed in half.

"Then why hasn't she told me?" He frowns. "You both usually tell me everything."

"Maybe we should have," I admit that, "but we didn't want you thinking about sex in that context, Moffy. It's complicated."

He weighs this knowledge.

"You love your mom?"

His eyes fill to the brim while he nods repeatedly. "It's why this is so hard, you know? I don't like thinking that she's struggling with something like this…"

I was wrong about him being ashamed of Lily. That's not the track he was going down.

Moffy just didn't want her to be sick.

Goddamn Hufflepuff.

"I can explain her addiction better, if you want me to." I don't know what it must be like for him. This is his mom. I didn't even have a mother.

He breathes easier and nods. "Yeah, can you?" He licks his dry lips, realization crossing his face. "Is this why you got so pissed over the pop-up porn on my computer?"

"Yeah." I bend my knees, both of us at ease. "Sex addicts can be compulsive about porn. We're just cautious."

"That makes sense…" He swings his head to me. "One more question."

"You can ask as many as you want."

Moffy almost smiles and he nods in thanks. "So…how bad is sex addiction? Sex is supposed to feel good, so it can't be that terrible, right?"

My teenage and college years with Lil race through my mind. I can't lie to my son. I can't tell him it was easy when it was fucking hard. So I say the truth, "She's at a healthy place now, Moffy."

He lets out the deepest breath. "If I think of something else…?"

"You can *always* ask me or her or us."

He nods to himself like he's more content again.

I stand and help him up. "You want some hot tea?" He drinks a cup almost every morning.

"Yeah, that'd be good." He hesitates before we leave the vending area. He nods to himself again and then says, "Thanks for trusting me."

I hug him to my side, and he hugs back.

I know, soon, we may need to trust him with a lot more.

< 57 >

July 2027
DISNEYLAND
California

Daisy Meadows

I'm in charge of three little rambunctious girls today.

I'm the only one who likes the spinning teacups, and this morning, three-year-old Winona and Kinney declared that they wanted to "spin until they puked" and two-and-half-year-old Audrey nodded like *me too.*

Rose told me not to put puke on the agenda, and I planned to cross *puke* out and put *fun*. Like total mind-blowingly awesome *fun*.

Well, it's been horrible stomach-curdling *un*-fun.

We've been at the Mad Hatter's teacups for over an hour, and we've only whirled on the ride once.

I have all three wiggly girls barely seated on their strollers by the teacups attraction. I place my arm to my mouth, almost gagging, and then I chug a *second* water bottle. My stomach roils and cramps.

Bodyguards surround us so safety isn't a monstrous issue, even with the growing crowds and people sneaking photographs.

Winona hops off her stroller with a devious laugh, wearing a tiger onesie. Her tail flaps behind her.

I pick up my toddler and set her back, my stomach caving in on itself. *Suck it down, Daisy.* I breathe through my nose, and Winona tries to dart off again. She thinks it's a game. It might be if I didn't feel like death just crawled into my stomach and died.

I'm sweating, dizzy and nauseous.

I'm going to puke.

I swallow the feeling. I don't think the teacups are to blame. I've never felt nauseous on rides or car trips or even boats.

"Girls," I say, squatting in front of their strollers. Redheaded Audrey sits in the middle, wearing a pink princess gown, hands on her sides like it's what she's meant to do. Kinney inspects a booger on her finger, dressed as a Jedi Knight, while Winona hangs upside-down in her stroller.

"What if we got *ginormous, humongous*"—I gasp like it's the craziest thing in the world—"ice cream cones."

"Huh?" Winona gapes.

"Ice cream isn't teacups," Kinney Hale says like it's just known.

Audrey nods and mumbles something that sounds like, *exactly.*

Exhaling a steady breath, I struggle layering on brightness when I don't feel well. I used to be great at this, and I don't know how. I can't remember the last time I painted on happiness when I felt sick.

It might be a whole nine years ago.

My phone starts ringing. "Ice cream is *better* than teacups," I try to convince them, but I have to put my forearm to my mouth while I stand up straight. I'm lightheaded for a second, and I shut my eyes.

"Mommy?" Winona is still upside-down.

"I'm okay. Ice cream," is all I can say before I answer the phone. I only realize it's *FaceTime* when Rose appears on screen. Shouts from park-goers crackle the speakers.

"Are the girls being little devils? How's Audrey?" Rose must see herself in the tiny window because she fixes her crooked Mickey Mouse ears.

Jane is wearing identical ones with Rose today.

"They're good." I chug more water.

Rose pauses, eyes narrowing towards me. "Are you pale or is that the light?"

"Definitely the light," I lie and then rotate the camera onto her daughter, the screen still on me. I tell Audrey to say hello to her mom, and Audrey waves like she's dusting the air.

Rose touches her lips as she smiles.

Not long after, she glances over her shoulder like she feels someone. I catch a brief glimpse of Connor. *Grinning.*

"You're infuriating," Rose snaps and then tries to raise a hand at his face.

He only grins more. Eliot and Tom suddenly jump out at Rose, trying to scare her.

Rose doesn't startle.

Then they both clasp her hand, tugging her towards a ride and talking over one another. Rose unconsciously points the camera at the cement.

It makes me so nauseous that I say quickly, "I'll talk to you later." I hang up and immediately call someone else.

I can't do this alone, and I don't want to try to push through this awful feeling. I just want to spend thirty minutes by a toilet and then curl up in bed.

Ryke answers on the third ring. "Hey, sweetheart." I'm not sure where he is with the older kids and Lily and Lo. They could be on another side of the park for all I know.

"Ryke—"

"What's fucking wrong?" Concern deepens his voice.

I don't even know *how* I said his name, but obviously it alarmed him. "I don't feel well…" I take a huge, cumbersome breath. I don't want to let these little girls down, but I can't be here.

"Are you still at the fucking teacups?" He adds something else, but his voice is muffled. He must be speaking to Lily and his brother.

"Yeah," I say, "we're still here."

"I'm not that fucking far away."

I remember how he wanted to spend time with his brother—after Lo had that huge talk with Moffy. Maybe it won't matter that much. Ryke said that Lo is in a good place mentally, and Lo told us bits and pieces about the conversation. Towards the end of the trip, we're all going to decide what to do about sharing more information with the kids.

I can barely even process pros and cons and what it all means right now.

"Daisy?"

"What?"

"I asked what you fucking ate this morning."

I think back. I left the park with my sisters for breakfast while the guys took care of the kids. Rose challenged me to eat something new. My lips part in realization. "Uh-oh."

Shrimp omelet.

"Food poisoning?" Ryke asks now.

"I think…so." I shut my eyes. *Don't puke.*

"Daddy!" Winona shouts but stays upside-down.

I spin around the same exact time that his hands clasp my face. Ryke absorbs my state of being which is *sickly sick sick.*

"Fuck, Dais." He looks over his shoulder and waves to Price like *we're fucking leaving.*

And then it just all comes up.

I tear out of his arms and puke into the closest bush. Cameras flash. Vomit is my new accessory. Yee-haw.

"Ew, Mommy." Winona wears a face like I'm stinky and deathly ill all at once. Then I puke again, and she slowly starts crying. "Mommy?" *Afraid.* She's really afraid.

It twists my stomach.

Ryke tries to approach me, and I push him away. "Nona," I tell him.

Ryke curses beneath his breath, but he listens and crouches to our daughter. I wipe my mouth with the back of my hand. He calms down Winona by hugging her to his chest, and then his dark eyes pin to mine.

"Bed, Calloway."

I can't even wag my brows and say, *you want to sleep with me?* I just nod thankfully. *Bed.*

I'd like that.

< 58 >

July 2027
DISNEYLAND
California

Ryke Meadows

I lie on a lounge chair at a hotel pool, phone to my ear. "Text me if you feel good enough to fucking eat something. I can bring up whatever you want."

Daisy has been in bed for four hours. I hate that she fucking feels like this. "Winona said she wants a big stinking smelly sandwich."

My lips tic up. I imagine Winona snuggling against Daisy. They've been together all day. "Yeah? Ask her where I'm supposed to find that fucking sandwich."

"The stinky smelly place!" Winona shouts over the phone.

"I'll get the fuck on that then." I glance at my brother, who's on a lounge chair next to me. Lo mouths, *everything good?* He was worried about Dais too.

I nod at him.

"Take pictures and videos?" Daisy asks, hoping I will.

"I already took a fucking ton of Sulli diving, so I'll send those to you." The hotel has two pools, and they let us rent the smaller one for the day. It's the only place our kids can relax (besides the rooms) without being hounded by people they don't know—or even just recorded on someone else's phone.

Daisy and I say short *see you laters*. I scroll through my phone and start sending her some videos. Ten minutes pass and I set my phone aside, lower my Ray Bans. Sun beating down on my bare chest. My worn paperback open and splayed on my leg.

Lo seems content, his dark sunglasses on and listening to music in his earbuds. If I strain, I can distinguish the heavy bass and pulsating electronics. Sweat glistens on his abs, and he brings one of his fucking knees up. I find myself scrutinizing him a second longer.

I fucking worry about my little brother, but he doesn't always need my worry. That fact won't change how much I care.

"I've got an idea," eight-year-old Eliot Cobalt whispers to Tom, thinking we can't fucking hear. They dragged a lounge chair towards the edge of the pool, but it's closest to Lo and me.

Their parents are far across from us, hidden inside a shaded cabana. Lily joined Rose and Connor with the youngest girls: Kinney and Audrey.

Truth is, Lo and I stay under the sun just to keep an eye on the rest of the fucking kids. We don't trust some of them to be on their own.

My head tilts to Lo at the sound of *I've got an idea*. His head tilts right to me, and he pulls out one of his earbuds, listening with me.

"What?" Tom asks his brother.

Maybe they think we're sleeping. We've both been pretty fucking motionless on the lounge chairs.

"Swim to the deep-end," Eliot continues his plan. "Then pretend to drown. Don't actually drown, but stay beneath the water so it looks it."

What the fuck.

Lo and I sit up some.

Skinny little kids, Eliot has straighter brown hair, but not as golden-brown as Tom's and not as lazily slumped on the fucking lounge chair. Eliot sits straight, his feet skimming the pool.

"If you do that, he'll jump in to save you." Eliot briefly glances at the lifeguard, a *teenage* boy in red swim trunks. "Then keep your eyes closed and pretend like you're dead. He'll use mouth-to-mouth for CPR...and go for the *kiss*."

"Dude," Tom counters, "you just described *Sandlot*."

Eliot extends an arm. "And it worked."

Tom mulls this over, eyeing the lifeguard, and then he whispers, "Okay, I'm in."

Fucking A. Their chairs creak, and I immediately start standing to physically keep them from pretending to *drown*.

My brother is faster with his words. "You two, sit down."

Eliot and Tom swing their heads to us, not startled by being caught, but they both look seconds from jumping into the water. "We were just about to swim," Eliot says innocently.

It's in his eyes. The twinkle of deception. I fucking see it. My brother sees it. *Everyone* sees it.

"Bullshit," I say, still standing.

They laugh at my swear word and then they sit their asses down. I do one further and drag their lounge chair closer to ours. Their laughs morph into groans of dejection.

"Uncle Ryke," they complain.

My brother straddles his chair and lifts his sunglasses to his head. Their focus veers to him while I return to my seat.

"First of all, you should be afraid of *me*." Lo points to his chest.

Eliot and Tom smile like they're afraid of no one.

Lo holds up two fingers. "Second of all, you're not fake-drowning to get the attention of someone."

Tom takes a peek at the lifeguard stand. "What if he's really cute?"

We're not suddenly surprised that Tom is attracted to boys and not girls. Rose and Connor cultivated this safe space for their children. Inclusive of just about everything and fucking anything. So when Tom started feeling an attraction towards guys, he didn't make a speech. He didn't worry his parents would disown him or fucking hate him or try to convince him to love someone he can't.

After a while, with casual, everyday mentions of crushing on a boy at school, we all just knew he liked guys.

And it never fucking changed a thing.

Lo squints at the lifeguard and grimaces. "*Thirdly.*" Lo raises three fingers at Tom. "He's too goddamn old for you."

"You owe me a dollar," Eliot says since Lo has been put on *swear jar* this week by Lily. He's said "goddamn" more times at Disneyland than he has in five months.

Lo glares at me like it's completely unfair. I can swear as much as I want, and no one gives a shit.

I tell him the consequences. "You want a nine-year-old girl who has lunch detention all week for saying *fucking fuck*?" That's Sulli.

Lo winces. "Yeah, no."

The boys whisper quietly, their foreheads nearly pressed together.

"Hey," I shout and then kick their chair, jolting them awake.

Tom crosses his arms. "You and Aunt Daisy have an age-gap."

Fucking really?

Lo is quick to respond. "He didn't start crushing on Daisy when he was *seven*." Cobalt kids believe they're adults, so they literally scoff at Lo.

Then Tom and Eliot cup their hands to each other, whispering again. This time more blatantly in front of us.

"Fourthly," Lo continues on and points right at Tom.

They stop whispering.

"If I see you at the deep-end and you're under the water for longer than ten seconds, *Uncle Ryke* is going to jump in, save you and give you

CPR. Not the cute little lifeguard, so think about that before you start recreating a scene from *Sandlot*."

Eliot drums his lips in thought. "At what age would Tom be allowed to do it?"

"When I'm dead and buried." Lo pulls his sunglasses down. "And if you start plotting my death, remember I have friends in hell."

Eliot and Tom smile. They've always liked Lo.

"No fake-fucking-drowning, okay?" I ensure that they understand the important part.

"I won't, Uncle Ryke," Tom says, sincere enough.

Eliot looks between me and my brother. "Just so you know, you could be stopping an epic, whirlwind romance like Uncle Ryke and Aunt Daisy's."

Lo rests his hands behind his head, sunbathing. "My heart is crying."

I lean back, my lips curving upwards as I see our lives, our fucking memories. These kids have no clue just how much Lo didn't want me with Daisy. And how fucking much he truly loves us together now.

Eliot and Tom spring up and race towards the mushroom waterfall where Luna has been standing for about twenty minutes.

"Dad." Sulli collapses on the empty chair beside me, soaking wet. Her drenched hair hangs over her black one-piece bathing suit. "Can you time Moffy and me? We want to race." She rests her chin on her knee and tugs at her ankle bracelets.

"Sure." I set my book aside and sit towards my young daughter. The previous talk of crushes fucking flares in my head. I'm trying to prepare for that day with Sulli.

Lily once asked me why I didn't like thinking about Sulli dating.

She's nine, and I want to stay in the moment for as long as fucking possible.

I still don't want her to grow up fast.

For a while, Lily and I talked about our girls and what sex means for them in this fucking world. She told me, "I sexualize men. You can't just be afraid of *men* that sexualize women when I do practically the same thing, and I'm a woman."

I told Lily the honest fucking truth. "You can't physically overpower a fucking man the way that a man can overpower you."

It doesn't matter who's thinking about sex. We all are.

It matters who's in a position of dominance. Who has the chance to abuse that—and it's mostly men. Bad fucking men. Rose never gave pepper spray to Lo, Connor, and me. Because she didn't have to. Women are the ones who walk alone in fear at night.

"Hey, Sul?" I say. "What do you think about the lifeguard?"

Sulli reroutes her attention and blocks out the sun with her hand. "He's okay."

I rake my fingers through my hair. "Yeah?"

"He's alert, I guess." She pushes my shoulder as she stands. "Don't worry, Dad. Moffy and I can watch out for the little kids. We'd beat the lifeguard to them anyway."

I know she fucking would.

I stand and walk with her to the pool ladder. She didn't understand my question, but that's the fucking point. She's nine. She's young. She's unconcerned about that.

I take the moment for what it is.

Sulli hops into the pool, and when her smile grows, causing mine to appear, I just fucking think, *swimming is her true love.*

[59]

Connor Cobalt

The six of us—Lo, Lily, Ryke, Daisy, Rose, and me—sit around an iron table on my suite's patio. The sun just now begins to set. Inside, most of our children are tucked in bed, fast asleep after a week-long tiring vacation.

And by *tiring*, I mean for everyone else. I'm nowhere near exhausted.

I slowly sip my red wine, my hand on Rose's thigh. Sitting beside me, she takes measured gulps from her own glass. My lips rise to Rose. She sears me with a torrid glare that burns me inside. I grin wider, yearning to go home so I can fuck my wife.

"Focus, Richard," she says, voice like frost.

We're in the middle of a conversation about our oldest children, and the discussion only halted because Daisy remembered she bought churros for Lily and Lo. She's felt better the past two days after a bout of food poisoning. Daisy left and brought them the dessert about two minutes ago.

Now Lo embraces his wife on his lap, arms around Lily, seated on the same iron chair while they dig into the box of churros.

Daisy and Ryke unsurprisingly ditch the *many* available chairs for the patio railing. Close enough to the table that Daisy reaches forward and sets down a can of Fizz Life, all while still balancing on the iron rail. Ryke keeps a hand on her knee, just in case she careens backwards.

My gaze strokes Rose's caustic, piercing eyes. "You've forgotten that I can multitask better than the above-average individual."

She gathers her glossy hair on her neck. "Maybe I just believe you're *average.*"

"Then you wouldn't be as intelligent as I believe you to be."

Rose tries hard not to smile, our back-and-forth rousing us, but she remembers the severity of our previous conversation and abruptly tears her gaze off me. I grin into my wine, and she snaps her fingers at her sisters and their husbands.

"We have to make a decision before nightfall."

The sky is orange, the sun lowering quickly.

"Christ, Queen Rose." Lo glares. "Wait until I've eaten my churro. Just put down your broomstick and cast spells at your husband."

Rose narrows her eyes. "Choke and die."

Lo points his churro at Rose. "You're wasting your spells. I'm already *dead.*"

Lily nearly chokes on her dessert.

Lo's face falls, his humor trampled immediately. "Lil?" He pats her back.

She swallows, and Rose and Daisy push their glasses of water to their sister. Lily takes a big gulp and says to Lo, "You're not *dead.* I thought we agreed that you just went to hell and now you're back."

I hear Ryke mutter, "So fucking weird." He's smiling with Daisy.

"I'm not dead, love. I promise." Lo holds his wife tight in his arms.

I see the sunset as passage of time, and the longer we skirt around the issues, the more time we lose. Rose is right, so I resurface the topic too.

"Moffy, Jane, and Charlie will be in middle school," I remind everyone, their bodies relatively at ease. I attribute it to my easy-tempered tone. The way I speak. The way I act as though whatever may happen, we will succeed. "We let them know as much about our histories as the general public. They deserve the answers from us, not strangers, not peers or school faculty."

Rose and I wanted to tell the children sooner than this, and what happened with Lo and Moffy could've been different. I'm not a fortuneteller. I can't predict whether the outcome would've been better, but I know if we don't begin to open up now—as their curiosities rise—we'll lose the chance.

Lily inspects her churro, thinking.

Lo swishes his ice water, jaw sharpened.

Daisy and Ryke stare between the sunset and us.

Rose rests her hand on top of mine—the one I keep on her thigh. As though to say *we're together in this battle, Richard.* Undoubtedly, we are. I lace our fingers, and she tells them, "If they feel like we're hiding from them, then they'll begin to hide from us."

Lo shifts in his chair, edged. "They're allowed to have *privacy*, even from us."

Rose scowls. "I'm not talking about knowing *everything*. I don't need to hear whether or not they ate lunch with so-and-so and what's-his-fucking-face—I just need them to trust us. Say a cameraman harasses them, would you rather them tell us or keep it a secret?"

Ryke shakes his head. "I don't fucking see how one equates to the other. So we don't show the kids *We Are Calloway*, they could still tell us that a cameraman harassed them." He outstretches his arm like *come on.*

He's not right. He's not wrong either. It just depends on certain variables and the child in question. "Some of them will feel like we didn't share with them, so they won't feel as forthcoming to share with us."

"Which ones?" Lo asks, his shoulders more strict because he knows one of his children is in this mix.

"For right now, Maximoff and Charlie, but if we tell Moffy, we have to tell Jane." He'd explain to her everything, and we'd rather just tell Jane ourselves.

We allow the children to watch *their* segments of *We Are Calloway*. They've never seen the episodes where Lily speaks about sex addiction or where Ryke, Lo, Daisy, and I talk about the Paris riot. My sex tapes with Rose are also discussed, but that particular in-depth episode focuses on *consent*. I'd rather them hear this than read an internet post about the sex tapes concentrating on Rose's body and the size of my cock.

They know nothing about our turbulent histories with the media.

I want to open their minds wider. I want to illuminate the world in vast, bright colors, but Rose and I can't do that without a unanimous decision. Our children are too close to each other, and what one may know, they may share and spread.

We've been at a standstill for years, but Moffy's acknowledgment of Lily's sex addiction has changed everything.

Ryke scratches his unshaven jaw. "There are some fucking things kids just shouldn't know." He lets out a long animalistic groan, knowing that we've already publicized intimate portions of our lives. We shouldn't forbid our children from viewing what strangers will.

Lily puts her half-eaten churro back into the box. "We wanted to wait until they were older. High school, at least."

She's taken the news with Moffy better than I imagined. Lily might've prepared herself for the moment he'd learn about her sex addiction, and when it arrived, it blew like the wind and not a storm.

Rose taps her nails on the iron table. "Maybe we can let the little kids wait that long, but the older ones are already finding out information before we've had the chance to tell them ourselves."

The sun has almost completely fallen, darkening our surroundings. We're quiet, and their minds click and turn rapidly.

Lo is the one to stand. "Moffy, Charlie, and Jane?"

Just three for now.

Daisy and Ryke nod, both at ease keeping Sullivan in the dark a while longer. Lily joins in, nodding decisively.

He already knows my stance and Rose's, so he flicks on the patio lights and disappears inside to bring out the children.

Rose finishes off her glass of wine, eyes pierced. Our children may see us differently after this, but I'm content with a simple fact. They'll learn our reality, the truth, and that matters most to us.

Rose raises her chin, my hand tightened in hers, and she looks to me with eyes made of fire and warfare. "Our children are growing up."

"I would be more concerned if they didn't."

She glares at my lips. "I was attempting to be sentimental, Richard."

"I believe we were speaking truths—"

She covers my mouth with her palm. My grin is extraordinary. She tries to murder me with her yellow-green eyes, but I'm unbreakable. And amused.

I put down my wine, just to pry her hand off my mouth. I lose time to speak. Lo enters with Moffy, his son in plaid pants and a Spider-Man pajama shirt. Jane is next, more ruffled like she was woken from sleep. Her collared, pastel blue pajamas are wrinkled, a sleeping mask on her forehead.

Charlie trails behind and stays leaning against the wall. My oldest son looks more interested in this event than every activity from the past few days. He stuffs his hands in his gray pajama pants, his plain white shirt ironed and crisp.

"Why us?" Charlie speaks before we do.

"Why do you think?" I return the question.

Charlie tilts his head in thought. "We only have one commonality. We're in the same school grade."

"That is a variable," I say in agreement.

Charlie is deeper in thought, more curious. He shifts his full attention on us. To acquire Charlie's attention to this degree might be even harder than acquiring mine.

Moffy and Jane sit side-by-side on a patio ottoman, my daughter stifling a short yawn. She sneezes.

"Bless you," Moffy says.

"Thank you." Jane gestures to the wine. "May I?"

"No," Rose and I say together. Jane knows the reasons why.

"That's indisputably fair, but just to prepare you, I may ask once more." Jane sneezes and then smiles.

I don't need any preparation, but it's sweet of my daughter to believe I do.

Jane might appear more disinterested than Moffy and Charlie, but she's not. Her mind travels quickly. She juggles topics, thoughts and actions like one has plenty of room for the other: ask for wine, be concerned, share in Moffy's curiosities, and peek at the churros.

And smile at Rose.

And smile at me.

Lo returns to his seat, Lily on his lap. In seconds, our expansive view of the theme park distracts them—and also Ryke and Daisy.

Everyone looks outwards.

In the darkness, the castle is lit and glittering. I have no problem with this kind of fantasy for my children, but I don't *feel* magic in the setting like Lily and Lo.

I do see innocence. Purity. It's just at a distance, sentiments not attached to me.

"They should build a Neverland theme park," Lily ponders.

Lo hugs his wife to his chest. "And we could stay there forever."

"And never grow up."

"You're already grown up," Moffy tells his parents with a fleeting smile. When his throat bobs, everyone focuses intently on Moffy, Jane, and Charlie.

Rose pulls back her shoulders. "We want to show the three of you *We Are Calloway*. You deserve to know more, and we trust all of you."

"Even me?" Charlie wonders, as though he's given us ample reason not to trust him. He believes he can wander as far as he wants to wander, but it's an illusion. He's restrained by society, and he's restrained by his own self-beliefs. *Don't upset my mother.*

Don't hurt my brothers and sisters.

Don't disappoint my father.

We grounded him for wandering from Lily and Lo. His punishment was a two-thousand word letter on the consequences of his actions before the morning. While three-fourths was satirical, he stated one sincere truth in the end.

> When and where I go disturbs the ground beneath certain feet. Ones that are not my own. People I know, and people I love. It was not my intention, and now I see.
>
> Signed,
> Your wisest son

We trust Charlie.

Rose tells him, "Even you, my gremlin."

Charlie begins to grin at the endearment.

Moffy looks between every one of us. "I want to know everything." Resolve centers his gaze, green pinpoints that refuse to fissure.

"You will," Lo nods, assuring his son.

"How much more is there?"

Years.

Lifetimes.

On a different occasion, half of us might frown. The other half might recoil. I'd always stay impassive, but tonight, in this moment, we all just smile.

Our histories may contain darkness, but there is great light.

I found love in that time. *Love* that extends to these five people.

"You'll see," Lo tells his son, and Moffy takes a breath, ready for it all.

Fireworks explode. Bright, glittering and sparkling above the castle, we all watch. *Innocence. Purity.* Vibrant colors flash across our faces, and my gaze drifts to Rose.

She turns to me. A rare, sentimental smile at her lips. I take it all in.

[60]

July 2027
DISNEYLAND
California

Rose Cobalt

"Please let me." Audrey speaks relatively clear for her age. She hikes onto her strawberry-pink suitcase, carrot-orange hair in a tiny braid, and she attempts to shut the luggage closed.

She's horrible at this.

"If you must." I raise my hands, watching her failure with a tortured heart. "If you need help, I'll be in the next room."

I leave Audrey be, and then pass an adjoining door, Connor inside. His wavy brown hair looks better today, and most days it looks too good. *God.* I'm complimenting him in my head.

What has Disneyland done to me?

I also blame the fact that he's shirtless and folding *my* clothes. He lays every garment into my suitcase while I make rounds to all the children. I cross my arms, my eyes burning hot up and down Connor. Just watching him fold my clothes.

It's sexy.

I could scoff, but it's hard to deny. So I breathe in this fact. *Connor Cobalt folding my clothes almost makes me wet.* When he straightens up, his head turns, and he arches a brow at me, a smile lifting the corner of his lip. As though he's known *forever* that I'm attracted to his folding, his hair, his abs—all beneath his words.

I walk further into the room like he does *not* attract me. "Keep folding." I wave at him like he's *nothing* to me.

"It's still amusing that you think you can order me around." Connor faces me, deserting our luggage for a moment. "Come here."

"And who said *you* can order *me* around?"

Connor grins. "Rose."

I don't add the perfunctory, *Richard.* I march to the dresser and pretend to inspect the star-shaped knobs. I plan to annoy him like he's annoying me, but he knows just what to say to completely startle me.

"You asked me something years ago, and I never gave you an answer."

My mind traces back, and I search for the long-lost memory. *What did I ask? What did he not answer?* He waits for me to question him, and then the moment from many years' past jolts me. The tea party in Jane's room.

When you were a teenager, did you ever fantasize about me?

I turn and face my husband, my neck tight. "Have you been waiting *nine* years with this information, just to use it as arsenal?"

Connor shakes his head once, his smile never diminishing. "No. I just remembered the moment yesterday. Jane was reminiscing about her tea parties, and it hit me."

"And?" I cross my arms again, waiting. *Nervous.*

No, I am *not* nervous. I've made love with this man. I've made *seven* children and listened to his every word the way that he's listened to mine. We've had war and peace, and there is nothing that could shake me.

"And I have an answer for you, darling." He reaches for the pile of clothes on the bed. *My clean panties.*

I try not to shift my weight. He's studying me. "It's taken you *nine* years to form an answer." I try to make him feel inferior, even when it's impossible.

"I've always had the answer. I just waited nine years." He picks a black lace pair of panties and *slowly* folds them, still facing me.

My collarbones protrude. "You're neglectful then."

"I'm patient," he rebuts, his fingers brushing the intimate fabric like they're on me.

I heat. "So what's the answer?" I cannot be horny right now. Lily even confessed that she abstained *all week*—and if she can be that epically self-controlled at this theme park, then so can I.

Connor places my panties in the suitcase, and his deep blue eyes flit to me. "Did I ever fantasize about you, sexually, when I was a teenager?" He steps towards me, until his hand brushes the bareness of my neck. "I don't live in fantasy, Rose. I live in vivid reality, and in my reality as a teenager, I thought most often and most fondly and most *passionately* about you."

I inhale strongly, my skin tingling beneath his hand. "More specifically," I challenge.

His lip rises more, his smile inching closer to me. Towering. Our bodies draw together, his other hand on my hip. "More specifically," he breathes, "I would masturbate to these realities."

"No fantasies?" My hands are on his waist, gripping like my knees might buckle.

"One or two," he says deeply, "but they would all come true."

Sudden, abrupt, annoying clatter alarms me. I flinch and break apart from Connor. I fix my hair like he just fucked me.

He grins like he did.

Honestly.

I touch my stinging lips. His words kissed me.

Get it together, Rose.

I shake out of my stupor.

"I'll check on the boys," I say with purpose, strutting to the door. I feel Connor's unbridled confidence all around me, as though he's still right beside me. I push out, into the suite, and towards the room with all of our boys.

I'm excited to finally go home. I miss my own bed, peeing in my own toilet, and curling up on my own couch. I even miss the spirited Lady Macbeth and that exasperating little Pip-Squeak. Being on vacation is nice, but sometimes it's more comforting to be surrounded by my own things.

I grab hold of a new door frame and skirt into a *disastrous* room. I do *not* enter further. I scan their progress, which is pitiful.

Only Charlie and Beckett packed their bags, and they're no longer in this room. That leaves Eliot, Tom, and my youngest, Ben, all standing on the bed.

I spot the casualty: an overturned lamp.

"One of you will be picking that up before we leave." I point a manicured nail at the fallen lamp.

Eliot laughs and starts bouncing on the bed, Tom following suit. Ben falls to his ass, but his brothers keep jumping.

Their clothes are wrinkled *everywhere*, most thrown haphazardly into the suitcases. "Did I not teach you how to fold?" I ask them. I most certainly remember that lesson because Tom face-planted on the clean clothes by the end of it.

"Mommy, I need help," Ben says, sliding off the bed.

"Me too, Mom!" Eliot calls, leaping onto the floor.

"Me too!" Tom now lands beside his brother, both rushing to their suitcases.

I don't care what their true motives are—at least they're beside their luggage. I grab one of Tom's black shirts, a gravestone on the front.

He never grew out of these prints.

"I'll demonstrate," I tell them, "and then you can finish your suitcase yourselves."

Eliot drums his lips. "What if I opt to forgo the folding?"

"Then when you're twenty and in college and you have no idea how to iron or fold, you'll wish you listened to this lesson."

"Go ahead, Mommy." Ben crawls into his suitcases like he found a new home, laughing like he made a joke. "I'm listening." He's five, and I cherish all the ridiculously strange things my children do. In a blink of an eye, they'll be grown and gone.

My bones are rigid as I fold Tom's shirt.

"But..." Eliot frowns.

"But what?"

"I can call you when I'm twenty and in college, can't I?" he asks. "You'll still be around to teach me how to fold?"

Tears brim, and I nearly shed an actual tear. I skim my finger beneath my eye, avoiding smudged mascara. Having children has been like viewing the *Titanic* a million times in succession. I could cry at the stupidest, silliest, most inane and nauseatingly adorable moments. I could cry at the sight of any of them, for any reason, for anything.

I take a deep, vital breath that grips my heart. "Whenever you need me, I'll *always* be here."

< 61 >

December 2027

THE WOODS OF THE MEADOWS COTTAGE
Philadelphia

Daisy Meadows

I swing my axe and split a log in two.

Ryke places another log on the tree stump where we've been chopping. A secret spot in our woodsy backyard. Yesterday's sudden snowfall layers the ground and trees in white. Coconut has been tired lately, so she's inside staying warm. Our girls are currently at school, which leaves me alone with Ryke.

We've been silent for the past fifteen minutes, exchanging coy glances here and there. Ryke skims me from head-to-toe again, and I draw out the heady tension, staying rooted to this place. I'd like to just slink forward, to run my fingers through his thick hair, his scruff.

My wolf.

I smile with the next swing, but I barely split this log. I try again, the wood too tough. Ryke extends his hand, and I go to pass him the axe. He tries to grab, then I playfully retract.

He raises his brows.

"You want this axe?" I hold my axe towards my crotch. I stroke up and down the wooden handle.

Ryke Meadows is indestructible, barely batting an eye. It drives me wild. My smile constant, never receding. I'm the one who steps forward. About three feet away. I nearly pant, winter air rushing cold through my lungs.

Ryke stares darkly down at me, and when we're an arm's length away, he tears the axe out of my hand.

And throws it aside.

What is he doing? What does he want? Where is this going? The mysteries light my eyes, and I rise and fall on the tips of my toes.

So suddenly, so swiftly, Ryke shuts the distance, his hands on my cheeks. Lips on my lips. I lose breath, my fingers scraping through his soft hair. His tongue wrestles against mine. Our animalistic energy snaps the air.

I quickly kick off my boots, and he yanks my jeans down my legs, along with my panties. He pulls me closer with a feral kiss. My body sings a song of love, affection and *happiness*. Ryke kneads my head like *hey, sweetheart.*

My hands speak back, the same motion on his head.

And then he breaks apart and effortlessly hikes me up onto his shoulders. My lungs eject, and my legs dangle down his back.

I cup his rough jaw, my smile out-of-this world.

The danger of it all.

Ryke stares up at me while he kisses between my legs. The cold nips my skin, and mixed with the warmth from his mouth, all my nerve-endings shriek in delight.

"Ryke," I cry, gripping his hair.

He sucks hard, and I tremble on his shoulders. *Oh…*

My head lolls, *ahhh…* I cry out, his hand on my thigh, the other on my bare ass. *Fuck.*

His tongue. *That tongue.*

My fevered moan pitches into the air. I contract, dots blinking in my vision. Skin on fire. My eyes roll back, *fuck fuck.*

"RYKE! DAISY!"

Connor Cobalt.

We're close enough to the tree line that he might be able to see me partially naked on Ryke's shoulders.

Oh God.

It takes me a second for my world to realign. Ryke slides me down his body, his head whipping towards our cottage. I see the outline of Connor's body, but thankfully his back is to us—and he's not walking further into the woods.

Ryke starts helping clothe me, rapidly, while I descend from a mind-numbing orgasm. Panties first. Then jeans.

"Fuck it." Ryke says midway through, abandoning my boots. He picks me up to save me from the snow, and he cradles me in his arms. Where I've been so many times before.

I couldn't discern Connor's tone of voice. Worried? Panicked? Angry? Elated? It remains to be seen, which is why Ryke *runs* with me.

We break through the tree line to our yard and then just stop. Connor stands right there, poised in an expensive black woolen coat. His gaze sweeps us, landing on my bare feet, and then his blue eyes flit to Ryke.

"Where are your phones?" Connor asks calmly, but I have trouble reading his gaze.

I pat the pockets of my jeans and sweater.

Ryke lets me down and touches his pants.

Nothing.

"Fuck," Ryke curses. Maybe we left them inside or maybe we dropped them somewhere in the woods.

"They might be inside," I tell Connor, my soles freezing. "What happened?"

"The school called Lo since he was your first emergency contact. Sulli needed to be picked up."

"Oh my God." My hand flies to my mouth.

"It's not serious," Connor says. "Lo is already on his way here with her. He called me to find out what happened to you." Connor flips his cellphone in his hand. "I told him you two were most likely fucking in the woods. To no one's surprise, I was right."

Ryke rolls his eyes. "Fuck off, Cobalt." His muscles are flexed, concerned for Sulli.

It's not serious. I hang onto this.

"Not today," Connor replies, tightening his leather glove. "And really, we must stop meeting like this." He heads towards the street.

"Fuck you!" Ryke yells.

Connor raises a hand as he walks away. "In time!" I hear the grin in his voice.

Worried, Ryke and I spend not a second longer outside. We race to our cottage, pressure on my chest.

What happened?

I GENTLY SHUT THE door to Sullivan's bedroom, exiting to the hallway. She sleeps like a brick. I pulled her covers up to her neck, and she never stirred. Apparently this is the fifth time she's fallen asleep in social studies, and after *five* warnings, they sent her home to nap in her own bed.

I feel responsible.

Sulli has a habit of mimicking our random sleep schedules. Some months, I nap more and sleep less straight through, but I always try to clock in at least six hours.

It isn't just fucking you, Calloway. I can almost hear Ryke's response to my thoughts.

He wakes up at the crack of dawn (or earlier), and she'll push herself to be wide-eyed and cheery by then.

What's not up for debate: her bad sleep habits created problems at school. I pull my blonde hair into a high bun as I descend the stairs.

"Connor was right; you two were fucking, weren't you?" I hear Lo from the kitchen.

"Can we decrease the use of that fucking phrase?" Ryke retorts.

"I know. I get hives whenever I talk about you two fucking," Lo banters, knowing full-well Ryke meant the other part. *Connor was right.*

I've heard Ryke say those three words many times before. He might be stressed about Sullivan too, and grumbling about Connor is a good distraction.

"Hey, guys," I greet, slipping into the kitchen. Ryke leans against the sink, arms crossed. I climb up on the countertop nearest him.

"At this…" Lo grabs our bag of Tostito chips, and he yanks open the refrigerator and steals our salsa. "For the trouble."

I watch Lo shuffle out the garage door, and it shuts closed. "You're paying your little brother in chips?"

"It's the only fucking currency he accepts." Ryke spins towards me, his hands on my knees, my legs swinging back and forth.

We're quiet for a long moment, a different quiet than before in the woods. His brown, hazel-flecked eyes search mine, and we both try to process our feelings into words. We're both not terrific at it, but we try.

We try all the time to say what we feel.

"We have to figure something out," I breathe. "She can't keep sleeping in school."

He removes a hand from my knee, just to rake his fingers through his hair. "I don't know how to fucking fix this, Dais." Ryke has *always* struggled telling Sulli no to things she loves.

We fall silent again, thinking. I rest my chin on his shoulder, his hand stays comforting on my head. I suggest, "What if we tell her that she *has* to clock at least seven hours of sleep at night? *Straight sleep.* That way she won't nap."

His brows harden. "What if she fucking doesn't?"

The hard part. "We can't reward her—so if she wakes early, she can't run with you. If she asks for pancakes, you can't make her any."

He grimaces. Ryke has such a soft heart, even the thought of carrying out a punishment pains him, especially when it's directed towards one of his girls.

"She'll fail social studies, Ryke." At least that's what Lo told us. The teacher explained the situation to him when he picked Sulli up. "You've always been a hardass when it comes to everyone's health. Just think that if she keeps going down this path, she could end up like me."

Ryke glowers. "It's not fucking possible, Dais." PTSD was one of the causes of my sleeping problems.

"Just think it," I say, straightening up. "Think that if she doesn't stick to seven straight hours, she might sleepwalk. She might scream with night terrors—think whatever you need to think to enforce this rule."

His muscles strain, but clarity and persistence fills his eyes, the look Ryke wears at the base of thousand-foot rock faces. Assured, he says, "I can fucking do that."

I tug at his shirt. "Hey, one day she'll be ten. Then the next blink of an eye, she'll be twelve. Before you know it, she's sixteen driving that Jeep outside and we're waving her off to go to college." I planned for that to be a funny speech, but I smile tearfully at my husband.

He holds my cheek, the one with the scar. "Today she's nine." His thumb dries my fallen tear. "Live in the fucking moment with me, Calloway?"

My smile stretches.

Every single day, Ryke Meadows.

2028

"I just want everyone to
be okay."

- Maximoff Hale, We Are Calloway

(Season 9 Episode 13 – Fairy Dust & Superpowers)

< 62 >

January 2028
UPPER EAST SIDE PENTHOUSE
New York City

Ryke Meadows

We rented an expensive penthouse for New Year's Eve, not to host a fucking party for anyone but us. The ball dropped about an hour ago. Confetti cakes the ritzy modern furniture and carpet. The walls are mostly glass, a clear view of the city lit up at 1:00 a.m.

Most kids are passed out on the couches, chairs, and Rose starts sweeping some confetti. Lily, Willow, and Daisy attempting to help, but they fling the paper at one another.

Lo, Garrison, Connor, and I find the four littlest girls piled on a beanbag, conked the fuck out. We all quietly and gently pick up our daughters and bring them to bed.

Audrey drools on Connor's shoulder, and he only grins by the fucking fact. Winona is in a dead sleep in my arms. Vada stirs in Garrison's, but he rubs her back and she easily relaxes. And Kinney—she's the only one who really opens her eyes.

She looks up at Lo, and he kisses each of her chubby cheeks. I've never seen my little brother love anything more than he loves his children and his wife.

Kinney rests her head on his chest, hugging him like a fucking stuffed animal.

When I return to the penthouse living room, I try to help clean since we plan to make breakfast tomorrow morning. I grab a trash bag and collect any paper cups and paper plates, pizza crusts left on most.

In the near-empty room, I notice Moffy in a Spider-Man long-sleeved shirt near the window. By himself. Reading on a stiff white chair. I tie the heavy trash bag, my eyes flitting to my twelve-year-old nephew. Lo told me the full extent of his conversation with Moffy at Disneyland.

He said that Moffy thought about dyeing his hair. Thought about wearing higher SPF sunscreen. To look less like me. I'd be fucking lying if I said it didn't hurt. It hurt because I love this kid. I was there when he was fucking born. I babysat him more than I did any other kid in our families.

And my existence in his parent's life caused him pain—*pain* that I'd willingly take away. I wish I could've saved him from that.

"You should talk to him." Lo is by my side, trying to stuff a paper plate into my already tied trash bag.

I'm not fucking good with words. It hasn't stopped me before, but since Disneyland, my relationship with Moffy is different. We don't talk as much. He doesn't ask to run in the morning with me like he used to. When I drive him to swim practice, he mostly makes conversation with Sulli.

"You sure?" I ask Lo.

He nods assuredly. "Who knows, maybe he'll surprise you." Lo gasps with his fingers to his lips, trying to make fun of my wife. It's a fucking poor imitation.

I shove the trash bag to his chest.

"I love you too, big brother."

My lips start lifting at the sight of his smile. Then I leave Lo and cross the living room to Moffy. I sit in an identical chair in front of my nephew, and he looks up from his paperback.

His hair is still dark brown.

His skin isn't as tan, but mostly because he swims indoors in the winter. I travel out of the country, constantly in the sun, so I hold a tan all-year-round.

"Do you want to fucking talk?" I unconsciously crack one of my knuckles.

"What about?" The paperback cover folds closed over his hand, and I go completely still at the sight of the title. At the sight of that book.

Knowing he liked to read, I gifted Moffy *Atlas Shrugged* by Ayn Rand for Christmas. I read that book around his age, so I thought he might enjoy it. I never saw him open the fucking present. I just thought he trashed it.

Off my stunned silence, Moffy says, "I know I've been…distant but…" His gaze drops to the paperback. "My dad said that I can love you and him at the same time, and I want you to know…that I do."

I rub my eyes, tears just sliding.

Moffy wipes his with his forearm. "And…thanks."

"For what?"

His tears fill to the fucking brim. "For taking care of my dad."

I pinch my eyes, nodding repeatedly, unable to fucking speak. *Fuck.* I believed he'd do *everything* to erase me from his life. Lo is his father—in every fucking way. I could never take his spot. I'd never try to. I'd never want to.

I'm just the uncle, and Moffy could've easily cut me out if he fucking desired.

When my hand falls, I nod to my nephew a few more times, peace exchanged between us. "You like the book?"

He sniffs loudly, rubbing his face dry before he talks. "It's cool." He opens it. "I like this line so far…" He passes me the philosophy novel and points.

"If you don't know, the thing to do is not to get scared, but to learn."

Yeah.

I like that fucking one, too.

[farewell]

April 2028
THE COBALT ESTATE
Philadelphia

Rose Cobalt

Connor grins at me from the head of the dining table, his fingers to his conceited lips. I envision his elbow slipping and his face falling into the bowl of mashed potatoes.

Do not smile, Rose. Don't offer him the satisfaction.

Ankles crossed, chin raised, I sit poised at the *other* head of the table. Equal distance. No chair larger than the next.

I inhale the extravagant atmosphere.

Crystal goblets, a roasted goose, two dishes of cranberries, green beans and potatoes rest on an elegant tablecloth, the chandelier twinkling above.

It's not a holiday.

We prepare the same meal every Wednesday night, and most of our children forget to eat by the end of dinner, goose becoming Thursday leftovers.

I return my focus to Connor.

His burgeoning grin tells stories of self-importance and superiority in mind and spirit. It's as attractive as it is obnoxious. "Are you ready, darling?"

"To carve out your heart and stick a knife through the center." I rise to my feet at the exact same time as him. My eyes blaze. I wanted the height advantage for at least a second. "I've been ready my entire life to *defeat* you."

He clasps his goblet of red wine, again at the same moment as me. "I hate to disappoint, but your triumph will come another day."

Translation: *I always win.*

If we were on the same team tonight, I'd say that his win is my win, but we're pitted against one another in an arms race that *I* plan to win.

"Say goodbye to your heart, Richard." I confidently pick up my knife, about to clink my goblet.

"You already have my heart," he says so smoothly. "So your goal is pointless."

"Then I'll take your eyes and your brain and shave your head."

Our seven children burst into applause by pounding the table with fists, some silverware, others with goblets.

The room rumbles to life.

Every dining chair is occupied. The table is so very full.

I almost smile, but as soon as Connor sees the glimmer, he *grins* like he won something already. I raise my hand at his face, and with this, the children settle.

Connor arches a brow. "So you love my sight, my mind, and my hair."

The children roar in delight, pounding the table once more.

"Mother and father look so beautiful," Audrey, just three, nearly *swoons.* Her red hair peeks from beneath a Victorian hat, everyone dressing as extravagantly or as plainly as they prefer. She's also our only child who calls us *mother* and *father*.

I thought it'd remind me of my own mother and I'd bristle at the title, but Audrey speaks with robust sighs. Not stilted or icy like when I mention Samantha Calloway. And I refuse to imagine this table without Audrey—or without any one of our little gremlins.

They've all acquired their own equal, profound, and *endless* place in our hearts.

I lift my chin, not denying my love of Connor's sight, mind and hair. I clink my goblet with my knife. "As with every Wednesday, it is what you make it."

"And someone will win." Connor sips his wine and seizes my gaze.

That someone will be me, Richard. I channel the promise through my glare and then state, "Opening remarks have commenced." Connor and I take our seats.

Eight-year-old Eliot raises his hand before his brothers and sisters. Whoever captures the moment first goes *first*. It's always been this way.

Eliot covets this role nine times out of ten.

Empty pipe in his mouth, his old-fashioned black suit snug and tailor-made, Eliot chooses to sit on the frame of his chair, *shoes* on the cushion.

I hide my smile in a sip of wine, not in the least bit horrified at the dirtied chair. I don't fixate on the little things because I *refuse* to control the setting like my mother tried to control mine.

I let everyone be who they want to be, and I love my children more than a fucking chair.

Eliot stands on the cushion. When he was seven, he fell backwards to the floor. Connor used the moment to remind him that freedom of expression, like most things, comes with consequences.

Now he's found a way not to fall.

His eight-year-old brother Tom—slouched and plainly dressed: black ripped shirt, daggered-heart print—grips the frame of Eliot's ornate wooden chair. All to keep Eliot from tumbling backwards.

Knowing what's to come, my gremlins swiftly grab their goblets. As do we. Just then, Eliot sets his foot on the edge of the table with a loud *thud*. Dishes rattle, and silverware clanks.

Our littlest gremlin is too slow. Audrey's cup quickly tips over as the table shakes. Water soaks the tablecloth.

"Oh no," she sighs, nearest me on her booster seat.

I easily help mop up the spill with my cloth napkin.

Jane, now twelve, leans forward across the table, adorning cat-ears and a sequined sweater and smiling wide at her little sister. "Take note, Audrey, this one likes to step on the table like it's the bow of a ship and that one"—she motions to Tom—"will forever and *always* be his accomplice."

Audrey looks entranced by all of Jane's words. Whether she understands—no one could know. Not even my narcissistic husband. We might have seven children, but babies are still unintelligible little monsters. They absorb what they can, and that's enough for us.

I clasp Audrey's hand in affection, and she places her other tiny palm on top of mine. My iced-over heartstrings tug. She's our last little one. If they slowed down from growing older—for just a second or two, maybe even three—I wouldn't mind.

"Accoomplace?" Audrey tries to pronounce.

"*Accomplice*," Jane says clearly, stroking a purring Lady Macbeth on her lap.

Audrey mouths the word and then nods.

Jane laughs, love flushing her cheeks.

I have to press my lips tight together to smother my smile. Connor is watching *me* out of everything around us. My eyes flit more subtly to him, and then I sip my wine.

Eliot removes his empty pipe, never filled. "Gentlemen. Ladies." He gestures to the entire table. "'This *above all*.'" He pauses dramatically. "'To thine own self be true, and it must follow, as the night the day. Thous canst not then be *false* to any man!'"

After this passionate monologue from Shakespeare's *Hamlet*, he returns to the top frame of his chair, pipe in his mouth.

Dear God.

My smile is betraying me. *Stay poised.* Connor is beyond grinning at this point and we've only just started.

My pride for Eliot arches my shoulders and lifts my head. He has memorized far more than just that scene. No one is allowed books, computers or cellphones at the table.

Connor has told them many times before, *"You bring your minds. That will always be enough."*

Tom raises his hand next. Like Eliot, he stands on the chair, mischief clinging to their vivacious souls. Then he looks over to Eliot and says, "Dear brother."

Eliot grins. "Dear brother."

Tom plops back on the cushion, seated and slouched.

"Was that it?" Audrey gapes, as though he's insane for not occupying more of his time.

During opening remarks, they can bring up *literally* anything they want and for as long as they want, which fascinates Connor more than they even realize. I enjoy learning about their week in open remarks, but not all are willing to share.

Eliot points his pipe towards his sister. "He's a boy of brevity, little Audrey."

Before confusion crosses her face, Connor says to me, "Brevity, darling."

"Shortness," I define.

"Conciseness," he adds.

I burn a hole between his eyes. "My love towards you."

Charlie Keating laughs, ten-years-old, and the most amused when Connor and I argue. I recognize as well as my husband that Charlie is one of the only ones who can mentally keep up. Jane, too. Charlie is also the only one who is consistently kicked back in his chair, polished black loafers *on the table*, dressed in a dapper, modern suit.

Connor called him *ostentatious* the other day. I called our son a smart-ass. We agreed that he's equal parts of both.

Connor swishes his wine, his grin overtaking his whole face as our previous words consume him.

Conciseness.

My love towards you.

Very smoothly, he says, "Rose."

"Richard," I snap.

"I adore when you define a lie."

I scoff. "I was defining *brevity*. Restrain your ego."

"It can't be restrained. If you haven't learned that by now, then maybe you need a new tutor."

"If you suggest *yourself*, I'll carve out more than just your heart."

"I suggest myself," he challenges. "I am the best, and you deserve the best."

I roll my eyes, but I never attempt to actually hurt him and enact my threat, so I'm not surprised he has a rebuttal for it.

"And thank you for defining a hyperbole."

Ben, six-years-old, looks horrified. He stares up and down the table. "Stop," he whines. "Stop it."

I go rigid.

Connor is calm, but his grin fades. Before he explains to Ben that our words are layered with figures of speech, idioms, and hyperbolic prose, Jane leans forward again. She sits on the side with Eliot and Tom, all her other siblings are seated across.

"Pippy," she says. "It's all in good fun. They mean no harm."

"I hate when they fight."

Charlie cuts in, "You only hate it because you can't understand."

Ben gawks. "I understand. Mommy wants to cut out his heart! And Daddy thinks it's funny. It's *not* funny." He rises from the table.

I meet my husband's gaze, and in our eyes, we both tell each other, *wait.*

In the next second, Beckett wraps his arm around Ben's shoulder. At the comforting touch, Ben sinks back in his chair. "They love one another, Ben. If you ever doubt their love, then look at all of us. Look at Wednesdays."

My eyes burn, tears threatening to well.

"They could be *working*," Eliot professes.

"They're here," Tom pipes in.

Wednesdays became their favorite, not for the goose or the grandeur, but because they saw Connor and me at each head of the table. This is the only day of the workweek where we're home together, the only one where our children know for certain we won't be stuck at our offices past a meal.

It's the day where our wit and our words battle for hours on end, and as they've grown older, they've become more and more a part of it all.

Ben looks to me for affirmation.

I sigh, knowing I'll have to *compliment* my husband. I loosen my jaw like it hasn't uttered this phrase in years. "I love..." *You can do this, Rose.*

I am the fucking lioness in a den of little cubs.

I clear my throat, feeling the heat of my husband's arrogant eyes, and I announce, "I love Connor Cobalt."

There, I said it.

Connor raises his goblet to me, his grin more affectionate than conceited. His love stampedes his narcissism so much that my claws recede.

Charlie cocks his head to Ben. "*Connor Cobalt* is Dad, in case you've fallen further behind."

"I know that's Daddy." Ben huffs.

I snap my fingers. "Moving along with opening remarks." Five children still need to speak up, even if they only want to say *no*. That's fine with us.

Charlie lifts his pointer finger in the air. "I invoke my right to pass."

Audrey gasps. "Why, Charlie?"

Beckett smiles up towards the chandelier. "It's like asking why the contrarian wears a suit and tie to a pool party." He didn't pick the example out of thin air. Charlie *actually* wore his most expensive suit to a neighborhood pool party.

Then he left after five minutes.

Audrey's hand shoots into the air.

"Audrey," Connor calls on our youngest with a broadening smile.

Our youngest child opens her mouth to speak, but with every eye on her, she forgets her words. "...I..."

We all wait patiently.

"You?" I try to help her without making her feel inadequate.

"I am..." Her cheeks suddenly flush, and she plops back to her bottom, clutching tight to her Victorian hat.

The three oldest children drum the table for Audrey.

"Such wise words. *I am*," Jane tells Audrey.

Audrey perks up. "Thank you, Jane."

I try to drink my wine to hide a smile, but Connor sees. *Defeat thy husband.* I can make him *ache* just as much as he can revel in my smile. I collect my hair on one shoulder and tilt my head, bare neck in his direct view. He rubs his lips and then drops his hand to his goblet.

You can't have this. I channel through my eyes.

We'll see, he replies back.

I take another sip of wine, just as Beckett raises his hand.

He confesses, "I Google-searched my name."

I choke on my wine.

"Careful, darling," Connor says.

I give him a look before planting my fiery eyes on Beckett. "In this entire ugly world, what compelled you to do such a thing?"

Connor and I have sat side-by-side in bed and Google-searched *all* of their names. If there are any particularly defaming articles that we think lawyers will squash, we unleash the hounds upon the unethical journalists. So for Beckett, I know what would've cropped up in his search.

All the stereotypes related to boys in ballet.

Beckett explains, "At school, Geoffrey Stanford showed me in computer class."

Charlie shakes his head at his brother. "Geoffrey Google-searched your name. Not *you*." It upsets Charlie when Beckett confesses to actions that aren't his own.

My warrior side flares, just to protect them in whatever shape they need, piercing eyes darting to each of my boys.

"I still saw," Beckett tells his twin brother.

"Geoffrey is an idiot along with the rest of the world." He pauses. "Except you." He *only* tells this to Beckett.

"Beckett." Connor's even-tempered voice catches everyone's attention. "We're all labeled. Every day we step outside, we're stereotyped. You let that affect you—"

"You let them win," Charlie finishes.

My chin rises once more. Beckett sees me, and his intensified confidence permeates like a spritz of perfume. He nods, assured.

"Anything else?" I ask him.

"That's all I needed."

Lady Macbeth springs off Jane's lap. "Would you prefer to go next or last, Pippy?" Jane asks Ben, both the only two left for opening remarks.

"Last." Ben eyes the mashed potatoes. He breaks tradition and scoops them on his plate before opening remarks have concluded.

No one chastises him, but Charlie cocks his head again to his little brother. I point my knife at Charlie. "Holster *this*," I say icily. By *this*, I mean any smartass remarks he thinks to fling at his little brother.

Charlie wears entertainment and pretentiousness like they exist in his marrow and bone. He nods like *so I will, but only for you, Mom.*

Jane raises her hand while standing. "Well then…" Her glittering blue eyes sweep her siblings and us. "I've chosen to pursue a love."

Audrey gasps. "Jane is in love!"

"Yes, Audrey, I'm in *so much* indisputable love."

I observe my husband, his fingers to his lips. Since we're in the introduction of a battle, I'd hope he'd crumble at this new discussion, but he remains unperturbed.

Connor arches a brow at me.

I narrow my eyes, just as Eliot asks, "Have we met your love?"

"Because if we haven't," Tom says, "I believe we should." Their loyalty to one another curves my mouth. Her brothers believe her love is a *someone*, but Jane has confided in me. I know her love is a *thing*. I also know that she's searching for romance as hard as someone searches for their own foot.

"You've met my love many times before."

Beckett questions, "Is love a person?"

"No," Charlie answers before Jane can. "Her love is common." He's being factual. I know *what* her love is just like Connor and Charlie, but she hasn't shared her future plans with us until now.

"Very common," Jane agrees. "We use it constantly without realizing."

Ben and Audrey's faces scrunch at the riddle.

"Are you terribly confused?" Jane asks them, and when they both nod, she explains, "*Numbers* are very common. We use *numbers* daily, sometimes subconsciously."

"Sub...what?" Audrey frowns.

Connor clarifies, "*Subconsciously*. Unknowingly."

"Unaware," I add.

"Your mother's love for me." Connor grins into his swig of wine.

I snort at that *inaccuracy*. Connor is the one who never acknowledged love. That he could love, that he did love, that it was *all* inside of him. If anything, *he* was unaware.

I always knew.

"So your love is numbers?" Eliot asks.

"Her love is *math*," Charlie is the one to answer fully.

"Precisely." Jane smiles. "I've signed up for competitions next school year. I'm joining *mathletes*."

Her siblings clank dishes, goblets, and Tom drums the table.

I have my hand to my chest like I can't breathe. Obviously I'm breathing. I'm alive, but this is the first time Jane has professed a dream, a goal—a passion in life. Even if it lasts a year or only two, I plan to encourage her any way I can.

Even if her aspirations consist of things I love and hate.

Academically competitive worlds? *I love.* Not just because I met Connor there. I loved competing and learning long before him.

Math? *I loathe.*

I will be at every motherfucking competition. Come hell or high water.

Before she sits, Jane looks to her father and then to me, and we both express our pride through our eyes. We ask questions that she answers with delight.

Do you have to tryout? Yes.

How many people per team? Unsure at the moment.

When she takes a seat, smiling more than I do annually, everyone's focus plants on the littlest boy, his mouth full of mashed potatoes.

"Your turn, Pippy."

Ben swigs his water and then stands. "I think we should start planting trees for every *tree* a human touches." We let him talk out his proposal, but Connor rubs his lips the longer Ben believes his fantasy is real. "We'll put them all in our backyard, and we'll invite people over to look. They can't touch or else they'll *kill* the trees. Trees help the planet, so it's important."

Charlie says first, "You believe a billion trees can be planted in our backyard."

"Why not?" Ben shrugs.

His father explains, "It's idealistic."

I quickly add, "Which is *not* a failing."

Connor swishes his wine. "In certain situations, idealism can be a failing."

"So can *narcissism*."

The children clank their dishware and pound the table at my rebuttal.

Connor raises his glass to me, as though conceding, but I know my husband. He never surrenders this easily. "The accuracy of your second statement doesn't eliminate the inaccuracy of your first."

Our children drum their feet with laughter.

I will burn you, Richard.

Eliot takes out his pipe. "Isn't idealistic another word for naïve?"

"Yes." Connor sips his wine.

Ben crosses his twiggy arms "I know trees and what they mean. It's important."

I catch his gaze. "What's important to you is important to me, my gremlin."

"We don't doubt your love for trees," Connor tells his son truthfully.

This appeases Ben for the moment, but he sinks to his chair, deep in thought. Connor studies him for an extra moment or two. Ben is our only child who believes he can soar to the moon via a tomato soup can. The only child who mentions freeing dolphins by parachute and plane.

In a household full of critical thinkers, he's an outlier—a little lamb in our den of lion cubs. We protect him and nurture him and *never* wish to change him, but sometimes lions bite harder than they intend.

I rise with my goblet—Connor step-for-fucking-step. My growl scratches my throat but never escapes my lips.

I read his amused gaze: *are you ready to be defeated, darling?*

Prepare yourself, Richard.

I speak. "This concludes opening remarks. Now the game truly begins." I clink the crystal with my knife. Our children dig into cranberries and green beans, plating food, but besides Ben, they hardly eat more than a bite or two.

We sit.

Eliot beats everyone to ask the first question, "What is Mozart's opera called, 'The Magic ... what?'"

"Flute," Connor says, just as the answer lands on the tip of my tongue.

"One point to Dad." Jane always keeps score with a notebook. We play a variation of the same game we created at Model UN.

The day we met each other for the first time.

This nostalgic fact passes between Connor and me, intimate and warm amid cold thoughts of defeat and losses.

"What is the Roman numeral for one-hundred-and-fifteen?" Jane asks.

I know these letters, in the very least. "CXV," I say, right as Connor begins. I stake a slice of goose and scrape it on my plate. The *screech* of metal knife on knife sounds violent. I eye him the whole time, aiming the noise towards Connor.

He replenishes his wine.

We could throw out questions, but it'd mean that we'd lose the chance to gain a point. We're too competitive, even amid our children. The rules of the game: anyone can ask a question, from any category, but they must provide it without reference material.

First to answer receives a point.

We never sit out. We never let our children win because they're children. Maybe one day they will beat us, but for now, the battle is Connor versus me. They like to see if they can stump *both* of us with questions they've memorized before dinner.

Which is why the next set of questions comes in a quick flurry, and I clip the start of Connor's answers as fast as he clips the start of mine.

"Mom and Dad are tied," Jane announces thirty minutes through dinner. "Twenty-two points to you both. Charlie has three points."

"Who was the captain of the Titanic?" Beckett asks, feeding me a question he knows that I know.

Connor senses this, but I've already answered, "Edward John Smith."

"Using your resources, darling?" Connor asks me. "Or are you cheating?"

I flame at that *fighting* word. "I never cheat." I didn't ask Beckett to join my team, but clearly he prefers Team Rose in this instance—and I would *never* kick a little gremlin off my side. I have enough room on my bench for them all.

There's even enough room for Connor.

We play for another ten minutes, our children asking questions in the subjects they enjoy: math, science, dance, drama, music, the world and love. Once again, we're tied.

Connor stands, as though expecting the incoming end. I follow suit, tall in my heels, our table full of lively children that may physically separate us, but our minds touch and intertwine, as close as can be. Closer than if we threw the table aside.

I have everything I've desired. I have him. I have them. This dining room breathes *life* the way that I only imagined.

What else left is there to say and do?

I'm already triumphant. I'm already proud of him, of them and of me.

Connor stares intently, longingly, seeing and hearing every victorious thought that roars inside of me. His deep blues thunder with unyielding promises and affections and that conceited, burgeoning grin.

And deeply, he says, "Here's a secret, darling."

I listen, poised for anything with him.

"I've always loved winning, but I would lengthen the time it takes us to reach the end, just to spend one more second with you."

[farewell]

April 2028
THE COBALT ESTATE
Philadelphia

Connor Cobalt

There are many truths in life, but as I stand opposite Rose across a table with our many beautiful children, I wield one that I condemned for years on end.

I'm in love.

With so much *more* than just myself.

This truth will never fracture.

Not even when our youngest son stands from the table. Our children believe Ben is about to ask a question. I don't subscribe to this belief. Neither does Rose, her pierced, sentimental eyes leaving me and rooting on our six-year-old.

Ben has been distant the last twenty minutes, his gaze continuously traveling to the door. I'm not surprised that he's about to digress, but I am truly surprised by his statement.

"I'm running away."

Rose inhales, her collarbones jutting, and questions wring her gaze. Similar ones try to cross my gaze.

I let them. I let Ben see. "Why?" I ask.

"I don't want to say why."

Rose and I desert our places at the head of the table, a rarity. We near our son as he pushes in his empty chair and tugs down his aquamarine shirt that says *Plants are Cool.*

I sidle beside Rose. My hand slips into hers, and I thread our fingers. My tranquil, languid water next to her raging, ardent fire. We don't block his exit. Whether it's illusion or reality, he has the ability to leave if he wants to leave.

He has feet. He has a brain. He can walk out the door and leave us behind—and *no*, I would not want my son to run away. At the mere thought, I have a heart that might be breaking.

I have a mind that might be splitting.

Before we handle this situation, Charlie interjects, "He's not serious."

Ben's face grows red with hurt, *ire*, and frustrations, and I know— immediately I understand my son.

I sense a similar acknowledgement pass through Rose. We stand directly on the same page of the same story in the same book.

I ask Ben, "Would you like us to help you pack?"

His mouth opens, surprised.

"It is what you want, isn't it?"

Ben hesitates and then nods.

Stilted but fiery, Rose tells him, "You *can't* forget your toothbrush. I don't care if you refuse to brush, but at least pack it in your bag. Do I need to make you a list?"

Ben thinks harder. "…I'd like a list but with pictures."

"Then pictures it will be," Rose says so affectionately that she might as well be hugging our son.

"Would you like a map?" I question. "What else do you need from us?" *We would give you the world if we could.*

"I have a map. I drew one yesterday, and I'm walking, so I don't need much."

Eliot and Tom snicker, not meaning to be cruel, but by laughing they unknowingly disregard his opinions.

Ben rotates to his brother that teeters on the frame of a chair and the other who slouches beside him. "I'm *serious!!*" he yells from his core, his neck beet-red. "I'm leaving! I'm leaving and *never* coming back!!"

Their faces fall. Understanding in this moment the true meaning and gravity of his words. It does not matter whether he *can* leave. It matters that he *feels* like he should.

"Pippy?" Jane calls out.

"Ben?" Eliot and Tom say together.

When Ben crosses his thin arms and turns his back to the table, our children fall into hushed whispers.

Rose and I guide our son towards a teacart, close to the door. He breathes heavily, frustrated tears welling. We crouch to his height. Rose dabs his cheeks with a clean cloth napkin. I whisper a few soothing sentiments in French while he catches his breath.

Ben wants to be heard.

We hear him and listen to him every day. He may believe tonight we've shot down his ideas, but I'm not drowning each one. I'm challenging them, and he has every right to stand by his convictions. However outlandish and fantastical they may be. Rose and I would still be here, with him, no matter what he thought in the way that he thought.

I take his opinions seriously, even if they're grounded in fantasy. I never call them *nonsense.* I never label him as absurd. He's my *idealistic* son that dreams in undiscovered colors.

That is fact.

He sniffs, cheeks dried and breathing more at ease.

And I tell him, "If your motive is to truly leave, we'll help you."

Rose combats tears as she says, "Our hearts would break *every* step of the way, but we'd help you."

Ben rubs at his watery eyes, dismayed.

"You have choices," I say gently. "You will always have choices. We respect yours, and it will pain us to watch you leave. We would let you go because that's *your* desire. Is that what you truly want?"

There's a fear that he will say *yes*. I can tell myself that realistically and logically he will never run away, but walking through the illusion will be excruciating. I can't separate the sentiments, and I don't try to convince myself that I can.

I know that I can't. He's *my* son.

He's a piece of this family.

He's not expendable.

And we'll go as far as packing his bags. We'll watch him roll his suitcase down the stairs, down the street. We will pretend our son has left us until he recognizes his ideas live in neon castles and clouds.

If he didn't reach that point before he reached the neighborhood gate, we wouldn't let him leave. We'll play into desires for as long as we can, but we'll *never* risk his safety.

All so he feels heard. So he feels understood. We'd do this out of love.

Ben wavers, face splotched red.

"What is it?" I whisper.

His head hangs. "I don't fit in here."

With hot passion, Rose says, "*Yes*, you do. Ben Pirrip Cobalt—you fit in at the table. You fit in my heart." She clutches his hands and tears drip down his cheeks with an entirely new sentiment. "You fit in this *family*. I promise you my skin and bones, you do."

Ben rubs his nose with the back of his hand.

I awaken at her fervor, choked with *real* emotion.

My throat is closed. I wait a second to process, and then with these feelings trembling beneath, I tell my son, "You're *necessary* in our lives."

Ben takes a short breath.

"I love you," I say without a shadow of a doubt. "We all love you. For your differences, for your similarities, for who you are."

"We, too, brother," Eliot says, drawing our attention to the table. Rose and I straighten to a stance, and Ben slips around our legs to see what we see.

All of our children rise. Not only to their feet. They rise to the table, pushing dishes aside, goblets tipping over, but their eyes are only on Ben. Staring down at him, as though he is the only one who matters. He matters above a dish. Above a chair. Above a glass, above themselves.

Charlie is the one who extends his hand. "We, too, love you, Ben."

Rose is a fortress of love and loyalty, her yellow-green eyes glassed at the sight of our future that's no longer *future*.

It is present moment.

And we are living inside of it.

I clasp her hand. My heart—a heart that cared for logic and practicalities and selfish pursuits—that heart is on fire.

Ben takes his brother's hand, and Charlie helps him stand on the table. Every child meets our eyes, smiling as though they've obtained knowledge and secrets of the world.

Each individually unique.

Each with a mind of their own.

Each proud and in love with who they are.

I expected no less.

Jane looks between Rose and me, and very strongly, she says, "Ensemble."

"Ensemble," our children then exclaim at once.

My lips pull upward into a blinding grin. Rose is moved, fingers to her own lips, and her fiery yellow-green eyes meet my calm deep blue. I skim the base of her neck with my hand.

We draw our gazes to our children. Fire and water upon them. We tell all seven the one word that has breathed inside of us from the moment we met.

We say, "Ensemble."

Together.

‹ so long ›

April 2028
Zoo
Utah

Daisy Meadows

For many, *many* years, we've strayed from any and all zoos. The one time we did visit, way before we had Sulli, the experience ended with crowds pressed up against us. Snapping photos, yelling our names. We never considered putting our girls through that mayhem.

Not even as Winona begged for the past year. "Let's see all the elephants and the turtles and the zebras and the unicorns!"

"Fucking unicorns," Ryke muttered, shadow of a smile peeking.

I explained that unicorns live in majestic meadows off in majestic lands, not zoos.

"Let's take a boat there!" Winona exclaimed.

We have not taken a boat to a majestic land with majestic meadows, but we finally planned a trip with a zoo pit stop. Only because this particular zoo let us slip inside on a *closed for employees only* day. No crowds. Not many people. Just some zoo attendants, animals, and us.

"Let me know if you want anything, I'll open the register," Bethany, our really nice zoo guide tells us. She first leads us into the gift store, saving the exhibits for later.

As our kids enter ahead of us, I come up behind Ryke, hugging him around the waist. I playfully try to ground his stride, but he easily walks forward, just with me in tow. I catch him eyeing my flower crown, and I playfully bite his arm.

Then our energetic four-year-old *giraffe* races into the depths of the store. Hopping up and down like this is heaven on earth. She lands at the towering wall of stuffed animals. Winona Briar Meadows is a giraffe, not just in spirit but in costume. I helped her put on an orange and white giraffe onesie this morning, hood concealing her messy brown hair.

Our ten-year-old daughter darts in the opposite direction, towards a bucket of silver pendants and rope jewelry.

I gasp. "Our brood has separated. Where will we go? What will we do?"

Ryke ruffles my blonde hair, my flower crown at a tilt. Then he faces me while I rock on the heels of my feet, my palms on his firm chest, lean muscle beneath his gray shirt. I'd steal his green baseball hat off his head, but flower crowns it is today.

Sulli wears an identical one, and she asked if I would wear mine with her.

My wolf stares down at me, his brown eyes flitting to my yellow shirt every few minutes. It says *here comes the sun*.

Ryke tells me, "Wherever you go, I'll go."

I smile tenfold and place my hands on his unshaven jaw, rough beneath my palms. I just stay here, liking how I'm in direct line with someone mighty and strong, daring and dangerous, and most of all— *kind* and *caring*.

Is there anyone in this world who cares more about me than this man? Has there ever been someone out there who loves me so *entirely* other than him?

I don't think there is. I don't think there could be.

Ryke doesn't wait any longer.

He kisses me, holding the back of my head, deepening our natural embrace. My smile grows beneath his lips.

"Daddy! I need help!"

"Mom, can you come here?"

We break apart, and he kisses my cheek before we physically separate.

"Looks like I'm going this way and you're going that way." I walk backwards towards the jewelry where Sulli digs into a clear bucket.

"Don't get into too much fucking trouble, sweetheart." He scans me once before setting his gaze on Winona, who jumps repeatedly. Trying to reach the highest shelf of dolphin, sea turtle, and penguin stuffed animals.

We never really tire from Winona's bounciness, her crazed energy in good company with the rest of ours. I slip next to Sulli and hip-bump her.

She hip-bumps back and shows me the rope necklaces she picked out. "Can I get these?"

Each has one silver animal pendant: bird, dolphin, wolf, and otter. I smile at her choices, knowing which one represents us. I'm the bird. She's the dolphin. Ryke is the wolf. Winona is the otter. "Definitely."

"I want to keep the wolf, then give you the dolphin, Dad the otter, and Nona the bird."

Sulli always thinks about us, and I was never really anyone's *number one* growing up. I was the *number two* or *number three* sister. Sometimes even *number four*. Ryke and I are number ones to our girls, and it's an insane feeling.

I just want to make sure that she *always* thinks about herself too. "You don't have to share if you don't want to."

Sulli adjusts *my* off-kilter flower crown with a smile and says, "I really, *really* want to, Mom."

"Then I'm totally wearing mine out." I wag my brows like this is an A+ daring act, even though it's so normal.

"Higher!" Winona's laughter lights her voice. The little giraffe sits atop Ryke's shoulders, already in line with the tallest shelf.

"You want to hit your head on the fucking ceiling?"

"Yeah!"

Ryke has his hand on her ankle. "Not fucking happening, sweetie."

"Watcha looking at, squirt?" Sulli skips over to her little sister.

"The sea turtles!"

Sulli glances over her shoulder at me, waiting for me to catch up, but my phone rings in my pocket with a familiar tone. I wave my cell at my daughter, and she nods, darting straight to Ryke and Winona.

I rest my arm on the checkout counter, our zoo guide Bethany texting by the rack of key chains, but I don't worry whether she's in earshot.

Phone to my ear. "Hey there."

"Okay, hey, so I'm at the store," Willow whispers like she is sneaking down aisles unseen. "And wait, we're still on for breakfast when you get back?"

"Totally, it's been too long." I haven't seen my best friend in an entire week, which seems short, but when she's in Philly, we usually drop by and see one another every other day. The biggest sadness of the summer: when Willow leaves for London with Garrison and Vada, their daughter who'll turn four soon. It's the longest span of time they're not around any of us.

"Agreed..." Willow trails off, making a thinking noise like *uhhh*. "I forgot why I called...hold on a sec."

I smile and push dolphin magnets around a display. "I'm sending you all the remembrance vibes."

"Got it."

I mock gasp. "Lily was right. I *do* have powers."

Willow laughs. "If it were up to Lily, we all would."

I smile wider at that truth. Absentmindedly, I thumb a silver ring on my finger, a square etched in the center. I haven't taken it off since the day Willow gave me hers, and she's never removed her matching one.

Quietly, Willow asks, "Winona hates banana muffins or blueberry pancakes? Vada said the blueberries, but Garrison is pretty sure it's the banana muffins."

Vada and Winona are best friends, along with Audrey and Kinney, so if one girl has a play date, chances are all four will be there.

"She hates blueberries," I say. "Sulli doesn't like banana muffins, but only when people put nuts in them." Sullivan is still the pickiest eater around, but she makes do.

"…awesome, okay, I'm about to make my way to the pancake aisle. No blueberries. Tell Ryke I said hi. See you when you get back."

When we hang up, I remember all my theories about friendships. Somehow, someway—I managed to keep this special one close, despite distance and years of time.

This one survived.

"LOOK, WINONA." I POINT towards the giraffe habitat as we approach the wooden fence. With each step, I try to tie the rope necklace around Ryke's wrist. It's too small to fit anywhere else for him, mine is more like a choker.

Winona sprints elatedly to the fence, her hood falling backwards. Sulli jogs after her sister.

Ryke uses his teeth to loosen the knot on the bracelet, finally secure and not too tight. He has the bag of stuffed animals crammed in his backpack. Simon the sea turtle for Winona and then she picked out three others for her best friends and a dolphin for Sulli.

I've never been to the zoo without crowds. Without so much congestion and *people*. The pavement is barren of bodies, the exhibits more visible from farther away. It's not this sight that swells inside of me.

It's the sound.

Birds chirping, lions roaring. Hooves and paws pounding the earth. The human noises we make never overpower the song of nature, and I could shut my eyes and just listen all day.

I catch Ryke staring down at me for an extended moment. "What?"

"You look really fucking happy." His eyes nearly glass.

"I really am." I can say it with certainty. With utmost ease. I'm almost so happy I could scream. I playfully bite his arm, and he kisses the top of my head.

When we reach Winona and Sulli at the fence, our teeny tiny giraffe tries to climb *up* and *over* the fence and into the habitat.

Ryke pries her off and sets her on her feet. "That's fucking dangerous."

Winona gapes. "But…but how do we see the animals?"

Sulli makes a wincing noise. "This is about to go pretty bad," she whispers to me before hopping up on the bench. She sits on top and absorbs the peaceful surroundings—while Winona swings her head from side to side like we've brought her to the wrong place.

I wondered if she understood what a *zoo* was, but I just didn't think it needed an explanation other than *it's where you see all the animals.*

Ryke glances over his shoulder at me. I know that look. It's the one that says, *I can't think of the right fucking words. I need you, Dais.*

I've never been needed, not before Ryke either. I've never been wanted or *truly* loved in the way that I know I deserve to be loved.

I'm quick.

Next to Ryke, I bend down to Winona's height. "You see the animals right there." I point through the slats of the wooden fence. Two giraffes amble across dry bush and sandy dirt.

Winona clutches the rungs and sticks her head through.

Metal fence also separates wildlife from us, and every ounce of excitement she had starts plummeting like an anchor sinking in an ocean.

I look up at Ryke as he runs his hand through his thick hair, putting his baseball cap back on. He outstretches an arm. "We should've taken her to a fucking petting zoo."

"I don't know…" I'm not sure it's just about Winona wanting to *touch* the animals.

Ryke squats beside me, his hand hovering on Winona's back in case she decides to fit her body through the fence. She's completely silent, not facing us.

With Ryke really close, I whisper, "She never mentioned touching animals, just *seeing* them."

"Maybe she was fucking confused."

It's possible. I rest my cheek on his arm while we wait for her to turn around. "Guess what?"

"What?"

"We made a baby giraffe."

The start of his smile slowly dies as Winona finally spins. Tears drip down her soft cheeks and slide along her delicate nose.

My lungs bind. Whenever one of our girls cries, Ryke's muscles tense, his brows scrunch, and he edges an inch closer as though to say *I'm fucking here for you.*

"Shh, it's okay." I wipe her tears with the corner of my shirt.

"How do the giraffes leave?" Winona asks tearfully. I watch Ryke watch me for a moment, both of us understanding why she's upset. The fences. The exhibits. Not because they keep her out, but because they keep the animals *in*.

Ryke shakes his head at our daughter. "They don't want to fucking leave."

"But what if they do? What if they want to roam the *whole wide world* but they're stuck?"

"What if they're all happy and they *never* want to leave?" I ask Winona.

"But they're not free!" she sobs, voice cracking.

I instantly pull Winona to my chest, and she wraps her arms around me. I lift her up and stand at the same moment as Ryke. I whisper in Winona's ear, "There are *millions* of animals all over this great big world, and the ones in the zoo are loved by people. These people even rescue them, nurture them, and *protect* them. This may be their home for now or for later, but they're safe here."

Winona sniffs. "They're safe?"

"Very, *very* safe."

Winona nods, still tearful, but she stares out at the scenery more like Sulli did. Ryke distracts Winona by taking out her stuffed sea turtle.

She hugs Simon like she's protecting him from the zoo's fences.

Sulli hops off the bench. "Can we see the monkeys before we leave?"

"Sure thing," I say.

Bethany left us with a map, so we find our way around the zoo alone. It's easier for Ryke to carry Winona, so he props her on his side with only one hand. She rests her cheek on his arm, a little mopey and downtrodden.

In time, she'll feel better, so we don't push and prod and try to yank a smile out of Winona. I walk backwards with Sulli, our smiles rising, and Ryke directs us which way to go.

"Fucking right," he says.

"Not fucking left?" I tease—then I accidentally trip over my own feet.

Ryke catches my wrist, keeping me upright, and his brows rise as my smile appears.

"So you didn't say *fucking down* then?"

Ryke eats me alive with his gaze.

"You're in L-O-V-E," Sulli singsongs, still walking backwards, the monkey and ape exhibits in sight.

His arm slides across my shoulders, and I clutch his hand that drapes down. "Did you hear, we're in L-O-V-E?" I ask him. "What will my husband say?"

Ryke almost smiles. "That he's in fucking L-O-V-E with you too."

"My husband would've said it just like that."

He pushes my cheek lightly with the same hand that I hold.

Sulli rotates as we reach the noisy monkey and ape habitats. Trees rustle, dark green foliage cascading. We all stand by the glass, silent as we watch. Ryke lets Winona down, and she puts her nose up close, fingertips against the window.

"Look." Sulli points to four chimpanzees swinging from branch-to-branch, squeaking to one another. "It's us."

We all laugh together, and mine transforms into an overwhelmed smile. I look to Ryke, but I can't do anything but nod at him—you know those moments where you're just *so* full you can barely breathe? So full of feelings you only hope to meet.

They crash against me like freefalling. Like cliff diving and bungee jumping. Like screaming at the top of my lungs. Like *one-hundred-and-fifty* miles per hour.

All with Ryke Meadows.

He holds my cheeks with both large, rough hands, and I reach up and hold his with my small, soft.

Ryke laughs into his own beautiful smile, and he says, "This is our fucking life, Calloway."

Every *moment* is wild, even the quiet ones.

< so long >

April 2028
Zoo
Utah

Ryke Meadows

In another fucking lifetime, in another world, Daisy is alone.

I'm alone.

We have no girls, no fucking kids to call our own—and it's just not what's here today. It's not what I feel when I wake up in the morning. It's not what I feel when I go to fucking bed.

I'm not alone.

I have a fucking family.

Daisy radiates beneath my hands, holding her face like she holds mine. And I kiss the most beautiful fucking thing on this Earth. Her smile pulls one from me, from the dark, lonely crevices.

Winona gags, and our eyes open on her—just as she says, "Old people kissing are *so gross.*"

Sulli smiles, but she's busy clucking her tongue at the four chimpanzees.

I rest my arm on Daisy's head while she nuzzles against my ribs like a fucking bear. "You think we're fucking old?"

"So old," Winona says, her stink-face ending with a smile. I'm glad she's not as fucking sad.

"How old?" Daisy asks while I slip my hand up the back of her shirt. Winona kicks a twig. "Eighty-four." That's incredibly fucking wrong.

Daisy looks up, and very quietly, only audible to me, she says, "You've been fucking an eighty-four-year-old. How does that feel?"

"Feels like we're finally the same fucking age."

Daisy laughs a full-bellied laugh. "Touché."

We spend the next thirty minutes hanging around the monkey exhibit. Winona plops down by the glass and captures the fucking attention of an orangutan. "He's orange like me!" Winona exclaims before watching intently as the animal inspects her from afar.

The orangutan might be fucking confused by her giraffe onesie. While our girls do their own thing with the animals, I film them with our video camera—and I fucking flirt with my wife.

In the last ten minutes, we watch Sulli who has grown *really* fucking quiet, no longer clucking or whistling. She searches left and right and scratches at her neck. Then she finds a bench nearby the *staff exit* and takes a seat, pulling her legs up to her chest.

I turn the video camera off and stuff it into my backpack. "Let's fucking ask," I tell Dais.

She nods, her flower crown halfway off her head after I messed her hair. I catch her wrist before she rushes ahead, and I situate the crown on the fucking *top* of her head while we approach our daughter together.

"Sullivan?" Daisy slides next to our daughter on the bench. Sulli rests her forehead on her knees, and Daisy rubs her back, searching Sulli as fucking quickly as I do.

I take my baseball hat off and run a hand through my hair—*fuck.*

I know this position. I've seen Daisy in it more than enough times. I put my hat back on. It's not *casual* legs-to-chest—it's a fucking *pained*, upright fetal position.

Sulli mumbles something.

"We can't fucking hear, sweetie." I stay standing above them, and Winona starts hopping over to us. She hangs onto the armrest of the bench, peering up at Sullivan.

"Sulli?" Winona whispers.

Sullivan lifts her head, fucking *pale*. I put my hand on her forehead while she mumbles out, "My stomach hurts."

She's not warm.

"How about we go to the bathroom?" Daisy says. "Maybe it was the extra whipped cream on your pancakes."

"But Sulli always eats extra whipped cream," Winona says, open-mouthed in confusion. Then in a quick fucking flash, she crawls beneath the bench and out the other side, racing to our backpack.

"Winona!" I yell. *Fucking A.* "Don't go any fucking farther than that backpack!" When it comes to their safety, I'm a bigger hardass. To this day, we've never let them do anything dangerous that I didn't do at their fucking age.

She screeches to a halt and waits there.

Daisy helps Sulli stand, our daughter nearly doubled-over.

I shake my head, thinking this is more than a stomachache. *Her fucking appendix.* "Sul, do you want me to fucking carry you?"

"No," she sighs like *Dad* but winces again. "I'm ten…I'm not a baby anymore."

She fucking reminds me at least once a week. We regroup and locate a bathroom about two minutes back. In agonized determination, Sulli walks to the bathroom on her own, Daisy rubbing her back all the way. Winona holds my pinky finger while she hops.

I must only wear dark fucking concern because Winona asks, "Is Sulli okay?"

"Yeah." I nod a few times, but the truth is, *I don't fucking know.*

We reach the bathrooms, and Daisy tries to open the women's door. She jiggles the *locked* knob. Fucking really? I try the men's door.

"It's open."

Besides employees, the zoo is still fucking empty and so is the men's bathroom. Four urinals and only two stalls. Sulli quickly slips into one, and I keep an eye on Winona who drifts from my side.

"Why are there strange looking water fountains?" Winona asks, hopping over to the urinals. I fucking scoop her up in my arms.

"Those are fucking urinals." I flip her upside-down, hanging my daughter by the feet.

She shrieks in laughter, and I concentrate partially on Daisy, who asks Sulli if everything's okay through the stall. Dais glances back to me, worried.

Really fucking worried.

I upright Winona in my arms, and she spits hair from her mouth. I keep her close, supporting her against my chest with only one hand.

"Mom, can you come here?" Sulli asks, fear pitching her voice.

I want to fucking go, to *help*, but she asked for her mom, so I wait. Daisy disappears inside, and Winona grows quiet, blinking at the blue stall.

She whispers up to me, "I don't think Sulli's okay, Daddy."

Fuck this. I near the stall and knock. "What the fuck's going on?" I need to know if I should call 9-1-1 or if it's mild like puke.

"It's okay," Daisy calls out to me. "We'll be out in a second." She sounds hurried, and I might be fucking pushy, but I don't push here.

Winona has other thoughts. Before it registers *what* she's doing, she's already boosted herself in my arms and tries to peer over the stall. She inhales. "Is that blood?"

"Nona!" Sulli yells like *shut the fuck up.*

I go rigid. It all makes fucking sense. Why I thought the position was so familiar—and maybe I knew. Maybe I just didn't want to think that today of all fucking days, she'd go through this. Because she's *really* young.

"Did she fucking start her period?" I ask bluntly.

None of us are abashed. We're open. We curse. Winona will fart on fucking cue if you ask. We gave Sulli a sex talk without batting an eye. This shouldn't be any fucking different, right?

The door swings open, and I back up so they can exit. Sulli is first, sighing heavily. "This sucks." She washes her hands in the sink. "You're so lucky you've never had to deal with this, Dad."

She started her period.

Daisy slips beside me. "We need to make a drugstore run."

"She's only fucking ten," I whisper to Dais, shaking my head repeatedly.

"Some girls start early."

It's what rings in my fucking ears while we exit the zoo. While I drive our green Jeep to a tiny hole-in-the-wall drugstore, the closest nearby. Sulli unpacks a change of shorts and underwear from her luggage with Daisy's help, and Winona, buckled in her booster seat, plays with Nutty.

We've been on a fucking road trip, all four of us, plus our husky. And Price, who follows the Jeep on a motorcycle. Sulli needed to take off school for a swim competition, so we just extended that time by an extra two days and took off out west.

Minutes later, Winona and I peruse the drugstore aisles while Daisy and Sulli are in the bathroom. Winona carries our shopping basket, and I have pads in my hand, only putting light fucking things in her basket—like a bottle of pain meds.

I pick out about five or six fucking chocolate bars and toss them in.

"Do girls on periods like chocolate?" Winona asks.

"Period or no period—girls like fucking chocolate."

Winona shoves three bags of chocolate kisses into the basket, and I catch the fucking handle, just as it weighs her down. I hear the *creak* of the bathroom door, Sulli and Daisy exiting, still wearing identical flower crowns.

Six-foot-three, I stand above every shelf here, and they both meet my gaze. Sulli is the first to give me a thumbs-up, and Daisy smiles like everything is okay.

These girls are my life, and all I want is good health and fucking happiness for *each* one of them. I'd trade places with Sulli in a second like I would've traded places with Daisy back then, but I couldn't. All I can do is be here. Be caring.

Be loving.

Hold them when they're fucking sad.

I'd do it every day.

When we check out, Sulli adds four bottles of root beer. I pop her bottle open on our way to the car, and she takes a giant swig. We pile the couple drugstore bags in the trunk.

Then we're on the road.

I drive the green Jeep down a scenic two-lane highway, the faintest ache in my right knee. Sandstone cliffs rise in brown and green gorgeous fucking hues. Some rust-colored crags up ahead, spiked in unique shapes that can't be found anywhere but right here.

Right now.

Daisy rolls down the windows, wind whipping through the Jeep. There's no car in sight down the lengthy stretch of highway. I look to my wife, to the road, and back to my wife, her lips upturning playfully.

"What do you fucking say, Calloway? Fast or slow?"

Daisy smiles so brightly, so fucking heartfelt—it's hard to stare for long, but I always take the fucking risk. My eyes burn like I'm meeting the sun.

And she says, "I love you."

In ten years, our love has never fucking waned. I raise my brows at Dais and feel my smile touch my lips. "Fucking fast then." I step hard on the gas, her smile flooding the car, and the Jeep races down the highway.

"Whoa," Sulli says and immediately sticks her head out the window. Nutty joins, tail wagging.

Winona shrieks in glee, bouncing in her booster seat. "Faster!"

Already flying, I pretend to go fucking faster but keep this speed. Daisy stays in the car, her long legs extended across my lap. With her hand, she draws waves in the wind.

No words need to fucking pass. No radio needs to be flipped on. Our music exists right here. *We're alive. We're alive.*

God, we're all fucking alive.

In this present moment.

In this place together.

{ goodbye }

May 2028
THE LAKE HOUSE
Smokey Mountains

Lily Hale

"I'll pick up where I left off." Luna flips through her journal, multi-colored stars doodled on the cover. Inside I spot pages and pages of scrawled words. Eight-years-old and so smart already.

I told Lo that she'll turn out to be a Ravenclaw like her namesake.

Lo told me that Ravenclaws don't forget to brush their teeth and flush the toilet.

I snapped back, "You just want her to be Hufflepuff."

"So what if I do." He pinched my cheek.

I smile at the memory, but Lo isn't with us this late morning. Luna and I share a pillow, lounging on the bottom bunk in a lake house bedroom. I split a Pop-Tart with Kinney, my three-year-old tucked up against me, her elbow on my bony shoulder as she eats.

"How far through are we?" Kinney asks, crumbs spilling from her lips.

I glance at my hair. *Yep.* Tart crumbs are all over my shoulder-length strands. I brush them away but give up when they break apart into crumbier crumbs.

My hair has seen so much worse than this.

"We're at the end," Luna tells us, her Hulk slippers swaying with her feet. I'm quiet, but I like listening to my kids just as much as talking.

Luna finds the correct page, and then with an alien headband, she pulls her long, light brown hair back, little green bulbs swinging.

Kinney finishes off her Pop-Tart faster than me, and she wipes her mouth with the back of her hand. She also has my round face, but unlike Luna, she has my big green eyes and shade of brown hair. Where Luna is outlandish and spirited, Kinney appears thoughtful and attentive.

Sometimes I wonder if they've taken after the two sides of me: goofy but introspective.

Luna begins reading, and I'm engrossed, not even realizing I've eaten my whole Pop-Tart until I try to shove an invisible piece in my mouth.

"Zhora forgot her ray gun and fluffy mallows on the hovercraft," Luna reads loudly, "and she needed to hurry. Dash was waiting."

Kinney scrunches her nose. "Where are the ghosts or the trolls? Is there a witch at least?"

"Just aliens." Luna taps Kinney's nose. "*Beep, beep.*"

Kinney barely flinches. She says matter-of-factly, "Ghosts are better than aliens."

Luna shrugs and flips a page in her journal. "Everyone likes different sorts of things." She glances at me, and when she starts smiling, I realize that I've been *beaming* at my eight-year-old like she's the empress of an intergalactic universe—and I'm just a little astronaut floating by, witnessing *this* beauty.

Luna Hale might not have any friends outside of relatives, but she has more confidence at eight-years-old than I did when I was *twenty*.

Never ashamed.

My daughter is *never* ashamed.

"You made Mommy cry," Kinney says and starts drying my tears with her Darth Vader pajama shirt.

"Happy tears," I tell them, wiping at my wet eyes, tears overflowing.

Luna touches her Hulk slipper to my Thor slipper and singsongs, "Fan *fiction*." She makes a smooching noise, Hulk kissing Thor.

I laugh at the Hulk-Thor alternate universe. Kinney scoots higher, sitting up on my stomach. I hold her waist, bony like me. Like Luna, too.

I squint at Kinney. "So you're not scared of any ghosts?" *I'm* scared of ghosts and all the horror movies Lo watches with Garrison. They act like they're *comedies*.

The only funny thing about horror movies is my petrified face in the black credit screen.

Kinney tells me, "I'm scared of nothin' in the world." For being three, she says this *very* seriously—to the point where I think I believe her. I try to recall any frightened Kinney moments, but most are just content Kinney moments.

"Uh-huh, not true," Luna says, tapping Kinney's nose.

Kinney swats her hand away. "Is too."

"Then ask Eliot to tell you a ghost story and see what happens."

"Let's not," I interject while Kinney says, "Okay."

"Nonono," I slur. "Not okay. We're in the middle of a *fun* story about aliens." I like these aliens. There are marshmallows and lots of chaste naps on the hovercraft. I almost think I could exist somewhere on Luna's planet.

"Mommy's scared," Kinney says with a *devilish* smile.

Now I'm scared.

Luna annoys Kinney with another *beep beep* nose tap, and the devilish smile seems less *Children of the Corn*.

I convince them to return to the story by just pointing at Luna's journal and asking, "What's happening?"

Luna starts reading again, and Kinney listens as intently as me. Only one page left and the door flies open.

"Mommy!" Five-year-old Xander races into the bedroom, floppy-eared Gotham hot on his heels. Xander's smile is more apparent at the lake house than anywhere else. It's the one safe place void of media attention.

No cameras in his face. No one shouting his name. We like bringing him here, especially when he needs to mentally relax and recuperate.

Xander tugs down his green Power Ranger shirt that rides up. Maybe he forgot what he wanted because he just stands still, smiling, pieces of his brown hair falling over his forehead. Gotham pants beside him.

Before I ask, my oldest son jogs into the bedroom, not out of breath, but smiling too.

"Hey, Mom."

"Hi…?" I switch on *Lily investigation mode.*

Moffy lightly squeezes Xander's shoulder in affection before tapping his sisters' heads like bongos. "Luna, Kinney." Then he pats mine. "Mom. Ready to go?"

"Wha…?"

Luna shuts her journal.

"Waitwaitwait, we have one page left." I might have whined that. I'm just deeply invested in what happens to Zhola and Dash. It was a *devoted* whine, a whine that every person in every fandom may understand.

So there.

Luna says robotically, "Later." She mimes a robot as she stands off the bed. Kinney slides off me and then the mattress before darting to Xander's side.

I try to dust away the cobwebs of my brain, but confusion still crinkles my nose and brows. Moffy grabs both my hands and pulls me to my feet.

"What's going on?" I ask my four kids. They're *never* this sneaky. Luna has trouble keeping secrets from me; Kinney will rehash her entire day, including the driest details: *I walked down the hall. I turned the doorknob. And then I sat on my bed;* Xander lied once about doing his homework and two seconds later made a tearful confession; and Maximoff—he likes being treated like a grown-up, like if anyone is doing the *sneaking*, it'd be all the other little kids. Not him.

"It's about my bike," Moffy tells me.

I frown. "What about your bike?"

Moffy jabs his finger towards the door. "I left it on the west bank of the lake."

How'd he get his bike over there? "Okay…" I trail off, my gaze drifting to the doorway where Loren Hale stands. I'm instantly distracted by *him*.

Cheekbones that cut like ice. Eyes like liquid scotch. He's much more than an alcoholic beverage, and he knows it.

Lo flashes his iconic half-smile, and he says, "Never trust a bunch of Hufflepuffs to do a Slytherin's job."

Our three youngest kids pipe up at once, shouting about how they haven't been sorted yet.

"I'm not eleven!" Kinney decrees.

"I'm a Hufflynclawdor," Luna says.

"We gotta wait, Daddy. It's too early for that," Xander exclaims.

Lo cups his ear. "What was that? I can't hear any of you. I'm immune to huffle-talk."

They all groan like he's the corniest dad in the entire universe.

I smile from ear-to-ear, gliding towards my best friend with gangly arms that ache to fit around him. Lo accepts the invitation, pulling me into the warmest, tightest hug.

He feigns a wince at our four children. "Christ, what is that on their faces? They're smiling, Lil. Make 'em stop."

I peek at our kids, all four smiling big, standing in an uneven line. Wearing superhero and pop culture paraphernalia. Lo squeezes me, no longer teasing. He sees each one, each kid, his nostalgia brimming with mine.

Between years of missteps, fuck-ups, and setbacks, something beautiful and pure happened, and we're viewing every little bit.

"Huh?" Kinney cocks her head at us. "This isn't part of the—"

Moffy covers her mouth with his hands, crouching behind her.

"Ha!" I point at my kids. "Something *is* up."

"I swear, Mom, it's about my bike," Moffy *lies*.

"Lying liar," I start, but Lo swivels me around.

"Did you call our son a lying liar, Lily Hale?" Lo gives me a look while he guides me into the hallway. Lo is a good and bad distraction. Good: he's *Loren Hale*. Bad: I've left our kids behind, and I only realize when we're halfway down the stairs.

"Lo," I complain, about to turn back.

His hands plant firmly on my shoulders, leading me forward. "This way, love."

Cobalt boys zip past us to the living room. Most of the lake house chatter originates from the kitchen, everyone probably gearing up for lunch. Kinney and I always eat Pop-Tarts in the *late* morning as a snack.

"What'd you put them up to?" I question.

He opens the backdoor. "We have to get Moffy's bike off the west bank."

My brows scrunch. "That's a real thing?" I thought for sure he made up a story.

Lo never answers, bending slightly and lifting me on his back. I hook my arms around his collar, legs around his waist. He carries me past the red chairs on the grassy hill, and we head towards the...dock?

"Wait—we're *rowing*?" One of our wooden canoes sways in the water.

"*I'm* paddling, love. You're sitting and searching for the bicycle."

My hazy mind only slightly clears when he drops my feet on the dock. "Waitwaitwait," I say quickly, hands up. The canoe is bound to tip over with me inside of it—I know because I went canoeing with Daisy, and we were in the water in two seconds flat. "This isn't a Lily and Lo thing. This is a Ryke and Daisy thing."

Lo glares. "It's *our* kid's bike. That makes it a Lo and Lily thing."

"Lily and Lo," I correct.

"If you're such a smarty-pants, then you should know my older brother doesn't have a monopoly on recreational activities. We can do them too, Lil."

"But we usually avoid these types of things, don't we?"

He pauses for a second, *cagey*. Knowing I'm right. "What I think? Today is a new goddamn day, and I'm not doing this without you, Lily Hale, so don't make me."

I succumb to Loren Hale's pouty, pleading gaze. "Okay." It takes me a wobbly few minutes, but we're in the canoe. It hasn't tipped over, sunk, or flooded.

Successes.

It's not so bad. The light breeze on the lake cools the tiring summer heat, and the further Lo paddles from the dock, the quieter our surroundings become. Lush green mountains landscape the vast, rippling water. Calm and slow compared to the hectic bustle of Philly.

Lo sidetracks me more than the rolling mountains. His muscles carve beneath his charcoal crew-neck shirt, his arrowhead necklace flat on his chest. It's not just his body, though that's definitely nice—it's this cutting but loving look in his eyes.

Like he could wipe out a species of ants if they nipped at me. Lo would also be the first to tell you that he's more bark than bite.

"We could've brought another oar," I realize. "I could've helped."

He reaches out and squeezes my puny bicep. "Huh, I could've sworn this is where muscles are supposed to be."

I slug his arm.

He feigns a wince. "Ouch."

"My upper-body strength has vastly improved these past few years," I defend while he resumes paddling.

"That Spider-Man weight is five-pounds, Lil. You haven't upgraded in the past few years."

"Because it's Spider-Man," I say, "and it's cool."

His smile dimples his cheeks.

Before I'm lost to those dimples, a wasp buzzes around us, and I freak out—sliding to the far right of my canoe bench. "Lo! Wasp!" I duck, careful not to swat. I swatted at a bee once, and it fought back and stung my hand.

Lo stands up, the canoe swaying.

We're going to tip over. "OhmyGod." I duck again.

Lo sits beside me, and then he stretches out his shirt. "In you go."

I know what to do. Seeking safety from the wasp, I stick my head beneath the bottom of his shirt, sharing the fabric with him. Right up against his bare chest. I sense Lo swatting the wasp with his oar.

"Is it gone?!" I shout like he can't hear me. *You're pressed up against him. Of course he can hear.* It's hard to forget where I am. My arms are tight around his waist, the warmth of his bare skin like home.

The canoe steadies as Lo goes still. He peeks down at me, through the collar of his shirt. His genuine smile begins to swell my heart.

"What...?" I breathe, slowly slipping out from beneath the fabric. I glance around, the wasp gone. We drift lazily towards the west bank.

Lo holds me to his chest, our limbs tangled up together. His face is sharp like steel blades built upon years and years of battles lost and won.

"These years..." he starts, and I know this is much more than a wasp. This is more than a bicycle. Whatever this is, it exists in our decades together. "These years have been epic, and not because it was easy—because it wasn't always—but because you and me, we flew."

My tears brim, and I see *us* fly beyond our lowest expectations for ourselves, all the hard parts where our addictions tried to weigh us down.

We flew.

"You made that possible, you have to know that," Lo says, his voice lowering. "Without you, I just don't know, Lil." When his dad died, it'd been his lowest point in years.

"You've made it just as possible, Lo. I wouldn't know what I'd do if you weren't here," I repeat the same sentiment. He helps me every day in ways that no one else could. No one else knows. It's not just sex. It's every emotion that's tied to a low, to a really bad day.

I always turn to him like he turns to me, and we're not enablers. No one says that we shouldn't be together. No one tells us to split apart. Our souls are still wound together, still wound tight.

"You know what I tell your brother?" I take a deep breath, remembering the conversations I've had with Ryke. "I tell him, 'Lo's ice in the winter now. He won't melt.'"

His eyes redden, welling, and he says, "Thanks to you."

A tear rolls down my cheek. "I think you give me too much credit." His brother has been a bigger force in his life.

Lo shakes his head vigorously. "Not enough. *Never* enough." He rubs his eyes before his tears fall. "*Christ.* I told myself I wasn't gonna make this emotional."

My confusion spikes. "What do you mean...?" *There's no bicycle.* My sleuthing skills did not fail me.

Lo digs a hand into his jean's pocket and reveals a delicate silver chain. A red heart-shaped ruby encircled with diamonds dangles at the end.

The shape, the style—it's an exact replica of my engagement ring.

"Lo," I breathe, more tears surging.

He unclips the necklace. "I gave you my heart a long time ago, and I'm not sure I remind you enough that you still have it. All of it." Lo leans into me and fits the jewelry around my neck.

I start to cry, clutching his waist. In the middle of this quiet lake. They're snot-nosed tears.

"Lil," he whispers, wiping my face with his shirt. "Why are you crying?"

"Because I don't have anything for you."

He laughs at me.

"It's not funny," I cry but that morphs into a tearful laugh that rattles my heart.

Lo kisses my cheek, smiling, and he whispers, "You've already given me everything, love."

And then an electric song full of heavy bass blares across the lake. Side-by-side on the canoe bench, we look out towards the west bank.

Our four kids and floppy-eared basset hound stand on the hillside, a common spot because of the rope swing tied to a maple branch. Moffy raises a set of portable speakers, *Bangarang* by Skrillex booming. Luna, Xander, and Kinney—they wave out to us and lift up a sign together that reads: **WE LOVE YOU!**

They were a part of this surprise all along.

I laugh and cry simultaneously again. As we watch our kids, joy coating their faces, childlike wonder in their eyes, I remember every moment I spent with Lo where we said *we can't.* Where we said *we shouldn't. Not people like us. This isn't meant for us.*

I realize something. So I tell him.

"I think we finally deserve this."

Tears spill out of his eyes, and he says, "I believe it, too."

{ goodbye }

May 2028
THE LAKE HOUSE
Smokey Mountains

LOREN HALE

M^{*ove.*}
     Run.

Today will be a good day, fresh air outside the biting morning with my older brother. I just have to crawl out of bed first.

Lily's limbs intertwine with mine, no beginning or end. I shift only one of her arms, and my soul wrenches like I should be closer, nearer. The desperate need to be with Lily still exists, still lives inside of me.

I lick my lips, another body wedged against me. My three-year-old daughter, dressed in a panda onesie, sprawls partially on my chest. How the hell am I going to move this little adorable thing? Kinney sleeps with her mouth shut. Dried tear tracks line her chubby, round cheeks.

She was scared last night, crying about some goddamn ghost or boogey monster. It was so late; we just let her sleep in our bed.

I sit up now.

Move.

Run.

When I step off the mattress, Lily's eyes flutter open at the absent extra weight. "What's…?"

I kiss her nose while her sluggish mind processes the early hour and what I'm doing awake. Then I make a crude gesture with my two fingers and tongue.

She makes a *humph* noise and slothfully pats my cheek. "You're such a tease," she whines.

"I'm also an asshole," I whisper back with a half-smile. I wasn't carefully tiptoeing around. I wasn't *that* quiet. I selfishly wanted Lily to wake up—so I could hear her voice before I go. So I could kiss her nose and see her brows wrinkle.

Just like they do now.

Christ, she's adorable.

I put on track pants and my running shoes, and the confusion in her face starts to vanish. "Lo," she says, eyeing Kinney who turns onto her left side. Lily glances at the clock and then at me. "Bring a light, okay?"

I already grab my handheld light off the dresser.

"Be careful." She lowers her voice to whisper, "The bears."

My dry smile crosses my face again. "We've had this lake house for over ten years, Lil. You haven't seen one goddamn bear yet."

"There could always be a first," she notes, and our gazes shift to our little girl, who props herself up with a yawn.

"Daddy?" Kinney squints at me.

I don't go closer. If I do, I'm going to stay. There are some things I need. For them. For me.

Move.

Run.

"Kinney Hale," I reply, lightness in my cut voice. I never thought it'd be there, but it exists with other unexpected things.

Kinney rubs at her dried tears, and she tells me with certainty, "I'm scared of nothin' in the..." she yawns tiredly, and Lily scoots closer to Kinney, both sprawled out. They have this whole "be the pancake, act like the pancake" routine—it's not as cute as rolling Kinney in a blanket burrito, but it's goddamn close.

I go to leave.

My soul tries to wrench me back. *Lily.*

Forever Lily.

Her green eyes flit up to mine, and she makes the Spock symbol.

I almost laugh, my smile less dry. I flash the gesture in return, and Kinney tries...but fails. She's a Hale. So that means one day, someday—she'll thrive.

Just maybe not today.

I find the strength to exit, but down the darkened hallway, I stop by a bedroom. Door cracked.

I'm responsible for *four* kids. *Four* lives. Not four shackles. Not four burdens. I want to do right by them like I wanted to do right by Lily. Like I wanted to do right by my brother.

In a way, my four kids helped free me from self-constraints. Reminding me why I need to get up. Wake up.

Just stand up.

When I check on Xander, it's not because I'm flooded with paranoia. *He's not okay. He's going to drink when he's older. He's the unhappiest kid in this house.*

It's not true. None of it. He's okay. He has the same odds as his brother and sisters. He laughs during Power Ranger marathons; he likes piggyback rides and snow cones. He might be painfully shy, but to his siblings, he'll open up. To us, he'll open up. To the youngest Cobalt boy rooming with him (his best friend), he'll open up.

I peek inside Xander's bedroom, nightlights illuminating the wooden bunk bed. I check on my youngest son because I passed his room. I thought about him. I love him—there's just nothing more than that.

Ben Cobalt snores lightly on the top bunk. He talks a lot to Xander, and Xander likes that Ben never pressures him to talk back.

I walk further in their room. Xander isn't alone on the bottom bunk. Pillows and heads on either end—Luna is with him. I squat by the wooden bedframe and nudge Luna's arm, the green quilt halfway off her shoulder. My eight-year-old daughter stuck washable planet tattoos all over her cheeks.

She looks scrawny. Like *so* young—younger than her age. I told my brother his girl is aging up and mine is aging down. Connor interjected, "Look at your wives."

Lily looks younger than her age. Daisy looks older. I didn't really think about how our daughters might go through the same thing.

Protect this one. Protect them all. Lily said I needed a mantra, so there's mine.

I nudge Luna again, and she tiredly squints at me. Before I ask, she mumbles, "He was scared." I look to Xander who sleeps pretty easily.

I say softly in Luna's ear, "Back to your bed, Luna."

She stretches out one hand, and I roll her into my arms and kiss either cheek. I lift her up, carrying my daughter to her bed. In her own room. I pull the red and green quilts to her shoulders, tucking her in, and she falls into deeper slumber all over again.

"Night, Luna," I whisper.

It's morning. I'm still processing what's up and down. It's goddamn *early.*

By the time I reach outside, I find Ryke stretching his hamstrings by the red Adirondack chairs. Handheld lights strapped to his knuckles. I strap mine, the woods dark. The sky dark.

At least it's not cold.

I stretch my quads beside Ryke. Birds waking. Chirping. I might complain—okay, I *definitely* complain more than my brother—but it's not bad. These mornings with him. After his rock climbing accident, before Sulli was born, I remember faintly where *this* stopped.

It was forever ago.

But I know it sucked. I know I would've given *anything* to wake up with my brother. To be here.

To run right next to him.

So I bite my tongue about the early time. I can't promise I'll bite it tomorrow or the day after, but Ryke won't care. My brother is amazing like that.

Both of us shirtless since it's a hot summer, I tower above him while he sits and reaches for his right foot. "Can you keep up with me, big brother?" I taunt.

I feel nothing but love and gratitude for Ryke Meadows.

He rises to his feet and lightly shoves the back of my head. "See if you can fucking keep in line with me." Not a second after, he *runs* like he was born to run in any weather, any place—any goddamn time. He looks back and adds, "Little brother."

I run after.

I'm not dragging. Not weighted. I catch up and fall in line with Ryke, disappearing through the mountainous woods. Along a dirt path, spruce trees on either side.

Our lights guide us ahead.

He taught me how to run. How to breathe. How to reach physical peace. It's what I think most of our way through. It's what I think even when I trip over a goddamn root.

Eight miles through the Smoky Mountains. I feel the power of my body beneath my soles. Our return towards the lake house, I go hard. Muscles *burning*. Heart *racing*. I lengthen my stride as far as I can go, and Ryke matches me with ease.

Step for step, we're there together.

I slow immediately as we break through the woods, Ryke in sync. The cherry red lake house is in sight. I let out a heavier breath than Ryke, sweat coating our lean muscles. My lungs adjust to our new pace.

His tough gaze matches his jaw. "I'm digging up that fucking root."

I watch him comb his hand through his damp, sweaty hair. Even when we're gray and eighty—he'll still *care* too much. He'll still treat me like the little brother I am.

I'm more than okay with that, but it doesn't mean I'm not going to tease him about it.

"The root didn't commit murder, it just fucking tripped me," I tell him. "Why don't you worry about more important things like your constipated face." I catch his eyes and flash him the driest half-smile.

He flips me off.

I laugh—*that's my brother.* He's never really changed, and the world would be worse off if he did. His brown eyes traverse through me, like he's seeing something I'm not seeing. Something *good*, something *happy*—and I wonder what Ryke is thinking.

I don't ask.

He just roughs up my hair, and I attempt payback for once, trying to mess his. Which is already a goddamn mess. Ryke pushes my shoulder. I push his.

We smile, back on the grassy hill by the red chairs. Prepared to stretch again.

The backdoor flies open, and we point our lights onto the wraparound porch. *Of course.*

It's one of the baby raisins.

Tall, ten-years-old, skin tanned from the sun, dark brown hair in a tangled, drooped pony—Sullivan Meadows tries to put on her sneakers and run toward us at the same goddamn time.

She mutters, "Fuck," and hops into a shoe onto the grass. I shake my head once and twice when I think she's going to face-plant.

"Careful, Sulli!" Ryke shouts.

I shut off my light and pat my brother's shoulder, *hard.* "Good luck with that one."

Ryke rolls his eyes.

I try not to imagine a baby raisin earning a driver's license. Sitting behind a wheel, having *Ryke* as their fucking teacher. We should all fear for our lives.

"Wait up!" Sulli sprints to us while we stand still. She wanted to join, and my brother used to let her—but she slept through school, so he actually made *rules*. Rules that literally could apply to no one but a Meadows kid.

My niece halts in front of us, face falling at our post-run sweat. "Dad," she says to Ryke. "You could've woken me. I was in a half-sleep, and I could've been ready really, *really* fast." Then Sulli spins to me. "Uncle Lo, tell him."

I feign seriousness towards my brother, crossing my arms. "Yeah, Ryke. Why didn't you wake her up?" My smile peeks as I remember that time I picked her up from school.

Napping in class. I thought for sure that would've been one of my kids before Ryke's.

"We've been through this, sweetie," Ryke tells her.

She sighs. "Sleep is so fucking boring. Why can't I just use an alarm clock and wake up earlier? Just one hour?"

I shake my head at Ryke. "Only your kid, man." Mine would be *begging* to add five more hours of sleep, not shave them off.

Ryke puts his hand on her head, and she stares up at him as he says, "Go to bed fucking earlier, and you can run with us tomorrow morning."

My brother, the diplomat.

"Will you wake me?" she asks. "Please." I think that'll do him in. The *pleeease* and the giant green eyes.

"Seven fucking hours." He stands strong. *Good job, bro.*

She nods, understanding. "Seven fucking hours. I'll do it."

The backdoor swings again, my oldest son sprinting out in sneakers and a backwards Spider-Man baseball hat. Sometimes I scan Moffy for any signs of being *encumbered* with shit he shouldn't be dealing with—but responsibilities involving his cousins and siblings never weigh him.

I don't get it all the time.

Then again, I really grew up as an only child. I didn't even know what it was like to have a brother until I was in my twenties.

Ryke has bent down to tie Sulli's shoe.

"Dad," she says like he's babying her—which he is. He's Ryke. He'll baby her all the way through high school and college. "I can do it." Sulli squats to tie her shoe, both exchanging smiles, and Ryke messes her already messy hair.

Moffy reaches me, thirteen in two months. *He'll be a teenager soon.* It's insane. I'd say *I'm not ready* but what have I been *truly* ready for? Not much—and I've done okay.

I think—no, I know. I aged up my son at Disneyland, to the point where he stands in front of me, and he looks like he's prepared for anything.

I clasp his hand, and then bring him in for a hug. He pats my back and says, "I can run the trail with her." *Not going to happen, Mof,* I think as I let go of his hand, but he keeps talking. "We'll bring bear spray and lights."

I nod to my son. "Apparently there's a murderous goddamn root on the trail right now, so think of this as me saving your life." I give him a smile that's less sardonic than all my others.

Moffy laughs, cheeks dimpling. "Alright," he says, easygoing, and he's understanding when it comes to rules. "I don't want to die yet, especially not by the Murderous Goddamn Root."

I don't want to die yet.

When I was twelve, I was already building my grave with bottles of booze.

I don't want to die yet.

I nod, trying not to show how this gets to me. "Horrible way to go out."

Moffy smiles and then nudges Sulli's foot with his. She's busy tying her shoes. "Sorry, Sul, I tried," he says.

Sulli stands. "Do you want to play checkers on the porch?"

"Yeah, sure." Moffy nods to her. "Race you there." He darts off with a growing smile, and Sulli tries to catch up and pass him.

After Ryke and I finish stretching, we enter the house through the spacious kitchen. Lights are on. Someone else is definitely awake, and my guess is Connor Cobalt. He's the right answer to most things.

Ryke gently shuts the door. I'm already inside, passing Connor on my way to the fridge.

He plugs in a coffee pot, shirtless and wearing drawstring pants. Hair perfect. Body perfect. The guy is a god—I call it as *fact*.

I bet you my brother would even hesitate to shout *fiction*.

Connor supports his sleeping daughter with one hand against his chest. Little three-year-old Audrey, dressed in strawberry-pink floral pajamas, drools on his shoulder. It's not the first time she's used Connor as a pillow.

I'm thinking she knows something that we don't.

I yank open the fridge door and find a water bottle. Out of the corner of my eye, I see Ryke helping Connor with the coffee pot. They're friends beyond their relationships with me—I'm glad for it; they both deserve more friendships.

They deserve every goddamn thing.

Ryke fiddles with the coffee machine that won't start. I search the fridge for another water bottle, and I strain my ears to hear him whisper to Connor, "She okay?"

Connor rubs Audrey's back in a circular motion and pries a strand of carrot-orange hair off her lips. "She was afraid last night and didn't sleep well."

I shut the fridge, two waters in hand.

"Scared of what?" Ryke asks, giving up on the coffee machine.

I edge closer, brows knotted. This story is starting to sound familiar, especially since my toddler is friends with his toddler.

"*A great and terrible boogey*," Connor whispers. "Her words."

Huh. I hand my brother a water bottle. "What's up with this boogey? My kid was crying all last night because of the same thing."

Ryke uncaps his water. "Which kid?"

"Kinney." I'd never seen her that afraid, but as soon as she said *boogey*, it was hard to be concerned. It sounds like booger.

"The monster is fictional," Connor explains, "from the imagination of Eliot Alice Cobalt."

My face scrunches at this truth, processing this, processing—and by the time I come to a conclusion, Ryke swigs his water and nods to us as he backs away. Leaving.

I whisper to Connor, "We need to have *words*, love."

His lips rise. "What kind of words, darling?"

"The kind that says *your son scared my daughter*." I lean against the counter, toying with the coffee pot with no intention to fix it.

"My son also scared *my* daughter—so your argument falls short."

I let out a laugh. "I'm used to that." *Falling short.*

Connor leans against the cabinets next to me. I stare at my hand that grips a water bottle. I'm not shaking. I'm not sliding down to the floorboards.

I'm upright. I'm standing.

I'm alive.

He tells me, "Very few people don't fall short of me. It's just a fact."

"Fact," I say with the cock of my head. "You're a conceited prick."

"Fact." He grins. "You're a good looking asshole."

I almost smile. "I keep waiting for you to replace *asshole* with *bastard*, and still, after all this time…you never do." I touch my chest. "I'm wounded."

"You're both," Connor says quietly, "but I prefer to call you whatever you identify with more."

I'm mostly a bastard in the literal definition. I'm an asshole any way you flip it. I take a large swig of water while Connor reaches over and tries to fix the coffee pot again. Still holding Audrey.

He has seven children. Seven goddamn children. A billion-dollar company and more reasons to have headaches than all of us combined—and still, he has *none*. In this world there might be another *me*, another angst-ridden guy who just needs someone to care.

I know in this world there will never be another Connor Cobalt.

I want to say that he keeps me smart, but he's done so much more than that. He loved me at my lowest—when I thought no one else but Lily could love someone spiteful like me. He always saw beyond my addiction, beyond the angst and the hate—I never had to explain. He just knew me.

I needed that kind of friendship, and I think he knew that too.

Connor resigns from the coffee pot.

I quip, "Just drink me, love. I'm bitter. I'll wake you up."

"Ugh," Rose gags at me on her way into the kitchen, knotting the strands to her silk black robe.

I give her an ugly dry smile. "Choke a little harder, maybe your missing soul will come out."

She snorts into a short laugh. "One day I have a soul. The next day I don't. Make up your mind, Loren."

You have a soul. I think it instantly. Without question. Without doubt. Rose has possibly one of the best hearts in this house. In her lifetime, she's done incredible things for people. Not just for her sisters, but *people*. Hale Co. has more female executives than it ever did, and she did that.

She grimaces at me. "What? Why are you looking at me like that?"

I layer on my usual glare, and her shoulders loosen. She's glad that I act like I hate her just as much as she acts like hates me. In reality, I love her as much as Lily loves Rose—it's just the way it turned out to be.

Rose whips her hair at me and glides towards her husband.

"You're fraternizing with the enemy," Rose whispers, her eyes softening on their daughter.

Connor says smoothly, "Your enemy is my best friend."

I smile smugly at Rose and finish off my water.

She rolls her eyes at both of us, but Connor draws closer and murmurs something against her neck. I let them flirt-fight in private. Though it's hard to miss the one consistency, the one unbroken exchange—you know it'll always be there. Reliable. Unfaltering.

"Richard." She glares.

"Rose." He grins.

I almost smile again. I open a cupboard, trashcan beneath, and I toss my water bottle in the bin. The darkened sky slowly begins to lighten. I shut the cupboard the same time Lily pads into the kitchen, Kinney dead asleep in her arms.

There's nowhere I'd rather be.

I'm beside my wife in an instant. By the fridge. My fingers on her waist. Lily blows out a strand of hair stuck to her lips.

Beautiful.

She whispers, "Luna told Kinney to listen to a ghost story from Eliot. That's how all this happened, Lo."

I love how Lily's nose crinkles and how she uses every last ounce of strength to hold up our three-year-old.

"Lo?" She frowns. "Did you hear what I said?"

I gather what words I remember while pulling Lily into my chest. "Ghost stories, girls." I put my lips to her ear. "*Boo.*" Then I stick my tongue in.

"Lo!" she whisper-hisses and slugs my arm.

I feign a wince. "Lil." I pout, and her green eyes flit to my lips.

My humor fades, and I float through decades. As kids, as teenagers, as adults. Staying up late reading comics, sneaking to parties—all the plans we never made in college. All the lies we told. I touch these memories. I can go as far back as I want, to the gravest depths.

The past can't drag me under.

I relive the better parts that are intertwined with bad. Because I look back and think, *Christ, we were so goddamn fragile.*

Look how far we've come.

Look at us now.

Lily's eyes flood, sharing my emotion. Ache for ache. Smile for smile. I only ever wanted to live this life with her.

"Hey, guys," Daisy whispers, just barely shaking my attention. "Did you see which way Ryke went?" I never saw my brother pass through the kitchen again, but Connor points towards the side door to outside. I glance out the window over the sink.

My brother sits on the grass by the red chairs, knees bent. He stares out, the sky morphing from dark to light blue. And I know.

He's waiting for the sun to rise.

Lily breaks from my side, just to put Kinney in a bouncer beside Audrey, both girls still asleep. I grip the sink counter, the side door clattering as Daisy heads out. She walks across the grass, light on her feet—going towards my brother.

I'm proud of Daisy. For never listening to me. Or her mom. Or her dad. I'm goddamn proud of Daisy for becoming the woman that she wanted to be.

My lips lift just slightly, and I turn my head. "Lily." She's not far, her hands on my waistband. I clasp one in mine, and I nod towards outside. She nods back, and silently, we leave through the side door, following my brother and her sister's footsteps to the hill.

Daisy sits between Ryke's legs, back against his chest, his arms wrapped around her frame. Their eyes touch the horizon.

I take a seat on the grass only a few feet from Ryke, and Lily plops next to me. I hold her as she holds me, her cheek resting against my shoulder. My eyes fix ahead, and I try to see what my brother sees in the sky. Orange colors that melt into blue.

My gaze breaks when Connor walks outside, hands in his pockets until Rose reaches him. Side-by-side. He laces his fingers with hers, and their heads turn. So does mine. To look back ahead.

Just as the sun rises.

With the six of us on this hill and the packed lake house behind us—I feel sentiments far beyond this sunrise, this morning, this moment. We filled an empty house.

I'm thirty-seven.

Just yesterday I was twenty and meeting some of these people—people that I'd spend my life with, that'd become my home.

Just yesterday I was twenty—still deeply and desperately in love with my best friend.

I grew older.

We all grow older.

In a blink of an eye, our children will grow old too.

And I'll think: just yesterday they were twenty. Headed for college. Falling in love. Memories will flood behind us, the lake house no longer filled to the brim. As quiet as the moment we first walked in—and we'll sit on this hill. Feeling the stillness that exists.

And then we end—we end where we started.

Just us.

All six of us.

Acknowledgements

Deep breaths.

Where do we even begin? The Addicted/Calloway Sisters series has been a journey from start to finish, and if you've reached this point with us. If you have read all 10 books, you have read over 1 million of our words.

Let us repeat that, in case you missed it. You have read *over* 1 million of our words. It's a staggering thought to know that you have loved these books enough to make it this far. We are so humbled to be given this opportunity. And make no mistake, these books exist because of *you*. We planned to end them at 4 simple books. There are 10 because of your love for these characters and our words.

So thank you from the bottom of our hearts. Thank you.

To our mom. You have been the superheroine behind these stories. You read them before anyone, you put on your proofreading cape and catch so many ugly mistakes, all while dealing with our crazy deadlines. But even more than that, your love and support have championed us far beyond the start of this series. From the moment we began writing stories, you have encouraged all our fantastical dreams. We never doubted that we could get *here*, even if we knew it would take immense amount of persistence and work, and that's because you instilled in us the belief that we could do anything. Be anything. It's a gift you have given us, and one that we will never take for granted. So thank you. Thank you for being our very own Rose Calloway.

To Jenn, Lanie, Jae, and Siiri. Words cannot describe how much the four of you mean to us. Every day we are blown away by your commitment and love to the Fizzle Force. Thank you so much for running, organizing, and putting your energy into it. We honestly do not know what we'd do without you…maybe have minor panic attacks. You calm us, listen to us, and fill this world with dazzling, brilliant color. You all are very magical in our eyes.

To Alice Tort & Olivia Danieli. We extend our biggest thanks for your help with the French and Italian. This book wouldn't glow nearly as bright without the translations, and we owe it all to you.

To Kimberly. You are a super agent, and we're so grateful to have you on our side. You may not know this, but we believe in fate. All things happen for a reason, and you're our biggest proof. Thank you for reading our books; we're still amazed that you love them.

To the Fizzle Force. We really want to name every single one of you by name, but I think we'd need a bigger book—and this book is already mammoth. We may not name you specifically, but just know that we know who you are, we love you, and you mean the absolute world to us. There is something strong and mighty in the Addicted series fandom. It's kindness and love and power, such great power, all wrapped together. Even if you've never spoken to us and just lurked around, we love you all the same. Because you've read our books. You've made it *here*. Thank you for sticking with one long series. One giant ride.

This may be the end of the series, but it's not *the* end.

We'll keep writing. We hope you'll keep reading.

And just know that these books will never go away. There's over 1 million words of Lily, Loren, Connor, Rose, Ryke & Daisy. That's more than a lifetime.

We won't officially say goodbye because as J.M. Barrie's *Peter Pan* said, *"Never say goodbye because goodbye means going away and going away means forgetting."*

Until next time.

xoxo Krista & Becca

ALSO BY
Krista & Becca Ritchie

ADDICTED SERIES
Addicted to You

Ricochet

Addicted for Now

Thrive

Addicted After All

CALLOWAY SISTERS SERIES
Kiss the Sky

Hothouse Flower

Fuel the Fire

Long Way Down

Some Kind of Perfect

STANDALONE ROMANCE
Amour Amour

WEB SERIES
Willow & Garrison: Whatever It Takes

CPSIA information can be obtained
at www.ICGtesting.com
Printed in the USA
LVOW10s0755230518
578180LV00003BA/24/P